Fire and Steel

The Soldier Chronicles Books 1-5

Also by David Cook

The Soldier Chronicles novella series
Liberty or Death
Heart of Oak
Blood on the Snow
Marksman
Death is a Duty

Battle Scars: A Collection of Short Stories Volume I

Fire and Steel

The Soldier Chronicles Books 1-5

David Cook

Fire and Steel: The Soldier Chronicles Books 1-5
Copyright © David Cook 2015

This book is for my mum & dad; the best parents a son could ever have

Liberty or Death

Lorn Mullone and the Irish
Rebellion
May-July 1798

LIBERTY OR DEATH
*is dedicated to the people of Northern Ireland and the
Republic of Ireland*

Horror came to *Uaimh Tyrell*.

It was a poor village, as it had been in Tudor times, and had never expanded like neighbouring Blackwater or Skreen. Richard Tyrell had been a *buanadha,* an Irish mercenary, who had fought for Hugh O'Neill during the Nine Years War against Queen Elizabeth's English troops. It was Tyrell that led Spanish mercenaries sent from Phillip II to assist the Irish uprising en-route to Ulster, and the meeting place was in one of the dark coastal caves that gave the village its name.

It lay along the east coast of Wexford about six miles north of the town bearing the same name as the county. A small stream named *Banna,* meaning 'goddess', flowed out to sea through a gully to a shingle beach where fishing boats worked the deep waves. The rest of the villagers herded sheep on the hills and farmed the land. *Uaimh Tyrell* was a collection of thatched huts huddled around a small stone church where Father Ciarán prayed to the bones of Saint Brigid. The Saint had visited the original village church before founding the great abbey at Kildare sometime in the fifth century. The converted church in her name was given the sacred bones when she was exhumed in order to prevent Viking invaders plundering them from the convent many years later. Her head was taken to Lisbon, her remains were scattered, and the four bones that kept in the hamlet's church were from her hands.

'They're not the bones from her hands,' Lochlann the Elder would say to anyone that enquired. 'Father Ciarán is a pious soul, but the man's mad! Utterly mad! They're the bones from a red fox! By the love of God, he prays to a fox!'

11

The bones were small, thin and ochre-brown in colour, and could have come from a red deer, or indeed a fox, but the elderly Father Ciarán would have none of it. He made his daily prayers to them underneath a Saint Brigid's cross, a cross-shaped symbol made from tied rushes containing a woven square in the centre and tied off ends. The children of the village had made this one for the Saint's day, and Ciarán proudly hung it above the open box containing her consecrated bones.

The sacred village was a place of worship, fish, cattle, rain and wind-swept hills. Where dreams were wished for and prayers rarely answered.

And on this day the redcoats came.

The first thing Ciarán heard was the sound of the cockerels crowing loudly in alarm, horses hooves thumping the ground like distant peals of thunder, growing instead of dying, and young Dónall's dog barking madly. Then there were screams that split the morning air; sounds that chilled his heart. His pulse quickened. He opened the church door and instantly a pair of scarred hands shoved him violently back inside the nave.

'Get back, you bible-humping turd!' a man spat at him, a great drip of spittle fell from thick lips to glisten on his coat. 'Back with you!'

Father Ciarán tripped on his cassock and landed on the hard stone floor. Three men, dressed in the red coat of the military, stepped over him; steel spurs jingled with each step. Their looming shadows reached the far wall to touch the altar.

'Please,' the priest begged, 'this is a house of God.'

'Better start reciting your prayers then, you piece of filth,' said the thick-lipped one, giving a lupine grin. He had immense shoulders, and powerfully-built arms and legs.

Manic prickles raced across Ciarán's skin. 'Why have you come here? What do you want?'

None of them answered. Next to the muscular one, the other two looked of the same mould; rough of face and of a similar age. They were cavalrymen who wore topped black leather boots, white breeches, black bicorn hats with a tall black plume and their single-breasted red jackets were faced black. Ciarán had not seen these men before, but they were fellow Irishmen and served the Crown. They also carried carbines, which were still hooked to their white shoulder belts with a clip, but it was the long straight-bladed swords that gave them the fearsome edge to their appearance.

These men were killers.

Outside, the villagers were being brought out of their homes by dismounted troopers. More horsemen, maybe thirty, were encircling the village. One man tried to resist and was punched to the ground. A woman howled, bright blood streamed down her face, as she was brought outside.

Long legs climbed the few stone steps of the church and a figure blocked the doorway. The silver-haired priest had to shield his rheumy eyes from the low sun in order to see the newcomer's face. A glint of gold buttons and a crimson sash revealed that he was an officer.

'I knew of a leper that once lived in this village,' the silhouetted man said in a clear and precise voice. He took off one of his long white gloves and slapped the front of his immaculate scarlet coat with it to dislodge invisible lint.

One of the two similar troopers took a step back. 'A leper, sir?' he swallowed hard.

All men fear the grey and rotting gnarled flesh of lepers. Most were treated in hospitals, but some were sent out into the wilds to live as they must, begging for food and clothing, hoping for salvation.

Father Ciarán nodded. 'Gerrit used to live up on the bluff. But he died five winters past.'

'What the hell was a bloody lazar doing here?' the trooper seemed to tremble. He scratched his white powdered hair at the neckline. In this heat, the men, except the officer who did not seem to follow procedure, found their hair itchy from the lice, grime and sweat.

'Gerrit wanted solitude and found it here,' Ciarán replied. 'He was a gentle soul and a good man.'

'And the kind and charitable Father Ciarán looked after him?' the officer said with a touch of sarcasm. 'Isn't that correct?'

Ciarán stiffened. 'I did. It is my duty to help the sick, the needy and the poor. We are all God's children.'

The officer snorted through his long canted nose. 'I understand that you look after all of your people. Isn't that true?'

Ciarán didn't reply, he swung his craggy gaze up at the man who took a step forward into view. He had raven black hair, a thin mouth and piercingly cold eyes.

'Where is the blacksmith?'

Ciarán guessed there would be no appeasing the man, for he looked bitter and sinful, yet he had to protect his people. 'I don't know.'

The chill eyes matched the officer's expression. 'I want the truth.'

13

The priest remained mute. He could hear shouting and sobbing, and he made the sign of the cross on his chest.

The officer signalled with a dip of his head and immediately the muscular trooper kicked Ciarán in the ribs, hard enough to fracture bone. Ciarán was propelled along the stones by the force of the vicious attack. He lay clutching his thin chest, gasping and wincing in pain.

The officer smiled. 'I've seen Seamus kick a man to death, Father. It didn't take him long, but every second for the victim was agony. So I'll ask you one more time.' He was calm, almost chillingly composed, as he moved into the church, spurs jangling with every step. 'Where is the blacksmith? I know he's called Scurlock. Where's his boy? Dónall, isn't it? Sable hair, freckles and he's got a scar underneath an eye from an accident with a hoe. Where are they?'

Father Ciarán gaped at the officer's knowledge. 'Please, sir,' he pleaded, making a mewing sound as the officer then ordered the thatch-roofed smithy to be torched. He reached forward to grab the tall officer's thigh, but Seamus stamped his boot on Ciarán's back and then kicked him in the face, dislodging a front tooth.

'I don't think he knows where this fellow Scurlock is, sir,' said one of the two troopers, staring at the blood streaming through the old man's fingers.

The officer swivelled resentful eyes on the man, who could not keep his gaze and, instead, looked down and fingered his carbine's trigger.

'Nonsense,' the officer said dismissively, 'we all know the people trust and confide in their priests. They are the ears, eyes and mouths of the rebels. They are the scourge of the land. They are the source of this insurrection. Breathing it, preaching it. They fan the fires with their sermons. They serve the Cause first and God second.' He turned to Seamus. 'If he won't talk, cut off his ears; then cut out his eyes and if he still remains silent, cut out his tongue. You may then do as you will.' He gave the priest a look of revulsion. 'Let's see if the rebels miss one of their own.' He turned away to walk outside.

Ciarán stirred. 'Please,' he said, his voice barely a whisper and thick with blood, 'we have nothing to do with the unrest. Scurlock is a good man. I've known him since he was a boy. He'd never hurt a soul, or get himself tangled up in the insurrection.'

The officer stopped to turn around and face him. 'He's a blacksmith, and the smiths are the weapon makers for the devious traitors. I want to question him in connection with the murder of two of my men.' His

14

face was a rictus of anger and sharp teeth. 'For the last time, where is he?'

The old man trembled, eyes glinting with tears. 'Have mercy!'

There would be none.

The officer stepped away and the last thing Father Ciarán saw was Seamus lean over him, and the wicked knife went to work. The peacefulness of village life suddenly became one of unimaginable torment.

The village was filled with more screams, for most of the women and children were still alive and their ordeal had scarcely begun. All the young women were saved from immediate slaughter, because they were raped first. The older ones were herded with the men and cut down. One auburn-haired woman was crying, not because a man with yellow teeth and rancid breath had dragged her near the *Banna* by her hair, but because her two boys were still inside her home that was flickering with flame and smoke. The man had lifted her skirts and was on top, rutting like a wild hog, impervious to her tear-stained pleas.

A few shots rang out from carbines as one or two men tried to fight back, but the bullets killed them. A man rolled on the ground and two horsemen leant down from their saddles, taking it in turns to slash his body with their swords. Another, dressed in a white shirt and tan knee-breeches, managed to break free and scramble up the road towards Blackwater, but a pistol banged from the church steps to send him flying in a spray of crimson. The body twitched. Blood trickled obscenely over the stones.

An officer, mounted on a ghost-grey horse, trotted over to the church as a piercing scream echoed from within. He wiped his forehead with a handkerchief and looked down to the tall dark officer. "Tis a fine pistol, sir,' Captain McGifford said appreciatively.

Colonel Black glanced at the weapon. It was rifled with highly decorative hunting scenes in silver mounts running along the walnut stock to the barrel. It was an exquisite piece of craftsmanship, and one he highly treasured. His servant, a trooper, held onto his horses reins.

'The quicker they fall, the easier the end shall be,' he said smiling, which was as welcoming as a blizzard.

'I do hope that wasn't our man Scurlock, sir?'

Black's lips tightened in anger. 'Then I wouldn't have fired my piece, Captain,' he said, giving the officer a venomous glare. 'Do you take me for an imbecile?'

15

'No, sir.' McGifford coughed to cover his embarrassment at the rebuke. 'None of the villagers knew where the blacksmith and his boy have gone.'

Black stared up to where the stream fell gently over dark rocks and thick grass covered in marsh thistle. He could see a pair of white legs and the auburn-haired woman appeared to be wearing a necklace of red gemstones.

'That one revealed earlier that Scurlock has a brother in New Ross, so that's where we'll go next.'

'I see, sir. She was pretty wee thing,' McGifford commented on the dead woman with the slashed throat. 'A shame that.'

'Careful McGifford,' Black warned, lifting his gaze. 'One must remember that they plot to overthrow our government and murder our people. I'll not have a man under my command think otherwise. We have those that were close to us to avenge in this bloody affair.'

'Yes, sir,' McGifford spoke ruefully. 'Of course, sir. I was only talking about her beauty.'

Black watched as two draft horses and one fine horse that could serve as a trooper's spare mount, as well as silver from the church, was being collected by his exultant men and packed into a covered wagon. He was pleased with their work today. No losses to the ranks. Another victory, so easily achieved. A pity the smith wasn't apprehended, but no matter. Time was running out for the man.

They left behind a smouldering, stinking ruin. Bodies lay in heaps, cherry-red embers glowed and seagulls circled high over *Uaimh Tyrell* like carrion birds.

The horsemen rode south.

*

It was a week later.

Fists pounded down on the desk, ink spilled, and cream-coloured papers swept down onto the polished marbled floor.

'The whole village was destroyed!' said a voice that made the half-dozen officers in the room all jump at once. The man who spoke was a tall Scotsman called John Moore. 'The people were massacred! Butchered into offal! Is this what this wretched conflict has become? A slaughter yard?' he asked and no one answered him. 'Is this the work of Colonel Black?'

'It appears so, sir,' replied an aide, braving Moore's unusual temper that flared sudden like black powder in the priming pan.

'It could well be the work of the rebels, sir,' suggested another. 'Trying to incite more unrest?'

Colonel Moore gave his opinion of the matter in the shortest terms. He stared out one of the windows of Dublin Castle, the thick-walled seat of British rule, where sentries, bayonet-tipped muskets and polished cannons guarded it from enemies. There was a curfew, still in effect after rebels planned to storm the Castle a fortnight ago, but the men were ill-led and had no cohesion, so the attack had failed. However, the threats of other attacks were still on everyone's mind, so only servicemen and state officials could be allowed out after dark and all had to have signed papers. He sighed to expel the temper raging hot inside him like a forge's fire.

'While we try and instil a sense of diplomacy and stability to the people of this land,' he remarked, turning to the men, 'we allow men like Colonel Black to haunt the thoroughfares in order to murder and butcher at will,' Moore continued, glancing down at the table where a list of atrocities were said to have been committed by this particular man. 'I am utterly appalled.'

"Colonel Black" was just a name coined by the press for the unknown, shadowy figure that roamed the highways inflicting torture and death in the name of the king. The government had put a price on his head at a thousand guineas, but he remained at large, and no one who had seen his face had lived to tell the tale. Religion has played no part in this. Black was a malevolent spectre; a bogeyman that preyed on the rich and poor, and so far his crusade of blood and terror had hindered any peaceful resolution between the government and the insurgents.

Moore gave a weary sigh and rubbed his temples with his fingertips. It was a swelteringly humid night and he undid the buttons on his white waistcoat to let it fall open and reveal a white silk shirt underneath. The back of it was soaked with sweat. 'Bring me Mullone,' he asked exasperatedly. 'Send in the major now.'

The aides shuffled out and a moment later the wide doors opened and a blond officer was seen into the room. The twin doors closed silently behind him. Lorn Mullone was dressed in a uniform style based on the British Light Dragoons; his scarlet coat had green facings, the colour of spring grass, and buff breeches, which on closer inspection were stained and worn with age. His Tarleton helmet with its white over red plume and black crest was battered and tucked under an arm.

'Have a seat, Lorn,' Moore gestured hospitably to one of the chairs.

'Thank you, sir,' Mullone's voice was soft and warm. He was a slim built man, with a wide-jawed freckled face. His green eyes revealed intelligence, warmth and trust. He shook Moore's proffered hand.

'How was your journey? Not too troublesome, I hope?'

'Not at all, sir.'

'You have your reports?'

'I do,' Mullone had brought with him several detailed reports of his findings; firsthand accounts, Militia and Yeomanry information, rebel dispositions and eye-witness descriptions. He read them all to Moore who appeared tense throughout the reading.

Tea, bread, butter, ham and cold chicken were brought to the room, mainly for the major who was tired and famished, having spent the last two days in the saddle riding down from Ulster.

'You may remove your coat, neck-tie and undo your waistcoat like I, Lorn,' Moore gestured with a ghost of a smile. 'It's devilishly muggy.'

'Thank you kindly, sir,' Mullone said, his hair at his temples and back of his neck were darkened with sweat. He undid the buttons on his scarlet coat, revealing a red-collared waistcoat underneath decorated in silver lace and buttons. He loosened the white silk neck-tie and dropped it into a pocket. He placed the helmet on the floor and draped his fraying coat over the back of the chair as no aides were present to take them.

Moore waited until Mullone had finished his supper. 'Colonel Black and his marauders have been terrorising the people of Wicklow and Wexford, and so far have not been apprehended. In fact, he has eluded every arresting party sent to find him. He's one step ahead every time.'

'How so, sir?'

Moore scratched his chiselled face. 'I really don't know how he does it. Damned good luck?' He shot Mullone a stale look. 'It has been reported that Black is English and his men are English Dragoon Guards, but that is a source of speculation having been solely reported in the press. It also seems there are conflicting rumours on his namesake. Some will tell you it's because he rides a black horse, some say it's because the troop he commands have black facings, while others will claim it's because his heart is as black as the Devil. I even heard one of the Castles' guards say that storm clouds herald his attacks.' He scornfully shook his head. 'Preposterous! He's just a man!

18

Yet, his name is whispered in fear and the people are cowering whenever it is mentioned. He's a damned canker that needs cutting out. Peace will not come until the day he's stopped.'

Mullone dipped his head with agreement. 'Do we know what his motives are?'

'Apart from slaughter?' Moore said, lifting a wry eyebrow. 'Nothing that I'm aware of. There's nothing that points to his intentions, so we've not been able to second-guess him. He makes no demands.'

Mullone took a sip of tea, savouring the taste. 'When did the first atrocity occur?'

'Three weeks ago a Militia captain from one of the garrison towns at the foot of the Wicklow Mountains is said to have allowed Colonel Black to release six prisoners from the gaol. Black and his men then hunted the felons down like foxes. The prisoners were apparently all arrested before the unrests had started and were not, as the captain testified at his court martial, conspirators or United men. It was cold-blooded murder and nothing more. And it seems Black has a taste for the sport.' A clock in the room struck twelve and Moore paused until the chiming stopped. 'Do you know of Torrington?'

Mullone's brow twitched a touch. 'Captain Ennis Torrington?'

'Yes, the very same. A contemptible fellow. He's now of the North Wicklow County Militia Regiment, and recently went on a bloody rampage with Black that, according to Sir Edward Clanfield, a local Wexford landowner, yielded five hundred pikes and thirty muskets taken from the rebels. Sir Edward's chilling account confirms that at least fifty were killed. I deduce that they were all rounded up and shot, or cut down where they stood. There are no indications that any of them were rebels, though. Torrington insists otherwise.' Moore sighed, as though he found what he was about to say disturbing. 'But it was last week that Black's savagery has caused this country new grief. It was a place called - '

'*Uaimh Tyrell*, sir,' Mullone interposed, knowing what the colonel was about to say. 'It's all I've heard about in the last two days. I can't quite believe it. It's despicable, so it is.'

Moore sighed heavily and stared into Mullone's pensive eyes. 'It was a hallowed place and he just butchered those poor people.'

'I know, sir,' Mullone said, voice tinged with sorrow.

'The village was a mix of Catholics and Protestants and he murdered them all. The women were abused in the most grotesque manner. The priest was found mutilated beyond all recognition.' Moore paused

19

momentarily because it genuinely upset him. 'We don't know why he went there. In the weeks since the new insurgencies started, Black's attacks have worsened. A Wexford barrister was found hanging from a tree yesterday morning. Disembowelled and his eyes gouged out.'

An image of a young man with a rope tied around his neck instantly shot into Mullone's thoughts as Moore carried on talking. A cold wind blew. Snowflakes twirled and danced in the air. He could hear the creaking of the rope as the man slowly rotated to face him. He was dead. That was obvious. His neck was horribly distorted, face bloodless, eyes bulging and tongue exposed through purple lips. Mullone shivered at the image. It wasn't the first time; it usually came to him when he was dreaming.

'Lorn?' Moore asked, seeing his expression.

Mullone blinked and shook his head. 'I'm sorry, sir.' He paused, trying his best to get the image out of his mind. 'Please continue.'

'Apparently, Black is supposed to have been responsible. If you ask me, I think the rebels did it. The barrister was a loyalist and unfortunately, out of favour. The same goes for that magistrate that was shot by his own gamekeeper. It's not the first time the rebels have killed in revenge. And I'm afraid it won't be the last. But Black, in my opinion, was responsible for *Uaimh Tyrell*.'

'Is he a government man, sir?' Mullone asked.

'No,' Moore said vehemently.

'Is he English?'

'I suspect he's Irish gentry, but the rumour is that he commands English Dragoon Guards, which is nonsense. His men are said to wear red coats, but there's no mounted regiment that I know of with black facings.'

'Yeomanry? Fencible?'

'Nothing in the records,' Moore said.

The government had raised and equipped numerous Yeomanry corps of both horse and foot, but these were smaller formations than Militia, and usually confined to their own territories for garrison and patrol duties. The Fencible regiments were raised in defence against the threat of invasion in order to free up the regular Foot battalions fighting abroad.

Mullone grunted. 'Yet, Black dresses in the scarlet coat of an officer in King George's army.'

Moore thought he heard an accusation in the Irishman's tone and looked at his face for any signs of insolence, but there were none.

20

'I don't even know if he holds a colonel's rank,' Moore said. 'I suspect it's self-styled. The press have started to call him 'The King's Wrath', or 'Cromwell's Ghost', but they easily forget that Black murders anyone, regardless of their convictions. I want him caught before he strikes again. Earl Camden is putting pressure on me to bring him in. We can't have peace while he still operates. I want you to find out who he is, and stop him.'

Mullone sat upright. 'Sir?'

'I know you're tired, Lorn,' Moore said compassionately. 'God knows we all are, but I need your help. I don't have anyone else I can ask that I trust. You come highly recommended by Castlereagh. Camden has given me the powers in order to hunt Black's irregulars down. I've had some difficulty already from command. You've heard that Sir Ralph has stepped down?'

Mullone was surprised. 'No,' he gasped.

Sir Ralph Abercromby, Commander-in-Chief of the British Army, was regarded as an extremely compassionate man. His plan was to disarm the populace as quickly as possible by sending troops to live in those districts that were still actively rebellious. The aim was to frighten the people into handing over any weapons and to nullify them. It had worked hitherto in Kildare and Kilkenny, but General Lake was a ham-fisted, tactless individual, who had taken the reins of command with his usual unsympathetic aplomb, discarding Abercromby's plans of empathy for brutality.

'Sir Ralph resigned due to clashes with the Whigs. Parliament wasn't happy with his views on the gentry being "troublesome", and so rather than face any more opposition, which have deluged the press of late, he simply quit. General Lake is now in command,' Moore said it as though it was a warning. 'The Irish populace is treated worse than the slaves of Saint Lucia,' he said bitterly, knowing as the once succeeding Governor of the Caribbean island, how appalling behaviour can quickly instil resentment. 'It's not in my nature to criticise a senior officer, but his methods are purely barbaric. How can we win the people's affections when we're treating them like war criminals?'

'I agree, sir. You can't.'

'But you are a sympathetic man and a damned fine officer. Empathy will win this war, not bigotry and obstinacy. Do you have your men with you?'

'Yes, sir.'

It was a delicate question to ask, but Moore asked it anyway. 'Do you trust them?'

'Of course, sir.'

Moore gave a brief smile. 'You've certainly earned their trust.'

Mullone was a major in Lord Maxwell Lovell's Irish Dragoons. The regiment was only two years old, having been raised by Lord Lovell, a member of the Whig party, and who was currently in London. It was once a hundred men strong, but now Mullone commanded less than forty. When he had arrived to begin his duties as major, he discovered that the men were extremely lax and uncaring. Desertion was ripe. He considered himself a fair man and a good officer and immediately investigated as to why the men were so unhappy. It became apparent that Colonel Pennyfather was skimming money from the regiments pay chest, so in an eye-blink, Mullone had him arrested and the men immediately paid all back payments. They had cheered him like a king, and from that day he had earned their trust.

'And if you're wondering about your appointment,' Moore saw the slightest hesitation in the depths of Mullone's eyes, 'it was your reports that alerted the government to Bantry Bay.'

Mullone was currently employed by the War Office to spy on Theobald Wolf Tone, a protestant lawyer, and his acquaintance of a French agent called De Marin. In Jersey, Mullone had intercepted a despatch from Tone to De Marin who was hiding somewhere in Cork. The codes revealed that thousands of men waited in flat-bottomed barges and troop ships. Mullone had quickly alerted the government to the French armada which left Holland for Ireland, and the army managed to repel the French landing at Bantry Bay, a small village on the south coast of Cork, during the bitterly cold winter of '96.

'Thank you, sir.'

'And if I'm not mistaken, the French calamity at Fishguard?'

Mullone smiled self-deprecatingly. 'I played a minor role, sir.'

A smaller French invasion fleet had stormed the Pembrokeshire coast in February '97, to which Mullone had managed to help defeat with the aid of local forces.

'Nonsense, I don't believe that for a moment. I have the utmost trust in your skills to find Black. You've got a natural talent for rooting out troublemakers. You've guile, tenacity and instinct. If anyone can find this black-hearted devil, then it's you.'

'Thank you for your kind estimation, sir.'

'Good. In the morning, I want you to take your men and head to New Ross. It's a town on the Kilkenny border, about forty miles west of Wexford.'

'Why New Ross, sir?' Mullone said cautiously, still thinking that he wasn't the right man for the job.

'I've received a letter from Colonel Robert Craufurd, who is the garrison commander of the town. Do you know the colonel?'

'I know of him, sir,' Mullone replied prudently. Bob Craufurd was said to be a difficult man and a strict disciplinarian, but a fine soldier nonetheless.

'He writes of a strange troop of cavalry outside the town. When they are questioned, they claim to be on an important mission from the government. There is no such standing. I've told him you're on your way.'

'Sounds rather odd, sir,' Mullone said suspiciously. 'Can we be clear on the matter of *modus operandi* if these fellows turn out to be Black and his irregulars?' Moore looked into the Irishman's eyes. 'Black and his men must be stopped. At all costs,' he rapped the table with his fingers. 'But he is to be apprehended alive! I want him to face a public trial. He must be made accountable for his crimes and punished in a court of law. The people need to see him brought to justice.'

'I understand.'

'God be with you, Lorn.'

'I hope He is, sir.' Mullone drank the last dregs of his tea before shaking hands with Moore and departing the room.

To hunt a killer for the sake of Ireland's future.

*

The first light of a new day blazed bright over County Wexford for a few seconds, lancing through the thin clouds like a glittering explosion.

A dawn mist hung between trees. Bark glistened. The air was already sticky, hazy and sparkled in the pooling mist that seemed to have washed away the stain and dust of the previous day. And yet, despite the dampness, it promised to be another beautiful summer's day in an otherwise wicked world.

And then the horsemen came.

They came out of the mist like creatures from a nightmare. They were dressed in the red finery of British Dragoon Guards, and the big horses thundered down the green tangle of sunken lanes with reckless abandonment. There were fifty of them, faces grim underneath black bicorn hats, and they cantered fast in pursuit of their prey.

The prey was in fact a man, who unknown to the troopers, had already negotiated his horse up the steep banks of the lane to lie concealed in the undergrowth's wild chaos. He watched them pass in a blur of horse, uniform and dust, waiting a few minutes until he was satisfied that he was safe, and then gently eased his horse up.

'There, there,' he said soothingly, patting its neck where the thick veins throbbed beneath the skin with large blackened calloused hands. He was a big man with broad shoulders, and a flat, hard face. The horse whinnied and jerked its head with fondness at his gentle touch.

He looked around. The patch of ground was covered in ferns and wood horsetails, skirted by ancient-looking trees with gnarly boughs. A red deer watched his movements, ears pricked, before bolting away. Hearing a soft trickle of water, he carefully negotiated up towards the high ground, feet snapping on old twigs and making a dull sound as his thighs brushed against the verdure. He reached the small bubbling stream, half-hidden by the ferns, and bent down to take a long drink. It was good and he cupped some for his horse. A blackbird sang its beautiful birdsong and a robin redbreast joined in; its call was louder despite its small stature. He pulled out a handful of corn from his long grey coat, and the horse munched noisily with big yellow teeth.

The man wiped sweat from his forehead when the corn was all gone, leaving husks on his skin, and yanked out a scrap of paper, which had an address on it. A slit of sunlight from the green canopy above dappled the clearing. He had risked his life to get this far, but the leader of the cavalry was a methodical and persistent bastard. One slip up, and the man knew he would be in loyalist hands and it would all be over. He had the address of a man who would help him, and now he just had to survive long enough to reach it.

Scurlock put the paper back in his pocket and followed the path through the woods to the town of New Ross where his brother, Pádraig and his son, Dónall would be waiting for him.

*

'Where exactly are we heading to, sir?' Sergeant Seán Cahill asked, before spitting a thick jet of chewing tobacco onto the roadside. His white breeches were spotted with spittle stains.

24

Mullone steered his horse around a charred shell of what appeared to have once been a mail coach. The rebels intercepted mail coaches and set them ablaze as a signal on the roads for the men to snatch up their pikes and green cockades, and meet at dedicated rendezvous points. The air was still and the horse's hooves kicked up dust, so the men and their mounts were grimy and dusty.

'New Ross, Seán,' he said, pulling at his neck-tie that seemed to choke him. 'We're to find this man, Colonel Black, and bring him back to the Castle.'

'Ah, that'll be nice,' Sergeant Cahill replied in his customary unbothered way. As usual Mullone was struck by the sergeant's ability to take everything in his stride, as though their hunt for a shadowy killer was just another adventure.

It was just after nine o'clock and the twenty-five-mile journey from Dublin had taken them three hours. They would have to rest properly soon, for the sake of their horses; having rode on and off for two days straight. Besides, the men were sore with chafed thighs and numb arses.

It was a beautiful June day. The sky was a brilliant corn-flower blue, speared by a dazzling and glittering sun. It had been the hottest May on record; certainly no one could remember a May that blisteringly hot, and now June too burned like an open kiln.

The dragoons made their way to the town across verdant fields and skirted great swathes of dark woodland. They discovered a moss-fringed stream where Mullone let the men fill their canteens and allowed the snorting horses a thirst-quenching drink before setting off again.

Tack and weaponry jangled and clinked and hoof beats thudded; those sounds were the only interruptions to the silence across the hazy fields.

Mullone gazed at the hedgerows, bright with flowers that edged along the wheel-rutted and hoof-churned road. A hare hopped onto the roadside a few yards away from the horsemen, then quickly disappeared back into tall grasses that were thick with catchfly, monkshood and corn cockle. Past the hedges, the warm morning sun seemed to hug the gentle fields. *Tintreach*, his grey stallion named Lightning in Gaelic, loped steadily, and he whispered soothing words into the beast's tall pricked ears. *Tintreach*, named because of the white lines that resembled sparks shooting from his hocks, was a sturdy horse and reliable as any trooper. It could also be stubborn and hot-tempered, which is why Mullone also nicknamed it *Tintrí*: Fiery-tempered.

25

'Good boy, *Tintrí*. Good boy.' He patted its neck and ran a hand through its mane. It whickered a contented reply.

There were some livestock being herded across a field and women and children planting seeds and picking early berries.

'They just carry on as if the uprising was somewhere else,' Cahill observed with a disdainful shake of his head. Like the rest of the dragoons, the peak of his helmet cast pools of shadow around his eyes.

'Why shouldn't they?' Mullone answered. 'They still need to eat, to feed their families and cattle, and make money at the markets.'

A tall woman, face partly obscured by a wide slouch hat and the hem of her skirts caked with mud, momentarily glanced up at the horsemen, and Cahill gave an appreciative grunt at her natural beauty.

The sergeant then began to whistle a tuneless rendition of The Rambling Labourer, which Mullone knew was also known as The Girl I left Behind Me. He stopped, face bright with sudden mirth, and then went serious. 'I know someone in New Ross who could be Black, sir. Yes, they could well be the one we're after.'

Mullone tore his gaze from the glorious landscape. 'Oh?' he said, with a raised eyebrow at the sergeant's dubious statement. The horses' hooves thumped dully in the still air.

'Aye, sir, I've been married to her for many years,' Cahill replied with a cackle. He was gap-toothed, small, but stocky and well-muscled and could outride, outshoot and outfight any man that Mullone knew.

'Is that right?' Mullone said with a straight face.

'Aye, sir,' Cahill insisted. 'She's a wee wicked witch, so she is. Mouth like a knife and that woman could talk the teeth out of a saw.'

'Marriage is a sacred virtue, Seán,' Mullone sounded disappointed.

'Aye, and so said the priest that married us,' Cahill replied with another cackle, 'and he was drunk as a lord.'

'You must have loved her once then?' Mullone said drily.

The veteran grinned. 'That's funny, because she says that too.'

'I see that Coveny has the beginnings of a black eye,' Mullone turned to the sergeant. 'Do you know anything about that?'

Cahill shrugged. 'Well, sir, you see that Trooper Coveny has a rare taste for the ladies, and when he's had a few drops of whiskey in him, he becomes very amorous. I was lucky enough to find him in the early hours before he caused any mischief.'

'So how did he get the black eye?'

'He took a tumble on the path back to his quarters, sir,' Cahill said innocently. 'A very nasty path in the dark. Especially treacherous when your mind is swimming with the local moonshine.'

'It was lucky you were there to help him.'

'Aye, sir. A proper blessing, so it was.'

'Coveny needs to be more careful, Seán,' Mullone said.

'Oh, he knows that now, sir. Drink is a curse, I told him. It makes you fight with your good neighbour. It makes you shoot at your landlord and as sure as there is a God, it makes you miss him. I'll tell Coveny that you asked after him, sir.' He gave the major a surreptitious grin at the levity, before hawking and spitting a thick gobbet of green-brown phlegm over the hedgerow.

Mullone knew full well that Cahill had dragged the trooper away before he had made a nuisance of himself in the inn last night that Moore had established for billeting, and for punishment had thumped him. Mullone would let any further recriminations pass, because Cahill was a good sergeant who kept the men in order.

Mullone was the senior officer and the only other subaltern that the regiment now possessed was Lieutenant Michael McBride, who trotted silently behind the two men. Mullone recognised that his young lieutenant had sympathies with the rebel cause, but he was content to leave him alone respecting another man's opinions. Besides, McBride was no threat; he did not openly praise the insurrection, or was swept away with French Revolutionary ideals. He had proved himself an able officer and the men liked him.

'We're just about to come to the town of Naas, sir,' McBride said, crinkled map in hand. 'It's been in all the papers. Utter bloodshed.'

'I heard about it,' Mullone replied to his hollow-cheeked junior officer. A force of rebels, a thousand strong, stormed the town, but were defeated by cannons that blasted grapeshot into their packed ranks. Unable to outflank the soldiers, the insurgents retreated outside and lost a great deal of men to a vengeful troop of sabre-armed cavalry. 'If the Militia hadn't brought up the guns, we'd have lost the town.'

'That's not what I meant, sir,' McBride answered respectfully, but somehow managed to convey that the major's answer was unsatisfactory.

'I know what you implied, Michael,' Mullone said, snapping his head around to address the lieutenant. 'What about Prosperous? The Militia were hacked to death in their beds. One of the officers was younger than your brother Hugh.'

'Repression brings out the worst in people, sir,' McBride muttered, bright sunlight reflected in his spectacles.

Mullone understood that perhaps he had been wrong about him. He would try to talk to him and get the truth out once and for all. If he confessed to being a rebel partisan, then he would be expelled from the regiment in secret in case any rank and file harboured thoughts of mutiny.

'The fields look so charming and green,' Cahill interrupted. 'It is only when you ride through them that you realise they're covered in shit.'

Mullone considered that Cahill understood McBride's feelings too. 'I think you'd better save your breath, Lieutenant. We've still a way to go yet and trouble may interfere with our mission.'

McBride could not meet his gaze, or bring himself to vent his views, and so he stared back at the map.

'What do we do if we come across trouble, sir?' Cahill asked, slapping at a fly. 'As much as I enjoy giving the rebel turds a walloping, it should be down to the Militia to keep the buggers in check.'

'They are doing their job,' Mullone said, glancing at a free-standing Celtic Cross that had once been a prominent feature beside the road, but was now strangled with weeds, besieged with dark moss and deeply pitted with age.

'If you call plundering, fighting and torture work, sir.'

'You don't have much faith in the peace talks then, Seán?'

'No, sir. There's more chance of me taking holy orders and becoming the Pope than there is of peace,' Cahill replied. 'The negotiations that spout from the politicians mouths are nothing but wet farts.'

Mullone chuckled.

'Some men don't want peace,' McBride uttered before he could stop himself.

Mullone scratched at an insect bite on his neck. 'Aye, that's true.'

'People just like Colonel Black, sir,' Cahill muttered. 'He's poked the shit with his sword and raised a stink. So what do we do if there's trouble?'

But then before anyone could answer, a musket shot echoed from the vicinity of Naas and the sergeant grinned like a fed fox.

Mullone closed his eyes. 'Too late.'

*

28

'Where are the pikes, croppie!' a gravel-voiced sergeant said, as he hauled a man up towards his grizzled face. The man gasped and tried to wrench himself free, but the sergeant was a powerful man, and he could not force himself away.

'There are no weapons here,' he said in desperation, 'not since the fight.'

'You lying croppie bastard!' the sergeant replied and thumped the man with his right fist. 'Do you take me for an idiot? There was a copse here five days ago, and someone has felled the trees to make the pike shafts.'

'No!'

The sergeant was a dark-eyed bullock of a man, and his chin was blue-black with a week's stubble. He took the man over to where the redcoats had boiled up a foul liquid in a squat cauldron above a fire. The town's square was packed with civilians, soldiers and horses. A woman screamed as she was being dragged by her hair away from her house. A dog was barking madly. A musket banged and two mounted officers ordered a platoon of redcoats into the tavern where more men were pushed and hauled out.

A young officer with a cleft chin emerged from the inn with the angry landlord in tow. A young boy, with a running sore on his cheek, darted out of the way. 'This fellow claims that none of the ringleaders have come back since the fight, sir,' he said to an observing grey-haired officer mounted on a well-groomed chestnut horse.

The single gold epaulette on his right shoulder indicated the older officer was a captain, and he urged his mount forwards with a touch of his steel spurs at its flanks.

'Where's the priest?' he bawled, through a bushy gun metal-grey moustache.

The innkeeper, who had thick side-whiskers and receding hair, shrugged.

'We are after a priest who calls himself Father Keay,' the captain revealed. 'Red hair, beard to match and he carries a sword. I know he was one of the ringleaders who led the attack on our outposts here, and I know he was seen at Ballitore two days ago and here again yesterday. Now where is he?'

'I don't know of that priest,' the innkeeper replied. 'I see lots of new folk on the roads. Some stable their horses and leave the next day, but I don't know of that man, sir. I've not seen him here.'

The captain stared into the man's fearful eyes and he knew he was telling the truth. But someone here had seen the priest, or knew of him, and this man would serve as an example to the onlookers.

'Sergeant Nolan.'

'Sir?' the dark-eyed soldier answered.

'Bind this man and take him to the cauldron. Let's see if the hot tar loosens some tongues around here.'

Nolan grinned wickedly. 'My pleasure, sir.'

The wretched man was dragged away and taken to where the black liquid bubbled and spat. The landlord, a rope-maker and a wheelwright had their hands bound behind their backs and positioned on their knees by a Militia private each. Nolan then began the terrible torture known as 'pitch-capping'. He ladled hot pitch into three waxed paper caps and, as the men tried to resist their captors, Nolan forced a cap onto each of their heads. They screamed; heads twisted in agony, tears rolled down their cheeks. Nolan stood grinning as the sticky liquid simmered and cooled upon their crowns.

A woman, possibly one of the victim's wives, screeched for clemency, but she was ignored and fell weeping to the ground. An old man, white-bearded and skeletal, tried to push past the redcoats to help the three kneeling victims, but was knocked down and kicked into unconsciousness.

A moment later, amidst the tormented shrieking, Nolan stooped over the wriggling men and ripped off the caps; tearing away hair and skin in the process. Their crowns were blistered and raw and would leave them disfigured like victims of scalping.

'Now bring me the shears,' Nolan said in a harsh, throaty voice. A grinning private brought him a pair of crude scissors. 'This is what happens to lying croppie bastards,' he said using the moniker that had been first given to Irish rebels who had cropped their hair in the French Revolutionary style in protest at the aristocratic long hair and wigs. Now it was now applied to all suspects of the rebellion. The scissors made short work of the remaining stubs of hair. Nolan drew blood as he sheared the heads, clipping the top of the wheelwright's ear, and raking the sore skin without deliberation.

'Bring the innkeeper's daughter forward,' the captain demanded, 'and we'll see if that will loosen some tongues.' The officer behind him, a lieutenant with brown crooked teeth and warts on his chin, grinned.

'What's going on here?' a voice bellowed with such irrefutable authority that the lieutenant twisted in his saddle, saluted immediately.

The moustached captain looked across the road, scowling at the interruption. 'Who the devil are you?' he asked with much intended impudence. He saw a blond-haired officer with a red sweat-stained face and perhaps forty dragoons. They wore Tarleton crested helmets with a turban in the same grass green as their facings. The men looked like a Yeomanry unit, who, in the captain's mind, were not proper soldiers. However, the horsemen were hard-faced, grim and looked as though they had honed their skills in battle.

'Major Lorn Mullone of Lord Lovell's Dragoons,' replied the officer who trotted towards him. His plume bobbled in motion to the horse's stride. 'Who are you, sir?' he asked coldly.

'Captain Torrington.'

Mullone stared at the pale yellow facings on the men's coats. 'Ennis Torrington of the North Wicklow County Militia?'

Torrington seemed to brighten up as his reputation was evident. 'Yes,' he offered a slight bow in the saddle.

'Lieutenant James Foote, sir,' said the brown-toothed officer.

'Be quiet and leave us,' Mullone snapped and the lieutenant's gaze swivelled to his captain as though seeking approval. Mullone leaned in closer. 'Are your ears full of straw, boy? I ordered you to leave.'

Torrington twitched as the lieutenant made a feeble departure.

Mullone looked past him and shook his head at the mayhem beyond. He could see the fear in the people's eyes.

'What's that ungodly smell, sir?' asked Cahill, sniffing like a hog.

'Pitch-capping, Seán.'

'Sweet Jesus,' the sergeant crossed himself at the stench of burnt flesh.

'I've seen far worse than this,' Mullone said. 'I've seen them sprinkle gunpowder, or soak the pitch in turpentine first, and then set the caps alight.'

'It's certainly an effective method,' Torrington replied with apparent satisfaction. 'I also use the travelling gallows when I can,' he pointed at a horrid contraption next to two wagons. It had two solid wheels and two frames that resembled a simple farm cart but up-ended. A thick strip of rope was nailed between the frames so that a noosed prisoner could be lynched on the spot. Two redcoats would steady the frames and up to four privates would pull on the rope, thus pulling the bound man up over the nailed rope to slowly choke until he confessed. 'A throttling sets a good example, but it's the hot tar that everyone fears. It's the tried and tested method to get results.'

31

Mullone said nothing. Instead, he seemed preoccupied with the hanging device, for his eyes glassed over, staring at it in deep thought. 'It's utterly barbaric.'

Torrington sniffed derisively as though he found the major weak. 'I know that trees were cut down to make pike shafts and the pike heads will be buried under the gardens, or in false graves and walls, or tucked up in whores' filthy skirts.' He gave Mullone a foul grin to make him uncomfortable. 'I'll dig up the gardens, I'll pull down walls, and I'll force the whores' legs wider apart to inspect their notches. I will find the weapons. I can assure you of that.'

'What about simply talking to the people?'

Torrington scoffed. 'What use is that? Might as well converse with animals, or the moon. You can accomplish more with a stout shillelagh than you can with words.'

'"*For all they that take the sword, shall perish with the sword*",' Mullone recited the parable causing the captain to scowl at him. 'Torrington, just because there are one or two bad apples in the crop, it doesn't mean the whole orchard is rotten.'

Torrington gave a guttural grunt of amusement. 'You men from the Castle are as soft as fresh butter.'

'We're certainly more compassionate.'

The captain wrinkled his face, pulled out a canteen of brandy and guzzled it back without offering any to Mullone. 'Life does not exist without authority,' he said, wiping the spirit from the ends of his drooping moustache. 'Out here it is men like me that give the government its power. I keep the peace and punish the guilty. The government in return pays me. I am rather shocked at your naivety on the matter.'

'The word, Torrington, when you address me,' Mullone said menacingly, 'is "sir".'

Anger sparked in the captain's eyes, but he bit his lip at whatever he was about to quickly retort. 'Sir,' he said with displeasure.

Mullone smiled at him triumphantly.

Cahill watched Nolan pull an attractive woman from the crowd towards the bubbling cauldron. Her hands were tied. He clicked his horse forward.

'Now, my pretty one, hold still while I put this nice cap on you,' Nolan said, as the woman screamed and begged him to stop.

'Da! Help me!'

Nolan chortled. 'Your da's not in a position to help you.'

32

A private handed Nolan the cap, but suddenly a horse knocked him flat over and the sergeant craned his neck up to look into a weather-hewn face that marked the cavalryman as a seasoned campaigner. 'Who the hell are you?'

'A man who's about to beat the seven casks of shit out of you,' replied Cahill. 'Let the pretty lady go,' he said, dismounting.

The prone redcoat tried to get to his feet, but Cahill kicked him in the face. Nolan pushed the woman to the ground and reached for the sword hanging at his left hip.

'If you draw that, you bastard,' Cahill warned him, 'I'll kill you before you can scratch your shrivelled prick with it.'

Nolan brayed as the blade rasped free. 'I'll use your stinking corpse for shooting practice after I spill your rotten guts.'

'Are you going to permit this, Major?' Torrington reeled. 'I won't have my men made fools of.'

Mullone patted *Tintreach's* sweat-lathered neck, his eyes jumping up to Cahill. 'My sergeant is only defending himself, Torrington,' he said icily, 'or do you have no stomach to watch when fighting someone who is not helpless and unarmed?'

Torrington's shoulders went taut. 'Damn you,' he murmured.

'I will not be a party to torture,' Mullone said. 'There is rarely any reason to torture women.'

'They can tell me something that may help with my enquiries.'

Mullone shot Torrington a look of disdain. 'Do you care about nothing?'

'I care about apprehending rebels.'

Nolan lunged and whipped the dull iron sword up towards his foe's face, but Cahill dodged the attack with fluid ease and let out a laugh. He had not drawn his own blade yet.

'Christ on His bloody cross, no wonder the croppies have got you running around in circles.'

'A friend to them, are you?' Nolan sneered, slashing again.

'Better them than you,' Cahill retorted.

'I've killed enough of 'em,' Nolan boasted to which Cahill scoffed at the man's hyperbole. Nolan growled. 'So what's one that wears a redcoat worth? I wouldn't wipe my arse on your stinking rags!'

The crowd, swollen by people who had come from their houses, cheered Cahill, and he returned their appreciative shouts with a wave.

'Always the entertainer,' Mullone muttered.

Nolan grunted as he feinted left, cut right and was pleasantly surprised to slice open Cahill's left forearm. He laughed at Cahill's look of indignation and surprise.

Cahill staggered backwards as though he had resigned himself to early defeat and Nolan roared as he sprang forward. But it was all a feint and Cahill kicked him hard between the legs. Nolan collapsed. Cahill punched him in the throat and slapped the sword out of his hands. Then he grabbed Nolan by his powdered hair and ran him over to the simmering cauldron.

'No!' Nolan gasped and although he was taller and bulkier than Cahill, he did not possess his strength. Cahill tipped him over the cauldron's rim pushing his face closer to the steaming liquid. Nolan gripped the rim with his bare hands and screamed as his fingers and palms were seared.

'Stop this at once!' Torrington ordered Cahill, ignoring Mullone.

Cahill expected to be dragged off by now, but no one came to Nolan's aid, which proved that he was not liked by his own men. A man from the crowd swore at the Militia. Their faces stirred with nervousness and remained inactive even when one member of the crowd threw stones at them.

Nolan attempted one final push to break free, but Cahill punched him in the kidneys and banged his head hard against the cauldron's thick rim, which rang like a bell. His screams were cut off as his face plunged into the scolding liquid. Cahill held him there with his iron-muscled arms until Mullone ordered him to let him go.

'That's enough, Seán.'

'Aye, sir,' Cahill obeyed and Nolan dropped to the ground like a heavy stone tumbled into a well, writhing in agony, with smoke coming from the pits of his boiled eyes and shrivelled nose. Cahill blew the horrid stench away from his face. He cut the woman's bonds with a knife, mounted his horse and waved to the woman, who in turn blew him a kiss.

'Are you all right?' Mullone asked his friend as he trotted back.

'Aye, sir. Blade just cut the sleeve.'

'I'll have you cashiered for this!' Torrington said furiously.

Mullone said nothing for a moment, but then seemed unable to control the anger, his blood up. 'You'll do not such thing, sir! I know who you are! You should be patrolling Wicklow, not Kildare. What are you doing this far north?'

'I was ordered here, Major,' Torrington replied as though he found the questions insulting.

'By whose authority?'

'I have written papers.'

'From who, damn you?'

'General Sir Ralph Dundas.' The Militia captain pulled out the said papers from inside his jacket. 'He has exercised caution and consolidated my men with Militia from Kildare and Queens County in rounding up a known ringleader called Father Keay. A villainous priest who preaches seditious sermons. He was seen here yesterday.' He handed the orders to Mullone who read them eagerly.

Sir Ralph, the district commander, had signed the papers and there was nothing Mullone could do to stop Torrington's movements. But there were questions that he could certainly answer.

'You were recently acquainted with a certain person in Wicklow. Is that correct?'

Torrington snorted. 'Colonel Black?'

'Aye.'

'Has the army gone soft and sent you to round him up?'

Mullone's face was taut. 'I asked you a question.'

'And I asked you one,' Torrington said obstinately. 'Don't try to play games with me, Major. I was killing the king's enemies when you were still sucking your mother's teats. When I wasn't employed by His Majesty, I was killing enemies in the name of William, Prince of Orange. Now, are you after Black?'

Mullone bit his lower lip, sighed and went against his better judgement. 'That is my assignment,' he replied levelly, thrusting the papers back.

Torrington ordered his company to form up. 'I met the man south of a village called Shillelagh when we caught cattle-boats loaded with arms as they made their way north to Hacketstown,' he revealed. The hanging contraption was noisily loaded onto one of the carts with the seriously injured Nolan. 'I know nothing else about Black.'

'Could you describe him?'

Torrington played with the ends of his moustache. 'Black hair, blue eyes, and not loquacious, but when he did, he was well-spoken like a true gentleman.'

The one thing Mullone had learned from his years of campaigning was that there was nothing gentlemanly about war. Nothing whatsoever.

'How many men did he have with him?'

'Fifty,' Torrington hazarded a guess.

'Dragoons?'

'Aye.'

'Anything else you can tell me about him?'

'I never caught his first name if that's what you're asking for,' Torrington mocked. 'As I said, he wasn't very talkative. He asked me to assist him in dealing with some of the rebel scum.'

'Did he say what he was doing?'

Torrington studied Mullone for a moment. 'No, he did not. But...'

'But what?'

'I overhead him talking to his captain about losing two of his men in the mountains near Oldbridge.' Torrington took off his bicorn hat, which had left a greasy rim-mark in his hair, and scratched. 'Something about pursuing a blacksmith who had some dealings with Father Keay, the priest I'm after. Maybe the smith had something to do with the deaths of Black's men?' He shrugged and rammed the hat back on. 'I don't know.'

'Is that all?'

'Aye.'

'A cavalry troop been spotted near New Ross,' Mullone said. 'I think it's Black. Do you know why he would travel all that way there?'

'To find the blacksmith?' Torrington sounded exasperated. 'Or the priest?' He pinched the bridge of his nose as though the conversation was testing his patience. 'Whatever Black is doing, Major,' he said with a crooked smile, 'it's for the better of Ireland.'

'What?' Mullone said incredulously.

'Death to all traitors of the king. Is that not what Pitt wants? I wouldn't hand him over for a thousand guineas.'

Mullone gave that comment the look it deserved before leaving.

'Jesus and all the saints,' Cahill remarked, as he reined in on the grassy crest of Corbet Hill, overlooking the towering walls of New Ross.

The town was pretty; set in a picturesque location on the banks of the River Barrow that was bursting with plump cargo boats, gun boats and skiffs. Mullone could see the quay where a long wooden bridge spanned over the glassy, smoke-coloured river to the neighbouring port-town of Rosbercon. New Ross was protected by an imposing semi-circular wall that included five great gates and nine flanking towers. If there ever was a siege; it appeared to be hard-pressed to break down those unsullied defences.

Cahill whistled. 'That'd be a tough bastard to storm.'

'Thankfully, we won't have to,' Mullone replied.

But as Mullone followed the winding grassy track down the precipitous hill, he noticed that the mossy walls and turrets were crumbling, and the gates were defenceless. He also realised Corbet's Hill dominated the entire area, so that any enemies could see where the defenders were placed in any part of the town; almost a bird's-eye view. There was nowhere to conceal the troops unless kept hidden in the small houses. He wondered why no redcoats garrisoned the hill and no artillery batteries were emplaced to guard the roads. Surely that was key in the defence of the town?

About a hundred labourers, supervised by an officer, were digging trenches outside the most easterly gate. Mullone saw that his scarlet coat had two gold epaulettes revealing his rank was either a major, a lieutenant-colonel, or a colonel. He looked up, hearing the hoof beats and watched their arrival with suspicion.

'Major Mullone, sir,' he said, saluting, having an inkling that he was the officer, Moore had asked him to report to. 'Lord Lovell's Dragoons.'

The officer replied the salute almost guardedly. He was a small man with a thin face, in his mid-thirties and the sight of the horseman seemed to bother him, for he was silent for a moment as he studied faces, equipment and horse furniture.

'Where are you from?' he asked, sizing Mullone up with a look of irritation laced with bewilderment. His accent betrayed that he was Scottish.

'Colonel Moore sent me from Dublin, sir,' Mullone replied. 'Would you be Colonel Craufurd?'

'I am,' he said, scowling. 'Moore wrote to me to say he was sending a government man. He also said you'd arrive two days ago. I assumed you were dead. What the devil kept you, Major? Got lost?'

'Apologies, sir. Business in Ulster,' Mullone said as carefully as he dared.

Craufurd gave an imperceptible nod at the uninformative reply. 'There's always business in Ulster,' he snapped. 'You can stable your horses at the old blacksmith's on Neville Street.' He pointed down the cramped road that was packed with a Militia regiment marching north towards where the spire of an abbey loomed above thatched roofs.

'Take the first left. You'll find the smithy near the barracks on Michaels Lane. Major-General Johnson commands this city. I will inform him of your arrival. He'll want to know why. Not sure why Moore would send us more cavalry,' he said ungratefully. 'No bloody good against pikes. What we need is infantry and guns. Do your men know how to fight?'

'Yes, sir.'

'Good. Dinner at eight at the Quayhouse Inn.' He said the last sentence as a command rather than an invitation.

'Thank you, sir.'

'Ignore the band of fools with the firearms inside the gate; the eldest sons of prominent land owners. Keen, but no common sense of their generation. Don't let me keep you,' Craufurd dismissed him to supervise the placements of two six-pounders near the entryway, which Mullone heard him call Three Bullet Gate. It had been widened with pickaxes and chisels to allow two lanes of wagons and carts to pass through it.

A hail of pistol and carbine fire shredded the air as young men on horseback discharged their weapons skyward. They whooped and laughed. They were watched by a unit of blue-coated horsemen with very grave expressions. Mullone shot the commander a look of pity.

'Idiots,' Lieutenant McBride muttered at the youths in their wealthy clothes.

'They just need a good thrashing with a strip of birch,' Cahill replied. 'I'd do it for nothing.'

Mullone led his men on; the horses' hooves were loud on the cobbled street that was stained with horse urine and dung. A lieutenant marching a platoon of men towards the gate saluted Mullone. A woman looked down on them through a window as they trotted past. Cahill looked up, saw her and waved. She shot him a withering look, made the sign of the cross, and went back inside.

'You've got that effect on most people, Sergeant,' Mullone said.

'That's the wife, sir,' Cahill said and cackled. He took a lungful of dung-filled air. 'Home sweet home.'

'She reminds me of my girl,' said Corporal Brennan, a long clay pipe clamped between his teeth.

'Jesus. How so?' Cahill raised an eyebrow.

'Feisty-looking, Sergeant,' Brennan said with a wink. He was nicknamed Black-Eyed Brennan, for his eyes were like polished orbs of jet. He blew a large pall of pungent smoke into the air above him. 'My Nora took care of herself when the croppies tried to take Clondalkin.

One tried to have his wicked way with her, but he never saw the knife she used to geld him with.' The dark-eyed corporal laughed. 'Gelded him like a pig. Aye, a pig! She's a lovely wee thing.'

'And maybe one day she'll cut out your tongue and do us all a goddamn favour,' Cahill replied dryly.

Brennan looked wounded. 'Now where would you be without my heart-warming stories, Sergeant?'

'Happy,' Cahill remarked with gap-toothed grin. A woman was walking up the road carrying a basket of bread and the sergeant whistled. 'Now that's a fine form!'

'She can shine my privy member anytime,' Coveny sniggered and the woman blushed.

'Quiet back there,' Mullone's voice shattered the gales of laughter.

'Some fine ale and a soft bed will do me tonight,' a pox-scarred trooper named O'Shea said, rubbing his sore behind.

'Never mind that,' Cahill grumbled. 'I want some decent hot food for a change. No more salt beef and hard bread.'

A boy and two girls played in the street ahead of the dragoons and their mother dashed out of her thatched home, clutching all three in her arms, before taking them inside. The boy broke free and gave Mullone a salute. The major smiled, and happily returned the greeting.

'They say the people of New Ross are very loyal to the king,' McBride said, as they passed a row of simple wooden houses where a Union Flag had been crudely etched into one of the beams.

'More loyal than you Dubliners, sir,' Cahill replied proudly.

Mullone said nothing, because as they rounded the street, something caught his eye. A corpse was hanging from one of the street lamps opposite the barracks. He was long dead, and as they trotted closer, Mullone could see a strip of parchment was tied around his neck. Remnants of clothes hung ragged from the yellowed bones.

Cahill leaned in. '"A just end to a traitor",' he read out aloud. He stared at the cadaver and grunted in disgust. 'Got what he deserved. Bugger was a turncoat,' he pointed a dirty finger at the tattered coat that was turned inside to show the mark of dishonour.

Traitor.

Mullone knuckled his forehead. The image of the young man swinging from a gallows pierced his vision again. It was too much for him. He turned away, a sourness showing on his usually affable face.

'Move on,' he barked, tugging savagely on *Tintreach's* reins.

It was beginning to have an effect. The past was plaguing him. Mullone had to tell someone soon. Cahill would be the first to know.

But for now his mission was his only purpose. He was also painfully aware that the horses needed a proper rest; he was tired and saddle-sore, and would need to freshen up for tonight to dine in unfamiliar company. He groaned, thinking of the small talk and, if Craufurd was the martinet he was renowned for being, tonight could be even more draining than the long journey from Ulster.

In the morning he would ride out to find Black and complete his mission.

For Moore had sent a killer to catch a killer.

In the early hours of the morning, Mullone returned to his billet which was a spacious airy room in the Customs House overlooking the quay. His head was swimming with claret and his belly aching from rich sumptuous food that was served on best china. He had eaten a delicious stew, a breast of mutton and wolfed down delicious sugared cakes for afters. The officers had then smoked cigars, drank brandy, talked about the rebellion and shared news from all corners of the country.

Cahill and the other men had been content to drink ale, eat oysters, salt-beef and oatcakes. They were not permitted to leave the smithy. Mullone did not want any of them to get drunk and aggravate the townsfolk. Craufurd would be on him like a terrier on a rat.

General Henry Johnson turned out to be an energetic, pleasant man of fifty with a fleshy face and generous mouth. He had fought with Cornwallis against the Americans and was pleased to find that Mullone had also fought there and wanted to know more of his military background, much to Mullone's chagrin for he disliked talking about that particular conflict. Craufurd was present, as well as a host of Militia officers from Kildare, Donegal and Lord Mountjoy. Luke Gardiner, Viscount Mountjoy was a colonel of a Dublin Militia regiment, and had entered the town ahead of his marching column, two artillery pieces and a Scottish mounted Fencible regiment, to the excited cheers, waves and whistles of the townsfolk.

Morale, Johnson pompously exclaimed, was extremely high and Lord Mountjoy said he was honoured to be present.

'God, will let us prevail,' he said piously.

'I hope He will, sir,' Mullone said.

40

Lord Mountjoy thought he was being mocked. His head spun to fix a drilling stare at the major. 'Do you believe in God, sir?'

Mullone paused before speaking. 'There are times when I believe in nothing more than a loaded carbine and a newly-honed blade, sir. But to answer your question, yes, I do.'

Mountjoy pursed his lips. 'Good,' he said curtly and decided not to press Mullone any further. He turned to Johnson. 'The good Lord will protect us behind these stout walls. God is our refuge and our strength from any attack.'

'An imminent attack,' Johnson commented to the dozen or more men.

A Militia captain, brandy in hand, seemed to stagger with the threat. 'I thought we had a week at least, sir?'

Johnson shook his head vehemently. 'I wish that were so. Thousands of insurgents have reached Carrickbyrne Hill.' Carrickbyrne was ten miles to the west, a day's march away. 'They've had the audacity to request that I surrender the town.'

The Militia captain's neck convulsed as he swallowed quickly. 'God preserve us!'

'Be quiet,' Craufurd admonished him.

'They say that only by surrendering will it save the town from rapine and plunder to the ruin of the innocent,' Johnson continued, and gave a small ironic laugh. 'They came under a flag of truce. So I allowed the messenger to leave with a firm and unequivocal 'no'.'

'And damn their nerve, sir,' Craufurd rose a glass to him.

Johnson paused and looked serious. 'In truth, I've lost all communication with Captain Tait and his men at Scullabogue. Alas, I do not have accurate numbers. A thousand have been spotted north crossing the River Nore, so I have placed gunboats to watch the estuary for movement and as many men as I can spare to watch the roads, hills and outer villages.'

'How many rebels were counted at Carrickbyrne, sir?' Mullone enquired.

Johnson cleared his throat and sipped rich claret before answering. 'Between fifteen and twenty thousand.'

The room went deathly silent. One of the long candles popped and uniform wearing servants returned with more port and claret.

Mullone imagined the hordes of pikemen storming through the gates, the lightly-numbered red-coated lines firing into them, volley

41

after volley. It would take nerves of steel to stand firm against such a horde.

'Confirmed, sir?' Mullone asked.

Johnson chewed the inside of a cheek. 'Fairly mixed reports, but there you have it.'

It was dispiriting to know the enemy possibly numbered ten times their own number, but Craufurd looked calm and a couple of the officers were staring at him for inspiration.

'Our men will beat them,' the small colonel said with easy confidence. 'I have no other convictions on the matter. Disciplined troops will always beat an untrained mob. No matter how many of them there are.'

'Agreed!' replied a captain of a blue-coated Yeomanry attachment. He was ruddy-faced with raised veins on his cheeks and nose. 'They won't stand.'

'There will be women and children in the rabble,' said another, a young man, barely into his twenties, but swayed with an air of confidence that Mullone knew immediately was born of wealth and privilege. 'You can't include them in that number who can fight.'

'Agreed,' Craufurd said, his mouth pressed into a hard line.

The officer turned to the Scotsmen. 'What you need is to funnel the rest into the streets where there will be no hope of getting out alive. Only that way will we win.'

'Don't begin to tell me what to do,' Craufurd growled. 'Leave the strategies to those with merit, and not their parents' money.'

The young officer, seemingly unconcerned by the retort, turned to his companions with a smile and a shrug.

Johnson turned to Mullone. 'I am aware of your duties, but will you stay and fight with us, Major?' he asked, and the rest of the officers waited eagerly for Mullone's answer. 'You command a troop, I know, but we could use the help of your rogues. What do you say?'

Mullone sipped claret. Truthfully, he did not want to stay and help defend the town. He had a mission to complete, an order from the Viceroy himself. However, he was a soldier at heart, and had fought for king and country for over thirty years.

'Of course, sir,' he said.

Johnson slapped his shoulder in joy. 'Capital, my dear friend, capital!'

'Concentrated volley fire and artillery support will see the insurgents off,' Craufurd commented further, and Mullone had felt he had said it to

42

counter any negative thoughts in the room – particularly to a handful of Militia officers who seemed to still be cowering from the reports. 'We'll teach them that insurrection buys the price of a grave. The others will melt away like snow fall on a hot spring day.'

Returning to his billet, Mullone had not felt Craufurd's confidence and now as he tugged off his boots, stripped naked and climbed wearily into his bed, he felt anxious and wanted nothing more to ride out with his men to hunt down Black.

It was stiflingly hot, even with the windows open, but Mullone still shivered. He pulled the covers closer and tried to sleep.

The next morning he was roused by a cheerful Sergeant Cahill who brought him breakfast of cooked eggs, bread and a pot of coffee. He dressed before venturing outside on the wooden balcony, taking in the crisp sweet air.

'Morning, sir,' Cahill said. 'A grand day, so it is.'

Mullone rubbed his eyes and groaned. 'It is?' An oxbow moon was visible above the tiled roof and the sunlight glimmered on the river's surface like a mirror.

'Yes, sir.'

Mullone had not slept well. He had dreamt of the town burning. Of his men cut down, of Black laughing and of the hanging man again.

'I have brought you some papers, sir,' Cahill said, wafting the creased papers under Mullone's nose. 'They're both three days old, but I know how you like to read them with your breakfast. There are some terrible stories that Black has struck again. A family including their three children nailed to a barn door whilst they were still alive. Not far from here too.'

Mullone fixed him a shocked look. 'Dear God!' He fought against a yawn and lost. 'I'll read them in a minute, Seán.'

'Late night, sir,' Cahill said with mock sympathy.

'Something like that,' Mullone shared a smile and watched the fishermen out on the water. He couldn't see the gunboats and reckoned they had left for the north in the night as Johnson had advised.

'You weren't still thinking about that deserter, were you?' Cahill asked.

Mullone rubbed his cheeks, and glanced awkwardly at him. 'What do you mean?'

43

Cahill shrugged. 'It's just that it's not the first time I've seen you bothered by a hanging corpse.' The sergeant leaned closer and Mullone smelt ale on his breath and stale pipe tobacco on his uniform. 'I never mentioned it before, but I've heard you mention the name Solomon under your breath a few times. Who is he, if you don't mind me asking, sir?'

Mullone drank some coffee and said nothing for a moment, as though the very thought of answering choked the breath from him.

'Solomon was my brother,' he said eventually. 'He was my twin and he died.'

'I'm sorry, sir,' Cahill suddenly regretted his enquiry.

Mullone sipped the coffee. 'We had enlisted together. When we were fighting the Americans he fell in love with a girl and deserted to the rebels to start a new life.'

'Oh,' the sergeant pursed his lips and blew a lungful of breath. 'Turned his coat for love, sir?'

'Yes.'

'And they killed him?'

'No,' Mullone said recalling the events. 'Solomon had run away to be with her and I had gone as far as I could with them before saying goodbye. I was angry and upset, because I couldn't change his mind. But he was happy and that's what all that mattered.' Mullone took a breath to cover the sadness. It had been sad to see Solomon leave, because they were very close. They had both been sent to Seville to study for priesthood, but had gone against their parent's wishes and decided to join the army for adventure. 'We were fighting Washington's army in Philadelphia when Solomon was caught trying to escape across the lines. He was hung as a traitor.'

Cahill softened his tone. 'Jesus, I'm sorry, sir.'

'It was twenty years ago,' Mullone said, 'but I can't stop thinking about him of late. I should have stopped him. People said he was weak, but do you know that he was actually the strong one? He left everything behind for love. I couldn't have done that. He knew what he wanted in life. I regret letting him go, in my dreams I cling onto him, but when I wake up, the truth hits me. It's as though I sent him to his doom.'

'It wasn't your fault, sir,' Cahill said loyally. 'Your brother knew what he was doing, he knew the risks. And ever since you've been beating yourself up over that?'

Mullone's eyes were riveted to the ripples in the swirling water below. 'Yes.'

'I think you need to let him go, sir. It's unhealthy to keep blaming yourself for something beyond your control.'

'I should have stopped him, Seán,' Mullone said, voice loud enough to startle two coots and moorhens that splashed away in alarm.

Cahill scratched the bristles on his chin. 'You weren't to know what would happen to him. We can't change the past, sir. No matter how wonderful it would be to do so.'

'I see him a lot now and I think he's trying to tell me something.'

Cahill's expression was as wrinkled as an old apple. 'Sir?'

'This,' Mullone said, holding out a hand. There was a small silver cross on a chain. He couldn't explain it, but it had something to do with it. After his brother's death, he had questioned his faith and walked a very rocky path for many years. At the beginning of the war against France, he started to look for salvation and now he reckoned that Solomon was telling him not to give up, to hold onto his faith. It would take some time, but he was healing slowly.

'Sir,' Cahill struggled to find the words. 'I...'

'It doesn't matter.' Mullone drank some coffee, feeling its richness stir life into his limbs. He noticed that the sergeant's left sleeve was crudely stitched up from the scuffle with Nolan. 'Our objective is to find Colonel Black.'

'The man's gotten under my skin like a burrowing tick,' Cahill said.

'I can understand that feeling, but we have to help defend the town. The general reckons that the rebels will be here soon. We can't abandon the women and children, so we stay and fight for them. Then, we'll get Black. Tell the men to get themselves ready.'

'Oh, I will, sir,' Cahill said. 'The lads will be looking forward to a wee scrap. Sir?'

'Yes?'

'Let's hope we break some skulls.'

*

It was late in the afternoon when the first rebels were spotted on Corbet Hill. Their arrival had been pre-empted by a huge dust cloud that whitened the sky. The picquets had returned back to the town before noon to say that the entire horizon, mile after mile, was darkening. The rebels were moving inexorably towards New Ross like the slow-flow of lava.

In truth, the rebel force was swollen with local villagers caught up in the fervour of the march. Thousands of women and children; the camp followers brought up the rear with carts full of oats, mutton, bedding, cooking pots, whiskey and beer. There were scores of home-stitched flags held aloft in proud hands. Drummers, flutists and pipers played their instruments. A few priests marched with their extended congregations, some armed with a myriad of hand weapons, others with simple crosses. The army pressed on towards New Ross like a terrifying pilgrimage, armed with musket and pike, and breathing nothing but vengeance and hatred.

That night Johnson convened a council of war in the Court House, knowing that his rebel counterpart, a man called John Fitzstephen, would be doing the same on the hilltop. He was a descendant of Norman nobility that had arrived in Ireland in the twelfth century. He was passionate, resourceful, beloved, and one of the United Irishman's most charismatic leaders.

Johnson's force of two thousand was mostly Militia with a few hundred regulars, Yeomanry and some cavalry. The horsemen would guard the bridge to Rosbercon, and some would act as aides. He was generally sure of success, but worried about defeat and the safety of his people. His main concern was that enthusiastic men would rush into battle without the true knowledge of its realities. Most recently a force of the North Cork Militia had been wiped out at a place called Oulart Hill, because the men had been eager to engage the enemy, and then were overwhelmed and ripped apart by pikes. Johnson could not afford any losses from over-zealous men.

'Any news, sir?' Mullone enquired. The assembled officers, some thirty or more men, seemed only interested in drinking the fine claret and smoking cigars. Craufurd would join the council later, having spent another day inspecting the defences.

'The latest reports say that the rebels haven't advanced anywhere else,' Johnson replied, as he sifted through the messages sent by commanders and loyal people outside of the town. 'The west is quiet too.'

'No news is good news,' chirped a captain of blue-coated dragoons.

Johnson winced.

'So they're all up there,' breathed the Militia captain that Craufurd had hitherto chided.

'They won't come,' said another officer, voice distorted and face swollen because of an infected tooth. He sipped whiskey in the vain hope of dulling the pain. 'They won't break our walls.'

'They have no firepower,' an artillery officer stroked the ends of his moustache. 'They can't breach the walls.'

But, in their thousands, they could easily swarm the gates, Mullone thought.

He stared down at the crude map of the city that the general had brought with him. It was difficult to make out the town in the spidery ink-drawn lines.

Johnson tapped New Ross with a finger. 'I suspect, along with Colonel Craufurd, that Fitzstephen will launch the first assault against the eastern defences,' he said, jabbing a digit at the Three Bullet Gate. 'I wonder if that priest is up there with him now.'

'Priest, sir?' Mullone asked.

'A clergyman called Keay,' Johnson scoffed.

Mullone's eyes narrowed, recalling the use of the name from Captain Torrington. 'Keay?' he repeated.

'Aye.'

'Do you know much about him, sir? In my lines of enquiry from the Castle, this priest has been mentioned before.'

Irritation flashed on the general's face for an instant, as though he didn't want to be interrupted with unimportant matters. He had a town to save. He rubbed his temples. There were bags of exhaustion under his eyes. 'He's believed to be leading the rebels in this area, and now jointly leads the mob. I don't know much else about him other than he's French, he's a damned upstart and that he is certainly no priest.'

Mullone knew instantly who this was.

De Marin.

Mullone brushed a hand through his hair, convinced even more that he was supposed to be here. De Marin was the French spy that he had tracked to Ulster, but he was more slippery than a wet rat in a gutter, and had somehow evaded capture. He had known of the Frenchman for a number of years and he was a true enemy. The last time he had seen him was at Fishguard and he had escaped before Mullone could apprehend him. And now he was here in Wexford, stirring discontent, and adding fuel to the fire. Mullone would do everything in his power to stop him.

'Sounds like De Marin, sir?' McBride whispered and Mullone gave a determined nod.

Johnson traced a finger down the town's wall, past Mary's Tower to the Priory Gate. He was sure that no rebels would be able to reach that part of the defences, or bother with it, so he would leave it virtually undefended. He positioned the main bulk of the troops and guns at various strong points; the Three Bullet Gate, the barracks, the marketplace, the street known as Main Guard which housed the gaol and the Court House, and finally, the oak bridge which provided a safe retreat out of the town. He would also leave a contingent of reserve troops at the North Gate where they could be brought forward to enforce any weak points or to defend any retreat.

Colonel Craufurd entered the room, calm and quiet, and Mullone studied his eyes that twinkled with intelligence and understanding. He poured himself a drink and edged over to the map whereby Johnson gave him a curt nod.

'The cavalry stays at the quay,' Johnson enforced his previous order to the assembled commanders. 'I don't want the horses clogging up the streets. They won't be able to charge the rebel pikes. Swords have proven useless. They'll be slaughtered, so they're to stay and guard the bridge.'

'Once you get past the point, won't it be easy?' Lord Mountjoy asked and a Militia officer grunted with agreement.

Craufurd, eyes bright in the light, smiled wolfishly. 'But getting past the point is the difficult bit.'

Lord Mountjoy gave a small laugh.

'Unless advised otherwise, the cavalry is to remain at the quay,' Johnson reinforced his order by thumping the table with his fists. 'No cavalry and no goddamn heroics.'

'My men can fight on foot, sir,' Mullone said without boasting and two officers at the back sneered at the remark. Craufurd scowled at them into silence. 'They're dragoons and they can fight as infantrymen.'

Johnson smiled crookedly. 'We'll make use of your carbines, Mullone.'

'Some of the townsfolk have requested to leave their homes, sir,' Craufurd said.

Johnson put up his hands in a sign of peace. 'Let them go, if they so wish.'

Craufurd scratched the blue-black stubble on his chin. 'I've removed the two-dozen 'glory-men', sir.' They were loyal volunteers who were just too hot-headed to have around, so they had been disarmed and confined to their homes for everyone's safety.

'Excellent. I'll not have anyone killed for misplaced bravery.'

'I've also enforced the probation of selling strong drink after nine in the evening on account of the pugilists. Two men have already been arrested for brawling.'

Johnson grunted in abhorrence. 'I may decide to close the liquor shops down until the threats have passed.'

Someone clapped his hands at the order, while another groaned.

'Very good, sir,' Craufurd rejoined, face expressionless. 'What do you want to do with the prisoners in the event of an assault?'

Johnson bit his lip. 'How many does the gaol hold at present?'

'Thirteen, sir,' replied an aide, who was a bylaw-man; an official of the manorial courts who enforced the courts orders. 'The figure includes that fellow who was arrested on Saturday as a potential rebel.'

'Ah. Yes, of course.'

'Who was that?' Mullone interjected, suspicion narrowing his face.

The aide, Coilin, was a rakish fellow whose coat seemed far too big for his frame. 'His name is Scurlock, sir, and he was caught trying to sneak into the town.'

'How do you know he's a rebel?'

'When he was apprehended, he was trying to digest a piece of paper, which was found to contain an old address of John Fitzstephen.'

Interesting, Mullone considered. 'Has he talked?' he asked, wondering if Johnson had allowed the use of torture to extract information, but had to be diplomatic in his approach. One wrong word and he would lose the general's co-operation.

Coilin shook his head. 'No, sir. I believe he was initially questioned on the day, but due to the reports of local insurgency, he remains locked away.'

'We need to have a word with him, sir,' McBride said.

'Agreed.'

'Perhaps this Scurlock may know Father Keay, sir?' Mullone turned to Johnson.

The general shrugged, but looked thoughtful.

'May I have your permission to ask him some questions in the morning?'

Mullone would also question him first thing about Black. Was this the man running from him? Mullone could only hope this trail goes somewhere.

'Of course you may, for what little use it may prove,' Johnson agreed and then added, 'however, if we are not attacked.' He sighed and looked at the officers intently, deciding that everything useful had been said. 'Gentlemen, you have your orders for tomorrow, and with any luck, we may be safe in New Ross for another day. Dear God I hope so.'

Mullone and McBride wandered out towards Three Bullet Gate where two regiments flanked the defences with two field guns, and yet more men waited in the trenches. They were quiet, solemn and Mullone stopped to stare up at the night sky where an orange radiance pulsed from the immense black mass of the hill to touch the stars. Campfires: the summit was ringed with so many of them. Mullone could hear voices coming from the glow, laughter, and the sound of a tambourine and a fiddle playing energetically.

'Sounds like they're already celebrating a victory,' Mullone remarked.

'Aye, sir,' McBride agreed. 'I don't blame them.'

Mullone turned to him. 'You'd rather be up there, wouldn't you, Michael?' he asked him without accusing him. He'd let Solomon turn his coat, why not his lieutenant? He stole a glance up to the summit where he was sure he could see figures, like pencil drawings, glare back. His brother had wanted a better life and to be happy, why couldn't McBride do the same too? 'Goddamn conscience,' Mullone muttered.

'Sir?'

Mullone adjusted his neck-tie. 'I almost wish I was up there with them.'

McBride's jaw lolled. 'Sir?'

'They're up there drinking, talking, laughing, sleeping and making love with their sweethearts under the stars, while we're down here quaking in the gutters, waiting for the moment they charge down for our blood.'

'Then, you agree, sir?'

'About what?'

McBride adjusted his spectacles. 'That we're *not* on the winning side.'

Mullone gave his young officer a look of sadness. 'Ah. I never said anything about that, now did I?'

McBride's top teeth worried his bottom lip and he awkwardly shuffled his boots. 'Do you think the prisoner knows anything about Black?'

'I don't know,' Mullone said thoughtfully, 'but we can only hope so. Perhaps the trail will lead us to Black.'

McBride bobbed his head. 'Do you think the garrison is ready?'

Mullone sucked in a breath of night-air. 'As ready as can be,' he said and smiled as a loud lingering laugh from the enemy camp hooted like a crazy owl. 'More so than the poor souls at Prosperous. Some say they deserved it. Their captain was a swine, probably like Torrington, but nothing justifies attacks like that. We're not all like that.' He turned to McBride. 'Go back to your lodgings and wait for me as per your orders. Try to get some sleep.'

'Thank you, sir.'

'Oh, and Michael?'

'Sir?'

'It may not seem it sometimes, but you are on the winning side.'

McBride gave the merest hint of a smile. 'Goodnight, sir,' he said, and walked away into the gloom of the alleys.

Mullone threw a searching look up at the hill. The garrison was ready. The muskets were primed, the guns loaded and the swords sharpened.

The soldiers were ready to fight.

The first thing Mullone knew of the attack was when a musket shot echoed out in the half-light of daybreak. Another musket banged, then another and suddenly hundreds of voices were roaring.

He had to give up his spacious quarters to Lord Mountjoy and had slept for three hours in one of the tiny houses that faced eastwards, overlooking the steep rise of Corbet Hill. He blinked and a shot out of bed as adrenaline coursed through his veins. Buckling his sword belt and risking a quick glance out of the dusty window, he could see thousands of rebels descending the hill in the dawn light, cerise with the blush of summer. It was as though someone had disturbed an ant nest. Bullets hummed and one hit the house with a splintering thud.

'Sergeant Cahill!' Mullone jumped the last flight of stairs to run outside into the street, slipping in horse dung, but managing to remain on his feet. He saw Cahill with a few of the men by a series of barricades cut from timber that some pioneers had lashed together in the night. 'Get the men to their positions,' Mullone said, peering through the gate where a fusillade of musket fire crackled outside the walls.

'Sir,' the sergeant barked and turned to a group of them at the rear. 'Get your arses here! Now! At the double! Jesus, you slow-witted buggers! I can piss faster than that! At the double! Trooper Coveny! You point the muzzle at the enemy, you useless bastard!'

Three riders cantered past them and Mullone saw that the leading horseman was General Johnson and the other two were his aides. Coilin saw Mullone and waved a hand and Mullone dipped his head. The general looked calm and rode out to where the two guns were emplaced by the gates and where the battle raged at the slopes. His horse was a fine steed with a diamond-shaped patch of pristine white against the roan coat and dark mane.

Mullone's dragoons cocked their carbines and slid the barrels over the barricade. A platoon from the Wexford Militia joined them and a white-haired major shook his hand fervently. He spoke with an accent so thick that Mullone had difficulty in understanding him. Mullone just grinned back, and the old major shook his head at the flaccid response, muttered something, and went down the line of his men, checking that bayonets had been fixed.

'He speaks the old language, sir,' Cahill said at Mullone's confusion. 'He's from Forth and Bargy. They speak a different tongue to the rest of us.'

The baronies of Forth and Bargy spoke in a dialect that was of mixed race. The language had grown over centuries from the Viking, Old English and Flemish settlers who had mixed with the Irish and stayed in Wexford.

'What did he say? Was it about me?'

Cahill's face split with a grin. 'You don't want to know, sir.'

Mullone pulled out his fob watch, it was just after five o'clock. Today was Wednesday and the fight to save the town had begun. He wondered if Black would go free if he was killed today? Would someone else catch him? Or would the wretch continue to slaughter? He suddenly became angry and told himself that he would live to see the monster apprehended even if this was the last thing he ever did on this mortal world. His fingers grasped the cross about his neck; Solomon's cross, and he did something that he hadn't done for a long time.

He said the Lord's Prayer.

The two field guns suddenly rumbled to life and Mullone was deafened as roundshot screamed over the forward redcoats to slash gaps in the enemies' front ranks. Mullone saw men punched backwards, pikes and hats snatched away as the two iron balls ploughed into them just like a terrible game of skittles.

'I can hear cattle!' Cahill said over the noise and sure enough a large herd of black cattle were being driven at the defences.

'They tried this at Enniscorthy last week!' Mullone told him. 'The cattle smashed the defences down, sending the garrison into confusion.'

Cahill grinned admiringly. 'Crafty buggers, sir!'

But at Enniscorthy the defenders had not entrenched the ground and the cattle, wide-eyed and stampeding, saw the bayonet-tipped men in the trenches and veered away. The leading redcoats in skirmish order shot at the men who tried to drive them on with staves.

'Fire!' The two battalions began firing by companies and the bullets tore into the rebels as they advanced against the first trench. Many fell, but there were thousands of them coming and the Militia were dangerously threatened with being overrun by the momentum of the advance. Mullone saw an officer flung backwards by a musket ball.

The sound of horses galloping along the cobbles made Johnson turn in his saddle. A score of blue-coated dragoons on chestnuts and greys reached the gates seeking glory with blades glimmering like rods of lightning held high.

'No!' Johnson screamed at them. 'Get back!'

'The damned fools!' Mullone snarled.

But the dragoons were not listening and thundered out to the enemy like avenging angels seeking glory. The horsemen's sabres were excellent for slashing and cutting, but the rebels were armed with ten-foot pikes and Mullone could see death in the long spears. Some were simple spear-like heads, others also had an axe blade like a halberd, but most had a curved blade below the main spearhead which could cut through a horseman's reins and straps, and hook men off their mounts. The horsemen charged straight into the packed lines and were immediately impaled by the block of pikemen. Men fell from their saddles and were soon set upon with clubs, billhooks and hammers. Others were stabbed in their saddles, or pulled down and mercilessly butchered with knives. An officer cleaved in a man's head with his sword, turned to bring the blade up through another enemy's chin to his nose, but a rebel with long black hair swung his pike into the horse's mouth, breaking its teeth. It tossed its head, shrieking, stamped its hooves and blood splattered the lines of pikemen. Whilst the officer struggled to control the beast, another rebel armed with a long handled axe chopped through his right leg at the thigh. He screamed as the limb fell away, and then a pike sliced up into his armpit to end his chance of glory. Within minutes all the dragoons were dead and the rebels advanced with a keening blood-cry.

'Gone! All of them!' Johnson thumped his fist hard into his thigh, face red with ire and frustration. 'A senseless waste of life!'

'A bit like this stinking war,' Corporal Brennan voiced. No one replied, which he took for assent.

Johnson twisted in his saddle to Coilin. 'I don't want any of our horse east of Neville Street or north of the barracks! Relay that message to Captain Buckley. I don't want his Fencibles anywhere in goddamn sight. The cavalry are part of our reserve.'

'Yes, sir.' The aide had to shout over a ripple of gunfire. He plugged an ear with a finger for the sound seemed to reverberate through his body.

'And Coilin, you tell him that if I do, I'll have him on a charge of insubordination.'

Coilin saluted, kicked his heels back and galloped down the street.

The cannons belched flame and the puffs of smoke momentarily blotted out Mullone's view of the battlefield. He heard the blue-coated artillery officer give the order to load with canister and realised that the rebels were closer than he imagined. Johnson then rode up to the gun teams, gave the hill a measured stare, and then ordered them batteries to be pulled back to the first barricades inside the gates. He could not believe his eyes as the rebels ignored the musketry from the walls to push back the forward posts and charge the trenches. The columns were soaking up the bullets like a sponge. Johnson muttered a prayer. It was too late for many of the redcoats. Some of the lucky ones managed to clamber out, but most were trapped. Rebels hacked with swords, clubbed with lumps of wood and speared with pikes.

'Back!' Johnson shouted at the two battalions outside the gates and immediately, his fine horse was shot in the head. The air misted crimson for a brief second. He kicked his heels out of the saddle and jumped free of the dying beast. 'Pull the men back to the secondary positions! Go! Go now!' he ordered, without breaking his nerve and the first Militia battalion shouldered their muskets and the files withdrew quickly like scalded fingers.

The remaining battalion continued firing their volleys towards the trenches as well as the light company men from the Kildare Militia who were firing from rooftops, walls and makeshift firing platforms. Red-coated bodies were stripped of cartridges, boots, shirts and anything the rebels could make use of. A lieutenant, barely seventeen, tried to crawl away and a woman cut his throat with a fish knife. A grenadier wearing a fur cap cried for his mother as men took it in turns to stab him to death as they passed. A group of musket armed rebels opened up on the battalion from the trench works and the bullets tore into the Militia's ranks. Men tumbled, bleeding and dying, their screams were drowned out by the savage salvos of musket, pistol, cannon and the crash of battle.

Johnson's remaining aide, seventeen years old and wearing a brown suit and an old-fashioned tricorn hat, brought up a spare mount. The general lifted himself into the saddle and cantered back past the barricade to assess the defences at the junction of Neville and Michaels' Street and at Bunnion Gate. Colonel Craufurd was in command of the detachments at Main Guard and he had two guns facing down the South Street and east towards the Barracks. If the rebels succeeded in driving in Johnson's defenders at the Three Bullet Gate, he reckoned that they would be stopped at Main Guard. *They would have to be*, he said to himself, for it was the heart of the town and if the heart was taken, then New Ross was dead.

The last battalion complete with the Colours filed in through the gate in reasonable order, but at the last moment the men's courage broke and they began to scatter in droves.

'Jesus!' Cahill shook his head in disgust at the redcoats who bolted past the barricades despite the best efforts of the officers and NCO's who tried to inculcate order. They could go nowhere else because Johnson had strategically blocked various roads throughout the town with stone, timber and wagons and would funnel any attacks in one direction from the gates to where the armed detachments waited.

The gun teams had finished pulling back the two cannon with ropes as the Militia bolted and the captain, a barrel-chested man with bow legs, ordered the iron killers to be double-shotted with canister. Both muzzles pointed at the gates and, if they could be loaded in time, would obliterate the assault in an explosion of flame and smoke.

The light company skirmishers on the walls and roofs gradually moved away from the gates for fear of being hit from behind. The air was thick with smoke as they fired at the enemy on the plain.

'Here they come!' one of the redcoats shouted from his position on the wall next to the gate. Mullone took a deep breath, bracing himself like a man striding into a storm. His sword was drawn, but he kept thinking of sheathing it. He was a soldier, but it did not feel right to fight men; Irish men, who were not wearing military uniforms. It was a rare and terrible thing to fight your own people. How had it come to this? Then, he found that he had forgotten to bring his helmet from the billet and thought that it was unlucky. For a heartbeat, he considered that he would die unless he retrieved it, but then ridiculed himself for that notion.

'I'll shoot the first bastard that shows his face!' Trooper Coveny boasted loudly, fiddling with the trigger guard that hung loose because the screw was lost. 'I'll send the croppie to an early grave.'

'You couldn't hit a target through an open window, Coveny,' Cahill replied, 'so still your bullshit!' The dragoons laughed at the swollen-eyed trooper.

Mullone knew that Coveny's flippant remark was because of nerves. The sound of the rebel army approaching, the great seething mass of men bristling with weapons could put ice-cold fear in a man or turn his bowels to water.

Behind them a mounted Militia officer was trying to control his horse. Its eyes were bulging wide and wet nostrils flared black. It snorted loudly and whinnied. 'There, there. Calm yourself, Rascal,' the officer said soothingly. 'It'll soon be over, boy. There, there.'

'Ready yourselves!' Mullone heard himself say, which was strange, he thought, for he knew his men were prepared.

A great cry came from beyond the walls that were punctuated by musket blasts and Mullone readied himself for the guns to leap into action. Mullone felt a tremor. The ground shook and then the first rebels poured through the gates like an oncoming tide. Mullone saw the leading man; both hands gripping a green banner, face contorted with zeal. The flag had a white cross in the centre of the green field and the initials JF below it. John Fitzstephen. Then, there were more men behind him, tens, then scores. Pike heads glittered. And then time seemed to slow.

The guns erupted barely twenty feet from them.

Later on, Mullone would remember the great streaks of flame leap from the muzzles to lick the air and all of the charging rebels were shredded and riven in one terrible, sweeping instant. Balls ricocheted on stone and great chunks were gouged out by the bullets. Blood sprayed on the walls as far back as the arched gateway, limbs were shorn off, and Mullone watched in horror as a bloodied head tumbled down the sloped street towards the barricade.

'Jesus sweet suffering Christ!' Cahill gawped at the carnage as the echo of the big guns resonated like a giant's beating heart.

Trooper O'Shea bent to one side and vomited at the sight of the twitching, bleeding and unrecognisable lumps that had once been human beings. A man staggered with both arms missing. A rebel buckled to his knees, holding his own entrails. Another crawled back to the gate with a shattered legs spurting blood. The stench of burnt flesh and the iron tang of blood hung ripe and nauseating in the oppressive air.

One of the low wooden cabins by the wall was aflame. A blast of musketry outside the walls rattled against the stonework and a redcoat toppled backwards with a gasp onto the roof.

'Here they come again! Ready your firelocks! Do not waste a shot!' Johnson shouted in a steady voice as the gateway became thick with more enemies. He took a deep breath.

'God forgive us,' Corporal Brennan said.

'Liberty or death!' A rebel, armed with a blood-stained pitchfork, shouted over-and-over.

'Fire!' Johnson yelled and muskets and carbines crashed from the barricades, doors, windows and roof tops. Whole lines of the attackers were jerked back. The pitch-fork wielding rebel went down, his blood thick on the cobblestones. Another tripped on a body and was shot in the mouth as he scrambled to get up. One attacker holding a banner with one hand burst forward and brought out a large horse pistol to shoot dead a gunner. The redcoats let loose another volley and more rebels fell from the bullets. The rear rebel ranks were pushing the front forward and one man shot in the thigh fell backwards and was slowly crushed by the sheer weight of attackers.

'Load!' Johnson wanted the men to have one last volley before the insurgents reached them en masse.

The wounded soldier on the roof began to scream as the flames fanned across the wood.

Cahill tracked a man holding one of the flags and put a bullet in his brain. The rebels able to bring their captured muskets from the dead Militia to bear began to fire at the barricades. A bullet splinted the wood next to Mullone's hand.

'Bayonets!' Johnson ordered once the guns were loaded. 'Gunners fall back!' He waved at the teams to move behind the barricades. 'Let the rebels dash themselves on our cold blades!'

The United men reached the fleeing gunners and those that could not get away were killed where they stood. Then scrambled to the barricades with a roar of triumph where steel waited for them.

'Fire!' Johnson waved his sword down in one snapping arc.

Muskets coughed and the first ranks of the enemy were thrown back in a maelstrom of lead and blood. No sooner as the foul-smelling powder smoke cleared, the next ranks came forth. The clamour of their voices was tumultuous like many waves breaking upon a rocky shore.

'Swords!' Mullone shouted and the dragoons slung their used carbines across their backs and withdrew their 1796 issue cavalry sabres. They were well oiled, so that they slid free with barely a sound.

'Now kill them!' Johnson screamed savagely. 'Death to traitors!'

'Let's break some skulls!' Cahill shouted as he swept aside two pikes with his sword. He chopped down and the cavalry sword cleaved down through an opponent's head as thought it were a hen's egg. Brain glistened and spilt like runny yolk. The other assailant reacted quicker, bringing out a broad-bladed knife, teeth bared in a grimace of pure hatred. He was dressed in dirty peasant smocks, his body thin and face pitted, but fury and zeal had transformed him into a formidable foe. He swept the blade at Cahill; a series of arcing swipes, forcing the sergeant back as another man with hooded eyes that were wide in terror and excitement, came at him with a rusted cutlass. The sergeant stayed out of their reach, but stepping ever backwards, he suddenly brought his sword forward and the blade flashed through the peasant's wrist, severing the hand that still gripped the knife. He staggered and then the sword struck again, this time cleaving his face in two. The second man brushed past his compatriot and thrust his old sword at Cahill's chest, hoping that one quick, hard blow would work. Except that the sergeant had seen the attack in his enlarged eyes and flicked his sword up, parrying the attack, to scythe across the man's throat. He sunk to his knees, blood gurgling and hands clasping at the hideous wound.

'Jesus, this one stinks like a dead hog left out in the rain,' Cahill said, giving the dying man a kick.

The defenders fought with ferocity, stabbing and cutting with a vicious frenzy. It was a street fight; a gutter brawl where men fought like animals for the need to survive. Mullone saw a tall man with black hair in a long green coat working his way towards the redcoats from the

58

gateway, pushing the men forward and rallying the gaps where men's courage failed. He was a brave man and it was at that moment that a rider from the garrison galloped to the barricade, vaulted it clear and urged his mount towards him. The horse ploughed through the mass of rebels, knocking them back, but the red-coated officer had not drawn his sword. It was Lord Mountjoy. Mullone could hear him trying to persuade them to surrender peacefully. He appealed to them with arms outstretched, he spoke of being kin, but they would not listen to him and he was pulled from his horse and dragged to the gateway where a pike ran through his chest to touch the stonework behind. Blood pumped from his open mouth as he died.

'Major!' Johnson called down to Mullone as a surge of Militiamen swelled the bayoneted ranks. 'We can hold them here. Take your men to Colonel Craufurd. Assist him at Main Guard!'

'Yes, sir,' Mullone replied. He twisted to his men. 'Follow me!' The dragoons broke from combat to follow him back down the street where more Militia were pressing forward with bayonets and charged muskets.

They ran down an abandoned Neville Street and turned left into Marys Street which was very steep. A man, trying to shelter from the assault, ran into an alley seeking solace. Mullone wasn't sure if he was a redcoat or not. Their boots echoed loudly as they reached the cobbled crossroads at Main Guard, which were strong with defenders.

'You bring orders?' Craufurd called, resplendent in his uniform, as several Colours rippled in the gentle breeze behind him. Men stared at them wondering what dismounted cavalry were doing here.

'No, sir,' Mullone said. 'General Johnson is holding Three Bullet Gate. He ordered me to assist you.'

'Assist? Well, find a position and try not to get in anyone's way,' he said irritably.

'Yes, sir.'

Suddenly, the two guns facing South Street roared and Craufurd immediately went to investigate their discharge. Mullone followed.

'I spotted movement down by the gardens, sir,' said the gun team captain.

Craufurd rounded on him. 'How do you know they weren't ours?'

The captain ran a powder-smeared hand across his forehead, dislodging sweat-matted hair that hung loose from his hat. 'I saw pikes, sir. Lots of them.'

Craufurd frowned. 'They must have somehow breached the Priory Gate.'

Mullone scanned the cobbled street. How in Christ's name had they achieved that? He heard shouts and men yelling and became all too clear that the rebels had found a weakness and were already converging to the towns heart. 'They must have, sir,' Mullone told him. 'No rebel had got past the defences at Three Bullet Gate.'

'I had shored it up tight with timber and stone,' Craufurd said, in a disgruntled tone. 'Captain O'Dwyer and his men should have sent word of any attack. I fear the worst.' A bullet snicked the wall beside him, fired from the captured gate. He returned to the defences stretched across the road where the Glengarry Fencibles held them. 'Wait until I give you the command to fire!' his voice boomed at the Highlanders who wore kilts, yellow-faced jackets and bonnets without the black ostrich feathers that usually embellished such headgear. 'Do not fire until I give you the word! Fellow men of Scotland, you will wait for my command!' The small colonel repeated his order until his voice was hoarse with the strain.

He knew full well that Militia and Fencible battalions were not as disciplined as the regular line troops and he did not want them to waste a volley. One error of judgment and the defence would be thrown into tatters. Craufurd would wait until the insurgents were at least thirty yards from the barricades and then, and only then, he would give the command to fire. And then they appeared at the slight bend in the road, stalking and moving cautiously. They could see the blockaded street. They knew muskets waited for them and yet, they still approached.

'Load!' Mullone yelled at his dragoons.

The rebel commanders were dressed in their Sunday best, and their hats were furnished with green plumes and white hat bands. Around their waists, or slung over shoulders, were green sashes and on their breasts, green badges showed the golden harp. The rest were dressed in their work clothes, or peasant smocks adorned with green bushy twigs in their flowerpot shaped hats. Some even wore Tarleton helmets, grenadier caps and bicorns plundered from bodies. The lucky ones carried muskets.

'*Erin Go Bragh*!' the rebels shouted. Ireland forever.

'Liberty or death!'

And then they came at the defences; fearless and with absolute conviction for their cause. They sprinted and they ran. Mullone saw that they were armed with all manner of pike, sword, knife, club and

60

axe. He could also see two priests, one was armed with a mace and the other carried a blunderbuss. Neither of them were De Marin. A pair of hands somewhere in the mass held up a large wooden cross. Mullone unconsciously touched the cross at his neck hoping that his prayers were answered too.

A rebel, his mouth torn wide in a battle cry, waved his sword. 'Kill them all!'

Craufurd was calm. 'Present! Fire!'

Two hundred and fifty muskets and carbines exploded and it seemed to Mullone that the rebels were suddenly jerked back by invisible ropes, and then were completely obscured by a bank of filthy smoke.

Ramrods frantically scraped down the barrels as the Highlanders and dragoons reloaded. The rebels jumped their fallen and immediately the long-reaching pikes thrust and stabbed at the redcoats. But Craufurd had piled so much on the barricades that the rebels found even their ten and twelve foot pikes were too cumbersome here. Men kicked at the obstacles and pulled at the great stones, broken cart wheels, carriages, boxes and barrels. Hands and arms bled from crude *chevaux de frise* as they tore at the barricade like frenzied animals. A rebel armed with a musket rammed it between a gap, pulled the trigger and a Scotsman fell back with a ball through an eye. Mullone knocked a pike back with his sword and then saw that the musket-armed rebel was a woman. She was dressed in a green satin dress and was startlingly beautiful. Their eyes met; and he could do nothing but stare at her. Then, the soldiers brought muskets to their shoulders and through the openings and suddenly, Mullone's vision was fogged with gritty smoke. A bullet smacked against the iron hoops of a barrel and he instinctively ducked. When he looked up, the woman was gone, leaving him to wonder if she had died from the volley, or was safely aside.

'Fire!'

Mullone's men knelt with loaded carbines and poured bullets at point-blank range into the innumerable enemy. 'Fire!' Cahill was keening with battle-joy. 'Keep firing, you bastards! Send them to Hell!'

'Hold the Colours!' An officer shouted as a rock hit the sixteen-year-old ensign carrying it. A sergeant helped up the bleeding junior officer and the Union Flag was raised high again.

A rebel threw his pike like a javelin and the weapon lodged between the spokes of an upturned cart. A woman wearing a green shawl hacked at the barricade with a set of spurs, a young man who had never seen a pike two weeks ago, now lay next to her with blood-roses blooming on his frayed white shirt. Another was coiled like a foetus from the bullet wound to his groin.

Craufurd waved his sword. 'Highlanders fire! Drive the blackguards back!'

'No quarter for the king's dogs!' A rebel countered.

Those Scotsmen who could reload, as most were defending the barricades with bayonets, did so and the steel ramrods twirled in the air so that they skimmed their knuckles on the long blades. A light company soldier, drunk before the fight had started, mistakenly left his ramrod in the barrel. He pulled the trigger and it shot out to skewer an attacker in the face. The soldier laughed like a crazed man. Ball after musket ball ripped into the rebel horde that pushed and fought against the musket-tipped blockade. The dead were piling up and the living were choking in the throat-drying acrid air.

'They'll never get through these tough bastards, sir!' Cahill shouted, raising his helmet and dragging an arm across his face, smearing grime and sweat. 'They can't get over their own dead!'

Suddenly, from Michaels Lane, Mullone saw a block of advancing shadows and, for a second, he could not believe his eyes. Panic bubbled in the back of his throat.

'Look out! Get down!' he screamed and managed to the sergeant down as a protracted volley slammed into the defenders. Fifteen dragoons and Highlanders were killed by the musket armed rebels.

'Christ! Watch them!' Craufurd exclaimed, stunned that the enemy had penetrated this far into the town. 'Load! Running fire!' he added to allow the men to fire at will.

Cahill bent down to one of the dragoons, closing his lifeless eyes. One of them was swollen and bruised blue-black.

Mullone looked up from Trooper Coveny. 'They must have broken into the barracks, and stolen the arms and shot,' he said, staring at the sixty-odd armed rebels.

Craufurd brought his reserves to fight off the new attackers and Mullone saw a flicker of worry cross his face.

'I'll go back and check Main Guard, sir,' he said, understanding the situation. There was a narrow street that led from the barracks to the cross junction and the Scotsman was wondering if the enemy had got behind them, thus cutting them off.

'Hurry! And report back to me immediately!' Craufurd said, before turning back to supervise the men where one Highlander screamed pitifully as a pike had sliced open his belly. Another coughed up blood.

'Push them back!' he crowed at the redcoats. 'Give them the steel! Go on! Push them back all the way! They won't break us!'

Mullone remembered from the officer's mess that Craufurd had stubbornly refused the idea of withdrawing from New Ross, or the possibility of surrendering. He considered that Craufurd was like Moore, both Scottish, confident and experienced, but Moore would always consider and respect other men's opinions whilst Craufurd could be obstinate and tough to deal with. But now here in the fight for survival, Craufurd could be relied on to manage the garrison and lead the troops. There was no one better.

Mullone sucked in a sulphurous breath that stung his throat. 'Lord Lovell's Dragoons! To me! To me!' His voice snapped sharp and crisp above the din. The dragoons, their faces sooty with powder, hotfooted to the junction. A terrified lieutenant wearing an ill-fitting coat met them near the gaol. It was deserted.

'Someone sprang the prisoners in the night, sir,' he said, jerking a thumb at the stone building. 'They're all gone.'

Mullone looked at Cahill. Scurlock, the man he planned to question, had vanished. It all seemed too convenient.

'Did anyone see who was responsible?' Mullone asked, chest heaving.

'No, sir.'

'It's a gaol!' Mullone threw up his hands. 'It's supposed to be guarded! Where were the guards?'

The lieutenant looked as though he was about to break down. 'I don't know, sir. I'm not the gaoler.'

'Where is he?'

'If he had any sense, he'd be on the way to Waterford by now, sir.'

'Here they come!' shouted a voice from the Court House and Mullone pushed past the lieutenant to see two long columns of rebels coming straight at them; one smaller group from the barracks and the other worryingly from Neville Street from the direction of Three Bullet Gate.

'The buggers have probably come from the two western gates,' Cahill suggested, as he finished loading his carbine. 'I doubt that they've beaten the general.'

A bearded priest led the smaller column and Mullone stared at the face, recognising the man instantly. The hair was cut short and the beard was full, and the last time he had seen this man, he had been

63

dressed in the uniform of the French *Légion Irlandaise*. At his hip hung an expensive sabre, sheathed in a simple cloth covered scabbard.

'De Marin!' Mullone hollered, unsheathing his sword.

The Frenchman looked utterly astonished for a second, withdrew his sabre and then offered his nemesis a huge grin, like those reserved for old acquaintances meeting after being apart for some time. He hauled free his sword, pointing it like a steel finger at Mullone, and then moved aside. Mullone saw a cannon muzzle. A man wearing a red Phrygian cap waved a black flag emblazoned with the mocking words stitched in white 'God Damn The King'.

'Give this to your poxed king!' A gunner shouted.

Mullone pulled down Cahill as the cannon roared and belched fiery smoke. The iron ball smashed into the barricade, ploughing straight through it to cut a man in half, disembowel another, and showered a dozen men with wicked debris. A private staggered back with a foot long splinter sticking out of his chest.

Mullone was dazed. He shook his head and saw that a shard of wood from a carriage wheel was sticking in his right boot-top. He pulled it out and groaned. He peeled back the leather to see that his knee was gashed open. A splinter of jagged wood was sticking out of his flesh and he tugged it free, feeling the wood scrape bone.

'That's twice now, sir!' Cahill rasped, as he helped Mullone to his feet. 'I hope to God you don't want this paid back in whiskey?'

Mullone took of his white necktie and tied it around the wound. He pressed his foot down and despite the pain, found that he could at least stand.

'De Marin's here!' he uttered and turned to see if the Frenchman was in sight, but could not see him in the great press of men.

Cahill looked incredulous. 'That bastard?'

The rebels were clawing at the barricades. A loose volley of musketry smashed into the redcoats killing three men and wounding a half-dozen more. A private, arm shattered by a musket ball, tried to bayonet a rebel who was clambering over the barricade, but a woman wearing a green bonnet jumped on him and swung a small hatchet into his forehead. Dark gore sprayed up into her face, but she was screaming in Gaelic and hacking wildly as the man twitched and died beneath her. A grenadier corporal of the Londonderry Militia shoved a man back, kicked the legs from under another and bayoneted both men with such force that both times the steel went through cloth and flesh to pierce the stone cobbles underneath.

64

'*Erin Go Bragh*!' De Marin shouted from somewhere in the throng and immediately tens of voices cried out the same chant.

Swords lunged and sliced, crossed and scraped, bayonets stabbed and pikes speared. The rebel dead were making their own barricades. A dog tugged intestines from a corpse. A little girl ran over to fallen redcoats and cut off their cartridge boxes with a knife and returned them to where the armed rebels were waiting in lines, desperate for ammunition.

'Death to the king's men!'

De Marin cut one man down and then speared the young terrified Militia lieutenant through the heart as he charged him. 'Fire!' he shouted while he was still killing the officer. The rebel lines flamed brightly, bullets hummed and buzzed and redcoats tumbled backwards onto the cobbles, or collapsed at the blockades. A rebel managed to dart up the barricade and aimed his blunderbuss. One of Mullone's dragoons saw him and put a carbine ball between his ribs. The dying rebel still managed to pull the trigger as two redcoats climbed up to stop him. They were instantly torn apart by the mixture of lead balls, nails and stones that exploded from the weapons' wide muzzle. Mullone was splattered by droplets of human debris.

Men kicked at the barricades, others dropped their weapons to heave aside the stones, the wagons and cut trees, all the time the redcoats shot at them and gouged with bayonets. Pike heads pricked the air in staccato thrusts. A big man wielding a hammer made a gap and the rebels poured through it.

'Seán!' Mullone yelled, pointing his sword at the threat. He shouldered a man wearing a black shirt to the ground, and kicked him between the legs when he tried to get up. A man wearing a top hat brought down a lump of timber in the hope of crushing his head, but Mullone leapt aside and punched his sword arm forward to break the man's nose. Another rebel armed with a scythe tried to slice Mullone across the belly, but he managed to parry it, grunting with the impact. The blades met, clashed and the shock jolted Mullone's fingers, palm and wrist. Gripping his sword in two hands, he drove both blades to the ground.

'You pup!' The man snarled and Mullone could smell the foul stench of decay wafting from his gums. The muscles in his arms looked like knotted rope. 'I've killed plenty of you king's men today with this. I'll tear out your stinking guts.'

65

Mullone, teeth clenched, found he could not hold his grip for long because the man was evidently stronger. He slapped Mullone away with a muscled arm, thundered forward and then Cahill shot him plumb in the chest.

'Are you all right, sir?'

'Yes,' Mullone clutched the sergeant's forearm as a thank you.

'So we're even then?' Cahill gave a wry, lop-sided grin.

Mullone saw that the makeshift bandage was soaked through with blood. 'We need support,' he said, knowing that they would be soon overrun. And if Mullone lost here, then Craufurd and his defenders would be flooded with attackers and massacred. He saw movement to his right. A boy snuck through gaps in the barricade and dodged through legs to reach him. The boy was not even ten years old, but was armed with a sharp iron rod and suddenly brought it towards Mullone who easily parried the small attacks with his sword.

'Go back home, boy,' he said, flicking the rod away.

The boy slashed wildly. Cahill cackled with laughter which seemed to incense him even more.

'Go home!' Mullone said and slapped the back of the boy's head with the flat-side of the sword. The boy cursed him before running to disappear behind one of the houses where a Militia drummer was slumped against a wall, drunk and oblivious to the fighting. Somewhere a man spilled the contents of his stomach and then made a gurgling sound.

The rebels, exhilarated by the victory, surged towards the larger group who were trying to hold Main Guard. The clash of steel on steel and steel on wood was louder than any musketry, for few men had time to load their muskets, and so used their blades, or heavy stocks of their guns instead of powder and ball.

Craufurd had brought back the Highlanders from South Street. 'There's no hope in holding them back,' he said disappointedly, as the files of redcoats extricated themselves from the killing field. Their faces were streaked with gunpowder and sweat. 'We'll hold them here and then fall back to the secondary position at the North Gate, if we need to.'

'What about the bridge, sir?' Mullone asked and ducked as the cannon fired again and its roundshot went high to smack into the corner of one of the houses. Stone and mortar tumbled onto the roadside.

'Would you see how they're faring, Major?' Craufurd asked. 'We must hold it at all costs!'

66

'I understand, sir,' Mullone nodded, as Cahill closed the lids of a dead trooper, a ragged mess where the lower part of his face had once been.

The remaining troopers ran to the quay, where the streets were narrow and twisting, until they came to the actual harbour that stank of fetid water and shit. Mullone half-limped and gritted his teeth at the agony of his exertion.

The bridge was full of townsfolk hurriedly retreating to Rosbercon. There were scores of mounted men and several canvass covered wagons too. He looked around to see if McBride was at his position near the North Gate but, pushing past scores of people and horses, he could not see him or their mounts. Mullone had posted McBride with six men near the abbey and all the mounts. Gulls cried over the buildings, smoke from several house fires to the south rose high above the harbour to drift across the Barrow. Where was McBride? Or the six troopers?

'Perhaps he's gone over the bridge, sir?' Cahill suggested, seeing the major's expression.

Mullone did not know. It wasn't like the lieutenant to disobey him. He gave the order for the men to load their carbines. There were six men missing, Cahill gave him the names. A splintering crash of musketry from the direction of South Street followed by a woman screaming caused Mullone to investigate it. If the rebels succeeded in breaking the defences here, the quay would be lost along with the bridge. A surge of panicking folk swept through the dragoons.

Mullone battered one man away and Cahill punched a man who tried to grab his carbine. The major hobbled around the corner to see a group of redcoats fighting with insurgents at the top of the road. The Militia were beaten down and the enemy swarmed over the bodies.

'In here!' a man shouted and Mullone looked up at the buildings, searching for the caller. A grey-haired man waved at them from one of the houses down the road. 'Get inside, you dullards!' he shouted as a large group of rebels converged on the road. They were surrounded.

'Jesus, you can't be serious, sir?' Cahill asked Mullone.

'Have you a better idea?'

'Once the mob knows we're inside, they'll tear down every wall to get to us. We'll be trapped like eels in a basket. It's a stupid idea. It's like taking a whore to meet your mother.'

This was not the time for indecision.

67

'Inside!' Mullone ignored Cahill and pushed the men towards the doorway. A young man wearing a pale shirt and an ammunition belt let them in. The dragoons fired at the two groups and a handful of rebels went down. A pistol shot killed one of Mullone's troopers as he attempted to reload and another was struck in the face with a rock.

'O'Shea! Get inside, you whoreson!' Cahill pushed the bleeding trooper and a rebel armed with an old broadsword ran up to the sergeant and stabbed it through his thigh. Cahill hissed through gritted teeth and thumped the stock of his carbine into the man's jaw, breaking it with a sickening crack. Another, sliced down with an axe, but the sergeant twisted nimbly aside despite the sword still stuck firm in his flesh, and knocked the rebel to the floor. Cahill then rammed the carbine's muzzle into his open mouth and pulled the trigger. It exploded and the back of the man's head seemed to vanish in a spray of bloody gristle that fanned the cobbles.

'Get him in!' Mullone ordered and two troopers grabbed Cahill inside. Hands clasped the door shut, but a sudden pressure was forcing it open.

'Jesus!' said O'Shea, rivulets of blood streaming down his ragged cheek, as he tried to help close the door. 'They're going to break it down!' He had to shout over the pounding, cursing and kicking.

Mullone took a lungful of sulphurous breath. 'Open it!' he said, bringing his sword to bear. 'Ready your blades!'

The trooper stared at him and then obeyed. The door swung open and three rebels tumbled inwards onto the stone floor and were immediately butchered with blades. Mullone charged over the dying men with a roar. An astonished rebel, sword outwards, found himself facing the major's own blade which skewered forward so savagely that the tip struck the far wall after it had gone clean through his body. Mullone withdrew it, and muskets banged to send two more rebels backwards, turning the alley slippery with blood. A carbine fired from the alley and the bullet struck Mullone's scabbard to ricochet with a hum. A rebel whose pike blade was dark with congealed blood, rammed it at Mullone, who twirled himself clear, and grappled the shaft to pull the man forward, hammering the sword hilt into his eyes.

A giant of a man whose face was all beard tried to pulverise Mullone with a long-handled hammer. 'I'll break you apart like old bones in a grave.'

Mullone saw the threat, ducked and the big iron head whipped through the air to smash into the wall, gouging a crater as though a twelve-pounder had hit it. He twisted away as the rebel swung the hammer with enough force to knock over an ox. Mullone stabbed his sword into the man's flank and he stumbled backwards with a dark stain appearing on his shirt. It must have hurt, but the man was frenzied and refused to die. The hammer swung again and Mullone's sword flashed in the blood-reeking alley to send three fingers spinning onto the ground. The man spluttered and Mullone opened up his chest, thrust the hilt to jar against bone, and he was down on his knees. Behind the dying giant, more rebels appeared and Mullone saw jaws set and faces sour with hatred.

Red arms seized Mullone, dragging him back inside the house where the door slammed and was bolted shut by a young man with two pistols tucked in his belt. Two more civilians put up four lengths of timber and quickly struck them across the door with long nails as it rattled and thudded from the enemy outside.

'You're dead men! All of you!' A voice threatened from the other side of the door.

'Well, that was closer than I'd hoped,' Cahill wheezed, trying to stem the flow of blood with his ragged sash after he had pulled the reddened blade free. A chair was fetched and strips of pale cloth were tied around the wound. 'Watch that door!'

The house was owned by the harbour-master and it was he that had accosted them from upstairs. He was called Sawbridge and walked with a wooden leg caused by a boating accident when he was sixteen. He proudly showed off his two sons, his brother and three friends who had taken shelter and had hitherto killed and wounded a score of rebels from the windows upstairs. Sawbridge kindly shared what little food they had, as his wife cleaned Cahill's wound with bandages and boiled water.

Shapes moved outside along the lanes and alleys. The rebels were lighting thatched roofs with pike heads tied with flaming rags. Mullone could hear men howling and screaming like feral beasts down the streets and alleys in search of more butchery, but it seemed they were left alone. The injured coughed and groaned. Sawbridge wanted to kill as many rebels that appeared, but Mullone told him to save his powder in case the house was attacked again and he reluctantly agreed.

They had survived for now, but Mullone wondered how long they must stay here and endure as the guns hammered on, their discharge ringing the town with orange-flame and smoke.

General Johnson had ridden down to survey the attacks at Main Guard and arrived no sooner than to see the redcoats be pushed back to the North Gate. He kicked his spurs back to see the bridge full of frightened townsfolk and rattled Militia. The rebels had now taken the quay and there was no hope of rallying the men here, so he joined the swarm of people in the hope of assembling them at Rosbercon, waving his sword, the reflected fires dancing at its tip like molten silver. But for now it was over. The rebels were victorious. They had beaten the king's soldiers.

New Ross had fallen.

It was eight o'clock.

Mullone waited in the house, hearing the rebels outside, but there were so much battle smoke that he could not see anything, even when he peered out of the window. *It was like London fog*, he reflected. He could hear the constant sound of musketry to the east and north and reckoned that the rebels had not completely taken the town. Even the group outside had given up and dispersed. Then, at noon as the sun burned from above, the shouting became a murmur of voices, the musketry a dull ragged tearing sound, and the caustic smoke thinned to leave the town washed in destruction.

The rebels were exhausted. The cauldron of blood-letting had boiled over and the flames had been doused. It was then that Johnson rallied the troops who stormed back across the bridge and through the North gate, and the tired rebels could not hope to turn aside the counter-attack. A great deal had fallen where they stood from exhaustion and some had broken into cellars and quenched their thirst with hidden kegs of ale and whiskey. The fight had gone from them.

The redcoats advanced with a savagery that the general could not control, for the men wanted revenge, and would not stop until the last of the rebels were dead. The Dublin Militia, hearing that their commander Lord Mountjoy had been killed, cut bloody swathes through the narrow streets in revenge. A group of redcoats found a house where wounded and exhausted rebels had taken shelter and they shot and bayoneted them all without mercy.

'When we've retaken the town, we go after Black,' Mullone said loud enough for all the men to hear. 'That is our mission. It still stands.'

'Right, sir,' Cahill said and attempted to stand, but Mullone eased him back in the chair where his foot rested on a keg. Sweat beaded the sergeant's pale face and his eyes were red-rimmed.

'No, Seán,' Mullone shook his head. 'Time for you to rest. Same goes for the other four.' He glanced at O'Shea's face, swollen with a great weal under an eye. 'The injured stay here. Mister and Mrs Sawbridge will take care of you.'

Cahill reluctantly agreed and Mullone shook his hand. 'Go break some skulls, sir.'

'You need to heal up before you can make a journey so stay put. What about your wife?'

'She can take care of herself, sir,' Cahill said dismissively with a grin. 'She's got a musket and a fowling piece and a temper to match. The Croppies won't go near her, if they know what's good for them.'

Mullone edged to the door, wound throbbing. He cast a look back at his bandy-legged friend. 'Take care of yourself, Seán. I'll come back.'

'Make sure you do, sir,' Cahill saluted him.

'And you still owe me,' Mullone said, giving his friend a grin.

The major led his remaining dragoons out into the streets where homes smouldered red, wounded crawled and blood dripped; the signs of tragedy. There were bodies everywhere, stiff limbed, punctured with musket balls or laid open by steel. They lay like seeds tossed to the wind. Black smoke was roiling up to the heavens. A troop of Scottish Fencibles galloped past, eager to hunt down the insurgents, shifting tendrils of the pungent smoke that stung Mullone's eyes. He blinked the tears away. Symbols of the harp with an absent crown were etched into walls, painted on doors and chalked on floors. Groups of redcoats drifted away to look for plunder and drink. The liquor shops had been destroyed to protect the men from temptation, but it didn't stop them from ransacking what was left. The lucky ones rolled out hidden casks of port, guzzled spirits and carried away joints of ham and sacks of oats. A civilian tried to stop a Militiaman from looting his house and was shot dead. A companion, laughing at the murder, was urinating against the broken down door. A powder-stained officer, with a tethered mule flanked by two armed confederates, tied more stolen goods onto the beasts back before leaving in search for more plunder.

Mullone went back towards the abbey where he found Black-Eyed Brennan looking after the horses. *Tintreach* whickered a greeting and Mullone patted its face with affection. The numerous fires made the air so hot that it began to sear their throats.

'Have we won, sir?' Brennan enquired.

A team of artillerymen, led by a sergeant with a syphilitic mouth, were pulling recaptured guns with ropes, straining hard with the effort. The cannons were splattered with streaks of dark gore.

'I'm not sure to be honest,' Mullone replied with a shrug. The world as he knew it had been flipped on its heels and now everything that he knew had changed. 'Where's Lieutenant McBride?'

'I don't know, sir,' the corporal looked pained. 'He went in the night. Me and the boys stayed here like you ordered us to, but we had to take cover in one of the houses.' A group of redcoats were shooting pigs that had broken free of their pens and began butchering their corpses for the cooking fires. More were running past laughing madly and crowing at the jugs of wine, shirts, pipes, shoes and silver plate that mirrored the dull-orange fires in their grasp.

'Boys, I've been fishing!' one of them shouted. 'Care to see my catch?' Raucous laughter echoed down the blood-slick road.

Mullone rubbed his tired face and fingered the tight bandage around his knee that Sawbridge had insisted on replacing. He saw several canvasses scattered on the cobbles, all of them riddled with musket ball marks. The paintings had been cut from frames and the portraits used for target practice.

'I don't have the time to look for the lieutenant, so we gather our equipment and find Colonel Black.'

Tintreach would ride like the wind and Mullone vowed that he would not give up searching for Black and De Marin until Judgement Day.

'You're going after Black?' called a voice and Mullone spun round to see a heavyset man with a boy approach him from the abbey. The man was armed with a blunderbuss and an axe was tucked in his belt.

'Who are you?'

'My names Pádraig Scurlock, and I'm the brother of the man they imprisoned here. This is his son, Dónall.'

'I'm not after your brother, or his son,' Mullone said, 'but I hear Black is after him in connection with a killing up in Oldbridge. Do you know anything about that?'

Scurlock bobbed his head curtly. 'My brother and his boy are the only survivors from *Uaimh Tyrell*. You heard about that?'

'What Irishman hasn't?'

'He came after my brother, because he and some United men killed a couple of his dragoons during a raid on a farmstead. Nothing else.

72

Don't believe anything else you hear. Black's men were about to murder the people when my brother stopped them. I guess Black wants revenge.'

'Was this near Oldbridge?'

'Yes,' Scurlock replied cautiously. 'How do you know that?'

'Through lines of enquiry, my dear fellow. Do you know where I can find your brother?' Scurlock shook his head. 'I told you I'm not after him,' Mullone reiterated. 'I'm only after Black. I want that bastard stopped.'

Scurlock watched his nephew for a second before answering. 'Clanfield Manor. South of Enniscorthy. You'll find him there.'

The name rang a bell. 'Is that in any relation to Sir Edward Clanfield?'

'Aye, it's his home,' Scurlock sighed. 'My brother says the United men want him for something. I don't know what for. It's none my business.'

Mullone climbed up into his saddle. 'Why are you telling me this?'

Scurlock looked at the Barrow, the mass of civilians and redcoats and to the sails of boats returning from across the water. 'Because I'm loyal,' he said simply.

Mullone thanked him and the dragoons rode out of the burning town.

They followed the roads north always keeping west of the retreating hordes of insurgents that fled the fires and billowing chaotic smoke over the towers and spires of New Ross. The sky was splashed orange and soon the warm evening turned to night and, as they came within five miles of Enniscorthy, the wide road was clogged with the fractured mass of fleeing rebels. They could not hope to reach the town, or find Sir Edward's manor in the ruddy glow of the sunset, so Mullone took them back to a tiny village they had passed to wait until dawn's first chink of light.

Mullone left sentinels to guard the road and slept an uneasy sleep in a farmer's tumbledown house. The villagers had offered his troopers their barns, byres and spare rooms that smelt of dust, dry fodder and the tang of animal dung. Mullone settled down to sleep in a tiny room laced with spider webs that shivered slightly from a breeze that cut through the rot beneath the windowsill. Shafts of light poured in from holes in the thatch and walls, where tiny motes danced. The farmer and his wife slept next door and both snored and grunted deafeningly.

Despite this, Mullone soon drifted off to sleep. He dreamed of those white frosted fields of a winter long gone by. He dreamed of Solomon who for once was not hanging from a tree, but was standing with the girl he had become a turncoat for, smiling and Mullone could see how happy he looked. He was how he remembered him when he was alive, and Solomon hugged him, told him how much he loved him, and with that last embrace, he ran away to where shapes moved in the dream-fog. Solomon waved once more and Mullone opened his eyes.

He got up and blinked away the tears that had fallen to soak his shirt. He put on his boots and walked outside to check on the sentries. His timepiece showed it was just after four o'clock. It was quiet outside, and poisonous plumes of cloud continued to drift from New Ross. Down in the meadows was an old stone church, a ruin, and it looked like a jutting black rock amongst the tall grass. He took a lungful of breath, happy of the dream. He felt light, as though a burden was gone. Solomon had found peace. It was time that he did too.

The first blow struck his temple, and his vision exploded in showering stars. Mullone stumbled backwards against the house and hands grabbed his arms tightly. He made no attempt to draw his sword, knowing it would be futile. Another blow smacked the side of his head and Mullone knew nothing more.

A bucket of cold water splashed over his face and Mullone woke from his unconsciousness to a cold, bleary and pain-filled semi-darkness. Blood crusted his hair and had dripped down to stain his shirt underneath his open scarlet coat. He was on a chair and his hands were tied around his back.

Shadows took on weight and form. They watched him, and he could hear them whispering.

'Who are you after?' a voice said in Gaelic.

Mullone shook his head to clear his eyes, but that made the pain in his head even worse. The man asked him the same thing in English and when Mullone did not reply, a shadow stepped forward and a fist struck his face.

'Answer the question!' the man who had hit him bellowed.

More pain and more explosions of stars. 'In Gaelic?' Mullone asked, as water dripped from his chin.

'Answer the question!'

'Black,' Mullone said in Gaelic, tasting the salty tang of blood in his mouth. 'My orders are to find Colonel Black. We're not here for revenge, or to seize any one from the United Irishmen. I just want that bastard Black.' There was a silence in the room that caused a chill to go up his spine. 'Where are my men?'

No one answered.

'Where are they?' Mullone shouted.

'Dead,' said a voice in English and Mullone recognised it instantly.' There was a silence.

'Michael?'

McBride stepped forward. He was wearing civilian clothes and a green sash. 'Sir,' he said in acknowledgment. His eyes showed defiance but also a sense of sorrow.

'Dead?' Mullone couldn't believe it. 'Y-you let them be killed?' he said accusingly. He shook his arms, tearing at ropes around his hands and the man hit him again. 'You treacherous-!' he shouted, his voice was thick from the springing blood in his mouth, and he had to spit to speak. 'You had them killed, Michael? Our boys? You had them murdered?'

'No, he did not,' a voice said. 'I did.' Another man, tall, blue-eyed and handsome, stepped forward.

'Why?' Mullone asked. Sweat prickled the back of his neck.

'They died because they were wearing the red coat and nothing more,' the man said matter-of-factly. 'Michael was the one that spared your life; otherwise, you'd have died in your sleep like your men.'

Mullone recognised him from New Ross. He had been the brave man who had rallied the attackers at Three Bullet Gate. He was wearing the green coat which was faced red, and decorated in gold lace. He wore a bright green sash and on his coat were two epaulettes of gold. His uniform was dazzling and immaculate compared to everyone else.

'My name is Fitzstephen,' the man continued. 'I'm sure you know who I am.'

'A United man,' Mullone replied.

Fitzstephen took several steps towards Mullone. 'We all are,' he said, gesturing at his men. 'And I know you and your dragoons were at New Ross. I had some trouble asking my men to stop from killing you too. You see they lost a good number of their friends and kin, but I

75

know you're Moore's man and you've not come to stalk us revolutionaries.' He grinned widely when Mullone frowned at his knowledge. 'I knew that even before Michael joined us. I know a lot of things.' He bent closer to Mullone so that he could smell the blood. 'You see that we have acquaintances all over the country. In Belfast, Dublin and even in London. I even spoke with Lord Lovell in Parliament once. And of course we even have the same enemies.' Mullone knew who he meant. 'Colonel Black.' Fitzstephen dipped his head at the man to Mullone's right and the next thing Mullone felt his bonds cut. 'We're after the same man, Major, only for different reasons. Where were you heading?'

Mullone rubbed his wrists and asked for some water. A jug was fetched and brought to him. He drank to swill out saliva and blood. 'Enniscorthy,' he lied.

The rebels began to talk amongst themselves. Mullone could not believe his men were dead. He rubbed his battered face.

'You said that you were after Black?'

'I did,' Fitzstephen said.

'Would it have something to do with him hunting down men in the Wicklow Mountains?'

'How did you know that?'

'Colonel Moore told me that he had set them free from gaol, only to let his men charge them down.'

'One of them was a young cousin of mine and they were not charged with anything. They were locked up because a Militia captain picked them out of a crowd. My cousin was not even twelve years of age. Black simply slaughtered them,' Fitzstephen grew angrier until he took control of his feelings. 'You have been charged to bring him in to the authorities,' he said, then laughed scathingly. 'What are they going to do at the Castle? What punishment will he get? Where's the justice?'

'He will be tried publically in a court of law,' Mullone told him, knowing that it sounded weak.

'The man will get proper justice. The Irish way.' The hubbub of agreement echoed around the room. 'What do you know of a man called Sir Edward Clanfield?'

'I've heard of him,' Mullone answered. 'I don't know the man personally.'

'He rides with the devil,' said a large man stepping forth. 'We're going to expose him publically for his crimes against the Irish people.'

76

Mullone eyed him, noticing a familiarity in the man who had approached him in New Ross. 'Expose him for what?'

'The true man that he is.'

'Are you Scurlock?'

The man grunted. 'I am.'

'You escaped the slaughter at *Uaimh Tyrell*, but Colonel Black was tracking you. You then tried to find Fitzstephen in New Ross, but your luck ran out and you were caught.' He cast an eye over his young bespectacled officer. 'You broke Scurlock out of gaol, didn't you, Michael?'

'Aye, sir.'

Mullone rubbed his sore temple. His gaze rested on Scurlock. 'Your brother approached me and told me that you were going after Black.'

Scurlock shifted as though he was offended. 'My brother and I don't see eye-to-eye much these days. But the one thing we do agree about is the murder committed by both sides. Sir Edward, a man of noble birth, is as guilty as Black. He will be punished. Liberty or death!'

The gathered men chanted the axiom loudly.

A thought fluttered into Mullone's head. There were some rebels still in shadow. 'Where's De Marin?' The room went silent. 'I know who he is Fitzstephen. I am fully aware of your association with him. You're a supporter of Tone and Bonaparte, and De Marin is your wee French messenger. I knew that before Bantry Bay.' Now it was time for Fitzstephen to gawk in surprise. 'De Marin!' he shouted the name. 'Show yourself, you wretched devil!'

There was another stiff silence.

De Marin stepped out of the gloom.

'*Bonjour, mon ami*,' he said with a grin and an elegant bow. He was dressed in his priest's garb.

Mullone wanted nothing more than to reach for sword and stab this man through his conniving heart. He stared at the Frenchman who had eluded him for so long. Now, he reckoned his chances of leaving this barn were now nonexistent. De Marin would not let him live, but have him tortured for information first.

'You're a murdering bastard,' Mullone spat at his foe, whose lips twitched with amusement and he bowed again. 'You wear those robes as though God can protect you. Only He can know what you've done to stoke this country's rage. You've whispered and plotted and planned and deceived. Men, women and children have died. One day I'll see you dead.'

The Frenchman's lips pulled back from his teeth. 'I wouldn't bet on it now, *mon ami*.' He laughed. 'You're going to die.'

'Someone is,' Mullone shot him a malevolent look. 'Well, Mister Fitzstephen,' he mocked, 'what will you do now that you have me?'

'Run the bastard through where he sits,' suggested one of the rebels.

'Aye, death to the king's men!' another uttered.

The United leader listened to the remarks. He rubbed the stubble on his chin and looked at the major with thoughtful eyes. 'You are released,' he said with a wave, and Mullone was so startled with the reply that he did not move.

De Marin gaped like a village idiot. 'Surely you jest? *Non?* You can't let him go! He's working for the British government. He is a spy! He is worth a lot to me dead!' He burst into hurried French and Fitzstephen pushed him away with distaste.

'Moore sent him to find Black, so let him continue his wee quest to Enniscorthy. He is alone, his men are dead, and I have no use for him. He poses no threat. Go!' he said to Mullone.

Mullone rose as De Marin and Fitzstephen broke into a heated argument. He made for the door, a man handed him his sword belt. It was McBride.

'You are a good man, sir,' he said. 'I didn't want them to kill you. I just wanted you to know that.'

Mullone offered him a wounded look before turning to leave.

'All roads lead to the same direction, Major,' De Marin said as Mullone walked past. His eyes shone like two cruel gems. 'We shall meet again, *non?*'

Mullone wiped his lips of blood. 'Indeed we will, Father,' he said and then thumped the Frenchman hard in the stomach. De Marin doubled over in pain, writhing and gasping for air. 'God punishes false prophets,' Mullone spat.

Fitzstephen followed him outside.

'I truly hate that man,' Mullone said to no one in particular.

'Fetch the Major's horse,' Fitzstephen ordered one of his men. The man, wearing a captured Highlanders bonnet and a musket slung over his shoulder, disappeared momentarily before returning with *Tintreach*, much to Mullone's utter delight. The United men had allowed Mullone to take his carbine and sword, as well as all his possessions with him. 'He's a fine stallion.'

'He is,' Mullone answered curtly, and grasped the reins tightly.

'Are you a patriot?' Fitzstephen asked him as he climbed up into his saddle. Mullone pushed his left boot into the stirrup, grimaced from the wound, and then lifted his body to flick out the tails of his scarlet coat. He clapped *Tintreach's* muscular neck and the beast snorted and bobbed its head with affection.

'I like to think so,' he said bitterly, because he could see naked legs and feet poking out from behind the barn. His men. Murdered in their beds, or where they stood and now dumped in a pile where flies feasted on the blood. He fought back a surge of tears.

'So am I, Major, but you wear the scarlet coat. Why is that if we are the same?'

Mullone let his gaze fall upon the rebel commander. 'I have worn this for more than thirty years. I wear it because I'd rather serve the British Crown as a free man, than be a slave to the French.'

Fitzstephen looked solemn.

Mullone glanced at the bodies again and his heart thumped in his chest, whilst theirs were growing cold. 'Give them a proper burial. It's what they deserve as Irishmen.'

He gave *Tintreach* his heels and rode north to warn Sir Edward.

Clanfield Manor was a spectacular sight. It was nestled above a small wood of pine and alder. A long gravel drive spiralled up from the road to Enniscorthy, and dotted with all manner of wild flowers. Outside the gates Mullone was stopped by a group of hard-looking men armed with swords and carbines. They let him pass by calling down a pleasant young man who introduced himself as Aengus, Sir Edward's major domo.

'Sir Edward sends his sincere apologies for the reception.' He saw the blood and bruises on Mullone's face. 'Are you in need of attention, Major? Shall I send for Dr Dalton?'

'No, I'm fine.' Mullone waved the empathy away. 'I've come from New Ross to warn Sir Edward of an attack.' Sunlight flashed on a pair of large rectangular windows overlooking the courtyard. He couldn't see anybody inside.

'My lord has received death threats in the last forty-eight hours,' he said, gesturing to the guards, 'so we've placed men at the gates and we're taking every precaution.'

'Who are they?'

'They all work for Sir Edward,' Aengus shrugged as if there was no other way of answering the question. 'Things haven't been the same here since Sir Edward's brother's death. Sir Charles. Poor man,' he sighed as though he found it too much to explain. 'A gang of rebels ambushed him and his servant on their way to Dublin. Both were robbed and murdered. A dreadful act of violence. The whole family is still in shock.'

'I was unaware of that. I shall pass on my condolences.'

'Thank you.'

A man with huge arms and thick lips led *Tintreach* to the stables while Aengus took him up several steps to the main entrance. Something was trying to get his attention, but Mullone was taken to the foyer where polished tiles gleamed, and then dully escorted to a room nearest the winding stairs. It was his lordship's private study.

Sir Edward was a handsome man, slim, dark-haired with a long sloping nose. He had none of the usual cold arrogance of the gentry and welcomed Mullone to his home as a friend and then shuddered at the bruises and dried blood. 'My dear fellow,' he said, 'what has happened to you?'

'I'll explain in due course, Sir Edward.'

'Then, please do have a seat.'

Mullone quickly eyed the many volumes with their rich covered bindings that adorned the shelves and tall cases. 'Thank you.'

'Now, what brings you here?'

'Firstly, please accept my condolences regarding your brother.'

'Thank you, Major,' Sir Edward said appreciatively.

'This conflict has seen the deaths of so many people. Any indication as to why he was targeted?'

'My brother was a staunch patriot and a loyal servant of the king.' Sir Edward suddenly looked as though he would wring Mullone's neck, but the major recognised the pain of losing kin and having to speak about it. 'That's why he was slain by craven murderers.' He blew out his cheeks. 'Charles was a good soul and his needless death in these volatile times has shattered my family. My eldest sister has miscarried and my ailing mother now confines herself to her house due to depression and fear. I loved my brother as any man could. Poor Charles was set upon like hounds taking down a fox. He never stood a chance. Now, why have you come to see me?'

'I believe that your life is in danger.'

Sir Edward did something that Mullone certainly did not expect. He laughed.

'My dear fellow, since this insurrection broke out I've had death threats nearly every week. I've had the odd tenant come to me with his complaints, and I've even had one threaten me with a hammer, but I take it in my stride as their landlord. I have come to expect it.'

'It's no laughing matter, sir,' Mullone said. 'I have first-hand accounts to say the rebels are coming here in force.'

'How could you possibly know this?'

'Because my men and I were stabled a wee way from here and a group of rebels murdered them all in their beds. We had just left the devastation of New Ross. They questioned me and let me go when I told them I was going to Enniscorthy, but I've come here to warn you instead.'

Sir Edward looked pained. 'My God! They couldn't have picked a better night for it. Most of the men working for me have returned to their homes. I have my wife, my three oldest friends and their wives staying with us. They are in the dining room right as I speak. I shall ask them to leave immediately.'

'Very good, and summon your guards, sir,' Mullone said. 'I need to talk to them first.'

Sir Edward shot him an inquisitive look. 'What for?'

'To make sure they're willing to fight.'

Sir Edward opened one of the drawers of a desk and bundled something into a pocket. They then hurried to the dining room, boots thumped loudly on the wooden floors down two long corridors to the back of the house. Sir Edward flung open the large door, startling a man examining the silver cutlery. He was dressed in the finery of an aristocrat: a plain dark-blue coat, tight-fitting and cut away, forming curving tails. His waistcoat of the same colour was shortened to just below the waist and his cream-coloured breeches were worn tight. It would have been fashionable to wear a powdered wig, dressed high and tied at the back, but there had been a recent tax imposed on hair powder by William Pitt, and the landed gentry had promptly abandoned them.

Sir Edward opened his mouth, when there was a shout outside in the gardens, followed by a musket shot.

'What's going on, Eddie?' asked the man.

'Troublemakers, Iollan,' Sir Edward replied calmly. 'Nothing for you to concern yourself with. Take some more claret.'

Iollan gazed at Mullone, grimacing at the bruises and cuts. 'If there's nothing to worry about, then what's he doing here?'

One of the female guests gasped and Sir Edward went to the large double doors and for a moment he could see nothing on the cut lawn, but then in the shadows of the hedgerows, he saw the glint of metal and a cold sensation went up his spine as several unfamiliar faces stared straight back at him.

'Get back, sir!' a hand seized and pulled him back as a musket flashed and the bullet struck to shatter the window where Sir Edward had been standing. Mullone had seen the movement and had known immediately what would happen. Lady Ellen Clanfield screamed and one of the guests whimpered.

'The house is under-siege, Sir Edward!' Mullone told him hurriedly. 'Are the front doors locked?'

'No, I don't think so.'

'What about your men, Eddie?' asked Iollan, his voice distant as though he was struggling to comprehend the implication of being attacked. 'They were posted at the gates.'

'They're out there still,' said Sir Edward.

'A handful might still be alive, but the rest will be dead, or most likely gone over to the enemy,' Mullone said dismissively.

Iollan went wide-eyed. 'What?'

A man with a white shirt, brown breeches and a white neck-tie stood up. 'Are we under attack?'

Iollan shook his head in frustration. 'Yes, Bartley!'

Bartley tottered a few steps before crossing himself.

'My men are loyal to me, Major,' Sir Edward vehemently. 'They will fight for me!'

'Let's hope they can, Eddie,' said the other male guest. He was dressed in a white frilly shirt. He had a shock of fiery-red hair and seemed to be trembling. He emptied a wineglass and poured himself another drink, spilling wine over the tablecloth.

Mullone edged beside a window, but could see nothing outside. 'If they still live,' he said, matter-of-factly.

'Oh, Edward!' Lady Ellen cried.

Sir Edward strode over to her, arms grasping hers. 'There, there, my sweet. Calm yourself. Everything will be fine. Just some warmongers outside, trying to intimidate us with violence. I told you they would try something like this. But I have taken safety measures.'

'They're going to kill us, Edward,' she replied, tears threatening to spoil her cornflower blue dress.

'Nonsense, my sweet.'

Another musket banged and a man screamed. He began to gasp for breath; each exhalation a terrible, pitiful moan. Then, he went quiet.

'Are the doors locked?' Mullone didn't wait for Sir Edward to answer and went over to the door that led to the rest of the house. He opened it slowly and it creaked. He moved quietly down the semi-darkened corridor; his heart beating fast in his chest, but could see or hear no indication of a break-in. He wished he had remembered to unsheathe his carbine, but *Tintreach* and his other equipment were in the stables. Then, there was a thud and floorboards creaked somewhere down in the near hallway. Mullone instinctively sensed danger and flung himself aside as a pistol flamed brightly in the shadows.

A voice shouted behind him. 'Show yourself, you lowborn villains!'

'Get back inside!' Mullone snarled as Bartley had ventured into the corridor. One of the household had appeared from the kitchen with two hunting rifles and a flask of powder and shot. It was Aengus. 'Inside! All of you! Now!'

He pushed the men forcefully into the room as another bullet smacked into the lintel above his head. Voices cursed him. The door slammed behind and a large sideboard was dragged across the floor to reinforce the door.

'I hope that's enough,' Mullone said.

'Liam, stoke the fire,' Sir Edward told one of the servants. He turned to Mullone. 'I've bullet moulds and lead bars should we need to make more shot.'

'Good thinking, sir.'

'Liam, load the blunderbuss too,' Sir Edward said, taking the cumbersome weapon from its wall mountings. He turned to the women. 'Ladies, please remove yourself from the vicinity and relocate at the rear wall. My dear, Ellen, that means you too. Keevan, would you escort my wife?' The red-haired man nodded. 'Ladies, please find appropriate cover: chairs, the display cabinet...'

Suddenly, the door thudded and one of the women whimpered. Bartley took an old sword hanging above the fireplace, marched to the door and swore at the intruders. A bullet tore through the wood, making him jump aside. Aengus fired one of the two hunting rifles through the large paned window and was rewarded with a yelp. He passed the unloaded rifle to the servant known as Liam. A musket shot splintered a pane and the glass crashed on the floor. Mullone helped tip the large dining table over, plates, cups, glasses, bowls and cutlery clattered and smashed onto the floor. Mullone, Sir Edward, Keevan and Iollan dragged the table against the window. Bullets crashed through the glass to make holes in the wood. Shadows blurred outside and Mullone withdrew his sword.

'Watch out!' he snarled as a man wearing a green sash smashed the glass and a pike sliced into the opening. Mullone hammered the weapon away before it thrust up into Sir Edward's neck.

'Thank you, Major,' Sir Edward said graciously.

A blast of musketry shattered more glass and the women screamed. An oil painting showing an ancestor from the 17th century was shot through and collapsed in a broken heap onto the floor. An axe thudded into the table and hands clawed at the wood from outside. Mullone slapped them away and kicked at fingers.

'We'll burn your house down, you devil!' a voice shouted from outside.

'God damn the king's men!' said another.

'Give me a weapon, for God's sake!' begged Iollan.

Sir Edward reached into a coat pocket and tossed him a pistol. The guest caught it. 'It's loaded, so save your shot!'

Aengus brought up a rifle, aiming at a shadow and pulled the trigger. The gun rammed into his shoulder and blotted his view with smoke. The third servant was armed with a carbine and tracked a shape outside in the green chaos and pulled the trigger. He didn't wait to see if he had hit anything, he simply began to load. The air was hissing with bullets, endless with the noise of muskets firing and the dull rattle of ramrods.

'There's one!' Iollan shouted, aimed his pistol and wasted the shot because he'd fired too soon. Gun smoke was wafting over their heads to touch the high ceiling like patchy grey clouds.

A bullet whipped close to Mullone, tearing at a silver epaulette. The gun smoke was getting thicker now, and he strained to see the grounds outside.

A carbine cracked and Aengus was shot in the neck. The force knocked him backwards, astonishment on his face, and blood spraying over Liam. He tried to speak, but blood spilled from his slack mouth.

Sir Edward's eyes bored into Liam's for an answer and the servant shook his head gravely. 'You murdering knaves!' the aristocrat raged at the attackers.

The door shook. Hands and boots banged and thumped it. Then, an axe head smashed through the wood and a muzzle appeared.

'You cowardly wretches!' Bartley shouted and the gun flashed to send him sprawling.

The door trembled as men shouldered and kicked at it. The sideboard slid across the floor.

'Here they come!' Mullone bellowed, bringing his sword to bear.

The door burst open. Three men wearing green cockades in their hats stood at the doorway, momentarily confused at the new surroundings and in that pause Sir Edward grabbed the blunderbuss from the footman and pulled the trigger. The gun went off like a small cannon, its noise deafening the room, and the rebels were snatched off their feet by the charge. Blood and gore splattered the door and wall behind. One of the traumatised women was screaming incoherently until she was slapped across the face into silence by another.

No enemies entered the room as the sound of the gun faded away. Mullone took tentative steps towards the door, his boots crunched over shattered glass, plaster, broken chinaware and cartridge wadding. There was an eerie silence, punctuated by Sir Edward asking if everyone was all right. Mullone's pulse settled because no enemies charged, no priming pans flared and no pikes sliced at him.

'Stay where you are, Major,' a deep voice boomed from the doorway.

Mullone stopped instantly. 'We have women in here,' he said. 'Let's put away the weapons. There's been enough bloodshed. Let us talk.'

A big man stepped through the gun smoke and Mullone saw that he was unarmed. It was Scurlock. He wore his long grey coat and his white shirt underneath was blood-stained signifying that he had been wounded in the attack.

'There's nothing left to say,' he said grimly, 'but I will show you the devil.'

Something clicked behind and Mullone spun round.

'No!' he yelled, but the doghead snapped forward, the flint sparked and the pistol flared. The bullet drummed into Scurlock's chest and he fell backward, wide-eyed against the wall. Mullone turned, bent down to him, but the smith was already dead.

Sir Edward lowered the pistol and gasped an intake of breath. 'Dear God, is it over? Have they gone?'

The rebels did not attack the house again.

Sir Edward ventured out into the rest of the house with a handful of servants who had survived the attack in the gardens. The enemy had gone, patches of smoke still wisped and the dead were slumped like string-cut puppets. He thanked Mullone by pumping his hand energetically and promised that he would write a report and send it to the viceroy gratefully acknowledging his service and heroism.

'Thank you, sir,' Mullone said jadedly, his resolve dampened by the attack.

'Where are you headed now?'

Mullone looked distant. 'New Ross, sir,' he said. 'To see a friend.'

*

Two days passed by.

Sir Edward, dressed in a sober black coat, plain shirt and snow-white breeches, opened the front door of his house, the lantern's light casting flickering shadows. There were no servants left, they had been sent to Dublin with Ellen, and the manor was left dark, silent and bare. The doors and stonework were pockmarked by musket fire and scarred from axe, pike and sword blows. He entered through the heavy doors with a lantern, confident that no harm would befall him. He had sent out two of his footmen to New Ross to determine the siege to find that the rebels had failed and hundreds were said to have been slain. The town was in loyalist hands and it seemed that the attack on his house was also a crippling blow to them. The rebels had destroyed many of his ornaments and stolen a lot more, but he was grateful to have survived the attack along with his doting wife. The remaining servants had hurriedly loaded as much of their possessions onto the four coaches for the journey to Dublin, but there were a few things left for him to collect and take care of.

Sir Edward made his way to the dining room that had witnessed so much destruction that night. The floor had been scrubbed of blood, but there were still dark stains where men had died. His old friend Bartley had taken a bullet to the lung and there was nothing that anyone could do to save him. His major domo, Aengus McGifford, had died instantly.

He walked down to the study and put the lamp on his writing desk and gathered some paperwork from inside a drawer. He saw that his pistol, one of two, was still there when a noise from behind him made the hairs on the back of his neck stand on end. His hand went for the pistol, but a voice spoke and he went utterly still.

'I still never understood why the rebels came for you that night when there was an artillery train ripe for plundering on the Wexford road.'

Sir Edward did not recognise the voice at first until Mullone moved out of shadow. 'Major, my dear chap,' he sighed exasperatedly. 'What are you doing there in the dark? I presumed you were in New Ross?'

'I was just thinking how lucky we were that night when the mob came,' Mullone said distantly.

Sir Edward stared down at the major's half-shadowed body, his eyes were like white orbs in the light. He was sitting on one of the green chairs that belonged to Ellen's grandfather. He straightened and turned fully so that he faced Mullone.

'Quite so. I thank God for it. I owe you my life, dear friend. We all do,' he said, smiling. 'I'm about to finish that report. Do you want to see a copy of it?'

'Not now, your Lordship,' Mullone said calmly.

'Would you like a drink?'

'Yes,' Mullone rasped, 'more than anything in the world, but I'd better not.'

Sir Edward brought out a bottle of whiskey and a small tumbler emblazoned with his family's crest.

'I was sent from the Castle by Colonel John Moore on a wee errand. Do you know what it was? I'll tell you,' he said when the peer shrugged. 'It was to find the man responsible for the atrocity committed at *Uaimh Tyrell*. A poor fishing village of not much else. A few families lived there.'

'Yes, I've heard of it. It was in all the papers.'

'A horrific crime was committed there.'

'So I read.'

'There were no survivors, and yet, there was a rumour that Colonel Black was responsible.'

Sir Edward chuckled, shaking his head. 'That creature? A crime is committed from petty thievery to murder and the peasants blame it on Black. He doesn't actually exist, you know. It's a rumour made up by the press to sell their damned stories.'

'Oh, but that's where I think you're wrong. He does exist, Sir Edward,' Mullone said. 'He's as real as rainfall and sunshine. It was said that the people of *Uaimh Tyrell* were good Protestants and good Catholics. They certainly weren't slaughtered by rumour.'

Sir Edward seemed to shudder as though his shoulders had been hit with a cudgel. 'A heinous crime.'

'They had nothing to do with the rebellion. They were not hiding fugitives.'

'So the priest said,' Sir Edward replied, taking a large gulp of the whiskey.

'Perhaps he really didn't know.'

'Priests are the eyes of the rebels, Major. He knew. He was just being stubborn.'

Mullone stared.

'And how would you know that, your Lordship?' he said after a moment of silence.

Sir Edward said nothing as though he was replaying the last sentence in his head. He blinked, then brought out the pistol. He opened the frizzen and checked that the flint was in place. He brought the doghead back until it clicked. The sound was loud in the small darkened room.

'It's a beautiful instrument,' Mullone said.

'Yes,' the aristocrat replied, long fingers stroking the barrel.

'It must have cost a lot of money.'

'It's one of a pair. Rifled with absolute precision and made by a craftsman in Germany called Lang. Cost a fortune, but they're worth every pound.'

Mullone remained seated; he watched the pistol in Sir Edward's hands where he jiggled it from one to the other.

'It struck me that your footmen knew how to load firearms,' Mullone said.

'I prefer that they do. A score of them accompany me during the hunting season. Armed retainers are what keep this manor safe. Other owners have failed to understand that and have now paid with their lives.'

'One of your guards was even wearing regulation white breeches. Cavalry breeches. They screamed at me when I arrived here, but I was too preoccupied with trying to warn you. Ever been to Oldbridge?'

The nobleman did not reply. He appeared to be occupied by the silver design on the pistol's grip that were full of hunting scenes: horses, hounds and a fox.

Mullone rubbed an eye, as though he was tired. 'What happened to your brother?'

'I told you. He was murdered,' Sir Edward's voice was suddenly cold. 'What has that got to do with your errand?'

'Was he killed chasing rebels?' Mullone asked. 'He died at Oldbridge, didn't he? That fellow Scurlock was the one you were after. He had something to do with your brother's death and you tracked him all the way to *Uaimh Tyrell*. But he wasn't there, was he? No matter. The people there knew him by association so they had to die too. Isn't that right? But what about the others you've killed along the way in your quest for retribution? What about the prisoners you hunted down in Wicklow? The family the press say were nailed to the doors because it was said they once let Scurlock sleep in their barn. Was it a game to you? A blood sport?'

Sir Edward chuckled in wry amusement. 'You don't know what you are talking about, Major. You're babbling. I fear the tragic events of New Ross have disturbed your mind.'

'I've never felt so alive, or thought so clearly, Sir Edward,' Mullone said. 'Or do you prefer being called Colonel Black?' The aristocrat said nothing and stared back at the pistol, turning it as though it was a rare gem. 'But it wasn't your brother's death that spurned you on your vile task, was it? You were hunting and murdering people long before that. You were Black long before the news of *Uaimh Tyrell* spread from one village to another until the country knew the crime. But now Scurlock is dead and your quest is over. I am under orders to bring you to Dublin where you will be tried.'

Sir Edward laughed again; the noise sounding like a snort. 'And what makes you so certain that I would willingly agree?' He raised the pistol to Mullone's face.

Mullone seemed unfazed by the threat. 'So we meet at last, Colonel Black,' he breathed.

Sir Edward gazed at him with mock surprise. 'And when did you become so wise?' he said, mockingly.

'It is not wisdom, Sir Edward; it is truth. The path to fact is always clear, if you look straight at it. I wasn't looking clearly enough, but I am now.'

'The path you tread will get you killed, Major. I will not confess. I am no one's puppet!' A smile nestled on Sir Edward's handsome face as he pulled the trigger.

And to his absolute horror, nothing happened.

'I thought you'd say that,' Mullone said with a long sigh. 'So I took the liberty of swapping your pistol with its twin. You said it was one of a pair, and I knew where you'd keep it.' Mullone brought the second pistol up to Sir Edward's face. 'They are marvellous,' he conceded. 'There's a harsh beauty about them.'

The aristocrat looked outraged, then smiled like the cold embrace of winter. 'You won't do it. I'm too valuable alive. You will have to prove your accusations and I'll have the best lawyers defending me. English ones. I'll see you cashiered. Ruined. Your career left in tatters. No one will find out the truth.' He gazed at the door and then at the window that would spill glorious early morning light onto the desk, illuminating the parchments with a rich glow. Now, darkness cloaked the grounds outside.

'You wouldn't be expecting Seamus, now would you, Sir Edward?' Mullone asked innocently.

Sir Edward's defiant face cracked. 'He...' his voice trailed off.

'He was a bullock of a man! And he was a surprisingly good talker too, but then he wanted to murder me, so I spilled his guts on your neat lawn. He was easy to spot in his uniform.'

Sir Edward eyed the weapon's black mouth, his jaw clenched. 'You're not a murderer. You won't do it.'

'Oh, I will, Sir Edward,' Mullone said softly, 'and I hate you for making me do it.'

The shot echoed from the house and pounded across the fields.

*

The clock in the room struck twelve of the morning. It was July 1st.

Colonel John Moore eyeballed the man who had just walked into the room at Wexford and delivered news that stunned the Scotsman into silence.

'Are you telling me that you didn't find Black?' Moore said when the chimes had died and he had found his voice.

'Yes, sir,' Mullone said, looking up from his report on the desk.

Moore's eyes flicked left to right, taking in every detail of Mullone's green eyes, like hooks snagging flesh. 'Do you have any leads? Anything at all?'

'No, sir. In the week since the Battle of Vinegar Hill I've not been able to trace his whereabouts. It's as if the ground has swallowed him up.'

On the 21st June, British forces launched an attack on Vinegar Hill outside the town of Enniscorthy, hoping to encircle and destroy the large rebel camp there. It was a brutal battle that spilled down into the streets.

'Then Black is still at large and we have failed,' Moore stated, giving Mullone a look of despair, before staring at the report again.

Mullone said nothing. A bat flew past the window, fluttering in the moonlight before disappearing. The deep waters of the River Slaney seemed to shiver.

'You came recommended,' Moore said with a glare, not hiding the severe disappointment that was affecting him, 'highly recommended. I am surprised. I presumed you would detain him. There really are no leads?'

'No, sir.'

'You make it clear in your report that De Marin was one of the ringleaders.'

'Yes, sir. He was at Enniscorthy on the 21st, but alas, he got away when the rebels blockaded the bridge preventing General Johnson's advance. I'm sure we'll meet again.'

'Have you the same confidence about Black?' Moore said bluntly, then rubbed his tired eyes. 'I understand about men slinking off into the shadows.' A day before Vinegar Hill, Colonel Moore, with orders from the Castle, had encountered a rebel force on the road to Wexford and defeated them as the shadowy ambushers struck from the hills, woods and fields. The army survived and the rebels melded away. 'I understand you and your men helped defend New Ross against Fitzstephen's rebels. General Johnson's report is most satisfactory.'

'Thank you, sir.'

'I'm sorry to hear about the loss of your men. I understand that your sergeant was wounded during the assault and your lieutenant was killed in the fighting.'

Mullone cleared his throat. 'Yes, sir,' he said, feeling uneasy about the lie.

Cahill was recuperating and Michael had chosen his true allegiance. He felt for the boy, had mentored him and he honestly hoped McBride would one day find reconciliation.

Moore pulled a letter to him. 'Do you know that they found Sir Edward Clanfield dead?'

'No, sir.'

'You aren't shocked?'

'I didn't really know him,' Mullone replied innocuously.

'His manor was attacked twice by insurgents. It seems they came back sometime later after the first assault and finished the job. Probably by a group eager for plunder and destruction following their defeat at New Ross.'

'We live in sad times, sir.'

'His poor wife is related to the Under-Secretary. Tragic.' Moore put the letter down and sighed. 'You've no doubt heard about the boats docked at Brest and Toulon?'

'Bonaparte's invasion fleet.'

'Which we now know is not bound for England, or these shores. You have your orders with you?'

'I do, sir,' Mullone replied. Government papers, for his eyes only.

'Well, God speed in your new adventure,' Moore stood up and clasped his hand, sighing. 'I just wish we'd got him,' he was still gripping the Irishman's hand.

'I know, sir,' Mullone replied humbly.

'If there's a shred of something good to come out of this tragedy, I wanted him stopped. He's been absent of late, but maybe we'll get him next time. I truly hope so.' Moore relaxed and withdrew his arm. 'Goodbye, Lorn.'

'Goodbye, sir.'

Mullone left the room for his quarters. He would only have a four hours' sleep, because at dawn he was expected to be at the harbour where he was to join a ship bound for London.

General Bonaparte and the French fleet were rumoured to be sailing for India to ally themselves with the ruler of Mysore to help destroy Britain's trade, but this was another fabrication.

Mullone fingered the cross at his neck and before going to bed, he said his prayers; for his friends and for God to forgive him for his sins. He was going to a faraway place, away from friends, and he did not want to go. Ireland was still suffering and he had desperately wanted to stay, but an old enemy threatened, and so he had go where he was ordered to.

Mullone slept peacefully, and that night he dreamed of wind-blown temples, sun-scorched deserts, strange animals and a land as distant and exotic as any on God's beautiful earth.

Egypt.

The Emerald Graves

The Emerald Graves, was added to the print version of *Liberty or Death* and the ebook version of *Battle Scars: A Collection of Short Stories*, for fans wanting to read more about Major Lorn Mullone at the Battle of Vinegar Hill. The full story is printed in the following pages.

The officer curbed his horse in one of the many fields below Vinegar Hill, a large pudding-shaped mound outside the town of Enniscorthy.

The sun had burned as fiercely as the rebellion these last few weeks and the night-air had been cool to the touch. There was a thin veil of mist that pooled around the grassy slopes of the hill. It was just after dawn and the sun was already rising above the valley floor, promising another kiln-hot day to come in County Wexford.

The officer brought up an expensive eyeglass and traversed it past the silvery haze and up to where fires burned a dull-red. His green eyes saw figures move up there. Only a score, but he knew there were thousands upon that emerald crown.

'Are you sure the bastard is up there, sir?' A voice rasped from the officer's left. The tone suggested speculation rather than worry.

'Aye. He's up there. I know he is.'

Sergeant Seán Cahill put a dirty finger to one nostril and blew a string of snot into a patch of nettles. 'Then the bastard knows we're coming for him.'

'I'm counting on it.'

'Why's that, sir?'

Major Lorn Mullone turned to his friend, studying the hollowness and extra lines in his face caused by a recent battle injury. 'Because that way he's scared, and men that are close to losing their wits make mistakes.'

Cahill's face twitched in understanding and he looked solemnly up at the great mound. He rubbed his leg that was still bandaged from the desperate fight at New Ross two weeks ago. Thousands of United Irishmen had stormed the walled town and succeeded in beating back

95

British troops under General Henry Johnson across the River Barrow. But the rebels had tired after the long assault and without firearms needed to hold back the redcoats, Johnson and his men had returned, brushed aside the fatigued rebels and retook the town. It had been a bitter and bloody engagement, and the survivors along with many leaders of the rebellion, were now up on the hilltop.

'One mistake, Seán,' Mullone continued, 'and I'll have him. For all the blood that he's spilt, I'll have him at long last.'

Mullone was currently employed by the War Office to spy on Theobald Wolf Tone, a leader of the United Irish, and his acquaintance of a wily French agent called De Marin. So far the Frenchman had eluded capture having recently dressed as a priest and preached lies and rumour to the Irish people that instilled fear and anger. He had been chiefly responsible for the French landings at Fishguard and Bantry Bay, and for inciting the heavy attack on New Ross.

Cahill's voice cut into Mullone's thoughts.

'Let's hope these buggers don't put a shell up his arse first then,' the sergeant said lugubriously, jutting his unshaven chin at the battery of howitzers nearby, 'otherwise your wee mission is over.'

'I'm well aware of that, Seán.'

The British troops had arrived in the early hours. Their final pre-dawn flanking march had taken several hours, far longer than their commander, Lieutenant-General Gerard Lake, could have anticipated. But it was a formidable force with over ten thousand men, twenty cannon and over four hundred carriages and wagons loaded with ammunition and equipment. The columns of redcoats were now beginning to make ready for assault. Their objective was simple: encircle the rebels and destroy them. There were four great columns designed to win the battle. Lake commanded the central force, Generals' Duff and Loftus were waiting to strike from the side of the River Slaney, Dundas waited on the east and Johnson was ready to attack Enniscorthy. Only General Needham had not reached position yet, but he had assured Lake that he would be there by first light.

Mullone's gaze wandered to Lake and his countenance instantly soured. They did not see eye-to-eye. The commander had no empathy with the Irish people and there was a rumour spoken that he would not let any man, woman or child live if he found them alive up on Vinegar Hill. He was a cruel man with eyes like two shards of pale ice set with the expression of constant indifference. Mullone had asked to see him this morning to discuss his apprehension of De Marin, but the general had almost angrily rebuffed him. The major considered that the attack could turn ever so easily into a massacre. There might be a small chance to apprehend the Frenchman, but it would be difficult.

Lake was on horseback with several officers and aides, staring up at the rebel lines. The redcoats, a mixture of Regular, Militia and Yeomanry troops, eagerly waited for the signal to advance. Officers shared jokes and laughed. Some men were smoking tobacco pipes and chatting to the men in their files and one or two were honing their bayonets with sharpening stones. A tall officer wearing a white-faced coat of the Dublin County Militia slashed at knee-high weeds with his sword as though he was waiting for a picnic to begin.

At seven o'clock, the signal was given and the cold iron throats of the guns were blasted free. The noise was terrifying and ear-splitting. Swift fan-shaped patterns rippled the long grass under the long barrels. Banks of foul-smelling smoke drifted like low cloud. Birds scared from their nests flew from trees. *Tintreach*, Mullone's horse, stamped its feet and whickered. He patted his grey muscled neck to soothe it.

'It won't be long until our boys are up there,' Cahill said, as the long column of Lake's infantry began the advance. 'Skulls are going to be broken, that's for sure.' Mullone pursed his lips, but didn't reply. 'Are we joining them, sir?' he said at the major's taciturnity.

'You can stay here,' Mullone replied abruptly.

'What?' Cahill pulled a face.

The blond-haired major turned to him. 'You're injured and supposed to be resting. What am I to tell your wife if anything happens to you? I left you at New Ross so that you could mend.'

Cahill spat onto to the ground. 'And you think by leaving me with her I would be safe?' The sergeant laughed sardonically. 'Jesus and all the saints. Once she got wind that the Croppies were going to attack the town, she sold a silver ring to buy a musket. A musket for God's sake! The woman's madder than a bishop without his whiskey.'

'I thought you'd be safe.'

'I am.'

Mullone huffed and shifted his rump. 'I promised her to keep you out of harm's way.' Their many years together had formed a strong bond.

'You have done,' Cahill quipped with a grin. 'I'm about to ride to battle and she's twenty miles away. I'm safe.'

Mullone winced. In truth, he was glad of his friend's company, having no other person who he would have fought alongside him. They wore the uniform of Lord Maxwell Lovell's Irish Dragoons, a design based on the British Light Dragoons. Their scarlet coats had green facings, the colour of the rich grass beneath them. Mullone wore buff breeches that were patched and heavily stitched, and was bareheaded having lost his Tarleton helmet. One hundred men had once ridden in the ranks, but after various skirmishes, battles and disease, ten remained. Mullone had left the remainder of his troopers under Corporal O'Shea with General Johnson's force whilst the two of them scouted for De Marin. He had been certain that the Frenchman was at Enniscorthy, until a blacksmith, caught making pike heads, had revealed otherwise. Mullone had questioned the man himself rather than let him be taken into custody and the smith had seen the compassion in the major's eyes and had talked. He said a bearded priest with a half-dozen United Irishmen, had asked him to increase the thirty pike heads he could turn out to fifty a day. That priest had been the spy and had joined a rebel leader called John Fitzstephen up on the hill. Mullone had guessed that the twenty thousand rebels planned to burn Enniscorthy to the ground and march triumphantly on Wexford.

The batteries opened up again, pumping clouds of jaundice-coloured smoke into the air, and bombarding the hill's crown with lethal iron shot. Mullone thought he saw great clods of earth flick up into the sky denoting a ball's strike. The redcoat column, supported by cavalry, were making the steep climb up the hill. So far they were marching in good order and with no rebel counterattacks. They hadn't even sent out their Light Companies and Mullone guessed that the threat of the cavalry was enough to hold back the few musket-armed insurgents.

'I think we should join them,' Mullone said and clicked *Tintreach* forward.

'About bloody time,' Cahill muttered, following close behind.

'But stay out of harm's way.'

'You've not to worry about me, sir,' Cahill gave a look of innocence as he patted the carbine in its holster. 'And when all this is finished, you and I can put our boots up and find ourselves a place that serves rare ale.'

'If we apprehend De Marin, I'll buy you the bloody tavern.'

Cahill touched the peak of his tarleton helmet. 'What are we waiting for then?' He edged his horse further than Mullone's.

When they reached the ascending column, musket shots rang out and as they kicked their mounts up the hill, volley-fire was splitting the air raw. Aides cantered between the regiments that formed and wheeled from column into line. Mullone saw a host of red coats with yellow, green and blue facings and banners of matching colours. The nearest battalion was the 89th, a regiment with black facings raised in Dublin at the start of the war with France. Its commander, Lord Blayney, was a young aristocrat who despised the United Irishmen and, with a history of an untiring perseverance in capturing the rebels, the regiment had been given its unofficial nickname of 'Blayney's Bloodhounds'.

Through the drifting dirty clouds of smoke, Mullone could see groups of rebels firing down from the summit. Their fire was sporadic and ragged, but the first redcoats were falling. A line of pikemen appeared behind a screen of yellow-flowering gorse. There were scores of them. Green banners fluttered in the wind. Whistles blew and more skirmishers ran out to meet the rebels. The Light Bobs in skirmish chain were winning the battle against the scarce musket-armed rebels because they were loading and firing quicker. Men and boys tumbled to the ground in gouts of blood. A leader wearing a short brown coat and a hat wound with a green ribbon was yelling orders and the rebels retreated. He turned in his saddle, aimed his pistol, fired into the mass of redcoats and then kicked his horse up the hill.

'Do you see their pikemen, Sergeant?' Mullone asked.

Then the ridgeline, as though sown by dragon's teeth, sprouted men.

'Here they come,' Cahill said almost excitedly, as hundreds of pike heads bobbed with the march of the men above the peak. First was the long staves, then arms and then the mass of men came into view.

The pikemen marched down the lip of the hill to the beat of drums and fifes. The Light Companies returned to their parent units after a flurry of blown whistles. Mullone could see the rebels' mouths open and close as though they were shouting or singing to a tune. The iron tips in each rank caught the sun, gleaming with orange light and with each step towards their enemy.

'Brave,' Mullone uttered. 'Foolish, but damned brave all the same.'

'Aye, sir,' Cahill agreed. 'There are women and children up there with their fathers and brothers. Jesus, but these bastards will not care who they kill.' He said the last sentence loud enough for the 89th to hear. The sergeant didn't care who heard him.

An officer, not yet thirty years old with dark curls and brown eyes, trotted his horse to the left of the regiment, a thin smile on his face. '89th!' Lord Blayney, pistol in his hand, commanded. 'Make ready! Let's spill some Croppie blood! Present!' Four hundred muskets went

99

to shoulders. 'I want these bastards dead! Aim at their black hearts, boys! Send them to hell!'

Mullone watched the rebels close the gap. They broke from their ranks to charge the redcoats. A boy of twelve hefted a green flag showing the harp. He stared wide-eyed at the bayonet-tipped muskets and then closed his eyes. At thirty yards the musket was deadly in concentrated volleys. Firing en masse, that would blast the enemy ranks apart like a giant shotgun.

'Fire!' Blayney bellowed.

Four hundred muskets spat smoke, flames jetted from muzzles and the balls punched into the rebels. The fusillade was like the crack of doom; a death knell wrought to this green place. Scores collapsed and the green slope was suddenly awash with blood. The attack faltered and Mullone watched the survivors clamber away.

'Load,' the sergeants bawled.

'Jesus,' Cahill said in the tone that could either have meant with awe or horror.

An aide galloped past, the beast's hooves scattering clods of earth behind it, and saluted Blayney before giving orders. The man then saluted again and kicked his horse towards a Militia regiment from Sligo on the 89th's right. A troop of Midlothian Fencible Cavalry guarded the flank, trotting with their sabres sheathed for now.

'89th advance!' Blayney rode forward and picked his way through the wounded. A man wearing a grubby white shirt was coughing up blood. Another man staggered with an arm hanging useless by his side. Mullone saw that the boy was still alive, but the green flag had been snatched away. His legs were trying to move his body, heels digging into the grass, but he faltered, chest expanding. Blood dribbled from his slack mouth. Blayney watched him. ''Tis a shame you fell in with the mob,' he said, stopping above him. 'But the shame will soon be over.' He brought the pistol around and shot the boy through the forehead.

The redcoats confidently resumed their march as though they had encountered no resistance. There had been a rumour that the rebels had built a series of defence works and Mullone twisted in his saddle to see the lighter field guns were being pulled and dragged up the slopes by the blue-coated horse artillery in case that proved true. The cannon could destroy the fortifications that had been hastily thrown up, and fire grapeshot into the packed ranks of pikemen. The howitzers were still lobbing shells overhead that fizzed and screamed like banshees before exploding above the packed ranks of the rebels. Every so often he heard a voice cry out, before it was snatched by a faltering wind, or from the sporadic musket-fire. Some shells, fired too high, crashed over the summit amongst the rocks. The rebels came down the hill again. This time they appeared in one contemptible line instead of a rabble. Muskets went to shoulders and the redcoats walked into a hail of lead. A few men went down, including a couple of officers ahead of their companies, but the range was too great. An officer of the Longford Militia to Mullone's left was trying to control his rearing mount that was screaming from a bullet to its neck. The horse kept tossing its head. A sergeant ran forward to help and received a kick for his trouble. He landed heavily on his back, where he gasped and clawed at his chest.

'Stupid bastard ought to have known better than to run behind a nag,' Cahill said carelessly. 'Probably now has a rib or two broken. Serves him right.'

Mullone heard a rebel shout commands to load. A roundshot slammed into the slope and bounced high up into the air. Both sides saw the heavy iron ball spin, and hit the ground with a terrific thud again to roll back down the hill going past the cavalry on the flank.

'They're loading too slowly,' Cahill remarked as though he was disappointed with the enemy's progress.

'They're not trained, Seán.'

The redcoats halted perhaps forty yards from the rebel line and levelled their muskets. The quick-witted ones turned and took flight, just before the red lines sent another crashing volley into them. More men tumbled like skittle and the line dissolved.

'Here they go again,' Cahill said as another line of pikemen appeared.

They descended steadily over the crest and Mullone saw three groups behind the fifth ranks moving, or steadying something. A glint of light flashed briefly.

'They've got cannon,' he said.

Cahill chuckled. 'Now we're getting somewhere, sir.'

The pikemen did not wait for any orders and suddenly broke cohesion to charge the redcoats. Again the musket line exploded and the balls twitched the British ranks crimson. A rebel picked up a fallen banner and waved his men on. Mullone espied a pike thrown like a spear just miss a Longford Militiaman in the front rank. Another man staggered as though he was drunk.

The redcoats were advanced through the whirling powder-smoke and the wounded rebels found beneath their boots were bayoneted without any disinclination.

Two of the cannon were small and Mullone considered them to be puny one-pounders, but the piece facing the men from Sligo was a six-pounder. The left gun fired a one-pound ball down the slope. It hit a bump in the grass and bounced harmlessly over the attackers. The other gun fired by farmers and labourers slammed straight into the 89th, decapitating a sergeant and disembowelling an officer's chestnut horse. The beast shrieked and collapsed before the man could climb out of the saddle. The horse fell and the man, trapped by the weight, gasped as his leg broke.

The redcoats were thirty yards from the crest and the rebel gunners were waiting until the very last minute before allowing the glowing slow-matches to touch the quills. The redcoats collectively took an intake of breath at the cold muzzles in front. Then, a howitzer shell fired from the British lines, trilled and flashed before exploding above the six-pounder killing all its crew. The remaining gunners fled and disappeared out of view.

A deep throated cheer went up from the redcoats and the ensigns hoisted their flags higher. Victory was certain and the rebels would be defeated. On all sides of the hill, they came and the rebels had nowhere to go. The battle was already won.

Then, a single man appeared on the crest. He wore a long green coat and a black hat with a green cockade. He stared with dark eyes and from a hundred yards away, Mullone recognised him. Fitzstephen was one of the United Irish leaders whom he had met following the slaughter at New Ross. If he was here, then so was De Marin.

Fitzstephen gave an ironic salute with his sword, picked up the slow-match and put it to the quill. The powder fizzed a heartbeat before the six-pounder crashed back on its long trail as the grapeshot burst from the blackened muzzle. The shot jerked back a dozen screaming Sligo men, tearing bloody swathes in the ranks and sheeting the grass with blood, bone and gobbets of gore. The wounded stumbled away or lay in mounds and the battalion appeared momentarily stunned, but the attack did not falter and the drums hammered them on.

The first redcoats over the summit saw the entire plain was packed with thousands of rebels. The pikes bristled with defiance. Horsemen trotted along the lines shouting commands, whilst others were trying to push men into formation.

102

Mullone and Cahill trotted in between the mauled Sligo men and the 89th, making way for three guns brought up to be quickly unlimbered.

'They've had it now,' Cahill said, plugging his mouth with chewing tobacco. 'There's nowhere else to run to.'

The redcoats advanced and the great rebel lines seemed to contract. Among the pikes and banners, wooden crosses were held up. Mullone saw a priest riding a horse up and down the lines. He was shouting with great fervour. Mullone looked for Fitzstephen and De Marin, but could not see either of them. Drummers were still beating the phalanxes onward and the redcoats were cheering as they advanced, their voices enthusiastic and almost light-hearted, as though this was just a game. More and more redcoats climbed the crest and the situation for the rebels looked dire. The east side of Vinegar Hill offered no protection. There were no rocky outcrops, ridges and pockets here where the musket-armed rebels had offered insolence. British cavalry, sensing ease, trotted up the smooth grassy bank unopposed and wheeled into line. As Mullone neared the enemy, he could see that the ranks were not formed as one giant hollow square, but fragmented into numerous unsteady formations. That being so, the horsemen could not charge for the pike was a cavalryman's worst nightmare. The long blades would stab and pierce them in the saddles, unhorse them and the animals were frightened of the iron-tipped rows.

God, but we could die here today, Mullone considered. To be buried in mass pits. He imagined a series of emerald graves upon the summit that would be the only mark of the battle.

The forward Crown battalions halted fifty yards from the rebels and were met with more curses and derisory whoops. Mullone curbed his horse. He brought out his spyglass and scanned the faces for De Marin and Fitzstephen. Bearded, dirty and bold unknown faces blurred as the glass traversed the ranks. Mullone grimaced for he could not see either of them. Then, he heard a deep voice emanating from the ranks, and Fitzstephen stepped forth.

'Don't fear them. They have one shot. You have your pikes,' he urged. 'The blade is as sharp as your wits, broad as your pride and deadly as your courage. Stand tall. Stand strong. *Erin go Bragh!*'

A crescendo of voices rose up to repeat the declaration and the hairs on the back of Mullone's neck stood up.

'Words spoken by a brave man,' he said, turning to Cahill. The rebel had captured Mullone after New Ross, but had let him live rather

103

than turn him over to De Marin who would have killed him in the blink of an eye.

'The mutterings of a mad man,' Blayney shouted as the noise died down.

The redcoats brought their heavy muskets to their shoulders and the regular, Fencible and Militia regiments disappeared in white smoke and the air rippled with leaping flames like hell's horrors as the volley-fire thundered into the rebels. Scores fell to the turf. A man holding a coal-black banner with God Damn The King stitched in white needlework stumbled and dropped the flag, sinking to his knees. A man ran forward to haul another away, who had a small crimson stain on his ash-grey shirt. A riderless horse, sheeted with blood, cantered across the lines. Someone began laughing hysterically.

All the curses and threats have come to end on this grassy mound. *Such a waste of life,* Mullone thought. Such a waste of good lives from men he could have called friends or drank with in happier times.

'Load!'

'Send the Croppies to hell, boys!' shouted an officer of the Longford Militia. 'Send them back where they came from!'

Mullone couldn't see Fitzstephen or much of anything as the smoke clogged the air.

The British reloaded and fired another volley into the vague shapes beyond the smoke. When a battery of six-pounders were brought up, the infantry was ordered forward with bayonets fixed.

'That's the way!' a colonel of the Sligo Militia yelled. 'Take no prisoners! Do you hear? Let not one of them live! That's an order now! Today is the Day of Judgement!'

Cahill spat tobacco juice onto the grass. 'The Croppies have no place to hide. This is the end for them.'

'I'm not so sure of that.' Mullone had been staring at the press of rebels to the south and they were disappearing. He quickly surmised that General Needham's force had not yet reached the hill and Lake in his rashness had left a gap in the attacking lines, which the rebels were fervently exploiting.

The redcoats marched and the drummers' rhythm was more ragged, as they had to step over the dead and dying enemy. Pools of blood were soaking into the ground, darkening the grass. Wounded men begged for water, or for their mothers, or for sweethearts. A great bear of a man with a stain from an old powder burn on his right cheek pounced on a writhing body.

'Look what I've found!' he said to his companions of the Sligo Militia, clasping long hair in his paw-like hands. It was a girl, perhaps sixteen years of age, pretty with hair the colour of peat, and the big redcoat struck her across the face to quieten her screams. She fell back onto the blood-slick grass. 'Let's have a look at you, my pretty.' He cackled and ripped open her dress to expose small, round breasts. 'Oh yes, they'll do.' He fingered one of her nipples and bent down to suckle when a boot caught him in the side of the neck. He rolled over to see a sergeant pulling the girl to her feet.

'You get up again and I'll spit you with this,' Cahill patted his sword.

The private cast sullen eyes and wiped his mouth. 'You want her for yourself, Sergeant?' he said, voice raspy from the assault.

'No,' Cahill replied and pushed the frightened girl up into the saddle. 'I'll return her to her family.' The man laughed sourly at that. 'What's funny, you ugly bastard?'

'Her family are here,' the private said, still laughing. 'Dead like the rest of them. Soon to be crow food.'

The girl whimpered and Cahill hauled himself up, wincing because of his injured leg. He spat a jet of the remains of his tobacco plug that hit the wretch full in the face, and clicked the horse on.

Mullone was frantically studying the bodies. 'I can't see Fitzstephen.'

'He must be with the mass of them over there,' Cahill said, staring east.

Musket fire crackled from the rebels and a handful of horsemen who were circling the moving horde tumbled to the ground. Mullone watched a ramrod wheel through the air. A knot of pikemen led by a sword-armed man charged into the 89th. The blades looked wickedly long in the smoke-torn sunlight. They slashed at faces, cut arms and tried to disembowel, but a blast of grapeshot threw reinforcements behind them down in a welter of blood, and the experienced redcoats killed the others with bayonet thrusts. An officer whooped, shot a woman who was pushing children away, then charged with his pistol raised as a club. Another cannon, brought to face the slope to the south, slapped horribly through the retreating rebel files to slash quick bloody swathes on the grass. Men, women and children were dying from canister. Canister was a cylindrical tin crammed with musket balls which burst open at the cannon's muzzle to hurl a spreading cone of bullets at the enemy. Mullone could see the effect of the grape shot and canister from the mounds of dead, and horribly wounded groups of rebels snatched backwards from the attacks. It was a sickening sight.

'Sir!' Cahill called urgently and Mullone twisted back in his saddle. The sergeant was pointing at a body.

Mullone dismounted and knelt down by the rebel leader. His face was pallid, grey almost like it had been rinsed of colour. He had been shot twice; a bullet to his shoulder and another had pierced a lung. Pink bubbles frothed at the corners of his mouth.

'Where is he?' Mullone asked him.

Fitzstephen coughed and blood seeped from his purple lips. He recognised the major and knew who he was enquiring about. 'Why should I tell you?' he croaked.

Mullone watched the dying man whose face was distorting in a combination of shock, pain and disbelief. There wasn't much time. 'You asked me once whether I was a patriot and I told you that I was,' he said in a soft voice. 'I love Ireland as much as any man here. But I will not be a slave to the French. De Marin does not care for your ideals any more than the rest of them. He's using you and you've been a fool. Now where is he? Tell me so that he can't ruin any more Irish lives.'

Fitzstephen coughed again and a hand fluttered over his ruined chest. The light in his eyes was getting dimmer. Mullone shook him and he regained a little consciousness. 'If I tell you, will you... help a dying man on his last journey? I'll not give these other damned redcoats the pleasure.'

Mullone ran his eye over the corpse-strewn ground, then nodded, knowing what was being asked of him. His eyes returned to the rebel with solemn agreement. 'Yes.'

'Your word.'

Mullone sighed. 'You have it.'

Fitzstephen's mouth spread to a smile. 'He left for Enniscorthy... and from there he'll likely go north to Ulster. They're planning... something up there.'

'Thank you.'

A bloodied hand gripped the major's arm.

'You... promised me,' Fitzstephen looked pained.

Mullone got to his feet. 'I did,' he said. The rebel's once green coat faced-red, and decorated in gold lace and epaulettes, was ragged and grimy. His uniform had once dazzled, but now looked like a veteran's cast-offs. Mullone hazarded a guess that the last few weeks had been grim. 'Seán.' he uttered, jaw clenched. He could not do the deed himself.

The sergeant pulled out his carbine, cocked the hammer and brought the stock to his shoulder.

'*Erin go Bragh*,' Mullone said softly.

Fitzstephen showed his teeth. It was obvious from the uneven rise and fall of his chest that death was not far away, but he wanted a soldier's death, for he had looked after his men like any good commander had. '*Erin go Bragh*, Major.'

Mullone climbed into the saddle as the shot rang out. 'We ride to Enniscorthy. And find that Crapaud bastard.' He remembered the girl was still with them and coughed to cover his embarrassment. 'We'll leave you safe at the town,' he said, and the frightened girl nodded.

They were about to move away when an artillery officer rode up to them, his bay horse slick with sweat.

'Captain Bloomfield, sir,' he said, saluting. He was a stocky man with salt-and-pepper hair.

'Major Lorn Mullone and this is my sergeant.'

Bloomfield shot Cahill a friendly glance, saw the girl and his mouth opened.

'What do you want, Captain? We have important business to attend to,' Mullone said tartly.

'Apologies, sir,' Bloomfield closed his lolling jaw. 'I was going to ask if you knew who this man was?' The gun captain jutted his chin at Fitzstephen's body. 'Forgive me, sir, but I've heard there's a bounty on a man named John Fitzstephen. One of the Wexford leaders. I was hoping to claim it.'

'I'm afraid you're mistaken.' As he spoke, Mullone gazed at a patch of dry grass smouldering from the burning wads jettisoned from the musket barrels. 'This man just asked for water and so I gave it to him. I've no idea who he is.'

Bloomfield looked crestfallen. 'I see, sir.'

'I've seen Fitzstephen and that is certainly not him,' Mullone reiterated the lie. 'I'd look elsewhere if I were you. Good day to you, Captain.'

Mullone saluted, made sure the officer had left, and the three of them climbed down the slope to cross a ford two miles north. The cold water of the River Slaney reached their knees, but they had crossed the high grass-strewn banks without any confrontation with the pockets of rebels. They followed a track made of ancient wheel ruts to the town.

Scores were streaming across Enniscorthy's seventeenth-century stone bridge where shouting and heavy musketry echoed loudly. The Norman castle dominated the town, which was garrisoned with redcoats. The Union Flag flew tall from the battlements.

Mullone found General Johnson directing two companies of green-coated riflemen into the narrow, cobbled streets. They were Germans from the 5th Battalion, 60th Rifles, and they ran forward in skirmish order. Beyond the roof tops, a thick plume of smoke carried from two burning buildings obscured the savagery ensuing on Vinegar Hill. A volley of musket fire hammered at a group of Light Bobs from the Dumbarton Fencibles, a Scottish regiment who wore bonnets and kilts. The Scotsmen were crouched behind walls, gardens and houses. One spun away and another staggered, clutching his side.

'Major Mullone,' Johnson greeted him warmly, despite the obvious fierce resistance his force had encountered. A steady stream of wounded were making their way to a barn where a surgeon was plying his gruesome trade. Skeins of smoke hung between the buildings.

'Morning, sir,' Mullone wiped the sweat on his face with a sleeve. Cahill hung back with the girl.

'Has General Lake sent you down here?' Johnson's tone rankled with hate for the man.

'No, sir. I came here of my own accord.'

Johnson was a tall man; gangly and narrow-shouldered with a face lined with age and a long nose. In the recent weeks, his face had become somewhat pinched as though he was worn down with the stress of the rebellion. He looked sideways at Mullone. 'More government work, eh? What the hell brings you here? Your troopers are helping to guard the baggage. Have you come for them?'

'No, sir. I need to ask you something.'

Johnson lifted his chin. 'Go on.'

'When we first met I told you I was looking for a French spy by the name of De Marin. He masquerades as a priest; a Father Keay.'

'Yes, I remember. And?'

Mullone looked towards the houses. 'A source has confirmed he's in the town, sir.'

Johnson watched the Germans clear the houses, darting forward like professional soldiers, watching, aiming and covering each step. One pair spotted an enemy marksmen firing from a rooftop and put a bullet in him. The body slid down the slate tiles, leaving a trace of blood behind. One of the Germans whooped with glee. 'Enniscorthy is thick with the mob, Major. I fear you'll never catch him.'

'The bridge, sir. If your men can reach it, then perhaps my chances will increase.'

The general blew out a lungful of breath. 'That might prove impossible...' His voice trailed off.

'Sir?' Mullone prompted.

Johnson made an almost apologetic face. 'The rebels have already thrown my lads out once. They are hard-pressed.'

Mullone could see the men's lips were stained by black powder from biting cartridges and would be desperately thirsty from the saltpetre in the gunpowder. There were red bodies lining the road and slumped against houses. It must have been a tough fight.

Mullone's exasperation and anguish broke. 'I have to find him! I can't let that bastard escape!' Johnson looked shocked at the outburst and Mullone shifted awkwardly. 'My sincerest apologies, sir. De Marin is a slippery fellow and I've spent months trying to apprehend him.'

The crinkles around Johnson's eyes, became more noticeable when he smiled. 'No regret needed, Major,' he countered quickly. 'I understand your position,' he said with empathy. 'I had hoped to have taken the town by now, but I take my hat off to the Croppies. Their pikemen are made of stronger stuff. They've blocked the roads and the bridge and my lads have not been able to break through. I've asked Lake for reinforcements, but as every minute passes by with no answer, they slip away. I'm sorry.'

Mullone clicked *Tintreach* forward, his gaze drifted towards the bridge. He turned to Cahill. 'Tether *Tintrí* to the post over there,' he said, pointing to a broken gate. 'I'm going into the town.'

'Let me come with you, sir,' Cahill pleaded. The girl still had not left his side.

'Stay here, Seán,' Mullone was emphatic. 'That's a direct order. Look after the girl.'

The sergeant reluctantly obeyed. 'Be careful, sir.'

'It's not me you should be worrying about.'

Cahill grinned, exposing yellow teeth. 'If you see the bastard, be sure to break his skull.'

Mullone picked his way down through the cobbled road to the heart of the town. Green banners, ribbons and freshly cut boughs hung from windows declaring their true loyalties. Musket shots echoed not far from him. His nose wrinkled at the roiling gun smoke and from the burning buildings. A leaden ball smacked into a house's wall not far from him, making a buzzing sound as it spun away. He followed the street to where redcoats were firing sporadically at barricades. He went over to an officer on horseback who stiffened in his saddle.

'Major Mullone, sir.'

'Colonel Vesey, Dublin County Militia,' the officer said, mouth clenching a cigar. What brings you here, Mullone?'

'I'm tasked by the Castle to find a French agent by the name of De Marin, sir.'

Vesey chortled as though that had amused him. He took out the cigar and a plume of blue smoke erupted from his mouth. 'A spy? Here?'

'Yes, sir.'

Vesey remained silent for a few seconds as though the thought of French secret agents was the work of fantasy. 'I haven't seen or heard any Crapauds. Lots of Croppies shouting 'death to the king' and 'liberty and equality' and such like. Nothing in French. What does this villain look like?'

Mullone gave De Marin's description. 'He's known to dress in a priest's attire, sir,' he added, staring at the bullet-marked barricades and houses. He could see scores of pikemen and musket-armed rebels, but no priest. 'He may have abandoned the guise, though,' he added, knowing that was a possibility. He would have done the same in the Frenchman's situation.

Vesey paused for a moment to suck on his cigar.

Dear God, Mullone thought. *Time is running out.* He fixed the man a penetrating look. 'Sir?'

Vesey puckered his lips, then shook his head. 'No, I have not seen such a knave. In any case finding him would be like trying to find a musket ball at the bottom of an ocean. Impossible. I wish I could help you further.' He spread his palms in a gesture of helplessness. 'I'll put the word out, though, should my lads come across a Frog in these parts.'

'Thank you, sir. I briefly knew your predecessor. He died bravely.'

When the attackers had breached one of the New Ross' gates Lord Mountjoy, commander of the militia, had tried to reason with them, but his words had fallen on deaf ears. He had been pulled from his horse and piked to death.

Vesey's eyes clouded with sorrow, but not for long for he had achieved command of the regiment, which was something he had yearned for. 'Yes. A God-faring man to the end. You were there then? A terrible day and night that was.'

'I was there.'

Vesey shifted in his saddle, mouth turned down at the corners. 'I've never seen such blood-letting in all my life. New Ross was a butcher's yard. Men, women and children slaughtered. I can still smell the scent of death.'

But Mullone wasn't listening. He was staring at a man wearing a long brown coat with a green sash and a black top hat. The rebel leader was standing on the bridge's stonework as a mass of fugitives were crossing the Slaney to where the survivors of Vinegar Hill were continuing to flee.

Mullone's skin prickled.

'De Marin!' He ran to an upturned cart and stood up on it, nerves taut, shouting furiously. 'De Marin! You bastard!'

The Frenchman looked around and smiled. He had shaved off his beard and was now dressed as a civilian, but at his hip hung his expensive sword. He waved once and disappeared in the seething horde.

Bile rose into the back of Mullone's throat. He had failed and he knew it. He thumped a hand down on one of the iron-rimmed wheels and swore.

From the slaughter of New Ross, to the blood-soaked battle on the hill and here at Enniscorthy today, De Marin had escaped. The Frenchman had boasted after New Ross that their paths would cross again.

Mullone knew that to be true, but when that time came he would be ready. He vowed it.

Historical Note

The rebellion of 1798 was an uprising against British rule in Ireland lasting from May to September.

The Society of United Irishmen, a republican revolutionary group founded in Belfast, 1791, and influenced by the ideas of the American and French revolutions, were the main organising force behind it. They came together to secure a reform of the Irish parliament and did this by uniting Roman Catholics, Presbyterians, Methodists, other Protestant "dissenters" groups.

From the very beginning, Dublin Castle, the seat of government in Ireland, viewed the new organisation with suspicion, and with the outbreak of war between Britain (including Ireland) and France in February 1793, mistrust turned to naked hostility. The Society members were viewed as traitors and it was suppressed in 1794. Led by Theobald Wolf Tone, a barrister, he vowed to "break the connection with England" as the group was driven underground. A planned uprising with French military help resulted in a series of blunders and the first invasion faltered and the fleet sailed home.

The government responded to widespread disorders by launching a counter-campaign of martial law in early 1798. Its doctrines used tactics such as planting spies, half-hangings, house burnings, pitch-capping and murder, particularly found in Ulster as it was the one area of Ireland where Catholics and Protestants had achieved a common cause of revolt. A plan to take Dublin was thwarted, but just after sunrise on 24th May, pockets of insurgents rose and the fighting quickly spread throughout the country over the next four months.

The aftermath was marked by the massacres of captured and wounded rebels with some on a large scale such as at New Ross and Enniscorthy. Rebel prisoners were regarded as traitors to the Crown, and were not treated as prisoners of war, but were executed. County Wexford was the only area which saw widespread atrocities committed by the rebels during the rebellion. Massacres of loyalist prisoners took place at the Vinegar Hill camp and on Wexford Bridge. After the defeat of the rebel attack at New Ross, the 'Scullabogue Barn Massacre' occurred where between one hundred and two hundred mostly Protestant men, women, and children were imprisoned in a barn which was then torched. In Wexford town, on 20th June some seventy loyalist prisoners were marched to the bridge and piked to death.

On 22nd August, one thousand French soldiers under General Humbert landed in County Mayo. Joined by several thousand rebels, they inflicted a humiliating defeat on the British at the Castlebar, which became mockingly known as the 'Castlebar races' to commemorate the speed of the retreat. But luck ran out for the French who were defeated and repatriated to France in exchange for British prisoners of war. For the hundreds of captured Irish rebels, their fate was the hangman's noose or firing squad.

On 12th October, another French force, including Wolfe Tone, attempted to land in County Donegal near Lough Swilly. They were intercepted by the Royal Navy, and finally surrendered after a three hour battle without ever landing in Ireland. Tone slit his own throat rather than wait for the noose and died a week later.

Small fragments of the rebel armies survived for a number of years and waged a form of guerrilla warfare in several counties. It was not until the failure of Robert Emmet's rebellion of 1803 that the last organised rebel force finally capitulated.

The Act of Union, having been passed in August 1800, came into effect on 1st January 1801. It was passed largely in response to the rebellion and was founded by the perception that the rebellion was provoked by the brutish misrule of the Ascendancy as much as the efforts of the United Irishmen.

The rebellion caused thousands of deaths. Modern accounts estimate the death toll from ten to as many as fifty thousand men, women and children killed by battle, starvation and disease.

Liberty or Death is a work of fiction, but firmly rooted by actual events. Lorn Mullone, Sergeant Cahill and the rebel leader John Fitzstephen are inventions, but men like Colonel John Moore, Colonel Robert Craufurd, General Henry Johnson and the pious Luke Gardiner, Colonel Lord Mountjoy, did exist. Lord Maxwell Lovell's Irish Dragoon regiment is another invention but based on the number of Yeomanry and Fencible regiments created at this time.

All of the locations mentioned are real except *Uaimh Tyrell*. The Battle of New Ross (actually the Second Battle of New Ross) did happen as much described. The rebels, under the leadership of Bagenal Harvey and John Kelly, tried to break out of County Wexford across the River Barrow to spread the rebellion into County Kilkenny and the outlying province of Munster. New Ross guarded the borders. The town was first fought over during the Irish Confederate Wars and captured by Cromwellian troops in 1649. Artillery fired three shots at the east gate and it was subsequently known thereafter as Three Bullet Gate.

The huge numbers of the rebel army swept aside the small military outposts and seized the gate. They then attacked simultaneously down the steeply sloping streets but were met with barricades and musket-armed soldiers. Despite a terrible number of casualties taken, the rebels managed to seize two-thirds of the town by using the cover of smoke from the burning buildings. Nonetheless, their limited supply of gunpowder and ammunition forced them to rely on the pike. The soldiers under Johnson managed to hold on and following the arrival of reinforcements, launched a counterattack which finally drove the exhausted rebels away. The slaughter, plundering and destruction mentioned in the story are based on true eye-witness accounts. Rebel casualties have been reported at three thousand whilst Crown forces suffered about two hundred. Most of the rebel dead were either thrown in the Barrow, or buried in a mass grave outside the town walls.

By the nineteenth century New Ross had become a wealthy port, but thousands left to start new lives abroad. The most famous emigrants were the great-grandparents of John F. Kennedy, who visited his ancestral home in 1963.

The Battle of Vinegar Hill marked a turning point in the rebellion, as it was the last attempt by the rebels to hold and defend ground against the British military. The battle, as told in the short-story *The Emerald Graves*, was actually fought in two locations: on Vinegar Hill itself and in the choking streets of Enniscorthy.

The British had surrounded Wexford with an estimated 20,000 troops and were ready to pour into the county to crush the insurgency. The rebel leadership issued a call to all its fighters to gather at Vinegar Hill to meet the army in one great, decisive battle. The number estimated at 20,000, but the majority lacked firearms and had to rely on pikes and whatever they could get their hands on. The camp also included many thousands of women and children who were staying there for protection. The British plan, as formulated by Gerard Lake, envisaged the complete annihilation of the rebels by encircling the hill and seizing the only escape route to the west, the bridge over the Slaney. As mentioned in *The Emerald Graves* the force was made up of four large columns; three under the command of Generals' Dundas,

Duff and Needham were to assault the hilltop, while the fourth, under General Johnson, was to storm Enniscorthy and capture its vital bridge.

The battle began shortly before dawn with an artillery bombardment of rebel positions on the summit. Advance units quickly moved against rebel outposts under cover of the wafting smoke and moved artillery closer as forward positions were secured. The tightening ring forced the rebels into an ever-shrinking area and increased exposure to the constant bombardment.

Meanwhile, a detachment of light infantry under the command of General Johnson attacked Enniscorthy, but were met with fierce resistance. Buildings in the town had been fortified, and the initial attack was driven back, with the loss of munitions and men. A second attack commenced with reinforcements and the rebels were slowly driven out of the town but managed to hold the Slaney bridge and prevent the British from crossing.

When British troops crested the eastern summit of Vinegar Hill, the rebels were astonished to see a gap in the British lines and so escaped through it rather than offer battle. It later became known as "Needham's Gap", so-named because the late arrival of General Needham's troops that prevented a total encirclement of the hill. Although much of the rebel army escaped, many were left behind and killed in the rout, from both cavalry and infantry attack, but also from the advanced field guns firing grape shot to maximize casualties. Eyewitness of the engagement said that the rebel casualties were around 1200.

The rebel force streamed away. The defeat was not catastrophic, but it did alter the course of the continued fighting in the form of raids and hit and run operations.

Colonel Black is another creation, but derived from a group of looters who styled themselves 'The Black Mob' after the conflict coupled with the fear and murderous hatred that had sparked across the country. De Marin was invented as Mullone's nemesis; they have a history and will undoubtedly meet again as the Frenchman mockingly hopes.

For more information on the events of 1798, I recommend Thomas Pakenham's *The Year of Liberty*, a masterly telling of that violent and deeply unfortunate chapter of Irish history.

Heart of Oak

Simon Gamble and the liberation of
the Maltese Islands
December 1799 - September 1800

Come cheer up, my lads! 'tis to glory we steer,
To add something more to this wonderful year;
To honour we call you, not press you like slaves,
For who are so free as the sons of the waves?

Chorus
Hearts of oak are our ships, heart of oak are our men,
We always are ready: steady, boys, steady!
We'll fight and we'll conquer again and again.

We ne'er see our foes but we wish them to stay,
They never see us but they wish us away;
If they run, why we follow, and run them ashore,
For if they won't fight us, we cannot do more.

Chorus

They swear they'll invade us, these terrible foes,
They frighten our women, our children, and beaus;
But should their flat bottoms in darkness get o'er,
Still Britons they'll find to receive them on shore.

Chorus

We'll still make them fear, and we'll still make them flee,
And drub 'em on shore, as we've drubb'd 'em at sea;
Then cheer up, my lads! with one heart let us sing:
Our soldiers, our sailors, our statesmen and king.

Chorus

'Heart of Oak' was a very popular military song, and to this day is the
official march of the United Kingdom's Royal Navy. It was originally
written as an opera and sung for the first time in 1760. There is an
American version called the 'Liberty Song'.

It was dawn and three longboats approached the northern shore of Gozo.

A frigid wind whipped over the waves. During the night, they had smashed white against the coast, but the storm clouds had gone, torn ragged by a morning gale that had now subsided to a gentle breeze that allowed the boats to cut through the water with relative ease. Behind them, silhouetted and anchored offshore to the west, was the HMS *Sea Prince*; a third rate seventy-four gun vessel of the line. The huge square-cut sails, turned dirty white by the long usage of wind and rain, reflected in the sea.

The boats, manned by sailors of His Britannic Majesty's Navy, carried a company of red-coated marines; tough and versatile soldiers, who were led by a man who looked as every bit as hard as they were.

Captain Simon Gamble was twenty-nine years old, and had enlisted at eighteen as a second lieutenant. He was average-looking with a soldier's face; sun-darkened, harsh and scarred. If you were to pass him in the street, you would pay him no attention, but if you saw his sea-blue eyes, then you would see that they sparkled brightly, accentuating his rough exterior to give it an odd gentleness that made him memorable. His scarlet coat and crimson sash were patched and heavily stitched and he was armed with a cutlass, a straight-bladed sword of extraordinary ugliness. It had a rolled iron grip, a thirty-inch blade, and curiously tied to the pommel was a scrap of a tattered silk. It had belonged to his mother; a parting gift for her young son who promised to return home with enough money to pay for his father's grievous arrears that had cost the family their home. A bone-handled dirk and a large pistol were tucked into his belt, which were also hooked to it in case he dropped them overboard during a fight aboard a vessel.

Gamble trained his telescope east to a narrow beach where waves exploded in bursts of foam on the massive limestone rocks. Dim in the gauzy light from the spray that drizzled like fog, he focused on the dark, almost black enemy gun batteries high upon the bluff. He had recently been part of the marine force under the command of Sir Sidney Smith who had helped defeat the French army under General Bonaparte at Acre during the bitter siege. Now he was about to lead his marines up that beach to where, in the half-light, they were to storm a redoubt, and silence those great guns that guarded the great expanse of blue-green Mediterranean Sea. Then, once he was satisfied the redoubt was secured, he would take his men overland to capture a French held fort situated on the Gozo's south-west coast.

The French had seized the Maltese Islands a year before and garrisoned it with over three thousand prime troops. There were many coastal defences, but the local Gozitans and Maltese confirmed that the French garrisons were too few and, encouraged with the news, the British naval taskforce had arrived to blockade the French into submission. The local resistance fighters pledged to support any British land attack.

'How many of the Frogs did you say there were here?' Gamble asked his Maltese guide.

'Fewer than fifty,' Giuseppe Falzon replied softly in his accented English. He was dressed in civilian clothes, but a large blue boat cloak was draped over his shoulders. 'They will be asleep now. They watch the sea, but think any likely attack will come from the south. Over land. They will not suspect a landing here of all places.'

'They'd better not do, Zeppi,' Gamble warned, eyes still fixed on the enemy ship-killers, 'otherwise we're dead men. But we have speed and surprise in our favour, and my marines are the best fighters known to mankind,' he said proudly so the entire boat could hear. He meant every word of the praise. The battles had hardened them like a tempered sword, forged in blistering flame. The men grinned back. The captain switched his stare to the Malteseman. 'However trusting of my rogues to do the task, you know the rules.'

Zeppi sighed as though he was being harangued. 'I know, I know.' He worked for British Intelligence and had first alerted London of the French fleet sailing to the islands, but now on land served as a local guide and would not take part in the attack. 'I'm to stay out of harm's way just like your stinking, flea-bitten dog.'

'Someone has to keep Biter on his damned lead,' Gamble said with a laugh. In truth, Biter, the marines mascot, was still on-board the *Sea Prince*, because it was too risky to have him accompany the landing for fear of him alerting the sentries.

'Biter would love a go at the Frenchies, sir,' said a gruff-voiced sergeant.

'Aye, Sergeant Powell,' Gamble replied, 'but the lads need to earn their pay and I'm not sure King George would approve of Biter doing all the work.'

'In that case, sir,' Powell jutted his unshaven chin at the man next to him, 'Marine Bray should forfeit his entire pay.'

The men roared with laughter at the squirming soldier and Gamble allowed it because laughter counters naked fear, and besides, he thought Bray was the most incompetent man under his command. He was round-shouldered, and resembled a fish with his protuberant eyes and slack mouth.

'That ain't fair, Sergeant,' Bray moaned at the ripple of bawdy laughter.

'Hold your tongue, you useless cur,' Powell scolded, 'or I shall cut it out and feed it to the fishes!'

'Steady, boys! Steady!' Brownrigg, the *Sea Prince*'s boatswain called.

'Here we go,' First Lieutenant Henry Kennedy said, as the boats neared the beach. He was immaculately dressed in his scarlet coat with its long-tails, silver lace, white gloves and a silver gorget.

'Steady! Now!' Brownrigg thumped a calloused hand onto the stern's gunwale, as the water made a sucking noise. All of a sudden, the seamen were overboard, up to their knees in cold water, and expertly dragging the boats toward the shelving beach. 'You lobsters have fun,' he grinned at the nickname given to the marines for their red coat. He was a dark-haired man with a fierce temper. 'Bring back plenty of loot, and that includes any unhappy whores you might find. I'll soon make 'em earn their wage.' He gave a foul smile of small yellow teeth. 'And don't forget to kill the Frog bastards whilst you're there.'

'I certainly won't,' Gamble replied with a curt nod.

As the boats took to the sand, the war-like marines clambered out. They relished the chance for a scrap and, grinning like madmen, were eagerly anticipating the assault. Whetstones had kissed the steel

123

bayonets and their smooth-bore muskets had flint's-re-seated, locks oiled and barrels cleaned out. But Gamble knew most of his men carried dirks. You could fire a musket and pistol once, but a blade kept on coming. The marines were ready for anything.

'Form up,' Powell instructed as quietly as he could, which was a feat because Archibald Powell was stern, loud and could out swear any other man Gamble knew. 'Form up, you heathen sods. Quickly now!' His brusque voice was deepened by years of salt air.

Powell was like an oak, Gamble often reflected; his torso was like a wide-bellied trunk, his arms were like knotted branches and his weathered-face like rutted bark. He bristled with weaponry. 'It puts the fear into the enemy,' the Plymouth-born veteran once said. Powell carried a long-barrelled musketoon; a weapon that had a flared muzzle comparable to a blunderbuss, and recoiled when fired like a small cannon. He also carried a boarding pike with a hook on the reverse side of the blade instead of the regulatory sergeant's halberd. Curiously, he owned a pair of throwing axes, much like a tomahawk, which each had a spike atop the blades head. They had been a gift from a Shawnee Indian named Blue Jacket who had allied with the British during the war against the Americans. A young Private Powell had saved the Indian's life during a skirmish and Blue Jacket had given him the pair in gratitude, an act that had been acted out at almost every campfire and at almost any opportunity.

The marines were armed with Sea Service muskets, blackened to help prevent them from rusting at sea and were carried over shoulders with white slings. They were each equipped with sixty rounds of ball ammunition and bayonets, but at the moment, the weapons were not primed and the blades hung in scabbards at their hips. They were in light order for manoeuvrability, and so their blankets and packs had been left on the *Sea Prince*. Their canteens were full with water, and stored in haversacks was enough hard tack biscuit for a full three days.

Gamble watched all but one of the longboats return back to the ship.

'The lads are in high spirits,' said Kennedy.

'So they should be, Harry,' Gamble said, watching the rocky crest above them with his eye piece, 'they know we're about to do some killing.'

'Won't we take any prisoners, sir?' asked Second Lieutenant Samuel Riding-Smyth, with abhorrence at the thought of killing all of the Frenchmen. He was petrified and fought down vomit, which was souring the back of his throat.

'Oh, Sam,' Kennedy said, shaking his head with an act of despair.

'What happens if they surrender?' Riding-Smyth looked pained.

Gamble grunted in frustration. 'If you want to take any prisoners, then that's your prerogative,' he announced, but was still watching the limestone hills. 'Do you know the Frog word for surrender?'

'*Capitulez*, sir,' suggested the worried lieutenant.

Gamble lowered the brass tube angrily. 'Fine, Sam. You ask any Monsewer you come across to *capitulez*. You shout really loud though, as the buggers will be gunners and we all know that gunners are deaf. You shout and hope they lay down their arms and that they don't meet Sergeant Powell first.'

Riding-Smyth 's eyes slid to the grizzled, broad-shouldered sergeant who stared back at him intently, and for good measure, patted one of his axes with a long exaggerated growl.

'It suits me, sir,' Powell declared. 'The bastards will be easier to kill if they keep nice and still. Saves me the bother.'

'I will shout, sir,' the young officer said zealously. 'I will indeed!'

'Good,' Gamble said, turning to his men who were formed up and waiting with expectant faces. The ball was about to start. It was time to dance. 'Company! Forward!'

'We're not really going to kill all the Frogs, are we?' Kennedy enquired as they advanced up the narrow beach.

'Of course not,' Gamble gave him a sly wink. 'That's why a boat will remain here. I'll send the prisoners back to the Prince of Waves,' he said, giving the *Sea Prince* its nickname, 'along with any keepsakes.'

'Very good,' Kennedy said, then frowned. 'I thought you spoke Frog?'

Gamble scanned the grassy bluffs ahead. 'You mean *Guernésiais*?' he asked, of the language of his native Guernsey that had roots in Norman French. Kennedy nodded. Gamble's mouth twisted. 'I understand the words, but I choose not to speak it. It's the language of our enemies. And I will not foul the air by muttering it.'

'You truly hate them, don't you?'

'I hate them all,' Gamble said loudly. 'As every Englishman should. Death to the French and every goddamn last one of them.'

'I've heard that French is the language of love?' Kennedy said with an impish grin.

Gamble laughed sourly. 'The whores don't care where you're from. Just if you have coin to pay them.'

125

...you shall pay life for life, a voice uttered in Gamble's head. He'd heard the saying many times since Acre. Too many times now. A friend had died and the words kept coming back to him. He adjusted his bicorn and looped the scope over his shoulders with its leather strap, trying to force the words from his mind, but without much success.

'Why don't we turn the prisoners over to the locals, sir?' Riding-Smyth enquired, catching up with his two superiors.

'Because that's a death sentence,' Gamble replied brusquely.

Kennedy fiddled with the gorget at his throat, a purely decorative horseshoe-shaped piece of metal that harked back to the days when officers had worn armour like medieval knights. 'As civilised men, we could not simply allow that to happen. Even to our bitterest enemies. However, knowing that they will be fed whatever Slope the Ship's Cook can boil up in his infernal copper cauldron is punishment and revenge enough.'

Riding-Smyth chuckled. 'At every mess time, I pray to God that He will keep me safe from harm.'

'He must be watching over you,' Kennedy said, 'because as of yet you've not suffered from any of the maladies that frequent the decks.'

'The Lord has truly been kind to me,' Riding-Smyth replied vehemently.

'You've obviously not been introduced to the lower deck whores, young Sam,' Kennedy said wryly. 'When you get back on-board, I'll have a dose of mercury on standby.'

Gamble liked his two subalterns. Harry was twenty-four, a fair and amiable man from Saltash who had been his lieutenant for three years. Sam had spent a little over a month with his new company. He was sixteen, religious, very keen, but had not seen any action. His predecessor, Robert Carstairs, a popular officer, had died fighting French grenadiers at Acre in May, as they attempted to take the entrenchments outside the city's walls. Gamble missed him dearly.

He remembered the smell of death; a sickly, clogging sweetness of putrefaction from the bodies that lay for days under a burning sun and a cold night sky. The stench was unforgettable, and he sniffed thinking he could still smell it now, but he knew he was imagining it. A score of marines had died in the attacks and he himself had been injured; his face still bore the scars from an enemy blade that had lopped off most of his left ear and carved open his jaw. Acre had somehow held out and the French, plague-ridden and bloody, were forced to withdrawal. A coup for the history books, yet achieved at such a dreadful price.

126

'We're half a mile from the guns, wouldn't you agree?' Gamble asked Zeppi after marching for twenty minutes. He had noticed that his friend was looking solemn and was trying to make conversation.

'Yes,' the dark-haired man replied, 'and this path will soon take us to the hollow where it splits beside the redoubt. From there, you'll be right there under their noses.' He was leading the marines up a sheltered track from the beach, and moved with considerable speed as though he wanted the attack over with.

Gamble understood fear. Every day he woke wondering if it would be his last, and every night said prayers of thanks to whichever deity looked after soldiers.

'Soon be over,' he said confidently.

The hollow was where the company would split into its two platoons. The first under his command would move south to where a watchtower guarded the main road to Rabat, the islands capital. Zeppi had said the tower was a ruin with a long-collapsed stairwell that would offer no defence, and was only used to shelter from winter rains and cold winds. 'It is haunted with the spirit of a girl who was said to have fallen down the steps. No one came to her aid and her ghost walks the ruins. At night, or when the sky is still dark, you can hear her pleading cries for help.'

'We don't have to go inside the tower, do we?' Sergeant Powell, in his mid-forties, with a battered face from numerous tavern and alley brawls, suddenly looked concerned.

'I'll hold your hand if you'd like, Sergeant?' Kennedy feigned mock sympathy.

'I need both hands free for my axes, sir,' Powell growled the reply over the gale of laughter, 'but I thank you for your kindness, nonetheless. Touched by it, I am. Touched.'

'It astounds me how Sergeant Powell can make "sir" sound like a question,' Kennedy said.

'I've noticed it too,' Gamble concurred, 'but it's only when he addresses you.'

The main objective was to secure the road and neutralise the sentries there, and no better job was tasked than to two particular Marines. Mathias Coppinger, half-Danish, and claimed to be a son of 'Cruel Coppinger', an infamous Danish smuggler who terrorized the coasts of Cornwall, and The Dane had inherited his father's unpitying skill with a blade. The second was Nicholas Adams, a slim man with villainous hollow cheeks and quick intelligent eyes that showed little emotion.

127

The company had nicknamed him 'Adder' for his coldness and slender build.

The second platoon under Kennedy would approach the redoubt from the west which overlooked the batteries. By taking his platoon down the road and securing the few buildings, Gamble anticipated the stronghold would be in British hands within minutes. But he had seen enough of battle, of the chaos that descended when musket volleys shattered the air and how the ground tremored when cavalry charged with long blades, to know the simplest plan could go awry in the time it took a man to whisper his sweetheart's name.

The track led the marines above the tumble of sand dunes into the barren coastline, where the wind whipped cold, and Gamble shivered. Strands of sand blew about his feet, but he was glad to be on land, nonetheless. It wasn't the thought of going back to horrid rations where men gave names to the weevils that infested the ship's biscuits, or the boiled salt-meat, or the drinking water which was sometimes slimy. It was the thrill of being on enemy soil, and the impending fight. This was what the marines were trained to do, what they were paid to do, and the boredom of ship life was soon forgotten and replaced with unabated exhilaration.

When Zeppi took them to the basin, the sound of the waves crashing against the rocks dulled to a whisper. It was here the men split into their platoons.

'No heroics, Harry.'

'You know me better than that, sir,' Kennedy shrugged innocently.

The memory of Carstairs' death ran through Gamble's mind again, unbidden, and he clenched his fists against it. He did not want to lose another friend. But Kennedy was already turning away so his eyes flickered to the man to the right of him. 'And that goes for you as well. You do exactly what Harry says.'

Zeppi waved a hand in irritation. 'I'm no babe in need of swaddling,' he answered back, a trifle defensively. 'My countrymen have already rebelled triumphantly and the French cowards scuttled to hide in their forts. I can fight. You know I can!'

Gamble rounded on him, feeling a stab of irritation. 'You are here as our guide and you're no good to me dead. Leave the fighting to my marines.' He knew he had sounded harsh, but it was for his friend's own good.

Zeppi hesitated, then gave a sparkle of understanding before joining the rear ranks of Kennedy's platoon.

Gamble then took his platoon up the ridge. From here, in the distance, the watchtower was a dark silhouette against the rather austere skyline. He could see an orange light flickering at the base of the tower, which betrayed a sentry's fire to ward off the morning's grey chill. The ground dipped with jagged ruts, and was swathed in thick patches of white-flowered Star Jasmine, so it looked as though a blanket of snow had fallen in the night. The sentries walking the walls of the redoubt could not see the marines as they moved southwards below the great cracks of jutting rock. He watched the two chosen men, their red coats, white breeches and black gaiters in stark contrast to the pale foliage, skulk low towards the tower, grasping their wickedly sharp knives. They disappeared and he scratched at the pink scar tissue along his jaw line with a ragged nail, remembering the Frenchman that had cut him at Acre's battlements. He was now dead, but Gamble could still hear his triumphant laugh ringing out, deriding and scornful.

'All clear, sir,' Coppinger whispered when the two men returned shortly. Gamble's nostrils were instantly filled with the stink of fresh blood. He didn't need to know any facts; all he needed to know was that the job was done and the sentries were neutralised. The smirk on The Dane's face and the glint in Adams' eyes - like the scales of a fish just below the waterline - told him that they had enjoyed the killing. Coppinger's white cuffs were stained red.

'Good,' Gamble replied. He swivelled his head to the platoon behind, waving an arm. 'Forward! Forward!' he said in hushed tones.

They moved out like wraiths towards the tower that had been built on a slight rise beside the road, which ran straight to the barracks giving the redcoats a good vantage point. Creeping low, they made their way forward where again Coppinger and Adams hunted ahead. The sound of the waves breaking upon the shore was still muffled. Somewhere nearby a blue rock thrush gave a melodious call. Otherwise it was eerily quiet.

The ground was hard, but with scattered patches of loose scree. Both scouts stopped. Gamble ordered his men to halt and went ahead, keeping low. Hearing a sudden noise like a man's cough, he feared, for a heart's beat, that an unseen sentry was walking up the road towards them. He cast his eyes towards the enemy position and then relaxed. A Frenchman was bringing water from a well near the barrack houses. Gamble moved and dropped flat to count the sentries through his glass. After ten minutes, he counted two on the northern wall. No one else had moved. A wind, lifted off the sea, gusted past and he shivered again. He always considered the Mediterranean islands as hot and dry lands, and so they were in the summer months when the sun burned mercilessly, but in the winter the rains battered the land cold and the wind stabbed like a hunter's spear.

But in truth, he was nervous.

He gazed down at the defences. A single track led to the enemy lines along the neck of land, the sea to the east, where the early morning sun glimmered it gold. There didn't appear to be a gate as such, just a series of platforms that were unmanned. Three batteries faced north, west and east, and he counted a total of nine guns. Four of them looked like big naval beasts. Thirty-six pounders, he reckoned. Beneath the semi-circular wall were several small tiled huts joined together which he concluded were the barracks. He saw a stone well and a ruinous building where four sorry-looking horses that looked like Welsh cobs were stabled. It was a remote redoubt, strangely undermanned in a hostile land. A washing line hung from a window to an araar tree. The tree's thick, leafy branches obscured the roof of the barracks that would offer plenty of shade in the summer. A goat, tethered to one of its low hanging boughs, cropped its head at a tangle of grass. Gamble trained his glass on the western wall and, after a moment of seeing nothing but empty stone, he caught a glimpse of red and white. Kennedy was in place. None of the muskets was loaded. He had insisted on that, fearing an accident which would betray their presence.

Gamble waited a few more minutes and when no enemy sentries threatened, he gave the order to load. When the last man had finished, he waved the marines on down the track.

Now was the time.

Their boots were loud, but no one called out to challenge them. There was no musket discharge, no enemy ball struck his body. No one had seen them.

His muscles were tense and the wind gushed in his ears. He could smell the aroma of bay leaves coming from a laurel bush near the araar. The goat saw the men, watched them approach and bleated softly. His heart hammered in his chest. He didn't know why he was nervous, he'd been in far worse situations. Perhaps each action got harder for the soul to deal with. Gamble would lead his men into the barracks by bayonet point and take sleepy prisoners. He did not expect a fire fight this morning, merely a scuffle and an easy victory borne out of luck.

However, he knew that it could also mean death, or of the terrible wounds that prolonged life to that of nightmarish suffering.

But luck was fickle and the enemy saw them.

A sentry on the high northern wall had bent down to light his pipe and had caught sight of the white cross-belts in the shadows of the rocks. He staggered with the discovery and managed to shout out in alarm before a musket banged and he was flung back over the wall and down onto the rocks. The other sentry was more vigilant and took cover behind one of the broad thirty-six pounders. Gamble swore as French voices shouted to gather arms.

'Marines!' he shouted. 'Two lines! Make ready!'

'Two lines now!' Powell said. 'Form up, you lazy bastards!'

What Gamble needed was cohesion. He would form his platoon in two lines inside the redoubt to prevent any enemies trying to escape by the path and also the muskets faced the buildings. From above, Kennedy's platoon would clear the gun batteries and be able to pour fire down onto the square if needed. Gamble, pleased at their positions, hoped the French, seeing that they had nowhere to go, or with little choice to continue, would simply lay down their arms.

The wooden door of the barracks opened and several Frenchmen appeared, some half-naked in shirts, or in breeches and hats, but all with firearms.

Gamble unclipped his pistol, pointed at the door and pulled the trigger. The shot echoed across the courtyard. Moustached faces scowled.

'Lay down your weapons!' he shouted. 'And put your goddamn hands up!'

'*Capitulez*, sir!' Riding-Smyth said encouragingly.

But the French, led by a bearded sergeant, stubbornly refused and a half-dozen enemy muskets went to shoulders. Gamble, half-expecting the refusal, brought his sword down.

'Fire!'

Triggers were pulled, dog-heads snapped forward, flints sparked and set off the powder in the pans which flared and ignited the main charge. The noise and the flame and the burst of smoke were almost simultaneous as the volley blasted out at the Frenchmen.

'Load!' he moved to one side, so he could see through the rising smoke and saw that a dozen of the enemy were already climbing the steps to the batteries. A musket fired from the doorway at the marines, but the ball went high.

131

'Obstinate bastards, sir!' Powell said admiringly, as a crackle of musketry echoed from the batteries. He scratched a louse bite at one of his thick black side whiskers that framed his battered face.

The front rank loaded with some difficulty as a bayonet-tipped musket was harder to load and knuckles scraped against steel. The wooden ramrods thumped in the barrels. The British Sea Service musket was based on the Land Pattern version that the infantry used, but was notoriously even less accurate, and came equipped with wooden ramrods as steel corrodes in salty air.

'And we know what the Frogs hate the most, don't we?' Gamble said loudly, so that his men could hear.

'Aye, sir,' Powell replied with a lop-sided grin. 'John Bull's cold steel. The Yankees hated the sight of them too.'

More French emerged from the barracks. A loose volley of shots was fired at the marines and miraculously none suffered a scratch. A French bullet slapped Corporal Jasper Forge's black bicorn from his head, leaving him unscathed. Opposite the barracks was a small stone house and at the doorway a tanned officer appeared. His blue jacket was unbuttoned and his face showed that he was utterly shocked at this attack. He shuddered momentarily, like a beast tethered to a slaughtering block, then the realisation hit him, and the officer began to shout commands.

'Charge bayonets!' Gamble shouted. He would take his redcoats close to the enemy now. 'Advance!'

The thirty marines advanced into the courtyard as the French officer tried to rally his small command where there were already eight dead. He knew it was a lost cause for his command was scattered. He stared at the officer commanding the impudent redcoats, wanting to get a good look at his face to see whether he was a gentleman. The multitude of scars, his ugly straight-bladed sword and patched uniform proved unlikely.

'Surrender!' Gamble shouted at him, but his words were drowned out by another volley of musketry coming from the steps and windows.

A ball snatched a marine backwards. Gamble heard a ball hum past his head. He turned just in time to see a French corporal approach the nearest window of the barracks and lunge with a bayonet-tipped musket. Gamble brought his sword up and knocked the blade aside as the Frenchman, snarling with several gold teeth, pulled the trigger. The musket spat angrily, and sent a gout of hot smoke into thin air. Gamble lunged and the heavy cutlass scraped against the corporal's ribs. He let the man fall away onto one of the sleeping cots.

Somewhere a man cried pitifully whilst another gasped and breathed hoarsely like an exhausted animal. The goat was bleating madly and one of the horses had bolted free to entangle the group of French by the steps.

'Lieutenant Riding-Smyth!' Gamble called out.

His subaltern appeared immediately. 'Yes, sir?'

'Take ten men into the barracks and clear the rooms.' He didn't want any enemies threatening his rear. 'Go in with the steel, disarm them, and prod the bastards out like cattle.'

'Yes, sir!' Riding-Smyth blanched, but disappeared with Corporal Tom MacKay's section.

Gamble looked at the remainder of his platoon. 'Advance! At the double!'

The French fired again and a marine fell against the well, hit in the leg. He stood, hobbled a few steps, but then had to steady himself on the masonry for support as bright blood spread on his breeches above the knee. A Frenchman, barefooted, tripped on the araar's roots and as he was getting up, Corporal Forge shot him through the forehead, spattering blood and brain matter over the hanging washing. Marine Frederick Crouch laughed madly. Men slipped on blood or tripped on corpses. Marine William Marsh slammed the butt of his musket into the forehead of a foe, then shot dead another aiming a carbine at Forge.

'I owe you a drink for that, Bill!' the corporal said.

Gamble could sense that this tussle was almost over, could feel it in his instincts, and his blood and bones. He knew they had won. Then, he looked up to see Zeppi fighting desperately. The damned fool! What the hell did he think he was doing?

'Take command, Archie!' his voice boomed across the courtyard. 'Press them hard!' He dashed through the powder-stink of the volleys.

Five Frenchmen had already given up and each one had thrown down their weapons in submission. Two were bent down, hands touching the dusty ground. The officer still at the doorway pulled up a pistol and trained it on the tall marine officer as he surged through the smoke and pulled the trigger. The bullet smacked into the stonework of the barracks. The Frenchman cursed at his haste and saw that the marines were too close so he closed the door and bolted it shut.

Gamble jumped a body killed by the volley, and flicked bayonets away with his sword as he approached the steps. He saw a Frenchman, naked to his waist, aim his musket, but had to trust that the ball would not strike him. He heard a flint strike steel and saw the muzzle flash, but the shot missed him as he ran on. A French gunner tried to kick him in the face, but he let the leg come forward, caught the boot and tugged hard so that the man fell backwards onto the steps, hearing his bare head smack painfully on stone. The man attempted to move, but Gamble kicked him in the face for good measure, and he slid down the steps; jaw hanging loose and obviously broken. A musket exploded, and the flame was enormous because it was so close, and the ball took a chunk out of Gamble's right boot top.

'Zeppi!' Gamble saw Kennedy knock a Frenchman down and kept him prone with the threat of his drawn pistol. 'Harry! I thought you were watching the bastard!'

'I'm sorry,' Harry replied, 'but he just ran ahead without warning.'

His friend had managed to break free of Kennedy's watchful eye and, armed with a long knife, charged with the redcoats when they stormed across gun emplacements. Zeppi watched as a marine and a French soldier tried to bayonet each other, the clash of blades rang like smiths' hammers, and he ran up and plunged his knife into the Frenchman's neck.

'Die! You godless animal!' he hissed like a lit fuse. 'Die!'

Blood trickled from the enemy's mouth as he disengaged to stagger away. Zeppi, driven by hatred, pounced on the dying man to strike again, but an enemy appeared below him and, before he could twist away, a long French bayonet went up through his side. The guide howled and reeled away with hands pressing the wound. He stumbled and fell away. His enemy was a bearded man with an ugly, bony face. Zeppi knew death when he saw it and spat in defiance.

The Frenchman raised his bayonet, but then turned when he saw the Maltese man's eyes flicker past him. A British officer was running straight at him, cutlass gripped in two hands. He swung it with a roar and with such force that the heavy blade cut through the man's beard and neck like a scythe reaping grass. The head tumbled down the sand-strewn steps and the body crumpled to ooze like a broken wineskin.

Kennedy's platoon were still charging down the steps as Gamble reached his friend. Some were herding prisoners, but most of them were in search of plunder while they still had time to look.

'You stupid little bastard!' Gamble said harshly, as he stooped to inspect the bleeding wound. It was not deep, merely and thankfully, and not life-threatening. 'Pace!' he called over the marine who was good with injuries. 'Get your arse over here now!'

'Sir!' Marine Josiah Pace said, giving the barracks a look of sadness as he envisioned himself going back aboard the *Sea Prince* with plugs of tobacco and bulging wineskins. Pace dropped to look at the four-inch cut, spat on a grubby hand and rubbed the blood away. Zeppi let out a whimper and fresh blood flowed immediately.

'You'll need rum for that, or brandy,' Gamble said.

'I don't drink alcohol,' Zeppi replied. His face was spattered with the sergeant's blood. 'I'm a strict Catholic, or have you forgotten?'

Gamble snorted. 'It's not for you to drink! Pace will use it to clean the wound and his needle.'

'Needle?'

'I'll patch it up nicely, sir,' Pace said, grinning. 'You're a lucky bastard, because the Frenchie missed your kidney.'

'Thank God.' Zeppi could not stop himself from making the sign of the cross.

'What were you thinking?' Gamble said to him. 'I goddamn told you to stay at the rear.' The Malteseman just shrugged meekly. 'You nearly got yourself killed. Let Pace get to work. You're in capable hands. Just look at what he did to my ear,' he pulled back his long hair to expose the mutilated organ.

Zeppi gulped and went as white as cartridge paper.

The fight was over; all but one had surrendered. Gamble left his friend under Pace's care as the marines piled captured muskets, and brought out crates, barrels and sacks. They found artillery and engineer equipment such as handspikes, hooks, drag ropes, rammers, buckets, sponges, pickaxes, shovels, spare gun wheels, a few tool boxes and some farriers' kit. Two wagons containing twelve barrels of gunpowder were found underneath a shady white poplar tree. He inspected it to find it damp, fouled by animals and of very poor quality.

He calmly approached the door to the small house. He had brought Sam with him who had procured two cooked chicken legs, a hunk of bread and a basket of boiled eggs. A salty breeze played with the tall weeds that stood in patches around the redoubt.

'Get the bugger out of there,' he said to the boy, biting into a chicken leg.

'Yes, sir,' Riding-Smyth said and cleared his throat. '*Excusez-moi, monsieur. Voulez-vous s'il vous plaît rendre. Merci tellement.*'

'*Non!*' came the muffled reply.

'He said "no", sir,' Riding-Smyth said, meekly.

Gamble sighed. 'Sergeant Powell?'

'Sir!'

'Would you do me the honour please?'

Powell gave a broad smile and in a flash, his hand withdrew an axe and in a blur of handle and steel, the weapon buried itself firmly in the door with an almighty thud.

A moment later, the door unbolted and the officer came out with his hands raised in submission.

'I rather think we've spoiled their day,' Gamble said. The marines grinned back.

It had taken ten minutes of stealth, of fire, of death to take the redoubt. As coffee was brought to him, and he ate his chicken leg for breakfast, he thought that it was not a bad way to start a glorious new day.

Zeppi was stitched and bandaged and, although ordered to rest, was up on his feet and willing to lead the marines onto their next mission. 'My wound is nothing to what has happened to my people. For the sake of Malta, I will continue,' he said, waving his arms theatrically.

Gamble examined the guns which, to his utter surprise, were of poor quality. One was mounted on a hay cart; Powell reckoned it was an Austrian six pounder. The four thirty-six pounders were the only guns mounted on proper carriages. The rest were twelve pounders and looked as though they hadn't been fired for several months. They had certainly not been maintained; the paint was peeling, the barrels were unpolished and filthy, and most of the metal trappings were rusty.

There were dozens of different types of shot. Gamble wanted it all destroyed: powder, shot and the guns spiked. If the French ever returned, they would find it a ruin. The well was filled in with rocks and lengths of broken timber, the powder rolled and tipped into the sea, and the horses scattered to the hills. He did not want to shoot them; he didn't like killing beasts unnecessary. He had once had to shoot a wounded horse and although it whinnied in agony, he was shocked at what he had done. Riding-Smyth had also found crates of good Sicilian wine and the men cursed when Gamble ordered that they be wrecked.

'Throw them over the walls,' he commanded.

'All of them, sir?' Powell was dismayed.

'Every goddamn skin and bottle, Archie. I don't need our boys stewed when they have work to do. Is that clear?'

'As rain, sir,' Powell commented without much conviction.

'We'll get the job done, sir,' Corporal MacKay said in his usual Scottish methodical way.

The twenty-seven prisoners buried their nine killed. The marines had suffered only three wounded, but unable to continue, they were taken back to the boats to see the surgeon. The French were sent back along with the goat, foodstuffs and a handful of good ammunition under a watchful detail of six marines commanded by MacKay.

Two hours after the attack, Gamble took his remaining fifty men south along the main road to Rabat.

'One down,' he said gruffly, 'one bastard to go.'

'Do you think the next one will be as easy, sir?' Riding-Smyth asked, trying to hold his gaze under his captain's steely expression.

He was in awe, for it was said that Gamble had survived more brawls than could be counted. But his exploits were nothing compared to the greatest sea battle in history: the Battle of the Nile. He had boarded one French vessel and the marines had captured it after a hard fought mêlée under the watchful admiration of Rear Admiral Sir Horatio Nelson. The captain was a hero and Second Lieutenant Samuel Riding-Smyth could not shake the worry of death from his mind. His stomach twisted like knots of fire and he wondered, as they marched, whether his famed captain had ever known fear.

'The next one is a proper bastard,' Gamble replied, oblivious to his lieutenant's anxious thoughts. 'It will curdle your blood. Zeppi, tell our young friend here about it.'

The guide flinched inwardly as though the fort was too painful to talk about. 'The captain is quite correct. A real nasty bastard. It's protected by walls, ravelins, batteries, a ditch and glacis. There's only one way in, too.' He looked sorrowfully eastwards to a small fishing village where his father had said the best clams were found on the island. Many years of peace before the wars. 'It was built in my father's lifetime by the Order of St. John. It sits on a hill overlooking the channel. It was to become another Valletta, to replace Rabat as the new city of Gozo and reinforce commerce between the islands. It was never finished and was abandoned to bats, rabbits and lizards.'

'Until the French came,' Kennedy said.

Zeppi nodded. 'Until the French came.'

'What's it called?' Riding-Smyth asked.

'Dominance,' Zeppi said, crossing himself. 'An apt name, yes?'

Riding-Smyth licked nervous lips. 'And we're going to besiege it, sir?' he asked his captain.

Gamble ran his tongue over the front of his teeth. 'We've no time for that, Sam.' He broke into a laugh as though it was a preposterous notion.

Riding-Smyth dutifully began to laugh. 'I apologise for my naivety, sir. Of course, we fifty could not hope to do such a thing.'

'No. No, we're simply going to march up to it and attack it.' Gamble's eyes were bright and hopeful.

Riding-Smyth went white as pipe-clay, his heart hammered against his breastbone. 'March up to it and...?'

'We'll have help, won't we?'

The guide nodded. 'Two hundred men as promised.'

'Where's the rendezvous?' Gamble asked.

Zeppi stretched out his arm beyond the undulating hills to the south, dark with olive groves and crossed with vineyards. 'Not far from here. They will come tonight. They will come to the temples.'

'They say a giantess built it as a place of worship,' Zeppi said to the three officers, marvelling at the crumbling stonework. Firelight flared and danced brief eldritch shadows up the ancient walls and cast strange shapes in the long neglected grasses. 'It's named after her. Ġgantija.'

As far as Gamble could discern, the Ġgantija temples faced south-east, and yet afforded views of Rabat to the west where tiny lights guttered. Somewhere in the gloom to the south was the fort.

It was an hour after dusk and the redcoats had arrived in afternoon sunlight where, beyond a stand of holm oaks and rocks, the temples stood in eerie solitude. Beyond the age-old buildings there was a high plateau of scrubland covered with Common Myrtle - Gamble gave a lop-sided grin because it was the nickname given to one of the whores frequenting the *Sea Prince* - and the wind brought citrus scents from its flowering buds and the ever present salty tang from the ocean.

Gamble had trodden the neglected stone-lined forecourt into the temples northern entrance. The interior walls were made of rough boulders piled on top of each other. Pillars and upright stones had holes bored into them, like the socket for a protective doorpost, but any sign of the gates were long gone. Animal bones, drifted soil and debris littered the ground and large boulders blocked some apses which Gamble suspected held the skeletons of the ancient dead. Feeling a sense of wonder, he stepped over low stone blocks to find a dirt-covered circular hearth.

'There is a horizontal slab there at the back,' Zeppi had said, his voice echoed in the small space. 'I came here once as a boy and found flint knives.'

'Sacrificial?'

'I don't know. But I looked for human bones and found nothing.'

'What about treasure?' Sergeant Powell's voice was loud as he stepped in, the white NCOs knot on his right shoulder made his frame look oddly shaped.

'I'm sorry to tell you that there is nothing here, Sergeant,' Zeppi replied. 'Greedy men have come here hoping to find gold, but I have only ever found a single Roman coin in these hills.'

'I wasn't thinking of myself,' Powell sounded disappointed, then shifted uneasily. 'Just what the lads are asking. If I tell them there's no gold or silver, then they won't go looting the moment my back is turned.'

'If they do that, then they risk the guardian's wrath,' Zeppi warned, shooting Gamble a sly grin.

Powell, who had not seen the smirk, looked alarmed. 'Guardian?'

'Yes,' Zeppi said gravely, 'it is said that even saying its name will anger it. Many looters here have simply vanished without a trace. An old and dark magic protects these walls. Tread carefully, Sergeant. Tread wisely.'

Powell, eyes wide with terror, quickly disappeared leaving the guide and the officers chortling.

The marines pooled their tea leaves and it bubbled in a cooking cauldron they had taken from the redoubt. Clay pipes were lit. One or two men took advantage of the rest to sleep. Gamble eased back against the wall as the smell lifted his thoughts. It made him think of faraway home. Drinking black coffee on the tiled terrace over-looking the sea. The scents of thyme, rosemary and sage wafting from the herb garden. Sunlight flooding the solar room. Fire crackling on cold evenings. The cobbled streets of St Peter Port that sparkled in the rain. All was peaceful until he overheard two guttural voices nearby spewing vulgarity.

'He says the girl has a pair of tits too big for her dress. Sixteen and hungry for a white man to whet his blade in her,' said the first, hawking and spitting.

'How the hell would he know?' said the other. 'We ain't going to see her. We ain't passing the town, are we, you dribbling dullard?'

'Ain't a town, is it. Just a bunch of mud huts.'

'We ain't going to see her,' said the second man. 'It's a rumour, 'tis all.'

'Maybe,' the first one said, giving a small mad laugh. 'Maybe there would be a chance once the captain's got his back to us for us to go find out.'

'They'll hang you, you oaf.'

Gamble knew exactly who was speaking. Marines Willoughby and Crouch. Both troublesome devils who had been flogged in the past for petty crimes. Bloodybacks, those men were called. He had even struck Willoughby once during the Siege of Acre, where he was found rifling through a dead man's coat rather than be alert at his post.

Gamble swivelled his head and spoke loud enough for all of his men to hear, knowing it was nothing more than drink-fuelled gossip.

'One word of trouble from anyone, and I'll kill the man responsible for it. Understand?'

There was silence, broken only by a murmur of obedience. The two men in question gawped for they considered they were safe from his ears. Crouch nodded with agreement, but Willoughby, a hulking man even broader than Powell, offered a defiant smirk, before reluctantly accepting the order with a curt bob of his head.

Gamble looked at them both in the eye.

'Trouble, sir?' Kennedy enquired, sitting down next to him.

Gamble tore his gaze away from them and blew out a lungful of breath. 'No, Harry. Not yet. However, I want those two bastards under close watch.'

'More so than usual, then,' Kennedy gave a cynical smile. 'Willoughby is indeed a troublesome wretch.'

'If I catch him at his tricks again, I'll hang the bastard. And this time no one will stop me.'

He let his eyes fall upon the three freshly caught rabbits roasting over the blazing fire. The smell made his aching belly rumble with hunger. Rabbit stew was Timothy's - his younger brother's - favourite dish. His father's too. Dark gloomy thoughts penetrated his exuberance and a creeping sourness squirmed in his gut. His father had wagered the house and their business and lost it all. He had ruined the family. Law said he was not responsible for any of his father's debts, but Gamble would not have the family name tarnished. They faced penury and another winter where his mother and sisters' future was uncertain. Both brothers vowed to bring back money to reclaim their family estate. If this mission went well, then there was a chance he would return with a sizeable amount of prize money.

'It would taste better with garlic,' Zeppi advised, busily rubbing in salt and sage to give it more flavour. He tested the meat with a knife.

'I can't stand the stuff,' Gamble muttered, still reeling from the bitter thoughts. 'Give me a plate of roast mutton, or beef with potatoes and gravy any day.'

Zeppi shook his head at the captain's lack of culinary adventure. 'Fried rabbit with wine and garlic. Now that's a proper meal,' he said, the whites of his eyes glistening in the flame light.

'I suppose the guardian doesn't mind us lighting a fire, and eating and drinking then?' Gamble said, throwing his friend a wry smile.

'It's fine when it's an islander doing it,' Zeppi replied with a deliberate shrug.

'Have we got any wine?' Kennedy brightened up.

Gamble looked thoughtful for a moment. 'Sergeant Powell?'

'Sir?'

'Have we any wine?'

Powell bit his lip and tried to look innocent. 'Now if only you'd have asked me to keep some back, sir. Instead of destroying them like you instructed, sir. Then you could be enjoying a nice drop of the stuff.'

'Are you saying you didn't keep any?' Gamble asked him, knowing full well that Powell's wooden canteen would be filled with it, as well as those of half of the men.

'You know me, sir. A stickler for orders. Can't abide insubordination.'

'A pity then,' Gamble said in mock disappointment and sighed. 'I'll just have to drink the two I retrieved all to myself then.'

The marines laughed.

'Sir!' A voice called from above.

Gamble looked up to the top of the walls where a marine stood on watch. 'What is it, Nick?'

Adams, the flames accentuating his hollow face and making him appear to be a living skeleton, pointed to the east. 'We've got company.'

141

The first Gozitans appeared on the track flanked with purple-blue barked tamarisk trees. They were armed with muskets, carbines, pistols and a collection of crude hand weapons: scythes, billhooks, hoes, axes, and staves.

Zeppi went out to meet them. They numbered around forty and they greeted him with curt acknowledgements. Gamble strained to hear their conversation, spoken in quick Maltese.

'They look like keen fellows,' Kennedy muttered.

Gamble looked sceptical.

Apart from the few firearms, the men were nothing more than farmers, fishermen, shepherds, milk-sellers, labourers, and unemployed. The French had dismantled the institutions of the Knights of St. John, an ancient order dating back to the Crusades, including the Roman Catholic Church. Its property had been seized and looted to pay for the French expedition to Egypt, generating blood-bubbling fury amongst the pious islanders. They looked hard, lean and bitter. But anger wouldn't win battles, skill would, and Gamble suspected the Gozitans had never fired a musket in battle before, let alone help assault a fortress. However, deception was the key to this mission's success and the only way in.

'They ain't worth tuppence,' said a voice behind.

Gamble turned to the marines. 'Quiet in the ranks,' he commanded.

The islanders had brought women with them, all dark and slim. They began to build a cooking fire and Gamble suspected they were there to cook for their men rather than be part of the fight. One of them brought over a basket of nectarines, peaches, grapes and cheese made from sheep's milk as a gift. He thanked them for their generosity, trying not to notice the distaste etched on her face at his scars.

'Now that's a rare sight to tighten a man's nuts,' Bray said in wonder, the flame light making his face look uglier than normal.

'Then it's just as well you don't have any,' Coppinger replied.

Adams sniggered, earning a low growl from Bray.

'You want to say something, Adder? I've seen sticks bigger than your arms, you shambling corpse.'

'I've just whetted my knife, Bray. Want to try it out? We want to hear your girlish cries again,' Adams said with a grin. The marines laughed because Bray had been hit in the arm at Acre, a flesh wound, and he had yelped like a girl. The men had not forgotten it.

'Quiet, you ugly whoreson's,' Powell ordered. 'Enough of your coarse chatter when there's pretty ladies present.' The sergeant, never truly comfortable around the other sex, stood to attention, relaxed slightly and then gave the women an awkward bow.

One of the women had vivid green eyes underneath raven-black curls, and gave the officers a wry smile. Kennedy's mouth was lolling open until Gamble noticed and gave him a nudge with his elbow.

'What a strikingly attractive creature,' the lieutenant whispered, gathering a level of coherence.

'Certainly different from what we've been used to.'

'No doubt our men have similar thoughts.'

Gamble glanced at the marines who, starved of regular intercourse, eyed the women hopefully.

'Remember what I said earlier,' he said, loud enough for the ranks at the rear to hear the warning.

There was a buzz of furtive agreement.

Zeppi brought a delicate-looking man with angular cheeks and grey distrustful eyes who scowled at the two lieutenants, and made the sign of the cross at the sight of Gamble's scars. He wore good woollen clothes, a white shirt and reminded Gamble of a stuffy clerk.

'He looks as miserable as a Methodist in a brothel, sir,' Powell said and Gamble smiled.

'This is Baldassar Grech,' Zeppi said, making introductions, and turned to the Gozitan, 'and this is Captain Simon Gamble.'

'Pleased to make your acquaintance,' Gamble offered a hand, the other held a half-devoured peach.

Grech hesitated and then thought better of offending the scarred officer by taking the proffered hand. 'Captain,' he smiled showing small white teeth, but his tone was icy. He rubbed his palms down his sides. 'May I ask which regiment you are from?'

As miserable as a Methodist in a brothel being handed a drink, Gamble said to himself. 'Eighteenth Company, Third Marine Division,' he replied, wiping juice from his chin.

The Gozitan blinked, and then peered at the red-coated soldiers, eyeing them up as though he was a farmer selling cows at the weekday market. 'Marine? You are marines?'

'Yes.'

Grech blew out a lungful of breath. He turned to Zeppi and launched into a frenetic conversation in Maltese, eyes distended with ire.

143

'Something the matter, Zeppi?' Gamble asked, an eyebrow rose querulously.

Zeppi held up a hand to stop Grech's furious cannonade. 'He expected a full battalion.'

Grech rounded on Gamble. 'A proper regiment,' he said in English and there was a sudden intake of breath among the collective group. The words echoed between the stones.

Gamble suppressed the urge to flatten the man with his fist. 'You'll find that my men can fight on land just as well as any line regiment. They're tough bastards and they're commanded by one too. They can turn an enemy's flank. They've broken French veterans in Acre. They've boarded and captured a French ship during the Battle of the Nile. My marines are worth more than a battalion. I'd have them with me more than any other redcoat.'

Grech glanced at Zeppi who scowled at the offence. The Gozitan rubbed the small beard on his pointed chin. His mouth twitched. 'I apologise, Captain. I meant no insult. It's just that we were promised a full battalion to attack the fort. Not a company.'

'And?'

'Now I doubt now that we can achieve such a task.'

'Nonsense,' Gamble said, chewing on the fruit. 'The plan still goes ahead. You will assist with the attack and my men will take care of the rest. That is what was agreed.'

'Captain, have you read about the Great Siege of Malta?' Grech asked.

Gamble paused to swallow, wondering where the question would go. 'I have,' he replied carefully.

'Then you will realise that the Turks and the French are more alike than you could possibly think.'

'How so?'

'The siege taught the world that a population, thought as nothing more than peasants, could unite in the face of invasion. That they could show courage and honour in desperate times, and dispel the destructiveness of religious hatred. Boys, who had become battle-weary veterans of the Italian campaigns, had sailed here to conquer Malta. But Captain, let me tell you, they have not. Have you heard of Fort St Elmo?'

Gamble stuck his chin out, and threw away the stone. 'I have heard the name,' he said, wondering if Grech was trying to embarrass him by his lack of Maltese historical knowledge.

144

'The Turkish fleet arrived with men who had conquered the fields of Europe with their scimitars, elite cavalry mounted on giant horses and devil-men who wore the skins of beasts. Their artillery numbered hundreds and they battered the fort's walls for days. Inside were Knights of St. John. And amidst that hell-fire they refused to surrender. Wave upon wave of screaming Turks tried to capture the breaches, but the defenders repelled them all. They fought with pikes, swords, axes, blocks of stone, and their bare hands. The siege gave the Knights inspiration to invent new weapons: fire-hoops; wooden rings, wrapped in layers of cotton, flax, brandy, gunpowder, turpentine, and ignited and rolled to the enemy. Trumps; hollow metal tubes filled with flammable sulphur resin and linseed oil; and when lit, they blasted flame like dragon's breath. Many Turks with their flowing robes died from these new weapons. For thirty days, the Knights held out. Eventually, they claimed their prize. But the Turks turned to Valletta and committed an utterly despicable act which angered God. They mutilated the fort's defenders, stuck their heads on pikes and floated the decapitated bodies of their officers across the harbour on wooden crosses. It was designed to cause distress and it would have, had it not been for God turning the tide.'

'God?' Gamble said, raising an eyebrow.

'Yes, Captain. God,' Grech insisted scornfully. 'The sun burned like a furnace, and it was said the dead left unburied in the fort blackened and burst, spreading disease to the Turkish camp. They tried to take the city, but the defenders out-thought and out-fought them. God had blessed them with plenty of supplies and ammunition. Even when autumn winds brought rain the defenders muskets and pistols still felled the Muslim attackers. Then a relief force from Scilly smashed the Turks aside. They were pursued across the island, dying in droves at the hands of my vengeful ancestors. It is said the waters of St Paul's Bay turned blood red. The Knights won. Malta was saved.'

'God,' Gamble said again, this time sounding distant.

Grech's eyes narrowed. 'Am I to believe that you are not a Christian?'

'I believe in a good musket,' Gamble replied flatly, irritation creeping back into his voice. 'I believe in the British Navy. I believe in wiping the earth of the bastard French.'

Grech grimaced. 'I see,' his grey eyes flashed at Zeppi, before turning back. 'We have been sent one company of men. Godless men at

145

that, I might add, to do a battalion's job.' He rubbed the ends of his beard with long fingers as though he contemplated his next move.

'Godless men who'll free your country,' Gamble said with a menacing glare. 'What were you trying to tell me with your story?'

'I want to see the French defeated,' Grech said. 'I want our people free. I want the world to see our victory as a beacon for Christianity.'

'You're doing this for God?'

'Yes,' Grech said piously, 'and so should you.'

Gamble shook his head, momentarily confused. 'No, I'm doing this because I've been ordered here by my superiors.'

The Gozitans mouth tightened to a smile. 'And just who do you think told them to send you here?'

The French, Grech explained, sent an armed convoy every two weeks to the redoubt via Rabat to acquire more supplies. He made a crude sketch of the island in the soil with his sword showing the fort, Rabat, the outer villages and the roads. Gamble noticed that the blade was spotted with rust. 'They do buy flour, smoked fish, grapes and local cheese, but there is never enough food for them. There is not enough food for the islanders, let alone the bloody French.' The curse sounded awkward, as though he was not used accustomed to it.

'How many in the fort?' Gamble was making mental notes.

'It is said five hundred,' Grech answered, 'but I believe more likely three.'

'That's still quite a number to hold the place,' Kennedy said.

'Two months ago they sent several boat loads of men to Valletta,' Zeppi said.

'Why?' Gamble asked.

'Supplies?' Kennedy suggested with a shrug.

Zeppi wiped the ends of his moustache with the back of a hand. 'A sickness struck the fort.'

Gamble's eyes bored into his. 'What sort of sickness? I'm not sending my men in if the Toads have got themselves the pox.'

'No,' Zeppi's head shook fervidly, 'nothing like that. A sweating sickness. Perhaps fifty were sent to the *Santa Infermeria*, the main hospital in Valletta to recuperate. I heard from a fisherman that about six weeks after the French took the fort some of their men became sick. There must have been something in the wells. Some foulness. Probably

146

the Gozitans had been pissing in it,' he said, translating it for the islanders who couldn't speak English, who laughed.

'It's a cursed place,' Grech murmured. 'It brings bad luck.'

'That's good for us,' Kennedy put in. 'We don't want to live there. We just want to expel the Frogs. You can have it back afterwards, old boy.'

Grech didn't know if he was being mocked or not, so stared back at the drawing instead.

'So the French supply force will be on the road tomorrow?' Gamble asked.

'Yes.' Grech's gaze trained up to the eastern side of the island. 'They always go along that road and then follow it to Rabat.'

'Why?'

'I understand the French bathe at the beach there,' Grech explained.

'What?' Gamble laughed mockingly.

'The islanders say that the salt water in this particular cove cures all illnesses and so the French make trips there.'

Gamble shook his head, incredulous. 'And I thought I'd heard everything there is to hear.' He chuckled again. 'We're at war and the Frogs want to go bathing.'

'Will we get time for that, sir?' Riding-Smyth enquired.

'No, we bloody won't,' Gamble snorted. 'Our job is to take the fort and hold it until reinforcements come, not to frolic in the waves like bloody mermaids.'

'That's a shame, Captain, because you do stink,' Grech said, tugging his nostrils.

Gamble's eyes devoured the man, taking in his proud and scornful demeanour. 'I probably do stink, but when you were still fast asleep this morning, I was capturing an enemy stronghold.'

'Captain, I-' Grech began, but Gamble interrupted.

'I am a soldier and I have seen some truly ungodly things in my life. I've even committed some of them. What you need are men like me to do the job whether I stink or not.'

Grech pursed his lips, not willing to continue the conversation, but enough to have his say. 'Bathing in salt water is good for you,' he muttered, his nose still puckered.

'How many Frogs will there be on the supply run?' Kennedy said. He spoke in the confident tones of a man willing to change the subject to avoid confrontation.

'Usually fifty, Lieutenant,' Grech said. 'Sometimes more, sometimes less.'

'Cavalry?' Riding-Smyth asked.

'No, the French do not have any cavalry on the islands.'

'They have pack horses, of course,' Zeppi added. He peered at the dark hills. 'We've hard soil here and some small patches of woodland, so it is ideal for mounted troops, but they took all their good horses to Egypt.'

'Good for us then,' Riding-Smyth said.

'So after we attack their men out gathering supplies,' Kennedy said, 'what do we do then? The Frogs will no doubt hear the musketry. Won't they send out men to scout the hills?'

'No,' Gamble said, spitting out the end of a broken fingernail, 'because when we ambush the bastards, half of them will be in the sea and the others will be dozing in the sun.'

'They go fishing in the cove too,' Grech added and the marines laughed.

'There you go then,' Gamble grinned like a wolf smelling prey. 'This will be easier than catching crabs in a barrel.'

'If you say so, Captain,' Grech said dubiously.

It would be easy, Gamble added to himself, if Grech and his men don't bugger this up.

Fog wreathed the walls of the temples, utterly obscuring the low courtyard and apses where Gamble, at daybreak, paraded his men.

'Another warm welcome,' Kennedy said sourly. 'That fellow Grech is as sharp as a newly honed blade.' The Gozitans had gone on to drum up volunteers to assist with the attack and would meet at sundown.

Gamble gave his opinion of the Gozitan in the shortest term, which made his first lieutenant smile. 'The islanders doubt they really need us. Their Maltese cousins have already taken all the forts on Malta. As far as they are concerned we're turning up late to the dance as they'll no doubt force the Frogs to surrender anyway. Besides,' he conceded, 'they are none too fond of soldiers, even their allies.'

'That's a shame,' Kennedy brushed at his coat with a gloved hand. 'I have gone to all that trouble of looking so dashing for them.'

Gamble drew and let his cutlass slip home. 'All present and correct, Sergeant?'

'Yes, sir!' Powell replied.

'Then, let's go hunting.'

Their boots crunched and thudded on the road as they marched east into the morning's cold whiteness of the fog. Gamble sent Adams and Coppinger to scout ahead, both men could cross open ground like ghosts. The waylay was less than a half day's march away, but he wanted his men into position long before the enemy got to the cove. The chilliness brought out the pungent smell of wild sage that littered the plateau. There were no rivers or streams on the island, so they followed the road and hoped Grech's information was correct. Another morning's chaos and then after signalling to the *Sea Prince* for reinforcements, they would start their bold attack on Dominance. The French wouldn't even know the marines had landed.

But Gamble thought that he should be the happiest man under the aegis of the Admiralty, for he had been given a land command to give the French revolutionary rats a damned good thrashing. A command to carry cutlass and musket to reclaim a country back from a hated enemy. He was given the freedom to do that; no shackles to hinder. He could fight his own war and take his men into the annals of triumph.

The redcoats climbed a steep hill; the soft fog clung to their salt-stained coats as if they were amongst the clouds. Somewhere off gulls cried, but nothing stirred. It was difficult to see anything; the fog partially concealed the road itself, thick tendrils seemed to grasp at the men's boots as they marched. Their heads were held high because of the black leather stock clasped around their neck which dug into the soft flesh under the jaw. Gamble remembered that Bray had been flogged once because he had been soaping his to make it softer.

He noticed his second lieutenant was struggling with the march. 'Boots giving you blisters, Sam?'

'Yes, sir.'

'You'll get used to it. Your feet will get harder. Aye, it's not good advice, but it's because you're a marine and we don't go on marches. I'll wager that you're looking forward to being back on board, yes?'

'Not really, sir,' Riding-Smyth winced. 'I get terrible seasickness.'

Kennedy laughed loudly. 'What? My dear fellow, you are in the wars.'

'I'd much rather be on land,' Riding-Smyth established quickly, not wanting to appear completely hopeless. He had heard that Nelson suffered badly from it, but the great man could shake it off easily. Riding-Smyth tried to think of that when he was puking his guts out

149

over the side. 'I often went out on hunts with my father and eldest brother. We'd ride for hours and sometimes with our gamekeeper, we'd be out for miles with our fowling pieces in all weather.'

'Are you close to your father, Sam?' Gamble asked.

'Not really, sir. My family owns five hundred acres of fertile land around Tavistock and I purchased my commission rather than follow my father's wishes to manage the farm estates which does not interest me one bit.'

'I bet you're popular,' Kennedy mused.

'He hasn't spoken to me since,' Riding-Smyth said, cheerfully.

'They can ruin lives,' Gamble said. The agonising thoughts of his own father's betrayal and loss of everything they had once known didn't keep plaguing his mind. He chewed the inside of his cheeks, deep in thought.

'Very true, sir,' Riding-Smyth said. 'But the one piece of advice he gave me I ignored much to my chagrin. I should have invested in a pair of decent leather boots.'

'That's the secret to a trouble-free life, Sam,' Kennedy said in his usual amiable tone.

'My cousin is a cobbler, young man,' Zeppi said, 'and he will fix them for a good price. He is very skilled.'

Riding-Smyth's face brightened. 'Really?'

'Yes, he will make your boots feel like you are walking on air. No more blisters. No more pain.'

'Where does your cousin live?'

'Valletta,' Zeppi said. 'If you survive this island, then I would think your next command will be to take the capital.'

'I see,' Riding-Smyth said, shoulders sagging slightly.

'So it's a new pair of boots or a coffin,' Kennedy teased. 'A hard choice.'

The march was warming the men. By nine o'clock the air had become humid and heavy, and the marines sweated in their woollen coats. They had reached the east coast where fishing boats dotted the sea and where clouds sailed like smoky trails. Gamble halted his company and took in the crisp scents of the ocean.

'Does anyone live there?' He jutted his chin to the thin stretch of land situated in the angry iron-grey channel between Gozo and Malta, the latter an imposing block of jagged rock.

'A few hermits,' Zeppi shrugged.

'What's it called?'

'Comino. Named after the cumin plant that is found there.'

Gamble didn't know what that was, and turned his attention to the stone fort, visible above the limestone cliffs dotted with caves. The sea bashed white, sending spray high into the air. 'What's that keep?'

'St Mary's tower,' Zeppi replied. 'It was built long ago by a Grand Master of the Knights of Malta.'

`Do the French hold it now?'

'No, it is long abandoned. I've been there. You'd need a regiment of sappers for a full month to clear it of debris and to shore up the walls. There are some other ruins to the south and a stone church. The Romans had once farmed the island. It was once a prison for traitors, and it has seen its fair share of pirates and smugglers over the years. I heard many tales as a boy. I wanted to be a pirate,' he said with a grin. 'It is now a desolate place, but Comino has a quiet beauty. It is peaceful. I like it there.'

'You like it, because there are no foreigners there,' Gamble needled.

Zeppi smiled. 'Baldassar would agree with that. Although, as I'm Maltese, he's not keen to see me here either.'

Gamble knew of Gozo and Malta's fragile and sometimes volatile alliance. He turned to see two men walking across the dark vineyards to the south. To the east was a small farm where a woman hung out her washing between two trees. A boy played with his dog. The marines remained unseen. It seemed somehow incredible that they could be here with the redoubt taken and no enemy aware of their existence. In Gamble's opinion, the Navy had made this all possible. Nelson was Lord of the Seas and the Royal Navy's 'wooden walls', ruled the waves. After inflicting the crushing victory at the Battle of the Nile, the French had virtually no ships to transport a company of troops into British territory. British landing parties could strike anywhere they wanted and would be gone before the French could bring reinforcements.

'How far until we reach the cove?'

'We'll be there in less than two hours.'

'And the damned Frogs?'

'They'll be there before mid-day,' Zeppi said, holding his wound.

'Will you be all right?'

The Malteseman nodded. 'Yes.' He looked down at the road, before looking up to Gamble. 'It was my fault back there.'

'Yes, it was.' Gamble was serious, but concerned.

Zeppi took a sip of water and shook his head humbly. 'I was stupid. I should have listened to you.'

'There might not be a next time.'

'I couldn't stop myself. The French have murdered, stolen, lied and cheated. I hate them. As soon as I saw them I became so angry.'

Gamble clasped his shoulder in friendship, a decade old bond, made in St Peter Port when Zeppi had worked for his father's merchant company. 'Just do as you're goddamn told next time,' he said. 'I promise I'll make them pay. Leave the killing to me.'

'Sir!' Coppinger interrupted.

Gamble turned to stare over the rocky basin. Figures moved on the nearby hills.

'Horsemen, sir!'

'I see them! Everyone get down here! Now!'

The marines scrambled across the roadside and capered to where an ancient carob tree sprouted over a natural spring, an opening deep down in the rocks.

Sergeant Powell thumped a slacking marine into place with his pike before jumping down into the gap.

Gamble rested his spyglass against the rocks to steady the cumbersome device. His view was one of blurred hills, and he twisted the lens until the vision was clear. Four horsemen were walking, rather than riding their mounts, and perhaps forty men - a company - marched in front of a cart drawn by two oxen. They were heading towards the redcoats.

'Looks like the scoundrels happen to be early, sir,' Kennedy whispered ironically, although the French were still half a mile away and could not possibly hear a conversation.

'They are in a hurry to bathe,' Zeppi suggested with a shrug. 'Perhaps they stink worse than you?'

Gamble was deciding what to do. He would spring an ambush on the roadside, but all of his men were now hunkered down on one side of the road. Perhaps there was another way? He beckoned Kennedy to follow him where the land edged down to the sea cliffs. He gestured up at a shadowed depression in the rocks where twenty men could hide from the road above. If he could position twenty marines there and line the road with the rest to block it, then as the French formed up, the concealed marines might spring up and turn the enemy flank to red ruin.

He doubled back with his lieutenant. 'Harry, you see that tumble of yellow grass edging the road?'

'Yes, sir.'

'Take twenty of your platoon down to the hollow and wait for my signal. By my reckoning that is forty yards away. We let the bastards come close and we'll hammer them on two fronts. It will be like boarding a vessel.'

'Yes, sir,' Kennedy replied. 'What about the officers? I'm told that when facing horsemen you should hit the beast rather than the rider.'

'Who told you that?' Gamble grimaced. 'There are only four riders and I doubt they'll give us any trouble.'

The marines waited.

Gamble watched the enemy move inexorably closer. The mounted men were officers and their horses were skin and bone. They wore swords and blue coats, their faces dark underneath bicorn hats. The men were *chasseurs*, light infantry troops, dressed in mostly blue coats and trousers with olive green fringed epaulettes and white cross-belts. They carried a short sabre as well as their musket and bayonet. Coming closer, he could see that their uniforms were patched in a variety of drab coloured cloth. They sauntered rather than marched and he thought they looked like street beggars rather than prime infantry that had shattered the armies of royal Europe. Fighting in pairs, using cover and keeping no rigid formation, the light infantry had sniped at the enemy lines, eating away at them slowly until they had collapsed under the nerve-destroying French artillery, infantry and cavalry support. It was a simple plan and the French were masters of the battlefields.

Two of the officers spurred ahead of the convoy, doubtless wanting to reach the cove where sea bream, squid and whiting could be caught by the barrel load. Curiously, one wore a cavalry cap: a mirliton, and a dolman jacket, and Gamble wondered if the man was a Hussar. Zeppi had said there were no cavalry on the islands because they had all been sent to Egypt with the rest of the Army of the Orient. The officer kicked his mount forward and the other one did the same, and Gamble cursed because they would spring the trap too early.

'Archie!'

'Sir?' Sergeant Powell answered.

'Deal with the bastards, but only if they spot us.'

'Aye, sir,' he said, pulling free his axes. 'Reminds me of the time when I fought the Yankees on detachment duties at the Battle of Oriskany.'

'Not now, Archie.'

The two riders were past Kennedy's group, kicking up clouds of dirty-white dust, and so far the marines remained unseen. Gamble grinned. This would be easy. The *chasseurs* were now approaching a dip in the road and this was the chance of victory. The first rider looked straight into his eyes. He stared fleetingly, until the realisation hit him like a musket ball, and he opened his mouth in warning.

Sergeant Powell drew his right arm back and, in a flash of steel, the blade buried itself in the blue-coated rider's chest with an explosive grunt. The force of the blow knocked the man backwards in the saddle, nerveless hands releasing the leather reins. His eyes were wide in shock and blood trickled from his mouth as he swayed. The mirliton wearing one froze. His mouth went slack. He jerked free his sabre and went to raise it when Adams sprang up and plunged a dirk between his ribs. The marine twisted the blade and hauled on the reins to take the beast off the road. The horseman slumped to the side, hands lifeless, but sword still suspended from the strap around his wrist. Gamble climbed the bank and dragged the dying officer out of sight. Coppinger went to reach the other horse, but it panicked, kicked its hind legs, and reared. The Dane stepped back from its thrashing hooves. The dead officer fell from the saddle, but his boot caught in the stirrup and the corpse was towed behind the bounding horse as it galloped north towards the coast. Gamble watched the body slam into rocks, crunching bone and gashing flesh, until finally the boot unclasped itself and the body lay in a crumpled pile. It was hidden from the advancing *chasseurs* who had neither seen, nor heard the commotion.

The horse that Adams had brought down whinnied loudly and Gamble twisted from the Frenchman who had died. 'Keep that bloody horse quiet!' he hissed. Coppinger and Powell ran to the beast to soothe it. Gamble turned to the others. 'Stop gawking and eyes front! Resume your places!' He saw that the convoy had reached the grass. Now was the time. He stood so that all could see him. 'Form line! At the double! Advance!'

The Malteseman stepped forward and Gamble shoved him back. 'You stay here, you bastard.'

The redcoats scrambled up the bank to form two lines across the roadside. The horse screamed and Powell flailed at the reins. Gamble cupped a hand to his mouth. 'Leave the bloody thing, Archie! Close ranks!'

The *chasseurs* halted and stared with sudden confusion. Then, the officers and sergeants shouted for them to form up. The two-wheeled cart kept moving until the driver hauled on the beast's yokes.

'Get ready to spill some Frog blood, boys! Remember Acre! Forward!' Gamble bellowed. 'Hold your fire!' He wanted his men to be fully-loaded. He withdrew his cutlass. The two remaining horsemen looked like veterans of the wars, hard-faced with a grim confidence, but he wanted the French to fear his men. The two lines of marines walked calmly, and one or two *chasseurs* broke ranks in terror. So far, the enemy had not seen Kennedy's platoon, only to stand and fix bayonets. Gamble noticed some did not have any. 'Halt!' They were a scant fifty yards from the enemy. One of the officers waved his sword about his head as though impatient with his men's discipline. 'Make ready! Present! Aim! Fire!'

The platoon's muskets split the morning air with a sound like the dull tearing of heavy cloth.

'Load!' Sergeant Powell shouted over the din, musketoon slung over his back, and boarding pike in his hands. Sam, who had seen a score of men collapse from the volley, punched the bitter smoke-wreathed air with his sword in triumph and narrowly missed slicing open Corporal Forge's neck.

A marine fumbled his ramrod and received a customary berating from Forge who had witnessed the slip. 'Bray! I saw that! You useless blundering bastard! Pick it up now! You dare show His Majesty's enemy that mistake again, and I'll have you on a charge!'

The *chasseurs*, perhaps half their number as they were still trying to form into line, shouldered muskets and Gamble held his breath. The crackle of shots smashed out, the thrum deafened and the heavy butts leaped back into shoulders. A ball nicked a large stone in front of him. A musket exploded with flame somewhere next to him and he thought the man had fired without permission. A marine, hit in the abdomen, fell sideways and slid down the embankment. He did not move again. Another hit in the throat tried to ignore the wound, but he dropped his musket and fell backwards. Forge dragged him free from entangling the others.

'Close up!' Sergeant Powell shouted, then seeing a marine in the second rank trying to break free, he clasped him by the collar.

Crouch, hissing like a cat, held his right hand with his left. 'A ball has taken a finger away, Sergeant! And it's dented the breech! She won't fire!' He showed the wound and the damaged musket. Powell looked away, stooped and thrust him a dead marine's weapon.

'Now back to your file!' Powell pushed him into position, and patting his shoulder. 'Your trigger finger still works!'

155

'Take Aim! Aim low!' Gamble shouted.

He had seen the enemy line shudder. British muskets were larger-calibre than the French, and the lead balls lost shape impacting flesh. They smashed apart bone as they drove deep into the bodies. The rear ranks were being pushed into positions over their dead, dying and wounded by the sergeants. One man, lying on his back, was screaming like a vixen. Muskets tipped up as they began to load.

'Fire!' Gamble yelled and the muskets erupted in dirty smoke and the rank smell of black powder. It was another quick, violent, horrifying volley at lethally short range and the curses of the French were wiped into instant silence, or rather changed into screams and sobs.

'Reload! Don't waste your powder!' Powell shouted.

The marines fought on. They did what they were trained to do, and what they did was learn how to fire a musket. Load and fire, load and fire. Months of drill. Pull free a cartridge, bite the top off, prime the lock with a pinch of black powder from the bitten end, close the frizzen to keep the pinch in place, drop the butt, pour in the rest down the blackened barrel, thrust the paper down as wadding, ram it down hard, and inside was the lead ball. Bring the musket back up, pull back the cock, aim, and pull the trigger. Repeat. Mouths would dry out from the saltpetre. Tongues would swell. Faces and hands would blacken. Eyes would sting from the stink and ears would ring from the roar.

Gamble waited until the time was right. 'Now, Harry! Now!' he roared.

Lieutenant Kennedy's battle-forged men stormed up the verge, screaming like banshees eager for blood.

'*Tirez!*'

The *chasseur* line exploded, but because they had seen and heard a new enemy, it was slapdash as files twisted to face the threat. Bullets whipped the air and two marines of Gamble's platoon buckled onto the stony road. One moved and the other did not.

'Fire!' Gamble slashed the air with his cutlass and the torrent of balls slammed into the French ranks that were in the process of loading, or turning to face Kennedy's men. 'Cease loading!' he yelled, not wanting his men to fire in case they hit their comrades.

Kennedy knocked aside bayonets with his sword and stepped back as a large Frenchman wearing gold rings in his ears lunged with his blade. The lieutenant parried and brought up his pistol to the man's temple. The enemy glared with terrified eyes as Kennedy pulled the

156

trigger and the ball plunged into his skull, erupting from the other side leaving a hole the size of a saucer, and spraying gore over the man beside him.

One of the mounted officers spurred his horse towards Kennedy, beating aside heads with the flat of his epée. He slashed it hard across the face of one marine, taking an eye and the best part of his cheek, brought it up and chopped down through the bicorn of another. He wrenched his arm back, to find the hat was stuck to the blood-dripping blade, and went to hack again when a musket ball shattered his arm. Hands reached up and pulled him from his mount. He fell to the ground, where feet kicked him and bayonets thumped into his writhing body, ripping his flesh and saturating the cold ground with his hot blood. A *chasseur*, belly torn open lay screaming as men trod and slipped on his spilled guts. A knot of Frenchmen broke from their company to fire as skirmishers as they had been trained to do at Gamble's platoon. Their ragged flurry of shots threw one of his men down in a welter of blood.

Gamble, ignoring the small group, looked at his steel-tipped marines. 'Charge bayonets!'

The French company had not reacted well and now the rest of the red-coated enemy charged with muskets tipped with long bayonets as though they were taking an enemy vessel. If the enemy held, Gamble knew, he would lose a good number of men. It was a risk, but one that his gut told him to take.

'For God and King George!' Riding-Smyth chanted, sword held low just as his captain had shown him.

The French gawked through the rank musket smoke, saw the enemy come and broke. Some were too slow and the marines' spikes caught them. Others threw down their weapons and pleaded for quarter.

'Surrender!' Kennedy shouted, eyes blazed through his crimson-spattered face.

'Hands up!' Gamble snarled at one stubborn *chasseur*. He punched him in the face and kicked him down onto the ground. 'Get your bloody hands in the air!'

Powell jabbed his pike lightly at the throat of the last officer. 'Get off your nag, sir! There's a good fellow!' Sunlight reflected brightly on the weapon's tip.

The Frenchman, a captain, knowing he was beaten, cursed and shouted for his men to yield. He kicked his feet out of the stirrups, jumped down and offered his sabre to Gamble.

157

Gamble gawked, sizing him up. The Frenchman had brown almond-shaped eyes set over a hooked nose, and a strong-boned face. 'Sam?'

'Sir!' Riding-Smyth panted.

'Tell the Crapaud he can keep his blade,' Gamble said and, as the lieutenant relayed the message, albeit slightly altered for politeness, he turned to his men who were still forcing the French off the road. He heard a scream and pushed Sam aside. Two prisoners were crying out as a marine continued to bayonet them savagely. 'Cease that now!' he bawled. 'Marine! Cease what you are doing!'

'You bastards!' The marine was saying over and over, flicking the reddened blade and jabbing it hard. 'Bastards!'

'Cease!' Gamble ordered and was ignored. He tugged the redcoat away with so much force that the man fell to the ground. It was Crouch. His face was twisted into a thing of madness. The French captain jostled his way over with Sam and Harry. Gamble knelt down to the dying *chasseurs*, but there was nothing anyone could do.

The officer exploded in rage, his mouth a misshapen pit of resentment and anger. He spat at Gamble, who was taking the anger calmly. He sympathised, he would have done the same had it been his men who had been butchered. Sergeant Powell brought the pike up to keep the Frenchman back, but Gamble ordered him to lower it.

'Would you like me to translate, sir?' Riding-Smyth asked, hesitantly, but Gamble shook his head.

'I understand,' he said to the Frenchman, feeling sweat bead between his shoulder blades and slicken his palms. 'I will deal with my man accordingly. You have my word as a British officer.'

The captain stared into Gamble's eyes, made hard and almost cruel from the clash. He was still looking intently at him when he spoke.

The young Marine lieutenant looked grave at the Frenchman's hurried reply. 'He said his men were surrendering. They were murdered and...' he hesitated, 'he said you may not look like a gentleman, but there must be honour in war. Honour demands punishment.'

Gamble took a deep breath. He glanced at the mutilated corpses and let his eyes roam to the faces of his men; seeing resentment, guilt, triumph, weariness and horror. Crouch, who had his face in his hands, sobbed and babbled wildly.

'I apologise. I give you my word that he will be reprimanded.'

A marine burst through the gaping ranks. 'They weren't surrendering, sir!' Willoughby said. 'I saw it happen. They attacked him and he had to put them down.'

Gamble's temper flared and he reached out and grabbed the hulking soldier by the throat, bristles like a wire-brush dug into his fingers. 'You speak to me again without permission and I'll tear your tongue out of your goddamn mouth!' He hauled him up and pushed him backwards towards Powell who tripped him over.

'Marine Willoughby, you are on a charge! You beef-witted bastard! On your feet!' Powell kicked his heels hard. 'Get up, or I'll knock your bloody ears off and you'll be picking the sand out of them for the rest of the month!'

Riding-Smyth was translating this to the captain who still seethed. He stepped forward and said something to Gamble who told the Frenchman to keep his bloody mouth still. He looked back at the roadside that was splashed with blood, littered with burnt wadding and spent balls. Corporal Forge herded prisoners with his bayonet towards the press of men.

It had taken ten minutes of fire, blade, blood and sweat. The marines had won and their prisoners now sat under guard.

To the south, Fort Dominance guarded the island with its batteries of guns like a watchful sentinel, and whether God wanted it or not, it was where Gamble would take his redcoats.

'Four dead,' Kennedy read out the butcher's bill of names. 'Four wounded. Two severely, the other two have asked to stay.'

Gamble rubbed his eyes as though he was tired. 'Thank you, Harry. Tell the men they did well. Very well.'

Kennedy hesitated. 'I think it would come better from you, sir. After all, they won this fight for you.'

'It's because I mentioned Acre.'

'Aye.'

Gamble smiled. 'I will, but I'm getting a 'there's something else, sir', kind of feeling?'

Kennedy smiled knowingly. 'The lads also want to know what you're going to do with Crouch.'

'It doesn't concern them.'

'I know.'

'He deserves to be shot.' Gamble stared at his lieutenant who was biting his lip. 'What, Harry? What is it?'

'I don't know whether Crouch is guilty. I didn't see what he was accused of doing. He's a dolt and he's been a troublemaker in the past I grant you. But he's one of the more useful of our men. Even with one finger less. Certainly more so than, Uriah Bray,' he said condescendingly.

'I've seen barnacles prime a musket better than Bray,' Gamble said to which Kennedy chortled. 'I've seen seaweed with more intelligence. But where Bray is goddamn useless, Crouch is a vicious little shit. Both him and Willoughby.' *It was a pity they still lived*, he said to himself. They had survived Acre, and the Nile when other men, good men, had died. An image of Bob Carstairs flashed in his mind's eye. The lieutenant had been wounded at Acre and fought on as though it hadn't weakened him. But French grenadiers had caught him and bayoneted him to death during the last night of the siege. Gamble had been unable to help him and now he clasped his sword's hilt in anguish over the death that seeped from his memory like a putrid wound. Bob should never have died there. Willoughby and Crouch should have. Life was bitterly unfair.

'Our men are murderers, rapists, thieves and knaves-alike. Most have had a career change on the orders of a magistrate. Crouch is no different, sir. But he's also not himself of late,' Kennedy continued. 'The men have noticed that he's started to laugh like a lunatic. He talks a lot to himself.'

'I haven't noticed,' Gamble replied carelessly.

Kennedy said nothing of his captain's ignorance. 'He's a changed man. Willoughby says ever since Acre he's been having nightmares. He dreams of blood and smoke and bodies.'

Gamble grunted, understanding the man's secret agony of having to deal with the aftermath of battle. The smell of death, powder smoke and roasting bodies came to him like a living nightmare. He breathed in Gozo's air, which was as fresh as a sunlit summer meadow by comparison. Should he show empathy? Would that be a sign of weakness? What would the company think of him? Battle-scarred and battle-weary? Here comes Captain Gamble, a man affected by war. Would they smile and laugh at him? He rubbed his face, deciding that he needed to bury those thoughts, and that he needed sleep even more.

'What are you saying? That he should be forgiven?'

'No, sir. Just understood.'

Gamble gave his friend a sharp meaningful glance. 'Harry-'

160

Kennedy held up a hand to placate the interruption. 'I'm not trying to be impudent. I know my place. Crouch has been in his cups ever since that dreadful siege. I think he's been affected by it.'

Haven't we all? Gamble said inwardly. His fingers found his mother's silk handkerchief and twisted the cloth as images of the siege played over in his mind. Carstairs had mocked the chaplain's prayers on the eve of the fight. *"But if there is harm, then you shall pay life for life"*. They had laughed like idiots, but somehow he could not get the axiom from his mind.

'What do you intend to do, sir?' Kennedy sounded contrite.

Gamble was jarred back to reality. 'I honestly don't know. Keep him under a close watch. I'll have to consider the punishment once the mission is complete.'

'Thank you,' Kennedy said, clearly pleased. He was a clever man and liked to feel that anything could be understood, and any problem solved.

'But if he steps out of line-'

'He won't,' Kennedy interjected. 'I'll make sure he doesn't.'

'Perhaps a French musket ball might find him first,' Gamble said, earning a somewhat chastising grunt from his lieutenant.

The cart had long been examined, and disappointedly contained nothing of value; old crates, sacks and fish and eel traps destined to take back to the fort full of provisions. The prisoners of war dug graves with captured spades for their fallen and the marines dug for their dead.

By dusk the sun had paled to a shimmering gold disc, hovering on the horizon like a stone flung across the sea. The water twinkled with a molten light.

Zeppi had left to meet Grech and the rest of the volunteers and so the marines waited for them where they had destroyed the French convoy. Gamble had allowed the men to rest and now a half-dozen fires lit the coast where the redcoats ate, drank, smoked and where the prisoners sat in sullen silence.

'Sir,' a voice called.

Gamble looked up from the flames where he and Kennedy shared a skin of wine, the order being that his men were allowed to drink for the day's success, but not enough to get them drunk.

'What is it, Sam?'

The lieutenant limped past a cluster of rocks. 'The French captain, sir, he asked me to come and see you.'

'And?'

'He wants to know if you have punished Marine Crouch.'

'What?' Kennedy laughed derisively.

Gamble considered his reply whilst sucking the wineskin. 'What's the bugger's name?'

'*Capitaine* Tessier, sir.'

'You tell Tessier I said I would deal with Crouch,' he said with a stern expression, 'and anything more is none of his concern.'

'Yes, sir.' Riding-Smyth turned to walk away.

'And explain that I've allowed him as an officer to keep his sword sheathed. Tell him I'd appreciate if he could do that with his goddamn mouth too. If the bugger can't, then I'm more than happy to.'

Riding-Smyth hesitated, then smiled. 'I will, sir.'

'The cheeky bastard,' Kennedy said, when Riding-Smyth had walked away, wincing from his blistered feet.

'Most of the Frogs are,' Gamble said boorishly, glaring at his timepiece. He snapped the lid shut and got up to stretch his long legs. 'Zeppi better be back here soon. I gave him strict instructions to be back here by six of the clock.'

'He will,' Kennedy replied, checking his own timepiece. It showed ten minutes after.

'I'm going to check on the picquets.'

'Would you like me to do that?'

'No, it's all right. I fancy a walk.'

Gamble picked his way through the tumble of rocks to check on the prisoners first. Dark faces glowered malevolently back, but Gamble ignored them. Riding-Smyth and the French officer were deep in conversation further down so he ignored them too. Powell and ten marines stood on guard and Gamble shared a cup of hot tea and a joke with them before climbing up to the rocks where Coppinger watched the roads. A hundred yards away to the west, atop flat rocks where the dead French horseman had been dragged by his mount, Marsh gave him a nod.

'Things quiet, Coppinger?' he asked, thrusting a steaming mug of tea into his hands. The Dane gratefully accepted it, because the sea-wind was biting.

'Yes, sir. Quiet as a pauper's funeral.'

Gamble watched bats flit from the rocks, twirling and dancing as they hunted insects, until returning to their roost nearby.

'We'll be making our way to the fort soon enough.'

'That's good, sir. I can't abide the wait any longer.' The Dane took a long drink. 'What will happen to the prisoners?'

'I had thought about sending them back to the Prince of Waves, but on second thoughts, I'll turn them over to the Gozitans until the island is in our hands,' Gamble said. 'They can throw the bloody lot of them in one of the keeps.'

'And let them rot, sir?'

Gamble chuckled. 'Perhaps. Once we've won, they'll be quickly repatriated.'

Coppinger sniffed to signify that he did not understand.

'Sent home,' Gamble answered.

They listened to the sounds of the sea, the murmur of voices and the wind that caressed the land around them.

'Can I ask you something, sir?'

'Yes.'

'It's personal, sir.'

'Go on.'

The Dane took another long swig. 'Have you ever loved a woman?'

Gamble winced and shifted his feet in awkwardness at the question. 'I've had the odd infatuation, Coppinger. I don't know if I've loved them, though. I've bedded a lot of them, but can you ever love a whore?'

'I loved a girl once.'

'A whore?'

'No, sir,' Coppinger said reprovingly.

'Oh.'

'I've been thinking a lot about her lately.'

'True love, was it?'

The marine grinned. 'I was smitten with her. Drunk with her.'

'What happened?'

'She loved another and moved away when he died.'

Gamble stared at him.

The Dane drew the cup to his lips, eyes blinking with dark secrets.

Gamble searched for better, less conventional words, but could not find them. 'How unfortunate,' he answered.

There was a commotion of sorts below and he suspected it was Powell finding a marine drunk, or that two of his men had come to blows. There was a sudden cry and he leapt down the rocks, knowing it was more than just a scuffle.

'What the hell's going on?' he shouted as a musket fired down by the shore. Marines were sprinting past and another firearm pounded the air.

'The Frenchie officer, sir,' Corporal Forge said. His bayonet-tipped musket, and those of six other men, held back the prisoners who were wide-eyed and frantic. 'He's done a runner.'

'What?' Gamble was incredulous.

'Down here, sir! The bastard's broken his parole!' Sergeant Powell waved a hand urgently and Gamble ran towards him. There was a marine in the centre of a bowl-shaped hollow, clutching his belly. It was Riding-Smyth. 'I told him to stay back.'

'Jesus,' Gamble said at the blood.

'The Froggie was angry. I told the lieutenant to stay back, sir,' Powell sounded as astonished as he was angry. 'The lieutenant tried to stop the Froggie from running, but he ran him through with his sword. I couldn't stop him, sir. I couldn't stop him. I'm sorry.'

Gamble twisted his neck up at the rocks. 'Pace! Pace!' he called desperately. 'Harry!'

'I told him-' Powell began.

'I told him to stay back, I know! Now shut up, Archie!'

'Here, sir!' Kennedy panted.

'Sir...' Riding-Smyth said, but was unable to finish. His face was pale, his lips going blue.

'Don't talk, Sam,' Gamble said, watching the blood pool between the lieutenant's fingers. Riding-Smyth's eyes were staring up at the sky where a smattering of stars were glimmered. 'Save your breath, there's a good fellow.'

'He was livid,' Riding-Smyth said and coughed, 'and upset about the deaths.' He winced and could not help crying out in pain. 'I saw him unsheathe his sword, but I didn't do anything. I froze.'

'It's not your fault,' Gamble said, glancing up again. 'Pace! Get your arse here now!' He clasped Riding-Smyth's hand, feeling the hot sticky blood and the lieutenant's tight grasp.

'I'm here, sir!' Pace pushed his way through the gathering crowd. He dropped to the floor and tried to inspect the wound, but the lieutenant was clenching his hands over it. 'I need to see it, sir,' Pace pleaded and Riding-Smyth eased briefly. 'I need a light!' A marine quickly returned with a lantern, illuminating the gruesome wound. A heartbeat later, Pace shot his captain a grave look.

'Help him.'

Pace was solemn. 'There's nothing more I can do, sir. I'm sorry.'

164

Gamble, mouth twitching, reached out and grabbed Pace by the throat. 'You can save him!' he snarled.

'I can't, sir,' Pace replied.

Kennedy bent down to Gamble's height. 'Let Pace go, sir,' he said soothingly. 'Sam doesn't need to see this. There's nothing anyone can do now.'

Gamble searched Pace's eyes for hope, saw none and released his grip. His gaze turned to Riding-Smyth, who was trembling. Gamble unbuttoned his coat and draped it over his friend.

'Oh God, have mercy,' the young lieutenant said, his voice a whispering moan. 'Tell my family I did my duty.'

A prick of tears stung Gamble's eyes. Carstairs had said the same thing. 'You did your duty, Sam. I'm proud of you in the short time we've known each other.'

Riding-Smyth smiled. 'Friends, sir?'

'For life,' he assured him with a smile.

'The fort...I wanted to be there when you took it.'

'I'll take it for you and I'll kill Tessier.'

Riding-Smyth shook his head. 'He was angry. Don't take revenge.' His eyes widened, dark blood trickled from his slack mouth. 'My family...' He coughed up more blood.

'I'll tell them you're a hero,' Gamble cuffed away tears, unafraid who saw him. 'Ain't that right, lads? Our lieutenant of marines here is a goddamn hero.'

A chorus of hoarse agreement rose up from the men.

He gripped Riding-Smyth's hands and felt rosary beads. Pace had placed them there and Gamble thought it an act of wonderful consideration. The marine began to sing Heart of Oak, a popular song, and one Sam liked.

'I don't want to die,' Riding-Smyth said, tears flowed to mix with the blood, as Pace's voice echoed around the hollow.

I don't want you too, either, Sam, Gamble's voice collapsed with grief in his head.

Riding-Smyth closed his eyes, convulsed and a gurgling sound rattled in his throat as Gamble held him. And then, he was gone.

A moment passed where the only sound was the sea.

'Lord our God,' Kennedy said in a loud, crisp voice. 'You are always faithful and quick to show mercy. Young Samuel was violently taken from his brothers-at-sea. Come swiftly to his aid, have mercy on him, and comfort his family and friends by the power and protection of the Cross. We ask this through Christ our Lord. Amen.'

'Amen,' voices spoke in unison.

Gamble peered at Riding-Smyth's absurdly young face. Another death, and another promising friendship gone to oblivion. His hands balled into fists, blood boiling with rage – a fiery killing rage, before he managed to subdue it. He stood, blinking and stricken.

'Where did the bastard go?'

Kennedy's eyes were red-rimmed. 'He climbed down to the rocks and it was there we lost him. I presumed he jumped into the sea, but I could not tell. It is suicide to try to swim those waves. The current would take him out and he'd either drown, or be dashed upon the rocks.'

'The bastard is still alive until I see his corpse. Archie, take a dozen men and scour the coastline to the south. Harry, take a handful and search the north, just in case he tries to backtrack. The craven turd has broken his parole. He's a man with no honour and anyone who finds him will earn himself the contents of my purse! Find him and bring him to me alive,' Gamble said, the word 'alive' the ballast of the order. 'Careful, he's armed. Now go! Go!'

'What about you, sir?' Kennedy enquired, wondering what his captain would do to the prisoner.

Gamble looked down at Riding-Smyth. 'I'll stay here with him a while longer.'

*

He had not wanted to kill the young officer, but there was nothing else he could have done. Gamble had not listened and so there was only one other option. And now the redcoats were scouring every nook and cranny to find him. They looked impressive; grim and battle-hardened warriors, but though they might have a keen sense of doggedness, Tessier knew that it didn't make such men intelligent.

He had watched them scan the waves as they crashed and sucked at the tiny cove from his place of hiding. A tall redcoat stood watching the sea for movement, then jumped down to the next rock and repeated his patient observations. Another enemy jabbed at dark places, maybe just wide enough to conceal a man, with his bayonet. But an officer searching large rock pools called them on.

Tessier was about to move when he heard the tiniest footfalls behind him. He froze. Unable to fetch his horse, he had run as fast as his

166

pumping legs could take him. Muskets fired and the lead balls whipped past him, but he had clambered down rocks, scraping the skin of his hands and knees as he descended to where the sea lapped the shore. There was a stench of something dead. Fetid. It was so powerful that it made him gag. It was coming from where a tangle of animal legs and seaweed protruded in amongst a cluster of rocks. It was a goat, its body bloated with rot, its face half-skeletal. Flies buzzed over the eye-less sockets and in and around its drooping mouth. It must have fallen into the sea, or been injured and drowned.

Tessier scanned the area wildly. There were places to hide, but they were exposed and easy to find by the enemy if they did a proper sweep. Wind brought sand into his face. A voice called. He dropped low. He couldn't see them, but the redcoats weren't far off. He had to hide and there was only one place to go.

Holding his breath, he heaved the putrid corpse carefully aside. The air was rank, sticky and choking. Flies and maggots crawled everywhere. Tessier had pulled the dead beast and stinking seaweed over him, squirming, cursing and burrowing into the foulness. There was an old expression his father used to say to him, *you made your bed, now lie in it'*. Tessier grunted at the irony.

There wasn't much space to breathe, but there was no time to change that now. Time seemed to go slow. He couldn't hear anything, except for the buzzing of flies, rank liquid dripping and the wind buffeting the seaweed. No one came and he suspected the corpse was cutting off the sound of the enemy searching and had gone past long ago. Revulsion was forcing his fingers to move the corpse. The moisture clawed at his nose and throat, sand was filling his nostrils and he became frantic to breathe. The goat pressed harder and he wanted desperately to push his way clear, but then the first enemy appeared. Stalking as a hunter.

And now the redcoat was standing next to him. Tessier closed his eyes, unable to breathe in the noxious fumes and expecting an enemy bayonet to pierce his flesh. There was a tapping sound, and hot water trickled down his arm. The redcoat was urinating. Perhaps he was safe after all. No voices called out. No mocking laughter. After a moment, the last of the enemy moved away and Tessier tried to keep the exhilaration from bursting out of his body. He lived! He slowly pushed up and crawled free, uniform soaked with rot. He glanced around. The redcoats were going and he scrambled down to the sea, wiping jellied gore from his face. He laughed. Cool salty air was upon him and he lay on the surf, letting the water wash his body as he drew in huge gasps of breath.

He told himself he was free, but a voice in his head said that only when he had reached the fort was that true.

And when the captain of marines came, Tessier would kill him for permitting the butchery of his men.

Tessier went south.

*

The marines returned three hours later withdrawn and unable to meet their captain's gaze. They had not found Tessier. Gamble turned to stare out at the sea. He only turned back when he heard the sentries call out a warning. Behind him the road coming from Rabat was alive with armed men. Zeppi had brought the volunteers. There must have been a hundred of them.

'Baldassar will bring the others from the north and the west,' Zeppi smiled proudly. 'They will come and we will take back our island.' He noticed a cold emptiness in the camp. Gamble stood over a freshly dug mound, his breeches and shirt filthy with dirt and sweat. Kennedy explained and Zeppi stood appalled.

'Sam was a catholic,' Gamble uttered to his friend, 'so I want a proper prayer said for him. Can you do that for me?'

Zeppi swallowed hard. 'Of course,' he said, gripping Gamble's forearm. He stood over the grave and said a prayer in Maltese.

'I'm going to get him for what he did,' Gamble said when Zeppi had finished, not caring who heard him. Marsh had brought him a bucket of seawater in the meantime to wash himself of the filth.

'It wasn't your fault, sir,' Kennedy said.

Gamble growled as he washed. It felt as though he was manacled with heavy chains around his heart. With every move they tightened like a noose. 'I'll murder him. I'll goddamn slaughter the beak-nosed bastard.'

'You weren't to know he would break his parole.'

Gamble rounded on him, eyes full of accusation. 'And perhaps if I had strung Crouch up in the first place, then maybe Sam would still be alive?'

Kennedy looked full of remorse, knowing he had championed the marine's innocence. 'It doesn't matter what you did, or didn't do, sir,' he said, trying to mollify the situation. 'Sam did say not to seek revenge.'

168

'You think I'm going to let Tessier get away with the murder of one of my officers?' Gamble snarled as he pulled on his coat.

Kennedy knew better than to question his friend's resolve. 'No, sir.'

'Then why did you damn well say it?'

'I think Sam was trying to keep you from the torment of retribution...' Kennedy left the thought unfinished.

Gamble blinked bloodshot eyes. 'It's too late for that,' his voice sank to a whisper, as though he didn't want Kennedy to hear the words.

'He should not have murdered our friend,' Kennedy said. 'The blame is with him, not with you or me. Even the prisoners seem shocked by it.'

Gamble's jaw clenched in anger. 'Christ, Harry, but it was my decision to let him keep his sword!'

'It was a matter of honour.'

Gamble spat. 'Damn his honour! He preached that damned word to me! I'll show him how honourable I can be! Sergeant Powell! Form the men up!'

'Sir!'

'And Archie?'

'Sir?'

'Give the Frog's horse to the locals,' Gamble said. 'It'll give them something to eat.'

The Gozitans went first, taking the tracks across the hills to the south, ever conscious of the fort's watchful gaze over the last ridgeline. The marines followed them; the wounded lay in the oxen-pulled cart. Gamble was the last to leave. His eyes raked over the road to where a brave feat was soured by the needless death of his lieutenant. He had blistered his hands digging, but at least the grave had a cross, and his lieutenant's name carved into it and now a respectable prayer said for him. Other fallen soldiers had not been so lucky.

Gamble forced the march hard. The wind picked up a little which swirled dust into mouths and eyes. Feet became sore, muscles burned and soon, he heard the inexorable sounds of grousing from the ranks.

'If I hear any more whining from anyone, I'll beat the man to death with my bare hands!' Gamble snapped for no other reason than that he felt like shouting.

The mixed force reached the cove and lit a fire at the shoreline. He noticed that a handful of the Gozitans were leaning on their weapons, panting for breath. One man collapsed onto the sand. For a moment, Gamble wanted to savage them for their weakness, but he knew that was wrong and that they weren't even soldiers. He took a deep breath to dispel his irritation.

The *Sea Prince* saw the beacon, and by midnight, as a soft rain fell, two longboats were dragged up the sandy beach. The smell of stale breath, sweat and damp wool washed over him.

A group of officers formed the sailors up. Gamble had expected to see the landing party commanded by the charismatic Captain James Eaton or First Lieutenant John Greenslade, naval officers of senior rank, and both men always liked to be in the thick of action. He was pleasantly surprised to see Benjamin Pym at their head. Pym was a naval lieutenant, a rank equivalent to Gamble's rank as a land captain.

'Not here to step on your toes, Simon,' Pym said in his thick Cornish accent, stretching out his hand in friendship, which Gamble took warmly. Pym wore his plain blue naval uniform over white breeches and stockings. A pistol was tucked in his sword belt, and a curved sword taken from a Turk at Acre hung at his left hip. 'The command of this here landing party was the subject of a good wager on a ferocious game of cards.' Pym was accompanied by Brownrigg the Boatswain, Rooke the Boatswain's Mate and two junior Midshipmen keen to make a reputation for themselves.

'And you won?'

'No, I lost the bloody game,' Pym grinned, his hazel eyes glinting in his freckled face.

'Lieutenant Pym wanted to bring your damned leg-humping dog along,' Brownrigg scowled. 'I ain't having that mutt with me so it stayed behind.'

'It's a shame because it's certainly got sweeter breath than you,' Pym said with a shrug.

Everyone laughed.

'You got any advice for these young idiots with salt for brains?' Brownrigg gestured at the Midshipmen who blushed under scrutiny.

Gamble frowned. 'Just don't get killed,' he said, causing a wave of laughter. He turned to Pym. 'It's good to see you here, Ben,' he said with genuine affection. He considered both Pym and Kennedy as able and dependable friends.

'So what's happened? The mission going well for you bootnecks?' Pym grinned at the moniker the Jack Tars gave the marines, which they considered the leather stock as bits cut from boots. He craned to look over Gamble's broad shoulders to see Kennedy's crestfallen expression. There was no Riding-Smyth and Pym's gaze flicked back to Gamble who suddenly looked crushed. 'Sweet Christ,' he said, dipping his head in respect.

'A French officer, who I allowed to keep his blade, killed him with it before fleeing,' Gamble announced evenly, and was inwardly surprised by his calmness.

'Broke his parole, did he? The cowardly, contemptible devil!'

'Aye.'

'Where's he gone? To the fort?'

'Yes, and I assume the Crapauds now know we're here.'

Pym sighed with bitter understanding, because he assumed the mission was over and the men would have to go back on board. 'So now what?' He glared at the Gozitans and grimaced. 'Not exactly armed to the teeth, are they? Are they willing to fight?'

Gamble turned to them. 'They certainly are. My guide tells me when their blood is up, nothing on earth will stop them. This is their land and they understandably want it back.'

'Good for them,' Pym grinned cheerfully, then looked around.

Gamble caught him looking almost disdainfully at his uniform. He knew that naval officers were jealous that their land counterparts wore lace, gorgets, epaulettes and sashes. As Naval officers, they were not permitted to, and constantly grumbled about the dullness of their plain frock coats.

'You might even take a lovely Frog officer's coat with gold lace,' Gamble teased, 'if that would make you feel any better?'

Pym gave a lop-sided grin. 'Anything that would dazzle more than the scarlet rag of a ragamuffin you wear.' He gave Gamble's elbow and forearm a theatrical inspection. 'Where's the material gone? Have you lost it? There's more shirt on show than coat.' He let the mirth settle, then looked serious. 'Then we continue?'

Excited chatter came from the seamen until Rooke threatened them with his starter, a length of rope used for enforcing discipline on the ships' decks. They were dressed in round hats, their slops were blue jackets, light or striped trousers, stockings and buckled shoes. They carried muskets, pikes, swords and pistols. They certainly did not want to go back to the ship - and neither did Gamble.

'We still go ahead with the plan,' Gamble said. 'Vengeance is...'

'Golden,' Pym cut in. 'Like sunshine after rain. The lads are keen for a spot of killing. Aye, we're all here for that. Cooped up too long and my ears have heard some of the coarsest language known to man. I've told them the Toads are guarding strongboxes of gold and that there is a harem of buxom whores in the fort in need of rescuing,' he grinned. He cocked his head up to the hills where thin veils of rain drifted towards them. 'Maybe I'm wrong and perhaps there will be treasures inside? I could do with recouping last night's losses at cards.' He looked wistful. 'But in truth they don't need to be coaxed. They'll do as they're told. We'll take the damned fort and you can murder that French bastard.'

'Before I disembarked, I asked you to bring something.'

'I have it,' Pym patted a bundle underneath his coat.

Gamble nodded grimly. He stepped away momentarily to gaze up at the sky where until the moon rose, there had been only pale starlight.

Pym lit a cigar. 'I pity the man who did what he did to Sam,' he said to Kennedy, out of ear-shot. 'He's about to wish he hadn't been born.'

Kennedy peered at Gamble's back. 'He's got a heart of oak, sir. I don't know of any other man as tough.'

'He's hard all right,' Pym said. 'Like Cornish granite.'

'I know the captain's hurting. Losing Bob hurt him deep, but now losing Sam...' Kennedy's voice trailed away.

'That French bastard is a dead man.'

'Aye, sir.'

Gamble turned around, face impassive. 'Ready?' he asked Pym.

'As I'll ever be.'

'Then let's go.'

Gamble would take his cutlass to the enemy behind their walls and, in the oncoming fray, would slaughter Tessier.

*

Général Évrard Chasse, commanding officer of Fort Dominance, could not bear the reek anymore.

He left his desk where maps and parchments had transformed the plain stone room into a map room of sorts. A tapestry showing the construction of the fort by the Grand Master, hung along one wall. An ancient sword, all rust, hung from the other and it suited the general. Chasse was a proud, fussy man who harboured a suspicion that the French command did not appreciate his military brilliance. He had fought the Prussians at Valmy, the Austrians at Jemappes and Rivoli, and yet, he commanded the fort on a remote island far from home. Bonaparte had secured his involvement in the campaign and now he felt slighted. He had once been given the command of a division, but now a garrison of three hundred men. A third of them were conscripts and seamen with no fighting experience, another was mostly veterans and the others were sick; languishing in the hospital beds, or confined to their quarters. The damn islands were fever-ridden.

He sighed despondently and peered out of the windows with tired-looking eyes. Far across the water he could see Malta where *Général* Claude-Henri Belgrand de Vaubois commanded Valletta. Chasse gave the island a sneer. Damn Vaubois! Loved by Bonaparte, all because he had once been an artillery officer! When his commission as *Commandant en chef des Isles de Malte et du Goze* was announced, the toadying junior officers had crowded around him like flies on a turd. The old saying proved it: *"It's not what you know, it's who you know"*.

The peasants had risen up and now Chasse found that he was not a commander, or a governor of Gozo, but a prisoner. A damned hostage trapped in a bolthole, on a flea-bitten and fever island that nobody in their right mind would want. He had thought the islands were ripe for the plucking, but no more. He hated being here.

'Sir?'

Chasse sighed again and rubbed the whiskers on his chin.

'Sir?' This time the voice was more urgent.

Chasse looked back at the man with the raw-boned face standing at the door. He glowered with fierce eyes like an unruly hound.

'So who was this man?' he asked Tessier, with distaste because he could still smell the rankness coming from him from the far side of the room. The incense burning in a pot did nothing to alleviate the smell.

'*Capitaine* Gamble. An Englishman, sir.'

'What regiment were these *les rosbifs* allegedly from?'

Tessier's hands contracted in anger at the thought of the punishing volley fire. He had thought the English were supposed to be raw soldiers and badly led, but the marines were anything but. He straightened stiffly as he responded. 'They're not alleged, sir. They are marines. They have taken the northern redoubt and ambushed my men who were out collecting provisions.'

Chasse gave a small mocking laugh. 'How do you know it has been taken? Are you sure it's not just a local force? It's not the first time we've seen an armed insurrection.'

Tessier blew out a lungful of air. 'No, *Général*. They are English. Redcoats. I presumed they would have seized it before marching south for they would not want an enemy garrison at their rear. I would have done so. They captured me and I escaped.'

Chasse waved a hand as though he was finding the report a nuisance. 'Yes, yes, you already told me that. You managed to cut your bonds and flee.'

Tessier said nothing at the lie.

'What of your men?' Chasse asked.

'Alas, I could not free them, sir. It was a terrible decision to leave, but I had little choice.'

The *général* grunted and continued stroking his beard and moustache. 'Then you hid underneath a rotting sheep and escaped.'

'I said it was a goat,' Tessier corrected, forgetting his manners. He couldn't help but stare at Chasse's facial hair that looked like a vagina's fringe. It was thick and curly and the *général* had no idea of a cruel and offensive nickname that was bestowed on him by the garrison: *'la chatte'*.

Chasse twitched. 'Goat! Sheep! Whatever! What are English marines doing here, *Capitaine*? Why land here when Valletta is blockaded by their ships? How many marines was it? Fifty?' The *général* laughed unpleasantly and stepped forward to pour himself some wine, then remembered the smell so pretended to stretch instead. Fingers drummed the wall.

'They murdered two of my men in cold blood.' Tessier's jaw clenched. 'They were surrendering and a damned redcoat butchered them.'

'Awful things happen in war,' Chasse spat.

'They pounced like a pack of hungry wolves. They killed Prost, Raffin and Fievet,' he said of the dead officers. 'This Gamble has no honour like his animals,' Tessier was beginning to feel that the *général* wasn't taking his accusation seriously enough. 'He is a devil!'

Chasse watched him before speaking, and rubbed the soft bulges of skin under his eyes. He had already marked Tessier down as an impetuous man. 'I think you are a sore loser, *Capitaine*. I think you are still smarting from the ambush and the anger is clouding your judgement. Snap out of it! I asked you, why would the English land just fifty men here?'

Tessier paused, then frowned. 'I don't know, sir.'

'No, you clearly do not,' Chasse waved a finger at him, ignoring the details to concentrate on something far more important. 'The English would never send just fifty men. Are they here to take this fort? A company of them?' He laughed mirthlessly.

'Sir, more of them must have landed-'

174

Chasse slapped the wall with a hand, then glared with protruding eyes at the dishevelled officer who was clouding his favourite room with his foul odour. 'You're an idiot, *Capitaine*! There is no sign of any approaching English force. The hills are bare of marching troops and the coast is clear of warships. The English must have sent a scouting party to survey the island, or perhaps it was a local rabble dressed in the uniform to trick you. That's all it is, and I won't have another word said on the matter. You're safe behind thick walls. Stop panicking. You'll make our men nervous of shadows.'

'Shadows didn't kill my men.'

'Were you distracted?'

'Sir?'

'You must have been. You walked straight into an ambush. Or were you simply docile? Too much sun, perhaps?'

'*Général*?'

'Where were your men who should have been walking ahead of the convoy in order to expel such an attack?'

'It was not quite like that-'

'Yes, it was!' Chasse interrupted by slapping the wall again. 'You were careless. Your men were careless.' A lot of the men from the early revolutionary days had become ill-disciplined, or had become riddled with bad habits after the easy victories in Italy and Chasse considered Tessier was one of those men. 'You led your men into the trap,' he continued. 'It was nobody else's fault. If you want someone to blame, then look no further than yourself.'

Tessier's eyes narrowed. 'The English devils will come here, *Général*. Remember it was I who told you this.'

'They will not come here! They will go to Valletta! And you, *Capitaine* will go and take a bath! Take two and take a whetstone to your wits! They need sharpening! Now vacate this room before you bring in more flies! Go! Leave me!'

Tessier, an incandescent anger about to burst from every vein, slammed a hand into the wall outside the *général's* room. The damned *les rosbifs* were here and he knew they would march on the fort soon.

Then, let the marines come here, he said to himself. *Let them die against the walls of Dominance.*

*

175

It was Sunday and six monks climbed the road cut through the hill called Ras it-Tafal when the dawn light was nothing more than an orange glow above the western horizon. The sunken road straightened and then the huge limestone walls of Fort Dominance rose up from the rocky landscape, obliterating everything else. Weeds and wind-blown grasses, dark in the morning light, hugged the stonework. The French Tricolour flew high from the imposing battlements, but the Gozitan monks were allowed to say mass in the chapel dedicated to the Blessed Virgin Mary of Graces every Sabbath day.

Sentries watched the priests approach as they crossed the stone bridge over a wide ditch to the fort's main gate, a path designed for just one wagon to cross at once. The gates were of the Baroque style with an inscription in Latin above the archway commemorating the fort's completion. One of the monks, tall and straight-backed, carried a simple wooden cross, whilst two carried a long oblong box, decorated with gold crosses. They stopped underneath the gate's archway where a portcullis blocked their entrance. Dust, kicked up by their feet, wafted in the air. Beyond the curtain wall to their left, and towering above a gun emplacement that guarded the woodland to the east, was the Notre Dame Bastion. To the right was a huge counterguard where figures scoured the hills for enemies from behind thick embrasures.

A French guard, grey-haired and puffing on a lit pipe, walked over to the gate. Two other guards, watching the monks, their eyes full of scrutiny, returned to their conversation with coarse laughter. The leading monk spoke hurried French and the guard mumbled to himself before disappearing back into the fort's courtyard.

'Where's the bastard gone, sir?' Sergeant Powell growled from somewhere in his shadowed habit.

'To fetch the officer of the guard,' Zeppi replied. Immediately, Gamble wondered whether this would be Tessier and the French may have imposed stricter concessions for entering the fort. After all, the French had dissolved all religious activities and it was only the governor's whim that allowed entry. 'Don't worry, I know the man,' he continued. 'He is cheerful and polite. We will be let in without further delay. Monks are always allowed.'

'Good, because this robe stinks like a sick goat, and sooner I can cast it off the better I'll be,' Powell grumbled.

The fort was silent; a stillness that frayed nerves.

'He's been gone a long time,' Powell rasped, splintering the quiet. 'It will not be easy if this bluff doesn't work?'

'Not long now, Archie,' Gamble smiled, and the sergeant saw a flash of white in the recesses of the hood. 'Remember: wait for my word and be quick.'

'We're like avenging angels, come to the French with swords to smite them down,' Zeppi's lips curled like a fed cat settling into its basket.

'And axes,' Powell muttered.

Boots thudded and a young officer greeted them. It was not Tessier. He was curious to know what was in the long box. Zeppi said something to him and the officer smiled and stepped back. He shouted up to the gatehouse and a voice replied.

'I told him we carried the sacred bones of St Giuseppe of Nadur, and this is a portable shrine,' Zeppi whispered.

'Not heard of that saint before,' Powell said.

'I made it up, Sergeant,' Zeppi said with a smirk.

'Do you think he believed you?'

'Perhaps,' Zeppi replied. 'Depends how suspicious he is. Or how gullible.'

'It's going to work,' Gamble said confidently.

'If I were them, I'd have killed us all by now,' Powell said. 'Why didn't they send out a demi-brigade to see us off?'

'Perhaps Sam's killer didn't come back here.' Zeppi mused. 'Maybe he fled elsewhere?'

'He came here,' Gamble said. 'It's the only safe place for him on the island.'

'So why haven't I seen any Frenchies come after us?' Powell said, scratching his crotch.

Gamble glanced up at the main gate, fingers clenching in the delay. 'He probably feels safe behind these walls and knows we'll be coming for him anyway. Why make it easy?'

'Or maybe he told no one?' Zeppi hazarded a guess.

Gamble shook his head. 'Why would he keep our presence a secret?'

'They don't appear to be on alert, sir,' Powell said.

'Agreed,' Gamble replied. 'And that's good news for us. We should take heart for this isn't a trap.'

The sound of gears turning and chains jangling rent the air and Gamble wondered if the barracks would be alarmed by the din, but then considered this was normal practice and he was allowing nerves to give his confidence a full broadside. Fear was giving the attack a desperate impetus.

The portcullis juddered to a halt and the officer waved them forward. The pipe-smoking guard smiled pleasantly and stepped out under the great iron teeth to the stone bridge to see what the new day would bring.

'Now,' Gamble said.

Zeppi went first and Gamble followed. At the moment of passing the officer, Gamble stooped and the Frenchman thought the monk had stumbled. He reached down to help him up and never saw the dirk that plunged into his heart. Gamble twisted it free and left the enemy bleeding and twitching on the ground. Adams slunk up the steps to the gatehouse and Gamble heard a soft sigh and then returned giving a curt nod of success. Good, the gatehouse was theirs. Coppinger walked up to the grey-haired guard and cut his throat from behind. The body toppled over the stone walkway and fell with a thud into the ditch below.

Powell pulled free his axes, letting their short haft fall through his hands until he was satisfied he had better grip. He calmly walked over to the two guards to the left of the gatehouse. He glanced up at the huge ravine, shaped like an enormous ships prow, saw no one looking down from the slanted openings and thumped his right axe into the nearest Frenchman's back. The man collapsed, and Powell yanked it free with a horrid sucking sound. The other Frenchman stood gaping at the axe-wielding monk and then understood this was no priest at all. He tried to bring up his musket when Powell knocked it aside with his left axe and then chopped his other axe into the foe's breastbone. The force knocked the guard onto the dusty ground, letting out a horrid, pathetic sigh. Blood spurted from his chest and bubbled at his mouth as he groaned. Powell mercifully and swiftly chopped down through his throat, the second blow severing his spinal cord.

'Get the weapon's out,' Gamble ordered and Marsh opened the box to reveal muskets and swords. They threw off their disguises and buckled swords, slid bayonets from their scabbards, slipped the rings over muzzles and slotted them into place. There was something reassuringly determined at the sound of fixed bayonets. Powell pulled the dying men out of sight, tucked the axes in his belt and Gamble threw him his musketoon. They then cocked their firearms.

All was quiet.

No one had seen them, no one had raised the alarm; but there were still two more gates to access. Trusting his instincts Gamble suspected the first would be open, but the second would be locked. It would be

178

impossible to open, but Gamble had already thought of that. Deep in the shadows, he craned his neck up at the ravine. The opening was across a wide dry moat, and from here Gamble knew they would have to scramble through the ravine to likely cross another bridge to get to the main gate.

It was time for Kennedy and Pym to come. 'Now!' he called out and Coppinger waved from the outer gate to the road.

It was five o'clock.

*

'Not long now, lads,' Kennedy's voice called softly. 'We wait for the signal and then we'll rush the bastards!'

'That's right, boys,' Pym said, 'plunder and whores await your eager fingers! Tits so big and nipples so hard you can hang your muskets on them! Stay hidden now!'

The marines and landing party were crouched down on the road, some lying flat. A marine jumped at a running lizard. Another marine laughed at him, and Corporal Forge slapped him across the head. 'Quiet now!'

Men scraped sharpening stones down their blades. The sharp, grating noise made the hairs on Kennedy's neck stand up on end. Pym felt the edge of his curved sword with his thumb. Another prayed and one of the Midshipmen vomited.

'Nearly time,' Kennedy called out, checking the timepiece in his palm. A bead of sweat landed on the watch face and he carefully wiped it away with a finger. It had been his grandfather's and he would take it back home one day.

It would be good, he pondered, to go home and see the new century for it was only a few months away. Perhaps the eighteen hundreds would bring him a wife, wealth and a captaincy. Maybe the world would change for the better and all the wars would end. But he suspected, the politicians would always need men trained to kill; it was the way of the world. Peace would not last long.

Kennedy saw movement and his heart raced. Gamble had secured the outer gate.

'There's the signal, boys! Up! Up! Let's go!'

*

The six men ran to the ravine, a distance of thirty feet. Gamble expected an enemy to call out, but it was eerily silent. He slammed against the ravine's gap and peered around the wall. The entrance led to a set of winding stairs. Gamble, took the steps carefully, sword in hand. Shadowed light flashed bright and he edged to the entryway. Directly to their right lay the walkway to the main gate. Gamble could not see any enemies there. Up above on the firing steps were two Frenchmen. The first was playing cards on a block of stone next to a glowing brazier. The smoke wafted pungent scents down towards the marines. The second was staring across the outer walls to where, above the wooded slopes that edged to the sea, birds flew from the tree tops. Something had startled them and Gamble knew what that was. His eyes flicked up at the fort's curtain walls, seeing movement along the parapet but no faces peered curiously down. The card-playing one was the nearest and caught sight of Gamble out of the corner of his eye. Before he could react, Gamble prodded man's Adam's apple with his cutlass. The Frenchman gulped loudly and his colleague turned to the sound. He reacted more quickly and brought his musket to bear. Gamble hammered it aside as the weapon fired, its discharge echoing like a death knell. The ball ricocheted off the wall. Gamble knew their infiltration was over, but they still had the advantage for now.

The seated Frenchman stood to pull free his *sabre-briquet*, but Gamble swung his sword back across his body to cleave through the man's neck. The enemy slumped over the stone, twitching as the blood fountained over the fallen cards. The other man charged Gamble, hefting the unloaded musket to batter him down. Gamble dodged to one side, kicked at the Frenchman and lunged. The blade went under the guard's arm, up through his armpit and into his chest cavity. He gasped, fell and Gamble turned with his reddened sword, seeing a shape appear at the stairs.

It was Powell. 'The Toads know we're here, sir!' he said urgently.

'I damn well know!' Gamble snapped.

'*Qui vive?*' a voice called out. The challenge was repeated.

'Ignore them,' Gamble said.

Other French voices called down from the parapets and Gamble saw movement on the inner wall. The enemy was running down to a flank battery. Three cannons, their muzzles pointing at the trees beyond the ramparts, were stirred to life by the gunners. He knew why, but they did not concern him.

The French gathering at the main gate did.

'Merde! Les Anglais!'

'Fire!' Baldassar Grech shouted. Muskets blasted up from the trees, the shots pocked the thick walls and caused no injuries, but that was not the intention. 'Keep firing! Let our enemies know we're here! For God and Gozo!'

The Gozitans cheered and fired and reloaded as dirty white smoke fogged the woodland. Each man wore a cloth badge pinned to their chest showing a white Maltese cross on a black field. A Gozitan saw an enemy figure high up at the Notre Dame Bastion, and aimed his musket and pulled the trigger. He peered past the plume of noxious cloud to see that the enemy was still there.

'You're not going to hit him from this distance, Micallef,' Grech laughed sourly. 'Our objective is to keep the French busy whilst the British assault the fort.'

'I don't trust them!' Micallef growled back. He had grey hair, and skin the texture of leather. 'The British said they would land an army, but they haven't even managed to send a single regiment yet. Do you know what I think?'

'What?'

'I think they are bluffing. They will only land proper soldiers after we have done all the work!'

'You're forgetting about the marines,' a drover named Camilleri said reproachfully.

Micallef threw his arms up in frustration. 'The French are still here, you fool!' He stuck his thumb at the fort.

'The British supplied the muskets and pistols,' Camilleri said patiently, loading his musket with untrained slowness. 'They armed the Maltese and they took the forts.'

Micallef spat to show his indignation. 'So they give us the guns to do the work for them. That way we lose many men and they won't. Ask yourself why do they fight? For us? No. They fight for the gold of Protestant England.'

'What are you babbling about?'

'Have you ever been there?'

'No.'

Micallef crossed himself. 'It's a vile land full of people inclined to criminality.' The others were silent and given a voice, he continued.

'They will see us killed and they will steal our lands. They will rob us as the French did, and you are both fools enough not to see that.'

Grech understood the man's distrust. 'Give them a chance to prove themselves. I did not want them here either. I was ignorant and that allowed prejudice to speak instead of embracing them as allies. They have lost men for our country. Does that not speak to you of their purpose? Today is the Lord's Day and that is a good omen. Once I see red coats on the walls, we'll make our move. Until then, and with the grace of God, we keep firing and we'll have victory soon.'

*

'Open the portcullis!' *Capitaine* Tessier demanded. 'Open it!'

The redcoats had reached the ravine, but there was nowhere else they could go to. If they jumped or fell, they would find themselves in the dry-moat where they would have to find the handful of accessible places to climb out. Even if they managed this feat, they would then come face-to-face with a bone-shattering drop separating them from the outer ramparts.

A trumpet blared and the sound of musketry hammered the eastern walls. The French soldiers were piling out of the barrack block, sprinting to the gates, buttoning their jackets and loading their firearms. The enemy was here, but the fools in the gatehouse were not hauling up the portcullis.

'You imbeciles! Open them!' Tessier banged on the thick metal bars with his sword.

The redcoats had to be stopped quickly before they took hold. He saw men wearing naval dress and knew that he had been right all along. From the moment the first musket shot punctured the morning's air, he knew Gamble was here. The English had landed more men on the island. Goddamn Chasse's obstinacy! Tessier could see the officer and knew it was Gamble. Tessier would kill him and eject the impudent English from the fort. He would shame the general for his incompetence, and be promoted to colonel by noon.

But the portcullis remained down and Tessier could only watch helplessly as the redcoats swarmed the defences.

*

Gamble gazed north from the ravine to see the marines and Jack Tars sprinting over the lip of the road, bayonet-scabbards, cartridge boxes and haversacks bouncing with each stride.

Suddenly, a boom of gunfire rocked the air. Gunners stationed in the St Paul's Bastion had fired a cannon and he saw one of the sailors torn to bloody gristle by the ball's terrible strike. The projectile, spattered-red, slammed into the banks of the road, churning earth high up in the air. A second gun fired sending the ball too high and he saw the ball clip the embankment, spin, and plummet down the hill's incline.

'Come on, you bastards!' Gamble shouted at his men, as the fastest reached the first stone walkway. 'Move your arses! Move!'

The seamen were the slowest because they carried cumbersome ladders, required to scale the inner wall. Gamble knew there would be no way to get through the gate, so the marines had to climb over the walls and take the fort by escalade. Riding-Smyth had questioned the method and now he could feel fear sniping at his confidence, but if they could climb the walls, half the fight was done.

A third gun was awoken and had its throat blasted free, but the seamen were now clear of its shot, and the first redcoats had reached the ravine. A crackle of musketry fired ineffectively at them from the main gate.

'Sergeant Powell!' Gamble ordered. 'One platoon to form on the bridge, the other to grasp the ladders!'

'Sir!'

The seamen could not hope to bring the ladders up the stairway, so they were placed against the ravine's high walls and the marines hauled them up and over the parapets. The portcullis was still down and Gamble wondered if the French officers had ordered it. He could see a handful of officers there but wasn't sure if one was Tessier.

'Faster!' he bellowed, glancing at the main gate and up at the inner wall where musket muzzles flashed leaving the embrasures ringed with flame, but the bullets caused no harm. The gunners on the emplacement were busy firing muskets at Grech's men and packing the cannons with grapeshot. Then, the great guns jerked to life and the battery instantly clouded white. The air was shattered with the percussive explosions. Gamble knew he had to scale the ladder, climb down the parapet and silence those guns. For now, he had to hope that Grech was still alive and that he had to get the Gozitan-built ladders in place.

'Heave!' Rooke the Boatswain's Mate, called from the ravine as the seamen pushed two ladders up for the marines to haul.

'Come on!' Gamble pushed a faltering soldier to one side and gripped the top rung. He brought the ladder down over the parapet to where Kennedy waited. 'We can't wait any longer, Harry! Get the two ladders to the gate now! The other four will have to wait.'

'Sir!' Kennedy spun on his heels. 'Platoon! Advance!'

'Fix bayonets!' Gamble ordered, as there would be little or no time to do so later. He turned and cupped a hand to his mouth. 'Lieutenant Pym! I want your pikes! Now if you please!'

'You'll be getting them soon enough, Captain Gamble!' Pym replied as more of the landing party reached the ravine's upper level. 'Come on! Get those bloody ladders over the wall!'

Gamble jumped the steps. 'Marines! To me!' He sprinted after the advancing men. Muskets crashed from the ramparts above, which threw down a marine. Another volley crashed from the gate and two other marines were plucked backwards, one spinning over the walkway and down into the dried out moat. A ball scored Corporal Forge's left cheek, exposing his back teeth.

Kennedy halted his men thirty paces from the gate and the platoon hammered a volley into the Frenchmen.

'Advance!' he ordered, and they pressed on through their own powder smoke. Behind him, Gamble and the remaining redcoats closed the gap, still carrying the ladders. 'Halt!' The men were below the main gate's walls now so were safe from above. 'Load!'

They ran the ladders up against the shoulders of the curtain wall and the first men began to climb. Gamble pushed past the ranks to steer the third ladder against the wall. A musket fired through the portcullis and the ball tore a rent in his sleeve. He pushed men to the rungs. The marines fired another volley and the defenders twitched and died against the metal rods. The first seamen arrived, and they charged with boarding pikes and the wicked blades ripped into torsos, throats and legs.

'Push!' Pym was shouting. A seaman next to him was shot in the face and it seemed to him that the man's head just disappeared in an explosion of blood. 'Push the bastards!' He slashed his sabre at a Frenchman, trying to stab him with his bayonet, and put his pistol to the man's chest and pulled the trigger. Blood misted the tight space. The enemy hung against the bars, kept upright by the press of men from behind. A sword sliced and another musket spurted flame through the churning rill of smoke to send another Jack Tar to his grave, but the landing party was winning this fight.

'Up! Up! Up!' Gamble shouted as some of the men started to look for cover. A marine staggered. Sergeant Powell kicked a man who hung back. They could not falter now for it would weaken the attack. Every man had to climb, not knowing if the next second would be his last. The only way to survive horror was to win. Gamble saw Willoughby and Crouch at the rear and ran over to them, thrusting them towards the ladders. 'Get up there!' he snarled.

Crouch looked terrified, but they both climbed. Men scrambled up the rungs, but then a marine was hit by a shot from the flanking battery to the left. He slipped and toppled to the moat, body twisting as he screamed. More jostled to climb the ladders. Sailors waited the rear, all armed with cutlasses, muskets, dirks and pistols.

'Up! Faster!' Gamble bellowed for the line seemed to falter. He saw Kennedy about to scale a ladder, sword in one hand which would make the climb awkward. 'Harry!' he called. 'Bring your sword to bear at the top!' Kennedy understood and rammed his weapon home.

The marines climbed with their bayonet-tipped muskets slung over their shoulders. A redcoat slipped half-way up and knocked the five below him to the ground. They cursed him and picked themselves up to continue.

The defender's fire was continuous, a staccato drum beat of musketry, but Gamble could tell the walls weren't fully manned. He had expected larger volleys. Grech had said that the French numbered perhaps three hundred, but experience told him that perhaps a hundred were defending the fort. If that was the case, where was the rest?

His legs burned with the effort of the climb. Gun smoke roiled thick from the ramparts and shots echoed about him. He couldn't see the enemy; his world was a pair of dirty white legs, a ladder and a limestone wall. Steel crashed against steel. Bullets flayed flesh. A man called out in English for his mother. Gamble coughed from the acrid stink. Then Crouch, with his bandaged hand, disappeared, and Gamble knew he had reached the top. He unsheathed his sword and threaded through an embrasure to drop down onto the parapet.

Bright blood spotted the stone. Marsh lay dying next to a fusilier and Gamble stepped over them, slipping in glistening gore. A grenadier was cocking his musket. Gamble levelled his pistol and the shot dissolved the man's face in blood. To his right, the defenders blasted the walls from the central St Paul's Bastion, while to the left, French crowded the Notre Dame Bastion. A ragged line of musket-armed French spat malice from the courtyard, but their aim was put off by the group of seamen who still poured fire from the portcullis. The parapets were filling with marines and the seamen swarmed the ladders skilfully as though they were climbing ships' rigging.

'My platoon to me!' Gamble pushed men aside as he went right. A hail of musketry tore scraps of stone from the stonework as he ran. A ball snatched at his bicorn, turning it.

An enemy swung his musket like a club. Gamble ducked and unceremoniously tipped him over the side of the parapet, hearing his cries all the way down. A bayonet lunged and Gamble battered it aside with his straight-bladed cutlass. The steel clanged, sending sparks over the body of a dead defender who had been shot through an eye. The blackened wound still smouldered. Gamble kicked his assailant, punched and grabbed the musket's hot barrel, turning it to the left with all his strength. His fingers burned, but the Frenchman could not bring his weapon back and gave a high pitched scream as the long cutlass cut him through shoulder to breastbone.

'Kill the bastards!' Powell bellowed.

Pace shot a man less than three feet away in the face. A grenadier, with huge arms and a long flowing moustache, fired his musket but the ball went wide. Gamble rammed his sword at his face, and the enemy dropped his weapon to claw at the ugly blade. Gamble withdrew it and the man hissed, but held on tightly, as blood dripped from his cut fingers.

A long bayonet stabbed the air and Gamble stumbled backwards with the muscled enemy on top of him. His hands were locked with the weight of the grenadier's body, as heavy as solid iron. The Frenchman tried to bite his face with crooked yellow teeth, snapping from underneath the moustache. Another two enemies appeared above. One went to stab Gamble in the face with his bayonet when a musket ball drummed into his chest to throw him backwards. The grenadier managed to get a bloodied hand free and tried to find purchase around Gamble's throat, but Gamble jerked his head and the moustached man couldn't get a grip.

A marine, shouting something incomprehensible, stabbed the other defender in the throat with the spike atop an axe head and swung another onto the grenadier's head. The sharp steel cleaved through black hair with a wet crack. The Frenchman's grip immediately eased, and his eyes rolled up into his skull. Gamble threw off the body and Powell hauled him upright.

'Thank you, Archie,' Gamble said. 'Now let's tear them to shreds!'

186

The defenders retreated, but in good order. A musket flamed and a ball shattered a marine's collar bone, spinning him around. The soldiers screamed terrible battle-cries as they began their grim job of clearing the defenders off the parapet with quick professional close-quarter work. Gamble trod on a fallen ramrod and his boots crunched on burnt wadding. The French reached steps and began descending into the bastion.

'Bayonets!' Powell bellowed. 'I want bayonets!'

'Charge the bastards!' Gamble screamed, blinking another man's blood from his eyes. There was no drum to beat the order, but the marines and Jack Tars surged forward.

'*Tirez!*' The French had been waiting, and their muskets jerked a handful of attackers backwards. Their officer, dressed in a patched brown coat, was horrified to see the savage-looking men advance unperturbed by the musketry. His men were mostly conscripts and they had fired too high. Now they had only steel bayonets with which to defend themselves.

'Get in close, boys!' Powell ordered. 'A Shawnee Indian named Blue Jacket once told me that a naked woman stirs a man's blood, but a naked blade stirs his soul. So go in with the steel. Lunge! Recover! Stance!'

'Charge!' Gamble turned the order into a long, guttural yell of defiance.

Those redcoats and seamen, with loaded weapons discharged them at the press of the defenders, and a man in the front rank went down with a dark hole in his forehead. Gamble saw the officer aim a pistol at him. A wounded Frenchman, half-crawling, tried to stab with his *sabre-briquet*, but Gamble kicked him in the face. He dashed forward, sword held low. The officer pulled the trigger, the weapon tugged the man's arm to his right, and the ball buzzed past Gamble's mangled ear as he jumped down into the gap made by the marines' charge. A French corporal, wearing a straw hat, drove his bayonet at Gamble's belly, but he dodged to one side and rammed his bar-hilt into the man's dark eyes.

'Lunge! Recover! Stance!'

Wet blades made quick work and the bastion was awash with blood and mangled bodies. A redcoat kneed a defender in the groin and clasped his hands over his face, thumbs digging into eye-sockets. The men with boarding pikes thrust them at faces, quick jabs, one after the other, driving the enemy down where bayonets could kill them. Men grunted, shouted and cursed. A musket flamed, so close that the orange

187

tongue touched a Frenchman's chest as Willoughby shot him through the body. The huge marine barged past the falling enemy and stabbed with his bayonet at the French officer. The man slashed at the steel with his thin sword, ducked another of the marines' assault, but a boarding pike took him in the throat and he quivered like a landed fish. His head flopped back as he buckled to his knees. Willoughby kicked the body backwards.

'Crouch is dead, sir,' he said, over his shoulder. 'Caught a Frenchie ball between the eyes.'

Gamble didn't know what to say to that. Willoughby had not turned to face him and Gamble somehow felt he was entirely to blame. The marine had been trouble and he had wished him dead many times, but he had died doing his duty, and that was all that would be remembered of him. Now was not the time to dwell on such things.

'Remember Acre!' he screamed. A marine next to him collapsed, holding his stomach, dark blood oozing between his fingers. 'Charge! Charge!'

The blades had done their work, they had carved their way across the parapet and the tight-packed French ranks had been destroyed. His men had done it!

'Cannon!' A voice called and Gamble turned, horrified, to see the French had brought artillery onto the southern ramparts. A gun captain, seeing that the enemy had concentrated the attack on the doomed St Paul's Bastion, raised his sword to signal the attack.

*

St Paul's Bastion had been taken, but the fort had not yet fallen. The attackers clogged the blood drenched parapet above the main gate, but they still had not taken St Anthony's Bastion or the Notre Dame Bastion.

Tessier's men were fighting hard, shocked by the attack, but were offering a stubborn defiance. Tessier formed a thin line of sixty men across the courtyard and gunners ran to the seaward facing gun batteries to turn them on the redcoats. If they timed it right, and aimed true, the gun salvoes could win this battle.

Musket balls hissed about him. A sergeant was shot through the head at his side, and two more were maimed by the English sailors at the main gate, but Tessier's life seemed charmed and he remained unscathed. He picked up a fallen musket and shot a redcoat dead. His

188

men fired up at the walls and bullets pockmarked the stone. Thirty had been hauled from the hospital and given muskets to fire. A dozen inside barricaded the building and offered the attackers another obstacle.

'Keep firing!' Tessier ordered. Blood splattered his blue coat, but none of it was his. He lived and grinned because the guns would soon shatter the red devils at the wall and Dominance would be riven to spatters of gore. France would win today and the enemy would bleed out their lives. His men just needed to hold their positions for a little while longer. 'Keep firing! Keep firing! Keep fir-' Tessier's voice was suddenly drowned out as the whole world exploded in thunder, fire and dust.

*

'There's the Prince of Waves!' Gamble shouted and the men cheered.

The *Sea Prince* had sailed around Comino in the night, hidden by its great island cliffs, then sailed in the pre-dawn light to anchor facing the harbour of Mġarr. It had come to rest with its port broadside facing the fort, and had just silenced the French seaward guns with an ear-splitting salvo at the north-facing batteries. The cannons had been fired by masterful gunners, and Gamble could see all that was left of them were smoking pits of twisted metal and gore. A gust of scorching air blew over the fighting men, and scraps of stone rained down like a mighty hailstorm.

Only the Notre Dame Bastion remained to be taken and the fort would be theirs. Gamble turned back across the outer defences to see scores of Gozitans swarming across the bridges to the ladders. He could see Zeppi waving a black flag showing a white Maltese cross, shouting encouragement and death to the French. Marines had reached the flanking battery. The gun team went down under blades, but not without a fight. A marine was hit in the chest with a gunner's rammer and disappeared over the wall. One of Kennedy's men stepped forward and shot the Frenchman dead.

Gamble drew a sleeve across his forehead, mixing black powder, sweat and blood. The French troops had formed a line across the courtyard, but were now unable to concentrate because of the devastating cannonade at their rear. There was not a moment to lose if Gamble was to consolidate his victory. Then, he saw Tessier, sword bright in his hand, and he clenched his jaw.

The marines and landing party charged down to capture St Anthony's Bastion. Gamble and Sergeant Powell ran back along the parapet, across the gatehouse to the Notre Dame Bastion. Sand and weed strewn stone stairs led down the courtyard where Gamble would find and kill the Frenchman.

The parapets were thickening with Gozitans, marines and sailors. Gamble pushed past men, keen for revenge. He almost slipped on gore-covered bottom steps where one of his men lay dead, his brains splattered like spilled porridge. A callow-faced *chasseur* with blood oozing from his mouth aimed his musket, and Gamble shoved Powell aside as the ball smacked into the stonework beside him. The defender lunged his bayonet at Gamble who, with a well-practised reflex, dodged, tripped the man, and then chopped down through his windpipe. Two men came out of the nearest building which was the chapel dedicated to the Blessed Virgin Mary of Graces. Powell brought his musketoon to bear and the defenders were blasted backwards in an explosion of misting blood.

'Jesus, but I could do with a drink.' Powell wiped his mouth, his eyes searching for more enemies as he loaded.

'We'll drink ourselves stupid tonight,' Gamble said.

'Amen to that, sir.'

'There's bound to be plenty of wine.'

'I would prefer rum or a nice pint of beer, sir,' Powell said over a musket ball hitting the wall with a loud crack above him. 'They used to serve rare stuff at The Turk's Head.'

'I remember the brawls too, Archie,' Gamble said of the particular Plymouth inn. 'You never lost a fight, did you?'

The sergeant chuckled reminiscently. 'No, sir. And I won't be losing this one either.'

Pym's men had raised the portcullis and suddenly the defenders were being pushed back to the middle of the huge courtyard. Rooke had been shot in the shoulder, but waved the men on, regardless.

'Ben! Raise the flag!' Gamble shouted. Pym cut the halyard that held the Tricolour above the main gate and ran the Union Flag up it. Gamble watched it with pride. It had been the bundle that he had asked his friend to bring. It would show that the fort had fallen to Grech's men, the islanders, and most importantly, to the *Sea Prince*.

'Where did the bugger go, sir?' Powell said, watching the defenders throwing down their weapons and the officers begging the redcoats for protection before the Gozitans got there.

Voices cheered the raising of the Union Flag. The ripple of voices echoed across the battlements as the final shots rang out.

'I can't see the bastard,' Gamble's throat was parched and his voice cracked as he spoke over the noise. The stench of sizzling flesh coming from the destroyed batteries was overpowering. The air was filled with drifting patches of acrid smoke.

'Sir! We've won! We gave Johnny Crapaud a proper drubbing!' Kennedy shouted. He was red-faced, coated with grime, but exultant.

Gamble thumped his arm. 'I'm glad to see you, Harry,' he said, pleased to find his friend alive. 'You did well back there.'

'Coming from you, sir,' Kennedy said, 'that is a compliment in itself.' He gazed back at the battlements. 'My word, what an achievement to tell!'

Gamble's throat was raw, frayed and he had to swill out his dry mouth with brackish wine from his canteen before being able to speak again. He hawked and spat. 'Have you seen Tessier?'

'No, sir.'

'He's here somewhere. I want all our NCOs looking too. I'll ask Pym for help. Check the prisoners first and remember we must be quick! I don't want the bastard getting away!'

'He won't, sir!'

The men inside the barracks and hospital decided to surrender rather than prolong the fight. Marines, under a bandaged Corporal Forge, brought those who were not too ill outside and stationed guards at the doors. Pace and two others helped the wounded move to the hospital where they would be treated. Some would not survive the night. Men with their bone-dry throats, slaked their thirst from their canteens, or from those of the dead. Others went to look for the fresh water wells.

There is nowhere for Tessier to go, Gamble contemplated. He looked at faces, unknown, bloody, grim and sooty with powder. Water and wine was passed around. A man crawled with a trail of blood dripping from his mouth. The unwounded gathered in the centre, weapons discarded, a grisly remnant of the garrison. Men of the same height and build as Tessier were scrutinized, but eye colour, hair and features didn't match. Powell and Kennedy returned.

'No sign of him,' Kennedy said, exasperated. 'Perhaps he was killed by the ship's barrage?'

'No,' Gamble replied feverishly, 'I saw him here.' The bastard was dangerous and clever, but not as much as Gamble. 'We search the living and then we search the dead. We search the rooms again. I want the wounded looked at. Kitchens, storerooms, the chapel...'

The prospect of prolonging the search made Kennedy's exhausted face lengthen.

Gamble saw it and tilted his head. 'What is it?'

Kennedy sighed. 'We have no guarantee that he's still alive. We could both die looking for him.'

Gamble's eyes darkened. 'I want him found.'

'So do I,' Kennedy said, 'but...'

'What?'

'To what end will this accomplish?'

Gamble was also fatigued, bruised and his fingers throbbed from touching the hot musket barrel, but Sam's murderer had to be found.

'It's our duty to avenge a fallen brother,' Gamble said, glowering.

Kennedy's eyes twitched. 'You do not understand, sir. Sam is not-'

'Samuel Riding-Smyth is not Robert Carstairs. And both are now dead.' Gamble was angry, but let it pass. He clasped Kennedy's forearm. 'I know. I do understand. But it's something I have to do.'

Kennedy understood the torment of losing both friends, and so nodded. 'Then let's find the bastard and bury him.'

Gamble smiled and shook his arm in gratitude.

The buildings were combed, even the cemetery. Gamble resorted to naming him in the hope that one of his countrymen might give him away, but those that knew him had not seen him. A middle-aged French officer was brought to Gamble, Kennedy and Pym.

'I am *Général* Évrard Chasse, the commander of this garrison,' the Frenchman said haughtily, but in good English.

'Captain Gamble, sir.'

'How did you find the British greeting this morning, sir?' Pym asked, with much intended impertinence. 'You should have just left the door open, old boy.'

Chasse grunted. He turned away from the smirking Pym to face Gamble. 'Are you the senior ranking officer here?'

'I am, sir.'

'I'm to negotiate terms with a captain,' Chasse sounded aghast. He brought out a large handkerchief and placed it against his face. The smell of open bowels and the copper stink of blood flayed his delicate nostrils.

'No, sir,' Gamble said respectfully. 'I'm to escort you to Captain Eaton of His Majesty's *Sea Prince*, where you will discuss terms.'

192

Chasse gazed at the marines who were tending to his wounded soldiers. He suddenly felt rather humbled. He cleared his throat. 'I understand you have been asking about *Capitaine* Tessier?'

'I'm interested in acquiring the bastard, sir.'

'Are you the marine officer that ambushed him?'

'I am.'

Chasse's eyes narrowed at the recognition. 'I understand the fight hurt him more than any bullet or blade, *Capitaine* Gamble. He told me he had escaped his bonds and brought news of your arrival. I must confess I ignored him. I never liked him from the start. Perhaps if I'd listened to him, then you would not be here, and I would still have a garrison.'

Gamble smiled. 'I would have still beaten you, sir.'

Chasse pursed his lips and allowed a smile to touch them. '*Bon*. I wish I could help you with his capture. You seem awfully keen to acquire him?'

'He murdered my second lieutenant, sir,' Gamble said and the *général's* bearded mouth immediately lolled open.

'*Mon Dieu!*'

'I allowed Tessier to keep his sword and he murdered my officer and fled,' Gamble said. 'I will hunt him even if it takes me to the gates of Hell.'

'He made no mention of this to me. I expect my men to be honourable, even in defeat. Chivalry still exists in France. That was an act of cold-blooded murder.' He swore and leaned closer to Gamble. 'We are enemies, but I hope you find him, *Capitaine*. I really hope you do.'

'I will, sir.'

'*Bon*. I trust you will allow our garrison surgeon Vipond to stay? He is very able and will treat even the locals.' Chasse sniffed to show that he found that somewhat distasteful.

'Thank you, sir.'

Gamble left to check the outer walls, the destroyed batteries, the Guardian Angel Bastion which contained a stone powder store with a conical roof and a five-sided watchtower. The walls offered good defence, for most had firing platforms and loopholes to allow musketry, but the French had capitulated and no one remained there. Gamble walked to the watchtower overlooking the sea. The *Sea Prince* was still at anchor and to the east, the waters were dotted with fishing craft outside the harbour. Gulls circled high in the air. There was no one below on the cliffs and rocky shoreline.

Triumph was his and somehow he was unable to feel the elation of it. He slammed a palm into the stone in frustration and turned around to find Kennedy waiting at the foot of the watchtower. He looked grim.

'Tessier?'

'I think you'd better come down, sir,' he said. 'We've found something.'

They had won, men had died, but by God's grace, they had won. And whether Grech was right about winning a victory for God or not, Gamble swore, because Tessier had gone and none of this mattered one bit.

*

God damn all Englishman, Tessier cursed.

They had taken the fort effortlessly and all *la chatte* could do was to surrender. I bet he never drew his blade, or fired his pistol. The yellow coward! Tessier had watched the general from the Guardian Angel Bastion, knowing that as soon as the English flag was raised, then the war ship would not fire for fear of hitting their own men. The attackers swarmed into the buildings and Tessier saw Gamble hunting for him. Whilst the prisoners lay down their weapons, Tessier had crept under the shadowed wall to where a narrow set of stairs led down to the sally-port. The winch system holding the portcullis was rusty, but with enough effort the bars raised to allow a single man to escape outside at a time. He had been the first out and a few of the garrison had seen him escape and now a slow trickle of men stumbled in the morning light. All of them went west, but Tessier, a survivor, knew the most dangerous route was the only way to freedom.

*

Nine months later on the morning of 8th September, 1800, Captain Simon Gamble looked up at Valletta's ancient gates and sighed heavily.

Malta's capital city had remained all this time in French hands. It was the only foothold the enemy still had, but today at midday, the garrison would march out with the honours of war, and the country would pass to the British.

194

But there was one man inside who had no such morality or virtue as far as Gamble was concerned.

After Fort Dominance had fallen, half-hidden near the wreckage of the seaward batteries, Kennedy had discovered the sally-port. Gamble had climbed down there. Gozitans had caught ten men outside in the hills, but none of them was Tessier. He took a score of his battle-weary marines down the cliffs to the water's edge, scouring every rock and bush, and down into the port of Mġarr. By the next sunrise, Tessier was still missing and Gamble came to the conclusion that Frenchman would have tried to reach the final French held bastion: Valletta. It was where Gamble would have gone.

Upon landing in St Paul's Bay, Gamble had Tessier's name, rank and a sketch of him posted and distributed throughout the Maltese suburbs in case he had not reached the safety of the gates. Gamble had even offered a reward out of his own money, but no one had seen him and Tessier remained gallingly at large. Kennedy had voiced that he had been wounded in the attack and had died, or most possibly drowned crossing the sea, but Gamble refused to believe that explanation.

The French ship, *Guillaume Tell*, had sneaked out of the harbour during the spring in an attempt to break through the British naval blockade, but had been captured early the next morning. Gamble had hoped Tessier was on-board and had been allowed access on board. One Frenchman knew a Tessier, but he had been killed the battle of Arcole. Apart from discovering three British deserters, the captain was not present and he resumed his search for him in the city.

The sun was bright and Gamble had not known an autumn sun so powerful or felt so very hot. Sweat trickled down his back. *Perhaps I'm not well*, he thought. He'd not be eating very much lately, or sleeping and Powell had shown concern. He knew he had become obsessed with capturing Sam's killer, and until now, he could do nothing but sit and wait.

The marines and a regiment of newly formed Maltese soldiers would be the first to enter the city after the enemy had marched out. The Maltese Light Infantry with their blue coats faced red and black hats styled with a green plume waited with nervous expectation. And it was an anxious time. They had families, friends and relatives inside the city and the last few months of the blockade had been incredibly desperate. The city folk and the garrison had eaten every horse, pack animal, fowl, rabbit, dog, cat and rat that they could to ward off starvation. The cisterns had long been emptied, the granaries were bare

195

and even a frigate had been broken up for firewood. Disease had claimed hundreds of lives. Valletta, the most humble of cities, was a vision of Hell on Earth.

'They'll fly like bleeding sparrows the moment we march in,' Bray said sneeringly of the new regiment. 'They're not proper soldiers.'

'Quiet in the ranks,' Sergeant Powell called out.

'A bad omen having foreigners in British pay,' Bray muttered despite the warning, digging a dirty finger around a nostril and pulling out something foul and glistening. 'Especially from this shit-hole of a country. Cowards, the bleeding lot of them. Left it late to enter the fort, didn't they? We lost some good men there.'

'A pity you can't claim to be amongst them then, Bray,' Gamble said, walking down the depleted ranks.

There were just twenty men present. The marines had lost a total of eighteen in the attack, and the rest of the company were recovering from a fever that had swept through the island in the summer like wildfire. The main hospital, the *Santa Infermeria*, with its precious medicines, was in French hands and Kennedy, one of the affected, lay in one of the temporary hospitals set up in a church. Zeppi still lived and had returned to his home in Mdina, the ancient walled city that had once been the island's capital, to assist with the rebuilding of destroyed homes.

'That's unfair, sir,' Bray wailed. 'I did my duty. I earn my tuppence a day.'

'Keep your assumptions to yourself, Bray,' Powell said. 'It's too early in the day for your bullshit.'

You shall pay life for life, the voice said in Gamble's head. He gazed up at the gulls that circled the city's walls like vultures. Behind him, men of the 30th and the 89th Foot stood in line. Maltese folk watched from doors and windows. The smell of the sea was as powerful as the pervasive stink of sewage.

Gamble had been given a presentation sword in honour of the fort's capture. Pym had said Captain Eaton was going to give a generous amount to the officers for their efforts, but prize money could take ages to come through and, once the Admiralty and the lawyers had taken their share, there would be little left. Gamble could not wait for the money, no matter how much, and had pawned his presentation sword. It had fetched eight pounds and he had sent the money home to his mother to help with the debt. There was still a huge amount to pay, but

Gamble vowed that he would not stop until he did. He felt a catch in his throat as he thought of his family's plight.

It was time. He could sense it.

Gamble's neck muscles tensed when he heard the first notes of music. The French were playing *la Marseillaise*, the Revolutionary anthem. The gates juddered and opened slowly and Gamble automatically wondered whether Tessier would be the first to march out. French soldiers shouldered their muskets. Drums and flutes played and the first French troops marched out with their flags held high under a brilliant sun.

They had not eaten for days; their uniforms hung ragged and loose. However, they had done their best to smarten up their clothes. Rents were stitched up, boots, belts, buttons and badges had been polished, jackets brushed and hair, moustaches and beards had been trimmed. Some had yellow skin and most had lost teeth, but they marched with a cocksure swagger. Transport ships waited in the harbour for them to embark quickly because the British didn't want the responsibility of feeding them.

Gamble watched as Major-General Henry Pigot and a knot of other high-ranking officers saluted the enemy smartly as they passed by. The civilians had been kept back by the British regiments, but it didn't stop a few from launching scraps of rotten food or stones at the French over their heads.

'Bloody children!' Adams said in exasperation. 'Look at 'em!'

'Just conscripts,' Gamble suggested, noticing that some were indeed absurdly youthful.

'Hey, Adder,' Bray said, pointing with what could amount to a chin to a marching individual who was oblivious to the scrutiny, 'that one there is still wearing his pudding cap!' Adams and the men laughed rowdily. Toddlers wore a thick padding around the waist called a 'pudding', meant to protect them should they tumble while learning to walk. They also wore a protective helmet called a pudding cap. 'Go back to your mother's skirts!'

'How the hell did these milksops terrify Europe, sir?' Powell commented, face glistening with sweat.

'Aye, they look like dirty-looking weans not soldiers,' Corporal MacKay said over more jeering.

But Gamble wasn't listening. He walked forward, his eyes regarded the scores of faces that charily marched past. It was an endless task. Unfamiliar face after unfamiliar face blurred past, but none were

197

Tessier. He shouted out the name, but although enemy faces watched him, none responded. Frustration tugged his conscience and instead of waiting, he walked up to the gates, and sprinted inside.

'Sir?' Powell anxiously called after him. 'Sir!'

Gamble heard other voices call him back, most notably from Brigadier-General Moncrieff, who commanded the Maltese Light Infantry. He wanted Tessier. Damn their eyes! Couldn't they understand? Sam's murderer was inside!

The streets were empty except for the long column of marching French. The air was cloyed with the smell of death and decay. Nothing else moved.

'Jean Tessier!' Gamble bellowed, hatred etched on his face. The tiredness and maddening inactivity of the past few months were instantly forgotten. 'I know you're here! You hook-nosed, cowardly, son of a bitch! Show yourself!'

Suspicious eyes regarded him, and unknown voices cursed and jeered his appearance. He watched as hope for revenge began to dissipate like mist burning away under a morning sun. Goddamn the bastard! He had to be here! He had to!

Tears pricked Gamble's eyes at the thought of never catching the killer. The rank memory of it had festered like a battle wound. He had been put forward by Eaton to command the new Maltese regiment, but in the last few months he had trouble sleeping and focusing on his duties. Powell had found him wandering the streets one morning unable to fathom how he had got there. It was not all down to drink. Vengeance had consumed Gamble so badly that the command had passed over to Captain of Marines James Weir, from the *Audacious*. But Gamble didn't care about reputation and less about honour.

He wanted revenge.

His eyes, flicked up the column, and one of the Frenchmen hung back, causing a disturbance in the files. He was two hundred yards away, and although much thinner, there was no mistaking who it was.

Both men stared at each other.

Gamble's mouth twitched. 'Tessier!' he suddenly roared, and charged forward.

The Frenchman twisted to his right, fleeing down a shit-reeking alley where sullen, hollowed out faces watched from partially opened windows. Tessier had taken a risk by fleeing into the city burning with hatred for France, but he was desperate and desperate men will do anything to survive.

198

Gamble's boots thumped on the cobbles and he turned into the alley. A pistol flashed from the shadows; the ball shattered stone to his left, driving shards into his cheek. Gamble ran on, not caring if the Frenchman had another pistol, or not.

Ragged washing hung between the tall narrow buildings. No one could use a carriage here. Two beggars, huddled beneath filthy blankets slept on wide steps. Gamble ran past a group of children who looked like half-dressed skeletons. Starvation and poverty ruled these streets. Foul liquid squelched underfoot and tall weeds climbed up pillared doorways. He ran on, chasing the disappearing form of Tessier, heading further into the labyrinthine lanes, Gamble realised he was lost. The heat smothered the still air. He passed his hand across his sweat-laced face. Alleys became yet more alleys, and he could not see where the enemy had gone. Damn! He would not lose the bastard for the third time! He chose the darkest path simply because he assumed the Frenchman would seek out substantial cover. He saw shadows move, ducked behind a squat barrel covered in mould, drew his pistol and cocked it. He edged beside the wall and heard a murmur. Gamble peered around the corner to see a bone-thin whore at work with her mouth and nothing more. He ran on ahead. More tight corners, and then two gaunt-looking men blocked his way.

'A Frenchman!' Gamble told them. 'He ran into these alleys. Have you seen him?'

The tallest one, a rakish fellow that reminded Gamble of Adams, turned to his companion, dipped his head and beckoned for Gamble to follow. They turned left, crossed a garden bereft of fruit and vegetables, past a series of empty poultry coops, down a series of steps to a grand sixteenth century Baroque piazza. The facades of the buildings were designed so that light and shadow created dramatic effects as it playfully spread over the city. And despite the siege, the buildings here looked pristine and flowers grew up the balconies and flourished at the windows. The men grinned with yellowed teeth and pointed straight ahead. He thanked them before sprinting down the cobbles towards the harbour.

*

He had panicked.

Tessier cursed his own stupidity. He should have remained in the column where he would have been protected by his compatriots.

199

Instead, he saw an enemy coming for him like a revenant rising from a dark tomb, and he had run away like a coward.

Except this was no longer a French stronghold. The forts had all been captured and surrendered and the glorious revolutionary soldiers had been defeated. If the supply ships had made it through the blockade, Vaubois might still have been able to defend the city, but with no food, limited ammunition and disease rampant, defeat was inevitable.

Tessier remembered the gut-wrenching escape from Fort Dominance where villagers spat at him and threw rocks. One man had brought out a pistol and the ball had slapped the air as it passed his face. Another man had chased him with an ancient boar spear and Tessier, exhausted from the tussle, had jumped into the water. He had nearly drowned in that cold grey sea, only just managing to cling to a rock whilst the enemy searched the shoreline. The English warship was anchored outside the village, and although Tessier could see men on-board, no one had spotted him. Hours passed by. Then, when he considered it was clear, he swam ashore to hide in the malodorous marshland outside Mġarr. His body shivered violently and his skin was blue and wrinkled like withered fruit, but in the night-dark light he lived. He had crept to a fishing boat, donned a salt-stained boat cloak and rowed out to Malta's monochrome coastline. He had somehow managed to escape capture by abandoning the boat to swim into the harbour. From there, it had been easy to climb the city walls and to safety.

He had written his account of the marines ambush, the fort's surrender and his opinion of Chasse, to Vaubois. Tessier wanted Gamble cashiered and Vaubois promised to take his complaint to the senior English officer when he was in a position to. Weeks went past. Months. A burning hunger for revenge changed to a desire for provisions. And until today, Tessier reflected that he would never see Gamble again.

Sunlight twinkled on the water, dazzling like a million diamonds scattered across its surface.

Tessier loaded his pistol in the shadows where the air was still and cool. He had two of them, a knife and a sword, and, although starving and crippled with stomach cramps, he would fight as he always did

With everything he had.

*

200

Gamble could not see the Frenchman.

You shall pay life for life...

Gamble ran out of cover, but no shot assailed him.

Wind tugged the aroma of seaweed and shellfish from the sea into the streets. The roads zigzagged down to the deserted wharves. Waves crashed against the breakwater. Three French warships were docked, blockaded by the British in the harbour. They stood empty and forlorn with a smattering of merchant ships and smaller vessels. Wicker baskets, nets and hauling ropes were stacked up and tiny fishing boats and skiffs bobbed on the water. The Maltese were at work, allowed to fish the shallow waters. The womenfolk in thick skirts combed the quays for crabs, lobsters and clams. His eyes darted along road, up to the vast walls and down to where towering buildings gleamed gold and palm trees added to the exotic curiosity of the island.

A pistol banged from the shoreline and Gamble impulsively ducked. The ball plucked at his temple, scoring a slash by his right eye. He was dazed, but not disabled. Sea birds screamed at the noise that pounded across the water.

You shall pay life for life...

Gamble, feeling warm liquid dripping into his ear, brought up his pistol, and pulled the trigger. He knew it had gone high and was surprised to see Tessier stumble, clutching his head, blood rushing through fingers. Gamble jumped off the winding weed-strewn road, and unsheathed his sword. The blade flashed silver as it roared free of its scabbard in the quest for blood. The French captain managed to bring a second pistol to bear and Gamble saw the black muzzle. It was too late to get out of the way. The air burst with flame and smoke and noise. Gamble's right thigh felt as though it had been hit with a hammer, followed by pain that seared white-hot. His leg buckled and he skidded across the ground.

Tessier, blood running down his face, dropped the pistol and reached for his sword when black spots flashed in front of his eyes. He staggered, slipped and tumbled rearward onto algae-flecked rocks. Seawater and blood stung his eyes. He was blinded and he awkwardly pulled his slim sword free, slashing the air with wild strokes, suspecting Gamble was upon him.

But Gamble was still on his side, blood oozing from the wound. He undid his sash and tied it around his thigh. He felt light-headed; blood was crusting at his temple as he hobbled to where the stinking water lapped against the rocks.

Tessier scooped water onto his face, clearing his eyes to see a red hunter stalk above. He shook his head and droplets of bright blood pitted the water's surface.

'Get up, you coward!' Gamble bellowed and spat. 'You have no honour!'

Tessier felt like a cornered beast, the pain in his head threatening to split his skull in two, but his senses were still wickedly sharp. He brought his sabre up.

'You devil! You allowed your cutthroats to slaughter my men,' Tessier replied in French, oblivious to what Gamble had said. Blood and seawater matted his head and dripped from his chin. He wiped his face with a sleeve. 'You English are a disease! A pox on you!'

Gamble spat to show whatever Tessier had said meant nothing. He was no warrior of finesse. He fought without the airs and graces learned at the fencing schools; he learned his skill from battles. His cutlass was intended for cleaving rather than duelling. It was a bone-breaker, a flesh-cutter, and a killer. He thrust it at Tessier's tanned face, who swept it away with practised ease. Tessier slashed the air between the two of them in a series of lightning arcs that threatened to smash through Gamble's inelegant defences. Gamble, pain shooting down his leg, barely had enough time to react, recoiling and parrying. Both men were of the same height, but Gamble was bigger and Tessier knew it would be skill that would win. The Frenchman twisted, slipped and blocked a low strike that might have disembowelled him, but his sabre was no match for the solid weight of Gamble's ugly blade and he was fast losing strength.

Shouts came from the streets and redcoats were clambering down the steep steps and cobbled roads to where they fought. A score of Maltese, drawn by the sounds of pistol fire, watched the fight with nervous intrigue.

Gamble kicked with his good leg, but his wound exploded in agony and so the attack lumbered. Tessier sliced, but Gamble was already stepping away. Blood was filling his right boot. The Frenchman sprang up, and Gamble hauled his heavy sword across his body. Tessier dropped. He did not see the dirk in the scarlet-coated captain's off-hand. The curved blade easily penetrated through the flesh, sinew and muscle of his neck.

'You shall pay life, for life,' Gamble uttered, giving the weapon a savage twist, but the French captain did not understand, or would know the significance of the words.

Tessier reeled, the bone-handled dirk lodged in his neck. He made a perfunctory cut with his sword, but it was slow and clumsy. His hand dropped the sabre and reached up to pull the enemy blade free, but was too weak to do so. He tried to speak but blood filled his mouth instead.

It was all over. He knew it and as a soldier, he had to suffer a warrior's fate. But he felt at peace. Odd. Tessier barely remembered a world at peace. He had been a soldier now for over a decade. A conscript like almost everyone else, he had discovered that he liked the army, and had risen to become an officer. It brought him to adventure, to life, but he would not allow the enemy to kill him from behind, so he would face his killer like a man should do. Nevertheless, thinking of his first sea-voyage, Tessier craved to see the sea one last time.

The cutlass went through his body, driven there by a strong arm and by a hated enemy. The force was powerful enough to drive him towards the water's edge. The final ounce of breath rasped in his throat as he folded onto the blade, which Gamble still held there.

Gamble could still see the look of terror in Riding-Smyth's eyes as he lay dying.

'That's for Sam,' he said, yanking the blade free.

The French captain fell back onto the rocks below. His blood-stained hands touched the cold water. He stared up at the dazzling skyline for the last time, feeling the warmth before a black cloud misted his eyes and an eternal coldness gripped his body.

Boots pounded on the cobbles. It was Powell. 'You skewered the Frenchie proper, sir,' he said. Gamble turned and the sergeant gasped at the wounds. 'Jesus! Are you all right?'

Gamble, trembling with the exertions and despite the pain, smiled. 'Aye, Archie. I am.'

Sergeant Powell wiped sweat from his face with a red sleeve, and took hold of his officer's arm. 'Is it over now, sir? For the love of God, say it is?'

Gamble turned to stare at the corpse. Blood flowed out from the body like unravelling strands of red hair. Gulls cried overhead. 'Yes, Archie,' he said, the sun catching his ocean-blue eyes. He smiled, relief washing over him like a wave. He fought back tears, knowing that he had been narrow-minded, obstinate, selfish, and that blind anger had almost wrecked his career and ultimately his friendships. 'It's over. It's damned well over.'

A gun banged three times outside the city, a salute to the French and the start of a new chapter in Malta's history. A golden sun glowed on Valletta's domes, roofs and steeples.

It was a day in September on an island in the Mediterranean and for now the world was at peace.

Historical Note

Heart of Oak is a work of fiction, but nonetheless fiction grounded in fact.

Malta was a significant base in the Mediterranean that offered impressive fortifications. The French invaded on their way to Egypt in June, 1798. The islands were governed by Grand Master Hompesch who was a rather weak character, and many of the Knights of St. John were French and eager for it to be devoured by the ravenous appetite of revolutionary France.

The islands fell quickly and absolutely.

Bonaparte spent a few days on the island, establishing his headquarters at the *Palazzo Parisio*, today the Ministry of Foreign Affairs. He issued a number of social reforms based on the principles of the French Revolution, targeting social, administration, church and education.

Within three months, the Maltese revolted.

The causes of the uprising stemmed from silver taken from the Knights and from the churches and melted down to make coins. Property damaged in the invasion was not compensated, taxes rose, and there was no real freedom of the press which was owned by the government. Religious hatred also played a part.

By September the French had lost control of the countryside. With thousands of Maltese armed with muskets, pistols and agricultural tools, the troops shut themselves up in the forts and behind the city gates of Valletta. A French foraging party attacked the village of Zabbar. The plan was to encircle the village, cut it from outside help and steal as much food as they could. The French found the village completely deserted, but when they went into the narrow streets the villagers attacked them. In December, a small group of Maltese patriots in Valletta planned to open the gates to let in some two hundred armed villagers, but the vigilant French guards caught them and forty were executed by firing squad.

The Gozitans, hearing of the Maltese success, also rose up in revolt. A parish priest called Cassar was chosen as their leader and the French garrison was blocked in at the southern fort. In *Heart of Oak* I named it Dominance, but in reality the fort was named Chambray, after the Norman Count of the Order of St. John who had financed it.

Negotiations between the French and Captain Ball of the Royal Navy allowed the French to evacuate the fortress and be escorted to Valletta, but only after handing over two dozen cannon, ammunition and over three thousand sacks of flour. Ball had this distributed to the islanders. No assault by British troops or Gozitans ever took place, and what is described in *Heart of Oak* is pure invention.

Over the next year the Maltese set up cannon batteries around the harbour's to stop the French from bringing in aid. They constantly skirmished with the outer forts and by the end of 1799 the first British troops had arrived: the 30th Cambridgeshire Regiment and the Irish 89th.

Fever struck. It was thought that contaminated air from the marshes at the head of the harbour was to blame and many British were affected. Malta's main hospital, the *Santa Infermeria*, was in French hands so its facilities and medicines were denied to the British and Maltese civilian population. Temporary hospitals were set up in churches. All were vastly overcrowded.

In the spring of 1800, four companies of Maltese Light Infantry were formed from local volunteers. They were led by British officers, mostly from the marines and Royal Navy, and the regiment helped harass the outer French strongholds at Cottonera and Ricasoli with notable success.

The British blockade continued to prevent French efforts to resupply the city during the early summer, and by August the situation was irrefutably desperate: no horses, pack animals, dogs, cats, fowls or rabbits still lived within the city. The cisterns had been emptied and firewood was in short supply. So serious was the need for wood that the frigate *Boudeuse*, moored in the harbour, was broken up for fuel by the beleaguered and starving garrison. Vaubois evicted several thousand Maltese from the city in the hope of rationing his remaining food. With defeat inexorable, Vaubois gave orders that the frigates *Diane* and *Justice* were to attempt a breakout for Toulon. They slipped away in the night, but were immediately spotted. *Justice* escaped and was the only French ship to do so during the blockade.

On 3rd September, with his men dying of starvation and typhus now reaching at the rate of more than a hundred men a day and with no chance of relief, Vaubois sent envoys to the British (not the Maltese) to reach terms of surrender. The victorious British and the Maltese regiment marched into Valletta on the 9th September as described in the story.

There was no HMS *Sea Prince* and yet I could not write this story without having one of the Royal Navy's ships present. I have been in awe of them since visiting HMS *Victory* at Portsmouth's Historic Dockyards as a child. I am continually amazed at the workings of the personnel, the training and professionalism that went into making Britain's fleet superior to all rivals well into the twentieth century.

The ships of the line were 'rated' according to the number of ports through which a gun could be fired. Often the number of cannon on board far exceeded the rating number. It must not be forgotten that it was the masterful command of the ships gun teams that won battles. At Trafalgar the British lost one thousand five hundred men killed or injured, whereas, the French and Spanish lost seventeen thousand! British gunnery won Trafalgar and the countless other great sea battles of the time. I have often wondered what it would have been like to walk a ship's Quarter Deck, whether sailing under a clear blue sky, or in the smoking, screaming horror of battle where sometimes the cramped fighting took place in less than the range of a pistol. Most times I am glad I am free of such experience.

Lieutenant Pym and his landing party are fictitious; however, such operations conducted on land by naval crews are not. For example, in August 1807, fifty seamen from the *Hydra* captured shore batteries whilst the rest of the crew boarded three enemy ships anchored in the harbour.

Simon Gamble is sadly an invention, but the marines were used as troops for amphibious landings as well as their duties on board the ships. A secondary duty was to suppress mutiny. There were three divisions of marines numbered 1-3, but more often they were designated by their location: Chatham, Portsmouth and Plymouth respectively. They formed part of Cavan's brigade in Sir Ralph Abercromby's Expeditionary Army that sailed to Egypt in 1801 from Malta to liberate it from French rule.

They were granted the title 'Royal Marines' in 1802 by King George III in recognition of their outstanding service.

In *Heart of Oak*, Gamble orders his men into two lines before firing a volley of musketry. It wasn't until the fighting in Spain that regulations changed from three deep to two deep lines. A three deep line was considered more solid. However, the third rank couldn't see very well and their aim was less sure, so it became two through necessity. Gamble, it seems, is a man ahead of the times.

Having Malta as a fortress island base allowed Britain to control the strategically-vital central Mediterranean. After the victories won in Egypt, Britain was supposed to leave, a condition set in the signing of the Treaty of Amiens of 1802. Tsar Alexander I was the head of the ousted Knights of St. John, and requested that it be turned over to Russian rule before agreeing any alliance with Britain. Prime Minister William Pitt the Younger categorically refused. It was Britain's refusal to comply with this clause of the treaty that was instrumental in starting the Napoleonic Wars in 1803. Malta remained in British hands until it acquired full independence in 1964.

With the capitulation of the French, Malta would resume some degree of normality. More and more British troops would land there ready for the expedition to Egypt, which meant that more battles - both land and sea - would come, and so more stories will be told.

Blood on the Snow

Jack Hallam and the Flanders
Campaign
December, 1794

It was dawn in Holland.

Under a blue-grey winter sky, a column of soldiers marched across frozen crop fields. Snow had fallen during the night, and in the morning, the world had become a crunchy white bleakness. The wind whistled as it whipped across the fields, ice hung from fence posts and sheeted the tufts of grass so that each blade looked as though it was encased in glass. The bare furrows were hard and slippery, puddles were iced-over, and the men's breath plumed above their heads.

The soldiers were from a company of the 28th, a British regiment raised in North Gloucestershire, and their destination was a farmstead half a mile away. The feeble sun clung to the horizon, throwing their rushing shadows far ahead of them like a newspaper's exaggerated caricatures. The wind tugged snow from the ground, whirling it in a glittering dance, and straight into their faces. Most of them wore their thick issue greatcoats, but some were without winter dress altogether. The British army had suffered horrendously from the Flanders climate; the men's coats had literally fallen apart. Some redcoats had been issued with simple jackets without any lace and facings as replacements, some wore local homespun coats that looked crude and ill-fashioned, and some even wore clogs made from willow-wood, because their boots had rotted away. The unlucky ones, without the winter coats and gloves, had tied scraps of cloth around their hands and bare feet. The smart bright red of the uniform had long faded to a dull purple, or pink, and was now so heavily patched with mismatched cloth that the men resembled vagabonds rather than soldiers. Their unshaven faces were wrapped in scarves made from common sacking, or what they had looted and begged along the way. Some had lost their black round hats, and either wore forage, or simple peasant hats tied in place under the chin with twine.

Their vacant expressions and sunken cheeks, made dirty through weeks of campaigning, betrayed that they were exhausted and bitterly hungry.

The Duke of York's British and German Army had joined their Austrian and Dutch allies by landing in the Austrian-owned Netherlands, and had marched expecting an easy victory. But the French, swept away with their new republicanism, had turned on them with an unforgiving fury, speed and superior numbers. Defeat after defeat had left the British fighting alone, but the winter brought more misery, and they were forced to retreat across the frozen Gelderland in the fervent hope of reaching the harbours in the north where ships would take them home.

They had marched for days. It was a struggle with the roads being flooded, iced over, or left as glutinous traps. Time after time, they had stopped and waited while a gun carriage, or wagon was shifted by brute force. Rain and snow fell with barely a break, and the few Dutch they saw stared at them with suspicious eyes. There were no cheers of welcome for their allies. There was nothing but marching, pain and cold.

An officer, mounted on a black charger, trotted to the front of the company; the horse whinnied, hot steam pluming from its wide nostrils. He looked ashen and seemed to wince in rhythm to the horse's stride.

'Damn your haste!' he said angrily. 'What's the hurry, man? Do you need to void your bowels?' His sneering comments were directed to an officer who marched confidently ahead of the men.

'We're late, sir,' the officer said reproachfully. He was a lieutenant and just stared ahead rather than turn to face his superior. Flecks of snow dotted his bicorn hat and his long chestnut-coloured hair that was tied back with a frayed black bow.

Captain Andrew Clements hawked once and then spat onto the ground. 'Late? Late for what exactly? You have a whore waiting for you, Lieutenant? Is that it?' He had an insolent face, cold and antagonistic. He held a canteen to his mouth, gulped and then wiped his unshaven chin that bristled with black and silver hairs.

Lieutenant Jack Hallam ignored the remark. He knew that the canteen contained rum and that Clements was already drunk.

He usually was.

'Pick your feet up, Private Tipton,' Sergeant Abraham Fox bellowed. 'I've seen Dutch girls who are more soldierly than you are!' Fox was a dark-eyed, burly man, and his face was a horror of ancient scars. He turned to the rest of the company. 'Pick up your stride, all of you!'

'That's the way, Sergeant,' Clements said, hiccupped and then burped. 'Onward, you laggard scum!'

Hallam glanced behind; the men marched quietly and solemnly. They might look like beaten tramps, but the 28th had spent the last two weeks fighting a rear-guard that had astounded even the most cynical adversaries and brought praise from the generals. Men may have died in their dozens from the miasmic fever caused by the swampy countryside, and crippled by frostbite, but the despondency in the men of Number Eight Company was irrevocably due to Clements.

The forty-year-old captain frowned constantly as if everything bothered him. He had dark hair turning white, protuberant eyes, and such a languid demeanour that he always appeared to slouch. His family was exceedingly wealthy and owned a thousand acres of woodland in the Forest of Dean, but he was never one for sharing such personal information, especially to his fellow officers. A month ago the brusque captain had ordered Private Wheeler to be flogged for suspected thievery of a pocket watch. However, it turned out that the popular private had not been the culprit and died from his wounds, caused by the four hundred given lashes. It became apparent that Clements had simply misplaced his watch, and Wheeler had died for nothing. The captain was not reprimanded and that galled Hallam severely. Clements verbally abused the men, even more so when he was drunk, so the remarks were frequent and daily. And so by now, December 1794, morale, already strained, had dipped to an all-time low.

Hallam knew the men deserved better than contempt, and when Clements was indisposed, he personally took command and encouraged and praised them. The captain had once told him querulously that the ranks were filled with 'every deplorable piece of refuse imaginable'. To control and forge the men into the professional soldier's hours of monotonous drill and harsh punishments were relied upon. There had been a skirmish a few days back and the men had performed admirably; every movement had been a drill-master's delight and every command was obeyed crisply as though they were performing on parade for the Duke of York. Clements paid them no heed. He had sat scowling from his saddle, no doubt suffering from a hangover, but Hallam had congratulated them and witnessed a spark of appreciation. It wasn't much; a tiny flicker of gratitude, but it was a start and one he wanted to build on.

Footsteps hurried towards Hallam. 'Did the captain call your wife a whore, sir?' Ensign Julian Stubbington asked tentatively, as the captain had slowed his horse to a mere walk in order to top up his canteen with a small bottle. One of the horse's hind legs was wrapped in a cloth, and the beast juddered due to an infection.

'No, he did not,' Hallam replied irritably, although his exasperation was directed at Clements, now further down the line.

Hallam was from Wendover in Buckinghamshire and at twenty-nine was newly married. He had met Isabel at a ball held in her home town of Lyndhurst, in the New Forest, when the battalion was on standby to join the army in March of this year. He hated such occasions. He disliked dancing, had no interest in small talk, but as soon as they were introduced he had felt his heart strings being pulled. Soon, they had both fallen deeply in love.

Isabel was a thin girl, not yet twenty, beautiful, loving, and considerate. He absolutely adored her – physically and spiritually. They got married in a tiny parish church on a beautiful day, just six weeks after meeting, and just days before the regiment had sailed away. He remembered the parting; she had kissed him hard, her tongue shimmering, exhilarating and loving as she curled it around his. She drew back, eyes glinting with tears.

'Come back to me, Jack,' Isabel had pleaded. 'Please come back.'

He had held her tightly, not wanting to let her go. 'I will, my love. I promise.'

Hallam brought out a silver locket from his pocket. It gleamed brightly despite the morning's bleak sunlight. He had it made for the wedding. Inside was a small miniature of her portrait. He touched her softly painted face with a finger nail. It still felt odd being married, even after eight months, but it was a good feeling nonetheless.

The company numbered thirty-five and were alone in the silent wintry landscape. The other nine companies that made up the regiment were somewhere to the north, and somewhere behind was the vanguard of the French. It was a world of pitiless torture, empty bellies, and the daily slog of discipline-destroying withdrawal.

'Are we lost, sir?' Stubbington asked. His face was red and his lips were severely chapped from the biting wind. He had turned sixteen on

214

the voyage over and came from Deerhurst, a small village on the eastern bank of the River Severn.

'No.'

'It's just that I can't make head or tail of where we're heading to, sir,' he said, glancing at the brown ruined stalks of old crops. 'Every field, every village and every wood looks the same as the last one.'

Hallam pointed at the farm with a black-nailed finger. Early morning mist cloaked a stream in pale skeins that ran parallel to it. The sky was still dark to the west.

'See that, Mister Stubbington?' he asked. 'That's where we're supposed to be.'

The ensign strained to see the dwelling, because it was snowing again. He could make out the tall beech, alder and oak trees that surrounded the farm, but very little else. There was a dark glassy patch of ground and Stubbington considered that it was a lake of sorts.

'That's where we were supposed to be last night.' Hallam could not keep the bitterness from his voice.

Lieutenant-Colonel Edward Paget had ordered Number Seven, Eight and the Grenadier Companies to attack a French held bridge. Paget was just eighteen and wanted to make a name for himself and his new regiment. He personally sent the three companies forward in the dark, urging the men on in his usual high spirits. However, his hope of an easy victory turned, like the rest of the campaign, into a debacle. Clements had kept the company back when the assault started, then bungled the advance so that the company missed out on the initial attack. Luckily, the redcoats were eventually able to eject the minor French force from the bridge after sustaining a well-timed musket volley. The enemy then retreated east to their battle lines.

The young colonel wasn't best pleased. He congratulated the other two companies on their success, but Clements was ordered south to the farm to wait for further orders. Hallam knew that they had been dismissed as Paget had no valid reason to send them out from the parent battalion. He just wanted to rid of them as though their failure was infectious.

Number Eight Company was deemed a hopeless cause under the mismanagement of Clements. His ineptitude had left the company lost in the dark as they struggled to find the farmstead in the endless patchwork of fields. As night fell, Hallam had found a barn, and despite Clements' constant grumbling, the men had been able to at least find shelter and warmth.

Hallam was in a foul mood. He was looking to snap at everything, in Stubbington's opinion, and the young ensign was rarely wrong about his lieutenant. He knew well enough from previous conversations that the best notion was not to engage in one, but Stubbington was infectiously cheerful and difficult to be swayed by bad moods.

'Is it true that the farm is called Buggenum, sir?'

'Yes,' Hallam said wearily, as he knew what the ensign was going to say next.

'Funny name for a farm,' the ensign said after a while. 'Sounds a bit like 'bugger', doesn't it?'

Hallam ignored him.

'It's not the captain's fault, sir,' Stubbington changed the subject. He wiped a frayed coat sleeve under his runny nose.

'What?'

'It's not his fault that we got lost.'

Hallam turned and narrowed his flint-grey eyes on the young officer. 'Who's bloody fault do you suppose it is then?'

Stubbington shrank back under Hallam's scrutiny rather than his reply. He stumbled on the slick and treacherous road, but managed to stop himself from tumbling over. 'What I mean to say, sir, is that he drinks to forget a hardship.'

'What the hell does that mean?'

The ensign adjusted his felt hat. He had tied a strip of blue cloth around his head to stop the round hat from spilling over his eyes; the cloth was always visible underneath. 'My father, God bless him for his sins, is a physician, and he once told me that some men drink to overcome personal loss. Women and finances and such like,' he said, shrugging as though that explained the way of the world. 'He'd seen it many times. They always take to drink, he would say. I suppose the drink is a comfort in dark times. Personally, I can't understand why, when a mug of steaming tea does the trick.'

'The captain is neither hurting nor taking comfort, Mister Stubbington,' Hallam said quietly and dismissively, because Clements had spurred his horse near them. 'He's idle and bored. That's why he drinks.'

'Perhaps the colonel could impose a drinking ban?' the young officer suggested. 'It might help the rank and file too, who I notice spend every waking moment on the stuff?'

Hallam glared at him. 'Stop the men from drinking? Soldiers will drink as fish will swim. It's preposterous to suggest such a thing.' He

216

thought about asking why the ensign had not followed in his father's footsteps, but bit off any inclination.

Stubbington looked glumly at the farm where the lake was more visible. He wondered whether there might be any fowl in amongst the reeds, with the intriguing thought of catching the birds for tonight's dinner. The water was frozen and was the colour of ploughshares. 'I'm sorry, sir,' he tried to assuage his captain.

Hallam cast the ensign a fleeting look, realising he had replied too callously. 'Most of them only joined up for drink, Mister Stubbington. You'd have a mutiny on your hands if you took it away. It's a shameful thing to say, but it's true. Half the officers I know will be drunk as I speak. Good ones too.'

Stubbington suspected that Hallam was not referring to Clements. 'Yes, sir.'

'But things are going to change.'

'Oh? Why?'

'Because there's going to be a battle,' Hallam said, rubbing his cold hands with relish. The snow was falling thicker, and there was a silence only punctuated by the sound of the men breathing and boots crunching.

The ensign went as white as cartridge paper. 'B-battle?' he stammered.

'Yes, Mister Stubbington,' Hallam said. There was just enough light to see his eyes glow. 'A good old-fashioned fight that will sort the wheat from the chaff. I can feel it in my very marrow. It's what this company needs. It's what the battalion needs. Jesus, it's what the whole goddamned army needs. If we're not fighting then we're not winning. Our lads need a morale boost. A proper fight will give them that.'

Hallam welcomed a good fight. It's what the men were paid to do and it's what they wanted to do. After months of doing nothing in Flanders but retreat, dither and then retreat again, the army had moved from one calamity to the next. The commanders were too busy fighting over their laurels and trying to pull rank over one another. Senior battalion officers blamed everyone except themselves for their own mistakes, the sergeants seemed to run the companies because most of the officers were drunk, jaded and lax in their duties. The rank and file were simply depressed.

Ever since the Battle of Fleurus in June, where the French had defeated a tired and ill-managed Austrian and Dutch army under Prince Saxe-Coburg, the French Revolutionary soldiers had beaten and outflanked the allies in almost every skirmish. They fought like devils and it left the British Army a forlorn, dejected and dispirited mass of men.

'The Slashers will show the French upstarts how Englishmen fight!' Hallam said, using the regiment's nickname. The 28th had been on garrison duty in Canada and a malicious lawyer regularly upset some of the men and their families, so some of them broke into his home and slashed the man's ear off in retaliation. The lawyer never said another hostile word and the guilty men were never found. The regiment showed the world that everyone cared for each other, just like a family, and to this day they were proud of that ferocious nickname.

'Yes, sir.' Stubbington tried to sound confident, but somehow managed to only increase the pitch of his voice. Hallam glared at him briefly before turning away.

There was going to be a battle, and the company, Hallam reflected brightly, might well be his by tomorrow's sundown.

*

A black dog barked incessantly at the approaching redcoats from the farm gates until it was silenced with a brutal kick. It ran back to the house, whimpering. There was a clatter of hooves and Major Osborne, mounted on his fine bay horse, appeared at the gates.

'Ah, good to see you, Clements,' he shouted the jocular greeting in his usual hoarse voice, but his expression was hardly welcoming. He was pinch-faced, with heavy bags under red-rimmed eyes. 'We thought we'd lost you. Well, at least the colonel hoped so,' he added with a sneering guffaw.

'Not lost, sir,' Clements said. 'I just took the company on manoeuvres.'

'What?' Osborne was incredulous. His horse bared its teeth and pawed the air as though it was uneasy, and he instinctively patted its neck with a gloved hand. Clements, the major and the colonel were the only officers Hallam knew who had not lost their horses to the campaign.

'Yes, sir,' Clements continued the lie, then turned briefly in his saddle to order the company to halt, before turning sharply back to the major. 'It's always good to get the men up early for manoeuvres. It keeps them keen and alert.' He gave a sickly smile.

Osborne gave a bewildered shake of his head. 'What an appalling notion.' He curbed an urge to drink the fine claret, which he had just taken from the house and that made him feel irritable. He drummed his fingers on the stiff leather saddle's pommel instead.

In the courtyard a group of redcoats were handling several bags, and one or two paintings. A private with an angry red boil on his cheek, held something in his hands and Hallam saw a flash of silver before it disappeared into a sack. Two men were carrying a heavy oak chest with some difficulty. Pockets and haversacks were crammed with goods, bellies were plugged with whatever food was found and heads were foggy with plundered alcohol.

'What's going on here, sir?' Hallam asked suspiciously.

'Naught that concerns you,' Osborne said nastily.

Hallam growled.

Captain Pulmer from Number Four Company walked out from one of the buildings. He looked surprised to see Clements. A bolt of red silk was under an arm.

'Nothing left for you, Andrew,' he said cheerfully, but then was silenced by a grunt from the major.

'What about the owners, sir?' Hallam asked Osborne. 'Are they home?'

Osborne, his mouth tight, looked at him with a deliberate slowness. 'So what if they are?'

So he had been plundering the farm with Pulmer's men. Hallam thought it disgraceful. Clements, he noted, showed no objection, but was probably jealous that he missed out.

'It's not right.'

The major looked infuriated. 'What did you say?'

'I said it's not right,' Hallam repeated obstinately.

'I don't give a damn what you think, Lieutenant.' Osborne glowered at him. Pulmer sniggered at the rebuke. 'They are French sympathisers and conspirators. A troop of dragoons were seen leaving here yesterday. All the damned Dutch are in league with the Jacobins, so I'll not have another word said about the matter.' He turned to the swaggering Pulmer. 'Let us leave this place. Our young new colonel is expecting us and he cannot abide lateness,' he said scathingly. 'Besides, there's a wood nearby where deer have been spotted in abundance. I fancy a spot of hunting. Bring back some venison for my Christmas dinner, eh?' He trotted away, before glaring at Hallam.

Hallam could have strangled the major. 'We should leave them money,' he said sharply.

Pulmer, a notorious braggart and troublemaker, just grinned. 'We're not here to buy things; we take them. By force if necessary. They are the fortunes of war.' He walked away, laughing smugly.

Hallam scowled at his retreating back. 'You're just a damned pack of thieves.'

He turned to step through the gates into the courtyard as the last of Pulmer's men filed past. A corporal had a hen with its neck wrung tied to his pack and another was cutting the canvas away from a gilt picture frame with his bayonet. A Gobelin tapestry of the Virgin Mary was ripped in two to make ridiculous cloaks. Four privates were bickering over a bottle of brandy, their language coarse and threats brazen. It slipped from their grasp to smash onto the road. One of the privates bent down to guzzle up the liquid, lapping at it like a dog. A puddle of horse urine steamed on icy cobbles. Several books lay scattered about, the pages flapped in the wind.

Hallam walked to the far end of the courtyard, which led to what was once the stable block. It had been months since it had last been in proper use and only the faintest of odours lingered. The smell of horses, leather and dung was fresher upon standing in the stalls. Just a few days before it had served as a billet to another British regiment. They had chopped up the last remaining doors and shutters to burn.

The house itself was long and low and was painted red with green shutters and frames. A large barn faced southwards, the roof thatch now lost to folds of crisp snow. Hallam could make out a piggery and a large henhouse. Beyond the barn and nestled in amongst bare trees was a smaller barn, a dairy and a windmill. It was certainly a prosperous and busy farm; a wide track wound around the distant trees and onto the meadows where the dairy herd would be taken to pasture across the stream. Hallam turned back to the house. The front door was open, splintered, which revealed it had been forced. One of the windows was smashed. He could hear muffled cries coming from somewhere inside.

'Where do you think you're going?' Clements enquired as Hallam walked towards the door. 'Lieutenant! Come back here!'

Hallam ignored him and, upon entering the house, found himself in a long, white-painted hallway. To the right was the kitchen and pantry; to the left a parlour with a large stone chimney and windows that in the summer overlooked a large rectangular flowerbed where roses, rhododendrons and persicaria might bloom in magnificent colour.

'Hello?' his voice echoed.

He waited. There was no answer, but he could still hear crying upstairs.

'Hello?' he said again, louder.

The place looked as though it had been stripped of anything of value. Drawers from a small writing desk lay broken on the floor and papers were scattered everywhere. The scullery and kitchen had been raided of all foodstuffs. Pots and bowls were strewn everywhere.

Hallam heard footsteps. He looked up to see a young woman, who was obviously the maid, coming down the stairs. She was blonde with a high forehead and blood from a wound had crusted dark on her scalp. She was adjusting her clothes. He didn't know what to say.

'Miss, do you need help?'

The woman jumped because she had not seen him. '*Wat doet u hier nog? Vertrek!*' she shouted angrily at him.

'I'm sorry, Miss, I don't understand,' he said removing his weather-beaten hat. 'Do you speak English?' He heard another woman moan. He glanced upstairs, but could see no one. 'Does your mistress require assistance?'

The maid spat at him. '*Ga weg!*'

'Please tell your mistress that I am sorry.' Hallam stared at the blood that matted her hair. 'Can I help you? Is there anyone else hurt?' He wondered where the males of the household were.

The girl gestured for him to leave. '*Vertrek!*' she shouted at him again, then began to cry.

Hallam hesitantly moved to the doorway after deciding he was not wanted. Then he was struck with a thought. He removed his purse from inside his coat and jacket. 'Please,' he said kindly, 'tell your mistress that I leave this payment with my sincerest apologies for the damage and theft.' He placed the money, which amounted to little over three pounds, on the sideboard next to an ornament. It wouldn't cover the loss but it was the bulk of his available funds. He bowed once before leaving amidst another yell of hostility.

'You have a way with the women, Lieutenant,' Clements said, laughing at his ire. He burped loudly and clicked his horse forward.

Stubbington ran over to Hallam. 'What's going on, sir? Is there a lady in there?'

'We're leaving; that's what's going on,' Hallam said furiously as he strode across the courtyard taking in the smell of animal dung, leather tack and unwashed flesh. 'How in God's name will the men learn

221

what's right from wrong when the officers are corrupt! Goddamn Pulmer!'

'Sir?' Stubbington had difficulty in keeping up with Hallam's long stride.

'Sergeant Fox!' Hallam called abruptly.

'Sir!'

Hallam went to speak disrespectfully of Clements in front of the men, then quickly bit it off. 'Where's the captain?'

Stubbington gazed down the road. 'He's with the major, sir.'

Hallam swore fluently and impressively and didn't care who heard him. 'Get the men ready, Sergeant,' he said fiercely. 'We're leaving for Rotheheim, and any bastard that isn't on his feet in one minute will be left behind! The French love handling pricks so they'll be overjoyed to acquire a few more.'

The two sergeants and two corporals immediately rousted the men. Fox kicked Tipton. 'Don't lounge there like an expectant whore, boy! Get up like the captain ordered!'

Corporal Beckett slapped a man across the face to wake him, but the private was already in the drunken throes of unconsciousness.

'Leave the bastard,' Hallam said callously. 'And take note of his name and offence for the records.'

'Sir,' Beckett said, leaving the man on the roadside.

A private went to drag his unfortunate companion up, but Hallam stopped him. 'I said leave him!' Beckett pushed the other redcoat back into his file.

Stubbington bent down to the road to one side to pick up a blue feather that had been tossed aside during the plunder. The young officer had a penchant for anything coloured blue and seemed delighted to wear it in his hat.

'You're a regular dandy now, sir,' Private Daniel Tipton said as the company marched swiftly away. He sneezed and, pressing a finger against on nostril, blew a string of green snot from the other. 'Best dressed one I've ever seen.'

Stubbington, immensely pleased at the comment, bowed at the private. 'Me thinks somewhere there is a young Dutch girl in need of rescue,' he said, standing in what he considered a heroic pose. 'Come hither, girl, to your Romeo.' He puffed up his thin chest like a winter robin. A ripple of bawdy laughter reached the lieutenant.

'Quiet in the ranks!' Hallam snapped. 'Get back to your post, Mister Stubbington.'

222

'Sir!' the boy obeyed, but his cheerfulness was not quashed by Hallam's temperament.

'March, you bastards!' Hallam set the company a brutal pace. He could hear their complaints, but ignored them. He knew from experience, having tried one on once, how the wooden frames of the backpacks pressed painfully against the spine, and the tight straps constricted the chest until each breath was raw. 'Marching and a rare fight will banish the chill from your bones. You'll thank me one day. Why? Because believe it not, I want you all to live.'

If the army had been shattered by the dreadful weather; where the wind cut flesh like a dragoon's sword and men froze to death in their sleep, then there were still some men who marched, even in defeat, in good formation and with good discipline. Private Matthew Hulse was one. Tall, reedy and with thinning hair, he was always respectful and eloquent. An intelligent man ruined by drink. Caught stealing liquor, he had enlisted to save himself from the gallows. He helped Fox run the company books.

Private James Shawford was another. A big man, in fact so big, he should have belonged in the Grenadier Company. Shawford was a professional soldier, with a dozen or more years in the regiment, and the recruits looked up to him. Impassive at times, and brutal in combat, Shawford had beaten to death a man with his own hands before escaping to the army at fifteen years old.

It was men like these, Hallam considered, that kept the regiment from dissolving into chaos.

They soon caught up with Pulmer's men, but Hallam marched his company off the road to go around them so that Clements was left with Osborne, who shrugged and cursed him.

Hallam could just about see a pall of thickening dark smoke from two miles away. A farm was burning. Or was it a house in the town? He wiped flakes from his eyes; his eyebrows were frosted white. He peered again, but the sky was darkening and the snowfall was turning to a horrid cold sleet. He shivered, the raw wind sinking its teeth into his marrow. This was a land where snow clotted in the dikes and ditches and, when there was a thaw, it came as drizzling sheets that made the conditions even more unbearable.

They followed the road northwards. It was fairly straight and flanked by some of the tallest trees Hallam had ever seen. Mostly oaks and birch, and in the summer he considered, this avenue full of plump green boughs would be a place of beauty. He remembered the tulip fields in the west of the country. What a sight! There had been acres of them. A man had once told him that Lincolnshire was like Holland, flat with large open fens, tulips and windmills. Hallam had scoffed at the notion; declaring it too foreign.

Now the great trees stood like ghosts and the flowers long dead under a frozen blanket. The sun, a glint in the melancholy sky, spat bitter embers.

The men were quiet, no doubt dreaming of warmth, food and women. Hallam tried to remember the last time he had eaten a hot meal. A week ago? Or was it two?

The British Army had suffered appalling supply problems from the start of the campaign. Food was often delivered late and was inedible by the 'Newgate Blues', the mocking nickname given for the Royal Corps of Waggoners, who were considered to be criminals. They skimmed the best of the supplies and sold it at a profit to the markets at Amsterdam, Ostend and Antwerp. But now the commissariat had completely disintegrated because the French had savagely forced the British to retreat from the ports, and the soldiers were left ravenous.

'Sir?'

'What do you want, Mister Stubbington?' Hallam didn't bother to look over his shoulder. The wind instantly snatched his breath away.

Stubbington proffered Hallam a white-toothed smile. 'I wanted to ask about Captain Clements, sir.'

Hallam frowned. 'What about him?'

'Are we going to leave him?'

Hallam paused, then shrugged. 'Bugger him,' he remarked scornfully. He pulled out a timepiece that Isabel's father had given to him as a wedding gift. 'In thirty minutes, we'll be at the town where the colonel will be waiting for us. He can't abide tardiness and I want to show him how to run a company not ruin it,' he said.

On the outskirts of Rotheheim, the road dipped slightly and the company had to cross an ice-crusted stone bridge over a frozen stream to get to the town that was smeared with the haze of dark smoke. A smattering of skeleton-like trees edged the road where rooks croaked and mistletoe grew in clumps.

Redcoats watched their arrival. There were men from the 27th, the Inniskillings Irish rogues to a man who wore buff facings. A couple of them were drinking heavily, but they let Hallam and his men past without causing any trouble. A tall officer with sandy hair, a broken nose and sabre-scarred face nodded to him, and Hallam returned the

224

greeting. It seemed that he was keeping a close eye on his men and he certainly looked as though he could handle even the most disobedient of them on his own.

There were scores of civilians, horses and carts in the town's square. A blue-plume of smoke roiled from a burnt wreck of a large building far across the road that Hallam had seen earlier. A couple of windows were smashed on some of the houses. Icicles of varying lengths hung from lintels. Redcoats from another regiment were forming up ahead of the crowd.

'Lieutenant Hallam!' a voice called him.

Hallam swivelled on his heels. It was Colonel Paget who was mounted on his fine horse.

'Sir,' he saluted.

'Where's Captain Clements?' Paget looked severe as he trotted over.

Hallam jerked his head back towards the bridge. 'He's with the major and Captain Pulmer's company, sir.'

Paget said nothing for a moment. 'What was Captain Pulmer doing back there?' he asked, wrinkling his nose from the snuff he'd just taken. He was addicted to it. He paused, then sneezed violently.

'Sir?' Hallam said impassively, feigning ignorance. Was his loyalty being tested? He wasn't loyal to Osborne and Pulmer, and certainly not Clements, but he would not openly spread gossip.

Paget watched him for a second, just as a hawk might watch its prey, before deciding whatever he intended to say would remain unheard. 'I won't have any men from the regiment looting from the Dutch when they are our allies,' he said, glaring at Pulmer's men who were just approaching the bridge.

Hallam didn't know what to say. How had the colonel known?

Paget fixed them a hard stare that spoke of disapproval. 'I won't have the regiments' good name dragged through the mud because a few officers can't keep their men in check. Roaming and pouncing like a pack of bloody wolves. It won't do, Jack.'

It's not the men that are the real problem; it's the officers, Hallam said to himself. He liked Paget because he was morally strong and incorruptible, and although he was so young, he had the maturity and shrewdness of a much older wiser man. He might be new and thought unkindly by Osborne as a mere wet-behind-the-ears boy, but he cared deeply for the regiment and was more of an officer and gentleman than the pugnacious major could ever be.

225

'What's happening here, sir?'

'We're burning one of our depots,' Paget replied as a gust of wind caught the smoke to cloud the street black. 'Can't take the stuff with us and we certainly can't let the Crapauds have it, so we have no options but to burn it. All of it.' The acrid smoke was stinging his eyes. 'Are your men ready, Jack?' he asked, scanning his watery eyes over the company. Stubbington tried to look alert.

'Always, sir.'

'Good, because we're going north to bolster our defences and push the French back across the Waal.'

'They've crossed it?' Hallam was taken aback by the news.

Paget answered with a gentle nod of his head. 'Last night. It took our forward sentries by complete surprise. They didn't need the bridges after all. Crafty buggers just walked across the ice. Humbugged us, by God. So we're burning unwanted stores and leaving now.'

'Jesus,' Hallam said, aghast. The British had thought that the River Waal, a natural defensive obstacle that swept across the land, would halt any French progress until Spring. The main bridges had been destroyed, or those left standing were heavily defended, but the French now threatened to cut off the British rear-guard by a brilliant out-flanking manoeuvre. Hallam knew the French would close in around them fast.

'We're three miles from the main body. We have to make sure our last precious supplies and guns get through this damn cold winters maw. Bloody buggering artillery,' Paget cursed, 'always the last. We have to wait for one lot to cross and then we blow the bridge north of the town. Then, we'll have to march like the devil up to where we expect to face the French.' He turned in the saddle to watch a dog run past them, barking madly as it disappeared into the throng of people. A redcoat was sat on a barrel drinking from a stone bottle while two companions were hassling a married couple who were trying to leave the town. 'The townsfolk that are our allies are coming with us, but most will stay. They seem to prefer the Jacobins. We're also leaving the wounded, those that can't be transported of course, to the mercies of the French.'

It was a terrible decision to leave men behind, but the French would look after them as would the British if it was the other way round. The weather had claimed many lives and most were exhausted and suffering from frost-bite, but the French would do their best to treat them.

'What about our allies, sir?' Hallam glanced at the ash that floated about them like the End of Days.

'Can't expect much from the Prussians or Austrians,' Paget muttered dismissively. 'No help whatsoever.'

'What about the Dutch?' Hallam had to shout, as the Inniskillings were being ordered to form up close by. Two of the men were fighting on the ground and, most bizarrely, no officer or NCO seemed to have the inclination to stop them.

Paget snorted. 'Might as well let their women fight instead,' he said, sighing. 'No, they've buggered off, so we're on our own. We've got a battle to fight and ships to get home to.'

'They will come, won't they, sir?' Hallam betrayed what every redcoat was nervously thinking.

'Of course, Jack,' Paget scoffed at the notion that the ships wouldn't be there. It was unthinkable. No British army had been left behind. The Royal Navy was dependable. He looked skyward where all light was slowly being banished. 'We'll get home.'

'What's the name of the place we're marching to today, sir?'

'Grave.'

Hallam stared and then winced. 'How apt, sir,' he said drily.

Paget grunted at the irony. 'Probably not the way the locals say it,' he said, tersely. 'I sincerely hope we can send the enemy to early ones, though. It'll be a desperate fight, all right.'

And it would be too. The French would fight like fanatics while the British would fight because their lives depended on it.

At a place called Grave.

*

The 28th left Rotheheim in a terrible snowstorm.

They were the last regiment to leave the town. Two troops of cavalry: a Light Dragoon and a French émigré, protected the rear-guard, but in the driving snow it was hard to see the man in the next file let alone if the enemy were near.

The wind brought snow and ice into the men's eyes causing them to curse and stumble. One man who had lost his boots a month before, and whose toes had all turned black, collapsed from exhaustion. His body instantly spotted white and as the wind howled across the fields the British cavalry passed him unnoticed and forgotten. Men sobbed and

227

shuffled in the storm. They were benumbed with cold and bitterly hungry as no food or wine had been left for them at the town.

They passed frozen corpses lining the road, like markers showing the way to hell. They were humped grotesque shapes, like snow-covered barrows. Hallam stared at one. The man had been a redcoat and had been there for many days. His face was blackened by wind and half-buried in snow so that his grotesque face seemed to watch the men who marched past. Hallam's eyes flickered to another body and he almost wept at the sight.

In his long service career he had seen some terrible things. He'd seen men shredded into ribboned meat by canister shot, a friend decapitated by a roundshot and another die of a horrible wasting disease, but nothing had prepared him for this. The body was a young woman. Late teens. Her hair was copper-coloured and she resembled Isabel, for she had been strikingly good-looking in life. Her eyes were blessedly shut and her thin mouth closed. Her bodice was open, her breasts were exposed and the lower half of her was hidden under snow. Hallam bent over, not to gaze at her body, but because he couldn't make out what was lying next to her. He had to hold a hand to his eyes to shield them from the snow. Beside her, in a tight bundle and as though it had been tossed aside, was her child. Its little face was blue and its eyes were open. Hallam struggled to keep what little food he had in his stomach down.

'Nice tits,' said one of the redcoats who saw the woman.

'Eyes front!' Hallam turned on the man with a sudden fury. He stood and spoke to the rest of the company. 'If I so much as catch one of you bastards looking at her, you will be put on a charge!'

'Is that a..?' Stubbington started, but blanched.

'Yes,' Hallam said sombrely. 'Poor lass.'

Stubbington stood aghast. 'How did this happen? How?' he appealed.

Hallam could offer no reason. 'You best return to your post,' he could only think to say.

When the ensign had gone, Hallam wrenched a frozen saddlecloth from one of the horses to cover her waxen body. He tucked the baby underneath it and said a brief prayer, but because he was not a God-faring man, he couldn't recite much. When he finished, he stood for a while in solace. He shivered and pulled his scarf closer to his neck and mouth. Then, with nothing more to say, he gave the pale sour light behind a momentary look before walking on.

An hour later, they reached the bridge that crossed a swollen stream. It forked north and east. To the north, the road climbed to a thicket of birch trees, while to the east stood an old ruined mill that shepherds sometimes used to shelter from the weather. The mill was deserted now.

The Slashers marched over the bridge to bar the road, and once they were in position they were ordered to halt. There were just the eight battalion companies, because the Light Bobs and Grenadiers had been sent on ahead with the 27th. The baggage, the regiment's equipment, and their wives and children had all gone on ahead too.

Hallam stamped his boots on the ground, breaking a virgin patch of snow. Like the rest of his men, he couldn't feel his toes. The companies were forbidden to gather wood to build fires because they would be leaving soon, which caused the men to grumble. He noticed one of his men kept looking over his shoulder.

'What's the matter, Shawford?'

The private licked his lips nervously. 'I was just thinking about the wife, sir.' He had married a thin girl who had given him a son, James, known as Little Jim. Rose Shawford was one of the handful of company wives that had followed their men in the campaign.

'Something wrong?' Hallam asked.

'There must be if he's thinking of his wife,' Tipton said, and the men laughed.

Even Shawford joined in, but his gap-toothed laughter died easily and the uneasiness returned quickly. 'Rose and Little Jim aren't well, sir. My son was awake all night with a dreadful cough and Rose ain't herself of late.'

'I'm sure they're going to be fine, Private,' Hallam replied. 'Your Rose is tougher than Sergeant Fox.' The laughter started and faded quickly again. Hallam understood the anxiety of missing, or fretting for a loved one. He shot the private a long confident grin and slapped him on the arm. 'Rose and your boy will be fine. It's this damned country that's the cause of it. How many men have we lost to maladies?' He smiled. Shawford looked horrified. Hallam winced. 'That isn't what I meant.' He sighed, and then spoke carefully. 'What I mean to say is she's a strong woman and Little Jim will be as right as rain once we leave. It won't be long before we're on home soil.'

The private dipped his head. 'Thank you for your kind words, sir.'

'Not at all. And once we're at rest, you have my permission to spend the rest of the day with your family. I'll see to it that you assist Rose with your personal belongings too when the train leaves in the morning.'

'Thank you, sir. If it's all right with the captain?'

Hallam's eyes flicked to Clements, and then back to the private 'Don't you worry about that.'

Colonel Paget, along with Major Osborne, trotted over to the engineer who was making notes in a small leather-bound book. His black side-whiskers were coated with ice, which made him look older than his years. The wind plucked at their scarves and whistled about their muffled ears.

'Will it work in this weather?' Paget asked the engineer, who was called Munday.

'It should go bang for you,' Munday said irritably, as though his reply was to discourage further comment. There were two empty carts next to him, which had contained the gunpowder barrels. Their iron-rimmed wheels were rusted and spindles of ice hung from the axle.

The engineer was accompanied by a half-dozen men from the Royal Military Artificers and Labourers, who were just as morose. A squat sergeant, who carried a small hatchet, hawked and spat over the stonework. The men had finished with the gunpowder that they had packed in the arches and would join the battalion on the journey north once the bridge was destroyed. The sergeant kicked one of the mules on; the empty cart squealed horribly along the road.

'I understand a gun got jammed here,' Paget said affably. He was trying to be pleasant to cover his anxieties. 'Luckily for us, they've managed to get unstuck. Or at least I assume they have.'

Munday just shrugged and said nothing.

A small wind brought a flurry of snow along the bridge and Paget swivelled his head to avoid getting any into his eyes. He turned to Osborne who offered him no support. Instead, the major stared up at the mill, and tapped a hard-boiled egg gently against the pommel of his sword.

'I wish I had some salt,' he said longingly as he pulled some of the brown shell away. 'A little sprinkle of salt would go down a treat.'

Stubbington slashed at some tall yellow stalks with his sword and then walked to where Hallam was standing behind the last file of men on the company's right flank. He saw tracks in the snow, little ones.

Rabbit, he considered. He gazed expectantly at the thin, bare hedges, but could see nothing, and he rubbed his empty stomach. His coat was crusted with snow like the coats of the rest of the men.

'Where's our cavalry, sir?' he asked Hallam.

Hallam was just wondering that too. He explained how they would have to wait here until the horsemen were across the bridge, but how long would that be he wondered. The French vanguard would be cavalry too. They'd be just as cold and tired and neither side would have the advantage. Once the bridge was blown up, the enemy would have to find another way across. But all the same, he felt terribly exposed where they were, which added to the misery. It was like waiting for the hangman's noose.

It was an eerie place, Hallam thought. There was an abandoned round stone windmill to the east, the wooden sails creaked with the wind. Once or twice, a bird flapped in the trees or heavy snow fell from boughs, which caused the men to glance nervously over their shoulders. But other than that, he could only hear the slow trickle of water and the whistling wind.

'How long now?' Paget said to Munday after a few minutes of silence. He was clearly becoming impatient with the wait, shifting irritably in his saddle.

Just then a shout from Captain Richard Hussey Vivian's company alerted them to a single rider approaching from the dark tree line.

As the figure got closer, it became apparent that he was an officer of the Royal Artillery. He wore a black round hat with a huge black fur crest, a large crimson sash curled around his greatcoat and he wore white breeches with topped riding boots. A black scarf was wrapped around his face, which he lowered when he approached the officers on the bridge. Foaming white spittle flecked the horse's bit. He slowed his mount.

'Captain Francis Fyfield, sir,' he said, saluting. Fyfield had warm friendly eyes that betrayed an easy-going nature.

'Good afternoon, Captain,' Paget said cheerfully, pleased that he had someone else to talk to. 'What brings you back here?'

'I come to ask if you could help with a situation that has occurred beyond those trees,' Fyfield said, pointing a gloved hand up the crest. 'I'm in a dreadful quandary to be sure.'

'Go on, old boy,' Paget said as Osborne grunted in displeasure.

'Thank you, sir. One of my guns has broken a wheel. The driver did not see the verge in the road because of the snowfall and the drop broke its spokes. We're just waiting for a spare, but that could take one, maybe two hours, as the limbers were sent on. I wonder if you could send a few men to help my gun-team. They're exhausted from pulling the guns by hand. We've only got one horse left and the poor thing has got cow hocks.'

Paget wasn't sure what Fyfield meant by that and tried not to show it. 'How many guns do you have?'

'Only two now, sir,' Fyfield replied. 'Used to have three, but poor Lizzie cracked her barrel so we had to spike her at Rotheheim.'

'I see.' Paget paused for a second, before deciding that the British cavalry would not be far off and that they all had to march up the rise anyway once the bridge was destroyed. 'We will gladly help you.'

'Thank you, sir,' Fyfield said gratefully.

'The first six battalion companies are to assist with the gun team, while the last two companies can wait with Munday until he has completed his task.'

Osborne instantly snorted with derision.

Paget twisted in the saddle. 'Something you wish to say, Major?'

Osborne had a tendency to question his decisions lately and Paget was getting fed up with the disrespect. More so, because this was in front of a lower ranking officer.

'I wouldn't have expected you to understand our predicament,' Osborne flashed him with a smile that showed no warmth. 'I would not split the regiment up. You've already lent the Light and Grenadiers for some damn foolish assignment. No more, I beg you. It would be seriously imprudent to do that, and I don't think a colonel, especially a newly commissioned one, should continue making reckless decisions without consulting his experienced deputy first.'

'I do not require schooling like some dull-witted child,' Paget said, his nostrils flaring. 'I understand the situation. I do not require your consideration.'

Osborne gave Paget a stern look. 'I implore you to consider my reasoning. I'm sure we can pull the regiment through this mess of a campaign with some dignity if we just allow some common sense.'

Paget said nothing for a moment. 'Reasoning, eh?' he replied distantly, as though he was replaying Osborne's insolence in his mind. He thought he could smell rum on the man's breath.

The major nodded emphatically. 'Reasoning indeed.'

Munday shifted uncomfortably below them. Fyfield was also embarrassed and looked across the river to the dilapidated mill as though he suddenly found it interesting.

'Very well, Osborne,' Paget said nodding. 'I'll leave you in command of the remaining companies whilst I take the rest of battalion up the hill. As an experienced and rational officer, you'll know what to do if the Crapauds show up.' Paget flashed him with a similar smile, then turned to Fyfield. 'Time to rescue your guns, Captain,' he said happily.

And with that, they both trotted away leaving Osborne sour-faced and Munday grinning.

When Munday was satisfied with the charge, he walked back towards the two companies; then, after a few paces, he cast a look over his shoulder and gave a sudden yell in warning.

French dragoons.

The green-coated cloaked horsemen came out of grey-sleet like vengeful wraiths seeking to claim a soul. The dragoons were cavalry excellent for reconnaissance, screening, pursuit and with their pale-as-ice swords, buff breeches and cloth-covered helmets, and were part of the French vanguard.

The enemy had caught up with them.

'Company - make ready!' Hallam was the first officer to react.

'They are ours, you damned fool!' Clements shouted, typical rankness shaping his opinion.

'French bastards!' Private Hulse gave his opinion. A man on the flanks gasped at the shapes.

Clements put down his canteen. 'They-they can't be?' he said, distraught.

'They bloody well are,' Hallam said.

'Make ready your firelocks!' Fox bellowed at the men who were unsure and inactive.

The British were equipped with the 'Brown Bess', or Short Land Pattern musket that had a forty-two inch barrel, and a fifteen-inch triangular socket bayonet. Cold, hungry and bone-weary bodies were suddenly animated in unison. Rags were untied from locks, corks were unplugged from muzzles and the walnut musket stocks were brought straight up, perpendicular to the ground; the left hand on the swell of

233

the stock, the right hand pulling the lock to full cock, and grasping the wrist of the firearm.

'By God, they are French,' Clements said in a strained voice.

'No one ever listens to me,' Hulse said miserably.

Munday tried to run, but the leading Frenchman was already on him. The hooves were thundering and the horse's eyes were white and he slashed down with his sword to split the engineer's skull in two. Blood misted the air crimson. The artificers were running, but one slipped on the ice and the horses ran over him as he attempted to get away. The sergeant pushed the others on and threw himself down on the snow just as a long sword sliced open his shoulder.

'Present!' Hallam ordered. Muskets went to shoulders.

'Present!' Clements copied with a bark. 'I give the goddamn orders here!' His contempt could not be made clearer.

'Aim low!' Hallam ignored Clements. He had tried to drum into the company the care needed when levelling a piece, particularly to the men new to the company who always aimed too high.

The dragoons, perhaps twenty of them, were crossing the span of the bridge. Their mounts had rags tied to their hooves for better footing in the ice and their huge lungs sent great jets of hot breath that steamed in the frigid air.

'Wait for it!' Hallam repeated for the few nervous men who might be tempted to pull their triggers too early.

One of the artificers tried to stop one of the mules from bolting up the hill and gripped the reins, but tripped and was dragged along the ice past the redcoats where one man laughed hysterically.

'Fire!' Clements barked.

'No!' Hallam countermanded, but it was too late.

Perhaps thirty muskets fired, the rest were damp. However, the range was too great. Clements had wasted the volley for none of the horsemen were hurt

'Load!' Hallam ordered because the captain had seemingly forgotten what to do next. Hot gunpowder motes bit the inside of his nose.

Clements licked his dry lips. Vivian's company hadn't fired yet, but the dragoons would soon overrun the two companies. Better to save one than lose both. He looked back at the trees where Paget had taken the other companies. He reckoned that he could make it to the crest taking his company with him. It was better to fight on higher ground.

'Fall back!' he yelled, waving his sword towards the hill, spurring his horse violently. 'Fall back!'

'No!' Hallam grabbed the nearest man that tried to follow Clements. 'Stand your ground! Stand! Sergeant Fox!'

'Sir.'

'You may kill any man who moves without your permission!' Hallam ordered.

Fox grinned like starving man brought a plate of food. 'It'll be a pleasure, sir.'

Hallam turned to Captain Vivian who nodded at him as though he approved of his unwavering ability. Vivian was a dandy, but he was also a good officer. 'Load, you bastards!' Hallam bellowed at the stragglers. They gazed awkwardly, then returned to their files where they were met with growls from those who had remained.

'Carry on, Lieutenant Hallam,' Vivian said, smiling. He turned back to his men. When the enemy were thirty yards away, he flicked his sword down. 'Fire!'

The company's front blossomed into smoke as the musket's fired. Vivian's timing was lethal and the leading dragoons were all killed in an instant. Bodies slid from saddles. Horses screamed and stumbled.

The rest of the dragoons swerved, but as Hallam's men brought muskets to shoulders most took their mounts away. A few stubborn ones, still charged, because the redcoats were in line and not in a defensive formation. Hallam ordered platoon fire and, after the second volley, the surviving horsemen had retreated back over the bridge.

Stubbington's face was drained of colour. 'What about the captain, sir?'

Hallam was silent. He was just staring across the riverbank, where grotesque figures lurked and crouched in the sleet. Dismounted dragoons. He heard a shout from across the water and suddenly two dozen carbines flamed and three men from Vivian's company, who were the closest to the French, fell dead. One body slithered slowly down the ice leaving a ghastly trail of blood.

Clements returned, somehow finding his nerve. His usual surly face was now twisted in a mixture of fury, humiliation and terror. Hallam snubbed him. He was thinking. The bridge was still intact because Munday had not completed the task. The surviving artificers had joined the company and Hallam had an idea.

'His tinderbox,' the hatchet-armed sergeant said after Hallam quizzed him. 'He uses it to light the fuses.' His speech was like the hissing of a snake because he was missing his front teeth. 'It must be still on him,' he said, wincing as a colleague tried to staunch the blood pouring from the wound.

One of Vivian's grenadiers was shot through the bowels and was dragged screaming back behind the line before the space was filled.

'Mister Stubbington,' Hallam said. 'I am going down to the bridge to light the bugger up.'

'Sir?'

'To light the fuse!' Hallam snapped at the ensign's lack of comprehension. 'It's the only bloody way to stop the enemy from crossing.' He purposely ignored Clements who had sheepishly joined Osborne behind Vivian's company. Hallam gazed at them. Useless cowardly bastards, the pair of them. He would look after the men himself as Clements didn't give a damn.

'Let me come, sir.'

'No, stay here with the company.'

'But, sir-' Stubbington went to object, but Hallam cut him short.

'Do as you're bloody told!' Hallam turned to his men. 'Company - fix bayonets!'

The men slotted the blades and he saw that Vivian's men were doing the same. It was the proper directive when threatened with cavalry so Hallam ordered it.

'Advance!' Hallam led them forward, the bayonet points glinting. He would get the men closer to the bridge to provide covering fire, but out of harm's way if there was a premature explosion.

The higher-pitched shots of carbines snapped at the redcoats and a man in the front rank gasped before collapsing onto his front. He did not move again. Another man was uttering a prayer over and over.

Hallam knew there wasn't much time. In a few minutes, the French could launch a larger attack and the long straight swords would chop and hack, and moustached faces beneath brass peaks would grin and laugh at the slaughter.

'Halt!' Hallam saw that Vivian had understood what he was doing and so his company edged closer to the dark swollen river. A man stepped away and Hallam pushed him back into his rank. 'Take over, Mister Stubbington! Sergeant Fox!'

'Sir!'

'Keep him alive,' Hallam jerked his head at the ensign and Fox grinned. Then, Hallam took a deep breath and sprinted down the snow that reached the tops of his boots.

'Platoon fire!' Fox shouted.

The splintering noise of sustained musket fire hammered towards the French, the echoes pounding up the slope to the tree line.

'Thank you, Sergeant Fox,' said Stubbington. 'I'll take it from here.'

'Very good, sir.'

Hallam threaded through the French bodies and jumped a horse that was lying on its side, legs jerking. A bullet fluttered past him. He drew his sword. It was an old one that he had been given as a gift from his friend and mentor Captain George Milsum who had bequeathed him the sword on his deathbed. Milsum had carried the sword as an ensign at the capture of Quebec in the Seven Years' War. It was an old sword, ugly, straight-bladed and brutal, yet had a bluish tint and sparkled as thought it had just been crafted, and he would not go into battle without it.

Hallam slipped on the ice and from a puddle of blood that oozed thickly from a dying horse. His hat fell from his head and a bullet clanged on his scabbard. He could see horsemen off across to the west on the road, and dismounted dragoons who were stooping over frozen hedgerows, the river banks and across the lichen covered stonework of the bridge. He saw the long fuse line and then he saw Munday, his head was nearly cloven in two. Hallam could see brain amongst the glistening gore. There were dragoons on this side of the river and the nearest one saw him first.

Hallam slashed across his body to parry the attack, using the strongest lower third of the blade, nearest the hilt known as the forte. The blades rang like a bell. The Frenchman was gritting his teeth as his blade scraped down the steel to be stopped by Hallam's sword guard. Hallam threw off the blade and then punched forward with his cross-guard to shatter the Frenchman's front teeth and split his lips. Blood and splintered bone erupted from his ruined mouth as he fell backwards. The second dragoon, whose shot had struck Hallam's scabbard, now charged at him, swinging his sword and yelling as though he was gripped in terror. Hallam desperately brought up his sword and the blades crashed against each other. His assailant slipped, tried to regain his balance, but Hallam used it to his advantage and he disentangled his sword to thrust up between the Frenchman's ribs. He gave Hallam a look of surprise before he died. The injured dragoon, blood trickling down his chin, got to his knees and Hallam chopped down with his sword and the blade hit the side of the man's cloth-covered helmet, making a clanging sound, and ripping the canvas away to reveal a flash of naked brass.

The third dragoon was more cautious and took time to aim his carbine at Hallam's trunk. He pulled the trigger. The hammer went forward and there was a dull click. Nothing happened. The powder was damp and the dragoon swore for the weapon being useless. He dropped the carbine and fumbled for his sword, which hung from its wrist strap. He was a large man, clumsy with big hands and thick fingers and couldn't bring the sword up in time before Hallam kicked him massively between the legs. The Frenchman gave an odd high-pitched wail before clutching at his groin, falling sideways and rolling on the ground in agony.

Hallam saw more shapes from the road and more carbine fire snapped at him. Bullets whistled overhead and smacked into the stonework, showering him and the three dragoons with sparks and stone chippings. But none of the enemy approached. He bent down and went through Munday's heavy coat, until his hand touched something metallic in one of the pockets: the tinderbox.

Hallam heard French voices and he looked up. A handful of dragoons were now running towards him. He jerked aside from a puff of smoke and a bullet fanned the air by his ear. But then an explosion of musketry to his left threw the dragoons down in an instant. He could just make out Stubbington in the musket smoke and he smiled. The ensign appeared to be in control. *Good boy*, Hallam said to himself, *good boy*.

He opened the tin case and within was the fire-steel, charcloth and a piece of chipped flint. Good, that was everything he needed. He shortened the slow match by ripping it apart by the main charge, then struck the flint on the ring of steel. A tiny spark flew, but died in the wind. He tried again and the same thing happened. A bullet smacked into the arch above his head, but he didn't look up. He bent closer to the slow match. The spark caught the linen on the third attempt, but it went out. He tried a fourth time and he blew on it until the tinder flared up. A ghost of a smile lit his eyes when he put the flame to the fuse and the powder fizzed and smoked. One of the dragoons groaned in pain and Hallam hit him hard in the belly.

He could hear horses. Out of the greyness, the French were launching a larger mounted assault, perhaps because they had brought reinforcements. The bridge had to be destroyed now! Another crackle of musketry and Vivian's men threw down three dragoons, but it was the charging horsemen that worried Hallam. The fuse was still fizzing, but it was taking too damn long. The enemy were charging. Hallam heard a French officer screaming at his men. The fuse burned fiercely. He only had seconds. He turned and ran for dear life.

'Fire!' Vivian, resplendent in his fine uniform, shouted. Another volley tore into the French and a dragoon, hit, momentarily staggered, and then fell into the water. It swirled red.

'Back!' Hallam shouted desperately. 'Get back!'

Behind him, the mounted dragoons galloped past the charge, the hooves clattered on the ice and stone. One man saw the smoke and dismounted. He lifted one boot to stamp out the fuse.

But he was too late.

The fuse puffed once more and then the world exploded.

The fizzing, sparking fuse ate into Munday's charge and the powder ignited. Great flickering tongues of flame leapt into the air, where the smoke turned it instantly black.

Hallam threw himself onto the ground at the moment of the explosion. He was dazed by the overwhelming, ear-splitting detonation. He stood, slipped, and staggered towards the redcoats. Great chunks of stone and debris smashed down onto the snow, ice and water. Hallam slipped once more, but hands picked him up and steadied him.

It was Sergeant Fox. His mouth was open, but Hallam could not hear him.

'What?' he said, and rubbed his ears. The sound was dull at first, hardly audible, and then it was replaced with a high-pitched ringing.

'Are you all right, sir?' Fox was saying.

Hallam groaned. 'Yes,' he shouted.

The redcoats were cheering. Hallam turned to see the destruction that he had caused. The bridge was completely gone. The enemy horseman had been obliterated and the few survivors retreated dazed, confused and beaten. The bridge was nothing but a blackened stump. He had done it.

'Well done, sir!' Stubbington was almost jumping in joy. 'You're a damned hero!'

'Jesus, my ears.'

Vivian came over and slapped Hallam's back. Osborne was ignoring him, and was speaking to Paget's adjutant who had come down to investigate the commotion.

'You're a reckless bastard, Lieutenant,' a voice spoke from behind. Hallam turned. Clements, who had been hovering in sulky silence, gave a begrudging smile, which was more like a grimace.

'Congratulations, Mister Stubbington,' Hallam said, whilst looking directly at Clements. His voice was still loud. 'You kept your nerve and you never faltered. The men will respect you for that. You're now a far better officer than some I can think of.'

Clements looked as though he had been struck. His cheeks twitched violently at the contemptuous insolence. He was unable do anything, because he knew he had panicked, and shaking with vehemence, he let Hallam walk away, the hero of the hour.

*

Mr Thomas Carew, the 28th's quartermaster wanted to get moving.

The battalion, along with the rest of the 6th Brigade, was not due to set out until nine o'clock, but Carew had been marshalling the baggage train two hours before dawn in the hope that they would be ready at least an hour before nine. This was because the bullocks plodded and the baggage and transport always held up the main column. Carew wanted to change that. Colonel Paget had been furious with the last few days trundling pace and Carew wanted to show him how good a job he could do. It was going well until the damned children got in the way; weaving in and out of the bullocks, getting tangled in the chains and hanging from the carts to see who could last the longest before falling. At first, Carew threatened them with the whip, but begrudgingly saw the funny side and let himself warm to the laughter of playing children.

It was then that there were shouts coming from the wives and Carew signalled the train to stop. He was furious. He suspected a child had yanked boxes off the carts.

'What's going on here?' he yelled.

'Mrs Shawford and her boy are missing, Mr Carew,' answered one of the wives. 'They ain't been seen this morning.'

'I thought I saw her at the rear?'

'She ain't there!' Another wife said. A young baby fed at her breast.

Carew scratched his head. He could feel his entire scalp move from the lice. 'Where's Private Shawford? I thought he was helping you lot pack your things?' A couple of the company's married men had been allowed to help their wives and friends with the move. The woman was busy feeding her child. Carew swore. 'So has the private and his wife absconded from the army?'

'No,' the woman said and yelped as the baby bit her nipple. 'You little sod. You're just like your bleeding father.'

Carew, frustrated, ignored her and went down the line to inspect the carts himself.

Fifteen minutes went by.

The train was still stationary and a company officer came up to Carew. It was Lieutenant Hallam.

'What's the hold up, Tom? The colonel's not very happy. Rumour has it that Major-General Cathcart is on his way here.' Cathcart commanded the brigade and was a stern man with little time for incompetence.

Carew looked terrified. 'Oh, dear God!' Then he noticed Hallam grinning and knew he was being teased. 'Jack, don't play any more games with me. My heart won't take it. Private Shawford is in your company, is he not?'

'He is. What's he done?'

'Well, he ain't here and his wife ain't here either.'

Hallam shot Carew a serious glance. 'I allowed him to spend some time with his wife as she's been unwell. Have you seen them this morning?'

'I thought I had, but I haven't. What am I to do now?'

Shawford was a reliable soldier and one Hallam considered would never desert his post. There must be some misunderstanding. Some miscommunication. The usual army calamities.

'I'll find them,' Hallam said, gaping up and down the baggage train. 'You get going, Tom. He's bound to be here somewhere.'

He walked down the train until his curiosity was satisfied. A couple of women were dressed in heavy shawls and had their pinched faces drawn up, so he had to ask them to drop their garments just to be sure. They weren't Rose Shawford. One of them was singing a mournful tune that pricked the hairs on the back of his neck. He returned to his company.

He accosted Stubbington who was trying not to get in the way of Clements horse.

'He's in his file, sir,' the ensign said. 'All present and correct.'

Hallam frowned, feeling that he had wasted his time, and stumped over to the private who was indeed in his file.

'Why in God's name are you here? I gave you permission to help your wife this morning.'

The private looked aggrieved. 'You did, sir. Except that the captain found out and ordered me back here.'

'He what?' Hallam threw his head to the sky in disgust. He then gawked at Clements, eyes tightening with contempt. He didn't wait for the private to answer and walked to the captain's side. 'What's this I hear about Private Shawford?' he said, unable to curb his deepening anger. 'I gave him permission to be with his sick wife.'

Clements ignored Hallam's challenging glare for a moment, pursed his lips and then turned to him. 'You gave an order that was not permitted, Lieutenant. An order that is not given by me is thus not official. For that insolence, Private Shawford will be punished for deserting his post.'

Hallam spluttered in anger. 'You can't do that.'

Clements laughed at his reaction. 'Of course I can. I'm the captain of this company, and I'll damn well do what I like. I've thought about bringing back picquetting,' he said, smiling widely with satisfaction.

Hallam glowered at the thought of the old punishment of making a wrong-doer stand bare foot for a length of time on a tent-peg being brought back.

'Or perhaps I'll simply have the scoundrel flogged?' Clements said it as though he was questioning himself. 'Nothing like a flogging to instil discipline where it's needed.'

'You'll do no such thing,' Hallam vented, before walking back to the unfortunate private. 'I'm sorry to say that Rose and Little Jim are missing,' he said quietly so that Clements could not hear. 'Quartermaster Carew informed me. I checked and I couldn't see them either.'

The old soldier seemed to shudder. 'What?'

'Don't worry,' Hallam said calmly. 'We're not going to abandon them.'

'What are you going to do, sir?'

'I'm going to get help,' Hallam replied, before disappearing.

Twenty minutes later, and against Clements' wishes, Sergeant Fox, Privates' Shawford, Hulse, Tipton and Phelps were called out of the retreating line by Major Osborne. They were told to report to Hallam at the double, before leaving their packs behind with the rest of the baggage.

'Ready your firelocks,' Hallam grinned when they found him at the rear of the battalion with the trundling bandsmen.

'Sir?' Fox, knowing how to deal with eccentric officers had perfected every answer possible, but this request and situation was entirely new to him.

'Do as you bloody told, Sergeant,' Hallam checked his pistol was loaded. When the men were ready, he explained. 'I've got some news,' he spoke to Shawford. 'Your wife and son were seen on the edge of that wood,' he pointed to the smear of trees to the south. 'One of the wives of the 27th saw a mother and son match their description. Rose was wearing her dark-red shawl, was she not?'

'Yes,' Shawford said, frowning. 'What would Rose be doing there?'

'Collecting firewood?' Hulse suggested. He had lost his round hat and instead wore a woollen forage cap that was a damp shapeless mass.

Hallam brought out his fob watch to check the time. 'Perhaps your son ran in there and Mrs Shawford duly followed him?'

The private glowered. 'The little bugger,' he said. 'I'll tan his hide for the trouble he's caused.' Everyone present knew that he would not do such a thing, because he doted on the boy.

'It's eleven o'clock,' Hallam said. 'Let's find them and bring them back before it gets dark.'

They jogged down the road. Their bayonets, cartridges and whatever meagre foodstuffs they had in their haversacks bounced with each footfall.

Phelps wore two sack cloths over his jacket, because he had not been issued with a greatcoat. It made his body look ungainly. 'Any Frenchie bastards hereabouts, sir?' he asked.

'That's why the lieutenant ordered loaded weapons,' Fox answered, as though he was dealing with a difficult child.

Hallam scanned the trees ahead. The wind whipped cold. 'Our outlying picquets are a quarter of a mile away and we have the cavalry behind us protecting our arses.' The small detachment of men laughed derisively as was accustomed to the infantryman's usual scorn for their mounted comrades.

They jumped a frozen dike; Phelps only just managed to avoid tumbling into it. They ran on across a snowy field that had turned to slush from the rains. Tipton slipped, but kept his balance, and as every man held their muskets by the trail, no triggers were pulled and thus exposing their position.

'Here are some prints!' Hulse exclaimed.

Hallam studied the marks on the ground. Two sets. One definitely belonged to a child.

'This is where they went,' Hallam said with a growing smile. 'We'll soon find them.'

'How did you allow us to come on this special task, sir?' Shawford asked as they entered the woodland. It was eerily silent.

'I spoke to the colonel,' Hallam confirmed with a wink. 'I told him everything.'

Shawford let his eyes come accustomed to the darkness. 'The captain told me that I would be punished for leaving my post.'

'Like I said,' Hallam crept forward, free hand pulling away low branches from his unshaven face. 'I spoke to the colonel. The captain won't be doing anything.'

'Thank you, sir.' The private's relief was heartfelt.

Their boots crunched on snow as they hunched underneath boughs and threaded past thick bellied trees. Mistletoe dotted the knotted limbs. They couldn't see any footprints, but they followed the path into the heart of the shadowy wood.

'If we see a deer,' Tipton asked, 'are we allowed to shoot it, sir?'

'After we've made sure that it isn't Mrs Shawford, Little Jim, or any French bastards wandering about,' Hallam replied.

There was a sliver of water, black like a huge spill of ink upon the snow. Hallam saw something on its surface. It was a dog, swollen and hewn. Someone had killed it many days ago and tossed the corpse into the stream.

A woman screamed from somewhere in the trees, and immediately a great wave of dread swept over the redcoats.

'Rose!' Shawford hurried forward, eyes dwindling in fear.

'Rags off,' Fox ordered, and the men removed the strips of cloth tied around the musket locks.

'And fix bayonets,' Hallam added.

The track turned to thick mud, and beyond a tangle of brushwood that half-covered the track, was a farm. Its walls were coated in mould, the roof was dark with moss and rot. There was nobody outside, so the sound must have come from inside the farm.

'Smoke,' Hulse said, jutting his chin to the blue-grey covering amongst the dark branches.

'I'll find out who's inside. Wait here and keep alert!' Hallam rasped. He skirted the main path to skulk towards one of the shuttered windows on the building's eastern wall. There was a crack in the wood and he gently inched closer to peer inside.

There was a hearth-fire with a pot bubbling away and a crude table made of a length of wood over two pieces of cut timber. A joint of salted meat hung from the rafters, away from the rats and mice. He couldn't see anyone but there was a murmur of voices. Hallam leaned in even closer and a young boy with hair the colour of straw saw the movement. It was Little Jim. Thank God, the child was safe. Snot hung from his nose and he was pale. Hallam put a finger to his lips, but the boy, not even four, did not understand, and just gaped innocently back.

Movement near the window. A man wearing a blue jacket took up a stone bottle and wiped his long flowing moustache afterwards. His hair was shoulder-length, falling unruly over the red collar of his jacket. Tied around his neck was a filthy red neckerchief. A woman moaned and the man grinned with tobacco stained teeth at the sound. Laughter and French voices. The woman whimpered and Little Jim turned to watch unseen figures. His eyes glistened and his bottom lip dropped. The woman began to plead and Hallam instinctively growled.

The Frenchman, hearing the noise, pushed the shutter open and the pistol's cold muzzle pressed against his forehead.

Hallam watched the man's eyes narrow and then widen, before his mouth opened. Whatever he intended to shout was never heard, because the ball smashed through his skull to erupt in a bloody spray as it exited the back of the Frenchman's head.

There was a brief moment of silence.

'28th!' Hallam shouted, as he stepped back against the wall. 'Make ready!'

French shouts dizzied the air and the woman sobbed.

Before he had shot the man through the head, Hallam had seen figures in the farm's murky interior. Eyes and faces tinted orange from the flame light and there was the unmistakable image of Mrs Shawford. She was half-dressed and lying down. Whatever the French were doing to her, Hallam could only guess with disgust.

There was no time to load the pistol again, so Hallam tucked it into his sash, and dragged his sword free. His men were crouched where he had left them, their coats just visible in the cold dank undergrowth.

The shutters to the front opened with a loud thud. Hallam saw two muskets appear at the window. A musket fired and Hallam knew one of

245

his men had taken the shot. He also knew Fox would be berating the private, but his concern was for Private Shawford, who had sprung up to charge the farm. The French had an easy target.

Hallam rushed towards the window, boots slipping in the mud, and reached out to grab the nearest enemy musket. He drove it forward onto the next one as triggers were pulled to send stabs of flame and gouts of powder smoke into the air. The proximity of the discharge was loud in his ears, but the shots had gone wide. Hallam twisted back and thrust his sword into the open space and felt the honed blade bite into flesh. He yanked it back and side-stepped as another musket crashed to send the racing ball high into the scrub.

'They're both inside!' Hallam wanted to warn his men. They were all rising.

The door opened abruptly. A tall Frenchman, wearing a blue jacket with red epaulettes and a bicorn with a drooping red horsehair plume, stepped outside hefting a bayonet-tipped musket. Shawford screamed as he charged. The enemy lowered his musket, weak sunlight caught on the long blade. For a heartbeat, Hallam thought the private would impale himself.

'Bloody French bastard!' Shawford snarled, and jerked his trigger. The bullet caught the Frenchman in the gullet and blew out through the back of his spine. The body dropped like a stone in water.

Another enemy emerged. This one wore a long, stained coat and cavalry overalls. The man flourished a straight-bladed sword, but Shawford reversed his musket and swung it with incredible force. The heavy stock collided with the side of the man's face with a sickening crack that sent him sprawling into the mud. Two more Frenchmen dashed out of the farm. The first brandished a large horse-pistol and Shawford brought his musket back to its correct position and rammed the blackened muzzle into the man's Adam's apple with the force of a sledgehammer. The enemy staggered, choking and Hallam's sword slashed left-to-right across his belly, sending coils of guts spilling and steaming onto the ground. The other screamed like a madman, swinging a two-handed axe. Shawford ducked, the blade knocked off his mildewed round-hat, and he ran inside the farm. Fox slashed the air with his bayonet and the enemy rushed forth his broad blade to parry the steel. The sergeant brought his blade up and the Frenchman chopped down to meet it, twisted as he anticipated Fox's next attack, but Hulse's bayonet ripped into his flank. The Frenchman screamed.

Fox grunted as he stabbed his blade into the man's belly, who then collapsed, momentarily trapping both weapons with his dying body.

Hallam heard sobbing as he entered the farmhouse. Shawford was dressing Rose and Little Jim was crying. Hallam soothed the boy and picked him up.

'There, there, my love,' Shawford was saying over and over. 'No need to worry. I'm here now.' He heard his son and reached over and took him from Hallam. Squeezing the boy tight, the old soldier could not control his emotions. He grasped Rose and the family cried and hugged each other. Hallam decided to leave them to it and then, out of the corner of his eye, noticed a seated figure next the hearth. The Frenchman grinned at Hallam's surprise with crooked black teeth. He looked relatively unhurt, but a swelling on his cheek revealed that Shawford had just struck him.

Hallam stepped outside to check on his men who were already going through the enemy's pockets, feeling for hidden coins in the seams of coats. Haversacks and pouches torn off, some of the contents scattered about. The wounded man wearing the overalls had been bayoneted.

'They appear to be from different battalions, sir,' Fox was brusque, because he had been caught plundering and was embarrassed.

If Hallam was offended, then he didn't show it. 'Deserters?' His eyes fell upon the ragged uniforms.

'A motley collection of brigands, sir,' Hulse said, counting the tarnished coins, which they would share out.

'I suspect that this rabble had been hiding here for some time,' Fox said, gazing around. 'Quite a secluded spot for this den of thieves.'

'"*The robbed that smiles steals something from the thief*",' Hulse said to no one in particular.

'What are you going on about, Private?' Fox said, bewildered.

Hulse pointed and the men turned to the doorway. 'Othello,' he said.

Shawford, despite his wife's terrible distress, and the tears that glistened on his dark cheeks, beamed. 'Thank you,' his voiced wobbled. 'Thank everyone of you, for saving my family.'

'Think nothing of it,' Hallam said, extremely pleased that they had found Mrs Shawford and the boy in one piece, despite the dreadful ordeal. Rose was white and sweating, tell-tale signs of the illness she was suffering from. She wiped the snot from her son's nose with a cloth. Hallam went to add that they should return to the regiment when a shape moved beyond the farmhouse.

A musket banged and Private Phelps spun backwards dead with a bullet in his heart.

Hallam saw sinister-looking men coming from the brush. 'Get in here, now!' he jerked a thumb at the farm.

More muskets exploded, but the redcoats managed to make it clear through the door without injury.

'Jesus!' Tipton gasped.

'More of the bastards!' Hulse ran to the farthest window through to the sleeping quarters that stank of decay and stale urine. The glass had a crack running up the filthy pane, but the private could see men crouch outside.

'How many do you see, Hulse?' Hallam called as he and Shawford pushed a heavy chest to the door and pulled the remnants of a barrel on top to fortify the entrance. Little Jim was crying and Shawford took his son in his arms, brought out a little soldier carved out of wood and let the boy play with it. Rose's face was unreadable.

'I count eight, sir.'

'Are there any other weapons in here?' Hallam said, wanting to keep the men busy.

'Jesus,' Tipton was saying over and over.

'Private Tipton, count to five and report,' Hallam ordered him.

The private wiped his face, chest heaving and belly squirming with nerves. 'Two Frenchie muskets, and two dead 'un's in here, sir. One of them stinks like a latrine.'

'What are we to do with this one, sir?' Fox asked of the bruised Frenchman. He brought out his sharpening stone and ran it expertly up his bayonet, revelling in the lethal zing the motion produced.

Hallam was loading his pistol. 'I don't know yet.'

The Frenchman fingered a chain around his neck and started to laugh.

Hallam turned to him. 'What's so funny, you Crapaud bastard?'

The enemy wiped saliva from his chin, which had dribbled out of his foul-looking mouth. 'You're going to let me go,' he replied in perfect English.

Hallam finished ramming the charge home and slotted the ramrod back in the rings beneath the barrel. 'You're not going anywhere.'

'May I have your name?'

'It's Lieutenant Hallam to you.'

The Frenchman's expression changed from absolute hilarity to grave solemnity in an instant. 'My name is Tristan Benoit. My father

248

named me Tristan after the famous knight of King Arthur.' Benoit chuckled. 'He was such a romantic. I hated it as a boy, but I read *Le Morte d'Arthur* and I grew to love it. Have you read the book? No? I have had my own adventures. Like the chivalrous knight of the stories. Some worthy, most not,' he said, falling into laughter again. 'I am a *capitaine* in the -'

'You're a goddamn disgrace, that's what you are!' Hallam interrupted nastily. He was angered by the man's self-absorbance and cocksure bloody demeanour.

'I am *Capitaine-*' Benoit said stubbornly, but was cut off again.

'Deserters, murderers and...' Hallam paused to choose the correct word, 'defilers of women, have no rank!' He caught the Frenchman's gaze and held it. 'You may command the scum out there, but you have no military authority, or influence in here.'

Benoit breathed heavily, the inflammation on his cheek looked pulpy. 'My men will kill all of you. The only way to stop that is for you to let me go.'

Hallam watched him, hands fingering the loaded pistol. He could feel the heat of the fire begin to warm his bones, and despite the situation, it felt damned good. 'And then what? What happens if I let you go?'

Benoit showed his rotten teeth again. 'We will simply walk away. Leave you.'

'Walk away,' Hallam copied dubiously. Eyes still on the Frenchman he spoke to his men. 'Hulse! What are the bastards doing?'

'Just waiting, sir.'

'Tipton?'

'Same here, sir.'

Benoit looked about the room. 'There is nothing here for us anymore. We intended to move away before the snow's came, but it was early. So we stayed. It's been two months.'

'No wonder this place smells like a shit hole. What have you been doing all this time?'

The Frenchman shrugged. 'Surviving.'

Hallam laughed contemptuously. 'Surviving? Don't you mean robbing and murdering? What an honourable man you are. You have no virtues of a knight.'

Benoit coughed as though his lungs were coming loose. 'I don't care what you think of me, or my men. We have been through hell. Hell, I tell you. I have seen terrible things. Things that would make an ordinary man piss his breeches at and scream until the surgeon would have to cut out his tongue to quieten him.' He gazed at the flames. 'I was at Jemappes. You heard of that?'

'No.'

'We defeated the Austrians and took Brussels,' Benoit said proudly. 'I lost many friends in that battle. Good men. They were heroes of the Revolution. I was wounded badly by cannon fire. I lay there in the day, unable to get up, as the battle raged. I fell unconscious. I woke in the night to find black creatures stripping the wounded of their possessions and in most cases, their lives. They missed me and I managed, despite the agony, to drag myself away and was found and taken to the hospital.'

'Is that when you deserted?' Hallam couldn't help but needle the man.

Benoit paused to consider the reply. 'My leg was terribly damaged, but I was spared the surgeon's knife. I was part of the garrison that stayed here, but after we lost hold of this country, I found myself uninterested in the army. I drifted away to join others. I've been in command for six months. I'm a good man-'

'Piss off,' Hallam said.

'I am a good man!' The Frenchman looked outraged.

'That,' Hallam said, 'from a man who has murdered, robbed and raped, is rich. Don't tell me that you wanted to do good things, but instead ended up doing bad things. You're nothing more than a common brigand.'

Benoit did not answer.

Outside a voice called out.

'Your sweethearts are missing you,' Hallam mocked.

'They are asking if I am alive.'

'You can tell them you live.'

Benoit sighed. 'They will not be happy until I am free. Just let me go, and I'll give you my word that we'll leave in peace.'

Hallam leaned in closer to him, trying not to let the stink of the man's fetid breath affect him. 'How many men do you lead?'

Benoit puckered his lips. 'There were thirty of us at dawn.'

Hallam laughed. 'You lying bastard. I don't think so. There are eight out there, maybe another two concealed. At best you have ten men remaining. And you want me to lead my men, a woman and a child out there for you to shoot us in the back.'

'I give you my word that we will not do that,' Benoit said.

Little Jim, shivering, said something to his father and the Frenchman turned to look at the boy.

Hallam reached forward and struck Benoit hard across the face. The sudden attack startled everyone. 'If you look at him, or Mrs Shawford again,' he said menacingly, 'I'll cut your goddamn throat.'

Benoit looked defiant for a moment, but then understood the threat was real. 'As I said, we have been through hell.'

'So has every soldier of this damned campaign!' Hallam exploded. 'You think because you survived a battle and saw the horror of what it brings entitles you to a life of brigandage? No, sir, it does not! That is a piss poor excuse. Now you're going to sit there with your mouth shut while I talk to your men.'

'They don't speak English.'

Hallam glared at the man. 'Then it will be quick.'

He walked over to where Hulse watched from the window and studied the men outside. He counted eight. They were crouched low and were hard-faced. One man had an eye-patch and another wore an Austrian uniform, and all had muskets.

'They have stripped poor Phelps of his firelock and cartridges, sir,' Hulse said in a quiet voice. 'They were laughing.'

Hallam growled. He made sure Hulse was loaded before checking Tipton.

'They come any closer and I'll shoot them, sir,' the boy tried to sound confident.

'That's what you're paid to do, Private,' Hallam said. Tipton looked at him, saw the smirk on his lieutenant's face and grinned back.

'Very good, sir.'

'I was going to say shoot the ugliest one first, but you're spoilt for choice.'

Tipton chuckled.

Hallam made a mental note. They had four of their own muskets, the two French and his pistol. He checked the Frenchman he had shot through the window to find a clasp knife and a smaller pistol tucked into his belt. He went about loading the French 1777 Charleville musket when Rose came over and snatched it out of his hands.

'Mrs Shawford-'

'I can load a musket, Lieutenant Hallam,' she said truculently. She was pallid and sweat beaded her forehead and top lip. 'Even a Frenchie one.'

251

Hallam thought better than to disagree and left her to it. He walked over to her husband. 'Does she know what she's doing?' he asked. 'She might break the damn thing.'

Shawford grinned. 'Let her do it, sir. She won't give up until she does it. Stubborn like her ma. She'll do it until she breaks it. Or breaks a nail. And if she breaks a nail, then she'll definitely break it.'

Hallam turned when the musket cocked. Rose shot him a look of triumph. 'Thank you, Mrs Shawford,' he said, trying not to smile. She reached for the second gun. 'I think we have another volunteer, lads,' he said.

The men gave a ragged cheer, which provoked a hail of musketry from outside. Little Jim started to cry again, but Shawford hushed the boy.

'Do not return fire!' Hallam barked. The balls had hit the roof and walls. 'They're just trying to scare us.'

And they're doing a grand job of it, he mused. Hallam's eyes skimmed across to his men to gauge their reaction. Both Hulse and Tipton were trying not to let the threat upset them. Fox was his usual glowering self. Shawford's tough exterior was weakening with every minute of being trapped here with his abused, ill wife and son. He was fearful of what might befall them and Hallam sympathised. Benoit lapsed into silence, which was good. Hallam didn't want to hear him talk anymore; however, he half-wondered whether the Frenchman's offer was genuine or not. Could he be trusted? Would they really be allowed to leave without being attacked? It was pulling his thoughts like a loose thread. But he considered that having Fox and Shawford with him was enough to see they had the advantage. Besides, they were warming up whilst the enemy outside must be getting colder. They would stay here tonight and break out in the early hours when the enemy was frozen. A quick dash to safety against cold and tired men. That would work. They couldn't stay here long, otherwise they might run into the French vanguard. It was risky, but there was little choice. Nonetheless, Hallam felt confident of success.

A voice called from outside and Hallam was tempted to ignore it, but Hulse called him over.

'Bugger's speaking English, sir.'

Hallam considered Benoit a liar and everything he said was a game of deceit. He snorted his disdain. 'What did he say?'

'Sounded like he wanted to talk,' Hulse said.

Hallam watched the man with the eye-patch walk closer. His hands were up and he appeared unarmed.

Hallam thought for a second. 'I'm going to open the door, but you keep your eyes on these bastards. If any one of them moves you shout out.'

'I will, sir.'

He told Tipton the same and moved back to the door. Rose and Little Jim moved into a little room, barely big enough for a cupboard and Hallam guessed this was the pantry. Two stone jars were broken on the floor and he thought he could smell the tang of pickled foodstuffs for an instant.

'Watch that bastard,' Hallam said to Fox, as he moved the chest aside. The door creaked open.

The deserter calmly walked to the farmhouse, stopping about three feet away. He studied Hallam's partially shadowed face for weakness and was surprised to see none. For months, the group had raided local villages; stealing food, killing the menfolk and raping the women. They had surprised a British cavalry detachment, which had used a stable a mile to the west. The horsemen had not thought to check the woods for enemies, and Benoit's men had bayoneted them in their sleep. They had taken the horses, but a few of Benoit's men had ridden off in search of other employment, leaving four horses. The beasts had been eaten as the cold weather came in and food became harder to come by. No one searched for them and their confidence grew. On one occasion, they had captured a Hanoverian messenger, sent to bring a British brigade into the nearest town, but they killed him. Benoit's men remained untouched and untroubled, and free to continue their criminalities.

'You are an officer, *oui?*' the deserter enquired. He was confident and looked as though he had years of military experience.

'I am.' Hallam looked the man up and down too. His bicorn was frayed and without a plume and cockade. He had a goat skin pack, a short-bladed knife in a brown leather sheath at his hip and his long coat hung down to his knees. Hallam noticed his boots were held together with twine.

The man's one eye flickered to the windows. '*Capitaine* Benoit is inside?'

'Yes.'

'May I see him?'

'No,' Hallam said laconically. Behind him, the walls glowed orange from the fire.

The Frenchman shrugged. 'I would like to speak to him.'

Hallam was tempted to deny him, but considered speaking through the door would be the lesser of evils. 'Step forward and speak only in English.'

The deserter attempted to object. 'My English is not so good.'

'I think it is good enough,' Hallam said. 'Now step forward and speak, or bugger off.'

The Frenchman frowned in disagreement; cast a look over his shoulder, then deciding it was futile to stand his ground, walked towards the door.

Hallam did not see if the man had made a signal to the men, but considered the notion. As the deserter stepped up to the door, he could smell decay, sweat and smoke emanating from his clothes.

'May I see him please?' The deserter tried to see past Hallam's frame.

'I said no,' Hallam replied firmly.

The Frenchman licked his chapped lips. The skin on his face was stretched tight over wide cheek bones, and his blood-shot eyes hung with thick lids. '*Mon Capitaine.*'

There was silence.

'Speak up,' Hallam ordered the captive without turning around.

'I am here, Sas,' Benoit said.

Sas did not clearly know what to do. He scratched his face with dirty nails. 'Sir?'

Benoit hesitated as if mulling over what he might say next, and drew breath to speak. 'Wait for me. I shall be free soon.'

'I will, *mon Capitaine.*'

'You and I have been friends for a long time, *non*?'

One Eye smiled. '*Oui.*'

'You were at my side at Jemappes,' Benoit said. 'Remember the dawn light that morning?'

'I do. It was beautiful.'

Benoit sounded wistful. 'It was September, wasn't it? Crisp evening's with beautiful sunrises. And the battle started as the sun was still climbing. How many times did we attack?'

'I lost count, sir.'

Benoit chuckled. 'And we rallied at midday. Remember what we did then?'

A smile spread on Sas's lips. He patted his chest. '*Oui.*'

'Then go now, *mon ami*,' Benoit ordered. 'Go and wait for me.'

Sas went to move but Hallam leaned in closer to the door. 'What time is it now?' he asked politely. The Frenchman merely frowned in evident puzzlement. 'The watch you have underneath your stinking, flea-ridden coat. What time does it show?'

Sas's eye twitched. How had the officer known about the watch? He hesitated before opening up his coat to reveal a battered timepiece. He clicked open the lid and showed Hallam its face.

It was five minutes to noon.

Hallam grinned.

The pistol exploded to send the ball straight through the door, to pluck the Frenchman backwards dead onto the ground.

'They're coming!' Hallam slammed the door shut as a volley of musketry struck the doorway.

Benoit screamed and went to get on his feet until Fox stepped forward and smacked him on the head with the butt of his musket. He fell back against the wall, eyes glassy.

'Here they come!' Tipton called, ducking away as glass was shattered by a French bullet.

'Hold your fire!'

'How did you know they were up to something?' Fox asked, then ducked instinctively as a ball smacked through the thatch roof to hit a beam overhead.

'He asked me if I had heard about Jemappes?' Hallam said. 'I lied to him. The colonel likes to discuss battles in the Mess. He thinks it will educate his officers. And those that listen, like me, learn from him. I knew the French had attacked at noon. That's what he was trying to tell his men to do. Benoit has a watch on a chain around his neck. He's been planning for his men to storm the farm.'

Fox looked outraged. 'The conniving bastard.'

'We have to hold this farm,' Hallam said in a low voice, so the sergeant could hear. 'They won't let us live otherwise. So we kill them.'

Fox nodded, gripping the musket tightly so that his knuckles showed white. 'It's them or us, sir.'

Hallam slapped his shoulder. 'Aye, it is. Just make sure it's them.'

'I will, sir.'

Hulse ducked from a shot that thudded into the shutters. Musket smoke was clouding the air outside, and he could only see a couple of shapes. 'I can't see them now, sir!'

Hallam loaded his pistol again, grabbed one of the French muskets and ran to Tipton. He peered outside where a man wearing a green jacket was edging towards the farm, trying to flank them. Hallam brought the musket up and pulled the trigger. The noise was loud. 'If you get a clear view, take a shot!' he yelled to his men. Tipton had emptied the French cartridges into an enemy's upturned bicorn. Hallam plucked one out and began feverishly reloading. Once finished, he ran to Hulse as the door rattled with bullets. Shawford appeared and Hallam ordered him back to the pantry.

'You keep your family safe,' he told him, thrusting the French musket into his hands. 'Your wife knows how to load one. Perhaps she knows how to fire one.' The old soldier understood and disappeared. 'Can you see them now?' he asked Hulse.

A figure moved next to the window and Hallam didn't hesitate. He pointed the pistol at the shape and the ball shot the enemy in the face, wiping all features away. There were footsteps and a bayonet lunged through the window towards Hulse. The private saw it coming and twisted away as the blade flashed. Hallam kicked the weapon aside.

'I've got him!' Hulse yelled and his musket banged to shatter the enemy's ribcage.

The door thudded and shook.

'Bastards!' Fox snarled.

Hallam left Hulse loading. He tucked the pistol into his sash and withdrew his sword. It was cumbersome in the tight space, but he would use it to spear the enemy rather than slash. Benoit was still unconscious.

The door shook again and voices cursed. A man laughed evilly. Two bayonets ripped into the wood. Again and again they hacked until a large crack appeared. Boots kicked and Fox, sitting on the chest, moved a fraction. Hallam knew they would enter soon. He rammed his sword into the earthen floor, grabbed hold of Benoit's jacket and tugged it off him. The man stirred and moaned. Hallam kicked him in the face.

'I can't hold them back!' Fox shouted urgently.

Hallam, wearing the jacket over his hands, lifted the bubbling pot off the hook. 'Stand back!'

The door thudded and suddenly swung open as two men tumbled forward. Hallam snarled as he flung the pot's contents at the door where two more men stepped forward. The boiling stew splashed over them, soaking the bare flesh of hands and faces, and they recoiled as

256

though a cannon had fired grapeshot through the opening. The men shrieked in agony. Fox rammed his bayonet into the nearest prone enemy's neck, fought the sucking flesh by twisting it free, and stepped back. Hallam dropped the empty crock, and whipped his sword free to skewer the other Frenchman. A bear-like man, untouched by the redcoats' bullets or stew, charged through the gap, and brushed Fox aside with a paw-like hand as though he was made of straw. Hallam lunged, but the blade glanced off the man's musket to entangle itself in his patchwork coat.

Hallam let the sword go and drew the clasp-knife. The big Frenchman tried to beat him down with his musket, but Hallam ducked and plunged the knife into his thigh. The man snorted like a beast, picked him up and tossed him across the room. Hallam smashed into the far wall, to collapse on top of Fox, who was bleeding from the mouth.

'You ugly bugger!' Shawford exclaimed before shooting the grizzled giant with his musket. The Frenchman jerked backwards, but the bullet seemed to have had no effect. He bounded towards Shawford who had gone wide-eyed at the man's doggedness. Behind him Little Jim shrieked.

'No!' Hallam shouted, trying to rise up.

The Frenchman swotted Shawford aside. He turned, snarling and Rose shot him with the French musket. The man stumbled with the private clasping his legs. He thumped a massive fist down onto the old soldier's head, but the redcoat hung on. Rose calmly walked up to the colossus and put the horse-pistol to his chest and pulled the trigger. Blood sprayed over the wall as the ball tore a length of spine away.

Hallam staggered to the door, clambered over the bodies to see two men running away. Hulse and Tipton fired from the windows and the slower man fell dead with a bullet in the back. Hallam let the remaining man go. The wounded French he left, sprawled and screaming from the burns. He didn't care what would happen to them.

'I think we're safe,' he said and sagged back against the wall. He ran a hand across his forehead, smearing grime.

There was a strangulated cry and he rushed back inside thinking there was still was a threat when he found Shawford with his thick calloused hands gripped around Benoit's neck, wringing it like a chicken.

'This one ordered the men to abuse me,' Rose said to Hallam.

257

Hallam ordered the other redcoats out. Hulse was placed on picquet while Hallam, Fox and Tipton buried Phelps. By the time they had finished, the afternoon light was darkening. Hallam did not ask about Benoit. He had the dead French dragged inside and tossed a burning brand into each of the rooms. It took a while for the flames to spread, but as they walked out of the woods, he heard the roof collapse and turned to watch. It was a place of misery. There was a history of violence there and setting it ablaze felt like it was the right thing to do.

A fitting end to such evil men, he considered.

The sky was still smeared with the smoke of the burning as they walked north.

*

It was Christmas Eve.

Icicles hung from branches and redcoats broke through the ice with bayonets to get water from the streams for the cooking pots. Breakfast for some consisted of flour dust, cooked into little dumplings, stale bread, or acorns and old berries found beneath the oaks and bushes. Several officers shot at a plump of ducks passing over, the musket bangs echoed as men looked up in anticipation, but none of the birds fell from the sky and they cursed their poor luck rather than their marksmanship. The vast majority of men had nothing to eat. Bellies were painful and swollen from cramps. Some had to run into the hedgerows to void their bowels. Dysentery and fever were rife.

Grave was a small impoverished town about nine miles southwest of Nijmegen on the left bank of the River Maas. It had been heavily fortified over the centuries, often billeting military troops from Austria, Spain and France, who of late had added embankments, ditches and gun emplacements to the ancient walls that surrounded the town. The large castle was rebuilt and it was here that the Dutch had surrendered to the French just days ago after a brief siege, but it was a poor place filled with memories of destruction, sieges, starvation and misery.

'You see, they can't even bloody well hold onto one of their own towns,' Major Osborne grumpily gave his opinion of the Dutch as he and Colonel Paget espied Grave from a thicket of pine trees less than a mile to the south. He had spent his night in a grotty little farmstead and awoke covered in flea bites. Rain showed above the far hills as a dark stain. 'That's what happens when you arm shit-stinking, clog-wearing peasants with firelocks. They're not an army, they're a goddamn rabble.'

Paget did not reply. He was still smarting at Osborne's impertinence from the bridge. Instead, he looked to where General Sir David Dundas, commander of the British right, and his staff were talking, making notes and giving orders just ahead of the tree line. Paget had grown to dislike Osborne's company and so he clicked his tongue and trotted over towards the group of officers without saying a word to the major.

This wasn't to be Paget's first battle, but he was nevertheless anxious to make a name for himself and not to let the regiment down. It was a fine battalion and men like Captain Richard Hussey Vivian had paid good money to get transferred to the 28th. Vivian had made a name for himself in the last few years and now wanted to transfer to a cavalry regiment, but it was a damned good regiment with a proud history and Paget hoped to continue with its legend.

'Should be a decent day's fighting,' said a voice over to his left.

Paget turned to see an unknown officer trotting along a muddied track; he was also heading towards Dundas.

'So I hear,' Paget replied genially. 'Edward Paget, 28th,' he said, and outstretched his hand when he was close enough.

'Arthur Wesley, 33rd,' said the officer, taking the proffered hand. 'Pleased to make your acquaintance.'

'Likewise,' Paget said. '33rd, eh?' he said, staring at Wesley's red facings. 'I heard about Boxtel.'

Wesley grunted slightly from the mention of the name. The regiment had been part of the British and Hanoverian force that had launched a counter-attack after the French had pushed the Dutch from the town. But the manoeuvre had failed despite the regiment's superb volley fire, which had shattered the French attack.

'I overheard that Sir David reckons the French at Grave will try to keep us pinned back whilst Pichegru marches his army to trap us like fish caught in the nets,' Wesley said. 'There can't be more than a four thousand of the Jacobins here. One whiff of a volley and they'll retreat behind the towns walls and we'll have to endure another siege,' he added bitterly. 'What this army needs to do is consolidate. We're scattered to the winds and all that's left for us to do is drift away like autumn leaves caught in a breeze.'

Wesley was in his twenties, slim, straight-backed and Paget noted he had piercing eyes and a sharp, hooked nose. There was something strange in his manner, impressive in his tone and utterly decisive in his manner.

Paget gave a firm nod of agreement. The trick was to win this small victory, and still bring the British Army to safety in one piece. That would not be easy, and it was all down to other men's decisions.

'We can't endure a winter siege,' he said. 'We have to hope the locals lock the gates behind the French and then they'll be forced to simply surrender.'

Wesley brayed with laughter that caused a few of the older officers around Sir David to scowl. He turned to see a sullen company of redcoats march past.

'Driving rain and snow makes men careless, for they are too consumed with their own misery to care,' Wesley commented. 'Or perhaps they are wretched because of their own officers?'

Paget grunted. 'I agree, Wesley. But what to do, eh?'

Wesley pursed his thin lips and stared across at the flat landscape, almost as though he was mesmerised by the bleak beauty of it. 'Have you heard that Robespierre was toppled?'

'The Directory,' Paget said with disgust. 'One dictator ruling the country is removed so that a whole group of dictators can do the same job. We're fighting a mob, Wesley.'

'Agreed, but the damned mob has beaten us at nearly every turn,' Wesley replied with a wry smile. 'They've seen off the Austrians who have scuttled back across the Rhine and they've taken Antwerp, Brussels, and their armies are chasing us every day away from the sea. We're to help the eastern defences, but we're done here, Paget. We're heavily outnumbered, but still there's nothing right now to cause us undue concern,' he said calmly. 'I heard that the government wants to recall some of our regiments for the Sugar Islands.'

Paget stared. 'Good God,' he uttered, thinking of the West Indies. 'That will leave us with even less manpower.'

'True, Paget, true,' Wesley replied. He brought out an expensive telescope and trained it at the walls where the Tricolour of France flew high from the castle's main tower instead of the Dutch Tricolour. Tall pine trees hid the outlying land and the River Maas. Then, he traversed it across the fields to the west to a tiny village called Escharen. He watched dark streaks of smoke that betrayed home cooking fires.

'Grave should give the men spirit, Wesley,' Paget considered, 'but I hear that Pichegru is less than two days away. There will be no time to lay a siege, any blockhead can tell you that, so we've got to beat them with volleys and finish them off with the cold steel.'

Wesley smiled, liking Paget's comments. 'The French haven't tasted defeat yet. But we shall see, Paget, we shall see,' he said, smiling and closed his eyepiece. 'I don't know where we're heading, but I do hope our paths will cross again.' He touched his bicorn hat and clicked his heels to spur his horse forward away from the group of officers.

Paget watched him leave and turned to greet a couple of the officers he knew from his Westminster days. It was good to catch up with friends before battle.

*

Julian Stubbington was resigned to death.

He was shivering, sweat-laced and yet his mouth was as dry as saltpetre. He confessed his feelings of his own impending doom to Hallam who told him not to be so damned silly, and to go and get his sword sharpened.

'For whatever use it'll be,' the boy said forlornly, as he disappeared beyond the throng of waking redcoats.

Hallam inspected his own sword to find it dull and blunt. There was a new notch in the tip and he reckoned it was caused by the desperate fight at the farm. Ignoring the pangs of hunger, he too went in search of an armourer. His sword had not been sharpened in days and would not be useful in battle, and this fight today promised to be a big one, unless the French surrendered early. He found a cavalry armourer from the 11th Light Dragoons who gave the sword a razor-like edge. He tossed the man a coin for his trouble and walked back to the battalion just as dawn was breaking.

Hallam stared across a flooded field that was pitted with soft rain, where a short-eared owl glided silently in the gloom. Just above the horizon the first arc of sunlight flared orange despite the swollen clouds. He stared at the glorious bright light that seemed to pulse and flirted with the idea that it might be a sunny day, and then dismissed it as whimsy.

Smoke from the camp fires seemed to stretch up to the star-flecked sky. There were a lot of men around each fire where the wood crackled and spat and popped in the rain. Their faces were gaunt, drained and unshaven, but they were glad of the warmth. One man with brown teeth laughed at a poor joke, and another poked inside a bandage tied around

261

his head where a sword cut from a hussar had taken an eye. Hallam saw him wipe his wet finger on his jacket.

'Tea, sir?' Private Tipton asked him.

'Have you got any?' Hallam said dubiously.

'I managed to trade a silver knife for some tea leaves and a new pipe from one of the lads in the 33rd this morning, sir,' Tipton said as he poured some tea into a mug. 'It came with an ounce of tobacco as well,' he added happily.

'It's a good trade,' Hallam replied. He sipped the hot liquid, savouring the taste and letting its warmth seep down deep into his cold body. 'That's damned good,' he said appreciatively and Tipton grinned. 'Where did you get the knife?'

Tipton shuffled his feet and cuffed snot from his pointy nose. 'Found it, sir.'

'On its own, or was it with a set?' Hallam said wryly, knowing all too well that Tipton had stolen it.

'Wish I had tea back last week, sir,' Tipton said, changing the subject. 'When I was on picquet duty with Appleton. We could have done with a mug of it then. Poor bloody Appleton. It's not right for a soldier to go like that.' He shook his head in sadness at the memory of his companion who had frozen to death during the night.

Since the farm, the private looked older. They must all have aged in the campaign. *Cold, hunger and fear does that to a man*, Hallam reflected candidly.

'Let's hope we lose no more of our boys to the damned cold.'

'Amen to that, sir,' Tipton said. 'I should have known something was wrong as he was a talker. There were times you couldn't shut him up.'

'I seem to remember him being punished for talking on parade?'

Tipton chuckled. 'That was him, sir. Talked right under the ears of Major Osborne. The clumsy oaf.' The private looked awkward for a moment. 'I meant Appleton being the clumsy one, sir, not the good major.' A thin strand of greasy hair slipped out from underneath his hat that he tucked back with rag-wrapped fingers.

The men should have had their hair powdered white into a pigtail called a queue, which originally was to prevent long hair from impeding a soldier's vision. Each man's hair was hauled back, greased with candle wax, and then twisted about a small sand-filled leather bag that was secured with a strip of leather so that the hair hung stiff at the nape. The white hair looked neat and tidy on the parade ground, but was a haven for lice and caused misery. Like most things, it had been abandoned during the campaign.

Hallam wondered whether Tipton was being facetious on purpose, admitting that he thought Osborne incompetent and yet unable to voice that opinion. Hallam declined to comment. He stared at the glowing cinders and his thoughts turned to Isabel, remembering that she preferred lemon in her tea and how he had wrinkled his face at the taste and how she had laughed at him. Her sweet laugh echoed in his mind and he smiled. He wondered what she would be doing now on Christmas Eve. She had a large happy family and no doubt plucked pheasant, partridge and other wildfowl along with smoked hams would be hanging from the kitchen walls and Hallam's favourite: a haunch of mutton would be ready for the spit. More food such as brawn, potted venison, roast goose, stuffing, applesauce and well-buttered mashed potatoes would complement the main course. Dessert would be rich plum pudding, fruit cake, eggnog, spruce beer and the hot, fruity and spicy wassail drink. Christmas was a time to be at home, warming next a hearth-fire, surrounded by loved ones and thinking nothing of peace, drink and good food. Instead, this morning they would do battle and some men would never see another Christmas.

Hallam blinked out of his glorious dream. 'You didn't acquire any food by any chance?'

''Fraid not, sir.'

Hallam smiled. 'What happened to that cooked meat at the farmhouse?'

'I'm not sure what you mean, sir.'

'No, nobody does,' Hallam said sarcastically. 'I definitely saw it hanging from the beams.'

Tipton sniffed. 'Perhaps it went up in smoke like the Frenchies, sir?'

'Ah well, it was probably not pork, or beef.'

The private stared and wiped his nose again. 'What do you think it was, sir?'

'Probably not worth imagining,' Hallam said, with a lop-sided grin. 'Being that it had been in French hands for weeks, it could have been anything. Goat, horse, deer. Or worse. Far worse. It's not unheard of that men when they cannot get food turn on themselves to feed their empty bellies.' He let the thought sink in. 'Still as you said all up in smoke. Ah well. Probably for the best. Make sure you give Mister Stubbington a cup of your tea.'

'I will, sir,' Tipton said, face suddenly ashen.

263

'Are you all right?'

Tipton's jaw lolled, eyes widening and Adam's apple bobbing in a pronounced gulp. 'I suddenly don't feel well, sir. I've had too much...tea.' The private bolted from the fire towards the head-spinning stink of the latrines.

Hallam broke into laughter. He stayed longer than he wished because the fire was so inviting, thinking the moment that he moved away, the chill would return to haunt him like the freezing grasp of a spirit. He drained the cup and returned to find Stubbington who was still morose and subdued. It wasn't like him. He was always cheerful and Hallam realised that the imminent battle was infecting him with fear. He understood the familiar gut-wrenching, bowel-loosening feeling.

'I was like you on the morning of my very first battle,' Hallam tried to soothe him as the first battalions were being ordered to form up in the battle lines. The rain had ceased and a harrying wind blew raw.

'I'm not scared, sir,' Stubbington replied tartly as though Hallam had questioned his nerve. He flicked a piece of dirt from a faded yellow sleeve and ignored the writhing in his guts.

The redcoats looked like tramps. A private who had lost his hat had a strip of dirty cloth wrapped around his head to protect his ears. One or two privates had French, Austrian and Dutch infantry packs and one even wore outlandish Hungarian breeches. Hallam looked at his own uniform; one of his knees was visible and his frayed greatcoat was speckled with blood and grime.

Hallam watched three émigré contingents march past, their moustached faces showed that they were eager to prove their worth in the imminent battle; nevertheless, he watched them with suspicious eyes. He'd seen a few foreign units collapse in disorder on the march and even one who, frightened by their own volley, had fled the field.

The first was Loewenstein's *Chasseurs*, a rifle armed German regiment clad in a uniform of blue-grey with green facings and black round hats topped with dark green plumes that matched the tall thick forests of their country. They were preceded by more Germans from Hompesch's *Chasseurs*, a unit that had been mauled at Boxtel and suffered in the retreat so much that only a hundred men were fit for today's battle. They carried carbines and long rifles and were clothed in dark green coats faced red. The last contingent was a mixture of cavalry and infantry who wore sky blue coats with black facings. The Damas regiments, consisting mostly of French émigrés, were raised for Dutch service, and had fought in this campaign as hard as any British redcoat regiment.

As the foreign troops marched onto the field, the 28th was ordered to form up alongside the 27th and Loewenstein's Germans on the British right flank from line into column. The 80th; volunteers from Staffordshire, Hompesch's green-coats and the Loyal Emigrants; a red-coated regiment who had already gained an excellent fighting reputation, formed the centre while the 19th and 33rd; men from the Yorkshire dales, formed the left flank. The 42nd, tough Scotsmen from the mountains and wild glens, the infantry companies from the Damas Legion and a thinned regiment of yet more French ex-Royalists called Autichamp, were held in reserve. Damas' Hussars, Rohan's 1st Hussars, the 11th and 15th Light Dragoons covered the flanks whilst two foot artillery batteries were dragged behind the reserve, giving the allied force a total of nine thousand men.

'The first thing to do is to stay calm,' Hallam said. 'The men look to their mates, but they look to their officers first. You might not see them, but they'll be looking for steely courage. As officers, we cannot show fear.'

'I said I'm not scared, sir.' Stubbington felt his skin prickle with sweat.

Hallam was watching the regiment's form up. 'More often than not, they'll be just lines of men facing each other. Both similar numbers and both armed with muskets. You'll find no one has an edge. At least that's what they think. But we do.'

'Sir?'

'We get in close and at fifty yards our volley fire will destroy them. You'll be amazed at how easy it is to miss, but at fifty yards or less our practised musketry will punish them.'

'Because we load faster, sir?'

'Exactly.'

A thudding of hooves made Hallam twist round to see a slim staff officer galloping along the fields. The man curbed his mount as he neared Paget and Osborne. Hallam tried to read their lips, but the distance was too far. After a brief moment, the officer saluted and spurred his horse towards the 27th.

Hallam turned back to Stubbington. 'Do you know something? I'm scared,' he confessed, before flicking his eyes back at the staff officer. He was deeply nervous because he kept thinking about Isabel, a fear that seared through his veins. He missed her and kept thinking that it

265

would be cruel if he was killed when he had only just found true love and married. He had no intention of attending that Ball in Lyndhurst, but somehow he had gone and it was then that cupid's arrow had struck with the accuracy of a German rifle. It wouldn't be fair, to die so far from home, from Isabel, but he also knew it was a soldier's life that he had chosen and knew what fate might have for him.

'You're scared, sir?' Stubbington knew Hallam was trying to soothe him, but he could not get the vision of death from his mind. His stomach clenched like a fist. Last night he dreamt that he had died in the battle. He saw whole files of men blown to scraps before his eyes and then he was hit and he felt nothing. He saw his blue feather drift away. And that was it; he was dead, gone into oblivion.

'Of course,' Hallam said, 'and doubtless some will say it gets easier, but they've probably never fought a proper battle before, or they are bluffing to cover their own nerves. I've seen men, with years of campaigning trod under their boots, stricken with fear. It makes men cry, vomit or become petrified to the spot.'

'An officer should set an example, sir,' Stubbington said, gnawing his upper lip.

'They should.'

'So I've taken courage in the form of brandy. A sip or two, but I will remain at my post. I will not let the Slashers down. I will not let you down, sir.' He wore his issued greatcoat, which bulked up his frame and the sword at his hip showed that he was a warrior. However, the ensign knew he did not cut an imposing figure, for his shoulders were far too narrow, his skin was soft like a girl's and he could not yet grow facial hair.

'I never suspected for one second that you would, Mister Stubbington,' Hallam replied as he negotiated a large ice-rimmed puddle. 'I joined up as a youngster like you.'

'Why did you enlist?'

Hallam did not answer straight away. He looked to the company. Morale was certainly at a slump, but as they marched in silence, Hallam detected the old feeling of pride from them; a pride that would carry them through to the very end like it had always done so.

'I wanted to live a boy's adventure tale,' Hallam said. 'I wanted to lead men into battle. I wanted to know what pride, honour and sacrifice meant. I wanted to feel alive.'

'And have you accomplished that, sir?'

Hallam grinned. 'Oh yes.'

The army had brought him opportunities: promotion, enrichment, education and escape from a life of possible drudgery and toil. It had given him everything he had wanted.

Hallam stared up at the town's stone walls that were high and imposing. In front of them, the land was darkening and he realised the French demi-brigades were similarly advancing. He wondered if a seasoned officer was giving advice to a junior in the enemy ranks.

'We all get premonitions and omens,' Hallam continued, 'it's natural before a fight. Try to remain calm, stay at your post and you'll do all right.'

'I suppose so, sir,' Stubbington said gloomily, his thin shoulders drooped.

'Have you had your sword cleaned and honed?'

A troubled expression clouded Stubbington's usually happy countenance. 'I forgot, sir. I was waylaid by the hope of brandy. I apologise.'

Hallam shot him a grin. 'As an ensign, I couldn't walk into battle without running a whetstone across the blade every morning. I considered it bad luck. Just pray that if you have to use it, that it will do its job. And the first thing you do after the fight is...?'

'Get it sharpened, sir,' Stubbington grinned.

Hallam's stomach rumbled painfully. It already felt like a tight knot, but he was desperately hungry and had to force a hand across his belly to try to soothe it. His breakfast consisted of a lump cut from a flitch of bacon fat and a piece of hard dark bread coated in rancid butter. Grave was crammed full of wine, food and women so it was rumoured, which meant of course that it wasn't, but the lie was said to encourage the British. The cellars, it was said, were packed with casks, bottles and wineskins, the storehouses jammed full with boxes, sacks and barrels of food and the women; all beautiful and long-legged, were starved of sex.

'Now if you're still nervous when you see the bastards, just think about all the young girls waiting for you inside,' Hallam said. 'They're on their backs right now waiting for you to give them your British beef.'

The young officer laughed as he was supposed to, and then clasped his ears from the thunderous roar that came from outside of the town.

The French artillery had opened fire.

It was six o'clock.

Every gun outside the walls opened fire.

The salvo showed as an eruption of flame-speared smoke as if a giant fantastical beast had awoken from a deep slumber, roaring, angry and terrifying. The smoke pumped yellow-grey that mingled with the mist so that the gun batteries were instantly obscured.

A heartbeat or so later, the sound of the cannon was ear-shattering and slammed across the frosted fields like a giant's whip-crack. The sound was enough to fill the hearts of their enemies with dread and told them that the soldiers of the French Revolutionary army were no pushovers.

The battle for Grave promised to be a bloody one.

The majority of the guns were loaded with roundshot. The cold barrels dropped the heavy iron balls short of the advancing redcoats that skittered and skipped harmlessly along the ploughed fields. The howitzers were armed with shell and the burning fuses were extinguished in the puddles, dykes and snow drifts. Hallam watched one roundshot slash through the branches of a willow tree to bounce and smash apart a fence post and come to a thudding halt against the ruins of an old farm building.

Stubbington had never seen so many guns. He knew the French always brought more cannon, more so than the allies combined, and yet somehow nothing had prepared him for actually seeing the great banks of gun smoke where the host waited.

General Sir William Harcourt's ADC came to summon the brigade forward. Another rider galloped past the 28th, sending clods of earth up into the air. A small clump hit Stubbington below the ear. He wiped the mud away, but it left a dirty mark.

'Forward march,' Paget called. 'At the double.'

Captain Ingram's Light Company was at the head of the column, jogging across the snowy fields, packs and equipment bouncing as they went. They were already exhausted and the men panted and gulped for breath.

The glowing slow-matches of the port-fires touched the quills and the French twelve pounders crashed back on their long trails. The guns sent their missiles straight across the fields, the balls smashing and bouncing their way towards the redcoats. Every time a roundshot hit the ground, it churned snow and dirt as it bounced away in a blur. A cannonball missed Paget's horse by a hair's breadth.

Each column was separated by enough distance so that they could form into line if necessary. The redcoats ran on and then suddenly the damp air was punctuated with the screams of the first dying men as enemy gunfire found targets. A single shot bounced down the rank and took the heads off of a half-dozen men from Ingram's company. Battalion men coming up behind dodged the corpses and wet patches of glistening gore.

'Keep your dressing!' Sergeant Fox, sporting a bruised jaw from the attack at the farm, bellowed at a man who had bent down to loot a dead Light Bob. Corporal Beckett instantly grabbed the man and shoved him back into his file.

Roundshot flicked one private aside like a child's toy, and then skidded low to take the legs off of two men standing beside Hallam.

'Forward!' Clements shouted angrily, his head aching from the schnapps he had stolen from the house that the quartermaster had commandeered in the night. It was a small farm, but the man had a large cellar and the regiments' officers had all helped themselves to dozens of bottles and jars. His stomach felt like it was on fire and his bowels loose with water, but he stayed in the saddle and hoped it would pass. It usually did, and after the battle, he would finish off the last two bottles and everything would be all right until he could acquire some more.

The gunners swabbed and rammed after each shot, but the officers saw that although the missiles had slashed into the red ranks, the gaps had instantly closed and the ranks were still advancing, almost as though the missiles had caused no casualties. Drummers hammered frantically and the Frenchmen cheered. Men were singing *la Marseillaise*, the Revolutionary anthem. Quills were put back into the vents, the gunners ducked aside, and the guns roared to life again.

'Form line here!' The ADC raised his arm to indicate the spot.

The 28th wheeled into line. The sergeants kept the men moving and then jostled and shouted at them to redress the ranks. The bandsmen at the rear beat the drums in rhythm to the manoeuvre.

Roundshot could disembowel, decapitate, or take a limb off, but a shell, landing in the packed ranks could devastate. Hallam watched Tipton stop a shell with a boot and knock the fizzing fuse clean from the charge with a hard smack of his musket butt. Tipton was the joker of the company, likeable, sometimes disobedient and a prankster, but his quick-witted action had just saved lives.

'Well done, boy!' Fox said approvingly and Tipton grinned.

The guns flashed orange again, tongues licking the snowy ground. This was the French way of war, deluging the line with artillery bombardments, pounding and pulverising the enemy infantry. Hallam doubted that any of his men had ever seen or heard so many French guns blasting their iron throats free. Every now and again, there was a pause in the thunderous cannonade, and it seemed so unreal that Hallam wondered whether his ears were too beaten to hear anything until he caught the faint sound of drums, cheering and the thud of marching men.

'Advance!' The ADC spurred to the Colour Party. 'Brigade to advance!'

Paget echoed to command and the 28th rumbled forward with the rest of the brigade. The smoke from the French guns rolled across the fields, obscuring the great muzzles and the air began to darken and choke. The artillery fire was sporadic as the gun teams that reloaded the quickest were firing more often. Hallam watched the guns, the jets of smoke and the flame-points entranced him. But as they got closer, the shots screamed as the balls arced higher from warm barrels.

Could this be done? To break through the French lines, ignoring the hammer-blows of the guns. To shatter the French lines? Hallam gripped his sword tight, hoping that British resolve would be enough to win the day.

'Onward, you humbugs!' Osborne croaked, sword tip tracing manic circles above his head. 'Onward!'

Hallam could see people watching the ensuing battle from the houses and walls and one or two daring ones on rooftops. He could not see any Dutch flags and wondered if the townsfolk were on the side of the French and would help repel the British assault.

A shell plunged deep into one of the dykes and Hallam heard the fuse fizzle loudly as the iron-grey water doused the charge. Another landed in a snow bank and Hallam was surprised when it exploded. Fortuitously, the snow soaked up the blast, a piece of red-hot casing, trailing smoke, smacked harmlessly against his ankle.

A flock of jackdaws speared the air like a sudden torrent of arrows slashing down from loosed war bows to the British right. They shrieked and made their distinct raw sounding call. To some, it sounded mocking. Rooks and crows followed in loose formation, flapping and raining down amongst the oak and elm trees as though they were launching their own assault.

'Bastard birds are laughing at us!' Tipton said.

'A collection of crows is called a murder...' Hulse began, then faltered. Tipton gave him a withering look.

Bugles sounded and hundreds of French skirmishers ran out to meet the attacking red lines. Whistles blew shrill and the British Light Companies and those from the émigré battalions ran out to meet their French equivalents. At first, they came in a loose mass of men; running and firing, and some used the cover of the few trees, fences, snow banks, but most aimed and fired with their firing partners, and then ran on again spreading themselves into a chain.

Some of the German troops were armed with long-barrelled *jäger* hunting rifles and Hallam saw one shoot a French officer clean off his horse. One of the French émigré skirmishers was wounded and Hallam saw his hands go up in surrender, but was viciously bayoneted by his assailant. The Revolutionaries never took émigrés' prisoner, because they were everything that stood against their new found ideals. They despised them.

'*Allez!*' a French officer shouted and the skirmishers sprinted forward to shorten the range and overwhelm the émigré *chasseurs* with their slow loading rifles.

A German fired, and immediately ran back to where his firing partner was crouched, waiting and watching for enemies while he reloaded.

'Watch him!' a British officer warned, as a bullet tore up the snow beside him. 'He's a cocky bastard and I want him dead!'

A group of six Frenchmen dashed forward, but they were seen by other Germans and redcoats and the musket and rifle fire threw all the Frenchmen down to leave one crawling and another rolling over in agony.

Hallam was watching a French officer with a tanned face with long flowing blond hair. He was waving his men on with a grim determination. Hallam thought him confident and probably a hero to his men. Bullets plucked the air about him, but he still gave his men inspiring orders to achieve glory. His sword blade flickered with sunlight and then suddenly there was a broad red stain spreading across his chest and his arms went high and wide, head flopped back, as the man toppled to the ground. Dead. A hero dead, just like that.

Four squadrons of French Hussars suddenly appeared on a sunken road over on the British right and the Light troops were immediately called back. British Light Dragoons spurred towards them, bugles

271

sounding, and the French skirmishers returned to their units. The redcoats jeered them loudly, even though the allies had just retreated.

'Don't you know what day it is?' Lieutenant Colonel Paget asked no one in particular as he trotted his horse forward, swerving past a spent roundshot. He looked energetic and cheerful. 'It's Christmas Eve! Time to rejoice!'

'I'll celebrate when we leave this damned country, sir,' Hallam replied dryly.

The Slashers, the Inniskillings and the German riflemen advanced steadily until the ground dipped to where two French battalions were rushing towards them. A hedgerow, whitened and crusted with ice, acted as a natural screen between the two opposing sides: on the right, near the road, a collapsed house offered limited protection. A blackbird flew from the branches over to the exposed rafters of the ruin.

'Ensign Bennett!' Major Osborne shouted at the young officer at the front of the battalion whose job was to carry the Regimental Colour, the silk flag bearing the regiment's facings. In the centre of the yellow field was a padded red shield with 'twenty-eight' in golden Roman numerals and 'REG', surrounded by a Union wreath. 'Hold that bloody Colour high, man! I want the damned Frenchie-bastards to see who they face!' A second ensign carried the Kings' Colour, which was the flag of Great Britain.

Hallam saw both flags rise higher, both flapping in the buffeting wind. He felt proud of the regiment and his spine always tingled at the sight of the unfurled 28th's Colours.

A howitzer shell exploded some distance to the regiment's front; hot wind fanned Hallam's face and scraps of casing and other debris churned the ground.

The French infantry marched head-on with their muskets resting on their shoulders, as if they would just simply brush the impudent enemy aside. Mouths opened wide as the men chanted the anthem.

'Keep your dressing!' Fox's voice carried with ease and brooked no argument. 'Dress the ranks, you dirty bastards!'

'That's the way! Steady!' Paget was calm and his unruffled composure instilled confidence in the battalion. 'Forward, my brave Slashers!'

'Are you still with us, Mister Stubbington?' Hallam asked without turning his head.

'Yes, sir!'

'Good man.'

A shell exploded in between the two British regiment's and a handful of men in the rear file were tossed into the air like rag dolls. One had the side of his head shorn away, and another had his spine laid open. One of the men was screaming because an arm and a leg were nothing but bloodied stumps. Another shell fired too high exploded harmlessly in mid-air.

The gap closed to a hundred yards between the opposing forces and the British, faces red with exertion and hearts pounding, were still advancing and the French halted. They formed up behind the frozen hedgerow in line. Muskets poked through branches. Officers pushed more men into positions. Hallam counted the barrels, estimating there appeared to be about a thousand of the enemy, the same number as the three allied regiments combined.

The drums and chanting rose to a crescendo behind them. Hallam could see the moustached and bearded faces clearly now. Unknown faces stared back in hatred, terror, or the familiar look of utter coolness. The French were experienced soldiers and their victories had given them an edge as sharp as a well-honed sabre. One officer was on horseback and kept galloping up and down the French lines. He raised and pointed his sabre at the British, his long cloak flapped in the wind.

'Where's our bleeding cavalry gone?' Tipton asked.

The drums beat louder now because the enemy guns had stopped firing for fear of hitting their own men. Voices seemed to echo.

'Keep your mouth shut, Private!' Fox shouted.

At sixty yards Hallam heard the French officer shout, '*Tirez!*' and then instantly the whole line fogged dirty white; a split second later, Hallam heard the rattle of musketry.

Tipton's head was jerked back as a neat hole was punched in his forehead. The ball erupted from the back of his skull to spray the man in the rear file behind him with his blood and brains. Ensign Bennett collapsed with a bullet in his lung. A private wearing clogs, stuffed with straw, hobbled for a moment after a ball had slashed his calf, then after discovering it was just a flesh wound resumed his pace. Perhaps twenty men were felled by the massive volley. The French had expected to kill and wound many more, but Hallam simply put it down to the range, or damp, or poor saltpetre in the powder.

He saw Frenchmen trying to break down a section of the hedgerow, and heard enemy cheers and shouted orders from the gun smoke blanketing their front. More shadowed figures behind them made the enemy line more impressive and yet more terrifying.

A lone shell screamed overhead to explode behind Hallam's company. Debris showered the men and something wet struck his neck. He wiped it away, eyes still focussed on the enemy.

'Close up to the front!' Paget shouted.

The NCOs echoed the instruction all along the line. When men fell, the normal practice was to pull the wounded or dead behind the line and then edge towards the centre to fill the gap. If losses were heavy, this would keep the line three deep, but made the frontage even narrower. Paget wanted the front rank full at all times, so if a front rank man fell, the man directly behind was to step into his file.

Hallam saw Fox haul Tipton's body to the rear. The old sergeant laid him out gently, a look of sorrow on his battered face. Fox had been harsh on the younger men, in order to mould them into steady soldiers, but the boy's death had genuinely affected him.

'Halt! Make ready!' Paget ordered. The French saw the British line ripple, as though the men had turned to the right.

'Let's send the bastards our goodwill!' Hallam shouted over the sound of five hundred muskets being cocked.

Then something caught his eye; it whirled about his boots, dancing and skipping in the small wind. He bent down to pick it up. Strange, it was a blue feather. What the hell was it doing out here on this killing field?

''Talion! Present!' Paget ordered. 'Fire!'

A thunderous explosion jetted out that flickered and stabbed bright flames. The air was instantly engulfed in the wretched smell of rotten eggs and with a tangle of death. The disciplined fusillade ripped into the French, breaking through the hedges to twitch and turn the front ranks to red ruin.

'Load!' Paget steadied his horse. 'I declare them out!' he exclaimed, half-laughing, as if commenting on a cricket match.

Hallam was still staring at the feather when he realised what it meant. His fingers turned it over leaving it blood-smeared. He twisted around to where Stubbington should be, but the junior officer was missing. Hallam cast an eye on the red rags that dotted in the snow behind as the regiment had advanced. A man wailed loudly for his mother and the less badly hurt yelled for help or for their friends to come and fetch them.

'Mister Stubbington?' Hallam called, looking around as the ensign was never at his post preferring to be close to his side.

'To your place, Lieutenant!' Clements said.

Hallam caught sight of Corporal Beckett who had just run back from collecting ammunition and spare flints from the bodies and his eyes told him everything he needed to know.

Stubbington was dead; blown to pieces by the last shell in an instant. Hallam touched the back of his neck again and withdrew his fingers. They were sticky and glistened red.

'I said, to your place!' Clements shouted at him.

Hallam could not speak, he was in shock. The boy had known he would die and stood at his post. Hallam was suddenly hit with remorse and guilt for the ensign who had only wanted to learn. He had become impatient with the sixteen-year-old, often rebuking his remarks. He rubbed away the prick of tears, unaware his rough fingers left traces of blood behind.

'Stubbington's dead, sir,' he mumbled.

'Another loss with no one to mourn,' the captain said heartlessly. He drew his pistol, cocked it and aimed it at the French. 'Useless little blighter. His mother should have kept her knees together.' The flint snapped forward and smoke blotted his view.

Hallam shook his head to clear his thoughts; the grieving would have to wait until later. He could hear the ramrods scrape in barrels, could see their looks of alarm on the French faces as the allies brought their muskets to shoulders. There was a battle to win.

Another company of the green-coated riflemen were running up to extend the line. Their captain gave Hallam a smile as he passed. 'Send them back to hell, *ja!*'

The French managed another volley; it was weak and ragged because some men were looting bodies, or trying to back away, but one or two shots found targets. A private of the 27th was hit in the neck and he continued the motions of loading until he collapsed from the loss of blood. A sergeant from the 28th, armed with a halberd, was shot through the eye and the weapon spun away from his sprawling form.

'Aim low! Aim low!' Paget's voice was snatched by the wind. 'Fire!'

The redcoats fired another murderous volley and the musket balls buzzed, whistled and slashed into the French ranks. The officer on horseback was struck by a bullet that tore through an elbow, his curved sword dangled useless from its wrist strap. He bent over and turned his mount away.

Volley after volley turned the air thick with acrid smoke. The muskets slammed back into bruised shoulders and hands reached for the next cartridge. The ranks levelled their firelocks and fired when ordered too. They could not aim. The enemy was hidden by the banks of jaundiced white fog, so it was simply a question of pointing the muzzle and pulling the trigger.

Hallam saw some of his men were hit. Beckett was shot through both thighs as he stood pulling cartridges free from a wounded man. He staggered, then collapsed and was unceremoniously dragged away by Fox. Shawford lost part of his ear to a French ball. He hissed but continued loading and firing with blood dripping down his neck.

'We're hurting them! 28th!' Paget shouted, his voice betraying happiness brought by their success. 'Fix bayonets!'

'Now for some killing, boys,' Fox said darkly, over the sound of the blades being slotted. 'Butcher them like hogs.'

A few shapes loomed in the smoke in front of Hallam. He brought his sword up as a French officer lunged. Sparks slid down the blades as Hallam parried. A second figure appeared with a musket-tipped bayonet. Fox shot the man in the face and he was pitched back in a spray of blood.

'Kill the Frenchie bastard, sir!' a voice called behind Hallam.

The enemy officer was tall, lithe and strong and Hallam felt the blows were already weakening his sword-arm. The man withdrew his arm, then flicked it back to slice open Hallam's forearm. The blade flashed away. Hallam growled, lunged and kicked the man in the knee as he stepped forward. The Frenchman slashed the air in front of him to dispel any attack as he reeled. Hallam knocked the sword away, reached out and grabbed him by the collar. He punched the man in the face with the sword's guard, then bringing his sword up, tugged the enemy onto the well-honed blade. The steel sliced up through the Frenchman's belly, spurting blood as though it were a full wineskin. The officer let out a high-pitched yell as Hallam twisted the sword free and then chopped down through his throat to splatter the ground crimson.

'That's the way to do it, sir,' said the same voice.

The Germans, having loaded their rifles, fired a ragged exchange and more French tumbled to the floor. One man screamed so loud that it was all anyone could hear for an instance. A lieutenant was hit by a bullet that shattered a rib, and stumbled to the rear with his arm around the shoulders of one of his men, who had his hand shattered by a musket ball. Then, the Germans promptly slotted brass-hilted sword-bayonets before the regiment moved forward.

276

Paget trotted to the front. 'Advance!' he shouted, waving his sword. 'For England and King George!'

The allied battalions marched and the French infantry retreated, but men who controlled the urge to flee or those who were more disciplined covered their ground with a volley that spat venom at the allied lines.

Hallam heard the sound of the balls hitting flesh and rapping on equipment. He felt a sudden blow to his chest and he staggered for a moment from the impact. He looked down at his coat fearing he'd been shot and saw a smouldering hole. An image of Isabel flashed in his mind. Widowed at such a young age. But he felt no pain and undid the buttons. The bullet had passed through his jacket to strike his timepiece. The watch had shattered and was destroyed, but it had saved his life. He breathed a sigh of heartfelt relief.

'Not your time, sir,' Shawford said.

Hallam grinned. 'Very droll,' he said. 'Allow me to offer the same regard to you too.'

Breath plumed in the air like the billowing of cannon smoke as men grunted with exertion, pain, or fear.

'Close up!' The sergeants shouted the litany of battle. 'Close up!'

'Forward!' Paget said. 'Push them back, you rogues!' A ball snatched at his cocked hat. He had his sword drawn. The drummers were beating a frantic rhythm behind the regiment. 'By fire and by steel! We'll give the French a damned good thrashing!'

The French infantry scrambled away and the artillery, who had been waiting patiently, wanted to cause more casualties so resumed firing.

Roundshot scarred the plain, flinging up soil and stones and bloody fragments of the men caught in their path. Something thudded into Hallam's shoulder and then fell to the ground. He looked down to see that it was a piece of jaw, complete with ragged flesh still attached to the bone.

A bullet hit a private, who was wearing a horse blanket over his coat, square in the chest and he fell backwards to entangle himself with the man in the rear rank. Fox saw this and went to pull the two men apart, when a roundshot fired from a gun that had been angled to inflict as many injuries as possible, slammed into the group of men, tearing Fox's left leg off at the thigh. The sergeant, covered in entrails and blood, twitched as blood pumped bright red on the snow.

'That's the way! Push them! Don't let them stand!' Paget continued his hoarse encouragements. His sword reflected the reddening sun as it slipped towards the horizon.

The British artillery began firing and the first shells exploded in the French ranks outside the town's walls. A riderless horse galloped across the fields, another lay kicking and bleeding.

The same private who had stopped to loot a corpse did it again. This time Hallam saw him, kicked him, punched the back of his head, and led him back into his file.

The men from Staffordshire suffered at the hands of a forward battery of guns that fired canister; a whole file was mowed down as the tin cans exploded from the cannon's mouths, as though the bullets shredded the men from giant blunderbusses. A grenadier hit by a ball, spun, fell, then dripped blood as he struggled to his hands and knees. Another doubled up as a ball shattered his hip, but his sharp cries were lost as the battalion cheered. Yet, the regiment advanced unperturbed, and the French commander ordered the guns brought back rather than leave them to be captured.

The soldiers of the new revolution were also dying. The steady redcoat and allied battalions were leaving pockets of bodies behind, but their volleys were faster and so the Frenchmen died from lethal musket and rifle fire.

Paget's horse stepped carefully over the bodies, which were once red, but were now in a myriad of colours, the grim water-mark of battle.

There was a loud British cheer from his left. Then, the centre brigade fired a volley before going forward, bayonets extended.

'28th! Charge!' Paget yelled as loudly as he could, putting spurs to his horse as men ran past either side of him.

A light infantryman stumbled, blood spreading fast where his white cross-belts met in the centre of his jacket. Hallam felt a ball flick his sleeve as he ran. His boots squelched in guts strung blue from a disembowelled enemy. He jumped a dying German who was sprawled in that ungainly way that only those deep in sleep could ever match. A French skirmisher with ragged hole in his neck, lay on his back, staring up at the iron-grey sky. Hallam noticed that the man's eyes were wet with tears.

'Charge!' Hallam shouted, as he ran, sword reddened with blood, thrusting it toward the mass of enemy. Muskets fired. One ball plucked at the hem of his coat, tearing a piece of it away. A ramrod cart

278

wheeled overhead, making a strange thrumming sound. 'Come on!' A redcoat lay on his belly; blood had erupted from his mouth to stain a foot of melting snow.

The clash between the Light Dragoons and Hussars continued until the French demi-brigades shattered like a glass goblet and retreated back inside the town. Even an extra squadron of Hussars did not help the matter for they milled about in confusion as the fighting French horse thundered back past them, showering the ground with clods of rigid earth. The cavalry retreated behind the walls covered by blasts of canister that emptied a half-dozen British saddles before bugles frantically called them back to safety. There was a ditch below the town walls, rubbish-choked and filled with dark-coloured water in which foul things glistened and floated.

'Packs!' Men were shouting. Some of the French desperate to get away had dropped their muskets and packs to go faster. 'Food! Food!'

Then, a white flag hung from the dilapidated town walls and miraculously, incongruously, astonishingly, the battle was over.

And Hallam gasped with relief.

*

The French barred the gates. This allowed them to retreat unmolested west along the winding Maas. They had not wanted to surrender, but the townsfolk were unhappy about a siege and they could not take another blockade. The town had almost been destroyed by siege work some years ago and they had worked hard to rebuild it, so the French had slipped away without spilling further bloodshed. The British were surprised at that, but its battalions were in no state to follow them.

A portly mayor with an orange moustache and side-whiskers welcomed the generals and the British were cheered by the deprived Dutch townsfolk who lined the streets with meagre offerings of oysters, smoked sausages, cabbages, cheese, beer, mussels and smoked eels. There was little bread. It had been a ruinous harvest before the snow came. It had rained for weeks and the rye crops had just rotted in the fields. What little bread available was poor quality, or charged at nearly six times the price.

But as the survivors thanked them, bought food and loaded the wounded onto carts, cavalry scouts detected a huge dark smear on the horizon.

The enemy vanguard.

The British understood that the retreating French had simply joined the larger force and their army was less than five miles away. They would be here within the hour. General Harcourt made an agonising decision to abandon the town and withdrawal north-east fast across the waters of the Maas to the allied held town of Nijmegen.

Seeing and smelling the food, and then being ordered to march away, was enough to make the hungry sob. Some redcoats were so distressed that they broke ranks to drown their sorrows in the wine shops and cellars. Those men not able to be mastered, looted and plundered, and were made insensible from the alcohol that they drank to forget their grief. They were abandoned to the enemy like the wounded that could not be taken wept and called out for friends, or loved ones. Even those too exhausted to continue lay down with the dead.

The cannon-fire had left the landscape scarred and corpse strewn. The dead were left unburied and the British, phantoms covered in rags, continued their retreat.

By the early afternoon, thirty thousand French soldiers crossed the wide River Waal and marched along the banks to Grave where the vanguard pursued the British along the northern road. The allied defences were gone and so was its thinning army.

*

The tired, despondent and bloodied army followed the road north, which was heavily potholed with a myriad of ruts and cracks. Mud sucked at boots and hooves, and the wheels of the remaining wagons and guns, got stuck in the glutinous slime and had to be pulled free. Those that couldn't be dragged with ease were simply abandoned. Equipment became heavy on tired, aching bodies and packs and haversacks were discarded. The road was a deep ugly scar across the hoary wilderness.

Hallam thought of Isabel: timid, intelligent and yet so elegantly beautiful. In a field of snow and mud and under a grey sky, the image of her seemed to shine like a beacon. From the first moment of their introduction, his devotion to her was unflinching. He longed to see her again. Soon, he hoped, soon.

It was nearly midnight when the regiment limped into the town and as the men collapsed from exhaustion, the officers immediately hunted inns, wine stores and warm billets.

280

'This place stinks like a whore's crotch,' Hulse complained.

'It's the best we have at the moment, so be thankful for it,' Hallam gave the reproach. 'I'd rather have a whore's crotch on my face, stinking or not, than another night out open under the stars. At least it'd be warm.'

The officers responsible for quartering had simply given each battalion a selected part of the village for billeting. There were none of the usual chalk marks on doors allocating the residence to a set number of men from each company of a particular regiment. Instead, the men simply crammed into the tiny rooms and outhouses. Some properties were boarded up, or deserted.

Hallam had wondered if the Dutch had fled first, or were kicked out. Small lit fires did not warm the men. There was little talk, and scarcely any liveliness as exhaustion and hunger consumed their thoughts. The battalion's wives looked far worse; numb hands tried to prepare cold foodstuffs, repair their husband's uniforms, or look after the children. Even they were subdued.

It was another bitter night. A thin snowfall had stopped and gradually the clouds scudded in the eastern sky to reveal a brightness of cold stars. Hallam, seeking solace, found an inn in a little alley off a wooded park called *Kronenburgerpark* in the centre of the town. The inn was crowded with officers from the other regiments and, despite the day's soul-destroying retreat, were drinking boisterously and laughing in English, German and French.

A pretty serving girl, freckled and smiling, brought Hallam a bottle of wine, a steaming bowl of pease pudding, some cheese, bread and a length of smoked sausage. It was delicious and he ate the food ravenously. He was so famished that he did not notice he had swallowed one of his teeth that had simply come loose from malnourishment.

After finishing the food and drinking the best part of the wine, it became too noisy and a drunken lieutenant with green facings from the 19th roared a huzzah, fell onto Hallam's table and vomited red wine. Hallam stood up, grabbed him by his jacket and threw him onto the floor. One officer laughed at the spectacle and another, possibly a friend, strode towards Hallam to question his intentions. The look on Hallam's face and the dried blood that flecked his unshaven face deterred the officer from seeking violence, and so he crouched to help his friend up.

'We won the day! Cheer up, you morose swine!' shouted another officer. He was red-faced and sweating like a roast hog from the huge hearth fire.

Hallam snarled, but curbed his anger. He paid for his meal and, strode outside where there was a snowman dressed quite accurately as the French General, Charles Pichegru. Someone, possibly the same creator, had also urinated on it. A friendly officer from the Loewenstein regiment stopped him and congratulated him on the battle, offering a cigar. Hallam liked to smoke them and was grateful for the kindness. They talked a short while and Hallam savoured the smell and taste. Then, the German saw an old friend and so Hallam said his farewells, promising if they should ever meet again, they would share a drink and toast fallen friends. Hallam walked back to his lodgings that he unhappily shared with Clements.

He passed a building where rows and rows of wounded soldiers waited for the surgeon. A steady stream of orderlies brought amputated arms and legs wrapped in filthy rags to a growing pile outside. A few men screamed. Most sighed softly or moaned through chapped lips, and some lay still in their torment.

Hallam had been wounded once. A bullet had entered his shoulder and thankfully passed through the flesh not to cause any lasting damage. The surgeon had still probed for fragments of the ball and cloth. The pain of the forceps digging into the wound was worse than the injury itself. He had cursed the surgeon who reeked of rum who appeared to be in delight of his agony.

Outside the entrance, he had to step around a puddle of vomit thrown up by another British officer who was lying face-down. He lifted his head at Hallam, foul yellow liquid dripped from his cheeks. He groaned and then retched. Hallam ignored the man, and went inside. There should have been a small room for Stubbington, but it was empty and Hallam shot the closed door a look of sadness. He climbed the stairs to his quarters when a voice called him from below.

'What is it, Shawford?'

The big man held something in his hand. 'I've a present from the wife, sir.'

Hallam descended the steps. 'A present?'

Shawford shuffled awkwardly. 'Yes, sir. For what you did for her and my boy.'

'It was nothing really.'

The old soldier shoved the linen wrapped item into his hand. 'God bless you, sir, but you were the one who asked to go back for her. If it wasn't for you...' Shawford's voice trailed away.

Hallam undid the material to find a handsome timepiece. He was shocked at the gift.

'It's not stolen, sir,' Shawford told him upon seeing his expression. 'It's from that Frenchie deserter. I figured he wouldn't be needing it no more and I was going to sell it, but when your own watch was damaged, I spoke to Mrs Shawford and she came up with the idea.'

'I don't know what to say,' Hallam said, touched by the gesture.

Shawford rubbed his hands as though he was suddenly cold. 'A tough fight today.'

'Yes,' Hallam thought of all the dead on the field of Grave. Stubbington, Tipton and he wondered whether Fox and Beckett would survive the surgeon's knife. If they did, he thought, they would face the rest of their lives as cripples, beggars, or ruined men destined for the workhouses. It was no life for a brave soldier to end up.

'It felt like we were marching into hell, sir.' Shawford's voice had been hoarse with emotion and Hallam understood that. He had met many old soldiers who would weep at the battles they had endured, or of friends lost. The private was a tough man, but sentimental.

'We got burned, but we came through it,' Hallam said, then remembered what Paget had said. 'We'll get home.' He was still dumbfounded by the gift, his eyes gorged on the exquisite timepiece. 'I must give you something towards it, as it must be worth-'

'I won't take a penny, sir,' the private interrupted sternly. 'My wife and boy mean the world to me. If I had all the gold in the world I'd give it to you.'

Hallam outstretched his hand and the private shook it gratefully. 'They are both well?'

'Getting better, sir. My boy has a cold, but his shivering has stopped. Rose is as strong as always.'

'That's good.' Hallam thought he ought to enquire of her ordeal, but then decided never to mention it again. 'Merry Christmas to you and your family.'

'You too, sir. Good night.'

When Hallam reached his room, he was surprised to see the fireplace alight with a man stood next to a large wide-armed chair. He thought it to be Mr Carew, the regiment's quartermaster.

'Warming your arse again, Tom,' he said, grinning. His boots were loud on the wooden floorboards. 'Sir,' he gasped when he realised that it was actually Colonel Paget.

'Ah, Jack,' Paget replied. 'I hope you don't mind. I had my servant light it for you. Have you eaten?'

'Yes, sir,' Hallam said. 'I haven't written my report of the farmhouse yet. I was going to do that tonight.'

'All in good time.' Paget glanced down at the burgeoning flames that crackled noisily. A moment or two passed by. 'A shame about Stubbington.'

Hallam remembered the boy's cheerfulness and satisfaction at being part of the regiment. 'I'll write a letter to his parents tonight.'

'That's really for your captain to do, Jack,' Paget remarked slightly reprovingly.

'I'll do it, sir,' Hallam said. George Milsum had once told him that it did not do the mind any good to dwell on death, but Hallam remembered the feather swirling around his boots and the guilt of not having more tolerance with the boy snapped at his conscience. 'I want to.'

Paget grunted, knowing that Clements wouldn't bother, or would simply get someone else to do it anyway. 'Very well. Tell them he died a good death.'

Hallam bobbed his head. 'Yes, sir, I will. In time he would have made a fine officer.'

Paget inclined his head by way of agreement. 'Indeed.'

The fire crackled loudly, and both men stared at the flames.

Hallam was puzzled at the colonel's presence. 'Was there something else, sir?'

Paget raised his eyebrows, then clicked his fingers as though he had forgotten. 'Yes, I have something for you,' he said, drawing out two crumpled letters from inside his coat. 'Post.'

'Post?' Hallam frowned.

'The mail, Jack,' Paget replied wryly as he handed them over. 'Five months late, I'm afraid, but we're lucky to get any. I have managed to acquire a month old copy of *The Times* waiting for me in my quarters. I'm eager to catch up on the news at home and of course the day reports to sign off, so I won't keep you long.'

The first letter was addressed to him and Hallam recognised the lettering. It was from Isabel. His heart quickened with joy. The second letter was addressed to a 'Captain Jack Hallam'.

284

'There's been some mistake,' he said, tearing it open. The paper was thick and creamy, and sealed with a knob of wax that looked as though it had just been stamped. He hurriedly read the letter, which was signed by Paget and dated today. He took a step back in disbelief.

Paget was bemused. 'Are you all right, Captain?' he said with a chuckle.

Hallam looked at him. 'Sir?' he said, then could not find the words and re-read the letter again. Captain. It was something he had always wanted, but it was still a shock. 'What about Captain Clements, sir?' he asked, thinking that he would likely be moved to another company.

'Clements will remain as commander of the company,' Paget said gently. 'It is you that will be transferring out.'

Hallam suddenly felt as though freezing water drenched his heart. 'Sir?'

Paget grimaced as though he had feared Hallam's response. 'You'll be taking over the reins from Captain Vivian who has had his transfer approved.'

'I see,' Hallam hesitated.

Vivian was leaving? So he was being promoted and transferred to Number Seven Company. He felt some of the joy leave because he had worked hard to make the company better. This campaign had toughened them. They were hard men; faces and bodies scarred by violence. Their hair might be unkempt, their coats patched and frayed, and their boots dirtied, but they held their weapons like veterans. And Hallam was proud of them.

Paget saw the expression on his face and must have understood because he spoke gently. 'You've done sterling work, Jack. Don't think I haven't read the reports, or have been blind to your accomplishments in the field and off of it. I see and hear all,' he said, a smile tightening his mouth. 'I am also aware of what kind of an officer you are and have been.'

Hallam had once been put forward for promotion when George Milsum had died, but an altercation with Osborne and his nephew had expunged him from a captaincy. Hallam had caught Osborne's nephew, who was a lieutenant, filching from Milsum's possessions, and Hallam had to be restrained before he had beaten the man senseless. He was let off with a warning, because he was a relation of Osborne's, and who claimed that it was Hallam that started the fight. The damage to his reputation was done and he had remained as a lieutenant until now.

'You are a gallant man,' Paget continued, 'competent, and I need you take your new company under your experienced wing.' His eyes seemed to drink in the dancing flames. 'I am reviewing the status of certain officers in the regiment. I see a new future for the Slashers, and by God I will not tolerate disobedience, negligence and incompetence.' He had been getting angrier as he spoke, but took control of his emotions. He blew out his cheeks. 'There are some who think themselves above the law. For too long, they have been allowed to swagger around like bloody pirates; plundering and marauding. I will not stand for that. The regiment has a proud history; full of heroic deeds and valour. I do not want it remembered for knavish behaviour. I will not have the legend tarnished.'

'I agree, sir,' Hallam replied, nodding his head. This is why he liked Paget. He was young, had his temperaments and his odd ways, but Hallam thought him a kind, wise soul and above all, a damned fine commander.

'Good man. I'm pleased to have you, Jack. I hear the men are already calling you 'Old Steadfast' because of your nerve from the skirmish at the bridge. You've already improved the morale by rescuing Private Shawford's wife and child.' He smiled with approval. 'I'll see you at breakfast at six. We'll only be staying here one night and then we're to march to a place called Arnhem.'

'Well, you know the army, sir - keep on moving even if you aren't going anywhere.'

Paget gave a sardonic smile. 'Quite.' He pulled out a bottle of French brandy and handed it to him. 'Merry Christmas.'

'Thank you, sir,' Hallam said, taking the present. It was a lovely gift and he felt awkward to receive it because he had nothing to give in return. 'Merry Christmas to you too, sir,' he added hurriedly as Paget made for the door.

He waited for the colonel to disappear before putting the brandy on the mantelpiece and opening his wife's letter. He did it carefully because it was precious to him and found it contained two long pages written in her beautiful penmanship.

It was some time later that he emerged from his room with a huge grin. He was so happy in love that he thought his heart would beat out of his chest. He was still clutching the letter when Clements appeared on the stairs.

Hallam's smile disappeared.

286

'Goddamn Dutch are pleased to see us for once, eh?' Clements, his face flushed red and brow glimmering with sweat, swayed. 'Shame we're pulling out in the morning. Damned fine town. Not the usual hovels and the smell of shit everywhere. There's food, drink and there are some rather attractive women. Proper breeding. Not the sort that would take a penny to part their legs.' He saw the letter. 'What's that?'

'It's from my wife.' Hallam could smell wine on his breath from a few feet away.

Clements wrinkled his nose at the reply. 'I thought you had orders,' he muttered peevishly. 'It seems to me you're the colonel's favourite at the moment. I thought he might have another special duty for his new pet.' He laughed, pleased with himself.

Hallam did not rise to the mockery. 'No, it's just a letter from home.'

'I never knew you were married.'

'You never bothered to ask,' Hallam said, moving towards the stairs. He was in no mood to speak to Clements. He was going to congratulate Vivian on his transfer before retiring to his room for the night.

Clements scowled 'I don't really care if you're married or not, Lieutenant. In the old days, you had to ask the colonel's permission and even if he agreed, it was frowned upon. Married women make men feeble. A feeble man is not fit to be a soldier,' he said, 'even one such as 'Old Steadfast'.' He let out a long lingering laugh that Hallam instantly found irritating.

Hallam looked at him. The captain's shoulders slouched, his coat undone and his waistcoat wet with spilt wine. 'You're drunk,' he grimaced, as though talking to him left a bitter taste in his mouth.

'You keep that firebrand tongue still!' Clements spat the last word, whirling a length of spittle onto the floor. 'And so what if I am? What's it to do with you?'

'Drunkenness breeds ill-discipline.'

Clements face went red with ire. 'How dare you-'

Hallam moved away, finding him tiresome. 'I don't have time for this.'

Clements held up a hand to stop him. 'Your mouth will get you into trouble one day, Lieutenant. Careful you don't disappoint the colonel. The higher you go, the steeper the fall. Anyway, you don't seem the type to get married. Where did you meet her? Back of some squalid alley? Break her in like some barrack whore, did you?' he said, breaking into another laugh.

Hallam's temper snapped. His right fist struck Clements jaw, and the captain tripped over his steel spurs to topple down the flight of steps. He let out a great bellow of anguish before thudding onto his back at the foot of the stairs, where he lay sprawled, bleeding and groaning.

Hallam casually descended the steps as Paget's adjutant appeared from around the corner of a makeshift briefing room.

'Everything all right?' he said, looking at Clements and then back to Hallam.

'You–you hit me,' Clements said disbelievingly, blood showing on his astonished face. His eyes were glassy.

'The captain is three sheets to the wind,' Hallam said.

'I see.'

'He took a tumble down the steps. I'll help him back to his quarters.'

'You hit me!' Clements tried to get up, but swayed.

'Would you like a hand, sir?' the adjutant asked Hallam.

'No, thank you. Goodnight.'

The adjutant saw that he wasn't wanted and had far more pressing work to complete so he eagerly went back to his paperwork.

Hallam bent over Clements with a menacing expression.

'You goddamned hit me!' Clements snarled. One of his front teeth was loose, his tongue ran over his split lips. 'You've crossed the line now, Lieutenant! I'll see you broken, and on your knees like your whore!'

'That's Captain Hallam now, you bastard,' Hallam said and stamped on Clements nose, breaking it. Clements howled and whatever he was about to say came out as a gurgle because Hallam then kicked him hard in the side of the neck. 'Stubbington was a better officer and a better man than you'll ever be, you drunken piece of shit.'

Clements collapsed unconscious. Hallam took hold of his ankles and dragged the him back up the stairs where his head hitting every step with a thud. One of the spurs came loose and clinked as it tumbled away. At the top of the stairs, Hallam pushed open the door to an unoccupied room and unceremoniously dumped the bloodied captain onto the floor. He closed the door and turned the key in the lock.

He returned downstairs to find Vivian to congratulate him, and then retired to his room as the church bells rang out. He gazed out of the window. The stars were so big and bright, it was though he could reach up and snuff them out.

It was Christmas Day and it was snowing again, but Hallam didn't care. Pulling off his boots and socks, he sat down on the chair next to the still blazing fire. The chair was upholstered, tatty and much worn about the arms, but it was exceedingly comfortable. He moved the logs with the iron and the wood crackled and spat in defiance. He wiggled his toes on the aged hearth-fire rug, feeling the luxurious heat seep into his chilled bones, and yet, had to rub his hands that were thrumming with the pain of cold flesh warming.

Remembering something in his pocket, he pulled out the blue feather, and gazed at pensively at if for a moment before putting it on the mantelpiece where two beeswax candles guttered from the draughty floorboards. He would enclose it with the letter to Stubbington's parents.

He sat back in the chair, sagging slightly, and unfolded Isabel's letter again and smiled.

It was dated 25th May, and she wrote that she was two months pregnant.

The baby must be due any day now and Hallam could already be a father, and the feeling was so wonderful that tears pricked at his eyes. If it was a boy, he would name him William after his own loving father.

The sound of singing outside the room echoed up along the street. German voices and they were singing carols. Soft music played. It was Christmas and he was a captain and a father. A father!

Hallam took a long swig of the brandy, eyes glistening in the firelight.

It was a magical Christmas.

Historical Note

The Flanders Campaign of 1793-1795 was conducted during the first years of the French Revolutionary War by the allied states of the First Coalition and the French First Republic. The allied aim was to invade France by mobilising its armies along the French frontiers to bully it into submission.

In the north, the allies' immediate aim was to expel the French from the Dutch Republic and the Austrian Netherlands, then march directly to Paris. Britain invested a million pounds to finance their Austrian and Prussian allies. Twenty thousand British troops under George III's younger son, Prince Frederick, the Duke of York, were eventually tied up in the campaign.

Austrian Prince Josias of Saxe-Coburg was in overall command, but answered directly to Emperor Francis II, while the Duke of York was given objectives set by William Pitt the Younger's Foreign Minister, Henry Dundas. Thus, from the outset, mixed political machinations and ignorance hindered the operation.

The French armies on the other-hand also suffered. Many from the old royalist officer class had emigrated following the revolution, which left the cavalry severely undermanned and those officers that remained were fearful of being watched by the representatives. The price of failure or disloyalty was the guillotine. After the Battle of Hondshoote, September 1793, the British and Hanoverians under the Duke of York were defeated by General Houchard and General Jourdan. Houchard was arrested for treason for failing to organise a pursuit and guillotined.

By the spring of 1793, the French had virtually marched into the Dutch Republic and Austrian Netherlands unopposed. In May, the British won a victory at Famars and then followed up the success for the siege of Valenciennes. However, instead of concentrating, the allies dispersed their forces in an attempt to mop up the scattered French outposts. The French re-organised and combined their troops. Dundas requested the Duke of York to lay siege to Dunkirk who had to abandon it after a severe mauling at Hondshoote.

By the end of the year, the allied forces were now stretched. The Duke of York was unable to offer support the Austrians and Prussians, because the army was suffering from supply problems. Dundas was withdrawing regiments in order to re-assign them to the West Indies.

The French counter-offensive in the spring of the following year smashed apart the fragile allied lines. The Austrian command broke down as Francis II called for a withdrawal. At the Battle of Fleurus, the defeated Austrians; abandoning their century long hold of the Netherlands, retreated north towards Brussels. The loss of the Austrian support and the Prussians (who had also fallen back) led to the campaign's collapse.

The French advanced unchecked.

By the autumn, the Duke of York had been replaced by Sir William Harcourt, but with rumoured peace talks, the British position looked increasingly vulnerable. The only allied success of that year was that of the 'Glorious First of June', when Britain's Lord Howe defeated a French naval squadron in the Atlantic, sinking a ship and capturing six.

The winter of 1794 was one of the worst any one had ever imagined. Rivers froze, men died in the sleep, disease was rampant, and the soldier's uniforms fell apart. It was an extremely harsh winter, because the army was starving due to the collapsed commissariat. Troops started to steal from the local inhabitants. The officers were too lazy or indifferent to control them, and discipline amongst some units broke down completely.

By the spring of 1795, the limping British reached the Hanoverian port of Bremen. They arrived back in Britain, weak, ill and emaciated. Some never fully recovered and left the army.

The Flanders Campaign demonstrated a series of weaknesses in the British Army. The Duke of York was given the role as Commander-in-Chief and brought forth a programme of reform. It created the professional army that was to fight with much success throughout the Peninsular War.

The allies abandoned the Low Countries. Britain did attempt to undertake a second invasion of the newly proclaimed Batavian Republic in 1799 under The Duke of York, but it faltered and proved equally disastrous.

Notoriously, a children's rhyme about the Holland campaign mocked the leadership of the Duke of York:

Oh, The grand old Duke of York,
He had ten thousand men;
He marched them up to the top of the hill,
And he marched them down again.

And when they were up, they were up,
And when they were down, they were down,
And when they were only half-way up,
They were neither up nor down

However, there is another satirical verse attributed to Richard Tarlton, and so was adapted where possible, the latest being The Duke of York. The oldest version of the song dates from 1642:

The King of France with forty thousand men,
came up the hill and so came downe againe

Many officers who would continue to serve their countries received their baptism of fire on the fields of Flanders. Arthur Wesley, the future Duke of Wellington, was colonel of the 33rd Foot and saw his first action at the Battle of Boxtel. The Austrian Archduke Charles fought in Flanders, as did several of Napoleon's marshals: Jourdan, Ney, Murat, Mortier and Bernadotte. The Prussian General Sharnhorst, another great reformer of the Napoleonic Wars, saw battle under the Duke of York.

Lieutenant Jack Hallam of the 28th North Gloucestershire Regiment of Foot is sadly an invention, as are most of the characters of the story, except Lieutenant-Colonel Edward Paget. The regiment were part of the British 6th Brigade, and were active throughout the campaign; fighting rear-guard actions amid the retreat. Grave, a Dutch fortified town, was besieged by three thousand French during December. The Dutch garrison surrendered at the end of 1794. The battle depicted in *Blood on the Snow* is based on the skirmish at Tiel, where an allied contingent under General Dundas drove the French back south of the frozen River Waal. The allies could not hold the town due to an overwhelming French force, and so had to retreat past Arnhem and across the Rhine.

The Flanders Campaign may have ended in failure, but the 28th was one of the regiments that remained unwavering and dependable. Lord Cathcart wrote in his General Orders, *"Whenever danger is to be apprehended and difficulties to be surmounted, you have the 27th and the 28th to call upon"*.

The 28th returned home in May 1795, and later embarked for the West Indies. A gale known as 'Admiral Christian's Storm' sprang up when the convoy was at sea and four companies of the battalion made it safely to Barbados to assist in the capture of St Lucia in 1796. The other six companies returned home and were sent to garrison Gibraltar. The complete regiment went on to Malta and sailed with Sir Ralph Abercromby's Expeditionary Army to Egypt.

I am indebted to several people. Lady Elizabeth Longford's *Wellington: The Years of the Sword*, and Professor Richard Holmes' *Wellington: The Iron Duke*, helped me to see the campaign through the eyes of the great man. Holmes also wrote the truly wonderful *Redcoat: The British Soldier in the Age of Horse and Musket*. This is an excellent and comprehensive study of the British Army, which I found invaluable. For anyone wanting to read more about the campaign, I recommend reading Christopher Hibbert's *The French Revolution*.

Jack Hallam has more adventures to come.

Marksman

Arthur Cadoc and the Peninsular
War
Late Summer, Spain, 1810

Sunlight speared the Spanish countryside, dazzling everything beneath an azure sky liberated of cloud.

To the north was Valdecarros, a peaceful place of harvested fields, rich vineyards, white- painted farms with terracotta roofs and bright-red poppies. A winding stream, coiling itself in the grassy uplands around the hamlet like a snake, was suddenly spoilt by a galloping horseman that burst out of a grove of silver-trunked corks, splattering quicksilver water over parched soil. The rider tugged hard on the reins and jabbed steel spurs into the beast's chestnut flanks, pricking the tough hide with quick desperate prods of his heel.

Despite the bullying heat, he wore a plain grey frock coat over white, long-legged breeches. A sword sheathed in a black scabbard hung at his left hip and his knee-high leather boots were stained with dust and grime.

Captain Steven Kyte of his most Britannic Majesty's Army, raced down the slope towards Valdecarros, his coat undone exposing a heavily sweat-stained white shirt underneath.

'We can't stop, old boy,' he said breathlessly to his mount. 'When we reach Navales, I'll have you watered and stabled like a king that dotes on his favourite nag.' He glanced over his shoulder at the hills, and then down to the village. Blond hair matted his sweat-lined face. He would follow the swirling cool waters all the way to Alba de Tormes where his contact waited for him. The town was only part garrisoned by the French having been taken in the previous year after Spanish troops were routed by superior French cavalry on the banks of the River Tormes. 'You've damn well earned it. Just a bit more to go and we're free,' he said, angling his horse down through a copse of stunted trees. 'Just a bit more, old boy.' His horse stumbled, and Kyte was almost swept out of the saddle, having only just managed to hold on. 'Steady!' he said, trying to soothe the beast, 'steady does it.' The horse, hot foam dripping from the bit and flanks stinking of sweat, took Kyte towards the hamlet. It wasn't much of a place; a dozen houses, a tavern and a small white-painted church that blessed the vista.

A potter, making beautiful intricate tiles under the shade of a wisteria, gaped up at the stranger, before frowning because he had lost his concentration. Kyte edged his horse down the tiny dirt road. Washing hung between the buildings. Vivid colours of field marigolds, wild lavender and asphodels bloomed in gardens, where the infectious and vivifying sound of children played.

'*Inglés*,' he said to the smattering of suspicious glances from the folk who watched him from shadowed doorways and windows. '*Soy Inglés*,' he repeated. It was not good to be French, especially a lone French rider in this war-ravaged land. The guerrilleros stalked them and captured them, tortured and killed them. They were bitter enemies and the French would die a slow and horrible death.

The tavern's door creaked open. Dust motes billowed outside. A woman, with hair the colour of black pepper and carrying a basket, came over to him where he paid good silver for a loaf, a length of smoked sausage, bread, tomatoes and a wineskin.

'*Gracias*,' he said and the woman dipped her head to him. Kyte glanced behind again, but no one followed. The enemy was gone and he breathed a sigh of relief, taking in the air of fried sardines and spices wafting from the nearest house. He clicked his tired horse in the shade and a bow-legged man, with a head of silver wiry hair, showed him a trough where water sparkled bright.

As his horse slurped noisily, Kyte slumped against a kinked trunk of a carob tree, allowing a sudden breeze to stir his ruffled clothes. He was exhausted; having ridden for days, but as the minutes ticked away, he knew the dangers of indolence.

He had a secret and it could not wait.

Kyte hungrily bit into the tomatoes, guzzled the wine, tore at the bread and looped the sausage around his saddle's pommel for later. He had eaten like an animal, but he was too famished to care who saw him. He hadn't eaten anything for three days. His captors had left him with nothing except cuts, bruises and cracked bones. Kyte ran a sleeve across his mouth afterwards, and gazed up at the road where only a cat hunted in a small garden of tangled brown grass. Two old men chatted beside a collection of penned white guinea fowl. There were no enemies. His mount had finished drinking and he knew that the next part of the journey would be even more uncomfortable, for every stop made it worse. Still, he contemplated; he had out-thought his tormentors and would soon be free. He wearily clambered up into the saddle and urged the beast on with a gentle prod of his heels.

Kyte tentatively edged out from the huddle of houses, cool shadows replaced by fiery heat before gazing up at the southern crest. It was wondrously peaceful. A gentle breeze rippled crops and nudged the pale leave of the olive groves and prickly pears. No dust rising from the straggling roads that betrayed movement. He clicked his mount forward.

Then, there was a sudden flash of silver in the cork orchard and Kyte's heart raced like a hunted animal's. He fished in his sabretache and pulled out his telescope. He extended the brass tube, which was cloth-covered to prevent the metal from giving away his position and he scanned for enemies. A nerve twitched along his jaw.

Glints of metal revealed dark shapes emerging from the tree line. Green-coated killers with yellow facings and brass horse-hair plumed helmets on big war horses.

French cavalry. Dragoons.

'Oh God,' he uttered.

The French word for dragoon was *dragon* and Kyte's body shook with nerves as though he had actually seen a mythical beast. Damn! They were here! He wiped the sweat that dripped to sting his blue eyes and trained his glass on the leading files. There were at least eighty of them. He could see moustached faces, grim under peaked helmets. Their *cadenettes*; pigtails that marked them as elite, swayed to the stride of the horses. Reflected sunlight glimmered like tiny sparks on their buckles and stirrups. These days the dragoons had taken to wearing cloth covers over their helmets, hoping to hide the gleam of brass and so make it easier to surprise the partisans who they hunted. They carried straight-bladed swords and their short-barrelled muskets were kept in a saddle-boot for quick and easy skirmishing.

He searched for a man dressed in civilian clothes. That was the one he feared. His heart pounded and blood seemed to pop in his ears. He wasn't there. Good. No wait. He searched again. There was a man with a brown jacket. Kyte swore. He was here! Kyte watched the man stare down into the valley where his gaze seemed to wander to exactly where Kyte now waited. The enemy halted. Kyte remained motionless. The

299

man yawned, stretched out his arms and slowly as though he knew the Englishman was watching him, pulled out his firearm from the bucket holster. Kyte's eyes jumped to the walls, fields and to where the sails of a tower wind mill creaked. It was a long way from the dragoons. No musket could ever hope to reach that distance, but the man in civilian clothes did not carry a smoothbore weapon; instead, he carried a rifle: a British-made Baker rifle.

Kyte watched the man who had turned to the dragoon officer to talk. He could see their mouths opening and closing. They didn't seem to be in a hurry or concerned about anything. Kyte looked down at the windmill, back at the trees again and decided to take advantage of the distance. He collapsed the scope, put it back in the sabretache, and kicked his heels back.

He felt naked and unprotected as he galloped down through the fields. He twisted in the saddle to look up at the skyline, imaging threatening silhouettes coming, but no one came. The freshening wind blew his hair back as the beast took him with great speed to the structure. From there, he would use the terrain to his advantage, and get to Navales before sunset. A friendly band of patriots patrolled this stretch of land and even a full troop of French dragoons would still be a target for their ambushes, and hit and run tactics. The French invaders held the majority of the towns and cities, but they had never conquered the countryside. There, the guerrilleros were the true victors. They roamed the land like undaunted princes and kings.

'Faster! Faster!' he urged his mount.

Kyte nudged the horse with his knees which indicated where he desired to go and the horse instantly obeyed. He swept past the wind mill, where two women dressed in black gaped at him, and up a slight rise where lizards scurried clear of the thundering hooves. Curiosity made him glance over his shoulder again. The dragoons had not moved, not even attempted to pursue him. What the hell? He gently eased back on the reins to slow down. What game were they playing at? Then, the civilian dismounted and knelt in front of the others. The bastard was about to shoot him in the back.

Kyte witnessed a puff of smoke just before an echo tore through the air. Birds panicked up from the nearest trees, then circled and flew back to the branches as the powder-smoke dissipated. No lead ball struck him. He was alive! The rifle could not reach him and he would not die today! He would complete his mission and this man would be doomed. He tugged back on the reins and gave a huge exultant cry. His horse whinnied and rose up its hind legs. If Kyte had kept his bicorn hat, he would have given an ironic salute.

'Good riddance, you bastards! See you in hell!'

He stayed there for a moment, savouring the feeling of freedom. Then, a second puff erupted from the enemy line. This time, the echo sounded like the crack of a whip and the bullet punched its way through his body with enough force to jerk him clean out of the saddle. Kyte was thrown onto his back. His horse, frightened by the gunshot, galloped off. There was just enough time for him to realise the first shot had been a ruse and the second was from the feared rifle.

He let out a moan and blood vented his mouth to spatter his chin. Everything swirled and he suddenly felt a coldness creep into his shattered body before the world went dark.

*

'Welcome to Navales, *senōr*,' said a quick voice in accented English.

A tall British officer, wearing a blue jacket of the Ordnance, pulled his cocked hat down more tightly to shield his eyes from the molten gold sun. 'Thank you,' he replied, not looking at the man, but gazing up at the thickening crowd of Spanish onlookers. *Like they were watching a damned play*, he thought. One, on horseback, watched the wagons approach with a baleful expression. Another was kneeling down to a small wayside shrine with his back to them. *Some reception.* 'Is this Navales?'

'*Senōr?*'

'We're a day late. Our guide got us lost and then the rascal promptly disappeared. Probably on purpose.' The miserable officer waved the olive-skinned Spaniard away with a flick of his wrist. 'Oh, never mind.' He sighed and gazed up at the shuttered white-washed houses, the crop fields that edged all the way to the horizon, the suspicious townsfolk and grimaced at the dark-skinned children hardly clothed at all and crawling with lice. 'This must be the place,' he said, shuddering with distaste.

'May we look at the guns, *senōr?*' the Spaniard asked politely.

The officer clicked his fingers and a group of privates unfurled the canvasses on two thick-wheeled wagons. There were muskets and pistols, barrels and crates of ammunition and powder. A half-dozen mules, tethered to the rear wagon, carried more firearms and a private stood sullenly holding the officer's mount.

301

Captain George Israel Cotton reached inside his newly-brushed jacket, dragged out a red handkerchief and mopped his brow. His buttons and badges gleamed. 'I must say that the journey was atrocious. The roads here are either in poor condition or completely non-existent. I suppose you fellows don't know how to build them. No skills and all that. The weather must have something to do with it. I was supplied a map, but God knows what for. The hills on this drawing show them to be to the north, but in reality they are to the west. I don't know who is to blame. The cartographer, or the Almighty for creating such a strenuous and wicked country.'

'*Senõr?*' the Spaniard asked, baffled at the whining Englishman.

'Nevertheless, I'm here to present the guns to a...a...' Cotton paused to read his orders, 'Colonel Antonio Herrero.' He gave the mounted one an inquisitive glance, and wondered when he would have the nerve to ask the Spaniard to sign the papers for the receipt of the arms.

The Spanish, at the behest of the mounted one, began to take the weapons until a voice called out. It was almost guttural. They all turned to the man who had been praying at the shrine. He had long coal-black hair, turned grey at the temples, and tied back with a bow. He wore a moustache in the typical Spanish fashion. He was unshaven with a hard angled face that bordered leanness. They watched him descend the heather-haunted slope to the wagons where he picked up a musket and cocked it. He shook his head vehemently, threw the firearm down, smoke-coloured eyes scanned over the rest of the weapons.

'Rust,' the man said, holding another one up. 'Goddamned rust.' He shot Cotton a look of menace.

'I say...' Cotton started, but the man's truculent expression was so brutal that he failed to finish what he was about to say.

The guerrillero continued to manhandle the muskets. He lifted one up, shouldered it and aimed it squarely at Cotton who blanched.

The dog-head snapped forward with a loud click. The man tossed the weapon onto the pile. 'It won't do. It won't do at all.' In and amongst the stacks of muskets of all ages and conditions were carbines, ancient muskets, musketoons and even snaphances. 'This isn't what was promised.'

Cotton adjusted his bicorn. 'Who are you, sir?' he said in the tone of one trying to acquire self-respect in the face of absolute insolence.

The man ignored him. 'Firing plates missing, loose triggers, fouled barrels, missing flints, missing screws, missing mainsprings...' He

302

paused whilst he picked up a smaller firearm, seemingly taken away with it.

'That's a rifle,' Cotton said. 'Made by gun-maker Ezekiel Baker, and was selected by the Board of Ordnance for The Corps of Experimental Riflemen in 1800.'

'I know what it is,' the guerrillero snapped. He ran a hand up and down the barrel, and then down to the stock, fingers feeling the grain of wood like a lovers caress.

The Baker rifle had seven rectangular grooves in the barrel, which gave it its deadly accuracy because it spun the ball when fired. Like the German *jäger* rifles, it had a scrolled brass trigger-guard to help ensure a firm grip and a raised cheek-piece on the left-hand side of the butt for snug purchase. It also had a patchbox located in the rifle's brass bound butt where the Rifleman would keep greased linen patches, a cleaning kit and tools. In short, it was a beautiful weapon of lethal precision.

'Is this the only one? A pity. It will do, but only suitable for parts. The rest…' the stranger shrugged. 'Not worth the bother. What are we supposed to do with them? Some of the stocks are infested with woodworm. I haven't checked the powder and cartridges yet, but I'm guessing they're in a sorry state too. Now, you can take them all back to your depot and return with complete working muskets, oiled, polished and with flints.'

'I..er-'

'I want the guns back here in three weeks,' the man interjected. 'No later. And this time I want a score of rifles and our riders need good horse shoes. Britain makes the bloody best and I want a five hundred brought back with you.' He rapped on the lid of a trunk half-hidden by arms. 'What's in here?'

Cotton's eyes bulged at the demands. As the red mist of outrage passed, this amounted to him stomping a leather boot into the ground and grinding his teeth, he suddenly realised the man had been speaking fluent English, but with a Welsh accent. Cotton eyed up the man's appearance with this new knowledge. He wore a pair of brown leather half-boots and heavily patched dark green pantaloons the same colour as his jacket and a black leather belt with a bayonet frog that was wrinkled from harsh weather. One or two white-metal buttons were missing on the coat, replaced with bone or white-painted wood, but there was no mistaking the black cuffs and delicate white piping.

'What are you doing here, Rifleman?' Cotton exclaimed, face leering. 'Deserter, are we? I can have you shot for that.' The captain's men looked over with eager attentiveness.

The guerrillero let the silence drag as he looked back at the shrine.

'I asked you a question, damn your insolence,' Cotton's nostrils flared. 'As a captain of His Majesty's Ordnance, I order you to-'

The patriot turned and grabbed Cotton by the lapels, shoving him back against the wagon before he could utter a gasp. His black felt bicorn tumbled down over a shoulder.

'You don't give me orders,' the partisan said. 'Now, you've a job to do, so get your arse moving.'

Seeing his commander being jostled, a huge lantern-jawed corporal shouldered his way through the throng, drawing a muscled arm back. The partisan, seeing the threat, ducked as the thick-fingered fist harmlessly punched the air. He nimbly dodged the next attack and brought up his right fist, which caught the corporal clean under the chin, knocking him backwards into Cotton who made a sound like a bagpipe being squeezed. The moustached man swiftly followed it with a right jab, a left, and then a right. The NCO shook his head to clear it from the assault, but was too slow to stop a thump to his belly and a powerful uppercut that knocked him clean out.

Cotton stood wide-eyed with the corporal groaning and bleeding at his feet. The guerrillero had a mask of someone used to gutter fights and brawls that wouldn't be out of place at a dockside tavern. Cotton's legs buckled slightly.

The NCO gasped and twitched back into consciousness. Blood seeped into the dry soil from a cut above his right eye. He stared disorientated, tried to move his limbs, and failed.

'Are you all right, Corporal?' Cotton managed to ask.

The NCO blinked and looked up at his assailant who had not moved.

'You get up again, boy, and we'll have another go,' the guerrillero told him.

The corporal hesitated, thought better of it, and held up a hand in submission.

'W-who are you?' Cotton gaped.

The man adjusted the rifle to stare up at the tall captain. 'Arthur Cadoc,' he said, 'and I was once a Chosen Man of the 95th Rifles.'

Cadoc was twenty-nine years old and from Fishguard, Pembrokeshire. He was the eldest son of six generations of fishermen who lived in a tiny house near the cove's harbour. He had first fought the French during the invasion of his town, February 1797, aged sixteen. The French, on-board a ship flying a Union Flag, had deceived the local yeomanry who let them disembark thinking they were comrades. Cadoc had found out their plans and alerted the militia and a skirmish ensued. Adept at hitting target with slings and with his father's old fowling piece, Cadoc killed six French soldiers with a yeomanry carbine. Praised for his shooting skills, he was convinced that his talents lie elsewhere rather than fishing for the rest of his life. He enlisted in the Light Company of the 43rd Monmouthshire Regiment, and then through skill, joined The Corps of Experimental Riflemen three years later.

'So you've been soldiering for a while now,' Cotton said.

Cadoc was a dangerous-looking man. He reminded Cotton of the other campaigners; men as tough as old boots, and he was a Welshman; a born fighter, and a proper warrior. He had knocked out Leatherby in seconds. Cotton had seen the raging fire in his eyes, the intense look of a prize-fighter and a champion of knuckle fights. The captain adjusted his neck tie. He was twenty-five and had bought his captaincy after the British victory at Talavera, and had never seen action. The two of them were now seated and shaded under a thick canopy of wisteria vines that ran across a trellis outside the village's tavern. Wine, cheese, figs, bread and ham were served on plates. If it wasn't for the war, it could have been a blessed day in paradise.

The Rifleman merely grunted a reply and speared a cut of the meat with a knife, putting a thick piece into his mouth.

Cotton, feeling awkward by the confrontation and the fact that he did not know how to converse with the rank and file, shifted in his chair. He'd given his men permission to smoke and brew tea at the wagons, and that had at least been received with a satisfactory grunt from Leatherby. 'So, where have you seen action...?' His voice faded because he did not know how to address the Rifleman-cum-guerrillero. His stomach rumbled painfully, but he was too timid to take some of the food.

Cadoc watched a bee buzz between the beautiful purple flowers overhead as he chewed noisily. 'Copenhagen, Roliça, Vimeiro and Corunna.'

Cotton tried to hide his embarrassment from the green-jacket who had accomplished feats he could only dream of, and exuded competence, by casting his gaze down at his boots. A scarlet glow flooded his hollow cheeks. 'Copenhagen?'

Cadoc, apparently oblivious to the captain's misery, bobbed his head. 'Aye, peculiar bloody fight that was.'

'What happened?'

The Welshman picked a strand of meat from between two teeth with a finger. 'We landed, fired a few volleys and left. It was something to do with the Danish fleet. Strange, like I said. Same thing with Buenos Aires.'

'What in God's name were you doing there?'

Cadoc stroked the ends of his moustache. 'I haven't a clue. I was a soldier. I was sent there. I never asked any questions.'

Britain had sent an expeditionary force under General John Whitelocke to seize some of Spain's territories. It proved to be disastrous and after suffering heavy losses, the army had surrendered. It was a humiliating defeat and upon returning home Whitelocke was court martialled and cashiered.

'We could have fought on, but the general had us surrender,' Cadoc continued unhappily. 'General Craufurd was there and he said to me if I was to see the general I was to shoot him.' The Rifleman suddenly laughed at the memory. 'It's not the first time I've shot a bad officer. But this time I wasn't so lucky. My aim was off and the general lived.'

Cotton didn't know whether to believe the tale, so he grimaced, before glancing over to where his men waited with the parked wagons, stiff with bristling stoicism. The Spaniards seemed pleasant enough and looked content to smoke pipes, drink and talk amongst themselves. There were about thirty of them. Only the mounted one looked out of place. He was as hard-looking as Cadoc, same height, but more refined with a long aquiline nose and a carefully trimmed moustache. He was well-dressed in a short scarlet jacket, with dark curls and his cheeks were widened with bushy side-whiskers. His brown eyes met Cotton's, and yet, there was no acknowledgement. The captain considered that his presence was not wanted, so he would leave after taking refreshment.

'Corunna,' Cotton said, 'now that was a sad affair.'

'You were there?'

'No, but my commanding officer was in one of the last ships to set sail after the battle. He was there when they buried Moore.'

306

Sir John Moore, the commanding officer of a small expeditionary army, had been sent to Spain to sever the invading French supply lines. The French, who had pounded half of Europe, turned on Moore who, after a series of Spanish defeats that left the British alone, was forced to retreat through the Galician mountains to Corunna. There, they had to do battle in order to allow the men to embark on the waiting transport ships. The British, following their fighting retreat, were victorious, but Moore was killed in the final stages of the battle. It was a terrible loss to the army.

'I lost three toes to frostbite, nearly a finger, and was severely wounded in the battle,' Cadoc said, remembering that every day was another tortuous march of cramped bellies, pain and cold. 'In fact, a local doctor said I was at death's door and would not be able to travel. I didn't want to stay here. I thought once we landed, I would have been transported to Hilsea where the regiment has a hospital. But upon hearing that Sir John had died I wept like a babe.'

Cotton had heard of Sir John's reputation as an inspirational leader for having pushed the boundaries of new light infantry tactics, and of the national grieving that followed his death. 'By all accounts, you were lucky to survive.'

'Aye, I thought the retreat would kill me for sure. It killed one of my best friends. But we're a tough lot: us boys from the 95th. First on the field and always the last off,' Cadoc said proudly, scratching at the scar on his belly where a musket ball had nearly killed him.

Cotton knew of the Rifles status. In the decade since the regiment's early formation, it had won the admiration of every veteran battalion in the army. They were considered the elite.

'What happened to you after Corunna?'

Grazia. That was what happened after the retreat. He closed his eyes, because the image of her was strongest then. Beautiful Grazia, with her dark tousled hair, snow-white teeth, and slender body. He missed her. 'I was nursed back to health. I was dreadfully thin and my hair had turned grey. But I lived. The fleet had sailed home without me. I was stranded.'

Cotton still couldn't understand why the Welshman hadn't tried to re-join the army since his recovery. 'Is that why you became one of these bandits?'

'They are decent men,' Cadoc riposted. 'Not all guerrilleros are scum. These help the locals rather than intimidate and rob. They report enemy movements to our intelligence too. Spy for them. They do good work. Work that will help turf the bastard Frogs out of this country.'

Cotton reddened from the rebuke. The stories he had heard of their acts of vengeance on the French had left him in a cold sweat. It was strange to hear something respectable about them.

Rather than apologise, he said something else. 'So do you lead these men? Or is it left to that patriot on the horse?'

'Colonel Antonio Rai Herrero,' Cadoc chided him. 'He's a fine gentleman.'

Cotton wrinkled his nose at the gentle reproof, considering that he deserved it for being boorish. He sighed. 'He looks a bit brutish if you ask me.'

Cadoc grunted with mirth. 'You have to be to fight this war. Rai has seen tragedy. His home was burned down and his wife and children thrown to the flames by the French. Now he hunts them.'

'Dear God,' Cotton could only say.

'After the ships had gone home, nobody knew where our boys would be sent next. Some said Lisbon. Some said they were going to the Netherlands. By that time the whole north was crawling with the bloody French. So I decided to throw my lot in with them.'

Cotton narrowed his gaze. 'Was it because of the girl?'

Cadoc's eyes twinkled with the memories. 'You're a perceptive sod, if you don't mind me saying so. Yes. Her brother was a guerrillero. I spent much of '09 with them.' He remembered the savage attacks on the French, the ambushes, the raids, the sabotage and the torture of prisoners. The exhilaration, terror, anxiety and the horror of his new employment haunted his dreams. But not as much as Grazia's death, or her brother's at the hands of the vengeful French. Cadoc managed to escape the slaughter to drift down into the plains where he stumbled onto a skirmish between Rai's men and a Polish lancer troop. He picked off all the officers with his prized rifle and the lancers retreated. Rai begged him to fight alongside his men and he accepted. 'But I'm here now.'

'For good?'

Cadoc smiled, his teeth flashed brilliantly in contrast to his sun-darkened face. 'I'm happy here.'

'What about your regiment?'

And that was the truth of it. Cadoc did miss his old comrades. He didn't know who had survived the battle of Corunna and where they were now. He was proud of the Rifles and what they had achieved, but

308

would he be welcomed back? Would the Provosts come looking for him? If he was found guilty of desertion, then he would be hanged for sure.

Cotton continued seeing Cadoc's hesitation. 'You still wear your old coat.'

Cadoc nodded vehemently. 'With pride.'

'Even though you've turned your back on your regiment?' Cotton saw the Welshman's expression darken. 'What I'm trying to say is that even as a guerrillero you still wear your Rifle uniform.'

'I'll be buried in it too.'

Cotton slapped away a fly, frowning. The tiny insects seemed to multiply with every minute of the day. 'Where are your loyalties, Cadoc? I don't understand.'

Cadoc had wondered the same thing since Corunna. But he had helped the locals riding with Rai's group and he was highly thought of. Rai was a good leader and an honest man and although Cadoc's Spanish wasn't very good, he could communicate well enough with them. Besides, he didn't miss the constant orders, the marching, the peacock-strutting officers, vindictive NCOs and definitely the rations. Out here, he had at least found freedom. But he still yearned for his old friends company, their coarse humour and the larking about. By wearing his green coat, he thought himself still part of them; perhaps they wouldn't forget him as he would never forget them.

'I'm still killing Frenchman, and so I'll stick around and help these people out. When the bloody Frogs are defeated, I'll think again about what to do, or where to go.'

'Return home?'

Cadoc shrugged. 'Maybe.'

'A bit different than Wales, eh?'

Cadoc chuckled. 'I miss the green hills. I miss the rain. It rains here, but it isn't the same stuff. I miss the valleys and the woods. I miss lots of things. Aye, you probably think I'm a sentimental fool.'

'I pine for home too,' Cotton said. He pursed his mouth, sweat glistened on his top lip. He rattled fingers on the table as though he was anxious. 'When I turn in my report, I'm going to have to tell my superiors about you.'

Cadoc leaned back in the chair and blinked.

'My dear fellow, I have to,' Cotton replied earnestly when there was no reply. 'I have to tell them that your men refused the weapons. That'll send ripples into the pond. Ripples will cause waves and the top echelon will want to know what happened. They always do. Perhaps Lord Wellington of Talavera will hear about you? Nothing escapes his ear, so they say, and I know for I have a cousin in the Staff Corps.'

'That's a shame.'

'Indeed.' Cotton replayed the words in his head, then frowned. 'I'm sorry?' he said, straightening himself.

'No, I'm the one that's sorry.'

Cotton lifted his eyebrows suspiciously, but remained silent as the Welshman spoke.

'You, your men and your wagons, aren't going anywhere.'

The young officer jumped out of his seat, bare head knocking a cluster of the hanging wisteria. 'What the deuce? How dare you threaten-' he bellowed and Cadoc waved a dismissive hand.

'You don't understand, Captain,' he clarified. 'You're staying put, because we're going to kill the Frogs, and you're going to help us.'

Cotton took a gulp of air.

'The firearms aren't just for us,' Cadoc explained to the young officer, 'they are meant for an uprising.'

'After Bailén,' Herrero said in a tone of cold civility, 'it told the world that the French could be defeated and that the Spanish would not lie down like dogs and be forced into submission. It proved that we can fight,' he paused to drink from a wineskin. 'It proved to you *ingleses* that we can fight and it spat in the face of the devil, Bonaparte.' He sputtered the Emperor's name as though it were a piece of rotten meat.

Bailén had been a resounding defeat for the French two years ago. Their army tried to break through the city having been outflanked and driven back. Following this, they capitulated to the Spanish, losing eighteen thousand as prisoners of war. The victory spread like wildfire across Europe and it seemed that the French would be expelled, but the Spanish armies were no more, the government hid in Cádiz and Napoleon had installed his brother Joseph, as King José-Napoleon I of Spain.

Cotton shot a worried glance at the wagons. He knew the arms were old, rusted and no good. Any uprising with these weapons would be short-lived, but he dared not reveal that sentiment. His commanding officer, Major Edeson, a burly Yorkshireman, had chided him for his concern.

310

'They are only for the irregulars, Cotton,' he had answered back at the tiny depot on Portugal's border. 'Damned bandits with no morals and ideals. They care not for their people or for Spain's future, mark my words. They care about killing, looting and raping. No discipline, see? The Dons can't match the Frogs in the field and so all that's left for them to do is bite and sting like bloody gnats. Let them take the arms, and report back to me by sun down. I have something more important for you than cleaning out our stock piles. It seems the Frogs have sent an army to take Portugal. And so what remains of us here will pull back behind the Lines.'

Cotton had heard about the Lines of Torres Vedras, which were a series of redoubts, blockhouses and ravelins strategically placed on the top of hills and passes outside Lisbon. The forts were defended with artillery batteries, militia and regular troops. Below, the land was completely destroyed and turned into a huge glacis. Every ounce of food had been removed or burned, vineyards cut down, and wells were filled with stones or fouled with carcasses, livestock taken and homes demolished. The French, who famously lived off the land, would have nothing to supply them. In essence, they would starve.

Edeson scratched at an insect bite on his buttocks. 'So all Monsewer Bonaparte has to do is take Portugal. The dagoes have been beaten, the Austrians and Russians out of the war, Prussians dithering, which means only us left to beat.'

Cotton had ignored the major's summation of the Emperor's strategy. 'What happens if they refuse the arms, sir?' he had said.

Edeson had looked galled at the prospect. 'The devil take the ungrateful wretches!'

Cotton stared at the scarlet-coated officer. 'How can I possibly help you? I work in the Ordnance. My job is deliveries, stores, sometimes repairs. Drudgery.'

'Exactly the man we need,' Cadoc said.

This assignment is getting worse, Cotton said to himself. He gazed around, uneasy.

Rai ran long fingers through his luxuriant black hair. 'You want to kill Frenchmen, Captain?'

'Yes, they're my enemies too.'

Rai watched him like a hawk watching prey. 'I am a colonel in the Spanish Army, Captain. I would appreciate the courtesy given to my rank.'

Cotton could see no evidence of this on Rai's clothes, only taking a stranger's word on the matter. Besides, where was Herrero's regiment? Where were his men? His red jacket was modestly plain, patched on one elbow and he wore brown woollen pantaloons, stockings and *alpartarga* sandals. The only evidence of him being an officer was a battered officer's bicorn of a Spanish line regiment, and Cotton had seen several guerrilleros wear the same headdress. They all carried a *cuchillo*; a knife, pistols and muskets. Nevertheless, instinct, and what the Rifleman had said, told him to be respectful.

'Of course, sir,' he replied politely. 'I apologise for my incivility.'

Rai gave a tight smile, pleased that he had made his point, but did not revel in the reproach. 'I want the French expunged from my country. And to make that a reality, Captain, I have to kill every Frenchmen I see. By any means.' He leaned in closer to Cotton. He brought up a cigarillo and puffed a couple of times, the blue smoke drifted away with the breeze. 'Ever since the scum killed my wife and my children, I have hunted them. I am good at it. I specialise in it. And for those I capture I kill. Eventually.' He gave Cotton a wolfish grin. 'I have cut them in places that would make you sick. I have plucked out organs whilst they still breathed. I have burned them. I have shot them. I have strangled them and I've even drowned them. If it had not been for the deceit of the French, we Spanish would still be your enemies. It is not too long after Trafalgar, no? But fate has brought us together, and so together we will drive them back across the Pyrenees to their hellish cesspits where they belong. You can play a part in this, or simply walk away. Your choice.'

Cotton licked his lips. However inexperienced, he would not be called a coward. *From the pan into the fire.*

'I'll stay, sir.'

Rai watched him for a moment, before nodding. '*Bueno.*'

'I've got something to show you,' Cadoc said with a twitch of a smile, and tying back a black bandana in the customary partisan fashion. 'And bring your boys too. They'll need to see what we have up here. That corporal's a strapping lad, isn't he? A proper brawler that one.'

Leatherby was the biggest man Cotton had ever known, and hitherto, Cadoc had knocked him out in seconds. Somehow, he considered, bulk had nothing to do with winning a fight.

'Quite,' Cotton muttered laconically.

Cadoc and Rai led the seven blue-coated men to a huge stone barn situated on the rocky crest above the town. The doors were pulled open and inside were great hillocks of hay. Cadoc went over to one of the mounds and hauled at the dried grass. At first, Cotton thought the Riflemen had lost his wits, but then he caught a glimpse of metal, and suddenly there was a wheel and carriage.

'One of them is Spanish, two are French and there's one of ours here too,' Cadoc said.

Cotton looked stern. 'You brought us up here to help drag them out?'

'No, Captain, much more than that,' Rai was smiling. 'You're going to fix them.'

'Fix them?' Cotton gaped at the old clumsy pieces covered in dust.

Cadoc slapped the barrel of the nearest one. 'I believe this is a Spanish twelve pounder. Sebastiano says it is a siege gun. The carriage is split. So one charge and it's done for.'

Cotton, enthused by the different cannon, inspected it carefully. He saw the two cracks in the carriage, which had been damaged in an accident. His eyes scanned the bolts, fixings and screws. 'This piece has different wheels, which tells me they've been replaced by limber ones and not refitted. And you see underneath the barrel placement there are severe dents. The left trunnion is buckled. This one was dropped, or slid down onto rocks. Most likely because of the treacherously narrow roads that seem to frequent this country,' he said, a smile playing on his lips, saw Rai's expression and then peered with serious determination. 'It's seen some action, though, from the apparent scorch marks around the muzzle.'

'What else can you tell me about it?'

'Well, this Sebastiano, you mentioned, is wrong. This wasn't a siege gun, or for garrison use because it would be red or stained with black fittings. Spanish carriage colours of the year of this one's manufacture were blue-grey, so this was a field gun. The pigment in the paint is actually cobalt blue; derived from cobalt oxide and, when exposed to the weather for a long period of time, it has a tendency to fade to a wishy-washy grey. I've seen this before.' He looked at the barrel, running a hand down from the swell, the neck to the vent. 'The good news is that it can be fixed. You need a team to lift the barrel in order for a carpenter to mend the carriage. A wright should be able to sort out the trunnion, and it does need its iron fittings replaced too. A bit of work, but it could be done.'

Cadoc raised a black eyebrow at the captain's knowledge. 'I'm impressed. Now tell me what you know of these two Frenchies.'

Cotton caressed the two cannons, crouching and looming over them. 'The first one is an old four pounder. I can't see the mark, so I'm guessing forty years old? It's got a wooden axle, not an iron one, and the barrel is cracked.'

'What does that mean?'

'It means it's useless.' Cotton gawked at the second one, teeth gnawing his upper lip. 'This is a heavier piece, an eight pounder. Looks sturdy, except it has no wheels,' he said wryly. 'Barrel is clean. Carriage is firm. Should be able to get this one to work.' He examined the last one. 'This is a British six pounder. Iron barrel painted black to protect it from rust. It worked, to some degree, but the vent is blocked. It's possibly been spiked.' This meant that the gun team, or an enemy, had driven a barbed metal spike down the touch-hole to prevent the cannon from being used again. With great skill, the spike could be drilled out, if not, it was beyond repair. 'I'd also need to see what's in the chamber. That too could be blocked. So you have two guns, possibly three, at your disposal.'

Cadoc grinned widely at Rai who gave Cotton a curt nod in appreciation.

'Seems we may have your guns fixed now, *senõr*,' Cadoc said to the Spaniard.

'*Bueno*,' clapped Rai. 'I am very pleased. This will help ensure that the French will regret what they started.'

But just as the men celebrated, a voice called out a warning. There were frantic hoof beats coming from the west.

Rai raced to the doorway and an urgent message was relayed to him from the town's courtyard.

'What is it?' Cotton asked Cadoc, panic clear in his voice.

The Rifleman checked that his rifle was loaded. 'No. Our scouts have brought back a uniformed man from the plains.'

'French?'

'No,' Cadoc replied. 'English. And a friend.'

Kyte was barely alive.

He still breathed, but would die soon. There was nothing more to be done. Navales' doctor, Duilio Escarrà, had probed for the bullet, but he

314

could not locate it. The gun shot was too severe, and Kyte had simply lost too much blood. Escarrà muttered something as he washed his bloody fingers in a bowl. He cleaned his instruments and washed out his bleeding-cup; coagulated gore floated on the surface.

'What did he say? It sounded like he said catholic?' Cotton asked, craning over Kyte's form. The small room was heated by a fire, and because of the midday sun, Cotton found himself sweating profusely.

'Doctor Escarrà said another heathen protestant dead in a catholic land,' Cadoc explained, holding up Kyte's long coat to examine the bullet wound. It was sodden with blood around a ragged vent.

Cotton could feel sweat dripping down his back. 'Who is he?' he said, gazing at the dying man.

Rai had been praying silently; clasping onto one of Kyte's hands tightly as though God could heal him, got up from his knees. In his other hand, he held rosary beads. 'His name is Steven Kyte, and is a friend to me and my brother. He has helped us countless times. And now,' Rai, face contorted with emotion and voice thickening, 'he will die.'

'Captain Kyte worked in the Peninsular Corps of Guides as an Exploring Officer,' Cadoc revealed.

'What does that entail?' Cotton asked.

'Kyte had a network of contacts throughout the area and provided information on Frenchie troop movements, where they went, were going, how many of them, infantry, cavalry and guns. He knew the colonel here very well and he knew the land. He always rode in uniform, so that he would not be accused of being a spy, but it looks like someone captured him.'

'How can you tell?'

Cadoc stooped and raised one of Kyte's wrists, showing red welts. 'He was tied up. There are also marks on his neck. Strangulation marks.'

Cotton stared wide-eyed. 'You mean to tell me that Captain Kyte was tortured?'

'Yes.'

'My God! By whom?'

Cadoc gaped at the man's naivety. 'By the French of course!'

Cotton looked as though he wanted to sit down. 'B-but they're our enemies.'

'Yes?'

Cotton rubbed his face. 'But,' he paused, 'there are rules of war. Wasn't Kyte given parole? He's an officer, for God's sake. A gentleman. Gentlemen don't go around tormenting each other like that.'

Rai looked appalled, and then sighed despondently. 'You English are so naive. This is war. This is horror. At Évora, the French massacred men, women and children. They pillaged, they raped and they tortured civilians. That's right, Captain. They raped women and children. Young infants. Blood ran like streams and the screams of the violated echoed to the next village. Priests were bayoneted and nailed to doors. Church silver stolen. Men had their eyes gouged out and were butchered like winter hogs.'

'My God,' Cotton said softly, looking as though he wanted to weep.

'The French are men with no honour. They come straight from the devil's own backside.'

'Look sir, we need your help,' Cadoc said to Cotton. 'We need those guns working so we can slaughter the bastards and maybe the ones that did this.'

Kyte jerked awake. His face was greyish, his skin slick with sweat, his eyes crimson- rimmed, and he began to mutter incoherently. Escarrà spoke hurried Spanish to Rai.

'What did he say?' Cotton asked Cadoc, the heat prickling sweat on his cheeks.

'He says that Kyte has a fever. His mind is gone. We'll never know who did this to him.'

Rai took his hand again. 'Steven, my friend,' he spoke in English because he wanted Cotton to understand. 'We shall ride again someday. A day under a glorious Spanish sun that is free from all enemies.' Cotton thought he saw the Spaniard glance sideways at him. 'I will pray for your soul. *Adiós, amigo.*'

Escarrà grunted. 'He won't understand you,' he said in rather good English that surprised Cotton. 'I wish I could offer more hope, but there is none. Allow him to enter God's realm in peace. I shall bring in Padre Tos. He can give our friend what he needs now.'

Kyte whispered something and Rai went closer to the bed. 'Steven? I didn't hear you? What did you say?'

Kyte's eyes flickered, stayed on Cotton who stared aghast, rolled like a tormented beast and finally closed.

'He'll not make any sense,' Escarrà stubbornly insisted. 'I did warn you.'

'He just did,' Rai responded quickly. 'He said *colaboracionista.*'

316

Cotton gaped at the grim faces in the room. 'What does that mean?' Cadoc was solemn. 'It means betrayer.'

*

Chef-de-battalion Pierre Helterlin had a journey of nearly one hundred and fifty miles and had to be escorted by a squadron of his dragoons who clattered across the border and into the Portuguese city of Pombal long after nightfall. He climbed wearily from his mount, handed his helmet to an orderly, and limped to the house where a Tricolour flew proudly. Orange trees grew outside and the citrus scents teased his nostrils as he climbed the steps to the grand building. Ten sentries stood outside, their muskets tipped with bayonets that reflected the bright lights from inside.

Helterlin climbed the stairs, nudging his sore thighs with a gloved hand. He took a step towards the central door and pounded on it. Sounds of muffled voices came from inside, floorboards creaked and the door was opened by a smartly dressed orderly. Several men in a brightly lit room were engaged in conversation, drinking wine and smoking cigars. A blazing hearth fire gave off a ferocious blast of heat.

A man wearing an intricate patch over one eye frowned at Helterlin. 'Who the hell are you?' he asked coldly.

Helterlin cleared his throat and was interrupted by a tall man with a shock of red hair who appeared beside One-Eye.

'This is the man I was telling you about, your Highness,' De Marin said in flowery tones.

Marshal André Masséna, Duke of Rivoli and Prince of Essling, the commander of the *l'Armee de Portugal*, grunted and gulped back brandy.

Helterlin felt everyone's gaze upon him, and Masséna's seemed to be boring itself into his very soul. Sweat began to sheet his back. 'Your Highness,' he said, bowing awkwardly, which prompted a snort of laughter from the marshal.

Masséna beckoned him closer with a hand, eye traversing over the man's stained and weather-worn uniform. He had lost the other eye in a shooting accident while hunting with the Emperor, and, ever since, had worn a patch.

'*Chef-de-battalion* Helterlin fought at Jena–Auerstedt and Preussisch-Eylau, and received the *Légion d'Honneur* because of his

317

heroism. He is a man much like yourself, your Highness,' De Marin said. 'Capable. Resourceful. He commands-'

Masséna waved a hand in disinterest. He gazed back at the handsome dragoon officer who had blond hair and the palest eyes he had ever seen, so faintly grey as to be almost transparent. 'I just need to know if you can do the job. Are you the right man?'

Helterlin had no idea what he was being required to do and was reluctant to admit that, but nodded anyway. 'Absolutely, your Highness.'

'Good.' The marshal sucked on a cigar. 'You understand what you have to do and what,' he paused to consider his words, 'that might entail. You won't be popular, that's for sure. In fact, you will have a bounty on your head. Can you live with that? Yes? Good. Know that the guerrilleros will likely come after you. But being popular doesn't mean you'll win battles. This is war. War is brutal. Horrid.' He leant closer to Helterlin and jabbed a finger, painfully, into his chest. 'Just make sure you are more horrid than the peasants. You'll earn respect that way. You'll be feared. And with fear, we'll win this damn war before the year is out. Remember: adversity brings knowledge and knowledge brings wisdom.'

Helterlin looked at De Marin for support, but the red-headed man was beaming widely as though he was in awe of the Marshal. The dragoon officer considered there was only one reply he could give.

'I'm the man for the job. I'll see it completed. You have my word, your Highness.'

'You see,' De Marin said, patting Helterlin on the shoulder like a proud father.

Masséna sniffed at the remark and drew on the cigar, eye narrowed as it sought to discover if the dragoon was correct. There were so many young officers trying to prove their worth. He understood ambition. He had fought his way up through the ranks demonstrating merit. He was decorated and given the title of Marshal. The Emperor even called him *l'Enfant chéri de la Victoire*, the Dear Child of Victory. Masséna knew reputation was everything in life. Men had to prove ability first.

'Have you eaten?'

'Not yet, your Highness.'

'There is some cold chicken and bread. Plenty of wine. Eat and drink and then I want you leaving for the border by dawn.'

Helterlin bowed deeply. 'Thank you, your Highness.'

Masséna grunted and walked away to refill his brandy glass.

318

Helterlin's eyes quickly surveyed the scene hoping to catch a glimpse of his mistress who reputedly dressed as a dragoon officer, but she was not here. *Probably waiting in their bed*, he surmised with a smirk.

'Your mission is simple,' De Marin said, watching the marshal's retreating back. He turned sharply to Helterlin. 'What I'm about to tell you is strictly to be kept within these walls. Understood? You are to kill several partisan leaders before they increase their numbers. They will flee and scatter, and then we will destroy them. I shall provide you with their names and where they operate. If we are to be successful here in Portugal, we need our supply lines free from attack. I need men like you to make that happen.'

'Yes, sir. And thank you for considering me.'

De Marin's gaze became steely. 'I'm giving you a second chance. After the apprehension of the English spy, you were given strict instructions to acquire names of those who work for them. Alas, you did not.'

Helterlin swallowed. 'He proved to be very stubborn, sir. My methods of extracting-'

'You failed and that is the answer,' De Marin cut him short. 'I ordered you to escort him to me and it is deeply unfortunate that he escaped. We had one of Wellington's Intelligence officers, only to lose him from our grasp. Your grasp.'

'I apologise again, sir,' Helterlin's face burned. 'I corrected the grievous error before he could warn anyone.'

De Marin said nothing for a while. 'A pity.'

Helterlin didn't know if De Marin was saddened by the death or by the fact that he did not acquire contacts from the Englishman.

'The first name on your list is a Spaniard by the name of Herrero,' De Marin said. 'His men have been armed by the English. I want you to strike now and run the quarry to ground. Exterminate them; all of them.'

'Sir.'

De Marin inched closer. 'No more mistakes. Complete your mission and redeem yourself. Perhaps, you'll even get promoted. I know you seek advancement. That's why I chose you. I like men who are hungry for success. Bear in mind thousands of others are equally eager to make a name for themselves. I am not sentimental. If you die, you will be replaced. Earn it, don't lose it.'

Masséna, chicken leg in hand, came over as De Marin finished what he was saying.

'Are your men ready?'

'Yes, your Highness.'

The marshal bit into the succulent meat. 'Do they know how to fight?' he said, half-mocking.

'Yes, your Highness. And they know how to kill too,' Helterlin crowed.

'Very good. I like you, Helterlin. There's something about you dragoons that I like. Not the ablest horsemen in the army; not like the Hussars or the *Chasseurs-à-Cheval*. But you fight with unquestionable pluck, and I like that.'

'And he has help, your Highness,' De Marin said.

'Oh? You perhaps?' Masséna said, and Helterlin noticed a sneer in the tone.

De Marin gave another silky smile. 'I very much doubt I can offer assistance to our gallant *chef-de-battalion*. No, I was referring to another,' he pursed his lips before continuing, 'eager recruit.'

'My man carries a rifle. He is an expert shot, your Highness.'

Masséna considered the answer and spat a lump of gristle onto the floor. 'Rifle? I've no time for them. Too cumbersome to load. Like trying to undress a fat whore.' He laughed at his own joke. De Marin chortled and shot Helterlin a look that he had better join in.

The *chef-de-battalion* gave a boisterous guffaw. 'He's a marksman, your Highness, who will shoot the heads' off every partisan leader in Spain.'

Masséna laughed at the boast. 'Good and if that's the case, you shall be a *général de brigade* by the time we take Lisbon.' He thumped Helterlin's arm playfully, before joining the group of officers seated by the fire.

'Good, he likes you. Smoke this Herrero from his den,' De Marin spoke softly and intently. 'Kill him and fulfil your destiny.'

A smile creased Helterlin's face. 'I will, sir. You can count on me.'

*

Steven Kyte died as Escarrà predicted. The Englishman had clung onto life, but by the second day, he slipped away without a sound.

The sky at sunset was violet and the western clouds glimmered gold. And as the air cooled and mosquitoes hunted, more guerrilleros came to Navales.

The dozen men, dismounted, and tethered their horses at the stable. Cotton watched from the abandoned house opposite that Cadoc had said was theirs for the night. The tiled roof had partially collapsed and the windows weren't shuttered, but the men from the Ordnance had been given a delicious hare stew, wine and two loaves of fresh bread. The partisans saw Cotton's silhouette, and then with suspicious glances, entered the tavern. One remained with the horses. Cotton saw smoke pluming from a clay pipe and a tiny smear of lit tobacco lighting the man's moustached face framed by a large wide-brimmed hat.

Cotton, naturally inquisitive, left Corporal Leatherby in charge of the men whilst he ventured towards the tavern. He had washed his hands and face, brushed his coat and wore his blue coat buttoned up. He was a British officer and as such, it was imperative to be smartly dressed at all times. He was nervous, but wanted to know what news had the guerrilleros brought of the French. And, he cogitated, as a captain fighting the same enemy, it was his right to know.

He turned right into the alley when three of the new Spaniards appeared with muskets pointed at him.

'Lower your weapons. I am Captain George Cotton-'

One with a yellow coat and brown pantaloons stepped towards him. '*Inglés?* You look like a Frenchman.' Cotton licked his lips. 'I kill Frenchmen,' the Spaniard continued, gesturing with a hand drawn slowly across his neck like a knife.

Cotton could smell his stale tobacco breath from six feet away. 'Good for you,' he managed to say despite the fact that he was trembling.

The guerrillero spat. 'I have no love for you *ingleses* either.'

'I don't care who you are or where you are from,' said the tallest of the three. He had a gravelly voice, and a face decimated by the pox. 'But you should know that I'm the best knife-fighter throughout Spain.'

Sweat beaded Cotton's forehead. 'No doubt you spawned that rubbish yourself.'

Pox Face hissed, like a lit powder fuse. '*Inglés!* Give us your money!'

Cotton looked exasperated. 'You...you are robbing me?'

The Spaniards came closer. 'Are you deaf? Yes, we are. *Tonto del culo!*' They laughed mockingly.

'But we're allies?' Cotton wanted to back away, to flee in sudden fear. And he would have done if his right hand had not automatically reached for the sword sheathed at his left hip, and pulled it free effortlessly. The sound of it reverberated loudly in the small space.

The guerrilleros seemed undaunted by the threat, and merely laughed with contempt. 'You think you can touch us with that? *Que te jodan!*' Pox-Face stepped forward, his ravaged face breaking into a snarl. 'I'm going to stick that in your heart! You *ingleses* are gutless dogs! *Te voy a matar!* I'm going to murder you, Englishman!'

'No, you're not,' said a voice to his left.

The Spaniard swivelled his face in time to see a fist hurtle out of the shadows. The punch was powerful enough to knock out his front teeth and to send him crashing into his comrades.

Cadoc gave the other men no chance to stand. The first one to react was kicked in the ribs as he drew a pistol from his belt. The kick was massive, but he held onto the firearm. Cadoc slapped it away with his left hand to send it skidding into the shadows and then stamped down onto the guerrillero's face, feeling bone snap. The third Spaniard, entangled with the first one, was trying to draw his sword when Cadoc swung one of their muskets as a club and the heavy stock connected with his temple. Cotton thought he saw a mist of crimson in the gathering twilight as the man was flung violently back.

'This one's always trouble,' Cadoc prodded Pox-Face, who groaned through the new gaps in his teeth.

Cotton grimaced at the twitching, bleeding men. After a moment, he found his tongue. 'Thank you.'

Cadoc rubbed his blood-stained knuckles on one of the Spaniard's coats. 'You can put your sword away now,' he said with a grin. Shadow and light danced across his face.

Cotton, gripping his weapon tight like a dead man's final grasp, rammed it home. 'T-thank you,' he said, stammering. 'I-I was just...I was going to...to...'

The Welshman, realising the captain was in shock, led him away by the elbow to the tavern. 'What you need right now is a drink. A proper one. That'll set you right.'

'That wasn't very gentlemanly,' Cotton said of the attack.

Cadoc gazed over the bodies. 'No, it wasn't. And if you fight like one, you'll be on the ground spitting blood before you can say 'oh bugger',' he mocked in a well-spoken English accent. 'You fight hard and fight dirty. Every time. That's the only way to do it.'

'I think I need to return to my quarters. I suddenly miss it.'

'Drink first,' Cadoc said, pushing the tavern's door open and into the warm fug of tobacco, and blazing hearth fire. The rich smell of spices and oil from the kitchen made their noses twitch.

Rai was drinking at a table with another man. They both looked up.

'Is something the matter, Rifleman?' It was the first time Cotton had heard the colonel use that title.

Cadoc took a squat bottle off a table, wiped the rim with his grubby sleeve, and gave it to Cotton. It was *aguadiente*: Spanish brandy. 'Drink up.' He turned to his commander. 'Paz is up to his usual tricks. This time he threatened the captain and tried to rob him.

Rai looked livid and the man opposite him slammed a fist down onto the table. He got up and strode over to Cotton, thrusting a calloused hand into his. He saw that his right cheek was pock-marked with powder burns, his almond eyes were bright with intelligence. He wore a long brown cloak of homespun, draped over a shoulder. Cotton considered they all had brown woollen garments because the Spanish sheep had dark wool, which didn't need dyeing.

'My name is Adolfo, but my friends call me Fito. I apologise for this, *senõr*. This is not how we treat our allies. I shall deal with him immediately.'

Paz, one of Fito's men, had been an outlaw with his brother, but they were caught by the French and his brother was hung. Paz managed to escape to join Fito's men and it is said he carved every kill into his musket's stock as a grim reminder. He was a troublemaker and Fito only allowed him into his partisan band because of his hatred for the French.

Cadoc drank from a full wineskin. 'I gave him a tickle. He won't try that again.'

'Usually, I discipline my own men, but on this occasion I hope you did more than that?' Fito gave the Welshman an almost reptilian smile.

Cadoc had only ever met Fito once before and didn't take to him then. He was guarded, suspicious and standoffish, and was nothing like his brother who was cherished by the locals. Cadoc had seen women and men; tough creatures from the mountains, kiss Rai's hand in awe. They adored him. Fito was a cold fish, and Cadoc sensed a hunger in the man that was more than provisions. He wanted power. He wanted to be a general in the army, but he was not a Don, or wealthy enough, so became a partisan instead.

Cotton gaped at Cadoc's flippant remark. 'You did more than tickle the surly brute. I've…I've never seen anything like it.' He could not get the image of the fight from his mind. Cadoc had simply despatched them in seconds, sparing him from a rare beating, or worse. He gulped back the brandy and tried not to let it show that he found it too eye-wateringly harsh.

'My Rifleman does have unique talents,' Rai put in.

'So I hear,' Fito said, nodding with approval. He had the same eyes as his brother, but that was where the similarities stopped. It was difficult to discern age from a face heavily-lined around the eyes and mouth where there was a thick, pointed beard at his chin. Cadoc guessed Fito was in his late thirties. He carried a sword and a pistol and one of the long Spanish knives at his side.

'What is the name your men call the Rifles?' Rai directed the question to Cadoc.

'Green jackets, senõr.'

'Green jacket,' Fito said the word as though it was new to him, and smiled to indicate he liked it.

'Who'd have thought that enemies could become friends,' Rai happily puffed on a cigar.

'Come on, let's drink,' Cadoc said jauntily. He rose a brandy-filled cup. 'Success to grey hairs, but bad luck to white locks!' He repeated the ridiculing toast made following General Whitelocke's cowardice at Buenos Aires.

The Spaniards frowned at the unusual saying, but nevertheless repeated it in accented English and drank.

Rai beckoned them all closer. 'Let us talk.'

Fito had ridden down the plains from Salamanca, avoiding many French cavalry patrols. 'It is infested with the scum,' he said. 'There are not enough bullets in the world to kill all of them, or enough of our countrymen to pull the triggers.'

'You talk nonsense, hermano,' Rai chided him playfully.

Fito laughed and sucked on his cigar slowly, relishing the pungency. 'It's true. I have seen them with my own eyes. They still come in their thousands across the mountains. Their supply lines stretch longer than the Tormes.'

'That will be their undoing. They need a full corps to protect it. All the while we buzz about them like wasps after jam; killing their officers, intercepting their messages, diverting wagons and capturing their weapons and ammunition.'

'The guerrilla way, eh?' Fito grinned.

Rai bobbed his head. 'Always, *hermano*. We raid, kill, flee and survive to fight another day.'

'And wear out our boots if nothing else,' Fito said with a laugh.

'I will never tend a vine or again plough the field until the French are driven from all of Spain.' Rai's expression took on a solemn tone. 'Captain Steven Kyte was brought here today. He was found outside Valdecarros. He had been shot.'

Fito's eyes went wide with shock. '*Dios mio*. Dead?'

'He did not live long.'

'Who was responsible? The French?' Fito crossed himself.

Rai shrugged. 'I'm not sure. The only word he spoke of was *colaboracionista*.'

Fito gazed into his brother's eyes, into Cadoc's and finally Cotton's. 'Who was he talking about?'

'We don't know,' Rai said. 'He said nothing more.'

Fito drank from the wineskin and puffed on his cigar. 'I have heard of an *afrancesado* west of Salamanca, near the border. El Medico searches for him.' The Doctor, was another partisan leader who operated in La Mancha, but his band had grown to hundreds and now watched the hills and plains around Madrid, Salamanca, Avila, Segovia and Cuenca. 'As of yet, the French-lover has not been caught. But El Medico will find him and strip the skin from his bones when he does. Perhaps our friend Steven found out his identity?'

'And killed him because of that,' Rai breathed.

'Rope burns and cuts indicated that he had been a prisoner,' Cadoc added. 'I knew Captain Kyte well enough and he would have used every trick to break free and escape.'

'We must find those responsible and punish them,' Fito angrily declared. He stood up quickly and Rai ushered him down with a hand.

'What are you doing?' he said. 'Sit down. You have ridden hard to get here. Your men are tired and there is much to talk about. We have other news to share.'

'Every *afrancesado* and *colaboracionista* must be stopped if we are to see King Fernando on the throne again. Spanish lives depend on this. Gossip can wait.' Fito hurried to the door and beckoned his men to join him. He turned back to his brother. 'In five days come to our safe place in the caves,' he said. 'I will be there. We will talk. *Adiós.*'

Cadoc watched the retreating men. Paz and the two others climbed groggily and bleeding into their saddles and then they were gone into the night.

'What on earth was that all about?' Cotton said to no one in particular.

'Forgive my brother,' Rai said. 'He has never forgiven the French for the murder of my wife and children. He loved them like they were his own. Now Fito builds up his guerrilleros and soon we shall number two hundred. Now,' he said, banging the table with a palm. 'We must avenge Steven. Let us drink! *Viva* Fernando VIII! To our friends! And death to the cursed French!'

*

Firelight flickered through the trees to the east of Navales.

'No, fires, Juan! The colonel will roast our backsides if he finds out!'

The Spaniard called Juan stamped out the fire, scattering cinders and sending sparks into the night air. 'I'm goddamn cold!' He cursed and shivered, pulling his cloak around his body.

'You should have pissed on it,' said his companion. 'It would have been easier and less noisy.'

Juan chewed on his cigar. 'You would have me piss on a naked flame? Are you out of your mind? You know I've been drinking *aguadiente*. One drop, and I would have exploded.'

The two men laughed and resumed their watch. The moon was full and they observed the plains and roads for enemies.

Behind them, dark shapes shifted and slithered in the gloom.

*

If Cadoc hadn't gone outside to relieve himself he would never have seen a dull glint on the wooded crest that dipped all the way to the roadside. He dressed himself, staring at the dots of light. He rubbed his eyes, his clothes stinking of tobacco and alcohol, as the shadows melded into the forms of men. Scores of them approached the town like a gathering wolf pack. He ran back inside.

He kicked the door open, which slammed into the wall, grabbed his rifle, yelling a warning to the dozen men still awake. 'The French are here! Get up! Get your weapons!' He knocked out a lantern on one of the tables as the men roused. 'Extinguish the lights!'

A volley of loose musketry rattled the walls, splintered glass and three Spaniards were thrown bloodily back. Plates of beans and cups of wine clattered onto the floor. The serving girls screamed, except one wearing a red flowing skirt, who picked up a fallen musket and calmly approached a shattered window.

'Get down, Edita!' Rai shouted, as he tugged his pistol free from the belt. 'Down!'

Edita, a twenty-year-old with dark curls and a playful grin, shouldered the weapon as any good soldier, and pulled the trigger. Scraps of flaming powder debris singed her right cheek, but she did not twitch. Cadoc saw a shape fall. Then, there was movement to his right, a Frenchman aimed at her, but Cadoc edged his rifle barrel through the window and, using the wooden frame to steady it, shot the man dead.

Rai's men extinguished the last of the lanterns, overturned tables and fired through the windows, the weapons belching smoke that stank of rotten eggs. One or two hesitated, wondering where the best spot for cover was and Rai leapt up, grabbed their arms and shoved them forward.

'I want fire! I want fire!' Rai bellowed.

The Spaniards poured fire through the windows. One, wearing a sky-blue jacket of a Spanish Light infantry regiment, vomited because he was half-drunk, and then reloaded soberly.

Cadoc saw that Edita had wrenched free a cartridge holder from one of the dead men and was loading. He smiled with approval and a smile tugged her lips. Rai had given him Kyte's telescope as a present and now he trained the glass to the woods. He could see grim faces, muskets and swords. He assumed they were French *voltigeurs*, but he saw Grecian helmets and long black horsehair crests twisting with every motion behind them.

'They're bloody golden-heads!' Cadoc used the Spanish nickname for French dragoons.

'How many are there?' Edita asked.

'Perhaps a company strong, *senõr*,' Cadoc said, closing the scope. He pulled out a cartridge from his belt, bit an end off with the ball, pulled the hammer to half-cock, flipped open the pan and poured a pinch of powder into it. Then spat the ball down the muzzle along with the paper as wadding. He drew his ramrod. He could hear bullets whip in the air.

'Infantry?'

'I didn't see, or hear any horse,' he replied, thrusting the charge home with his ramrod.

'What are they doing here?'

'Trying to kill us,' Cadoc said glibly. He returned the ramrod and pulled back the rifle's hammer to full-cock.

The French were spread too thinly as they struggled to control all of the many villages and towns. There was no garrison of brigade size for twenty miles, and these men were braving the night when partisans liked to stalk. No Frenchmen left their forts unless they were sure of success, or led by men that feared nothing. But he wondered whether the French were nervous of being in Spain and Portugal, always watching over their shoulders, never sure if the enemy lurked in the shadows and if so, how many of them were there. He was glad he was not a Frenchman.

Carbines blasted at the tavern. The crash of so many incoming shots let loose in such a confined space was near deafening, and Cadoc could barely hear his own voice. He gawked at the walls. It would be dangerous to leave, but he did not know how many men waited for them out there in the darkness. To stay here, trapped, enemy bullets whittling them down one by one and chewing at their morale was a death sentence.

'We can't stay here.'

'My thoughts exactly. We don't know how many of them are here, or if others are on their way.' Rai looked grim. His men did not live in the village. They had no formal home of their own; preferring to live in the hills, gullies, caves and abandoned farmsteads. He did not want the folk here hurt because the guerrilleros stayed there. And now after the attack, they would not come back again. 'I need to see if Sebastiano, or Ciro have got our men from the homes. I wonder what happened to my men in the woods.'

Cadoc tap-loaded the rifle by thumping the stock against the floor, instead of using the cumbersome steel ramrod. It saved time, but reduced the rifle's firepower. 'Likely they are dead, senõr.'

Rai grunted because he had been thinking the same. More French lives his *cuchillo* would take in revenge. 'What about the captain?' He had to shout the last sentence as another volley crashed into the room.

Jugs were smashed and bottles fell to the stone floor. A bullet slammed through the window and struck one of the beams above Cadoc's head.

There was no light coming from Cotton's tiny quarters. Cadoc wondered if he had left a guard stationed near the door who had seen the attackers and they had taken precautions. Otherwise, the French, taking the sleeping British as Spaniards, would likely kill them where they huddled. He hoped Cotton would remain unmolested, or not do anything stupid. He liked the young man. There was a spark of bitterness when he first saw him. Cotton was the spitting image of a lieutenant from the 43rd who had made Cadoc's early life misery and the Rifleman thought Eurion Prothro had returned to haunt him again.

The French were shouting, '*Vive l'Empereur!*' It sounded mocking, as though it would easily strengthen their victory. Cadoc knew that the dragoons were extremely loyal to the Emperor, their cause and would carry out their orders to the last man. This would be no easy fight.

'We can't worry about him now, *senõr*,' Cadoc yelled over the sound of gunfire, taking aim at a grey shape and the rifle bullet took the man through his neck. 'I'm going to circle the town and go up to the barn. I need ammunition, so I'll go get my pack first and return. Up there will give me an advantage. I can see where the buggers are going.'

The Rifleman was gambling on instinct that the dragoons were attacking en masse in the hope of surprising their enemy, rather than assailing multiple points. He stared out where moustached faces with their odd pigtails fired back. He thought he could hear a Rifle bugle signalling the order to 'fire and retire', but he realised he was hearing things from days long gone past.

'Very well, *amigo*. I will regroup our men. Take Niguel with you. He's a good shot.'

Cadoc glanced at the young man behind the colonel who had eyes that burned with a keening anger, but he turned to Edita who had already loaded and fired again. 'I'll take her.'

'Come on, girl. Let's make some mischief.'

The two of them snuck out of the tavern's tap room and into the yard where the owner kept goats and mules. Cadoc slipped on fresh dung, but managed to keep upright. He edged to the stone wall. There were no enemies lurking in the shadows, or hiding at the alleys and he guessed that the French had not hitherto reached this far into the village. He tap-loaded the rifle again and tugged free his long sword-bayonet to slot it onto the muzzle. His dark green coat was black in the half-light, which gave the riflemen the nickname 'sweeps', because they looked like chimney-sweeps. There was another crackle of musketry coming from the trees. Cadoc tugged Edita's sleeve and she followed him as he sprinted watchfully down the road. He saw a figure lurch by the wall of the nearest house, blood showed on his pale shirt and then there were shadows with long blades behind him. Somewhere a dog barked incessantly. Cadoc pushed the girl down. The Spaniard collapsed as the blades did their death work. A moustached face below a peaked helmet laughed.

'You Toad bastard!' Cadoc snarled. The rifle flamed bright, and in the flash, he saw three Frenchman twisting aside as the bullet struck the laughing one in the chest to send him backwards.

There was no time to load and he stepped back as the dragoons rushed at him, steel flashing in the moonlight. The first one didn't see Edita and her musket took his life instantly. The next dragoon hesitated because there were now two enemies; a man in half-shadow, and a beautiful Spanish girl. And because of the indecision, Cadoc took the advantage by charging with his sword-bayonet. He was screaming incoherently as the twenty-three inch blade, honed razor-sharp ripped in between the man's ribs. He twisted the blade free, the alleyway stank of blood. The last dragoon, wearing brown homespun overalls, brought up his short-barrelled musket, pointing the muzzle at Edita.

'Look out!' Cadoc threw himself at her, pulling her down as the musket banged above them in an orange burst. The ball sang harmlessly overhead.

The dragoon threw it down, unsheathed his sword and sprang forward. He thrust the blade down, aiming at Cadoc's heart, but the Rifleman kicked his assailant's knee and the dragoon went off balance. The blade speared Cadoc's flank, ripping into his coat and slicing just below his hip.

The Frenchman swore at him as Cadoc grabbed hold of his collar. 'You're not going anywhere, you ugly bugger.'

Edita, her face contorted into something bestial, leapt up and grabbed hold of the dragoon's face by his forehead with all her strength. The knife gleamed silver before turning crimson in the blink of an eye.

Cadoc was sprayed with the hot salty blood from the enemy's severed throat. He heaved off the jerking, gurgling body. 'Good girl,' he said.

'Are you hurt?' she said in English.

His fingers probed the cut; they came stickily away. It was deep, however, there was nothing he could do about that now. He cut a strip of cloth from a dead dragoon and tied it around the wound. 'I'll be fine, love,' he said, wiping his face with a ragged sleeve. 'Let's go. We have work to do.'

They scurried through an orchard of lemon and lime trees and up to where the road touched the first houses. The musket fire was still sporadic, which told Cadoc the French had not given up, or that Rai's men had not been defeated. Opposite the house was the shrine where he had first encountered Cotton and his wagons. He checked for enemies first, then satisfied they were alone, led Edita up there.

Her brows arched, bridging bewildered eyes. 'Are you going to pray now?' she sneered. 'Rai always told me you were just another godless protestant.'

Cadoc scrambled up the slope to the shrine of Teresa of Ávila, a Saint who stayed in the village on her journey to Salamanca. It is said the villagers were struck down with an illness, and she found they were under a devil's spell. She located the creature in a cave and destroyed it with holy water, and thus saving the souls of Navales. Cadoc got down on his knees and shoved aside the statue of the Saint and baskets of flowers.

A dog padded its way down the roadside, seemingly obvious to the sound of gunfire. Goats bleated in one of the fields and a vixen cried somewhere. The rich smell of animal dung mixed with the roiling gunpowder made Cadoc's eyes begin to water.

'What are you doing?' Edita said angrily. 'This is sacrilege!'

Cadoc ignored her, pulling at something from deep with the shrine's niche. 'If I don't get what's in here, there will be blasphemy of a kind you've never heard the likes of before, girl.' He gritted his teeth, then his fingers found grip and he dragged out something heavy. Edita continued gaping at him.

'Here they are,' he said, bringing forth a pack of sorts and a belted box.

It was his infantry pack and black leather cartridge box, which contained his readymade cartridges. The box was issued with a wooden block inner that was designed to hold twenty-four cartridges. Each one contained a patched ball and a measured amount of gunpowder wrapped in greased paper to be used as wadding so the ball stayed in the barrel. Most Riflemen used the holders as kindling, preferring to have up to twice as much loose and the added weight. During the retreat to Corunna, the men had as much ammunition crammed into their packs, because of the worry of supply problems, but they discarded spare boots, shirts, box of blacking and shaving kits to keep the rounds. He had a score of gold Napoleons hidden in the pack as well as another twelve of the coins stitched into his coat, all taken from French corpses. The pack, rifle and clothes on his back were everything that he owned in the world.

Unique to the Rifles was the powder flask. It was made from cow's horn, fitted with a number of brass spouts for measuring precise charges of gun powder and contained fine ground gunpowder that gave a greater accuracy. It was usually suspended from the cartridge box cross belt by a length of green cord that allowed it to be moved easily from its carrying position on top of the cartridge box to the Rifleman's front for loading with loose ball ammunition.

'Why did you put it in there?' Edita asked, jutting her head at the shrine.

Cadoc flashed a roguish grin. 'No one would think twice to look there, now would they? There is a pistol in the bag and sixty rounds. Check it's loaded and load your weapons too.' There was sufficient light to load, but after years of training, he could load a firearm blindfolded.

When it was done, they snuck up to the barn, treading over the dry, pale heather that teased his nostrils with its warm scents. Cadoc went first, Edita trailed him. They heard the sound of rats scrabbling away. He edged along the side of the building, and, happy that no enemies lurked, went inside. He propped his rifle, pack and cross belt against the stone wall and moved two squat barrels to the entrance where he could steady the rifle's barrel against them and use them for additional cover.

'Keep the pistols and musket close by, just in case any of the bastards come up here,' he said, removing the bayonet because it made the rifle unbalanced.

'*Sí.*' She gave him an inquisitive glance. 'You have killed many men?'

He nodded. 'Aye.'

'You are a good shot?'

'The best,' he said, with a grin.

She seemed pleased with that answer. 'Then, you will kill more tonight. That is good.'

Cadoc stared down to the village. Weapons flared and shots rang out. He could see Spaniards firing from the church doorway and windows. Flames spluttered in the night air. From what he could comprehend, was that the French had now stormed the nearest houses, including the tavern, but had been checked by Rai's men. He remembered he now owned a telescope. He had an idea. He gave it to Edita to spot the enemy whilst he adopted a suitable firing position.

The men of the 95th fought ferociously, and were made even more deadly because they were trained, unlike other infantry, to fight independently. They would not look to an NCO or officer for instruction as privates would do in the red-coated battalions, but knew, thanks to their special training, just exactly what to do. On a battlefield, there were none better. And now, Cadoc, a man bred for war, and trained to be the best of the best, would fight and kill his enemies.

'There are six of them by the stables,' Edita said. 'One is now kneeling, and looks like he's reloading. There are two on the stables roof. There are…four maybe five running to the church. I can see a group trying to break the doors of Doctor Escarrà.' She smiled wickedly when the doctor fired a blunderbuss down into the green-coated men from an upstairs window that left the dragoons twitching and bleeding.

'Tell me if you can see their officers,' Cadoc said, staring down the barrel. 'If I can kill them and the NCOs, the buggers will retreat. Look for dragoons with gold epaulettes, or those that you can see giving orders.'

'It will be difficult in the light, but I will try my best.'

Cadoc risked a glance at her and could not help, but feel his heart pang for such beauty. He knew of Edita, but thought she was being courted by one of Fito's men.

Humberto, known as El Gigante, was six foot eight inches and the biggest man Cadoc had ever seen. It was rumoured that he had caught a French messenger by punching the horse in the face, knocking it out, and then proceeded to twist off the unfortunate man's head with his bare hands. 'There is one in the group around the stables.'

Cadoc trained his rifle down to the stables where enemy dragoons were gazing round corners, firing at unseen targets and loading their muskets.

'He is second from the right,' Edita said helpfully.

'Got him,' Cadoc spotted a shimmer of gold on the officer's right shoulder. He was directing the two on the roof when the Rifleman's bullet severed his spine.

'You hit him!' Edita cried out excitedly.

The Welshman was already loading. 'Secret is the patched ball,' he told her. 'It takes a bastard amount of time to load one, but in the right hands the rifle is truly deadly.'

'Like in your hands,' she said, giving him a smile.

'I was the best shot in my company,' he said, 'nay, probably the battalion. Tom Plunkett, a friend of mine, is a crack shot. Back in '07 when we were besieged in a convent by your lot in Buenos Aires, both of us were on the roof picking off every goddamned enemy we could spot. We tallied our kills; over fifty dead before we were ordered down. So what I'm saying, girl, is that tonight I'm going to perform miracles of my own. Now, what are the Frogs doing down there?' He could hear shouting and a bullet ricocheting somewhere.

Edita raised the glass to an eye. There were coats of green everywhere. There were puffs of smoke and she saw a Spaniard tumble out from a window. It looked like Ciro, the shepherd's uncle, dead. 'Two of them are carrying the officer away, but it doesn't look as though the others have noticed us.'

'Good.' He pulled back the hammer to cock the rifle.

Somewhere a man screamed and a dog kept barking frantically, until there was a curse and a sudden harsh bang of a French musket or carbine.

Edita resumed spotting. It had taken Cadoc twenty seconds to load the rifle. The next bullet found a sergeant who was leading a squad towards the road towards the church. The one after entered through the back of a corporal who was aiming at someone in one of the houses. The ball glanced off the stables stone wall, sending a spark into a patch of hay. The corporal slumped as the flames twitched and smoke billowed. Cadoc shot a man trying to climb a ladder, so that he seemed to hang there as blood dripped obscenely down the rungs. The rifle snapped at a dragoon pointing towards the church where it seemed the guerrilleros had made their bastion. The man pitched sideways behind a house, obscuring Edita's vision. She trained the scope down the road, up to Eduardo, the cooper's house, then down to the tavern where her heart quickened. A group of dragoons had noticed the rifle fire. A fearsome- looking officer with an eye-patch pushed five men towards them. They came crouching low.

'They've seen us!' Edita wailed. She was suddenly pale, but that could have easily have been just the moonlight. 'They're coming for us!'

'It's going to be all right, love,' Cadoc said calmly. In truth, he feared being cornered and the French blades would hack and slash their bodies to turn this barn into a butcher's yard. It would be a horrible death. 'Tell me where they are? Use the glass.'

'They are...they are coming up from the tavern in a...a zigzag way,' she said. 'Is that how you say it?'

'I understand,' he said and found them. He held his breath, felt the thrill of power and squeezed the trigger. Almost immediately after the rifle made its distinctive crack-like sound, he tap-loaded.

'One down,' Edita's voice was ominous. 'There is a really tall man. His shoulders are very wide.'

Cadoc brought his weapon up to his bruised shoulder. He found the next target. 'Is he as big as Humberto?' he asked clumsily.

Edita stared at him. 'No,' she muttered. 'Humberto is bigger.'

'Oh right.' He sighed slightly downheartedly. 'Are you two still sweet on each other?'

'No,' she said laconically.

'Good,' Cadoc said with renewed interest, glancing at the Spanish girl who smiled back.

The ball took the big man in the throat as he attempted to weave towards a jutting rock. As he knelt to load, muskets drummed up at the barn.

'They're firing at us!' Edita warned through the glass. She saw three puffs of smoke and heard the sound like buzzing bees as the balls slashed above the grass.

'They haven't the range,' Cadoc said coolly. 'And now they have to load them.'

The French corporal screamed as the flames found his flesh.

The dragoons had stopped to reload, lying on their backs or behind the large rock, but they had not yet warned their comrades of the Rifleman and so Cadoc waited until they showed themselves. The first one looked from behind the rock and fired up towards the barn, as another decided to clamber up the slope. Cadoc had expected the diversion, and the bullet spun the Frenchman backwards in a cloud of scarlet.

'Three left,' Edita said.

'If they charge now, I won't have enough time to fire again,' he warned.

Edita could see three shapes, like creatures coming from the earth, coming towards them. She snarled at their bravery. 'They will be here soon.'

Cadoc's eyes went to the musket. 'Grab the pistols and wait here by the other barrels. When they come in, take your shot.' He reached over for the heavier firearm and cocked it. It was smoothbore and would never hit a target more than seventy-five yards away and could be inaccurate at fifty.

But the dragoons had assumed that the marksman had been alone and was a guerrillero. They never thought that a British Rifleman could be the culprit.

'*Vive l'Empereur!*'

The dragoons charged. The musket spat fire to send the ball through the officer's remaining eye. He was lifted clean off his feet, sword flashed bright as it skittered down the slope. The nearest dragoon fired his musket and the bullet went so close to Cadoc that he felt its passage like a thump of air. Edita fired the pistols into the nearest dragoon; the first ball tore into a thigh, the second lodged in his pelvis. He fell to the ground wailing in terrible sobs before Edita calmly slit his throat. The last dragoon's nerve broke, and he turned tail back down the incline yelling and shouting. The rifle ball took him clean through his open mouth moments later.

A trumpet sounded, high and shrill. Cadoc took the glass and scanned across the village. It seemed the dragoons were retreating. Bands of Spaniards emerged from houses, doorways and from behind walls to fire at the withdrawing enemy.

'We did it!' Edita screamed in joy, planting a kiss on the Welshman's sun-scorched and blackened face. 'Thank God!' She clasped her hands and murmured a rapid prayer.

Cadoc smiled. 'Thank God for the Baker rifle and the Welsh.' The saltpetre from the powder was rank and dry in his mouth. He needed wine. *A pint of it would go down nicely*, he reflected.

The skirmish was over and, as Navales stank of blood and smoke, there were so many unanswered questions.

*

The remnants of the stable still smouldered even though the fires had long been put out before the new day's dawn. A silky brightness spread over the hills, lanced through the branches of the tall oaks, chestnuts and elms, and laid across the graves like a blanket. The charred remains of the dragoon had been dragged from the ash to be buried with the other twenty-two dead French in a mass grave north of the village. They were in a pile, stripped of all weapons and clothes. Flies blanketed the corpses. Padre Tos, his cassock swirling up dust as he walked had even said a prayer for them, not out of respect, but hoping their ungodly souls would not return to haunt Navales.

'Eleven of my countrymen died here,' Rai lamented. 'Eleven who will never see another Spanish sunrise.'

Cadoc was staring at the white-skinned bodies. 'We'll avenge them, *senõr*,' he said, half-grimacing at the blood-letting to come. He wore a black hat favourable with the Spanish infantry over a black bandana. It kept the fierce sun from his eyes, ears and back of his neck.

Rai spat to show that he was eager for retribution. 'Our *cuchillo*'s will soak our hands with French blood.' He fingered a discarded dragoon helmet. A bullet has ripped away a chunk of the canvass that covered the brass as protection and to prevent it from reflecting sunlight to betray the French position. The material was a cheap imitation of leopard skin, denoting it was an officer's headdress. He tossed it away, half-wondering if he should keep it as a memento. 'And you, *amigo*, what magic did you work with your rifle? Edita tells me it was perhaps fourteen or fifteen killed?'

'I wasn't counting.'

'She told me that you were very good with your hands too.'

Cadoc flushed. Images of the girl's naked body whirled about his mind. After the fight, the Spaniards mourned their dead and he and Edita had shared *aguadiente* and harsh cider before pulling off each other's clothes and making wild passionate love. They kissed with so much force that he was sure he had cracked a tooth. They made enough of the glorious sound with the cot creaking loudly to cause gossip. But they did not care who heard them. The horror and excitement and sadness of the fight had burned that night, and so their lovemaking was needed to slake it.

She laid back, back arched as he had given her pleasure and afterwards, she lay with her head resting on his muscled chest, her hair tickling him. But he did not move. He traced a finger up her arm, and down her shoulders along her spine. She moaned with content and kissed his torso. She clasped a hand around his forearm, studying the long red tattoo on his arm.

'What is it?' she had asked.

'The red dragon of Wales.'

She traced a finger down the spiralling tail and scales of the mythical beast that ran down his entire arm. She propped herself up to stare at the beast's armoured body and open maw. There appeared to be letters up and along the dragon's body. She angled her head, pulling back a tousle of dark hair from her eyes.

'What do the words say?'

'*Dihina'r ddraig sy'n cysgu a fydd well ganddoch gael achos l,*' he said and she grinned at the unfamiliar language. 'It roughly means in English, 'If you wake the sleeping dragon, you'd better have cause to'.'

'Why did you have it done?'

'The French attacked my home back in '97. They were dressed like British Fencibles and fooled us. But not for long and I had it inked in celebration of us beating them before I joined up.'

'Have the French woke the dragon?'

Cadoc reached down to a wineskin and brought it to his mouth. He offered her a drink: she titled her head back as the liquid squirted down into her open throat.

'Aye, they have, girl. More fool them. And they've stirred a hornet's nest over here too where even God can't help the bastards.'

'They will all die,' she said fervently, and Cadoc believed her.

They drifted off to sleep and he woke to find Edita still slumbering. He dressed and went to the woods opposite the town, where he found the ragged bodies of the two sentries.

'Padre Tos says that God blessed us last night,' Rai continued.

Cadoc chewed the inside of his mouth, thinking that Edita was indeed an angel sent from heaven. 'True, *senõr.*'

'She is a wildcat, *amigo.*'

Cadoc didn't know if he was being warned or not. 'She certainly knows how to handle herself. She killed two of them with musket and pistol and knife.'

Rai breathed a sigh of appreciation. 'Our padre said we could kill the 'antichrist' French with God's consent. Every man, woman and child is an enemy of France. They will die to protect it from invaders.'

Cadoc was not a godly man, but respected the views of others, careful not to show his own if they differed. 'We gave the Frenchies a drubbing they'll not forget, *senõr.*'

338

Rai gave a bitter laugh. 'The bastard French thought that they could walk over us. They thought because our leaders were corrupt and incompetent, they would find its people easy targets. But they underestimated us. They thought as King Fernando and the royalty were gone, our armies scattered like the windblown embers of a fire, that God had abandoned us too. No. He listens to our prayers and blesses us. Last night he showed that miracles do happen.' He gave Cadoc an appreciative look. 'Miracles in the form of a Rifleman. I would never have guessed. I have known you *ingleses* for a number of years. The rankers, dull, ugly men.'

'True,' Cadoc conceded.

'The officers: a collection of self-righteous preening idiots.'

Cadoc laughed. 'We call them Jack Puddings.'

'But with you,' he clasped the Rifleman's arm, 'I believe what I have always thought: God sent you to me.'

The Welshman was embarrassed with the praise. 'Thank you, *senõr.*'

'I must admit, she is quite lovely, is she not?'

'Perfect,' Cadoc said, his mind swirling with images of Edita.

Rai mumbled a disagreement. 'I would not say that. I am sure you know the faults of such a thing. After all, you told me you spent many years training with it.'

Cadoc realised that he was talking about the Baker rifle. He ran a dirty finger from the hammer up and along the barrel, which was fouled with black powder. Hot water would clean it out and he would do that shortly. During the lull in combat, it was common to see a man piss down the barrel rather than wait for water to boil.

Cotton emerged sheepishly with his men. They had been spared the attack because Cotton had seen the dragoons coming and had ordered his men into the shadows. The French seeing a lifeless, half-tumbled building did not expect to find anybody in there so left it alone. The captain's decision had saved their lives, but his eyes showed guilt. He saluted Rai and nodded a greeting towards Cadoc. He looked even more remorseful when he saw the bodies.

'I should have helped.'

'There was nothing you could have done.' Rai shot him a look of sympathy. 'If you had opened fire, the French would have swarmed all over you. You and your men would now be dead. So, as much as I value your keenness for killing the enemy, it can wait another day. And believe me, Captain, there will be many more opportunities. Besides, who else will fix my guns?'

'But, sir-'

'You live to fight another day!' Rai said firmly. 'Many others do not, so embrace that gift.'

Crestfallen, Cotton glanced at the bodies. 'I will, sir.'

Rai puffed on a cigar. 'Good,' he plucked it from his mouth, 'and perhaps you can tell me how the French knew we were here?'

'Sir?'

'They came here under,' he paused, teeth dragged a small portion of beard across his bottom lip, 'how do you say it? Cloak and dagger. Yes? So they knew we were here.'

Cotton chewed on his bottom lip. 'Agreed, sir.'

'So someone alerted them?' Cadoc cut in, eyebrows arched. 'Or more than one did.'

'Were they after the firearms I brought?' Cotton asked, half-disbelieving it.

Rai shook his head. 'No.'

'What about your inactive guns?'

The colonel looked up at the barn. 'No, not them either. They wouldn't know of them. No. They did not come here risking their lives to spike inoperative cannon. I overheard one of them say, 'Find him! He's here!' They came here for one purpose.'

Cadoc spat on the dusty ground. 'You, senõr,' he suggested.

'What? They came to assassinate you?' Cotton could not believe it.

'And they failed,' Rai grinned. 'For that small mercy, I will find out the truth. Come with me now.'

Cotton glanced nervously at Cadoc, because the partisan leader beckoned them to a house where once the door shut behind them, agonised and tormented screaming pierced their ears.

The one seated on the left was a *sous-lieutenant* and the other just a trooper. Both had their hands tied behind their backs, and both had been severely beaten.

'Do you speak French, Captain?' Rai asked Cotton who nodded. The tiny room smelt of dry grass and goat. Two sparrows flitted up in the rafters. The house was typically split in two; one for the owner and the other for the beasts. 'Mine is not very acceptable. Ask the officer who led them here last night?'

Cotton cleared his throat. He felt himself being drawn even further into the murky world in which Kyte had evidently been part of. Still, he also believed he should have played a bigger part in the night attack. He rattled off quick French to the man with bruised cheeks and lips that were split and oozing. The reply came as speedily back. 'He says *chef-de-battalion* Helterlin, sir. That will make him a major in our Army.'

Rai stared at the young man. 'What is his name?'

Cotton asked him. 'Tobias Woitsche, sir.'

'Doesn't sound French?'

'No, sir. He's actually from Hesse. He's German.'

Rai waved a hand dismissively. 'Another godless foreigner in Spain,' he said carelessly. The patriot known as Sebastiano, a short man with bushy, unkempt eyebrows and well-muscled forearms, prowled behind with bloodied fingers. He spat onto the floor, a string of it glistened in his beard. 'Ask the lieutenant what their mission was.'

Woitsche, with a slashed cheek from a musket ball, and two loose teeth from his capture, licked his lips. 'May I have water, please?'

Cotton asked and Rai shook his head. 'When he answers the question.'

The German, perhaps twenty years old, turned to his left as if seeking approval from the trooper in the hope that he would not be accused with cowardice, but the man had simply buried his neck in his chest as though he had given up all hope of a reprieve, so Woitsche continued. 'We were sent to find someone.'

Sebastiano cracked his knuckles, a sound that made Woitsche shiver.

'Who?'

'I don't know.'

'Are you sure?'

Woitsche nodded confidently that what he was about to say would suffice. 'Yes. I was not told.'

'I think you do know. Let me tell you anyway: you came to get me. And this whoreson Helterlin sends just a detachment?' Rai gave a sarcastic laugh. 'He mocks me! He should have sent his entire regiment. And you know what? We would have murdered the dogs all the same.' He stared into the terrified German's eyes. 'Tell me where you are garrisoned. What is your strength?'

'We're a mobile unit. On the move all the time. We...' his voice faltered.

Rai waited for the translation, paused to reflect it, and gave a short determined nod to Sebastiano who was relishing the chance to inflict damage. He grabbed hold of the lieutenant's hair with his left hand and punched Woitsche in the face with his right. The blow was powerful enough to knock the German backwards in his chair onto the earthen floor, so extraordinarily powerful, that Sebastiano was left holding a handful of hair. The Spaniard chuckled at the find, let the strands fall away, and then reached down to haul the prisoner back up. Blood was pouring from his shattered nose, but the assault did not relent. It became harder because the Spaniard seemed to revel in it. He knocked the air from Woitsche, bubbles and pink foam frothed from his open mouth as he fought to scream. Fists swung in from left to right, short, close hits that brutally pulverized the officer until the screams fell silent and he lost consciousness. Rai allowed Sebastiano to continue. The hammer blows pounded flesh to jelly and splintered ribs. He went on punching so that Woitsche's head flopped with every strike. The trooper had not moved, or reacted to the sounds of the lieutenant's muffled cries as his face was repeatedly battered, or the blood that spattered his own green jacket.

When he had finished, Sebastiano took off his sweat-soaked shirt, rubbed his knuckles and wiped them on the lieutenant's coat. There was the strong copper tang of blood in the air. Cotton looked absolutely terrified and sickened.

'You wish to give a better answer?' Rai then asked the other.

The trooper stared into his eyes, before spitting a mixture of blood and spittle onto the floor in defiance. Sebastiano growled.

Rai laughed mockingly. 'For that you will go straight to the knives.' He made a gesture with a hand and two of his men dragged the dragoon away outside.

'Where are you taking him?' Cotton enquired.

'To his death, Captain. That is all you need to know.'

Woitsche gasped loudly. He groaned, blood seeped out of broken nose and split lips to hang in thick tendrils from his chin. He gurgled something.

'What did he say?' Rai said to Cotton, but the captain was transfixed at the young German's terrible injuries. His face was unrecognizable; swollen, pulpy and broken. 'Captain! Captain!' That got Cotton's attention. 'What is he saying?'

Cadoc felt for the young Ordnance officer. 'Just ask him, sir,' he said with sympathy. 'And this will all be over soon.'

Cotton leaned in, but could not bring himself to look into the bloodied horror of his face. He had never seen such ghastly wounds before and a creeping sourness was spreading up from his stomach to his throat. He gulped back the nausea. Woitsche spoke in short rasps, but they were merely wordless whimpers of pain. Cotton spoke to him again and listened intently to the German. It was only when he fell into silence that Cotton returned to his upright position.

'Well?' Rai enquired.

Cotton cleared his throat. He swivelled around to face Rai. 'He said that a guerrillero rides with his regiment.'

The Spanish colonel staggered as though he had been hit by a roundshot. 'What?'

'He is the one who told the French of our position.'

Cadoc gaped. 'The betrayer that Captain Kyte tried to warn us about.'

'Yes,' Cotton nodded.

Rai snarled. 'Who is the traitor? I want a name!'

Cotton looked grave. 'The lieutenant doesn't know, but he does know that he carries a rifle: a Baker rifle.'

Rai slowly turned towards Cadoc, eyes dark with fury.

The guerrilleros numbered sixty. All were equipped for battle and rode their horses under a sun-blazoned sky.

Fields of wheat shone like gold in the sunlight as the men cantered along a dusty road north. They rode beside gullies of yellow gorse abundant with bird nests, ravines and rolling hills, then took their mounts across hay meadows almost ready for the scythe.

'I shall find the traitor,' Rai said, a cigar hanging out of the corner of his mouth, 'hang him, disembowel him and afterwards, burn his corpse to ash. The enemy shall hear of the man's deception and his death all the way from Santiago to Cádiz.'

Cadoc, riding on his flank, cautioned his commander. 'We must tread carefully, senõr. If there is one betrayer, there could be another. How well do you know Saturnin and Dantel?'

'I know them well enough,' Rai explained. 'Have I told you of my time in New Granada, or The Kingdom of New Spain?'

'No, *senõr.*'

Cigar smoke dribbled away from Rai's mouth. 'You are lying,' he said with a knowing smile and laughed. 'They were with me in the colonies for eight years. They are like my brothers. I trust them. Unconditionally. During the long years of garrison duties, we put down several revolts from the natives, fighting side-by-side. We even destroyed a British schooner who had wandered too close to our forts.' He glanced at the Welshman to see if there was a reaction at the said defeat.

The Rifleman was too shrewd to take the bait. Instead, he gazed up at the barren hills where a stand of pine trees were dark against the sky. For a brief instant, Cadoc thought he could see a figure standing in between the trees, but, as he continued with the journey, he could not be certain of what he had seen.

'When you looked at me earlier, *senõr,*' Cadoc said, 'I thought you perhaps considered I was the traitor.'

'Of course not.' Rai snapped, and shifted uncomfortably. 'I just think that a rifle in the wrong hands can do terrible damage.'

'In the right hands too,' Cadoc said with a grin. 'It's a bloody good job the French don't use them.'

Rai grunted. 'I couldn't agree more with that statement.'

'However, it would be easier if you'd let me go after the man,' Cadoc suggested. 'I'll put a bullet in his heart.'

Rai watched his friend. 'I've never doubted your skill, but *I* will kill the *bastardo.*'

They cantered along narrow tracks, away from the main thoroughfares, to keep away from the French cavalry patrols. By dusk they had reached a series of escarpments that obliterated the eastern and northern skyline. The track twisted its way up through the rocks, to where, partisan sentries watched them guardedly. There was the sound of a flute playing; its melody, soft and mournful. Cadoc could see a large cave smeared with dull orange light and yet more figures standing outside with muskets. Rai called up at the guards who wore cloaks slung across their shoulders, shared a joke, and allowed further up into the pass. There was enough space to leave their horses, so Rai took Cadoc, Sebastiano and Padre Tos, whilst the rest waited with their bivouacked countrymen.

Two men greeted Rai, clasping hands and hugging like kinsmen. Cadoc understood these were the colonel's friends. Saturnin was a brute of a man, bearded, hugely muscled and squat like keg of beer. He

344

was in his late forties, and gave the Rifleman a bear-hug of an embrace before thrusting a wineskin into his belly. Dantel was a slim dark man who reminded Cadoc of Fito; cold-eyed, and calculating. He greeted the others warmly, but purposely blanked Cadoc.

As they ventured up a muscle-burning climb into the lip of the cave, and as the firelight smeared their faces orange, Rai turned to the Welshman. 'Forgive Dantel, *amigo*,' his voice a mere whisper. 'He distrusts anyone who is not from Castile.'

Cadoc allowed a quick smile to soften his face, but he knew his friend was being genial. The truth of it was that Dantel despised anyone who wasn't Spanish and Rai was being polite. The Welshman stared north in awe at the distant peakless mountains of Zamora, because he had never seen such a thing before in his life. They looked like strange islands rising above a vast sea. The red sun was gently falling away to plunge the land into darkness.

The men ate a stew of goat, beans, bread and consumed wine by the skin. There were perhaps twenty of them, all fierce-looking and united in their oaths to destroy the French. After the meal, they drank and small talk changed to that of Navales. Rai spoke of Cadoc's skill and was rewarded by favourable grunts and nods. Dantel remained impassive.

Saturnin spoke to Rai, but Cadoc saw that he was looking at him. Rai turned to the Welshman. It all went quiet. 'He wants to know why you wear a green coat instead of the usual British red?'

The Spaniards chuckled when the translation was given. All eyes were on him. Cadoc fingered his beloved patched coat. 'I enlisted in a redcoat battalion before joining the Rifles.'

Rai translated and Sebastiano to his left mimicked firing a rifle. 'He wants to know why green? Have they run out of red dye?'

Cadoc ignored the round of chattering playful merriment. He stared up at the twisting tendrils of tobacco smoke above their heads. 'It's for camouflage, and it works damned well.'

The men nodded, apart from Dantel who sighed as though he was bored. The fire crackled and spat and Cadoc watched his eyes flare angrily when his gaze crossed the Welshman's. He could not hold the gaze and the Spaniard looked away.

Saturnin asked if it was true that all British soldiers were convicts, thieves and murderers. Cadoc tried not to show offence, so played with the ends of his moustache.

345

'Some join up because it is better than being unemployed and starving. Some join wanting adventure, or patriotism.'

'What about you?'

'It was either join up, or get bloody married,' Cadoc said.

The guerrilleros exploded with laughter and passed around blocks of tobacco for pipes, cigars and flasks of brandy. There was a piercing scream coming from somewhere outside. No one reacted and Cadoc went utterly still. The moon was a silver blur behind drifting clouds.

'Dantel's men captured a French courier earlier,' Rai expounded cheerfully. 'He's just helping them with enquiries.'

Cadoc glanced at the Spaniard but his expression was unreadable. *Poor French bastard*, he thought. A horrible death awaited the messenger.

A boy no older than ten came to the fire wearing a French shako on his head. One or two men laughed, but Saturnin, cuffed the boy around the head like a bear swatting a salmon out of a river. The boy began to sob and the big man leant over, kissed his face and sent him away with a hunk of bread.

'He doesn't like us to mimic the enemy, especially his sons,' Rai whispered to Cadoc. 'One of his men once wore a French coat and was shot by mistake. He didn't die, but my old friend fusses over his children like a mother hen.' He laughed.

Saturnin, picking meat from between big, yellow teeth with a knife, spoke in a deep booming voice. 'The French will come back to Navales once they hear of the defeat.'

'I expect them to,' Rai said. 'That is why I called you here the moment I could. I have men watching the roads from Salamanca and from Alba de Tormes. There are only two other available routes to Navales. One is a poor road, heavily rutted with deep holes and the other is sunken. If the French choose that road, then they are as stupid as they are ugly. The banks either side are steep, wooded and rocky. A hundred men could block it and hold off an army there. They will not choose it. They will take the other road.'

'We will be ready for them,' Saturnin vowed, relishing the butchery. He was grinning, the corners of his eyes creasing like a crow's foot.

Dantel got to his feet, raising a drink. 'For Fernando and for Spain!'

The men cheered and cursed the French.

And so in the morning, long after the wives danced with castanets and tambourines, and the sound of the music had faded, the guerrilleros watched the bare roads for an enemy to come.

Two days later and there was no sign of the French.

Rai rode to all the sentinels who reported inactivity. Only goat herders, shepherds and the occasional peasants were spotted. Nothing stirred and Rai was anxious.

'Maybe they won't come?' Sebastiano suggested. 'They are cowards with no honour. They were beaten and do not want another hiding.'

'They'll come,' Cadoc told him.

'If there's one thing I've learnt,' Rai said, 'is that the French do not give up without a fight. They'll be back in greater numbers. They can't afford a defeat in one of the towns. News will spread and they need to quash the resistance. They will come.' He thumped a fist into his hand.

Sebastiano, his brutal face twitched fretfully, ran calloused fingers across his chest in the sign of a cross. 'Dear God, *senõr*. What of the people there? We will draw the heathens' attention. Soon there will be thousands coming to Navales!'

Rai waved away his concern. 'I have already taken care of that problem,' he said, soothing the usually violent man. 'They are all safe. Trust me.'

'They'll come after us, *senõr*.'

'Good. Let them. Remember: a wise wolf hides his fangs. We'll be ready for them.' He smiled one of his long white-toothed grins and slapped Sebastiano on the arm. 'I want our men alert. I want to know if one of them sees hide or hair of a Frenchman.'

'*Sí, senõr*.'

'Colonel!' It was Padre Tos who interrupted with an excited shout. He was riding a fast horse, armed with a musket and an ammunition belt clipped around his brown robes. 'Colonel!'

'What is it, Padre?'

The priest was smiling. 'The French are here. They chose badly.'

*

Rifleman Cadoc whistled the tune of Over the Hills and Far Away, before switching it to Spanish Bride when he thought of Edita; the girl who turned his mind to smoke with her beauty. He thought of her nakedness, her soft skin, her dark curls and the shadowed lines of her muscles in the morning's half-light. She was strong, graceful and feminine. He felt the familiar pang of love.

Rai began to sing a song, his voice was soft and Cadoc noticed a glint at his eyes. The colonel finished it and laughed away the tears of happiness.

'What was it about?' Cadoc asked him, then cursed his curiosity.

The Spaniard stared down at the empty track. 'It is about a love that cannot be spoken because of such heartache.'

Cadoc knew that Rai was still mourning his wife and children. 'I understand, *senõr*.'

Some wounds were too deep.

Rai smiled, and wiped his cheeks of tears.

Padre Tos began a prayer and his voice echoed across the ravine. '*Ego te absolvo a peccatis tuis in nomine Patris, et Filii, et Spiritus Sancti.* Amen.'

Many of the Spaniards kissed crosses at their necks, or their knives and guns.

The rifle was Cadoc's talisman. He had oiled it, screwed a new flint in place and had given the barrel a clean. Cadoc traced a finger along the walnut stock amazed at all the scrapes and knocks it had sustained over the years when a shadow loomed. He looked up.

It was Dantel.

'Are you scared, Rifleman?' he said in English.

Cadoc smelt sour wine on his breath. He ignored the Spaniard and his needling words to stare down at the road where two butterflies danced above a patch of pale blue flowers.

Having his words disregarded seemed to make Dantel angry. 'You shouldn't be here. You aren't needed and you aren't wanted.' His voice travelled far and several partisans turned to stare. Rai watched, but kept a polite distance.

Cadoc hawked and spat over the edge of the embankment. 'I don't care what you think. I kill Frenchmen. That's all that matters.'

Dantel shook slightly. 'You have no right to ride with us. This is Spain's war, not yours.'

'Your war?'

'Yes, my war,' Dantel said defiantly. 'I have fought in almost every major battle for my country.'

Cadoc seemed to think hard about that. 'So you fought at Ocaña and Alba de Tormes, did you?' he sneered, knowing that the Spanish defeats would needle.

348

The slim Spaniard stiffened, but said nothing.

'Let me see now,' Cadoc continued, as sweat dripped onto his stained collar, 'you lost Seville, Granada, Córdoba, Málaga and Jaén, at the start of this year. Followed by Astorga, Ciudad Rodrigo, Lérida, Tortosa, Badajoz and Tarragona.' Dantel's face twitched with ire and Cadoc grinned at the intended impudence. 'The only places left under Spanish control are the mountains of Galicia and Cádiz. Will you fight there?'

'You English think you're so righteous,' Dantel spat.

Cadoc sighed. 'If you're going to insult me, at least give it some proper thought. I'm Welsh, not English.'

The Spaniard shrugged. 'I don't care what dung heap you're from. You're another heathen foreigner in my country.'

'A heathen foreigner fighting for your country, don't forget.'

Dantel ignored the rebuke. 'Has Rai told you anything about me?'

Cadoc was tempted with more insolence, but bit it off in time. 'Not much.'

'I was at Buenos Aires,' Dantel ventured, eyes searching for Cadoc's thoughts as he went still. 'Yes, that's right. Rai told me you were there, but I don't remember you. You were just one man of a foreign invading army. And what was it? Three years ago? But there was one incident that I have never forgotten.'

Cadoc glanced back at Rai who was listening intently. By the looks of his face he had not heard his friend speak of this before. 'Go on,' the Welshman said, still prone.

Dantel's eyes ravished Cadoc's uniform. 'I never forgot the colour of your coats. Green. Dark green. And a man wearing such a coat beat and raped a Spanish wife of a friend of mine.'

Cadoc had known scores of men who were rapists, and men who had escaped punishment to enlist instead. 'I'm sorry,' he could only think to say.

Dantel spat onto the ground. 'I care not for your pathetic regret. The woman could not live with herself and took her own life. As a Catholic that is a terrible sin. Shame and guilt destroyed them both. All because of an *Inglés* soldier sent to that city by a greedy and corrupt government. I found my friend hanging on the day your generals surrendered. He killed himself over grief. I have not forgotten it and I never shall. You *ingleses* are a pox on this earth.'

Cadoc stood to full height, giving the Spaniard a sorrowful and thoughtful expression. 'I am sorry, despite your distrust of me. Our

349

people were enemies. Once. I came here to help fight and I too have lost friends and companions along the way. How many unmarked graves have I seen from friends lost to a French bullet, a French sabre, or disease, or Spanish weather? I've lost count. I've even lost a loved one here. So don't tell me about loss, *senõr.*' His face changed to something brutal. 'Now I've no time for ill-mannered buggers like you. You address me like that again, and I'll knock you flat on your arse and send you straight to Saint James, or any other buggering saint this goddamn country has got. *Entiendes?*'

Dantel still glared at the Welshman, his throat emitting a low growl. He saw Rai stroll over, and strode away without muttering a further word.

Rai chuckled. 'You certainly have a way with words, *amigo,*' he said softly. 'But don't tell him I said that. If he asks, you tell him that I chided you and I've prayed for your sins.'

'He has balls like shrivelled plums.'

'I trust him with my life.'

'You're a braver man than me,' Cadoc scoffed. 'I wouldn't trust him with mine.'

'Dantel is a good soldier and a good friend,' Rai was enjoying the Welshman's anger.

'I don't care if he's a friend of yours or not,' Cadoc cracked his neck a couple of times to relieve the sudden antagonism, and rammed his black hat onto his head. 'If he speaks to me again, I'll hang the bastard upside down by his ankles until he chokes.'

The guerrillero leader sucked his cigar and slapped the Welshman's back, before walking way. '*Bueno!*'

The enemy came at midday.

Sebastiano and three men brought news. A troop of dragoons led four companies of infantry, four canvass-covered wagons and another troop of horsemen protected the rear. Cadoc could see a smear of dust in the sky and considered the numbers of men, close to eight hundred. The French were coming in strength, but the Welshman decided that surprise would nullify the advantage.

'To your positions!' Rai instructed, and the men hurried to the high banks where they crawled and lay unseen above the sunken dirt road in soft grassy patches that rippled with the wind and weed strewn gullies.

They let the French scouts go unhindered. These men were mounted on light horses and despite the imposing walls of the embankments, they trotted on without a care in the world. The wind swirled dust devils along the track they were taking. Rai had positioned his men with Dantel's men and Saturnin watched from the opposite side where the rocky edges were nearly double the height of Cadoc's position. Saturnin had a score of men, bristling with weapons that were ready to charge their horses from the wood on this side of the road to the scouts or use them to flee.

Cadoc's own plan was simple: kill as many of the enemy as possible, starting with the officers and NCOs.

He knew from experience that effective musketry could only be delivered at very short range; controlled and precise volley fire, not from each individual who skirmished. Smoothbore weapons were inaccurate and skirmishers, or men running about choosing targets, dallying, would never decide the outcome of a battle. The guerrilleros numbered one hundred and fifty. Rai had instructed the men, strung out all along the roadside to wait until the dragoons passed before starting the ambush. Only by surprise and one well-timed volley they might win the fight. Cadoc chewed the ends of his moustache in anticipation.

Hope for the best and plan for the worst.

Time went slowly.

Sweat dripped down Cadoc's spine. There were some animal bones nearby, yellowed with age. Shrew or mouse killed by a mink or marten. Soon there would be corpses and the beasts would have larger bones to gnaw. A shiver made the hairs on the back of his neck stand up. The sounds of insects buzzing equalled that of the hooves, marching feet and the squeal of the heavy wagons below. A nerve quivered in his gut and for the first time in months he was nervous. He glanced to his side. Rai was crouched over to his left, a young man with a gaunt face was praying. Cadoc could see a pulse beating along the line of Rai's throat. Carbines, muskets and rifles slid over rocks and grass. The Spaniards looked confident.

The French marched on, oblivious to the threat. It was certainly no Thermopylae, but it was an ideal choke point. The scouts had not signalled a warning, or the men were thinking of distant home, of their wives and sweethearts, or of food and drink. Whatever they were thinking, it wasn't death from above.

Like shooting rats in a barrel, Cadoc considered.

Rai took a massive intake of breath. 'Fire!'

One hundred and fifty bullets crashed out of one hundred and fifty muzzles.

The embankments were suddenly spotted with filthy powder smoke. Scores of French fell dead, and suddenly the packed column knew chaos. One minute they were a marching formation and the next their world had been flipped on its head and had become one of screaming, blood and death. Horses whinnied and a man was kicked in the head, breaking his neck. A horse, shot through the neck, twisted and pitched onto an infantry officer who was on his hands and knees coughing blood.

The French commanders shouted at their men to fire up the guerrilleros, but as they sent protracted volleys, the Spanish pulled away from the edges and the bullets were wasted. They were like ghosts; one minute there, the next gone. A man was screaming piteously. The leading dragoon officer ordered his men to break out of the road, then to dismount to hunt down the enemy. He waved his straight-bladed sword high over his head.

'Now!' Rai shouted and from both sides men pushed and heaved logs and boulders over the edges. The noise was horrendous. The heavy logs pounded the sides before slamming into the ground, creating a series of ear-splitting cracks as boulders and large stones smashed into the ground to send jagged fragments into the leading dragoons. A jagged splinter, two foot long, struck a dragoon sergeant shattering his breastbone. An officer's face disintegrated as a rock rebounded up from the ground to crush bone. A white-eyed horse veered into another and both mounts fell, crushing their riders.

'Don't waste a shot! Make every shot count!' Rai ordered as though the strength of his voice would add to their destruction. 'Aim low! Fire!'

Cadoc shot at an infantry officer who was wearing his bedroll around his waist and shoulders. The bullet passed cleanly through his throat. Blood, bright as dawn, fountained from the man's open mouth. The Rifleman edged back out of sight and reloaded. Beside him, the young man was jiggling on his heels as he excitedly reloaded his musket. An older man with greying hair and dressed in a dirty white jacket and pantaloons fired and re loaded his wide-muzzled blunderbuss with a bag of nails. He had a dozen crude bags laid out in front of him. The pan flashed and the gun slammed into his shoulder, sending a blast of shrapnel down into the packed ranks which snatched two horsemen from their saddles.

The crude barricade of fallen logs was stymieing the French advance and Rai whooped derisively.

'I've seen tougher nuns! You boy-lovers! Your mothers are whores!'

The French infantry, mostly wearing campaign dress of sandy-coloured coats, brown pantaloons and covered shakoes, were trying to break free. They scattered, but the dragoons were in the way, unable to move past the obstacle. The infantry in the rear ranks were unable to pass or see the cause of the delay, instead had to endure the enemy's cheering and jeering over the sounds of Frenchmen dying. Saturnin's men sent more logs and boulders tumbling down to trap the horseman at the rear. A score escaped before the avalanche of timber and stone slammed down into the road. The wagons blocked the infantry's view. Some of the guerrilleros were firing at them, the canvass was pock-marked with bullets hoping to hit a powder barrel to make it explode.

'Fire!'

Padre Tos was there, firing and loading musket like a soldier. He had made a large cross from two lengths of wood lashed together, which he had pierced the ground with. 'God is with us!' he cried out. 'He loves us and He will punish the French!'

The musket smoke was as thick as stew. The air blew hot, and the stink of blood mingled with the acrid powder-stench.

Sapeurs; huge, bearded men wearing bearskin caps and wielding great axes, shoved men out of the way to try to hack through the logs. Cadoc shot at one, but the man moved aside and the bullet passed through his thick apron. The French sent another volley upwards and Cadoc felt and heard the bullets whip the grass and ricochet from the rocky overhang. One struck the older man with the blunderbuss in the forehead. He grunted once, then crumpled like a puppet that had its strings cut. The embankments were clouding with so much gun smoke that it was getting impossible to see the enemy. The partisans just fired their weapons into the contracting, bleeding, shouting mass below, trusting they would hit something - anything to cause damage and pain. Blood spattered the roads surface and splashed up the banks.

Some guerrilleros, impatient and blood-crazed, emptied their weapons, before throwing rocks, knives and anything that could be used as missiles. A few over-keen stood too close to the edges, assuming that because the French were blocked and dying, they were perfectly safe. The French still maintained volley fire and those Spaniards were whipped back. Cadoc watched one, stumble, and teeter on the edge, before falling down onto the French infantry, knocking down four bayonet-tipped men.

'*Vive l'Empereur!*' the cry went up.

'Kill those bastards!' Cadoc shouted and pointed at the *sapeurs* who were hacking their way through the blockade. Great chips of wood were flying through the air. Some of the infantry had skirted the verge and horses to haul the timber away. A *sapeur,* with massive shoulders, was breaking a boulder apart with a pick-axe.

Rai, clasping hands around his mouth, relayed the command across the roadside. Another Spanish volley hammered down at the barricade, flaying the French. But it was not enough and the dragoons were minutes from breaking free.

A guerrillero staggered with a large rock and, using all his strength, veins standing out on his thick neck, tossed it over the cliff's edge. Cadoc watched it plummet to crush two men into piles of convulsing gore. The Spaniards jeered the French dead.

The partisans kept firing through their own smoke and the blacker smoke of the grass fires caused by their own wadding. Cadoc looked for officers. He found one on horseback with a drawn sword who was bellowing at the men to reform their lines. The rifle cracked and spurted yellow-grey smoke. Cadoc twisted aside to see that the man had dropped his sword, a blood-slick hand was clasping his flank. A bullet immediately thrummed back through the air close enough for the Rifleman to feel the wind of its passage.

'Keep killing them!' Rai urged. 'Fire! Fire with every weapon at your side!'

Dead and wounded men and horses lay beside the road choking the ones that still lived. A few hollows in the embankment offered some safety for small phalanxes of infantry from the bitter musket fire, but sergeants pulled men out and jostled them into files. The *sapeur* with the pick-axe still lived and more bullets thumped into his back, but he carried on breaking apart the barricade until Cadoc put a ball through the base of his skull. The pick-axe clattered onto the road, where French blood trickled.

Then, as the huge *sapeur* fell, the dragoons charged forward.

'*Vive l'Empereur! Vive l'Empereur!*'

'Back!' Rai hollered. 'Get to your horses! Back!'

Dantel, pistol smoking in a hand, waved his men back. 'Go!'

The partisans grudgingly broke their positions and hurried back down to where their mounts were tethered in a sheltered hollow. The sound of the French cavalry surging up the road shook the ground.

'Go! Go!' Rai kicked one of his stubborn men away.

'Let me kill more of them!' the man insisted and Rai slapped his face and pushed him forcefully away.

'Fool! You will not live if you stay! Now go!'

Cadoc waited for Rai and then returned with him to where the guerrilleros were hurriedly mounting up.

'Back to Navales! Back!'

*

The surviving dragoons formed up and followed the dust trail that whirled down the road towards Navales. The shattered infantry limped back towards the garrison at Alba de Tormes. There were so many wounded and dead that it was at first impossible to count them all.

The dragoons were led by a man who had fought in the Italian campaign, crushed the Prussians at Jena–Auerstedt, destroyed the Russians at Preussisch-Eylau, and received the *Légion d'Honneur* for his heroics before being sent to Spain.

Chef-de-battalion Pierre Helterlin took his squadron to the Spanish village swearing an oath of revenge for the slaughter that had occurred. He would hunt down the enemy and burn every settlement to ash until they were caught and killed.

'These pieces of rat-shit have no honour!' he remarked bitterly. 'I'll gut them, their families, and their friends for what they did.'

And for the failing to capture the partisan leader, Colonel Herrero, Helterlin vowed privately. The Spaniard was a *Jean-Foutre*. Helterlin still fumed at his humiliation. He had lost good men during the night attack, and only one officer had returned alive. This was not how French cavalry - the finest cavalry in the world - should die. Cavalrymen should die with glory on the battlefield, not succumb to Spanish knives or Spanish bullets on night attacks, or patrols.

The dragoons thundered after the irregulars and it seemed they were gaining on them. Fields blurred past. And then the road dipped to reveal the collection of tiled homes. Helterlin suspected that a few would hide in the houses, but leaving a detachment behind to seek them out, he would take the majority after the others who would be fleeing to the hills.

'*Capitaine* Jaillet!' he called to his subordinate.

'Sir?'

'I know this village. Take your troop around the western flank and I'll drive through it northwards. We'll pursue them on two courses. Leave a squadron behind to search the buildings.'

'Yes, sir.'

'We will crush them today. No survivors, *Capitaine*!' Helterlin commanded.

Jaillet nodded. 'Sir!'

It was then that Helterlin saw a puff of smoke blotting the ridge above Navales. Experience told him, that this was a cannon. But what were the partisans doing with artillery? He stared open-mouthed as a ball slammed into the road directly in front of them in a blur, bounced twice and Helterlin held his breath. It was all he could do. He heard the gun's discharge. It was feeble against the huge artillery barrage at Preussisch-Eylau, which seemed to cause ripples in the sky. He would never forget the sound; like peals of never-ending blood-seeking thunder.

The ball snatched the dragoon to his left out of his saddle, tore through the dragoon behind him, disembowelled the third horseman, and decapitated the fourth dragoon's horse, and suddenly men and horse of the rear ranks twisted, fell and collapsed screaming in blood, leather and steel.

'They have artillery!' someone in the ranks shouted the obvious.

Helterlin snapped out of his thoughts. No other gun fired. The guerrilleros must have captured a gun from a convoy, so he decided to continue the pursuit. The gun had caused damage, but would not fire again. The rabble would not have the skill of proper gun teams. 'We'll soon be out of range!' he called. 'I was at Marengo with the Emperor! I charged the Prussian guns with Marshal Murat at Jena–Auerstedt! I charged the Russian cavalry at Preussisch-Eylau and I lived!' Spittle danced between his lips. He withdrew his sword, like most dragoons', the blades were made with the famed Toledo steel, and he held it high. 'I lived so follow me! And together we will destroy the Spanish dogs! Glory and France! *Vive l'Empereur!*' His men cheered him fervently.

Helterlin kicked his spurs on, leading the chase. His mare, captured like so many of his men's horses from the battlefields of Prussia and Austria, offered a gruff snort as though the beast understood the urgency. A great roar went up. The dragoons were filled with the mad, terrifying joy of the pursuit. The hooves of the galloping horses beat a frantic and fierce rhythm on the Spanish earthen road.

The gun fired again and the ball tore through the air, this time going overhead. He wondered how they had fired so quickly, because it was the same gun in the same location. He considered that the enemy were made up with the broken fragments of the Spanish army so may there may have had some ex-gunners. Nevertheless, Helterlin laughed sourly. His men were safe now and would corner the impudent gunners and hack them into offal. He glanced over his shoulders, his men as though reading his mind. The Frenchmen whooped and spurred their mounts at the partisans.

The road split and Jaillet took his men west. Helterlin could see the guerrilleros flee on their horses and they were closing fast. He clasped his sword tightly with his gloved hands, raised it in salute and kissed the blade. Retribution was as sweet as a virgin's first intercourse. He laughed. He would bed women tonight as he had done after every fight. There was something in victory that was exhilarating as sexual intercourse. He craved it, and he would look for it. After Marengo, he had bedded General Graf von Morzin's Italian whore who was trying to sneak through French lines. After Jena–Auerstedt, he slept with two Prussian women, one of whom was dressed in a Prussian grenadier's uniform. He laughed at the memory. After Preussisch-Eylau, he slept with a Polish countess who insisted her maids watch them make love. Spain had so far brought nothing but sullen encounters and what Helterlin wanted now was a Spanish girl. He didn't care how old or how beautiful. Victory would give him what he needed and with those thoughts that aroused him in the saddle, he did not expect to see a strange contraption blocking the road.

It looked like a cannon barrel lashed tight with ropes and blocks of wood and mounted on a hay cart. It dawned on him that this was an improvised artillery piece, cannibalised from parts and a big blue-coated man rushed out from behind a wall with a piece of slow-match.

Helterlin could not believe his eyes, and as he hauled on his reins commanding his men to veer left, the gun exploded sending grapeshot straight into the dragoons.

Helterlin saw flame, smoke and then nothing more.

*

'*Disparar!*' a voice shouted and thirty muskets flamed from walls, windows, trees and doorways. Dragoons tumbled from saddles from the volley, horses collapsed and they slammed to a halt as a line of guerrilleros blocked the roadside.

Capitaine Jaillet had heard the cannon fire coming from his flank, but assumed it had been the same artillery piece. *Chef-de-battalion* Helterlin had given him an order and so Jaillet would obey. His men were disorganised and he brought his chestnut mare to face them. They would form and cut their way through the brazen Spaniards. Tack jangled, scabbards clanked, men shouted and horses whinnied. Jaillet went to speak but found that he could not. His men were staring at him. He heard a distinctive crack above him and something was stinging his throat. Hot, salty blood erupted from his mouth. He was shaking. A trooper snatched the reins from his hand. Everything was moving slower, dizzying by sunlight flashing in his face.

'Reload!' someone was shouting in English above him, but Jaillet did not recognise the voice. Instead, he slumped forward, mouth taking in some of the horses flapping mane. He was very cold, limbs feeling like heavy weights and he suddenly wanted to sleep for eternity.

Jaillet closed his eyes, welcoming it.

*

'Reload!' Cadoc bellowed, cursed himself, and then repeated it in Spanish. '*Recarger! Recarger!*'

He gazed down from the roof tiles, seeing the officer slump and the dragoons in chaos. A few of them snatched up their muskets and the balls smacked and whizzed harmlessly against the house. He cast a look across the tumble of roof tops to where Cotton's ingenuity had fixed two of the four guns in the short time the guerrilleros had been away. A crackle of musketry echoed and small plumes of smoke billowed to show that the dragoons were still present there. Another musket fired and the bullet cracked tiles to Cadoc's right. He lay back, reloading his rifle with blackened fingers.

The partisan line advanced rapidly and they shouted like most Spanish infantry when they did. They hefted an array of firearms, swords, lances and Cadoc even saw a boar spear waver in the air.

The dragoons were attempting to form. The enemy offered little defence against charging horsemen. Single line infantry on firm ground were a horseman's paradise. French blades would spill Spanish blood.

358

A shrill call echoed. The French turned in their saddles, thinking that it was one of their own, but the dragoon trumpeter wearing a white horsehair helmet and coat matching the colour of the trooper's facings signalled that it was not him.

Mounted guerrilleros thundered into the left flank of the French dragoons who reeled in shock. Colonel Herrero charged headlong into the green-coated enemy. One of his men even carried a Spanish flag tied to a lance and the point slammed into a dragoon who was trying to spur his mount away. The Frenchman was knocked to the floor, and the standard bearer rode the banner free.

Rai held his sword aloft. The blade, heavy with gold inlay, flashed in the bright sunlight. *'Fernando! Por Dios y por España!'* he shouted, drawing out the last word like a war cry.

For God and Spain.

Hooves pounded the ground, dust and clods of earth were flung high in the air. The dragoons were still milling and twisting when the Spanish cavalry crashed into them. Sword blades, pale as winter ice, chopped and thrust. Terrified horses screamed, hooves lashed and big yellowed teeth bit. Swords clashed, ringing like smith's hammers. A Spaniard shot a dragoon in the face, then he was himself hit between the eyes with a French bullet. The enemy advance was checked. The dragoon trumpeter was sounding the call to retreat when Cadoc and more guerrilleros slammed into the French rear. Saturnin and Dantel's men had feigned retreat and as Cotton's guns splintered the Spanish afternoon's air, they had wheeled left and swooped up the hill to where Rai's mounted men had hidden behind a sloping vineyard.

Cadoc stood up so that the dismounted guerrilleros could see him. *'Disparar!'*

Perhaps twenty-five muskets and carbines fired from the line and more Dragoons, a mere forty yards away, were thrown backwards. The Spanish then howled at the heavens and charged into the bloodied mess of men and horses.

There was nowhere else to go and the French knew that. Their only option was to fight their way to freedom. A few brought out their muskets and a smattering of partisans fell to their bullets, but they were being pressed from all sides. A dragoon speared a guerrillero's horse in the neck, causing its rider to haul frantically on the reins to control the beast. The Frenchman slashed into the man's neck and soon both were dying together, blood pumped bright onto the road. A pistol flared and a Frenchman grunted as he was hit in the chest. The dismounted guerrilleros reached the horsemen and they clubbed and hauled and stabbed more dragoons until a knot of blood-sheeted Frenchmen threw down their swords in the vain hope of surrender.

Cadoc scented victory and so decided to check on Cotton and the gun teams. He slung the rifle over one shoulder, jumped down onto a rain barrel as the murderous slaughter began. A dragoon drove his horse towards him and went to bring his sword down, but a bullet caught him in the flank and then screamed as Cadoc's sword-bayonet stabbed up into his belly, to be twisted and ripped free. The Welshman ducked as another blade sliced at him. This time from a man with epaulettes whose swordplay was quick and careful. The gleaming tip sliced open his forearm and a sliver of green cloth twirled to the dusty ground.

'You French bastard.'

Cadoc leapt forward to surprise the enemy, but the officer had expected the attack and the long sword almost cut him up through the chin. Cadoc ducked underneath the horse, sliced the stirrup's strap and pushed the man out of his saddle. The Frenchman managed to hang onto his sword. A guerrillero tried to bayonet him, but the officer got to his feet, slashed his blade across his face and the Spaniard fell away screaming, hands pressed against his face. Another partisan ran at him, slicing with his *cuchillo*, but the blows were easily beaten aside and the dragoon thrust once, the tip driving through an eye. The officer yelled, daring the enemy to come at him when a Spaniard on horseback put a pistol to the back of his head and the shot blew his brains out. Cadoc stared at the great glistening wound as the hair around it smouldered from the point-blank blast.

The Spaniards were fighting well enough and so he scrambled down the nearest alley. A dismounted dragoon saw him through the rills of dust and powder-smoke, and followed.

The sound of muskets firing still echoed but it was very sporadic, bordering on non-existence. Cadoc vaulted a wall, scampered through someone's garden. Roaming chickens clucked noisily and flapped out of the way. A spiral of thick smoke was rising higher. Cadoc saw streaks of blood bright on the earth. One wall of a garden was spattered with gore. A horse lay dead, its guts strung blue on the road, perhaps three feet from its corpse. A dead dragoon with no face lay at an odd angle on the street. Hooves thudded and men were shouting in English, Spanish and French. A musket fired and a man gasped. A carbine ball nicked the wall next to Cadoc, showering him with fragments.

'It's me, you dozy bastards!'

A man wearing a blue-coat of the Ordnance held up a hand in recognition. A larger figure behind saw him and shouldered his musket. Corporal Leatherby smiled like an executioner. Cadoc stared wide-eyed, heard loud boots behind him and threw himself sideways as the stalking dragoon was shot through the body. Cadoc twisted, sword bayonet flashing in his hand to strike in case the shot had missed, but the sprawled enemy was bleeding and dying. The Welshman turned and sprinted to a low wall that was crowded with musket-armed defenders. One Spaniard hung over the wall, blood dripped from his open mouth. Dragoons were firing their carbines from horseback and from behind walls and houses. The hay-cart and the French eight-pounder were on fire. A Spaniard next to Cadoc was wearing a British Light Dragoon cap. He grinned back with tobacco stained teeth and fired his musket into the throng of the enemy.

Cadoc slotted his sword-bayonet to the loaded rifle and shouldered it. He aimed it at a sergeant leaning out from behind a wall, pulled the trigger and the Frenchman collapsed like a sack of old clothes. A Spaniard pounded the skins of a drum nearby until Cadoc shouted at the man to put the damned instrument away and pick up a musket. A small dog lapped at blood.

A carbine ball struck a partisan in the thigh and he fell back with a grunt. A helmetless dragoon charged with suicidal courage and was instantly flung back by musketry, blood jetting in a great fountain from his mouth.

Cotton heard his voice over the din and ran over to him.

'My God, we've trounced them!' he said exuberantly. He wiped his blackened face, crossed with trails of sweat with his handkerchief. 'We gave them a drubbing they won't forget!' He ducked as a ball smacked noisily into the pock-marked stone wall.

'Well done, sir.' Cadoc thumped his arm and Cotton hissed in pain. 'Are you hit?'

'Took a bullet earlier,' he said as though it was all fault. 'Cornered by two of them. Shot one fellow with my pistol and Corporal Leatherby took care of the other.' Cadoc glanced over his shoulder at the muscled NCO who had joined them.

'Hauled the turd off his saddle and cracked him one across the jaw just like you would have done,' the corporal shouted. 'Then, I dashed his skull in with my musket stock.'

Cadoc was impressed. 'I owe you thanks for back there,' he said. The corporal waved a hand as though dismissing it. Cadoc inspected the captain's wound to find the carbine ball had passed through the flesh without breaking bone. 'We'll get that fixed up after this, sir.' He looked for more targets, but the dragoons were edging back.

'I think we did a good job here, wouldn't you say?' Cotton enquired, wanting praise. He moved and then winced from the pain.

The Welshman grinned. 'You bloody well did, sir.'

'A pity the charge set the cart on fire,' Cotton remarked plaintively, 'but we only had enough grapeshot for one blast anyway. The Spanish twelve-pounder fires like a dream, though. I hope Rai keeps it. Still, we did well, all of us.'

They had done extremely well. The British and Spanish men jeered the survivors, shot their weapons in one final sporadic volley, and then clasped each other in celebration. Some pounced on the wounded and knifed, shot or clubbed them. Sebastiano, a man who beat other men to death with his bare hands, kissed Leatherby on the cheek and danced with tears in his eyes. Cadoc laughed, and lowered his primed rifle, because it was not needed now.

The ruse had worked, the French had been defeated, and Cadoc was smiling like a fool.

They had won, but there was still one more enemy yet to kill.

*

A single horseman took the steep rocky path up to where grey caves looked like fiendish maws. It was a high climb. When the peak was still touched red by the last daylight, the valley below would already be dark. There was no sound here, apart from the hooves and the slip of a rock which slid over the side of the precarious path. The track was only wide enough for one horse, mule or men on foot.

A gentle rain had fallen in the night. The wind freshened again and blew ripples across the puddles. The horseman, nostrils filling with cool air, brought his plain brown cloak closer to his body. A hawk circled in the bruised sky, gliding freely in the currents.

As the horse climbed to where the ground levelled, Colonel Antonio Rai Herrero dismounted and led his horse to the entrance to the largest of the caves. Four horses were tethered to a dying oak tree, the trunk a mass of rot and white fungi. He looped the leather reins around a jutting rock, then glanced at the diluted outlines of the far sheltered

362

hills where a thin veil of mist still loitered to mingle with low clouds. The air felt crisp and brittle like the first breath of autumn.

'Welcome, *hermano*,' a lone voice rose up from the cave's gloom.

Rai turned and smiled as his brother stepped out to greet him. They embraced.

'You are well?' Rai asked him.

Fito smiled. 'Of course, and I am so glad to see you safe. I heard about the French attack and of your victory two days ago! A dragoon squadron smashed apart!'

'I had help,' Rai said self-depreciatingly. 'It wasn't all my doing.'

Fito waved an admonishing finger. 'I hear it in all the villages. They speak nothing but praise. You won a great victory! You've made a reputation for yourself. I hear that El Medico wants to meet with you. What an honour!'

'The victory goes to Spain.'

'Our father would be very proud. I am proud,' Fito said, beaming. 'I want to hear more.' He clasped his arms around his brother's shoulders. 'I have the best French wine, our *aguadiente* and even some British Rum that needs our most urgent attention,' he said, breaking into a laugh.

'French wine?'

Fito grinned. 'Plundered two days ago from a supply wagon. I have crates of the stuff. It's rather palatable.'

'You like the taste?'

Fito frowned. 'It's a good wine,' he conceded. 'You know me I'll drink anything.'

Rai shrugged off the embrace. He walked towards the steep hills, expression of someone deep in thought.

'*Hermano*?' Fito enquired of Rai's sudden remote behaviour. 'Is something wrong?'

'Do you remember the last time we met?'

Fito rubbed his unshaven chin. 'Yes, in Navales,' he said warily, knowing that his brother would have known the answer.

Rai looked down at the bottom of the gorge, face unreadable. 'The French attacked that night.'

Fito growled. 'I know. I wish I'd stayed a little longer. My *cuchillo* would have found many throats to cut.'

'And yet you left,' Rai uttered the sentence as a question.

'Yes?' Fito gave his brother a lop-sided grin. 'Where are you going with this?'

Rai was silent for a while. He gazed at the cave entrance knowing eyes watched him from within its cold darkness. 'Do you believe that Saint Teresa fought the devil here?'

'What Spaniard doesn't?'

'How many of your men do you have here now?'

'Two.'

Rai hoisted an eyebrow. 'Where are the rest?'

Fito scratched his neck with long, bony fingers. 'There are watching the northern roads. I understand that there is a large French convoy coming up from Ávila. Have you heard that the *ingleses* are falling back across the border?'

'Yes. It seems that we're going to have to save Spain ourselves.'

'I fear it won't be enough.'

'How so?'

Fito walked towards the slope's edge, where thick weeds grew amongst the rocks. 'We have no armies left. The guerrilleros are tiny against the French armies. It is said they number more than a quarter of a million men.' He shook his head. 'We're a grain of sand against the tide. We haven't the firepower to defeat them. We haven't the manpower. We are running out of money. Half the partisan bands I know haven't horses, weapons or even the clothes to put on their backs.'

'We haven't been beaten yet!'

'Our regulars have. There will come a time when even the guerrilleros cannot win.' Fito stared out to the distant peaks, his face glowing by sunlight that had appeared through a tear in the clouds.

'Our people need to know the war is not lost.'

'It is only a matter of time.'

Rai growled, 'I never thought you were such a defeatist.'

Fito was silent for a while. 'Not a defeatist, brother. I'm just considering the future prospects.'

'For Spain, or for yourself?'

'Both.'

'What about your kin?'

'What do you mean?'

'Do you see me in your future?'

Fito hesitated before answering. 'Of course. Don't talk such nonsense.'

'I think I'm making perfect sense,' Rai said. 'How long have you allied yourself to the French?'

'What?' Fito frowned in puzzlement.

'I never would have imagined this as possible. It makes my body tremble just to speak it and God forgive me for saying it, but you are a liar and a traitor. A better traitor than a liar, I grant you. I know when you are lying to me. I am your brother, after all. But why whore yourself to the French dogs? I think I understand. You've always worried about money. Land, money and titles. We are from poor stock and the French have taken everything else we had. We have nothing now except the clothes on our backs, the weapons at our side and the ground our boots tread on. But that's not enough for you, is it? You want more. You've always wanted more. And the French offered you that, didn't they? What was it? Riches? Titles?'

Fito shook his head and gazed at the horses that whickered softly. 'I think perhaps,' he said thoughtfully and carefully, 'that the victory has blunted your wits.'

Rai grinned wolfishly. 'The only thing that has been dulled is my sword. I need to sharpen it and work out the notches. It could so easily have been defeat.' He laughed sourly. 'Now I sound like you. But since the victory, one thing is certain; the French will come back to Navales.'

'They will.'

'But this time they will find it empty. The folk have long gone.'

'Where did you send them?' Fito asked.

'That is not your concern. From the moment the French dragoons attacked Navales, I knew it would not be safe for them to remain. But in truth, the French that night weren't after our people, were they? They came with one purpose and that was to kill me.'

'How can you be so certain?' Fito fiddled with the pommel of his sword, hanging at his hip.

Rai sighed. 'Because the dragoon major told me so.'

Fito did not answer. He just watched his brother, fingers fidgeting.

'*Chef-de-battalion* Pierre Helterlin was in a bad way,' Rai said. 'He suffered terrible injuries, but Doctor Escarrà worked his magic, and saved his life. Funny that, don't you think? He's an enemy of Spain, a killer of our people, and yet I made sure he lived. I prayed he would and God listened. Do you know what the Frenchman told me?'

'Go on?'

'He said that a Spaniard rode with him and his men. In fact, it was the same story that I beat out of another French officer. A Spaniard rode with them,' Rai said, shuddering as though the notion was too much for him to contemplate. 'He said that this traitor was employed to

365

spy for him, to help root out patriots, name the leaders and have them destroyed. He said they would target the leader's families if they could not get to the man they wanted. What a despicable being that traitor is. And I think that our good friend Steven Kyte found out who it was only to get captured. But Steven was resourceful, even for a heathen *ingleses*, and he escaped.'

Fito glanced up to the horses again and Rai's eyes followed.

'I think Steven came to warn me, only to die by the traitor's bullet. A bullet fired from a British rifle I would imagine. Both the officer and Helterlin told me that my countryman carried a rifle.'

Fito turned his attention from the rifle holstered and strapped to his horse's saddle to his brother. 'You know the *ingleses* supply us with muskets and rifles. We both know the Baker rifle's are highly sought after. Many of our men carry them.'

'You do.'

'I always have. So what?'

'But not all of them are traitors to their country,' Rai said, catching his gaze. 'A traitor to his own brother! I learned that you had told the French I would be at Navales. They came to kill me because you had warned them.'

'Nonsense,' Fito said angrily and walked to the horses. 'I will no longer listen to your babbling. Come back when you are feeling better.'

It was though Rai had been punched in the guts. 'I know in my heart it was you. You are no longer my brother.' Fito turned and Rai spat into his face. 'God forgive me, but you're a traitor and you're going to die.'

Neither man moved.

Suddenly, swords were whipped from scabbards and the two blades struck each other, the noise echoed down into the valley.

'Betrayer!' Rai hissed, spittle dropped from his mouth. 'My own blood a traitor!'

'I am no betrayer,' Fito exclaimed through gritted teeth. 'Is reason, intelligence, science and understanding cause for hatred? Our country is corrupt. The Church rules it. It is knotted in great tangles of superstition, ancient practices and suppression. Where is our liberty? Where is our free will? Why is it frowned upon to question our faith? The workings of the world? The French are free to do this, why can't we Spanish?'

'The French are invaders!' Rai gaped, incredulous at his brother's true thoughts. The blades were still crossed.

'They bring hope. They bring light.'

Rai's mouth twisted in rage, eyes a veritable blaze of hatred. 'They murdered my Ana! They murdered my children!'

Fito blinked. 'With progress there has to be casualties.'

'You bastard!' Rai howled and threw off his brother. He lunged and hacked with no great skill. The rising anger drove him on. 'You have no honour!'

The fight happened in a blink of an eye.

Rai barrelled into his brother with all the force he could muster, bringing his sword down at Fito's head in a great, bone-shattering attack. It slipped beyond the surprised Spaniard's guard, slicing a cut across above his left ear. Fito rushed aside, felt the wound and sneered. He brought his sword up sharply for the next assault. He did not wait long. Rai rained blow after blow at Fito's head, but each time he parried in a way that would have made a fencing-master proud.

And then Fito went on the attack, stepping in with sword high, tip angled like a silver snake, ready to strike. The sword flashed bright, darted and valley was ringing with the song of swords. Rai managed to turn the attack, chopped down, but Fito parried, back-cut, and turned the cut into a lunge that sliced deep into Rai's flank. He knew he had wounded his brother, for Rai stepped back, face grimacing and left hand grasping his ribs. Blood flowed through his fingers and began to darken his scarlet coat.

'Fate,' Fito sneered and Rai spat at him again.

Two men appeared at the caves entrance, both armed with muskets and pistols. Paz cocked the long firearm. Fito heard it, turned and waved them away. 'This is my fight,' he said. 'It won't take long.'

A crack seared the morning's air and the guerrillero next to Paz was thrown to the ground, leaving a small pink cloud in the air above him, which drifted an inch and then disappeared in the breeze. His musket spun away, clattering on the stone. The horses whinnied noisily. The weapon's mark still reverberated for several seconds after the shot.

The three Spaniards were astonished by the gun fire, and stood momentarily dazed. They stared at the man lying on his front, limbs twitching. A huge, ragged, hair-fringed hole had been punched through his skull, leaving a glistening hollow of blood and bone. Paz, coming to his senses, wiped hot gore from his cheeks, before bolting for cover. He slammed into a boulder near the path's edge. He had seen a puff of jaundiced-grey smoke from the nearest hill where a line of stones ringed the summit. He took a lungful of air, then positioned his musket over the rock, aiming below the gun smoke.

367

Fito stepped back from his brother. 'Hold your fire, Paz! You don't have the range! He has a rifle.'

'I can see him,' Paz replied, seeing a figure creep east along the stones. A dark shape, but it stopped and the Spaniard gripped the trigger, made smooth over the years. The enemy was reloading. It would be an easy kill. The rifle shot was still echoing.

'Keep out of sight, Paz!' Fito ordered, glancing at the enemy marksman. From experience he knew the distance to be just under a rifle's effectiveness. 'Hold your fire!'

The man moved again and the temptation was too much. Paz pulled the trigger and the musket banged. He was sure he had hit his target, for once the smoke dissipated, he couldn't see the enemy. 'I hit him, Fito!' he yelled triumphantly. 'I killed the bastard! I killed him! I kill-'

The rifle bullet snapped Paz's head back with the impact, and the body dropped like a lead weight, blood spurting over the uneven ground.

'You son of a bitch!' Rai shouted at Fito, lungs-heaving with exertion. 'Fight me like a man! You French-lover! You French whore!' He was weakening, fast, but he would not show it.

Fito drove his sword down onto Rai's, using both hands, down to his knees, then kicked him over. Rai fell backwards, still holding his sword. 'It's a pity it has to end like this.'

'It hasn't ended.'

'Not yet. Stay here,' Fito said, ramming his blade into his brother's leg.

Rai screamed, more in anger, and slashed wildly with his sword, but Fito had gone.

The Spaniard ran to his horse and dragged free his own rifle. He used the horses for cover, concealing himself behind the oak. He primed the gun, then slowly edged out from the trunk, scanning the hills. The dead men's blood was steaming in the cool air. He heard Rai scream out his name, but he would deal with the Rifleman first and his brother afterwards. He could see the hidden marksman. He knew it was that bastard Welshman. He had seen the man's pride of the rifle, noticing that his clothes were grubby and ragged, yet the weapon's mechanics looked well-oiled, polished and maintained. Rai spoke highly of him. And he had earned Fito's respect and not many men had done that. But still he was an enemy and would die all the same.

A shape moved and Fito was tempted to fire at it, but considered it to be deception. He was too shrewd to fall for such tricks, having used many to send countless enemies to their unmarked graves. His brown eyes watched the man in the dark coat like a hawk watching its prey. An age seemed to pass, then the moment he had been waiting for. Cadoc moved and exposed his upper body for an instant as he attempted to get a better shot.

Fito's rifle cracked and he sprinted forwards out of the foul-smelling smoke to see the Welshman sag. The Spaniard let out an exultant cry! It was so easy! He was still smiling when he saw another figure slowly rise up from the crest to his left. The man was aiming at him. A cold shiver went up Fito's spine. He'd fallen for a ruse and there was just enough time for him to acknowledge his momentous and irreversible mistake with a smile of admiration when the rifle bullet hammered into his body, exploding his heart into bloody tatters.

*

A calloused hand gently gathered Rai to his feet. His crimson sash torn to stem the bleeding wounds was sodden, but the Spaniard put a grin on his pale face.

'I told you I'd put a bullet through his goddamned heart,' Cadoc said with a ironic smile

'How did you know I would come here?' Rai groaned.

Cadoc fussed over the wound to his side. 'I saw you leave, *senõr*. I remembered Fito asking you to meet him.' He straightened. 'I'm sorry he was a traitorous bastard.'

Rai shook his head. 'I can't believe he would betray me. Not my own brother.' He took a step forward and winced. 'Thank you for coming. You saved my life. Again,' he said with a wry smile, despite the pain. 'Who did you bring with you?'

'Corporal Leatherby.'

'I didn't know he's trained to use a rifle?'

Cadoc shook his head. 'He's not. I brought him here with the rifle Captain Cotton brought. It's jammed, but Paz and your brother wouldn't know that.'

Rai looked puzzled. 'You used him as a decoy.'

'Yes.'

'Clever.'

Cadoc scratched his chin. 'Well, your brother shot him in the arm. Only a scratch.'

369

Rai grinned despite the pain. 'How did you persuade him to come with you?'

'A bottle of best *aguadiente*.'

The guerrillero laughed and looked down the path to where the hulking NCO waited for them. 'I guess there is only one true marksman here and that's you, Rifleman Cadoc.'

The Welshman was suddenly very proud and a pang of longing filled his mind. But for now there was plenty of rest ahead of him. Summer was coming to an end and the French were still marauding Spain, and so for now he would stay and fight.

*

Chef-de-battalion Helterlin woke from an agonised dream where sadistic men had sliced him with wicked blades, hammered bones until they broke and scalded his genitals with boiling water.

It was dark, wherever he was.

He tried to recollect recent events. His head felt like it was made of wool. He closed his eyes, remembering that he had been riding to a village. That was it. A village. But what was there? The guerrilleros. Yes. Goat-stinking peasants that had attacked him on that sunken road. Goddamn them! Helterlin's mouth curled into a snarl, then he saw flames. Flesh-searing heat and smoke. Cannon. Yes, that was it. A gun had fired at them. Had it hit anyone? Yes. Men and horses had fallen in chaos and death and blood. He could still hear the men screaming and horses whickering in terror.

He wanted move but he was unable to. Arms were stuck together. No, not stuck. Bound. He kicked his legs, but they were bound at the ankles too. His body throbbed.

Help me, he mouthed but no sound came out.

He remembered the questions voices asked him. It went on for hours or had it been days? Who was the Spaniard that rode with him? They repeated it over and over and Helterlin tried desperately to keep the name secret. But the pain became too much. He had revealed the one who was a true believer, or the *afrancesado*, the Spanish would call him, just to stop the torment.

And mercifully they did. He remembered thanking them, his hoarse voice turning into sobs.

Now his body was numb, but a terrible pain was lancing up from toes to his fingers. His eyes flickered, closed and opened into darkness.

He knew he was outside. He could hear a dog barking faintly, a soft breeze on his naked body and the low murmur of voices. Where was he? What was he tied to? He moved his shoulder blades apart, feeling hewn wood and the clotted-wounds on his back opening up. Would they let him go now he had given them Fito's name?

There was the sound of footsteps. He turned to see who was coming but there was nothing there. Not nothing there, he could not see anything! He let out an anguished cry.

They have taken my eyes!

A man was talking to him. Helterlin had not bothered to learn a word of Spanish so had no idea what he was saying. The voice was spoken intimately, final and crisp. Helterlin heard the man walk away, or perhaps climbed down, for the footfalls sounded like they had been on steps. Something struck something below him, but what it was he did not know.

Then, there was a faint sound like the tearing of cloth and smoke singed his nostrils. Helterlin screamed. They had given him prayers and were now burning him alive! He was tied to a stake. He would die after all. His mutilated feet caught the flames first and he screamed and the flesh withered, twisted and bubbled. This was not how a hero of France was supposed to die! He shouted it out. He had been given a *Légion d'Honneur* medal by Bonaparte himself. He was a decorated hero of France!

But no one could hear his words anymore as the roaring, rippling flames reached his torso and Helterlin was burned alive.

*

The British wagons were loaded and two men watched the final canvass cover be strapped down.

'Has it really been two weeks?' Captain George Israel Cotton said. His arm was in a sling and he was fully dressed in his usual pristine coat.

'It has, sir,' Cadoc replied. He waved a hand to Corporal Leatherby who returned the gesture, even with a bandage around his arm.

'I still can't believe Leatherby went with you to safeguard Colonel Herrero! And nothing for his trouble,' Cotton said with a mystified look.

Cadoc had given the corporal three bottles of brandy and as many wineskins as he could take, and the wily NCO had failed to register that gift with his commanding officer. 'He's a good man, sir.'

Cotton raised an eyebrow to that statement, remembering their first encounter. 'It's funny how adversaries can become friends.'

'Aye,' Cadoc said and noticed that Cotton had held out a hand. He grasped it and shook it. He suddenly felt awkward, not knowing at first what to say. 'Thank you, for what you did here, sir. Getting the guns to work. A grand job.'

'It was nothing. You had all the right tools and my lads did the work, so full credit goes to them. I just got in the way.' Cotton smiled self-deprecatingly. 'I've been like that all my life. Getting in the way and not making much use of anything. I bought my lieutenancy and my captaincy without seeing or hearing a shot fired. I simply didn't do anything of merit and I guess that's what I'll achieve for the rest of the war. You can buy advancement, but not skill.'

'You led your men like any good officer could and you helped make a difference here. If those guns had not been fixed, we'd have lost. The bastard dragoons would have scoured us out of here and we'd all be dead. What we did here has already made its way to Madrid and I hope every Don hears about this. Back home they'd call you a hero. Here: you're an officer, a gentleman and a soldier,' the Welshman flourished a broad smile. 'Even if you don't think you are.'

Cotton hoped the burning sun hid his blushes. They were ten miles from Portugal's border, safe with Rai's partisans watching the horizon for enemies. 'If I wish to be a soldier, then I would wish to be a good one, to prove myself, not just for advancement.'

'You've done that, sir. You can go back with your head held high.'

'That's kind of you to say,' Cotton said.

Cadoc shuffled his feet. 'There is something else I wanted to say.' He licked his lips. 'I was hard on you when you first arrived. I assaulted you. If I still marched in the ranks, I would have lost my Chosen Man status,' he tugged at the faded-white stripe around his right arm, 'arrested and flogged. You reminded me so much of a man from my past that I actually thought he was here. I hate him and I couldn't see past my own hate.'

The 'what happened?' died on Cotton's lips as he decided now was not the time for the Welshman to speak of past horrors. 'I'd forgotten about that,' he graciously said instead.

'What I'm trying to say, sir, is that I apologise for my behaviour.'

Cotton smiled. 'I accept it. I do hope whoever this man is gets what he deserves.'

Cadoc's face creased into a sly grin that spoke of promised retribution. 'One day, sir.' The wagons and mules were waiting for the tall captain. Cadoc straightened his back to stand to attention and gave Cotton a smart salute.

The captain saluted back. 'Pass on my regards to Colonel Herrero. I hope he recovers. I look forward to hearing more of his exploits.'

'I will, sir. Where will you go now?'

'I'm being sent to Lisbon. You heard that we're pulling back. Not for long I hope. I'd like another crack at the Crapauds soon enough.' They both laughed. 'Before I go, you never did look into that trunk, did you?'

'No.'

'Take a look. You might find something that,' Cotton said, and the pause was significant and quite deliberate, 'you might be missing.'

Cadoc watched the retreating wagons and Rai's escort until they were gone. Then, the guerrilleros spurred back to their new hideout some one hundred or miles north-west of Salamanca deep in a land of lush forests, rocky hills, impassable gorges, beautiful waterfalls and sweet-smelling meadows. Rai's force had grown to one hundred and twenty men since the victory and more men were joining every day. The French still lingered so more were needed if Spain was ever to be free again.

Cadoc reached the village of Masueco where Edita waited for his return. She stood on the balcony of their new home, waving at him intensely as the partisans' horses clattered noisily in the small square that stank of spice-smelling, wood-smoke. The weapons that Cotton had brought had already been divided into working, to be mended and beyond repair, but the trunk had still not been distributed. He had commandeered it for personal use and it was still unopened. He raced upstairs, kissing Edita fiercely before reaching the trunk in the cellar, which opened into the village square. The floor was littered with bales of hay because he kept his horse there. He undid the clips and opened the lid. There were piles of boots, pantaloons, jackets and belts. His hands pulled aside a simple coat and his jaw dropped.

'What is it?' Edita called from the stairs. She then hurried down to the cellar. 'What does it mean, my love?'

'Everything,' Cadoc said, marvelling at the thing in his hands. 'It means everything.' He pushed open the rickety doors to let bright sunshine stream in. The light caught metal, which gleamed brightly in his dirt-ingrained hands. It was a badge showing a bugle horn. His eyes pricked.

He held the felt cap high with its green tuft and cord. Cadoc threw off his bandana and black hat and replaced it with the regimental cap. Smiling broadly with utter pride, because he was a marksman, and at heart, a Rifleman of the 95th.

Historical Note

Marksman is a work of fiction, but nevertheless grounded in fact.

This story takes place during the Peninsular War (in Spain it is referred to as 'The War of Independence') at a time when the British had almost wholly withdrawn (apart from a strong Royal Naval squadron in Cádiz) to Portugal behind Wellington's ingenious series of fortifications to protect Lisbon: the Lines of Torres Vedras.

After defeating Marshal Soult at Porto on 12th May 1809, Wellington's army crossed the border into Spain, joined forces with the Spanish general, Gregorio García de la Cuesta y Fernández de Celis, and marched eastwards. On 27th-28th July, French armies under Joseph attacked the allies north of Talavera and were defeated. The victory had, however, been costly and, with Soult threatening to cut the road to Portugal, Wellington was forced to fall back.

By the end of 1809, the Spanish armies were crushed heavily at Ocaña and then at Alba de Tormes, while Sir Arthur Wellesley, now Viscount Wellington of Talavera, concentrated on the Lines. The value of these defences proved their worth (and cost) in the following year when Marshal Masséna led a French army through the fortresses of Ciudad Rodrigo and Almeida in a fresh attempt to re-take Portugal. Despite being repulsed on 27th September 1810 in his attacks against Wellington's position on the ridge at Buçaco, Masséna was able to force the allies to seek safety behind the Lines by his continued presence. However, he had no chance of breaking through, and a stand-off ensued until a lack of supplies and the imminent arrival of British reinforcements in the spring of 1811 led Masséna to fall back. But that is another year and by then, even after the victories, the war was far from over, and it had not even reached turning point.

In the late summer of 1810, when *Marksman* takes place, most of Spain was under French control, except that its army of over two hundred and eighty thousand men could not be concentrated. Three quarters of it had to fight against local insurrections, and contain and protect the supply lines from the Spanish irregulars - the partisans. Even messengers had to travel with an escort of sometimes as much as a regiment, or take the awful chance of being captured by the guerrilleros who would brutally torture and kill them.

Napoleon had been present in Spain, but left in late 1808. He ordered his marshals to achieve decisive battles against the regular troops, but was unable to grasp the power of the civilian's anger and the threat of the partisans. The Spanish villagers stubbornly refused to bow to the French. They burned crops, poisoned wells, and evacuated with all their cattle. Napoleon, having had his forces tied down, Wellington was thus able go on the offensive with the combined Spanish, Portuguese and British regulars.

The guerrilla forced the French into a terrible dilemma that they never overcame: how could regular troops fight against the enemy regular troops, while simultaneously fighting irregulars. Fighting on two fronts shattered the prestige of the French army, thought of as invincible, and it was ultimately a war that Napoleon could not win.

So why did they fail?

The French famously lived off the land, they robbed, stole and raped. Thus, they could never win over the civilians. There were those Spanish who supported French ideals and were a minority. Likewise, there were partisans who were self-serving, amoral and who terrorized their own people. But by invading Spain with the idea of forcing their own way of life and ideals, the French did not immerse themselves in the culture, traditions, religion and language. Instead, they violated the people and their principles.

During his exile on St Helena, Napoleon famously said, ''the Spanish war has been a real ulcer, the first cause of the misfortunes of France''.

It was not the killing-fields of Europe, or the disastrous campaign in winter Russia that ruined him, it was the Peninsular War.

And men like Arthur Cadoc fought in that conflict.

In 1800, The Experimental Corps of Riflemen was formed, becoming the 95th Rifle Regiment of Foot three years later. Abandoning the red coat, the Rifles wore the distinctive 'green jacket'; the British Army's first attempt at camouflage. Not only was the uniform and training different to that of the other line regiments, they were equipped with the finest firearm of the age: the Baker rifle. Accurate at 75 yards and capable of hitting a target at 200, the rifle, with its seven rectangular-grooved barrel, gave the regiment a distinctive edge over their French opponents. The Rifles were masters of the battlefield skirmishes, marches and were held in high-esteem by allies and foes alike.

Rifleman Cadoc is an invention, but I'd like to think that the ghosts of his regiment are pleased with his incarnation, and if I've done them justice, I can sit back in my chair a very proud man.

For further reading I recommend reading Jac Weller's excellent *Wellington in the Peninsula 1808-1814* and David Gates' *The Spanish Ulcer: A History of the Peninsular War*. For the 95th Rifles, no other books come to mind than *The Recollections of Rifleman Harris* and Mark Urban's *Rifles: Six Years with Wellington's Legendary Sharpshooters*. This is an absolutely breath-taking piece of narrative history, tracing the regiments origin and achievements throughout the Peninsular War.

There will be more stories of Arthur Cadoc to come.

Death is a Duty

Adam Bannerman and the
Waterloo Campaign
June, 1815

DEATH IS A DUTY
is for my old friend, Adam Palmer; who marched the field with me, June 2015

'Jesus, this is too bloody early,' Lieutenant Boyd Anderson exclaimed, before doubling over and vomiting onto the pavement.

'Aye, sir, it is,' Regimental Sergeant-Major Adam Bannerman replied not too unkindly, but without any sympathy either.

It was dawn in Belgium and the first sunbeam struck like a golden spear across the world's rim; a high hemispherical glow in the east, trembling, bouncing, weakening and strengthening. Bannerman blinked at the magnificence, the light reminding him of all those times he had slept underneath Iberian stars and woke to see the sun touch the land.

It was four in the morning and at this hour the city of Brussels would usually be tenderly asleep, yet today was different because it was stirred to life by the threat of battle. Staff Officers and messengers rode in every direction along its cobbled streets guttering with light. Drums hammered a persistent rhythm. Bugles called.

'Jesus,' Anderson muttered and spat onto the road.

Bannerman was still enamoured by the light that was slowly flooding through the dark sky chasms. He blinked again, welcoming it and sucked the cool air into his lungs. 'There are plenty more gentlemen far worse than you, sir.'

Anderson looked up into the senior NCOs black eyes and firm countenance. 'That doesnae make me feel any better, you know,' he said, and fell to his knees retching and spitting red-yellow vomit.

'It's nae supposed to, sir,' Bannerman said airily, walking off towards a tall brick house, neat and tidy with a sage-green door and shutters with bright lights emanating within.

'The devil with you, RSM-' Anderson managed to say before he was sick again.

383

The door opened and two officers descended the steps. Bannerman knew them of course. They were of his regiment, the 42nd Royal Highlanders or "the Black Watch", called that after the early days of policing and of the dark-blue regimental facings. The feather bonnet had a band of 'Highland dicing' of red, green and white and bore the red hackle plume of the battalion companies with a black cockade underneath. Their scarlet jackets sparkled with gold epaulettes, a crimson sash worn over the left shoulder and, at their flanks, they carried lethal basket-hilted broadswords. They saluted and hurried away, both reeking of whiskey and claret.

Good, thought Bannerman, because the order was that all officers were to report to their regiments at once. And even those Scotsmen with drink in them were better than most other men. Bonaparte had returned from exile and plunged the world into hell again, so the British Army under the Duke of Wellington were recalled from peacetime to fight once more.

This morning the army was going to advance to meet the old enemy. They were to march to Nivelles it was mentioned, or perhaps Mons. Prussian outposts were said to have fallen back under a 'great host', but there was so much tattle-tale it was difficult sometimes to pick the truth from the lies. Wellington was said to be worried that Bonaparte would strike east and turn the allied flank, leaving the army stranded. In the last weeks Bonaparte had closed the eastern borders, preventing travellers from crossing. Fishing boats were banned from leaving harbours, couriers were forbidden and the mail stopped. All of this was carried out for a week and the French were moving under a total blackout. 'Subterfuge', Lieutenant-Colonel Robert Macara of the 42nd had said grimly, and Bonaparte was the master of it.

The Black Watch had landed at Ostend in May and marched to Brussels where it had formed part of the garrison for the last three weeks. The men had enjoyed the town and certainly the gin and schnapps. Cricket had been played in the park. Bannerman had performed admirably at the batting crease and even enjoyed a winning share of a hundred guinea bet when the Highlanders had played against the 95th Rifles. There was no sign of the French. The Duchess of Richmond had given a ball in a rented coach house in the *rue de la Blanchisserie* and Brussels dazzled with colour and light. Music rang sweetly. Quails eggs, caviar, and pink champagne were brought out on silver dishes and in crystal glasses. Every officer of every regiment had attended to enjoy the sumptuous splendour, but Wellington had slipped away after supper and soon the call to arms had sounded. Men had returned to their billets to gather their belongings and change into their more comfortable campaign dress.

Bannerman entered the house where the soldier-servants and other orderlies were helping their officers with their dress. Bannerman cast an eye over the chaos. A young lieutenant, barely seventeen was staggering with a bottle of fine claret in his hand and wearing a Dutch officer's cap with its odd front and rear peaks, 'W' stamped plate, orange cockade beneath a tall white plume. Ensigns Gray and MacKenzie were deep in conversation and another officer, with a white-laced handkerchief over his face, was snoring blissfully in an armchair.

'Gentleman, please return to your posts forthwith,' Bannerman said in a firm and yet polite tone. Gray, from a very prominent family, scowled at the interruption. He was blond-haired with such pale freckled skin, pale eyelashes that he was nicknamed His Royal Whiteness. No one moved. 'Now, if you please!' Bannerman's voice thundered and the officers, most of whom were still recovering from the ball, twitched into sudden animation. The lieutenant dropped the bottle, which spilled all over the floor. The ensigns - new men to the regiment, as were most of the rank and file - rammed on their bonnets and made for the door.

'If you ask for my opinion,' Gray ventured, 'I dinnae think the Crapauds will turn up,'

'I didnae ask for your opinion, sir,' Bannerman replied, causing the young officer to look affronted. 'I asked for you to return to your post.'

MacKenzie sniggered and murmured a curse under his breath, which Bannerman considered was against him.

He stepped in front of the young subaltern, shadow looming over him, eyes narrowing with menace. 'I know from long experience when there is to be a killing. Today's going to be the day. And I was doing it when you were still tucked away in your wee mother's womb.'

'Killing Frenchmen?' MacKenzie said, quaking slightly.

Bannerman's face tightened. 'Nae always,' he said wolfishly.

The ensign's eyes were like two eggs as he realised for the first time that the RSM was holding his trademark halberd, an eccentricity he had carried with him through Egypt and Walcheren campaigns and throughout the Peninsular War. It was an old- fashioned weapon, having been long replaced by the spontoon, but it suited him. He also carried a musket, which was now slung over his left shoulder. MacKenzie gulped and Gray pulled him outside.

'All of you now, please,' he called as three ensigns tripped over each other to get out first. 'You dinnae want to keep General Picton waiting, now do you? No? Good. So be off with you. Go!'

Lieutenant-General Sir Thomas Picton commanded the Fifth Division of the Army's Reserve to which the 42nd was brigaded to. He was a burly Welshman with a legendary foul temper and an even fouler vocabulary. He had proved himself a very capable commander during Spain, but Bannerman had overheard that he had already irritated Wellington by being overly familiar, an act the Duke was keen to rule out, which had left Picton in an even worse mood.

'Where is Captain Reid?' Bannerman asked a tall, reedy private, who was Reid's soldier-servant. The captain of the Light Company was a devil-may-care kind of fellow, the son of a squire to a prominent laird, who, had joined simply for adventure.

'He's upstairs whetting his blade, Regimental Sergeant-Major.'

Bannerman stared into Private Miller's blood-shot eyes, knowing that the captain was entertaining a Belgian whore and that the private was being polite. But this was not the time for such activities. He stepped closer. 'You have thirty seconds to ask him to sheath it and be down here, or I'll go up there myself and do it for him. Kindly remind the captain that my hands are as rough as granite and I'm likely to snap the wee thing in two.'

'Aye, Regimental Sergeant-Major,' Miller said, unmoving.

'Get him now!'

Miller turned and darted upstairs. Bannerman casually glanced into the two adjoining rooms, saw that they were empty and walked to the snoring officer and lifted up the handkerchief.

'Time to move now, sir,' he said, shaking the man's shoulder.

Captain Hamilton grunted and sputtered to life. 'At ease, Adam,' he said, before laughing deliriously. 'No Frogs here today, thank you.' He settled back to sleep.

Still drunk, Bannerman said to himself. He thought for a moment. 'Mrs Hamilton is on her way, sir,' he muttered, hushing his tone. 'She has one of her faces on.'

Hamilton's eyes immediately snapped open and he stumbled to climb out of the chair, but seemed trapped by it. Bannerman pulled him free.

'What? She's here?' the captain said, panicky, face draining of colour. 'She's really here? Now?'

'I'm afraid so, sir,' Bannerman said matter-of-factly, ignoring the smell of stale food and spirits on the man's breath. 'But I'll deal with her for you, if you'd like?'

'You will? My God, Adam, that's kind of you.'

'My duty as RSM is to help the officers of the regiment at all times, sir. Discipline, training and advice. It would be remiss of me nae to help an officer with his personal duty when and where I can.'

Hamilton burped, shook his head, and then fastened the gold buttons on his jacket with some difficulty. 'Thank you. Much obliged, Adam, much obliged.'

'Very good, sir, and I suggest you leave now. I'll have Private Kelly bring you your things.' Hamilton was wearing gold-buckled dancing shoes. Bannerman shook his head at the footwear, hoping the captain would be reunited soon with his regulation boots.

Hamilton tried to salute, failed and Bannerman helped him to the door where the streets were awash with soldiers of all units, noisily spilling out from their billets. NCOs were chasing men down, kicking the drunks and those men half-asleep into ragged files. A troop of Hussars, who had been keeping the beggars away from the ball, were now helping to clear the road free for the army to march. Men were running and shouting. Wives and sweethearts were calling out their loved one's names, or were weeping.

'It's a damned circus,' Hamilton said, shuddering at the noise.

'It will soon be quiet,' Bannerman replied, staring up at the rising sun that slanted across rooftops. Smoke from chimneys rose to besmirch the magnificent sky.

The townsfolk were watching the spectacle with interest from high windows; some had lined the streets waving lace handkerchiefs and orange ribbons. Orange: the national colour of the Kingdom of the Netherlands. Signposts and gates were decked with the colour. The civilians knew history was in the making. Belgian blue jackets were filing up too alongside the redcoats. They spoke French and to the British units this was a strange allied force indeed.

Bannerman crossed the street. A lone Hussar leant down from his mount to offer him a drink to which he politely refused. The cavalryman shrugged and sat back, swaying in his saddle.

Sergeant Ranald Grant had his son Robbie on his shoulders and his dear wife at his side. Beth was a beautiful woman. Kind and loving that

387

a husband could know and Bannerman closed his eyes at the thought of her. He had known Ran for many years and when he married Beth after the disastrous Walcheren campaign, Bannerman had always been civil to them, but had had to hide his disappointment and, he was ashamed to admit, teeming with jealousy. He loved Beth, but could never tell her. Ran was an old friend, and despite his inner feelings, he loved the man like a brother.

The sky was pink and orange to the west. Dawn light glimmered and glinted from the windows, the iron-wrought balconies, and then on buckles, gorgets, buttons, bits and on brass plates of those caps that were not covered by the weatherproofing. The air was cool, refreshing, but even old soldiers shivered. Battle was imminent. The young recruits were pallid and one or two leant to one side to vomit.

The 28th, North Gloucestershire Regiment marched past the Highlanders, yellow-facings and wearing the old stovepipe cap that bore a back badge showing a sphinx, having won considerable acclaim at Alexandria in 1801. It was one battalion Bannerman was very familiar with over the years. He looked furtively along the ranks to see if he could see old friends, but most of the officers were currently without their mounts, and so hoped he would see them again soon. Their hobnailed boots ground the cobbles loudly as they went past.

Next the fellow Highlanders of the 79th, the Camerons, marched off. An officer saw Bannerman and gave him a friendly nod, to which he returned the greeting with a smart salute. The 79th wore kilts of deep green that matched their facings different to the 42nd that wore a dark 'government tartan' with a red over stripe. Neither wore their horsehair sporrans, which was used only for full dress occasions.

Ran was still saying goodbye when the 42nd were forming up, doing up the straps of their hard, wooden-framed back-packs, positioning their canteens and haversacks, checking bayonet scabbards and some were stamping their boots as though they were cold. They wouldn't be of course, just getting calloused feet ready for the march. Bannerman remembered the boots from years before that had clay insoles, which were comfortable, but would fall apart as soon as it rained, or if the wearer had to wade a stream.

'There, there, Beth,' Ran said, voice calm despite his wife's sobs and Robbie's tears. 'I'll be back safe and sound.'

'Will you be long, da?' said the boy. 'Will you be home soon? Come back, da.'

Ran, a sentimental man, was unable to speak. He stared up at the sky, tears pricking his deep blue eyes.

'Of course he'll be back,' Bannerman said, picking Robbie up. 'Aye, your da will be swinging you from your arms and playing piggyback before your supper tonight. The boy smiled and Bannerman handed him to his mother. 'Beth,' he said, giving her a nod. His heart fluttered as their eyes met. *Love,* he thought, *strikes as fast as cold steel.*

'Adam, as always you look strangely fierce and gentle at the same time,' she said smiling, her pale fingers wiping tears from her cheeks. She had a quiet dignity and was usually serene, but this morning he could feel the fear in her.

Bannerman was six foot five, a giant of a man, and solid with muscle, but he handled the boy with affection. Wee Robbie was like a son to him. 'Well, that's good of you to say so, Beth. You look lovely as always.' She was wearing a cornflower blue dress and grey shawl, tight fitting, which accentuated her slim waist. Her auburn locks, freckles and soothing brown eyes always brought a catch to his throat. He went to add another compliment, but he couldn't find the words.

'Let's go,' Ran said, after kissing his son on the head.

'Look after him please!' Beth pleaded to Bannerman, as the men stepped away.

Bannerman stared back and grinned. 'I always do.' He turned to his friend with his gleaming eyes, broken nose and lantern jaw. 'Come on, Ran. It's time to send Boney back to hell. Goodbye Beth. Goodbye Robbie. We'll see you soon.'

'Haste ye back!' she called, meaning 'return soon'.

'I could do with some of that local beer right now,' Ran said, as they crossed the road to where the 9th Brigade, commanded by Sir Dennis Pack, were forming up. 'Dark stuff. Looked and tasted funny at first, but what I widnae give for a keg of it.'

'Aye, me too,' Bannerman said firmly.

Ran gave him a long sideways look. 'You? By the sweet love of God, you are never scared.'

'Nae so,' Bannerman chided.

Ran laughed. 'When were you scared? We fought together in the shite of a place near Fleshing.'

'Flushing,' Bannerman corrected with a smile.

'Aye, that fever-ridden, louse-pit of a latrine. Jesus. That campaign was a bastard.'

'So was Corunna.'

'Aye, but we didnae lose men left, right and centre as we marched,' Ran said. 'They dropped like flies around us like they had the bloody plague. Corunna was different. We lost men, but nae like that. Jesus, I was shite scared of dying of that bloody disease. Damned Dutch air was to blame. I'm no physician, but damp weather is nae good for a man. It's foreign over there too. The air was different, could you nae tell? Even the midges looked diseased.' Bannerman laughed at his nonsense. 'It's true, I tell you. But in all that horror you were never scared. Nae once.'

'Hush your twaddle,' Bannerman breaking into a laugh. 'I've heard more sense from a hog's fart.'

'You dinnae need the drink. I do.' Ran looked up at the battered face of his old friend, expression suddenly anxious. 'I'm scared, Adam. I'm nae scared to die, of course. I've spent too many years in the army to realise a soldier's duty is to die. I know it can be a short life with a shallow grave. No, I'm scared for Beth and Robbie if anything happens to me.' He rubbed his unshaven chin. 'I cannae shake the fear.'

'You're worrying over nothing, Ran.' Bannerman waited for a mounted officer to guide his horse past a crowd of civilians, watching the 42nd. One or two of the women, pretty things, he noticed, were in awe of the men in their kilts. 'You're too shrewd and too bloody ugly to die.'

Ran grinned, then looked serious. 'But if anything does happen to me, you'll take care of Beth?'

Bannerman hesitated, not because it would be a responsibility that he wasn't pleased with, but his heart skipped a beat.

'Ran…' he started to say.

'Promise me,' Ran gripped his forearm. 'Robbie needs a father figure. But I dinnae want him to take the red coat. I want him to go to school and get an education. You're the man to see to that if I'm killed.'

'You're rather melancholy today.'

'We're going to do battle,' Ran said, sounding bitter. 'Men will die. Fate demands it.'

Bannerman watched redcoats longingly kiss their wives farewell. A private was hauled away by a sergeant and a woman collapsed onto the pavement, which provoked another to scream and wail in despair. 'Fate demands we do our duty,' he said dismissively, not wanting to get dragged into an argument about mortality.

390

Ran grunted. 'You've nae answered me.'

Bannerman let out a lungful of breath and nodded adamantly. 'I promise to take care of Beth and Robbie if anything happens to you.'

'Good,' Ran said, relieved. 'Thank God. That's like a twelve-pound shot lifted off my shoulders. Much obliged, my friend.' His mouth then twitched into a half-smile.

Bannerman, guiltily thinking of Beth, saw the movement and peered at him. 'What is it?'

'Remember that Spanish girl after Salamanca? The one that caught your eye?'

Bannerman answered with a cautious grunt.

'Do you recall when you went to ask her to court you, and her mother would have none of it and chased you off with her broom. A big bitch of a woman.'

Bannerman groaned. 'How could I forget her? She could take on the grenadier company by herself. Why are you asking?'

'I was lying,' Ran revealed. 'I have seen you scared.'

'You bastard,' Bannerman said over his friend's mischievous laughter.

Colonel Macara was riding his black gelding around the regiment watching the companies form up, and offering advice and jovial comments. 'Apologies for interrupting your evening's entertainment gentlemen, but it appears Monsewer would like your hand for another dance. So we're going to oblige him with our muskets and bayonets the best way the Black Watch can.' The men cheered him raucously. 'We'll give him a Highland greeting! All the way to Paris!'

'Has anybody seen Lieutenant Anderson?' A voice called out as the final ranks filed in. 'Anybody?'

'He was asleep on the pavement. Quite knocked up if you ask me,' came the reply from somewhere over a burst of laughter.

'I'm here, God damn it,' Anderson groaned. 'I wish I was nae here, but more fool me, I am.'

After the 79th Highlanders came the Rifles. Usually stationed at the rear of the column, but soon opened up to double time – the light infantry pace. Bannerman watched the elite green-jackets with their packs and sword-bayonet scabbards bouncing as they jogged. They looked a very fine unit of men.

The first regiment of the 9th Brigade was already marching; the third battalion of the 1st, the Royal Scots. The 42nd were next to leave, then the 44th, Englishmen from East Essex, and finally more

391

Highlanders of the 92nd, the Gordon Highlanders. The bands were playing *The Downfall of Paris* and *The Girl I left Behind Me*. Together with the sounds of drums and bugles, it was a cacophonous mess. But the redcoats were marching solidly and that was all that mattered.

Soon the 42nd began to march under the watchful glare of General Picton who was wearing a civilian coat and a shabby top hat. Bannerman, happy with the battalion's good order and discipline, glanced over to where Beth waited patiently. He was half-tempted a wave or nod, but knew that was an impossible thing to do. His eyes swivelled to Ran who was blowing kisses to a Belgian girl with an orange ribbon in her hair. She took it off and placed it in his hands. Ran laughed heartily and tied it around his forearm. Bannerman thought his friend was a damned rascal, so he took courage and waved to Beth. Lovely Beth. The woman with the face that haunted his dreams, saw him, waved back and blew him a kiss.

Bannerman, his heart screaming with excitement, thought about that as the battalion exited the Namur gate and headed south.

The land, Bannerman observed when they were four hours into the march, was good fertile ground. Crop fields of rye and barley grown for the straw was broken up into fields of rich grass and hedgerows where black birds and larks burst into song. The soldiers had passed sellers of cauliflowers, carrots, strawberries and cherries going to Brussels. Riders had galloped past frantically, but other than that the hours had passed peacefully. The men were in good spirits, apart from one or two voicing their opinion on the state of the roads, which had caused two men to stumble and one who sprained his ankle. The roads in Spain were far worse: villainous was a word often used to describe them.

'The road into Vitoria was marginally better, widnae you say, RSM?' Macara remarked. He had been in command for three years and was a good officer, well-liked, fair and was adored by the men.

'Just a fraction, sir,' Bannerman replied, eyeing a wide muddy hole in the ground.

The colonel rubbed his blue eyes and smiled confidently. 'Still we beat them then and countless times since. No matter how many times the Corsican Ogre comes back to conquer Europe.'

'That old dream,' Major Duncan Blackwood said scornfully. He was a small, impatient man with a perpetual scowl and little time for small talk and reminded Bannerman sometimes of Picton.

'I have a notion that we'll be marching south for two more days,' Major Charles Orr said. 'Boney is still in France.'

'You think so, Charles?' Macara twisted in his saddle to face his senior major, the leather creaking as he did.

'Aye, I do so, sir,' Orr replied cheerfully, seeing the colonel's brow crease in surprise. He was a young man, tall and heavy set, and had proved himself a capable officer in the dying months of the previous year. 'He may have humbugged us with his vanguard, but with the Prussians at our side and the Russians and Austrians approaching the border fortresses, the man's brilliance will prove to be nothing more than a damp squib. He'll nae make an entrance for some time now and then it'll be too late.'

'I hope you are right,' Macara said, but Bannerman noticed the tone wasn't entirely confident.

'Nosey will see us through the campaign well enough,' Blackwood said pointedly.

'Aye, he's nae let us down yet,' Macara replied.

The horizon was now a dark mass of trees and the Division passed through the Forest of Soignes where it was ordered to bivouac near a hamlet of drab-looking houses. Fires were soon lit for the camp kettles, food was eaten and the rank enjoyed a rest under shafts of warm light that lanced down through the branches. Long shadows of oaks and beech trees stretched across the forest floor and dappled the road. A villager, dressed in a smock, was grazing a dozen pigs. His eyes raked over the mass of intrusive foreigners before moving his livestock further away into the trees.

'We're to wait here as a reserve,' Bannerman heard Macara announce to his majors. 'I'd imagine for some time at least.'

Blackwood glowered up at the green canopy as though he dreaded the prospect of staying here much longer. 'I heard one of the staff officers say we may bivouac tonight at Waterloo and Genappe,' he said wistfully, and grimaced at the smattering of houses in and amongst the trees.

Macara chortled. 'I'm afraid Brussels quite spoilt us, Duncan. It might be days until we find another plump feather-down bed.'

'Aye, sir,' Blackwood said, bowing his head in agreement. 'I'll never forget that city in a hurry. Salamanca was beautiful, but there is something that draws me to Brussels.'

Macara sucked in his top lip pensively. 'I agree with you. A grand place.'

'It was the schnapps,' Orr muttered and the officers chuckled.

'The whores,' Lieutenant Anderson chipped in under his breath, which Bannerman heard and smiled at.

There was a murmur of voices. The speaker was Ensign Gray, while a handful of other ensigns stood around him grinning. 'Och, the Frogs willnae fight us. They're much too frightened,' he said, then laughed, which Bannerman thought curious, but ascribed it to youthful foolishness.

He was suddenly overcome with a creeping lethargy and wandered past the makeshift officers' Mess, where the orderlies were hurriedly brewing tea, to find a small ringed area of oaks. Five minutes, he decided. Just five minutes' rest. No more. He took off his pack, bonnet, propped his sergeant's halberd and musket against the trunk of a stag-headed oak and settled himself down where giant roots curled about its base. It was quiet, serene and only broken by pigeons clattering in the green sunlight of the high branches, and a cuckoo calling sleepily from a distant covert. He was soon asleep. For how long he did not know, but he dreamt of French cavalry charging, the ground trembling, bugles calling and men screaming. He was sweating and twitching as he slept. A friend was calling. Muskets fired and then the vision became one of fire and pain and Bannerman jerked awake. He was in the forest, where the air pricked his skin and where motes of light danced in the speckled haze.

He wiped his forehead with a sleeve, black hair matted his skull. He sat back, taking gasps of sweet air, wondering if he'd slept longer than five minutes. A spider crawled on his right arm, across the silver chevrons with the crown denoting his army rank. He flicked it off and got to his feet, half-laughing at the state of him. He always dreamt of battle when he was contented. Infuriatingly, almost every night in Brussels he had awoke to find his bed wet with sweat and Ran had told him that he shouted in his sleep. Battle dreams. Soldier's dreams.

His shirt underneath was soaked now. He and Ran had survived Walcheren, but ever since then, he had noticed a change in his body. He sweated more and found breathing sometimes uneasy to come by. He walked with a slight limp that stemmed from a wound he had received in faraway Egypt, some fourteen years ago. He had been wounded many times, but that wound had been most vicious. He had been stabbed with a bayonet whilst attacking an enemy stronghold and the blade had raked his hip joint. However, he had turned on his foe and killed him with the blade still attached to the musket sticking through his body. He could march well enough, but found it difficult to run.

Bannerman was forty years old now, an old man by some accounts. Silver had blanched the hairs by his forehead, but other than that he still looked a man in his late twenties. He always said to Ran that he would still have another twenty to go and that he had strength to do his duty no matter what.

He was moving from the oaks when a shout rent the air, a woman's cry, and he instinctively grabbed his weapons. He wasn't sure where the sound had emanated from. There was no actual clear path, but he knew the shout had come from the trees away from the road. Nothing seemed out of place. He could hear the murmur coming from the battalions behind. Nothing like the chaos of broken order. Bannerman, deciding to investigate before calling for assistance, picked his way down through the foliage, past a badger's earth to where a tiny brook gurgled over loose jumbled stones. The west bank was marshy and dank. There across a patch of water was a house of sorts. It was in a state of disrepair. The roof sagged and was thick with bird droppings whilst the ground around the entrance was a mass of knee-high weeds. Blue-grey smoke palled thickly from the chimney. He couldn't see anyone else. He waited and heard a shout again, this time muffled and then he caught a glimpse of red in between the oak trees to his left.

Blurred movement, someone running fast.

Did the French wear red? He'd seen red-jacketed Hussars in Spain. But could the enemy really be this far north? And if so, where were the horses? This seemed very unlikely. Perhaps they were some Dutch units camped here. It would make perfect sense, but then Bannerman heard a voice and knew for certain, that it was not the case.

The redcoat was laughing, a wild cackle in the trees, and chasing the woman who was struggling to get away. 'Come here, lassie,' he was saying. 'I willnae bite you.'

The woman, short with blonde-hair, kicked his legs and raked her nails down his face, which only seemed to increase his pleasure. She tried to run, but the man nimbly tripped her up. She turned onto her back, ready to bite his flesh if he dared come forward. He undid his kilt and let it drop, exposing his erect manhood.

'I dare you to take a bite of this, lassie.'

The woman did not scream, but her eyes flicked to the left. Private Coll Burrell was too shrewd to fall for her diversion. He had fallen for it in the past, but never again.

'Is that the best you can do?' he asked her with mock pity. 'Now, what would you like me to do to you first?'

'How about trying this?' A man's voice spoke in his ear.

Burrell turned to see Bannerman smiling at him. He had not even heard the big man approach. He felt a cold pressure on his scrotum and looked down to see a wickedly sharp blade press the skin. His gaze went up to the RSM who withdrew the blade and slammed the weapon's haft across his mouth, gashing lips and breaking teeth. The private fell backwards onto the leafy ground in a shower of blood.

'Up to your filthy tricks again, Coll? You shall nae harm another girl,' Bannerman said, as the private moaned clutching his ruined mouth. 'What you did after Toulouse was never dealt with, you wee bastard. You deserve a proper skelping! One strike of this and you'd be gone from this world and no one would mourn.'

The trouble with Private Burrell was that there were two of them.

There was a horrible crack and Bannerman's head was jerked violently forwards. He collapsed onto his front, lights flashing before his eyes. He managed to turn himself over onto his back, groggy and his vision was blurred. He lifted his head to focus, warm blood dripping down his collar. A boot pressed him hard on the forehead, pushing him painfully down.

The last thing he saw before darkness struck was the form of Sholto Burrell aiming a musket and the weapon's deep black muzzle pointing malignantly between his eyes.

Bannerman woke beside the roadside, muzzy-headed and thumping like the very devil. He opened his eyes and groaned because the streaming light hurt. He waited a while before opening them again. His head swirled and everything was out of focus. He lay there a while, trying through the pain to recall what had happened. A girl. Running scared. Chased by someone. Who was it? Coll Burrell. And Sholto had hit him. Yes, the Burrell twins.

'You're still with us then, RSM?' said a disembodied voice. It sounded surprised.

Bannerman groaned and suddenly felt a canteen at his lips. The liquid was cool and refreshing. 'Private Burrell...' he said and winced from the pain. His hands found a tight bandage around his skull.

'Steady, old boy,' Lieutenant Anderson said. 'You're in a lot of pain and in no condition to move.'

'I need to move.'

'You sure?'

'I need to move,' Bannerman insisted.

'Well, I widnae if I were you. You look a lot worse than me and that's rather shocking. You've nae even had a drink, which I think is the crux of the pain. I have a couple of bottles of brandy stashed away. When you're ready, I'll introduce them to you.'

'Jesus,' Bannerman said, trying to sit up.

'He willnae help you,' Anderson remarked cheerfully. He was smoking a cheroot, and blew out a cloud of blue-smoke. Bannerman had liked him from the very first moment he had arrived at the regiment because his smile was instant, his face open and guileless. And that he was a cheeky rogue. 'It's nae even a Sabbath day, so that's definitely out of the picture. In his stead, can I be of assistance?'

Bannerman shook his head to clear it which made everything worse. He groaned, coughed and sat up. 'I caught Private Coll Burrell chasing a wee girl by a brook,' he said, looking around, unable to comprehend where he was. He recognised the path he had taken down past the officer's mess.

'Really?'

'Aye, and his brother smacked me across the head with his musket as I put Coll down.' Bannerman had not heard Sholto approach, thinking that he must have moved as soundless as a cat's shadow. He got up, legs wobbled. Anderson, with some difficulty, helped steady him.

'Then the buggers will be severely punished for striking an senior NCO,' the lieutenant said happily, paused to suck something from a tooth, then spat it into a patch of nettles. 'The captain was telling a different story though.'

'Och?'

'Ah, RSM,' said a voice. It was Captain Neil Darrow of Number Five Company. Bannerman instantly recognised the tone spoken with its slight nasal inflection.

397

Darrow was a thin man. He was thin-lipped and thin-haired, had a thin nose, and his thin nasally voice was precise. His nickname in the regiment was 'the Surgeon', a nickname with no joviality or warmth, for he was cold, clinical and disapproving. His steel-coloured eyes gazed over Bannerman with indifference.

'I understand there was a...' he paused to consider the word, 'misunderstanding.' He guffawed at his own joke.

'How do you mean, sir?'

Darrow flicked invisible lint from his coat. 'Two of my men were out gathering water for the kettles when a local ruffian thought it wise to rob them.'

Bannerman's eyes fixed unblinkingly on the captain's. 'The two men being the Burrell twins?'

'Aye.'

Bannerman glanced at Anderson, who was Darrow's subaltern, and he shot back a meaningful glance. 'That's nae what I saw, sir.'

Darrow tightened his lips. 'They came to me to report the villainous act,' he said very stiffly. 'Coll Burrell said the brigand attacked him and of course I could see the damage done to his mouth. He is with the surgeons. Sholto said you came to help but were knocked to the ground. He immediately called for help. I informed the colonel and a section went out to apprehend the man, but he was never found.'

Because there was no man, you fool, thought Bannerman. The twins had lied to cover up the truth, which had involved Darrow and now the colonel. He winced not out of pain, but from the falsehood. He could not challenge the story when they had all believed it and he had no evidence.

'Well?' Darrow said, giving him a speculative look.

The captain's voice was grating Bannerman. 'Sir?'

'You said that's nae what you saw,' Darrow said anxiously.

Bannerman hesitated. A pheasant screeched loudly and a Highlander grinned and rubbed his belly causing his friend to guffaw. 'I'm nae sure what I saw to be honest, sir,' he said carefully, massaging his head, feeling the tender lump underneath the bandage that had once been bed linen taken from a Brussels home. 'I might be mistaken.'

'A blow to the head can do that to a man. Even for one as thick as yours.' Darrow gave a wan smile. 'Good, we'll leave it at that,' he said, eagerly trying to placate the situation. He looked into the shadowy tangle of trees. ' *"Light thickens, and the crow makes wing to the rooky*

398

wood. Good things of day begin to droop and drowse, whiles night's black agents to their preys do rouse.'"

There was an awkward silence until Anderson broke it. 'Macbeth, sir.'

Darrow's expression softened. 'Correct, Lieutenant. I see you are nae entirely uncouth.'

Anderson bowed elegantly. 'Perhaps you would do me the honour of explaining that to my father, sir.'

Bannerman was wondering why the captain was so eager to let this pass. Something wasn't right. Had Darrow known the truth and was keen to avoid the recriminations? If so, for what purpose?

Darrow gave him a curt nod and turned to walk away.

'Just one question, sir.'

The Surgeon stared querulously. 'What is it?'

'Did you find the girl?' Bannerman asked.

Anderson sucked on his cheroot and frowned, but nonetheless watched his captain for he knew something was strangely amiss about this situation.

'What girl?'

'I thought I saw a girl.'

Darrow's eyelids flickered, his expression darkening for a fraction of a moment. 'I thought you said you were unsure?'

Bannerman shrugged his huge shoulders in pretended innocence. 'Aye, well, in combat men tend to see and do strange things too. I thought I heard a wee girl scream for help.'

The captain watched him. 'Maybe you heard that after the attack? The mind can play tricks. The colonel sent Sergeant Grant's section down past the hamlet and recovered yourself and Private Burrell. He made no mention of a girl in his report.'

'There's a farm down there.'

Darrow blinked rapidly. 'There is indeed, but uninhabited,' he replied tautly. 'I myself checked out the building. Long deserted. No trace of any one.'

There had been a girl, Bannerman had seen her. Wood smoke had risen from the chimney: he could still smell the tang of it in his nostrils. It was not deserted and he knew Darrow was lying. But why? He could not prove anything, but there was something strange going on. He thought about the girl. What had happened to her? He would ask Ran if he had seen anything. Now he just needed the Surgeon to bugger off so he could think.

'Very good, sir,' Bannerman said. 'I just need a mug of tea and I'll be back to normality.'

Darrow forced a smile. 'Good. Thankfully, no one else was hurt,' he announced. 'I shall send a mug of strong tea over to you immediately. Rest well, RSM. We widnae want anything else to… happen to you.' He gave Anderson an admonishing look, was about to say something, thought better of it and then abruptly turned and walked away.

Bannerman watched him go. A thundering of hooves made him twist around to see a Staff officer in the blue-jacketed uniform of the Royal Horse Guards galloping towards the regiment.

'Och, hello,' Anderson said, a dribble of smoke escaping his mouth. 'Is it time for me to lay down my life for King and Country once again?'

'I think you're in luck, sir,' Bannerman answered, and saluted the officer from the Blues.

The officer curbed his horse, replied with a sharp salute and then frowned at Bannerman's bandage, perhaps thinking that the enemy had already been found. He was a handsome man with chiselled features, bright eyes and a generous mouth.

'I'm looking for Lieutenant-Colonel Macara.'

'I'll take you to him now, sir.'

'Much obliged,' the horseman nodded.

'I'll come too, RSM,' Anderson voiced, keen to be present when the order is given. 'I suspect we'll be leaving sooner rather than later.'

Macara took the new order sombrely. The brigade was to advance to the nearest settlement where it was to wait for further orders and soon the 42nd gathered itself and continued south through the immense forest.

Where blood would be spilt, because fate demanded it.

*

The battalion halted just south of the town of Waterloo and waited with the rest of the Division on the grassy embankments on either side of the road. Bannerman was seated next to a thick snarl of blackthorn and bramble amongst whose white flowers a thousand spider webs glistened with dew. The sky was a brilliant blue, dotted with lamb's wool clouds. He had taken off the bandage for it was more uncomfortable with it on. He wore the bonnet, but the leather-lined rim raked the bump savagely with each step and was glad of the

400

opportunity to take it off. He tipped a handful of cold water into a palm and wet his head, feeling the coolness work its magic.

The 42nd watched a sombre-looking brigade march past. The black-coated Brunswick contingent were proudly led by its Duke and the Scots cheered them as friends. The Germans, the grey-coated *jägers* of the Advanced Guard, had fought well in Spain and the Highlanders always applauded comrades who had fought alongside them. The Duke, with piercing blue eyes, waved to all as he passed by.

'Funny seeing them again,' Ran said to Bannerman, as he lit his long clay-pipe. 'Reminds me of Spain.'

'Aye, I was thinking the same.'

'Good days now long gone,' Ran said wistfully.

Bannerman wondered what had made him remember those far-off days, then realised he was thinking that his days might end soon, and a man facing death looks back on his life. 'You make it sound like this will be the end!' he chided his friend. 'They weren't always good. Marching in the rain, mud and snow. Hunger. Disease. If I recall, you spent most of Spain grumbling.'

Ran chuckled at that. He watched a dragonfly hover over a water-filled ditch. 'Do you think we'll get a chance to see the Grumblers?'

The Grumblers were Napoleon's grenadiers; veterans to a man, and heroes of no more than ten years as a fighting soldier. They wore earrings, moustaches and flour-whitened hair, their height increased by their tall black bearskins and shoulders made broader by epaulettes. The Emperor's Guard were feared throughout Europe, for they had never been beaten.

'I hope not,' Bannerman said, 'but if we do, we'll still send them back to hell with their master. This time once and for all.'

They sat in companionable silence for a while. A yellow butterfly fluttered past in the bright sun and a hare stood on its hind legs to watch the Highlanders, then skittered away before standing and staring again. Sparrows quarrelled in the nearest hedges. It was a sun-kissed day and Bannerman, like most of the Scotsmen, had attached the peaks to their bonnets to shield their eyes from the fierce glare.

Ran played with the orange ribbon around his forearm. Bannerman scowled at it and Ran caught the expression. 'I'm only wearing it in case I happen to meet the Prince of Orange,' he answered lightly.

Bannerman gritted his teeth. 'I conceived that it was a notch of sorts.'

'A what?' Ran asked, amused.

'Ran, you and I have known each other for many years,' Bannerman said tiredly.

'Aye, and we've been friends for a couple of them,' Ran teased.

'And when you married Beth, well, I couldnae imagine you'd ever be happier.'

Ran nodded and rubbed the dark stubble on his chin. 'I've never been so happy, Adam,' he acknowledged.

'But I know what sort of man you are,' Bannerman said with a stern voice.

Ran shrugged to indicate that the comment was negligible. 'How do you mean?'

Bannerman watched a young rider dressed in the uniform of the Life Guards gallop past, scarlet jacket flecked with dust and Grecian helmet with its black horsehair that flapped in the wind.

'After Walcheren you were a ...you became a...a rogue with the girls,' he said uncomfortably. He had known this conversation was going to happen and had practiced it in his head. But in truth, it was all coming out wrong. 'You're a married man for God's sake,' he blurted.

Ran looked away and a faint smile spread on his lips. 'Adam, you think I've been unfaithful?'

'I know you damned well have,' Bannerman turned on him. 'I know it! I watched you in Spain and France plunge your ramrod in and out more than once.'

Ran laughed. 'Jesus, were you watching?'

'You flaunt your adultery like a prize,' Bannerman said heatedly. 'Think of Beth and Robbie.'

Ran went to offer another witticism, but at the mention of his son he went quiet.

'In my defence, half the army was paying girls to part their legs,' he said with a shrug. 'I'm no different.'

'You're a married man!' Bannerman countered, fury of the unfaithfulness putting fresh blood in his cheeks. 'Beth deserves respect.'

Ran waved the issue away as if he were swatting an irritating fly, and then wished he hadn't when Bannerman growled. He blew out a lungful of breath. 'Jesus, Adam. I thought I was going to die. Look at me? Just look at me and hear me out!' Bannerman settled down. 'I was sure I was nae going to make it at Salamanca. So with a bottle of rum in me, I paid for a girl on the eve of the fight.' He paused in memory of the bloody fighting. 'It's no excuse, but I was scared. I wanted company. Beth was nae with us then and I needed a woman. I've never stopped loving her.' He gave his friend a lop-sided grin. 'If you didnae have such a strict up-bringing, you could have had some fun that night too.'

Bannerman grunted at the levity. 'Never mind me. I ought to snap your damned neck, you fool! Beth doesnae deserve this! She deserves love and honour!'

'She gets all the love she needs,' Ran exclaimed loudly, startling a few men to their immediate right.

Ran was a good soldier and an even better sergeant. He had proven himself an able man, trustworthy and loyal and Bannerman was glad of their friendship. However, he knew that a girl's smile could erode duty faster than flame melts frost.

'So tell me, were you unfaithful in Brussels?' Bannerman asked.

Ran adopted an offended expression. 'No.'

Bannerman shot him a quizzical look. 'You're sure?'

'Aye!'

'So why did that Belgian girl give you that rag?' Bannerman gestured a calloused thumb at it.

Ran shrugged that off. 'I honestly dinnae know, and that's the truth. A good luck charm? I'll keep it all the same.'

Bannerman, deciding that his scoundrel of a friend was telling the truth, let any recriminations pass. Their closeness was too strong to go into a fight with a broken bond. He felt as though he should tell Ran how precious he thought Beth was. How lucky was to have her, but Bannerman couldn't find the words and so stared glumly at the battalion. He'd fallen in love with Dutch girl once, but she had turned out to be a whore and it had broken his heart. He'd not found a girl since to equal Beth, despite being propositioned on numerous occasions. He knew he'd been a fool to turn them all down, but it wasn't what his heart wanted.

He wanted Beth.

'I still want you to keep your word,' Ran said, his grin returning.

Bannerman broke from his thoughts to consider the question for a moment, before letting out a sigh that sounded like a gale through oak branches. 'And you have it, you damned fool.' He relaxed with a smile. 'I just want you all to be content. You, Beth and Robbie are my family too.'

Ran playfully punched his arm. 'You are like a brother to me. Beth adores you.'

Bannerman gave a white-toothed smile at that, then looked away, face burning with embarrassment. He saw Sholto Burrell look his way, then turn to speak to Darrow. The twins were alike, in height and build, except that Sholto had a broader face, a nose that had been broken and a scar to his cheek that gave him a grim appearance. 'There's something I need to ask you,' Bannerman said, changing the subject abruptly.

'Oh, Jesus,' Ran said, feigning despair. 'What the hell now?'

'This isnae about you. This morning I caught Coll trying to rape a peasant girl and Sholto knocked me out with a blow to the back of my head.' Ran stared open-mouthed. 'Captain Darrow knew what they were up to and lied to the colonel when the story was brought to his attention.'

Ran, clay-pipe in his hands, frowned. 'Why did he do that?'

'I dinnae know, you blockhead,' Bannerman chided him. 'If I knew that, I'd hardly be asking you, now would I?' He shook his head. 'The captain said he ordered you into the woods after Sholto raised the alarm. Was that true?'

'Aye, he did. Sholto had come running up screaming at the top of his lungs that someone had been robbed and the next thing the captain was speaking to the colonel. Then he asks me to take my section and hunt the bugger down. Saw and found nothing, as you know.'

'Did you check the farm?'

'The captain had already done that. He said it was abandoned.'

'He's a lying pinch-faced bastard.'

Ran snorted. 'I've never liked the man.'

Bannerman was silent, thoughts rushing into his mind. A cloud of starlings flew overhead. 'Was Sholto with him?' Ran nodded silently. Bannerman cursed. 'There was a girl, Ran. I saw her. They lied and that can only mean they took care of her.'

Ran sucked on his pipe for a moment. 'Jesus,' he said, a plume of tobacco smoke erupting from a corner of his mouth. 'And they lied so that you couldnae report Coll?'

'There's something more going on. I'm sure of it.'

'Like what?'

Bannerman gave his friend an ironic glare. 'I dinnae know. But do you remember him after Vitoria?'

'A very wealthy man.'

The British, Spanish and Portuguese army under Wellington had broken the French army under Joseph Bonaparte and Marshal Jourdan,

404

which forced the French evacuation of Spain. After the clash, the allies discovered abandoned carriages and wagons containing many treasure chests. Many men became rich that day and no more so than Neil Darrow.

'But nae before the battle,' Bannerman pointed out. 'He made his fortune there, but I know for a fact that he owed a lot of money. A lot. Even the Burrell brothers are said to have found a jewel or two there. And they've been very close to him since then. Have you nae noticed that? Now they're at his side all the time. I remember that the captain got Sholto off a hanging for beating a private of another regiment half-to-death during some drunken fight.'

'I remember that,' Ran said. 'I was the one who escorted him from the property and into the hands of the Provosts. Gave him a smack round the head too whilst I could.' He flicked a ladybird off his sleeve. 'He frightens me,' he admitted.

'He's a frightening man,' Bannerman agreed emphatically.

'He's a canny bastard too,' Ran said. 'Canny, strong and fierce.'

'Like the rest of us Scotsmen,' Bannerman said drily. 'Sholto should have been hanged that day. So should Coll for the rape. I'm convinced the captain knew they were both guilty, but he still spoke for them. It's a strange world.'

'Do you think they have a haud over him?' Ran asked.

'It seems that way.'

'Then they know something that the captain doesnae want others to know.'

Bannerman nodded at his shrewd friend. 'Aye.'

'So what are you going to do?'

'I dinnae know,' Bannerman admitted.

'Are you going to tell the colonel?'

'No.'

'But best be on your guard,' Ran warned.

'Watt, you dirty bastard!' Sergeant Weir called from the mass of men. He was a stout man with shaggy eyebrows and thick dark sideburns. 'If you want to have a shite, at least have the decency to do it downwind! Jesus Christ, that stinks!'

'Sorry, Sergeant,' the private said meekly.

Ran busily sucked on his pipe. 'Lucky the captain didn't have you dead and buried then.'

'Lucky for me,' Bannerman replied, 'unlucky for him.'

'Handy to come across a chest full of jewels when you're desperately poor,' Ran said. 'What I could do with that now.' He sucked on his pipe wistfully then; feeling that the battalion would be moving soon, he extinguished the remaining tobacco with a dirty thumb and tucked it all away in his haversack. 'Do you think we'll come across Boney's baggage?'

Bannerman stood, having the same intuition as Ran that they were about to march again. It was an old soldier's instinct. 'That's if we get to fight him. The Prussians might well do the job for us.'

Their intuition for battle was as accurate as a rifle bullet and the Division was ordered further south.

'What's the next place called?' Major Blackwood asked.

'*Les Quatre Bras*,' Bannerman heard Macara reply. 'The Four Arms.'

*

The 42nd approached the crossroads in sweltering heat and, in the distance, could see the dark flecks of birds hurrying away in the garish sky. There was a broken stream of wounded Dutch-Belgians making their way to the handful of white-washed buildings of the village to see the surgeons. To the west was a narrow meadow shadowed by tall trees on which foxgloves, daisies, poppies and dandelions grew in abundance.

Bodies littered the roadside; some seemed to be sleeping by the way they were lain, but Bannerman could smell the familiar battle aromas: burnt powder, putrefaction and dung from whence they had passed the town of Waterloo to know that these men had died doing their duty.

A damaged Dutch gun limber lay broken on the roads verge. One of the team's horses had been hit in the belly and lay dead next to it. Flies were swarming over the glistening wound to feast.

'Jesus, have they lost?' Ran said, frowning at the Belgians in their French uniforms. A sudden gust of wind brought a sharp smell of blood with it.

An outburst of musketry came from the Dutch-Belgian front confirming that they were holding their ground. It was not heavy like platoon fire, but energetic snaps of skirmishers trading fire.

'I think we've arrived in the nick of time, though,' Bannerman said, sweat beading his forehead, but his headache had thankfully gone.

'Congratulations gentlemen,' Macara said to his men, 'we're the first British troops onto the field.'

'Wonderful,' Anderson said wryly.

Bannerman stared ahead at the stretch of gently rolling countryside where a large walled farm, defended by the Dutch-Belgians stood just beyond the near fields. It was the last bastion before the crossroads, where it guarded the thoroughfare east to Nivelles where the Prussians were, west to Namur, south to Charleroi and north to Brussels. Loopholes, like dark stains, had already been made in the walls of the barns which, like most farms, were joined together to form a stout stronghold. The farm had to be held. Musket smoke wreathed the walls south and Bannerman realised disappointedly that the blue-coats were in fact French firing at Dutch-Belgians in front of a great field of rye. There were other farmsteads dotting the fields to the south, but the smoke was thickening and hiding the enemy.

'There's Nosey,' Ran said, awe sounding in his voice.

Bannerman turned to see the Duke trot towards the regiment. He was dressed soberly in white breeches and half-boots, a dark-blue tailcoat and a white neckcloth. He was holding a telescope and gave a curt nod to Sir Robert, his cocked hat shadowing his strong beak of a nose.

'Your Highlanders ready to do their duty, Macara?'

'Always, your Grace.'

Sir Thomas Picton rode out to meet Wellington who began to traverse his scope south of the roadside. It appeared he had just arrived from the way he espied the landscape vigorously. The Duke's staff was bloated with the need to have liaison officers for all the many foreign contingents with the army, plus it included officials from Spain, Prussia, Russia, the Netherlands, Austria and the British government. Bannerman had heard that there was rumoured to be a reporter from *The Times* observing, a woman at that too.

'I have returned from Blücher, and promised to march to his aid, if we aren't attacked here first.' Bannerman heard the Duke say in his usual strong and serene voice. Field Marshal Gebhard Leberecht von Blücher led the Prussian army and was some way to the east. The Duke had sounded calm and his face betrayed nothing. He paused as his gaze flashed from the farm to the distant buildings and across to the thick wood of fir trees of the *Bois de Bossu*. It was a dark green wall, thick and imposing, and held by Prince Saxe-Weimar's Nassauers. 'It seems that the Prussians will have to fight without us today after all.' He lowered the glass to view his left flank with his own eyes. Sir Thomas saw the blue-coated troops he was looking at and snorted with derision.

'The Dutch there are raw boys called from the plough,' he grumbled. 'They won't stand for long.'

'Time will tell, Picton.' Wellington, ignoring the Welshman's blustering, turned to an Aide, and pointed at the big, stone-built farm nearest the road. 'The name of that farm?'

'Gemioncourt, your Grace.'

A thin-looking horseman riding an expensive horse trotted past the battalion with an entourage of officers behind. The leading man was dressed in a thick black Hussar coat and pale blue breeches. He was smiling widely.

'There goes Slender Billy,' Blackwood said, using the pejorative nickname given to William, Prince of Orange, because of his rather long thin neck.

The Prince greeted Wellington with a beaming smile. He gestured with a sweeping arm over the land. 'The crossroads are in firm hands and we've checked the French advance at the woods.' His English was perfect, yet spoken with the crisp sounds of court and pomp. 'We're holding here,' he insisted, face still joyful.

Wellington did not answer. The prince had held of the attacking French, but had not probed nor offered a counter-attack. The Duke brought up his scope again to the right to see the green-clothed force of Nassauers who had held off the French during the night. The foreign generals looked jubilant, but Bannerman could see Wellington surveying the land with shrewd eyes. The way the generals were smiling, it would seem that they had won a victory when in actual truth they had not probed the enemy, fearing they would be over-whelmed and so had made a stand at the crossroads.

Wellington looked to his left flank and breathed in through his nose. 'Your Division to hold there, Sir Thomas.' He tapped fingers against his note pad. 'Your men will advance and hold the front of the crossroads. Now if you please.'

Sir Thomas nodded and trotted with his Aides through the throng of Dutch Militia.

The brigade followed and the British and Dutch-Belgians watched each other with bemused expressions.

'Jesus, what a noise,' Ran said irritably of a band playing a ragged piece of music. 'They're playing like they've all been hit with grapeshot.' He stared ahead where there was a tall field of crops. 'I suppose there are thousands of Frogs out there then,' he said, fractious that he couldnae see the enemy.

'We'll move these bastards aside,' said Bannerman, knowing his friend was nervous. An irksome lock of his dark hair kept falling across his face. He pushed it back under the bonnet, but a few moments later annoyed him again.

Ran considered that his friend could manage that job entirely on his own.

The battalion halted. Flies buzzed above more bodies. A Dutchman lay on the chalky roadside spitting blood, another had walked away in the hope of finding a surgeon, but had passed out in a ditch instead. Bannerman had seen hundreds of dead in his time and this was no different; he tried not to look, but couldn't stop his eyes from being drawn to them. One man lay stretched across the grass, tongue lolling out, the blood at his neck already turning black.

Distant drums sounded.

'I never thought I'd hear Old Trousers being played again,' Ran said, wincing. It was the sound of the French infantry being drummed to the attack. 'I thought those days were over.'

'We all did,' Bannerman replied, stirred from his thoughts. 'And we did in '02, but the bastards resumed their threats the next year.'

'Beth asked me why we fight.'

'What did you tell her?'

Ran shrugged. 'I didn't know what to say.'

'We fight because we're born to,' Bannerman said savagely.

'I thought we'd hand over our guns and bayonets to be beaten into ploughshares.'

Bannerman was amused at the thought of melting his halberd down into a tool to till the fields. And it was unthinkable. 'We'll always be at war. They'll always need soldiers. Old hands like you and I.'

The old hands were veterans of the wars; immune to the echoes of battle. The new recruits watched the rye fields as though a fearsome beast was about to emerge from them.

'Just like old times, eh?' Macara had walked his gelding forward for the battalion. His handsome face was calm and cheerful.

'Never a dull moment when you hear them, sir,' Orr replied as he rode aside with Blackwood, the adjutant and Bannerman on foot. 'I've missed them if truth be told.'

'That's because, Charles, peacetime doesnae suit your Highland blood,' Macara remarked, grinning. 'You've spent too many years in the army fighting the Crapauds to grow accustomed to sitting on your arse looking at paperwork.'

'Aye, sir. That may be true, but I was thinking of my wife and that I'd rather face a French battalion than listen to another one of her damned stories.'

'She's still into her scribbling?' Macara asked.

'Aye, sir. Keen as a Highland blade.'

The corners of Blackwood's eyes creased. 'If my wife wasted her time writing stories, I would take the belt to her.'

Macara fished out his eyeglass and trained it on Gemioncourt directly overhead of the crops. 'Pretty wee farm. Now spoiled with Crapaud blood.'

'And Dutch, sir,' Orr said helpfully.

Macara nodded. 'Quite.' He paused to watch French gun teams bring more pieces from the crest above the farm. He guessed from the pall of musket smoke and the glint of light on French Eagles, buttons, bayonets and shako plates that the bulk of the infantry was concealed somewhere in the fields.

Bannerman thought he heard muffled sounds to the east. It sounded at first like peals of distant thunder, but the noise was continuous like distant cannonades.

Macara had heard them too. 'So the Crapauds are having a go at the Prussians as well,' he said.

'Sounds like quite a battle going on,' Bannerman replied.

'So who commands here then?' Blackwood said, crossing his own scope back and forth the fields. 'Is it Bonaparte?'

'Afraid not, Duncan. I heard Sir Dennis say from a captured messenger that it's Marshal Ney,' Macara sounded disappointed. 'I had hoped to get a glimpse of the Ogre and see Wellington give him a damned licking.' He chortled. 'However, I dinnae think Ney's forgotten the last time he fought us.'

Michel Ney, a brilliant cavalryman and known by his men as *le Brave des Braves*, was a veteran of the wars. He had fought the British before and lost heavily at Buçaco. The French had marched against a retreating enemy up a crest only to discover it had been a feint. Volleys tore into them and the survivors had fled the mercy of the British musketry with bayonets at their heels.

'Is that why the Frogs have nae taken the crossroads yet, sir?' Bannerman enquired, wondering if they were convinced that there were more British regiments concealed and that was why they were hesitant.

'That's what I think,' Macara said. 'They dinnae want another Buçaco, gentlemen. They dither and with every hour we grow stronger.' He watched the first batteries of British artillery reached the vital thoroughfare and ordered to unlimber. 'That'll do nicely.'

'More fool them,' Orr said, then jerked upright. 'I can see them! There!'

Great patches of rye were being trampled flat and that betrayed where the enemy were coming from. Solid formations aimed like a battering ram to smash apart the flimsy Dutch troops. With one smash, the might of the French would swat the British aside like a steel glove striking a fly and victoriously take the crossroads.

A loud crash of musketry off the right. Bannerman heard men scream.

'*Vive l'Empereur!*'

'Och, you lucky bastards!' Ran said to his company. 'You're about to earn your keep!'

The Dutch-Belgian lines seemed to shiver, even the bands paused to consider the rattle of drums. There was a collective intake of breath and, in that pause, the sound of hundreds of boots thudding at once could be heard. The drums were silent and then came the shout again.

'*Vive l'Empereur!*'

Just then a deep-throated cheer went up from the rye fields and the first French skirmishers dashed out of the crops and suddenly the front between the crossroads and the wood was awash with the enemy.

'Confident bastards, sir,' Bannerman said.

'Indeed they are,' Macara replied. 'But let's test their self-assurance and then we'll see just how cocky they are.'

The French had been sent forward safe in the knowledge that the small number of opposing Dutch skirmishers would be swatted aside and the crossroads would open up for the rest of Ney's force to take it. The sudden appearance of redcoats made some hesitant at the new enemy in front of them.

Macara ordered the Light Company forward and whistles blew from the other battalions. The British skirmishers ran forward to meet their French counterparts and suddenly the crushed rye and hedgerows were soon aloud with the popping sound of musket fire. Bannerman watched as the skirmishers fired by pairs, aiming and watching for targets. It seemed to be going well, the French were stopped but then even more of the enemy appeared and the small British Light Bobs looked to be overrun.

411

'Haud them!' Macara said, kicking his mount forward to offer encouragement. 'That's the way! Send them to their graves, my lads!'

'Careful, sir,' Bannerman said, edging forward as bullets fluttered and hummed by. Macara was an easy target on horseback, but was so far untouched.

Sir Dennis Pack ordered his brigade forward and the four battalions threatened the *voltigeurs* who slunk back, but when the regiments returned to their posts, the French came back again.

Bannerman watched the wounded return; faces already black and lips made dry by the acrid gunpowder. Hands clasping the injuries; some, unable to walk, were being brought back by colleagues. Cartridge wadding that still smouldered, and fanned by the wind, created small fires which added to the false mist of powder smoke.

Cavalry reached the crossroads from Nivelles. They were black-coated Brunswickers who dashed into the fields after the French skirmishers as though they were on a fox hunt. Their blades found easy targets. Sabres slashed open ribs, necks and heads. The German troopers carried on with the slaughter until they stumbled across a hidden French infantry brigade formed in square which fired a massed volley into the blood-stained horsemen. Riders tumbled to the ground. Others wheeled in confusion. Most returned to the crossroads, but they were in a state of mourning for their young Duke had been mortally shot.

Dutch-Belgian cavalry arrived and Bannerman watched them form up ready to charge the *voltigeurs* who were still sniping at the British lines. The surviving Brunswickers formed up behind the Dutch-Belgian lines, eager to avenge their fallen Duke. Soon the lines quickened into a trot. The horsemen went past the foot regiments who cheered them and jeered the French who saw the new threat.

'Off they go!' Macara called from the saddle. He was watching the horsemen disappear into the tall crops. The infantry had disappeared, but all for the skirmishers who were running past Gemioncourt farm up the gentle slope past French artillery batteries that had been pounding the fields and road before the British had arrived.

The order came for the brigade to advance into the rye field.

'Looks like this business is done for,' Macara said, trotting to congratulate Captain Reid of the Light Company. The colonel liked to give his men praise where it was due, and the company had proved itself against the horde of French skirmishers. Then he saw dark shapes appeared at the crest beyond the farm and Macara let out a groan. 'Christ no!'

'What is it, sir?' Bannerman asked.

'French light cavalry,' Orr declared, staring at the green, red and blue uniforms. 'Looks like Hussars and lancers coming this way.'

'Lancers?' Blackwood said brusquely, then growled. 'I hate goddamned lancers.'

'Here they come,' Macara continued the running commentary. 'They're forming into two lines now. Lancers in front obviously. I can see they mean business.'

'Will the Dutch stop them?' Orr sounded anxious.

'If they dinnae haud, then we're in trouble, sir,' Bannerman said, turning to the 42nd which like the rest of the brigade was advancing in line. 'Shall I halt the battalion and form square, sir?'

'Nae yet, RSM,' Macara glanced at the other British regiments, which had not moved either and he did not want to do anything rash. Beyond the curtains of grain, the furthermost Dutch battalions were still fighting hard. 'Our Horse seem to outnumber the Crapauds. They have the advantage of sabres.'

Even so, Bannerman would not like to face a charging lancer. Each lance, eight feet long, had a small red and white swallow-tailed flag attached beneath a razor sharp point. Some men reckoned that once you were past the blade, the threat was over. However, there was something terrifying in seeing them change from being held vertically, to drop for the charge and for the kill.

The British marched through the trampled rye. One or two men stopped to loot the dead *voltigeurs*, but sergeants pulled them into their respective files. Bannerman moved aside great stalks of crops with his halberd, gripping the well-worn shaft as though it was a comfort.

'Forward! That's the way, my lads! Keep your ranks now!' Macara exhorted.

Bannerman saw that once the rye cleared, a Dutch regiment was in full retreat and a French column was advancing nearly sixty yards away. General Picton with his Aides rushed forward and ordered the two brigades to halt. Picton had a deep booming voice, and shouted the order like a drill sergeant on the parade ground. Bannerman was impressed. The redcoats halted.

'Make ready!' Macara turned to his men. The French saw the British line ripple, as though the men had turned all at once to the right. ''Talion! Present!' A pause. 'Fire!'

413

The disciplined fusillade ripped into the French, twitching the front ranks to red ruin. The air between the opposing forces was instantly engulfed in the wretched smell of rotten eggs and copper tang of fresh blood.

'Fix bayonets!' Picton ordered. 'Time to go in with the cold steel!' he said over the sound of the two thousand blades being slotted. He rubbed his hands in anticipated glee.

The brigade advanced with the bayonet. The French fired a ragged volley that threw down a score of men, and some of the fleeing Dutch. Bannerman thought he saw Picton jerk in his saddle, but a bank of powder-smoke soon blotted his view. When it was gone, the general was with an Aide, pointing at the French.

'Och, dear God!' Macara gasped.

The entire Dutch-Belgian and mingled Brunswick cavalry had turned about and were galloping back towards the crossroads. Behind them the horde of lancers and Hussars were galloping fast.

'Are they Brunswickers?' Blackwood asked. 'I cannae see any flags.'

'No! They're Crapaud bastards!' Bannerman answered.

'Jesus, we must retire!' Orr yelled.

Macara shook his head as if he had just woken from a trance. He looked about desperately. 'No time for that!' A bullet struck his scabbard and pinged into the rye. 'Form square!' he bellowed.

'Form square!' Bannerman echoed the order.

They had to form square as every second was a delay and every delay made them vulnerable to the steel-armed cavalry. A horse would not charge an infantry square of four ranks bristling with bayonets. The first two ranks would kneel whilst the second two would pour continuous musket fire at the horsemen who would be forced to veer around the flanks of the square losing more men to the volleys.

The allied cavalry, hooves thundering, passed the redcoats and the 79th, thinking they were French, let loose a powerful volley. Two-dozen Dutch-Belgians crashed to the floor. Men wheeled and the Frenchmen closed in for the kill. Sabres and lances found unprotected backs. A Brunswick officer pulled out his pistol and shot a lancer in the face, the ball erupting bloodily from the back of his head. A Dutchman had his spine laid open. A blood-sheeted horse limped away. A Hussar cut through a Belgian's neck with such force that the head fell obscenely backwards to hang by a shred of tissue, hands still gripping the reins.

414

'Form square!'

'Four-legged bastards to the left!' Bannerman cried as the lancers wheeled between the British battalions and scattering mass of allied horsemen.

'They're German,' Captain Darrow voiced with the authority on such things. 'Uhlans, to be precise.'

It took time to form square and, before the last flank companies completed their movement by running into position, the lancers reached the battalion. Bannerman knew from experience that these men were not allies. Their hooves churned great chunks of soil in their haste.

'No, they're not! Watch out! Frog bastards!' he shouted; his knuckles were white as driven snow where he gripped his pole-arm.

The corners of Darrow's eyes crinkled at Bannerman's peremptory tone. 'Uhlans,' he stubbornly insisted.

Macara stood up in his stirrups. 'Dear God! Close the wings! Close the wings!'

'We're too late!' Orr cried, his hands raked down his cheeks, tugging at his side-whiskers, as though he suddenly envisioned a horror too awful for his mind to believe.

'Run!' Captain Reid galloped, hitting his men with the flat of his sword to hurry them up. One Highlander lost his boot, so Reid sheathed his sword and grabbed the man by the collar and hauled him to safety as the rally square continued to close.

'Close the wings!'

'Hurry! Watch out!' Bannerman shouted as the enemy swarmed in through the gaps, spearing Highlanders as they went. Lance points plunged into chests, necks and faces. They made quick jabs, smooth motions that killed men as swiftly as a heartbeat. Bannerman watched a lancer stab one grenadier in the back, withdraw the weapon and plunge it into the man on his left, then twist it free to kill another in the space of a few seconds. He threw off the body, shouting incoherently. They slashed and stabbed towards the centre where the bandsmen and the regiment's two flags flapped brightly in the wind enticingly. 'Pikes!' Bannerman shouted desperately. 'Pikes!'

Colonel Macara turned his horse around to meet the attack. A lancer thrust his weapon into the eye of one of the ensigns holding the Regimental Colour. The officer went down. He saw the Scottish colonel charge him. He withdrew the blade, made easy by giving the lance a twist, and thrust it upwards as fast as lightning strikes.

Macara, basket-hilted broadsword in hand, didn't comprehend the speed of the attack until it was too late. The lance punched its way underneath the soft flesh of his chin and up into his brain. Blood ran down the blade in a sudden flood and the lancer twisted and withdrew it.

'No!' Bannerman shouted, seeing the attack through the chaos. He shouldered men out of the way and beckoned the lancer to face him.

The Frenchman, many others around him forcing their lances into the Highlanders backs, grinned. He kicked his horse forwards. Macara's body tumbled lifelessly onto the crushed crops. At the last moment the Frenchman leaned forward to ram the lance into the impudent enemy. Bannerman had waited and then brought his halberd across his body that smashed aside the long spear. The pole-arm chopped through the wood and across the horse's face, slicing flesh and bone and the horse screamed, bucked and reared on its hind legs. The enemy dropped the shattered weapon, but before he could control the maddened beast or unsheathe his sabre, the halberd slammed into his ribs with the splintering wet noise of a butcher's axe striking meat. The force of the impact drove the lancer clean from the saddle. A French officer, tall in the saddle and with a black bushy moustache, kicked his horse to the attack, sabre flashing bright in the sun. The horse snorted and Bannerman turned to meet the threat, halberd dark with blood. When the officer stooped to slice the blade across the enemy's belly, the Highlander threw himself to one side, as the blade hissed through the humid air. The Frenchman tried to bring his mount around so that his sword-arm was not blocked by the beast, and Bannerman launched himself at the enemy, seized his booted leg and hauled him out of the saddle. The man gave a yell and fell heavily onto the ground. He tried to drag free his sword that had become tangled in the crops when a Scottish bayonet took him in the mouth and up into his skull. It was Ran. The cavalryman's legs twitched, his body heaved once and then he was dead. Ran gave the blood-spattered spike a savage twist before bringing it around to face another sword-armed horseman. The enemy screamed at him. Ran simply pulled the trigger and shot the enemy through the heart.

More lancers tried to take the Colours. A Colour Sergeant went down with two lances penetrating his groin. Ensign MacKenzie was blinded by a sabre that took both his eyes. A musket ball shattered a Frenchman's arm, so that the long weapon slipped from his grasp to hang by its leather strap. A Highlander ran his bayonet into the man's belly, screaming in Gaelic. A lancer rode over a drummer boy and grabbed the King's Colour, but Major Orr's broadsword flashed through his blue-cuffed wrist. The man screamed until Orr whipped the blade across his neck that silenced him for good. Another rider spurred his way forward and Bannerman readied himself. He was yelling curses, shouting the man's death, begging him to let his halberd drink blood. That was the way he had always fought; fierce, merciless and brutal. Bannerman noticed that time slowed, as it always did in combat. He moved quickly when everything else seemed to slow down. He watched the enemy approach. The lancer was young and keen to make a reputation. He lowered the lance to drive it deep into Bannerman's belly when a musket exploded to send a ball into the horse's flank. The beast twisted in agony and Bannerman was on the light cavalryman before he could react. The halberd ripped his gullet open so that blood spurted a blade's length into the air. He gasped and died clutching his ruined throat. The beast kicked and rode onwards, spilling the body down into a puddle made from recent rains.

'They will nae take our Colours!' Orr bellowed, which sounded like a challenge. A bloodied hand still clasped the silk.

'Nae while I have this, sir!' Bannerman said, hefting his trusty halberd across his chest in both hands. Some thought it was outmoded and unfashionable, but to Bannerman it was never obsolete. He would not go into battle without it. He should also have had a broadsword at his hip, but Bannerman was never comfortable with swords and preferred to fight with his musket and pole-arm.

Orr, Macara's deputy, saw a group of the enemy clustering around the fallen colonel, and ordered Captain Menzies of the Grenadier Company to carry him away in a litter to the surgeons. But the Highlanders were surrounded by lancers and the deadly spear points and sabres cut the unarmed men down in a flurry of blood-letting. They hacked, jabbed, stabbed and sliced, laughing at the carnage, for it was as easy as butchering pigs caught in a pen. The major watched the horsemen lean over and hew Macara's body with their blades.

'Bastards!' he snarled, and kicked his chestnut mare into the throng of enemy, screaming for blood. His straight-bladed sword beat a sabre away and he rammed the blade's tip into an enemy's face. A lance thrust at him, but he managed to parry it and cut the man from his horse. 'Kill them! Kill them!' he screamed over and over. A lancer coming from his right jabbed his weapon into the major's side. Orr, feeling the tip break a rib, brought his arm down, which cut through the shaft. The pain was excruciating and he feared he'd made the injury worse. The Frenchman grinned wolfishly as he brought his sabre to bear. Orr, the broken lance still trapped in his body, nudged his horse around to bravely fight the enemy, but suddenly, his vision became clusters of spots and he slumped forward unconscious. The cavalryman drew his arm back to finish the major off when Bannerman's halberd severed his spine.

'Major Orr is wounded, sir,' Bannerman said to Blackwood as he wrenched the gore-spattered weapon free. It made a horrible sucking noise.

Blackwood was now in command. He watched the two-dozen lancers who were still wheeling and killing his Highlanders. Men were screaming, arching their backs, staggering with cuts, bleeding and dying. Some horsemen carried carbines, short-barrelled smoothbore muskets, and pistols which cracked from the saddles. Horses bit men. A Highlander fell backwards with a lance almost through his body. He writhed on the ground, then went still, the lance still quivering. Sabres slashed and metal clanged. A lancer crashed his horse into a knot of men, knocking them over, and began stabbing them as they rose to their feet. The square was a place of men shouting curses, bellowing orders, crying for their mothers, or weeping on their way to the grave. It was a place of mud, blood and death.

'Now the Crapauds are trapped!' Blackwood said, grinning despite the butchery. 'The flanks have closed and they've nowhere else to go-'

The words died in the major's throat as a pistol ball took him in the forehead, snapping his head back and misting the air red. He fell sideways where Bannerman caught the body, held it fleetingly, before resting it down onto the ground. Three commanding officers dead or wounded in a few minutes was unthinkable. It was soul-destroying to a regiment. Bannerman couldn't believe it, but the enemy still threatened and so the mourning would have to wait.

'Platoon fire!' Bannerman thundered at the outer ranks. 'Platoon fire! But I want these bastards inside dead first!'

Muskets found targets and the Frenchmen were killed. Most were dragged from their saddles and ripped apart by vengeful bayonets. One man shouted for quarter and Captain Reid broke his helmet apart with his broadsword so that blood and brains oozed onto the jagged metal. The last few put up a brave defence. A bandsman was lanced; the spear point sliced into his lung, and he collapsed onto his bagpipes, the tune making a terrible shrieking sound as he died. Bannerman climbed over the red-coated bodies, far too many he measured and brought forth his musket. He pulled the trigger and the gun hammered a ball into a Frenchman's chest who had been trying to slash his way free. An enemy officer knocked aside a sergeant's spontoon to cut the Highlander down through the neck. A bayonet raked his thigh, but the officer was twisting his horse aside expertly parrying bayonets until a musket ball penetrated his liver and a musket stock took him in the side of the head. He fell to the ground and was immediately set upon by a half-dozen Highlanders who slashed, stabbed and kicked the body in a bestial frenzy until there was nothing left but a bloodied pile of gore.

'Close the ranks!' Bannerman shouted as the wounded backed away into the centre of the hollow square. 'Close up!' A blade stabbed the back of his right ankle and he turned to see a wounded lancer trying to hamstring him with his sword and the Scotsman stabbed down again and again, butchering him in the trampled rye with his pole-arm.

The first mass of French cavalry reached the roadside but British guns loaded with canister exploded at close range, and emptied a score of saddles. The gunners fled to the safety of the squares, so the horsemen wheeled away to hunt for easier targets.

Bannerman rammed the halberd's pointed butt into the soft earth and began to reload his musket, casting an experienced eye on the carnage. Men staggered, limped, bled and twitched. There were scores of injured. It resembled a butcher's yard. A man was panting somewhere like a wounded beast. Another sobbed in torment. Private Miller, Reid's orderly, lay blood-slathered in the grass with his neck half-severed, whilst his head had a dozen cuts to it. A lancer, guts hanging out on his lap, sat against his dead mount. He stared up at Bannerman with dull eyes as the halberd split his skull as though it were a hen's egg. The Scotsman stepped away, eyes casting over the scene again. A young Highland officer was shivering and vomiting, but he seemed otherwise unhurt. A private with the face the colour of pipe clay, kept loading his musket as if he was unaware of what he was doing. A corporal, his forehead a mass of blood, was trying to locate the enemy through blood-veiled eyes. Bannerman caught sight of bright orange amongst the sprawled collection of heaped bodies nearby. Had any Dutch cavalry mistakenly charged into the square? He then saw that it was a strip of cloth tied around the muddied arm of a Highlander and Bannerman suddenly shook with grief.

'Och no!' he said over and over. 'No!' He reached down and hauled a dead cavalryman away and a Highlander whose face had been

419

stepped on by a horse leaving it crushed and with an eyeball dangling loose. Bannerman dropped to his knees and held his friend in his arms. Lifeless eyes stared skywards.

The battalion was still being hunted by the lancers outside the square, but the disciplined platoon volleys were killing them. It was a chaos of blood, dust, screaming and burning rye.

Ran was dead.

But the Black Watch, like the crossroads, were safe for now.

Bannerman watched the neighbouring 44th being mauled.

The men of East Essex had been caught in line too, but had ordered his rear ranks about and the volleys had disintegrated the attackers, before closing ranks. The Hussars and lancers had tried to wrestle the Regimental Colour from the ensign, but the young officer despite terrible wounds, had grimly hung onto it long enough for the enemy to be killed by a cluster of vengeful redcoats.

The air was humid and stinking of rotten eggs. Burning wadding drifted like motes of volcanic ash that teased the nostrils. Bannerman was desperately thirsty. He had not moved from Ran's side, standing over him as though he was a ghillie: a servant on a hunt, protecting his fallen master. The French cavalry withdrew and had reformed out of musket shot from the Brunswick infantry which had sheltered in a wood on the British left. But the horsemen were still there and very much a threat.

'Use the Frog bodies for defence!' Captain John Campbell ordered. He was the ranking senior officer now. 'Pile them up!'

The Highlanders of the rear ranks took hold of the enemy dead and dragged them through the lines to dump them outside the kneeling files. Bannerman noticed that some were still alive but so near to death as to make no real difference. Those Highlanders severely wounded were carried away in litters of muskets and blood-soaked blankets to the surgeons operating in the white-washed houses of Quatre Bras. Already piles of amputated arms and legs were being piled outside. Some were naked, others displaying the colours of their uniforms red, black, blue and green.

Bannerman overheard a private exclaiming that he was sure he was going to die.

'If you are going to die, lad,' he said, 'then there's nothing you can do about it. You fight and kill as many Frenchmen as you can before the end. Do you hear?'

'Aye, Regimental Sergeant-Major.'

'Good. And that goes for every other man here. You murder the bastards! Every Frenchman is a veteran of battles. Half of you have never seen one before. But that's all right. Most of them have never fought Scotsmen before and today they will die in their hundreds. Now face your front like men, and prepare to avenge our fallen brothers. Give them blood!'

They cheered Bannerman. The deaths of the senior commanders and friends whipped through the battalion like high wind through dry grass, and the Highlanders were bereft and enraged. Bannerman remembered the first time he had worn the plaid and the feather bonnet. It was a mark of his heritage. He was fiercely proud of his ancestors. His first encounter with the enemy was at Boxtel, in Flanders. A campaign that had toughened him up. He recalled the sergeant next to him shouting orders to close the gaps when he got hit in the throat by a ball that pierced his neck to spin around the other side leaving a necklace-like-wound. He carried on giving orders but he could only gurgle and make nonsensical sounds until he was carried away. What was his name? Bannerman couldn't remember. But there had been scores and scores of men he had known who had died since Flanders. Men's faces, friends some of them, now consigned to memory that were fading away with every passing year.

Bannerman saw a Highlander by the name of Bruce make the sign of the cross. The private looked the same age when Bannerman had fought at Boxtel and, knowing what his business was, he stood like a block of granite against the flood to come. Bruce was a hulking great farm boy, strong as a bullock and ever cheerful, and it was men like this that gave the Black Watch their solid reputation. Soldiers were in the business of death. They were instruments of death. Politician's toys. Paid killers and their price was fate. One day it would come looking for them and that was a soldier's life. Ran had known that as Bannerman knew too. He thought of Beth and Robbie and fought away tears as he imagined their faces at the news. He would honour his oath to Ran and look after them both. They were his responsibility now.

Bannerman knew the French cavalry had come dangerously close to smashing apart the British troops and achieving victory. First there had been panic. Abject fear. It had been men shaking with fright, men pissing themselves, men grimacing and men crying like bairns. It was the chaos of battle, but the Scotsmen had prevailed. The enemy would come again, he was sure of that and when bugles sent piercing notes into the air, he knew it to be true. Only this time Marshal Ney had sent his best troops to crush the British once and for all.

Bannerman felt the ground tremble.

Cuirassiers.

They were the Emperor's heavy cavalry that were used when victory was certain, for *les gros freres*; the big brothers were armoured, carried straight-bladed swords and weighed more than a ton, man and horse. The mounted killers on black horses with the front-and-back cuirass, helmets and butcher swords charged for glory.

'Jesus God!' A private exclaimed. 'They're huge bastards!'

'Aye, but a man on a horse is still only a man,' Bannerman countered. 'We're ready for them.'

And the Black Watch was ready. They were tough breed of men. There might be new faces in the files; green recruits from the glens, but the veterans with their steel-hard nerves would bolster the battalion when men were losing their minds or their lives.

Highland bayonets promised no quarter, no mercy. French steel vowed to spill more blood for their beloved Emperor.

The cuirassiers, dressed in their shining war-glory, raked their spurs back for the final charge. Musket smoke crashed out and flames licked free of British muzzles, and the balls punched and tore their way through the armoured plate and horseflesh. Bannerman thought the sound of the bullets hitting the breastplates was like hail pounding against panes of glass. The giants crashed and tumbled onto the reddened fields. Horses twitched from bullets and fell onto fallen cuirassiers. Those that had plunged onto the ground had difficulty in getting back up. Some managed to unburden themselves of their helmets and plate before limping away, but not many. The Highlanders gave no mercy to them.

'Dung the fields with French blood, lads!' Bannerman yelled over the sound of ramrods rattling in the barrels. Muskets went up to bruised shoulders. 'Kill every last mother's son!'

'Fire!' Campbell slashed his broadsword down.

The big horses could not break the squares. Again and again they charged the redcoats, but were beaten off every time. Swords struck bayonets harmlessly, but the well-practiced musketry at close range was devastating. An officer tried to smash his way through the files, but bullets swept him backwards. A Highlander, unable to move because his spine had been severed by a lance thrust, tried to cheer and coughed blood instead. Bannerman had fired his musket at an officer, but could not see if he had hit the man through the roiling smoke.

'Fire!'

The cavalry staggered, limped and died. It was chaos. All cohesion and impetus was gone. The survivors wheeled away despite one officer shouting, *'Avancez, mes enfants, courage, encore une fois, Français!'*

'Cease firing!' Campbell shouted when he was certain they were retreating.

'Well done, sir,' Bannerman said to him, regaining his stance when a foot slid in a slippery tangle of guts split from a Highlander eviscerated by a French sabre. 'The volleys were timed perfectly.'

Campbell wiped his face. He was missing his bonnet and wore grey muddied breeches over his boots. 'Thank you, RSM, but we're all still at God's mercy,' he said in a hoarse voice. He was in his late twenties and had a boyish face that was spoilt by a long broken nose. He cast a look of sorrow at the heaps of bodies. A man sobbed pitifully, another crawled, his life leaking away through a bloody hole in his back. 'Why did He take the colonel? Why him? He was such a decent man.'

Bannerman took off his bonnet and mopped his sopping brow. He ran a bloodied hand across his skin, sweat stinging his eyes, which left behind a crimson stain. There was never a good answer to that question. Why fight in the first place? Why do people die? A man could go mad with such thoughts. It was better not to ask it in the first place.

The French cavalry withdrew back across the stream with a number of riderless horses joining them at the rear or cropping the clover-rich grass. Bannerman saw a horse pathetically trying to drag itself forward, its hind legs shattered by canister. The smoke-skeined air was dreadfully humid and was oddly silent, except for the regimental bands that had not stopped playing in the squares since the first attack.

'Dear God, is that it?' a voice asked from right wing. 'Tell me that is it for the day?'

The air popped with skirmish fire and Bannerman twisted to see the *voltigeurs* had returned to haunt the British battalions, creeping out slowly, kneeling and aiming. Only this time they were supported by the French batteries beyond Gemioncourt and the twelve-pounders opened fire. Unable to move away, the men in the squares had to stand firm and die.

423

'If it couldnae get any worse,' Lieutenant Anderson said, laughing hysterically. He then shuddered as a great boom echoed across the battlefield.

French roundshot slashed down making a whip-crack of a sound. The cannon balls ploughed through the mixture of straw, blood and the mounds of dead, churning the ground into channels and craters. Four men were tossed into the air like rag dolls. Another slapped down a patch of rye stalks to take the head off a man to Bannerman's left.

'We cannae bloody form up, because of those bastards!' Campbell said with impotent fury, thrusting his sword's tip at the French cavalry by the stream, which were watching the redcoats like hawks.

'The Duke is saving our guns for their infantry,' Bannerman suggested, glancing at the mute British artillery at the crossroads where the afternoon sun glinted off cold polished barrels. Counter-battery fire was frowned upon as a waste of ammunition.

'Bastards,' Campbell said and Bannerman didn't know if the major meant the French, or the British artillery.

A roundshot plunged into the crippled Highlander lying on his back and bloodied scraps spattered the men nearby, leaving behind a broken carcass of glistening offal.

Then, another British brigade was arriving on the Nivelles road, pre-empted by a cloud of dust. The men looked exhausted, sweat-stained and their red coats were patchy with grime. Battalion officers waited to find out where they were to be positioned. The men were allowed a provisional rest until the orders came and they fell about the roadside, with dry mouths, sore shoulders and blistered feet.

'I hope the buggers are ordered to make for those damned guns soon enough,' Campbell said, staring at the air smirched with smoke and rising from beyond the whitewashed farm in the centre of the line. 'Jesus Christ,' he uttered after a shot struck a file of the 44th knocking down ten men like they were skittles.

'I hope our cavalry arrives too, sir,' Bannerman put in as a Highlander gasped and stumbled out of line, a mass of bloodied gristle where there had once been an arm.

The orders were given and the new infantry battalions got to their feet and marched over towards the *Bois de Bossu*. The British batteries began to fire shell over field to where French skirmishers were fighting back and being drawn into the fire fight that was happening in the dense tangle of trees. The Duke was pleased as more troops had at last reached the crossroads. He began to secure his position as the air grew ever more acrid and muggy.

The battlefield was darkening, shadows were getting longer. Bannerman reckoned the time to be about six. It would otherwise be a beautiful summer evening. Pockets of blue sky stubbornly refused to surrender to the great roiling clouds of dirty smoke.

'Oh, God no!' Campbell suddenly breathed.

Bannerman, twisting aside thinking that a new threat was coming for the regiment, saw that Campbell was staring at the infantry to the west. They were advancing in line, but hundreds - perhaps thousands - of French cavalry were trotting from the folds in the land by Gemioncourt towards them. Cuirassiers, Hussars and the dreaded lancers.

'Sweet Jesus Christ,' Bannerman said, 'but our boys will be cut to pieces.'

'Form square!' Campbell yelled but it was impossible for the battalion to hear over the din of battle. 'Form square, you fools!'

A bullet hit a British gun and clanged loudly to Bannerman's right. And moments later an abandoned Dutch gun limber trapped in mud, was hit by a French shell and exploded in front of the Highlanders, showering fiery debris. Men watched for enemies, but the skirmishers had been ordered west to fight the new brigade so the squares remained as gunners' targets.

Bannerman heard the trumpets blare to order full charge and grimaced as he saw the enemy cavalry break free of their lines, the faster horses and the eager riders surging ahead. The Light Companies were racing back to their battalions like flushed hares before the hounds, but it was too late. The noise of the charge was like a drum roll of death. Sunlight, spearing that part of the battlefield, caught of the cuirassiers armour and swords so that they appeared to glow. A massive cheer went up and the trumpeters sent the men on to death and glory.

One of the regiments had formed square but the other three seemed frozen to the spot. Then, they broke as the cavalry reached them and Bannerman could only watch on in horror as the men disappeared under a sea of steel. Some men made it back to the shelter of the great forest, some even ran as far as the crossroads, but most died where they stood. The cavalry, unable to enter the trees, swerved aside and ignored the square to concentrate on a battalion that had neither formed square nor run. It had stayed in line and the men with green facings were

425

attacked from all sides. The battalion fired a volley and Frenchmen went down, but there were simply too many and the regiment was smashed apart. An Hussar, clasping the Regimental Colour, punched it high in the air with triumph. Men slapped his back as he made his way back to the lines. Men cheered and wheeled about the dying battalion, slashing and cutting at anything that moved.

The horsemen moved on towards the crossroads, hoping to inflict further damage but the British guns supported by more infantry twitched the roadside with French blood until the trumpeters called for the retreat.

More British advanced and Bannerman saw it was the Guards. 'Here they come to give the place a touch of class,' he said and Campbell grinned. Horse artillery and more units at the march of the drum advanced to extend the British line whilst the French, tired and battered, were pushed back. British cavalry, the first of the day, arrived in a jangle of dust, sweat and horse furniture. Suddenly men cheered as the French artillery stopped firing at the squares, to give the retreating infantry and cavalry cover. The British marched across the tiny patch of Belgium that was littered with the dead and dying that staggered, shivered, crawled and moaned. Pockets of flames smouldered next to pools of blood. The French abandoned Gemioncourt as the 92nd assaulted the pock-marked walls and retreated up the slope towards Frasnes. The *Bois de Bossu* was taken by the Guards, though not before a severe mauling from artillery. The western farms were captured and the Rifles and Brunswick troops stormed the eastern ones where in the distance the guns still boomed fire and threat from the clash between Blücher and the Emperor. But as twilight gathered, those too began to soften and fade.

'We've taken the field,' Campbell said as wagons approached with much needed ammunition. 'So that must mean we've beaten the bastards. God be praised.'

Bannerman thought he sounded unsure. 'Aye, sir. We've seen them off today, but I've a feeling in my bones that the job's nae done. Nae until Boney is defeated.'

Campbell wiped his brow of sweat. 'Unless the Old Prussian gave him a hammering.' He meant the Prussian commander, Blücher.

Bannerman stared at the Colours, both stained with blood, and riddled and frayed with shot. 'I hope so, sir.'

Quatre Bras was secured; the roads were open and the French gone. For now.

*

By nine that evening every inch of ground that Marshal Ney had taken was regained. The skies were dappled red as though God Himself was bleeding in Heaven. Wellington's army pushed southwards and stopped north of Frasnes where the delicate glow and slew of enemy camp fires betrayed their positions.

The surgeons, feverishly working in lantern-light, had not stopped at all, and even now wounded men with shattered limbs and smashed bodies waited in line for the bone saws, knives and probes. Some were in litters, some unable to move and had to be carried. They waited for more torture; every second the air around them was punctuated with screams of those waiting or those already with the surgeons.

The 42nd were too tired and too bloodied to move so they camped as night fell across the flattened fields. There were still wounded men unable to move who called out for their friends and loved ones from the dark. Some cried uncontrollably, some incoherently. Scores of arms were raised. Every once in a while Bannerman thought he recognised a voice, or a name being called out. He thought he heard Ran's voice at one point, but he knew that was impossible. Picquets formed around the battalion allowed the bandsmen to help the injured, threatened looters who descended on the battlefield the moment the guns had stopped, or hungry dogs searching for fresh meat.

At midnight the butcher's list was given to Campbell who had been made brevet-major. He took it solemnly. There were still over fifty men missing and Bannerman knew they were amongst those still out in the gloom. In the morning the searches would resume. The officers said goodnight and returned to the few tents available, but most collapsed onto the straw under the starry-sky with fatigue. A dog growled nearby and was rewarded with a kick. It yelped and scampered away.

Bannerman, hearing Gray weeping under his huddled greatcoat, slept an uneasy sleep.

*

As the sun rose shortly after four in the morning, Wellington's allied army was almost wholly assembled. A rent of orange showed in a thinner patch of the eastern clouds and it was suddenly daylight, though the dawn light exposed the grotesque number of bodies still lying in the

427

blood-fouled fields. Birds had feasted well. There were gaping hollows where eyes had been; flesh had been stripped from cheeks and lips gorged on.

The air was heavy and rank with the sick-sweet stink of death.

Bannerman woke to find his hands black with dried blood. He made some attempt at wiping away the stains on his crossbelts and coat, then washed his face in an upturned dented cuirassiers breastplate filled with water from his canteen. He then organised the first of the battalion's camp fires, for the morning was unseasonably chilly. Tea was being brewed, but there was no fresh meat to eat so the men had to rely on their rations until the commissariat arrived. The officers checked their companies before grouping together at the Mess where breakfast was eaten at a table made from a scorched timber board from a gun limber over two barrels.

'Two bits of good news,' Campbell said, giving Bannerman an appreciative grin for the steaming mug of tea. 'Firstly, it's nae raining yet and secondly, Blücher gave Boney a thorough hiding yesterday!'

The officers applauded and toasts were given to the King, God, Wellington and Prussian resolve. Bannerman noticed an air of relaxed cheerfulness as though the campaign was already won. He saw a line of Belgian Light Dragoons queuing to have their swords sharpened and he wondered whether he should take the opportunity to have his halberd blade kiss the whetstone. He rubbed his face thinking he should also have a shave. Sweat dripped down his spine, proving that today would be another muggy, humid day.

'We'll be in Paris by the end of the month!' Campbell said to more cheering. 'But of course before that we'll have to finish Boney first.' He spoke as though destroying the most influential and powerful Frenchman who ever lived was a small matter.

'It seems some of my brother officers have forgotten yesterday's bloodshed,' Anderson commented sourly after a ripple of jovial laughter split the air.

Bannerman, a ragged nail fingering a notch in the steel blade, instantly thought of Ran. What had Beth said to him? *Look after him please!* He fought back tears.

Anderson, knowing of the friendship, slapped his shoulders. 'I'm sorry about Ranald. He was a good sergeant and good man.' His thin face was suddenly lost to sorrow. 'We lost too many good men.' He turned to stare north where burial parties were beginning to dig mass graves. 'His bones will share the ground with all ranks and of so many others taken in this shite-hole of a Belgian field.' He paused, unsure. 'Ranald has a wife.'

'And a wee bairn.'

'Poor things,' Anderson said ruefully. He chewed his bottom lip and leaned in closer with a sigh. 'The captain is to promote Sholto to corporal,' he said in a low voice so no one could hear. 'A bloody corporal. Just when things get stranger, eh?'

Bannerman wanted to explain what he had told Ran yesterday, but there were too many others who could overhear them. He hoped to find the time later today to talk to the lieutenant. Gray wandered over. He looked paler than ever and somewhat cowed.

'And what's in store for His Royal Whiteness this morning?' Anderson asked him playfully. 'A wash, my lord? A glass of claret? A fondle from your seamstress?'

Gray offered a ghost of a smile and winced at a congealed puddle where blood had collected in a horse's hoof-print. He looked up as a shot rang out.

'Putting a nag to sleep,' Anderson said calmly. 'Cannae let the poor beast continue in pain. Good news is that there's plenty of horsemeat on the menu to plug our groaning bellies.' He gawked back over at the bodies that had been stripped and motionless as though they were just asleep. Some were strangely unmarked by wounds, others were dark with stains and twisted into grotesque forms. His throat thickened with bile and he stole a glance up at the sky where clouds were darkening with every second. 'If we have to fight today, we'll have to endure the damned rain.'

'It's good it's about to rain, sir,' Bannerman replied as he too stared at the heavens. 'It rained before Salamanca and Vitoria. Both times we won.'

'It rained before Agincourt too,' Gray commented, abstractedly.

'I dinnae know about that, sir,' Bannerman answered. 'I wasnae there.'

The men laughed raucously.

Captain Reid came over, smiling as though he anticipated joining in with the fun. He had a lean, intelligent face. 'What are you three rogues giggling at?'

'We're just thinking about the licking we gave the Frogs, sir,' Anderson said, grinning. 'The Emperor beaten twice on one day? That's one for the history books and yesterday's battles of courageous men dying are meat and drink to scholars.'

429

Reid's smile waned. Steam from his tea wafted over the rim. 'Havenae you heard? We'll be withdrawing today.' The men gaped at him with confusion. He glanced over his shoulder, as though fearing to be eavesdropped. He spoke in a hushed voice. 'I've just come from Major Campbell and the news now is that the Prussians were in fact beaten and that they're actually retreating.'

'Retreating?' Gray said, astonished.

Reid nodded austerely. 'Retreating.'

'Jesus,' Anderson was shocked. The excitement dissolved as quickly as it had come.

'We'll soon have orders to move.'

'Why are we retreating?' Gray asked as though he was dumbfounded by the idea. 'If we stay here and keep the roads free for the Prussians, then shouldn't that help our situation?'

'We must be pulling back because the Prussians have, sir,' Bannerman suggested, watching the eastern horizon to see if he could see the enemy. But the only shadows were from the thick clouds above the folds of ground.

'Exactly,' Reid agreed. 'They've taken quite a pounding and I suppose aren't up for a fight today.'

'What was their battle called?' Gray enquired. 'I heard ours was named after the village here.'

Reid clearly did not know and shrugged. 'The Prussians retreat and that means we're forced to as we're now quite a few miles apart,' he continued. 'Our armies are like a chain; break us apart and we're both vulnerable.'

'Jesus,' Anderson said again. 'I quite thought we'd won here.'

'Maybe we did, but strategically it doesnae look like it,' Reid said disappointedly, then made a face at the tea. 'We're doomed if we stay because the eastern road now leads to Boney's army.' He sighed. 'And poor old Miller is sorely missed. Private Bruce wants to be my orderly and going by this brew of his, I'll be dead before we do battle again.' He shuddered, offered Anderson the tin mug and walked away.

'I wonder where we'll go now,' Gray muttered in a small voice.

'That way,' Bannerman pointed northwards. 'We'll likely go back to Waterloo or find a road somewhere that'll link us with the Prussians.'

'If they havenae marched too far away, that is.' Anderson made a face at the tea. 'We need to be close because we cannae fight Boney on our own.'

'Nosey will take us back to the coast.'

Gray gawped. 'That far away?'

Bannerman shrugged and adopted a thoughtful air. 'Depends if the Prussians are worse than the captain says they are.'

Anderson looked eastwards. 'We need them like they need us.'

Gray blew out his lungs. 'It feels like our friends died for nothing,' he said, wretchedly.

Bannerman turned to him. 'They didnae die in vain, sir,' he declared, thinking of Ran's sacrifice. 'We'll no doubt be fighting Boney on the morrow, or the day after we've pulled back. We'll get our revenge by murdering the bastards good and proper. Their time will come.'

Gray's young eyes glinted. 'Good.'

As the battalions waited for orders to depart, the remaining wounded were loaded onto wagons. The sky was blooming into an angry grey and by noon the infantry and the heavier artillery were the first to withdraw up the single road, the *chaussée*, towards Brussels, while the cavalry and nimble horse artillery, acting as the rearguard, watched the roads and fields warily for enemy scouts. The lumbering column was like a vast serpent, its spine made of men, horses, wagons and guns, as it moved. There was some skirmish fire from the picquets on both sides, but Ney had still not stirred from his position and so the allied troops slithered away.

As Wellington's men approached the village of Genappe, the sky was black with cloud, while behind them where the French were, was sunlight. Bannerman gawked at the dark smudge on the landscape. It moved fast and he knew they were horsemen come to harry and molest, spreading out when the British light artillery fired at them, and because the leading troops were just emerging into the sun-touched fields, it seemed as if they had sprang out from the shadows. Swords, helmets, breastplates, lance-points reflected the light, a myriad glints of broken sunlight that seemed to grow as yet more cavalry came from beneath the towering clouds.

'Bloody hell,' Anderson said, in unabashed awe. 'I have never seen so many.'

Bannerman said nothing. Instead, he just glowered at the horses sweeping towards them, and at the British Hussars being pushed back, and turned to snap at the battalion's rear files that seemed to be dawdling. But it wasn't their fault for the *chaussée* was blocked with the army. The battalion halted and it was then that the first spatters of rain fell. A chill wind blew and the wounded in a wagon; taken off the road due to a broken wheel, shivered and groaned.

'Poor sods,' Anderson commented. He walked over to them and pulled out a bottle from his haversack and offered it to those who could take it. Rum or brandy, or whatever it was, Bannerman thought, was an act of kindness. 'They need it more than me,' the lieutenant said, walking back. 'Christ some of them won't live to see sundown.' He peered at the ominous inky black clouds above and pulled his great coat closer as the fresh pricks of rain fluttered over his face. 'I have this for you, RSM.' He held out a crumpled bit of paper. It was unsealed. 'The major asked me to give it to you. It's Sergeant Grant's letter to his wife. Would you...' his voice faltered.

Bannerman could see some of the words, paused to reflect what might possibly be written, then silently put it into a pocket as the rain began to thicken.

Look after him please! Beth's voice echoed in his head.

'Thank you, sir. I will see that Mrs Grant gets this.'

He had to shout the last sentence as the heavens rumbled with thunder and a spear of lightning split the air. Then came a torrential downpour; a rain that Bannerman had encountered once before as a young shepherd on the hills that spilled down towards the Moray Firth. He had been five miles from his home at Croy, a small village between Inverness and Nairn, and managed to find shelter in an hut of dark stone, moss and black thatch. He remembered the malevolent hammering, the fierceness, the noise. And now a similar flood of water drummed on bonnets, caps, packs and made the red dye of their coats run in rivulets down their kilts and legs.

Brevet-Major Campbell, on foot and wearing a cloak, splashed through the large puddles. He looked tired and sable-coloured stains lay under his eyes as if he had smeared charcoal under them. 'RSM.'

'Sir!'

'It appears some of our baggage is stuck in the village, which is causing pandemonium. Orders from brigade are that we march with discipline. It's a tactical withdrawal, nae rout and so I need you to make good of the chaos. I cannae have it known our boys are causing delays.' He held up a hand. 'It's nae our fault – it's the transport, but nevertheless I want it fixed now.'

'Of course, sir,' Bannerman replied, comprehending Campbell's nervousness at his new command.

'Therefore, I've ordered Corporal Buick and six men to assist you. Once it's sorted, join us up the road. We're going beyond that ridge to the north.' He twisted to show the way and water spilled from his peak. The nearest trees thrashed, shedding leaves as though it was an autumnal wind.

Bannerman stared over the major's shoulders and could just make out through the rainfall a wisp of bright sky beyond a dark set of ranges. 'Aye, sir.'

'Good man and dinnae be long. I need you,' Campbell grinned affably and turned away to disappear with the adjutant and a mounted Staff Officer waiting for him.

A clap of thunder crashed, a vast sound that consumed the heavens and was so loud that some of the men gasped and flinched. A crack of lightning splintered blue-white above the northern ridge line and Bannerman gawked at it wondering if it would be the place where they would defend or attack.

'Mont St-Jean,' Anderson said helpfully. 'I hope it's dry there,' he said wryly, before the battalion continued its march.

A dull boom echoed, a mile away, signalling that the British guns were continuing to fire at the enemy pursuers. Bannerman wondered if the rain hadn't come, then thousands of French lancers and Hussars might have swarmed the allied column, slashing and piercing as they went to turn the *chaussée* red with blood.

He found Buick, who was a rail-thin man, with diminishing fair hair and bland, unremarkable features, waiting on the roadside with his squad. They then marched towards the small village made up of white-washed buildings and smaller outer barns and granaries. Rain constantly dripped from his bonnet's peak. It ran down his cheeks, worked itself inside his thick coat and ran in shivers down his vastly muscled frame. Civilians watched from windows and doorways. A dog seemed to study him before slinking away into a shadowed archway. The streets were cramped and crowded with wagons and supplies. Bannerman couldn't understand why the transports weren't moving past the stranded vehicle and so walked to where a narrow bridge shouldered the thoroughfare over a gushing river. A wagon carrying packs and some wounded was the cause of the problem. It was at an odd angle and he knew it was another broken wheel that was to blame. Some packs had fallen down onto half-submerged cobbles. Wounded men with dirty bandages, crutches and even one watched the chaos from a wheelbarrow. Bannerman ordered his men to work. A mounted officer seemed to be arguing with another who was on foot. Blood dripped from the horse's whipped flanks and Bannerman patted the beast as he went by.

The rain pelted fiercely now, a cloudburst that assailed and soaked all who were caught in it, and more thunder rolled away in the distance. He saw lightning flicker beyond far hills. The fields were now flooded death-traps and the rye, oats and barley crops hung limp under the assault. The ditches ran like streams and the wind whipped the surface to scatter more water across the road and into the men's faces. Bannerman looked down at the river's surface that was pattering as though it was being hit by grapeshot. Cloaked cavalrymen walked their beasts across the fields, but no foot soldier dared break from solid ground to tread the mire. Another bellow of thunder and the rain had a new and vicious intensity. Bannerman shivered and decided he could watch proceedings from underneath a doorway from what appeared to be a small building attached to the local coach house. It was empty and smelt of horse tack, old sweat and leather. A mouse scurried amongst the debris scattered on the floor. The rain hammered noisily on the tiles. He piled the halberd and musket against the wall, placed his wet bonnet on a squat barrel, undid the first three buttons of his greatcoat and pulled out Ran's letter. He stared at it for a moment, unsure if he should read it or not. Curiosity got the better of him and he moved away from the commotion outside to a window with grime-smeared glass that let in mottled light. He opened up the paper and read as thunder boomed overhead.

Beth,
Let the recollection console you in your loss that the happiest days of my life were with you. Know that I die loving only you. I pray that our souls may be reunited in the Kingdom of Heaven and we will be together forever. Tell Robbie he'll grow into manhood knowing that I am proud of him. Every day, tell him I love him. My boy, how I will miss him. My darling Beth, I must tell you how much I will miss you too, but know that I fell at peace. My darling, my Beth. Your ever-loving husband, Ran.

Bannerman's eyes filled with unshed tears. *Look after him please!* Beth had implored and Ran was now dead and Bannerman had failed. 'I'm sorry, Beth. I'm so sorry, Robbie.' He could not stop himself now as the tears fell to mingle with the rainwater on his face and had to bite a hand in order to control himself. Loud laughter and voices filled the air and he pushed the letter back inside his coat and lurched towards the rear wall where a rickety door led to a narrow corridor outside. He shut it behind him, wanting to be away from onlookers, fearing he would be seen.

He stared out into a small courtyard. There were remnants of beehives and a patch of soil that might have once been an herb garden, but it was now a space of broken stone, weeds and horse dung. The rain tumbled from gutters, dripped from lintels and ran like a flood from gardens to puddle in the hollows. He thought of Ran's promise and how he had broken Beth's. What would he say to her? Would she blame him? Robbie had lost his father and his idol. It was heartbreaking. He straightened himself and rubbed his red eyes, ready to check on Buick.

The door creaked open. A wild cackle of a laugh sounded and Bannerman spun around instinctively knowing who it belonged to.

'Well, if it isnae my old friend, Regimental Sergeant-Major Bannerman,' Private Coll Burrell said mockingly, hefting his bayonet-tipped Brown Bess musket. He hauled back the hammer which cocked it and although held at waist height, the black muzzle was pointed at Bannerman's trunk.

Bannerman scanned the doorway and windows but there was no one else to witness this.

'You looking for your friend?' Coll sneered. 'Only I heard he was killed.' He cackled again but it was with some difficulty as his lips were still swollen and bloodied from yesterday's assault.

Bannerman growled. 'Put that damned firelock away before I seize it from your hands and beat you to death with it.'

Coll smiled horribly. 'I dinnae think so.'

'What you're doing is a punishable offence, Private Burrell,' Bannerman fell back on rank, but the twin did nothing than smile wickedly again. It was obvious what was going to happen. 'You're going to kill me,' Bannerman said to him, 'but how do you think you'll get away with it? We're in a small village. Our army marches beyond the houses and there are civilians everywhere. You pull the trigger and people will hear it.'

'Nae if I time it right,' Coll muttered airily, glancing up at the sky.

So he intended to use the cover of thunder to kill me, Bannerman considered. He would have to time it right and hope that no redcoats distinguished the sound and wander over to investigate the musket shot. Coll would never have thought of that himself as he was dim-witted. Someone must have given him instructions.

'Who ordered you here?'

Coll ran a wet sleeve under his nose. 'It doesnae matter. Now, you go outside. Go. Go on!'

Bannerman, weaponless, backed away, further until he passed the lintel and the rain immediately splashed his bare head and coat. His eyes darted left and right. The building's wall joined to a smaller brick house to his left where two large doors were shut. To the right of the courtyard was a small tumbledown cart, an abandoned dovecot covered in ancient bird droppings, the greasy remains of a manure heap and a cobbled path that lead around to Genappe's twisting streets.

Coll had not followed him outside and stood undercover. Bannerman knew that he did that to prevent moisture getting into the charge, but he seemed to be nervous. No, not nerves. He was waiting for something, or someone. Bannerman suspected Sholto would be coming here to assist with his murder.

'So tell me before you shoot me what this has to do with Captain Darrow?' he hazarded a guess.

'I dinnae know what you're babbling about.'

'Come on, Coll,' Bannerman said with mock-amusement. 'You can tell me. I'll be dead before the hour is out. I know this is nae about what happened after Toulouse, or yesterday, or the days when you were punished for drunkenness, disobedience, or plain stupidity! Tell me! What does the captain have against me? I know he sent you here.'

Coll shuddered. He glanced over his shoulder and wiped his face again. 'Vitoria, of course,' he said but a sudden hardness of rain almost made it inaudible.

Vitoria, Bannerman thought, *was two years ago*. There was the bloody encounter and the aftermath of poor men becoming rich men, but there was no other incident that marked out this sudden vendetta.

Bannerman frowned. Cold water dripped from his face and his coat was now soaked through to the lining. 'What of it?'

'The captain knows what you know.'

'What? You're nae making sense. You're either bullshitting, or lying,' Bannerman snarled. 'I'd go with the latter because you havenae the imagination to bullshit.'

436

'I'm nae lying to you!' Coll snarled, letting a dribble of spit wet his chin. 'He knows that you saw him put Captain Napier under the sod.'

Bannerman's eyes were enlarged at the revelation. Captain Kenneth Napier had been friends with Darrow and had died during the French rout at Vitoria around King Joseph's plundered baggage train. It was thought he had been killed by the enemy. Bannerman had not been at Napier's or Darrow's side during the incident and now he was saying Darrow had murdered a fellow officer. Officer's slaying each other. It was unimaginable. If this ever came out, it would stain the regiment's exemplary conduct. Would they have the Vitoria battle honour stripped from the records? Would Macara's legacy be tarnished? Would other men become embroiled in this scandal?

'What else has he said?' Bannerman enquired, hoping that some locals might appear and cause a distraction.

'Only that the bastard friend of yours, Sergeant Grant, was bothering the captain about it,' Coll replied.

Ran had not said anything about this, Bannerman brooded. Had he known about the murder? *Ran would have told me.* 'Asking him about the murder?'

Coll clearly did not know. He glanced over his shoulders again and scowled as his brother was still absent.

The fury in Bannerman was building and he knew he had to act now and quickly before there were two of the bastards. He could try to run away and hope he could twist free of the single shot the musket would hammer out, but that was a risk and he did not want to turn his back on this man. A thief, a rapist of women and a murderer.

'You raped that girl yesterday, didnae you?' Bannerman said, thinking of a plan. 'You raped her and killed her.' A smile slowly spread on Coll's lips and Bannerman wanted to hurt him. 'But you had help. Help to haud her down because you're a weak, cowardly piece of shite.'

The smile vanished as Coll's ruined mouth twisted. 'Shut up.'

Bannerman grinned. 'You're a prickless boy lover. That's why you needed help. Was Sholto there too? Of course he was. I bet he held her down, because you couldnae. She was too strong for you.'

'Shut up!' Coll yelled, stepping forward.

'I bet she sniggered as you fumbled with your prick. Probably seen a bigger louse.' Bannerman broke into a deep hearty laugh.

'Shut your stinking mouth!' Coll roared, spittle twirled between his lips.

'I bet ploughing a girl is different for you,' Bannerman continued the mockery. 'Different than fucking your own brother!'

Coll reacted to Bannerman's taunts exactly as he had wanted him to. The twin burst from the doorway, face twisted to that of some beast from hell, ready to rip the long bayonet into Bannerman's belly.

Bannerman let him come. He took a step backwards as the dull blade was splashed with rain and suddenly the two Scotsmen were in the courtyard. Coll gave another guttural shout, which was cut off as he slipped on a patch of horse dung Bannerman had been standing in front of. The private collapsed onto his right side, the impact tugging his index finger which made him pull the trigger.

There was a dull click and nothing happened.

Thunder was not needed to conceal the musket shot because the lashing rain had already worked its way into the pan and made the firearm useless.

Just the way Bannerman had hoped.

He sprang forward and slapped aside the musket as Coll attempted to bring the bayonet forward like a spear. Bannerman hit him and it was like the sound of a bullock being clubbed, wet and hard at the same time. Fury maddened him and he picked Coll up like he was a child's doll and tossed him against the nearest wall. The screaming private hit the brickwork with a thump, musket clattering on the ground, and he fell hard onto his front. Bannerman ran to him, picked him up and swung him casually at the opposite wall where he hit a jutting stone and Bannerman thought he heard a distinctive crack of broken bone.

'You bastard!' Bannerman screamed the words like a war cry.

Coll was bleeding and crying, but Bannerman strode over to him. He grabbed him by the collar and belt to throw him again, but suddenly his left arm lanced with pain. He stared down to see Coll had stabbed him through the forearm. Bannerman grunted as he clasped Coll by the neck and lifted him clean off his feet, banging him against the wall. His fingers dug into the white soft skin and Coll juddered and gasped for breath. He kicked, hammered a hand down to try to break Bannerman's nose but the giant of a man held him there. Coll's eyes bulged, his face was turning crimson, his tongue thrashed past his teeth and Bannerman felt him dying. Then, he slowly released the pressure until it was enough for Coll to breathe. His chest heaved and his breath came in ragged gasps.

'Did you rape the girl yesterday?' Bannerman asked him. Coll's head flopped forward and Bannerman shook him back into consciousness. 'Answer me, you bastard! I need to know!'

'Aye,' Coll admitted.

'What did you do with her afterwards? Where did you bury her?'

'We put her in...in the ground. Covered her... with bracken.'

Bannerman kept his gaze level. 'Your brother helped?'

'A...aye.'

'Who else?'

Coll hesitated, then Bannerman tightened the iron-grip around his throat. 'The captain told us to bury her,' he said swiftly.

'Captain Darrow.'

'Aye.'

Bannerman had been right all along. Now he had heard everything he needed to know. At least he thought he had. He needed Coll to talk more, so released the pressure again. 'Go on.'

'The captain ordered my brother to take care of Sergeant Grant,' Coll revealed. 'He said he knew that you and him were onto his secret, so... my brother knifed him before any more questions were asked.'

'What?' Bannerman let out a growl, his muscles trembling with vehemence. The revelation hit him like a blast from a twelve pounder. He forgot the pain of the blade still in his arm and let Coll drop to the ground. The private coughed, hawked and spat, watching him carefully, unsure of what was going to happen next.

Bannerman's face was not grizzled and fierce, it was usually open, affable even. His eyes were black and twinkled with intelligence and compassion. But at this moment he looked at Coll with such malevolence that the private trembled with fear. The image of Ran lying dead in that charnel house of blood played in his mind, and anger turned to rage that coursed through every vein. Bannerman made no sound as he pulled the knife from his flesh. He continued to stare at Coll as he brought his hand down and with one quick motion the knife sliced up into the twin's belly. Coll gasped and shook. Bannerman clenched his jaw and ripped the blade hard through his uniform, opening him up like a gutted deer, and the twin gave a strange mewing cry as he staggered away. His intestines spilled down onto the ground, his blood soaking his kilt and bare legs. He dropped to his knees, face drained of colour and then collapsed fully. His fingers clawed the wet ground, then he gave a great jerk and was still.

It took a moment for the red mist to dissipate. Bannerman had murdered a man, but he did not feel any guilt or remorse. He felt angry. He watched the blood pool and mix in with the rain before dragging Coll's body where he hid him under the mound of manure. He snatched up the musket, concealing it also, and looked up at the sky, letting the cleansing water wash his face and blood-smeared hands.

If Sholto and indeed Darrow were coming, then they didn't show themselves. Bannerman retrieved his weapons and bonnet and ramming the feathered cap on his head, he walked outside to find Buick waiting for him.

The road was clear of obstructions and the Highlanders joined the army on its retreat north to a shallow valley where Wellington hoped to make a stand.

And where Bannerman had a score to settle.

*

The rain continued to fall.

But whether it had been an act of God or not, some considered it a good omen because the torrent had obliterated the French pursuit. Wellington's army continued its march north, but the men were bone-weary and chilled from the piercing rain. Bannerman saw that they passed a white-painted tavern called *La Belle Alliance* and Ran would have joked about raiding the cellars and that thought made him smile poignantly. The road dipped at Mont St-Jean so that he could suddenly see a dull-green valley below where curtains of silver rain swept over rich fertile land, a marked difference than the rugged, open but breathtaking glens back home. The great sheets of rain were gradually moving away, but there was still dark clouds heaped in the sky. The long road shone as a ghost-pale ribbon stretching dimly towards the opposite ridge. To the west was a large farm; Bannerman could just about make out the dull-red brickwork and block of trees around it. Further on up the road, the Black Watch passed a white-painted farm with high-walls and then, over the flat-topped ridge, the army amassed.

The green fields had quickly been churned to mud as men brought wood from nearby hedgerows and copses to make fires, drove wagons and the artillery teams brought the Duke's heavy guns. Thousands of infantrymen crowded. Soon numerous bivouac fires smeared the air as the last of the cavalry and light artillery left the long road and the valley was at last empty and silent. Bannerman, hobbling with a large blister forming on his right heel, found a farrier who miserably told him he was too busy with horseshoes to sharpen the halberd's blade. Bannerman told him that if he didn't do the work then he would break his arms. The farrier went to work.

'I want it sharp as a razor, do you hear?'

'Yes,' the farrier said weakly.

'Good, so get to it.'

When it was done, Bannerman tossed the man a shilling before finding the major in conversation with Captains' Reid, Hamilton and Darrow. The officers murmured beside a large fire that hissed and popped from the rain. Reid and Hamilton greeted him affably except Darrow who looked affronted by his appearance.

'Good work getting the wagons moving, RSM,' Campbell said, which caused Darrow to shift awkwardly as though he objected to the praise.

'All in a day's work, sir.' Bannerman tried to ignore the lancing pain in his arm, the wound bound with linen made his limb feel stiff.

'You were lucky to get out when you did. Apparently, lancers trotted into Genappe shortly after our infantry passed it. There was a skirmish of sorts with our Hussars and the damned lancers threw them out until Lord Uxbridge sent in the Life Guards and gave them a bloody nose,' Campbell said with relish. Darrow cleared his throat noisily. The major glanced at him and then let Reid and Hamilton go, making sure they were out of earshot before speaking. 'Captain Darrow told me that Corporal Burrell asked his permission to assist with the wagons at Genappe.'

'Och?' Bannerman rose an eyebrow at that. He glanced at the Surgeon who stared with cold aversion. Darrow had no doubt sent the twins to finish him and was no doubt seething that they had failed.

'The corporal met Buick in the village, but he reported that didn't know where you were at one point,' Campbell said and it felt like an accusation of shirking orders. 'Burrell said that he couldnae find you either.'

No, but I found his brother, Bannerman thought wryly.

'I was there, sir,' he confirmed. 'I happened to step under cover for a wee moment during the downpour.'

'While our men worked tirelessly in it,' Darrow snapped like a dog, his eyes cold and sharp. 'Dodging the rain and your orders, RSM? Well? Have you nothing to say for yourself?'

441

Bannerman ignored the outburst. He stiffened and gazed at the fire, which threw strange iridescent shadows across the mud. The portentous clouds had brought about a premature eventide. 'I apologise, sir,' he muttered, turning to Campbell.

'Accepted, RSM,' the major remarked hurriedly, as if he wanted this confrontation over with quickly. 'It was a truly horrendous weather earlier.'

'No, sir,' Bannerman said respectfully, 'I am sorry for reading this.' He pulled out a crinkled piece of paper. 'It's Sergeant Grant's letter to his wife. You entrusted it with me for safekeeping until I can give it to her. I will do that, but shamefully curiosity got the better of me. I stepped out of the rain to read it so that it would nae get spoiled. I wanted to know if I could expand on Sergeant Grant's love to his dear wife.'

'I see,' Campbell said slowly in the mixed tone of dismay and empathy. 'Well, it was carried out with a good intention. So no harm done, I suppose.'

Darrow looked incredulous. He was glancing from face to face and Bannerman could tell he was scenting trouble with the eagerness of a hound smelling a fox's den. 'No harm done? The RSM has just admitted that he had read another man's letter to his wife and was avoiding his responsibilities, both of which you entrusted to him.'

Campbell rubbed his face. Bannerman was standing to attention and gazed over the officers' bonnets, expressionless.

'I'm appalled at your behaviour,' the Surgeon continued to chide with his precise voice, gusting wine-smelling breath over Bannerman's face. 'I thought with your years of experience you would set an example.' He glanced at the major. 'I'm sure there are other sergeants who could do a better job as RSM.'

Campbell sighed at the hostility, but remained looking at Bannerman. 'Sergeant Grant was your friend, was he not?'

'Of many years, sir,' Bannerman replied. 'He asked me to look after his wife and son should anything happen to him.'

'Did he tell you that, or did he write that down in the letter to his wife?' Darrow enquired with a scathing glare.

'He was a sergeant in your company, Neil?' Campbell asked.

Darrow, anger slowly abating, nodded abruptly. 'Indeed he was, sir,' he replied, but had nothing else to add to that. His face appeared hollow in the firelight.

'After yesterday's battle we've a shortage of good men,' Campbell said firmly. 'Men like Sergeant Grant who carried this regiment to glory and on to greatness.'

'I was just yards from him in the rally square when he was,' Bannerman paused, his face tightened with anguish and he momentarily glanced away before letting his gaze rest on Darrow, 'stabbed in the back.'

The captain blinked rapidly, but other than that showed no reaction to the accusation. Campbell had not picked up on the undertone. Coll had been since declared missing, but so had two others since the battalion left the field of Quatre Bras and it was presumed they were with the convoy of wounded. Darrow had not pushed his disappearance, but it was obvious to Bannerman that he suspected foul play and this exchange was intended to punish him.

'Our casualty list is nearly three hundred men. Three hundred!' Campbell let that figure hang in the air before speaking again. 'We're licking our wounds, but we've still a duty to perform at half-strength. I think we need to bed down for the night and leave our anger for the Crapauds in the morning. It's been a hard two days for us all. Understood?' He had been speaking to both men.

'Aye, sir,' Bannerman grimaced in half apology.

Darrow winced because his cause for complaint had been neglected, rubbed his face, nodded and stared at Bannerman as he spoke. ' *"Revenge should have no bounds."* '

'Very good, Neil,' Campbell was evidently pleased with the reply, but whether it was because it was from Shakespeare or the meaning, Bannerman couldn't tell. He watched the major walk away.

Darrow's eyes were boring into Bannerman's mind like fish-hooks, trying to latch on, trying to capture what he was thinking. The captain glanced at the sky as though he suspected a heavenly eavesdropper. He leaned slightly towards Bannerman and dropped his voice.

'I'm nae sure how much you know?' he asked, curious.

'Why dinnae you elaborate?'

'So if you think...' Darrow said, then checked himself. 'You will keep your mouth shut,' he warned instead.

'Are you threatening me?'

'I'm still your superior,' Darrow said, his mouth pressed into a thin white line. 'I outrank you, RSM,' the last word was a slur in his mouth.

'Are you threatening me?' Bannerman repeated, glowering dark defiance.

443

Darrow sighed at the insolence to his rank. 'Whatever you know, or think you know will nae stand up under scrutiny. You'll be a laughing stock if you involve Major Campbell, or anyone from brigade with your story. I have a cousin who is a lawyer. I cannae stand the man, but he knows his stuff. I promise he will ruin you.' He stared warningly for a moment, then brightened his face with a wan smile. 'I can provide you with enough money for you to retire and live comfortably for the rest of your life. As long as you haud your tongue, that is.' He wagged a long finger in Bannerman's face.

'Och?'

Darrow smiled as if he was pleased with Bannerman's expression. 'Give me your word that you'll retire after this campaign and I'll give you the funds,' he said in a very matter-of-fact voice. 'I dinnae suppose half-pay will provide you with enough substance to live on. But I can. Think about it. You'll be a rich man. Nae like me, of course, but still a rich man.' He gave Bannerman an inquisitive glance and let a condescending laugh fly. 'You rest on your halberd like a shepherd leans on his crook! You're getting too old, RSM. There's no fool like an old fool. Think about your retirement and what you could do with five hundred pounds.' He spread his hands in mock appeal.

'What I cannae understand,' Bannerman said, ignoring Darrow's assertion and insults, 'is why you murdered Captain Napier? Was it over the money? Was it greed that made you kill him?'

The Surgeon flinched as though he had been struck. 'Kenneth,' he started and paused to gnaw the inside of his cheek as he chose his words carefully. 'Captain Napier wasnae as honourable as folk believe him to be.' He shrugged irritably as though that was enough to say on the matter. 'How did you find out about it?'

'The murder?' Bannerman said with a snarl, hoping that saying it would needle him. 'Coll Burrell revealed it thinking he was going to kill me.'

Darrow shook his head. 'He was such a slow-witted oaf. How did he die?'

'Do you care?'

'Just tell me,' Darrow insisted.

'I gutted him.'

Darrow stared. 'Sholto will be upset at that.'

No remorse, Bannerman noted. *Probably did the bastard a good turn by eliminating Coll. One less mouth to fear the secret getting out.*

'You can tell Sholto to come and see me and I'll show him exactly how I did it.'

A smile flickered and died on Darrow's face. 'He still thinks his brother is alive somewhere.'

'Why did you order him to kill Ran?' Bannerman demanded, bitterness sharpening his tone.

Darrow rolled his eyes as though having to converse further was anathema. 'Because you knew my secret of course.'

'But we didnae,' Bannerman said, watching Darrow's expression go from arrogance to astonishment. 'I knew something was amiss when you hushed over Coll's rape and murder of the peasant girl on the Brussels road. I didnae know why you would do that, or why the twins bound at your feet like lapdogs. I told Ran my thoughts. He didnae know either.'

'So why did he ask me about Toulouse?'

Bannerman shrugged. 'I didnae know he was going to approach you. I can only determine that he wanted to know the truth about Napier so you killed him for the secret of baubles. Then you sent Coll and Sholto to murder me at Genappe. And you failed. And now, more fool you, I know the truth.' He watched Darrow who was trying not to let his disappointment show. 'Why didnae you buy a majority or a lieutenant-colonelcy? You have the money. You could have transferred out. You could be leading a battalion rather than a company.'

'I could,' Darrow said, then smiled, 'but I'd much rather lead a company. I have much more fun this way.'

'Fun?' Bannerman asked disbelievingly.

Darrow ignored the question. 'My offer still stands. I'll provide you with say,' he paused theatrically, 'five hundred pounds and you'll agree to keep quiet and retire forthwith.'

Bannerman clenched his jaw. 'You think you can buy my silence?' He spat angrily at Darrow's feet, the rage curdling his belly. 'You can keep your damned blood money. I want only one thing.'

'Which is?'

Bannerman stepped closer, looming over the thin captain, smiling like a wolf seeing fresh meat. 'Your death. I would kill you right now where we stand and so rid the world of a cowardly piece of shite, but that pleasure must wait, Captain,' he rasped, almost spitting the rank as though it had burnt his tongue on its way past.

'By God, we're nae finished here, RSM.' Darrow's indignant tone did nothing to hide the threat.

'For now we are, you murdering, dishonourable streak of piss,' Bannerman hissed. 'Now go and boil your head.'

He left Darrow in furious impotence and went to check on the companies. Edging his way through the crouching figures around the fires, Lieutenant Anderson must have sensed his approach, or else saw a gleam of light reflected from the halberd's tip, because he greeted him warmly. The lieutenant was sitting on a rather ornate chair beside a healthy fire that was made up of doors, casks, a wheelbarrow and what looked to be a tall clock-case.

'I paid the equivalent of three shillings for this.' He patted the chair, one that had been taken from one of the local farms. He looked happy to be sitting in the numbing cold misery of the rain, sucking a cheroot into fragrant life. 'Worth every bloody penny.'

'Saves getting your arse muddy, sir,' Bannerman said, gazing at the men around the nearest fires who were laying and sitting on straw and cut leafy boughs as crude mattresses. The unfortunate ones had to simply make do with the mud. Some looped blankets over pegged branches to keep out of the rain, but the material quickly became sodden, limp and was abandoned.

'Aye, it does.' A look of sadness suddenly crossed the lieutenant's face. 'I feel sorry for Captain Darrow,' he said humbly.

Bannerman stopped and stared at him in the semi-darkness. 'How so, sir?'

'He paid two pounds for requisitioning a chair from one of the larger houses in that village yonder,' he said, pointing east where tiny lights wavered. 'I think he said it was called Papelotte. Saxe-Weimar's Nassauers are down there. Anyway, two whole pounds! And unfortunately some idiot thought it was more fuel for the fire and so ...' he grinned slyly.

Bannerman saw the blackened shell of the former chair on top of the flames and he laughed.

Lightning flickered, followed a few seconds later by a cannonade of thunder that crashed across the far sky. For a second the thousands of voices upon the ridge were silent, nothing was heard but the rainfall, then as horses whinnied, dogs barked and the army went to work, peace was drowned out.

And Bannerman let his mind wander with vengeance.

*

Beth Grant had spent the afternoon and evening of the 16th shivering from the noises of the far away gun fire. She shared a small attic above a chandler's shop with another sergeant's wife called Dolina Anton and her three children, one of whom was ill with a vomiting sickness.

'Will da be back soon?' Robbie had asked, staring out of the room's narrow window.

'He'll come back when he's allowed to,' Beth had skirted the question. 'Dinnae keep asking me.' She sighed tetchily. 'He'll be bringing back some memento of the battle to give to you, like he always does,' she said with a smile. 'He promised you.'

'Aye,' Robbie had said. 'Maybe he'll bring me a pistol, or a French sword this time instead of buttons,' his eyes glinted with promise.

'No weapons,' Beth had said sternly. 'That's the rule. Your da said he will nae be bringing any back. Nae if he knows what's good for him.'

Robbie kicked at a loose floorboard sulkily. 'When I'm older, I might get my own,' he said petulantly.

I pray you willnae, Beth said to herself. She had listened to the echo of the guns and prayed to God. She had got down on her knees and wept and begged that He keep her husband safe. Only that the hours ticked on and there was no news. Beth waited anxiously.

Now on the evening of the 17th, the only noise was the thundering rain. Mrs Anton had left her children with Beth for a short while to purchase some bread and cheese, which Beth knew really meant more gin, for the woman drank more than a bottle a day. There was shouting outside in the streets. She moved quietly as not to wake the sleeping children and stared out of the window. Horsemen galloped past, the hooves clattering on the cobbles. She could hear men's voices, muffled by the weather. Beth crept down the ladder, down the next floor which was more spacious and rented by a captain for his wife and two children and down to the ground floor of the shop. The owner, Monsieur Rademaker and his wife, were already at the door and the commotion outside was loud. A carriage flew past and some men splashed through puddles as they jogged.

'Madame, what's going on?' Beth enquired as a woman's hysterical voice cried out somewhere.

Madame Rademaker pulled her shawl closer to her large form. She was a middle-aged woman with raven-black hair, wrinkles around her eyes and a warm smile. 'They are saying that there was a *grande bataille.*'

447

'A battle,' Beth said. 'And?' she urged.

'They are saying that the British lost and that the *Allemands*,' she tried to think of the English word and then spoke quick French to her husband. There was the sound of someone banging on front doors.

'The Prussians have been beaten by the Emperor and are fleeing,' Monsieur Rademaker provided the news in his usual deep voice, which belied his thin and wiry frame. He was smoking a cigar and the tip glowed brightly as he sucked on it. 'I am sorry to have to tell you this,' he said, his expression serious, 'but the British, Mrs Grant, have been destroyed.'

Beth stared at him. 'No,' she gasped.

'I'm afraid so. The people from Waterloo and Mont St-Jean, and the survivors of the battle are warning us now. There is a panic. The soldiers are fleeing. The Emperor will be here within the day.'

'My God,' Beth said, watching the stream of fugitives on the dark road.

Madame Rademaker hugged Beth. 'Please stay, you will be safe here. My husband and I will look after you.' Monsieur Rademaker suddenly erupted in rapid French to which Madame Rademaker looked reproved. 'My husband says that many *Anglais* and the exiled Bourbons are already leaving for Antwerp and perhaps there will be transport for you and your son.'

That was enough for Beth to hear. She hurried back to the attic and packed their belongings. Mrs Anton had returned by then, drunk, but there was nothing that Beth could do for her, or her children. She woke Robbie, dressed him and both of them plunged into the madness of wind and rain. Madame Rademaker hurried after them and kissed Beth on both cheeks, thrusting a cloth bundle, which contained bread, cheese and some smoked sausage, into her hands.

'You will go to Antwerp, *oui*?' she asked Beth.

'No,' Beth replied, glancing at the road north to the ports, before staring south where lightning split the night sky. 'I'm going to find my husband.'

*

On the morning of the 18th the rain had gone eastwards, leaving a rinsed sky ragged with hurrying clouds.

Bannerman had snatched what sleep he could. It hadn't been the rain, or the damp wind that had kept him awake, or the knife wound that ached foully, it was what Darrow had done. He had plotted and killed for the secret of a fallen king's treasure. He had paid, Bannerman presumed, the Burrell twins well enough to keep their tongues still. They had themselves got away with murder and rapes, protected by Darrow and his new found wealth, but now, they were involved in the murder of a friend and Bannerman would not reveal this to Campbell, instead he would look to punish the remaining two of them himself. He wanted justice; the Highland way, and one that was swift and definite. No army courts. No lawyers and note-takers. He had murdered Coll and that act had obliterated everything that he had strived for; decency and honour. He knew by taking revenge that he slid away from the light and down into the murky depths of chaos. He would be sacrificing everything, his years of service, his honour and possibly his life, but as he climbed up out of the wet straw-filled ditch that had been his bed for the night, all he could still think about was retribution.

Bannerman, his greatcoat, legs and boots slick with mud, began to wake the officers to life as the morning's first light flared to the east. Cocks crowed from the farms. The bivouac fires had long died and those that still crackled were requisitioned for brewing tea and soon he was holding a steaming cup of tea in a dented tin mug. It was strong enough to reanimate the dead and it thankfully brought life back to his long cold limbs. He crouched for a while, warming his calloused hands at the flames as if it were the dead of winter not a summer's morning. The Highlanders had slept against large ruts in the ground, or against hedges using their packs as pillows. Food had been cold rations. Private McKinley of Number Two Company had snared a rabbit and Bannerman had eaten a mouthful of it, the rest had been distributed amongst McKinley's platoon. Most men were awake though, talking and smoking their pipes in a land of cold shadows. A horse, broken free of its constraints, whinnied and galloped in and amongst the bivouacs, sending cursing men into the mud and wafting the tendrils of camp smoke. Bannerman watched it jump a hedge, and disappear down the slope toward the farm of La Haye Sainte.

'Lucky bastards are probably dry down there,' Anderson spluttered to life in his chair that had started to sink in the mud, so that he was slightly tilted over to one side. 'Spent the night warming their Sassenach arses while we're up here soaked to our bloody stitches! I begged the major to send me down there with my platoon, but it fell on deaf ears. But then again trapped in a room with my men I should be thankful of a cold wet night under the stars rather than intoxicate

449

myself with their foul breath and stinking arses.' He yawned, shivered and then groaned. 'Good morning, RSM. You smell like a wet dung heap.'

'Tea, sir?'

'Make it strong, would you? The kind of tea strong and thick enough to stand a ramrod straight in it.' Anderson yawned noisily. 'Dear sweet Lord,' he said, 'but it's a cold morning.'

'Did you sleep, sir?'

'Now who in their sane mind could after that deluge?' Anderson said, yawning again, having slept more than six hours.

The British picquets scooped out the damp sludge in their muskets and sprinkled dry powder in the priming pans. A few flashed and banged in the early hours, but most needed more powder to catch the sparks of the flint. Men watched the enemy across the valley, who were as wet, muddy and cold as they were. The sun rose and was visible above the ridge as a pearly glow beyond the cool brume and pungent smoke from the bivouac fires. Breakfast still consisted of the men's rations for the commissariat had failed to bring food. They grumbled and then cheered as barrels of rum were rolled across the rutted ground and distributed. Some were already drunk, having consumed wine, brandy and gin through the night, and their excitement at the victory of Quatre Bras had still not subsided.

The 42nd was positioned with the rest of Pack's brigade on the Duke of Wellington's left wing. Fellow Scotsmen of the 92nd were on their immediate left, and the Royal Scots and the 44th were formed thirty yards behind. A narrow path: the Ohain road, was heavily-rutted, water-logged and lined with blackthorn, hazel and hawthorn. The tall thick hedges could prove a tough obstacle to cavalry. It also ran west towards the allied right wing where the ground rose sharply and passed between embankments of five to seven feet high, giving it the appearance of a sunken road. To the east, it wound towards Wavre and it splintered to a collection of farms a quarter of a mile away, half-hidden by oak and beech trees. Far behind the horizon, a thin bar of gold light shone beyond the treetops and homes.

Bannerman stood on the brow of the rampart-like ridge and stared out in the golden dawn as the world stirred to life. The wind whipped droplets of water from the trees, hedgerows and lank grass. Birds circled in the sky. A hare darted into a tangle of green on the opposite verge. The French were absent. There was a low fog of dirty smoke hovering above the *La Belle Alliance* ridge, and a small group of

450

horsemen; mere silhouettes, watched back. The rest of Bonaparte's men were all but hidden.

Footsteps that made a sucking sound made Bannerman twist to see Anderson approaching.

'Bloody mud! Good news, RSM,' the lieutenant paused while he manoeuvred a tricky patch of the mire that came up to his shins. He sniffed the air. 'Everything I've ever seen always looks nicer after rainfall. Except this place,' he said, sniffing the fresh morning air again, but the heavy rain had gone and there were no clouds shadowing the land. 'The major says that the Prussians are definitely coming. It's come from brigade so it must be true.'

'That is good news, sir,' Bannerman replied ardently, the pale morning light sliding along the flat of the halberd's wide blade.

Anderson stamped his wet muddy feet and gawped at the empty ridge. 'Maybe they'll get here before the Frogs turn up?' he said, glaring around. 'Where the bloody hell are they?'

'They're there, sir.'

'Sabbath day today, you know,' Anderson remarked, glancing back at Ensign Gray who was dressed immaculately as though the fight might well be his last. He was wearing a fur-lined cloak over his coat that he had brushed so that the scarlet was as bright as new, his belts, buckles, buttons and sword-hilt sparkled in the cold, damp, smoky light. He was dressed for war. 'His lordship doesnae want to be buried in rags, nae like the rest of us.' Anderson plucked at his own damp, mud-smeared coat. He cocked his head up at the tall NCO. 'I bet you veterans dinnae fear dying. I can see it by the way you haud yourselves.'

'I dinnae fear it, sir,' Bannerman said. 'I've spent too long a soldier to worry about it now.' He had seen shot and ball mutilate horribly, turning a healthy man in a blink of an eye into a tormented remnant. He'd had friends killed without a sound, not even a mere gasp of breath snatched from dying lungs, and some left twitching in agony and invalided out of the army to spend many painful years of helplessness and suffering as a cripple. He knew every day, when the time came, that it might well be his last.

No, a voice said in his head, *you do fear dying. You fear nae ever seeing Beth again. You're worried that Ran's letter will never be read by her. You owe it to them to live. But you do fear it.* A ripple of unease ran along the back of his neck. Bannerman bristled against the words

451

and watched the sun rising to gild the clouds that stretched across the bright sky.

Anderson gave him a long sideways look. 'I would nae worry about death if I looked like you,' he said dryly, then blew steam from his mug.

Ran had mentioned something similar leaving Brussels. *Poor Ran.*

'Reverend Slora; our very pious chaplain, says that Jesus Christ rose from the dead,' Anderson went on. 'He died to give us life. He lived again in his dying. Death, it seems, is another path to more life. If that's true, then why do we then fear death? Is it because we expect a painful end?'

Bannerman shrugged. 'Maybe the ache of leaving loved ones behind,' he suggested, thinking of Beth and Robbie's plight.

'Och, well, I dinnae have any,' Anderson replied, taking a sip of tea. 'Lucky old me, eh?'

'A lot of men will die here today, sir,' Bannerman said. It would be death on a muddy ridge. He squinted at the knot of Frenchmen, guessing they were scanning the British ridge to determine where it was weak, but Wellington had concealed the army behind it to deny the enemy that opportunity. There were Belgians exposed in a crop field and some British 95th Riflemen in a large bowl-shaped pit next to the farmhouse of La Haye Sainte, but that was all.

'True,' Anderson allowed, then gawped. 'Why did you look at me when you said that?'

Bannerman ignored the levity. 'So is it a fair price to pay to make sure this battle will be the last one?'

Anderson blinked and then grimaced. 'Who said it would be the last one?'

'I hope it is, sir,' Bannerman breathed.

'I sometimes wonder who sets the value of life.'

'Only God Himself can do that,' Bannerman said, rubbing his thumb against his halberd's blade to check its sharpness, an old superstition. 'The good and bad will die today. So let's kill as many of the bastards as we can and let God sort them out.'

Anderson grinned and slapped his shoulder, the sound was like a man punching an oak tree. 'That's a better sermon than our God-haunted reverend ever gave. I think you've found your next vocation, RSM.'

By nine o'clock Wellington's army waited for the French to challenge them, but none came. The 42nd, like the rest of the army were ordered into columns of companies, their packs stacked on carts and taken to the rear where the baggage train waited at the edge of the Forest of Soignes. The Light Companies of the battalions of Wellington's first line formed a skirmish line, linking up with the 95th Rifles at the gravel pit, and divisional artillery were sighted behind the hedges. At the rear of Picton's division British Heavy Cavalry under Sir William Ponsonby were lining up in the fields, churning more of the damp stalks of crops to ruin.

Then a dark line spread at the southern ridge and suddenly the land was awash with the enemy. The Peninsular War veterans had seen the French come to fight many times. They had swarmed over Portuguese hills and Spanish vistas and that was expected. But this time the enemy flowed down the road in an endless display of power. Infantry, guns and cavalry. There were thousands of them. Battalion after battalion, battery after battery and squadron after squadron marched and wheeled and trotted to face Wellington's army under the smoke-patterned sky.

'This might well be a feint,' Bannerman overheard Gray wondering out loud. 'A trap to keep us here while the real one comes from the east; that'll split us from the Prussians for good. They call Bonaparte the Master Deceiver.'

The young ensign was decidedly wrong about that. Bannerman could not help but stare in astonishment as the minutes ticked by and more of the enemy surged down the slopes. This was Bonaparte's great army. British, Germans and the Dutch-Belgians watched the spectacle unfold. This was what the Emperor wanted. This was the might of Bonaparte, a man once thought crushed and defeated, but he had arisen and now would unleash his new army in the hope of achieving the bloody heights of *Le Grande Armée* of 1812. This was a dazzling display, an arrogant show of force as the regimental bands played jauntily, but this was no feint. Every pistol, musket, sword, lance and gun was there for one thing: to destroy Wellington's army.

'I hope the Prussians are hasting their way,' Campbell said, as the nearest French voices singing *la Marseillaise* got louder.

Bannerman stared down the files. Young faces. Most had never seen a battle before and Quatre Bras was their baptism of fire. But this was different. Bannerman watched the Dutch-Belgians and they too looked absurdly young. The Emperor's music was strangely hypnotic, but at the same time shattering morale even before the first shots had been fired. Fear was a battlefield killer. Then the sound began to fade and scores of voices called out together, '*Vive l'Empereur!*' Bannerman

453

watched a small man riding a light-coloured horse descend the road with an entourage of followers. The Scotsman blinked. His heart quickened a touch.

'My God!' Campbell exclaimed, witnessing the figure. 'Is that the devil himself?'

'Aye, sir,' Bannerman observed with awe. 'It's Bonaparte.'

The French cheered their Emperor until their throats were hoarse, as he swept along the echelon, trotting victoriously as though the campaign was already won. '*Vive l'Empereur!*' they chanted.

A drum of hooves and one of Picton's Aides gave Campbell the order for the regiment to lie down. Whistles blew and the Light companies returned to their battalions. Wellington wanted his infantry behind the ridge's crest to shield them from French artillery, but it also served a purpose for them not to see the mass of the enemy. Some of the Highlanders grumbled at being asked to lie in the mud and patches of rank grass, but a look from Bannerman was enough to cease their belly-aching.

'The only thing I require from you is dry ammunition, a sharp flint and silence,' he demanded.

Then a French gun fired.

The cold iron shot burst across the valley and smacked into the steep ridge below a solitary elm tree, churning a groove of mud. Campbell and those officers that had them, opened their pocket watches to see the time. A second shot sounded and its ball thudded harmlessly into a patch of lank grass.

'The time, sir?' Bannerman asked the major.

'Half-past eleven.'

A third gun fired and it hit a mound of grass and bounded just to the right of the forward Belgians who taunted when it came to a halt.

'Three shots,' Campbell said, watching the puffs of smoke rise high. 'The Emperor sends his greetings.'

And the blood-letting began.

The French guns opened fire on the large château to the west, which Bannerman had heard was called Hougoumont. He remembered seeing the mass of trees and tall-high walls during the night march, but now could not see it from his position. Nor could he see the thousands of French infantry eagerly sweeping down the valley to capture it, but he could certainly hear their efforts. The musket fire started as sporadic bursts, then intensified as the French found that the British Guards and the rifle-armed Germans defending were not so easy to displace.

'They'll never take it,' Campbell remarked confidently. 'The Guards against the Monsewers,' he said, making a scornful noise.

Wellington's infantry remained prone as time ticked by. A shower of cold rain fell, which softened the raging battle and partly-obscured the tree-lined hedges.

Bannerman felt clammy in his uniform. The air was warming up despite the rainfall, proving that today might well be the hottest day of the month.

Then there was a sound that he had heard before but never with such intensity. It was like the thunder god whip-cracking across the sky. Every gun on the French ridge pounded the air; its burst leaving a percussive beat as the muzzle spewed fire and hot air fanned the grass in front of each gun. One minute the gunners had been standing next to their pieces, and then the next the air was blotted with foul-smelling, yellow-grey smoke and ears deafened by the fury.

Eighty guns had opened fire. This was the Emperor's Grand Battery and now those twelve-pounders, his Beautiful Daughters, blasted their cold throats free to send the iron missiles straight at the allied centre. Roundshot smashed into the ridge, whipping mud and water ten feet into the air as the balls bounced harmlessly away or over the heads of the front line battalions. Some ricocheted to whirl and tumble down onto the Ohain road, but most were stopped by the deep slope. Shell burst along the summit, sending red-hot casing down onto the front lines of the redcoats, but the majority were left unhurt. But the French were gnawing at the allied infantry as the balls skimmed the crest and ploughed down into the crouching men.

An unlucky Highlander of the 92nd was decapitated by a roundshot and one private of the 42nd hissed as an exploding shell took away part of his right kneecap. A crouching sergeant from the 28th was struck in the chest and hurled thirty paces to the battalion's rear. What was left was a mess of splintered bone and flattened flesh. Parts of the trees and hedges were blasted to kindling and Bannerman watched one shell roll down towards him, fizzing iron-grey smoke, to plunge into a puddle where its burning fuse was thankfully extinguished.

But the bombardment was relentless.

Bannerman had never heard such a tremendous roar followed by a high-pitched scream of the missiles as they tore through the rain-snatched sky. It was never-ending. A private trembled and jerked whenever a shell exploded. Bannerman put a hand on his arm and tried not to let his nose wrinkle at the smell of excrement coming from the young soldier. Minutes went by as the French cannonade continued. A solid shot bounced to crush a man's leg and then take an arm off a young lieutenant who was gazing into his fiancée's eyes of a miniature portrait contained in a locket. Bannerman heard the dying scream of a horse at the rear; the cannon fire were causing casualties in Ponsonby's cavalry brigade. A trooper of the 2nd North British Dragoons, known as the Scots Greys, was decapitated by a roundshot, and it happened so quickly that the shattered body still sat upright in the saddle for a few ghastly moments. Another ball eviscerated a horse, then bounced to carry away a trooper in the rear file in a spatter of blood.

Bannerman guessed that three maybe four thousand rounds had already been fired at the ridge line and still the gunners let their weapons belch fire and cloud the valley with leprous smoke in the hope of slaughtering the enemy. But the French could not see Wellington's men and were firing blind.

Darrow turned his head and shot a look of hate at Bannerman who stared back unflinchingly. The captain's thin mouth half-smiled as if was hoping a raining shot would slam down into Bannerman and kill him.

I willnae die, you bastard,' Bannerman growled in his head. *I'll see you and Sholto dead first.* He wasn't a religious man, but prayed to God to give him the gift of revenge before his time was up.

Then the Grand Battery ceased its dreadful bombardment and the redcoats waited, expecting another tempest that would assail their ears, but the only sound was the intense musket-fire coming from Hougoumont and the explosions of shells lobbed by howitzers into the woods. Smoke, tugged by the wind, rippled and danced away to reveal a new threat.

The first French infantry advanced towards the allied ridge. Four great columns; each one some two hundred men across, marched down the slope, crushing the crop fields in their wake. Splinters of men left the four phalanxes, like clouds of flies departing a swollen corpse. They were *voltigeurs,* and these well-trained light infantrymen ran ahead to snipe at the enemy first before the heaving and chanting leviathans smashed the defenders apart.

The redcoats, who were still lying flat or crouching low, were quickly ordered into two ranks; a thin red wall to stop the assault. Sergeant Weir kicked a private.

'Get up, Private Bruce,' he shouted. 'You're wallowing in the mud like a drunken hog. Up!'

'I'm ready for them!' Private Watt announced.

'You shut your flapping tongue!' Weir quickly responded.

Whistles blew and the Light Companies sent their men out again to challenge the mass of *voltigeurs*. Muskets coughed and rifles cracked and soon the air was thick with skirmish fire. Bannerman could just about hear the thump and rattle of the French infantry drums inside the four columns. The drummer boys were emphatically beating the *pas de charge*; the old rhythmic sound that accompanied French assaults, with a new keening fire. The sound had once carried Bonaparte's warriors to the world's end, and now in a narrow Belgian valley, it was pulsing like the heartbeats of doom.

The skirmishers traded fire, but the French easily outnumbered their counterparts and so the allies were pushed back up the slope. The British Baker rifles were battlefield killers, but very slow to load. A soldier could shoot a musket three times while a rifleman reloaded. To fire it accurately a rifleman was supposed to wrap each ball in a small leather patch, then ram it down on the charge, and ramming a patched ball was hard work. With the skirmishes batted aside, the columns advanced boldly even when the British artillery opened up to send roundshot, each one weighing nine-pounds, into the packed formations. Men in their files were snatched back as though they had all been tugged by an invisible rope.

The sun was higher, but the artillery smoke still made it look a dirty yellow behind their veil. Below it, men were shouting emphatically as the drums paused and the men sang, '*Vive l'Empereur!*' The French had severely mauled the Prussians at Ligny, the first spark of a great fire to come. And now the attackers would hammer-blow the impudent redcoats aside and rightly give their beloved Emperor another blaze; a beacon, that would inform Europe that the master was back for good.

'*Vive l'Empereur!*'

The British and Dutch artillery were still firing and great gaps were showing in the phalanxes. As men were killed, the deaths caused ripples throughout the formations as the NCOs hauled and shoved men into those holes. Some lost cohesion as the soft ground was rain-soaked and the rye stalks tripped and officers shouted the order to close ranks.

The allied guns were double-shotted with canister and roundshot that twitched the front ranks to red ruin, and there was a strange rattling noise as the exploding balls struck musket stocks, yet the French formations soaked up the damage and continued their fervent advance.

'*Vive l'Empereur!*'

'Close up!' A sergeant shouted and a private next to him seemed to disintegrate as a roundshot hit him square in the chest. A drummer boy, guts ripped open by canister, sat in the mud and rattled his drum in even though he was slowly dying.

'Hoist the Eagles High!' An officer, mounted on a fine chestnut mare, shouted. He waved his expensive sabre up at the ridge, and tried to ignore a shako at his feet with half a man's head still in it. 'Hoist them! Let the bastards know we're coming for them!'

The Eagles were the French war standards, each one blessed in person by the Emperor, and they gleamed above the mass of mud-spattered men. The French were cheering with each step and their strong voices carried the tune of *la Marseillaise*. They always advanced in column and to the British officers it was the accepted attack mode. Most of the French infantry would not be able to use their muskets while every redcoat in two ranks could fire his weapon. Thousands of bayonet-tipped muskets now glimmered the ridge from La Haye Sainte to the farm of Papelotte to the east, and each flank was protected by cavalry.

For the Eagles and Tricolour flags had returned and the days of glory were in reach.

'Here come the ugly bastards!' Sergeant Weir shouted.

Bannerman could hear French voices clearly now over the sound of withering rifle fire coming from La Haye Sainte, the regimental bands, and gun-fire; the cacophony of battle. Then the crest seemed to shift and wobble as hundreds of plumed shakoes appeared and the rum dum, the rum dum, the rummadum dummadum dum dum of the *pas de charge* followed by a pause in which a rousing cry of '*Vive l'Empereur!*' made Bannerman's blood stir with memory. The air was dreadfully humid and he could feel a chill prickle of sweat lacing his back.

'Play louder!' Campbell ordered the bandsmen. He wanted pipes played to drown out the French chanting and war music.

The Gordons were playing *Johnny Cope* and now the Black Watch's pipers began to play *Highland Laddie*, which always instilled the Highlanders with a love of home, duty and loyalty to one another.

A brigade of Belgian infantry in front and to the right of the 42nd opened fire at the attacking French. Men fell, but it was not enough to stop them. The French, easily piercing the hedges that lined the slope, halted and Bannerman saw muskets level and a powerful volley tore into the Belgians from less than forty yards. Scores of men fell like stringless puppets and the remainder simply fled. The French cheered vociferously. Bannerman watched the Belgians leave, saw young frightened faces as they passed the veteran British battalions who jeered them, calling them milksops and girls, even when their officers beat at men to stand their ground and to return. One Highlander left his file to spit at them. 'You shite your breeks, you cowards!' he said. Bannerman clasped the private by the scuff of his neck and thrust him into his file.

'You stay there and keep you filthy mouth shut, you wee bastard,' he said to him before returning back to his position by Campbell.

'The Frogs are in line, RSM,' Campbell said, jutting his chin at the three deep ranks that flickered in the heat haze. 'I've never seen them come on like that.'

'They think to copy us, sir,' Bannerman replied. 'Spain taught them to fear our lines. However, a line always beats a column.'

'They dinnae look fretful,' Campbell said. 'They swagger. They look confident. They've just sent most of a Belgian brigade running after one volley.' He slid his basket-hilted broadsword a few inches to test that the oiled blade would not stick in the scabbard.

Bannerman watched the French finish reloading, but they did not move on afterwards. What were they waiting for? Cavalry support? Were they bringing up cannon to blast their way through?

An Aide galloped to Campbell, white breeches and polished top-boots all mud-splattered. 'Sir, you are ordered to immediately advance to the crest parallel with the 92nd and expel the French from the ridge. From there you will halt your men, careful not to advance any further and await further instructions.'

'Very well,' Campbell nodded, giving the Aide a salute.

The Black Watch and the Gordons advanced and Bannerman understood the immediacy of the order. More French infantry were joining the first French battalions, wheeling on the flanks to form a long thick line of troops. They wanted every musket to kill and the

459

British would try to deny them that initiative. Bannerman watched the enemy. At fifty yards muskets went to shoulders and the British still marched. He heard the French command of '*Tirez!*' and the French line spat flame and smoke and the first men of the Black Watch were killed. Not many, for the range was still far, but it was still saddening to see more Scotsmen die when the regiment was vastly under strength. A Highlander staggered groggily, like a man emerging from a drunken stupor. Another, still wearing a bandage around his head from a sabre wound at Quatre Bras, fell onto his haunches coughing up blood. The 42nd stepped over the wounded men and corpses as they marched on.

'Keep your dressing!' Sergeant Weir shouted the litany, as he forced a man back with a hand from going too fast. Each private was supposed to advance compactly with his elbows almost touching his left and right fileman.

A voice suddenly played in Bannerman's head. 'Advance thirty paces!' He searched his mind for the answer. For a moment he couldn't recollect it, but it spoke again and he knew the words had come from Lieutenant-Colonel James Stewart, his old regimental commander. *Funny to hear that now of all times*, Bannerman thought. *Was there any meaning in this? Was fate calling out to him?* The battalion had marched onto the sandy Egyptian plain at Alexandria in '01 and helped turn the tide of the battle. Thinking of that campaign brought back visions of old friends, deserts, weathered ruins and palm trees. He shook his head to clear those faraway days thinking that this might be life passing before his eyes.

But nae yet! Darrow and Sholto must die first!

The French, who had been ripped by the round-shot and riven by the appalling canister, gave a great cheer as they reloaded. They did not seem to fear the redcoats. They were confident that another volley, now with double the firepower, would do the job. One volley would clear the path and Général Jean-Baptiste Drouet, Count d'Erlon, would give the Emperor his victory.

At a distance of thirty yards, Campbell halted the Black Watch. 'You'll fire by platoons!' he bellowed.

Bannerman recalled that Stewart had said the same thing during the battle of Alexandria. *Perchance this was an omen that Wellington's men would win this day.*

'Ready,' Campbell took a deep breath. 'Present! Fire!'

A great thundercloud of musket smoke burst out as the volley fire by half-company's hammered into the enemy ranks. When the platoon had fired, it immediately began to reload, so that when the last platoon pulled their triggers, the first platoon would be loaded and ready to fire again. Men bit bullets from the tip of waxed paper cartridges, poured the black powder into their musket barrels, wadded the powder with the paper, spat down the bullets, and then rammed down the mixture with their ramrods. A Highlander swore, because he had mistakenly put the ball down the barrel before the powder, which meant it would not fire until he had extracted it. Bannerman thrust him his own loaded musket to use rather than try the tricky process in the heat of battle.

The French hit by the continuous onslaught staggered as the front ranks were felled like wheat chopped by an invisible scythe. Sergeants pulled men into the files, but almost instantly the new men were hit by bullets. A few backed away, but a wounded officer was bellowing at them to stay and fight.

'Fix bayonets!' The order was given and the British battalions halted firing to haul their seventeen-inch triangular socket-bayonet from their scabbards. 'Charge!' A loud hoarse voice called and Bannerman saw that it was General Picton riding beside the 92nd. He was wearing a black long-tailed overcoat and top hat, but there was no mistaking who it was. 'Charge the bastards!' He shouted readily, as though he was relishing the chance of slaughter. The drummers beat the Point of War. 'Charge! Hurrah!' And almost a heartbeat later, as two thousand redcoats surged forward against eight thousand French, a bullet punched its way through his forehead killing him instantly in the saddle.

'Charge!' Campbell roared. 'Avenge your fallen brothers!'

Behind the regiment, the bands played wildly, and the Highlanders shrieked like banshees as they drove their steel spikes into the French ranks. A few muskets banged to send a few Scotsmen to the grave, but the Black Watch and the Gordons plunged into the enemy and the French could not hold them back. They were frightened of the men in their kilts screaming a wild language and the fierceness in their faces. Bayonets stabbed and ripped into bodies, some used their muskets as clubs and blood spattered the ranks behind them.

'That's the way lads, spit 'em like hogs!' Weir exhorted.

'For Macara!' Captain Reid shouted, lunging with his broadsword to skewer a French Fusilier in the throat. 'For Scotland!'

Bannerman saw a Highlander jab his bayonet into a Fusilier's belly, rip it free, knock an enemy musket aside to thrust the blade up and underneath a grey-moustached grenadier's chin. It was Sholto and he

461

was shouting gleefully, enjoying the brutal killing. He gave the spike a savage twist, blood jetted from the man's mouth, and the corporal recovered, poised and thrust his gore-spattered bayonet into the next man.

Whatever Sholto might be, Bannerman knew he was an able and a fearsome soldier, nonetheless. He would be a difficult man to put down.

But suddenly there were more French approaching. The 92nd to the left of the 42nd looked to be overwhelmed and pushed back by superior numbers when the Earl of Uxbridge ordered Ponsonby's cavalry forward. The Scots Greys, on their huge white horses and wearing tall grenadier bearskins, had to walk across the muddy field, strewn with corpses, wet crops and a steep rise. Then trumpets blared; the sound shrill and haunting, and the heavy cavalry galloped down into the French line and smashed it apart. Bannerman watched one trooper cut through a Frenchman's shako down to his nose, and half-decapitate an officer who had brought his horse to intercept him. Some of the Gordons had dashed in with the horsemen, giving a great whoop of joy, and they slashed and killed with their bayonets shouting 'Scotland forever!'

The horsemen of the Union Brigade: English, Irish and Scotsmen, spilled down into the valley that shimmered in the afternoon heat, cutting through the packed French. A squadron of cuirassiers, who had just hacked apart a Hanoverian regiment by La Haye Sainte, had mistakenly spurred their way across the slope so that the British cavalry now smashed into their flank and so destroyed the armoured killers in a welter of blood and gleaming steel. Some of the wounded or unhorsed limped south, a few were shot dead by the expert German riflemen behind the farmhouse's walls in retaliation for killing their countrymen.

The Heavy Cavalry, whooping with glee, slashed and hacked with their straight-bladed swords at the French infantry that could not hold the press of horsemen back and broke apart like rotten wood. As men turned to flee, some threw down their muskets and held up their hands to surrender. Horses with brown-flecked teeth, bit and stamped, and the heavy swords reddened with the slaughter. The bugles were still calling and the horsemen, spattered with hot blood, were laughing like drunken devils because it was so easy. This was the stuff of dreams. Fleeing and scattered infantry on firm ground. Spurs raked back, the swords lifted high, and the riders shouted for more butchery.

Bannerman saw, in a clearing made by swirling smoke, a Scots Grey sergeant hefting a French Eagle. He was a hugely powerful man and had ridden his warhorse into the throng of the enemy and butchered the defenders who had tried to cling on to their sacred standard and now brought the prize back. Men cheered him and he carried it clear of the destroyed column where the enemy still died under hooves and by the brutal swords. There were so many heaps of bodies that horses tripped and stumbled. Sir James Kempt, senior brigade officer, who had taken control of the division after Picton's death, ordered his and Pack's brigade back across the reverse slope for fear that the French guns might cause considerable casualties.

'That was the most beautiful thing I ever saw,' Anderson said in wonder.

'Quiet, Lieutenant,' Darrow snapped at him.

Bannerman could hear the blare of the bugles call to reform, but from his position as the Black Watch returned, he could just about see that the cavalry were still hacking their way south and some had captured a battery of guns where they killed all the gunners, cut the traces and harnesses and sent the artillery mounts away. Bugles called again, this time frantically, but Bannerman knew the horsemen had their blood up and nothing would make them listen. There were now hundreds of prisoners under guard. They had been stripped of their equipment, muskets and possessions and were taken north by Belgian militia and survivors of the Inniskillings to the allied rear. The wounded, some with terrible slash words and deep cuts, filed to the small Mont St-Jean farm along the road, which was designated as the main field hospital.

Bannerman stood with Campbell in front of the battalion, which was less than a hundred yards from the crest. But the summit was obscured now by thick skeins of gun smoke which resembled sea fog sweeping over the coast and was difficult to see anything at all. He could hear the sounds of horses: hundreds of them, thundering across the valley, the metalwork sound of blades meeting and men screaming and dying. Groups of all sizes of the Heavy Cavalry returned, some missing their hats, some dismounted, but most blood-stained and wary of a great threat to their rear.

'Damned Crapaud lancers!' An Inniskilling Dragoon captain said to a friend who was trying to staunch a nasty wound to his neck. 'Quite spoilt the ball!'

'Looks like Boney's cavalry gave ours a bloody kicking,' Campbell uttered, then stared at a frightened horse as it had returned with the fragments of the cavalry.

There was also a fire fight to the south-east where one of the French columns had tried to dislodge the troops of Saxe-Weimar from the stout farmhouses in the tangle of lanes and hedges, but the Germans fought resolutely and the continued musketry proved their stubbornness. Bannerman looked to the east where the fields and woods were silent and empty. The French attack on Wellington's centre and left had come close to success and still the Prussians had not come.

A cannon-ball whipped through the veiled sky to smash into the Grenadier Company, sending three men into the air like ejected toys. One of the men had lost both legs and kept trying to rise until a sergeant ordered the private taken away in a litter. Bannerman could see the confused look on the man's face as though he couldn't comprehend his plight. Another ball thrummed in the air, but it hit a great puddle of water between the brigade causing no injuries.

A flurry of hooves caused Bannerman to turn around in time to see a Staff Officer galloping in front of the brigades. 'Pull back! One hundred yards! To your markers! Back and lie down! Back!'

Campbell turned his horse to face his Highlanders. 'Black Watch! We go back now, but this is no defeat! We walk proud and remain strong!'

The allies retreated back to the muddy fields and trampled rye where shells exploded and roundshot skimmed the crest, churning crops and furrowing the field like a plough-team. Howitzers lobbed shells over Hougoumont which started a fire, but the defenders still denied the French the château. Erratic musket fire sounded from the hamlet some way beyond Papelotte to the south-east, and still the French guns fired up at the ridge.

'Look at that,' Private Watt exclaimed at the rent in his kilt near his groin. 'The Frenchie ball went right through. I'm a lucky man.'

'It's lucky you never had much of a cock anyway,' Weir replied gruffly, causing the men to laugh.

A shell burst overhead the Black Watch, knocking down six men. Five remained motionless whilst the sixth writhed and coiled like an adder. Bannerman couldn't see the wound, but the private's red coat was darkening with blood and he gave a great shudder and then was still. It was then that Captain Hamilton fell from his horse. Bannerman and two corporals turned him over, but he was unconscious, and it was then that the wound was revealed. A fragment of shell casing had shattered his left shoulder and gashed open his neck to leave a hole where tendon's glistened and bone glinted white. They used Hamilton's sash to bind it and Bannerman ordered four men to carry him in a litter to the surgeons. He noticed that Hamilton still wore his buckled dancing shoes from the Brussels ball.

'How is he?' Campbell asked.

'He'll live, sir,' Bannerman said. 'Might lose the arm, but he's alive.'

Campbell, mounted on his horse, suddenly gasped. 'My God!' he said in astonishment, staring down into the valley. He fumbled to pull out his telescope tucked in his sash.

'What is it, sir?' Bannerman asked.

'The Emperor's sending every bloody horseman up here!'

Bannerman moved to the right where there was a lip of ground and saw a sight he had never witnessed before. He was stunned. The ground moved in one seething mass of cavalry. Through the palls of smoke, the afternoon sunlight glinted on breastplates, helmets, swords and lance points. Regiment after regiment of cuirassiers, dragoons, *carabiniers*, *chasseurs* and lancers were forming for an attack. More British officers trained their expensive scopes on the cavalry, all entranced by the glittering sea of steel.

'Where is his infantry?' Bannerman said, returning to his post. Campbell didn't answer. 'Boney's going to send them all up here unsupported?' he said, sounding dubious.

'His infantry appears to be reforming after the attack, but none are advancing.'

'Or he thinks we're so battered by the guns that we're unable to stand.'

Campbell rubbed his face. 'Even so, cavalry alone cannae beat us.'

'It's suicide, sir,' Bannerman said.

'They're desperate,' Campbell remarked. 'That's the only reasonable answer I can think of.'

Brigade officers galloped among the lines ordering every battalion into square, but marking them out so that every formation was staggered and thus unable to fire on each other. But the French guns, some brought close to the ridge when the army withdrew a hundred yards, were now able to fire roundshot and shell into the forming squares. Bannerman watched a roundshot skim the top of the crest, bounce and plummet straight at the 92nd, tossing eight men into the air like rag dolls. Bandsmen took the wounded away, the dead were used as barricades outside the kneeling front rank. The NCOs moved men into the gaping holes to keep the formation tight.

Bannerman could hear the thunder of hooves, the metallic chink of the horse furniture and the slap of scabbards. Gunfire sounded and the first of the French cavalry were dying. The gunners frantically reloaded before the might of France reached the heights.

A trumpet sounded and Bannerman could feel the ground shake even though the cavalry were in a mass of lines between the blazing fires of Hougoumont and the pock-marked walls of La Haye Sainte. They attacked the right wing, whilst Wellington's left merely looked on, grimacing and shuddering from cannon-fire still firing up from Bonaparte's centre. More blasts of British guns and then the cuirassiers galloped over the summit only to find the enemy army all in perfect squares.

'Prepare to receive cavalry!' the cry rang out.

Bannerman saw a side of a square suddenly blossom white smoke and the first cuirassiers were plucked from their saddles. Balls hammered into breastplates with the sound of hail striking glass. Horses screamed and fell, hooves thrashed, and riders tried desperately to extricate themselves, and behind them still more crowded the tight spaces. Men shouted and as the horsemen swerved and wheeled between the squares like water breaking against rocks, more musketry tore into them. Practiced volley fire stabbed the air and the horsemen could only suffer and endure the storm of lead. Men were hit and falling from their mounts. Others were ridden over and some had already limped or crawled south to look for more horses or to escape the dreadful butchery.

And still the horsemen came. *Carabiniers*, dragoons, lancers and *chasseurs* tried to pierce and stab the square's front ranks who gripped their bayonet-tipped muskets steadily, whilst the two rear ranks aimed and fired over their heads.

'Fire!' Officers shouted and immediately muskets kicked bruised shoulders and the horsemen could not penetrate the squares. It was chaos. The air was thickening with smoke and a man was only able to see a few yards in front of him. Shapes of horses and sword-armed men gathered and moved like phantoms.

'Kill the horses!'

A cavalryman was nothing without his mount and soon the spaces between the squares were clogging up with the dead and dying. Horses shook with bullets. A trumpeter's mare drummed its hooves on blood-sheeted crops. A *carabinier*'s horse reared and then fell back onto its rider crushing him to death. A dragoon fired his carbine into a British flank and was then obliterated when the redcoats fired a volley into him and at the mass of riders behind. Bannerman could hear the screams and could only look on in horror as the Frenchmen turned and wheeled back down the muddy ridge to charge up to the right wing again. The British gunners, who had found refuge in the squares, raced out to the empty guns out on the ridge, which the cavalry had not spiked, and the long barrels blasted double-shotted canister into retreating backs, or those charging again. A *carabinier* was hit by a roundshot and the man disintegrated in a spray of crimson. A *chasseur*, his face a mask of blood, slashed impotently at bayonets as he rode past. Horses tumbled and rolled. An unhorsed cuirassier ran at a square, brandishing his long sword, when he was stabbed in the thighs and clubbed to unconsciousness. A lancer, shot in both legs, was still riding in the sixth wave of the assault.

The churned ground was like a slaughter yard. Hooves slipped on entrails and dung. Men twitched, bled and died. And the French still reformed in the valley and charged again. Horses were panting and glossy with sweat. Blood dripped from spurs, lances quivered in the turf and men choked and drowned in puddles and channels of mud.

'Those brave souls,' Campbell said of the French.

'Mad bastards, sir,' Bannerman corrected.

'I dinnae think we'll ever witness such a splendorous thing ever again.'

'I truly hope not, sir.'

Another assault came again, only this time it was slower because the horses were tired and the French ranks were thinner because of loss. If a lancer could reach out and stab an enemy in the front rank on the first wave, by now he could not reach the same man with his lance-arm outstretched due to the mounds of bodies. A cuirassier, armoured breastplate dented by ricocheting musket-fire and streaked with mud, charged a gun. He kicked back his spurs, eager to reach the gun team that were hastily reloading it. But he was too late. The cannon erupted and the Frenchman was snatched back like a handful of chaff held in a palm and then blown. Bannerman had a vision of splitting metal, horseflesh and then nothing but a cloud of red gore that misted the air.

By the next wave Bannerman gaped on in utter disbelief. It was unnecessary. The Emperor was slaughtering his own men by sending

467

them again and again. They had lost, but pride would not back down. *Go back*, he found himself saying. He knew it was wrong, but it was ridiculous. *That's enough, you stupid bastards. Enough!*

Volley fire swept through the weary horsemen and again they could not break the squares. Casualties mounted in the defenders from pistol and carbine shots, and sabres managed to find victims, and as they fell the officers and NCOs replaced them with men from the rear ranks. The dead and dying offered a barricade against the hooves and enemy blades.

'Why the hell are they still attacking?' Anderson asked Bannerman.

'They dinnae know defeat, sir.'

Muskets flamed, burnt wadding glowed like motes of whirling ash and the volleys flickered orange in the smoke. A *carabinier*, weeping from the failure, limped south. A dying cuirassier called out the names of his children. A *chasseur* spat at the squares before wrenching his tired mount around and trotted away.

The French cavalry had been beaten and not one square had been breached. They withdrew broken, bloodied and bitter. As the last of them left the ridge, the guns were sighted and they were stirred to life again.

*

'Ma! Ma! Where's da?' Robbie Grant called out.

'If I knew where, my lad,' Beth answered, 'we'd already be with him, now widnae we?'

They were waiting at the edge of the Forest of Soignes, having walked all through the night and were now shattered. Rain had assailed their clothes, but they had at least found shelter underneath a wagon carrying a battalion's equipment. A benevolent Dragoon sergeant took pity and managed to acquire some straw which he spread on the mud and provided them with a thick blanket. They had been halted there by a troop of cavalry which had been tasked to stop the company wives, camp followers and even civilians from getting to the battle. There were so many wagons and carts and tents and streams of men walking north towards Brussels and even a line of French prisoners. They looked terrified and walked with their heads bowed to their chests.

The sky was dark and the air thick with the rumble of cannon and musketry. Beth gawked at a great pall of smoke lit by gun flashes, rising high above the village of Mont St-Jean. *Like sheet-lightning*, she

468

thought. The din of battle was almost deafening. All she could think about was Ran and where he might be.

'I miss, da,' Robbie said tearfully and then yawned.

Beth pulled him closer, watching a wagon of wounded men in all uniforms trundle up the road. 'I miss him too,' she told him, placing a kiss on his head. 'It won't be long now.'

Beth mouthed a silent prayer and tried not to let the claws of sleep take her.

*

The cannon-fire assaulted the entire ridge line. The crest was torn ragged by the gale of shot that seemed to be out of vengeance for the destruction of the cavalry. Some of the guns fired close and the shot hit ammunition wagons and gun limbers exploding in great gouts of orange-flame behind Wellington's men who had been ordered to lie down again once the threat of cavalry was deemed no more. Burning flesh, grease and gunpowder mingled with the stench of the dead. British guns were also targets and Bannerman saw a gun team destroyed by a well-aimed French shell.

And on it continued.

The bombardment was so intense that some men were sure the roar of the cannons was making them deaf for good. Bannerman could now feel the heat of the guns as the blasts punched their shots through the air. There was so much gun smoke that it was bringing on a premature dusk. Bannerman looked at the men about him. They were like the rest of the army; bruised and worn out. Their faces were freckled with mud, blackened by powder, and grimy with sweat. Buick was praying. Gray was hollow-eyed and numb. Reid was thinking of his children and the wife he had been unfaithful to. Weir just stared malevolently at the French. Anderson offered Bannerman a half-smile and shuddered when the next salvo came. Campbell gripped the hilt of his sword and gazed at the two Colours that were so frayed and torn by bullets that it was difficult to see the regimental number. The air was thick and men coughed and swilled out dry mouths with water from their canteens. Nobody spoke. They waited and endured the guns that belched sulphurous smoke and flashed red fire.

A shell landed in front of the regiment, where it fizzed brightly and whirled about. Men rolled and moved as far away as they could before it exploded killing ten men.

'Jesus, that was close!' Anderson panted. The jacket-sleeve on his right arm was in tatters, a graze to his hand, but little else.

He had been lucky. Bannerman watched as the bandsmen began to clear away the bodies, one of whom was Buick, whose windpipe had been ripped open by the blast.

The cannonade eventually weakened and brought about the sound of heavy musketry to the west where La Haye Sainte flanked the road. To Bannerman it sounded near. Very near and very desperate.

Somewhere a church bell was ringing wildly, the peal was coming from beyond the farms to the south where a village was situated in a hollow on the French right.

Major-General Sir Dennis Pack, mounted on his well-bred chestnut charger, trotted over to Campbell. Bannerman wouldn't hear the conversation, but they talked for a while, both twisting to gaze eastwards to which Bannerman, to his horror, saw shapes moving below a smoky ochre sky. Were they Prussians or French? He turned back to see Pack smiling and immediately realised they were the Prussian vanguard. He felt a surge of relief.

'RSM,' Campbell beckoned him over and saw his smile. 'So you dinnae need me to tell you the good news.'

'No, sir,' Bannerman grinned.

'The fight isnae over for us yet. We've been ordered to assist the Nassauers over there,' he said, dipping his head at Saxe-Weimar's men to the east. 'The French threw them out of a hamlet and the farms when the column's attacked earlier. The Germans havenae been able to reclaim their territory and now, as the Prussians are coming, it may cause them a delay on reaching Boney's flank. The Duke cannae have them delay any longer. They must fall on the French flank. We're to go down there and help Prince Bernhard's men turf the Crapaud bastards out for good.'

'Just us, sir?'

'No, the Gordons are coming too.'

'The division's best men, sir,' Bannerman said with a smirk, then watched a red-coated Aide gallop hard towards the Germans with the new orders.

Campbell chortled. 'Best of the army. I'm sending the Grenadiers and Light Company first. Battalion to go column of companies. Quarter distance.'

'Very good, sir,' Bannerman saluted, turned to face the regiment and took a lungful of breath. '42nd! Stand up! Column of companies!'

He bellowed loudly, but in a calm and precise manner. 'Quarter distance! Form up!'

Campbell wanted the battalion in the formation whereby each company would march in line a width of no more than twenty-two yards and a depth of fifty-five yards. The space between each company was about five yards. It was a very tight formation, but frequently used for initial deployment, the men being kept under close control of their officers and NCOs and it facilitated ease of movement perfectly in unknown territory.

The 42nd went first, glad to leave the awful artillery fire, and followed the land passing Dutch and Hanoverian infantry and cavalry guarding the left flank. The mud gave way to grass speckled with wildflowers and then more crop fields. The Highlanders followed the middle of three dirt roads south, which soon became a green tangle of ancient paths shouldered by high banks, some fifteen feet high and topped with tree-lined hedgerows. Bannerman could understand why infantry were kings here: the sunken lanes provided the Germans with excellent defensive ditches that made cavalry manoeuvring impossible and would greatly hinder limbering artillery.

Nevertheless, heading towards the sound of musketry, where at a junction of ancient oaks so close together they resembled a bucolic chapel, they were met by the first Nassauers, German troops in Dutch service. A tall man wearing a short green long-tailed jacket, black facings piped yellow, expensive boots and a hand casually placed on the pommel of his sheathed sword, half-leaped, half-skidded down the embankment, leaving a dozen men of his men eying the Highlanders suspiciously. More flocked like starlings at the opposite bank, impressing Bannerman with their vigilance. Campbell halted the battalion whereby Major Donald MacDonald, commanding officer of the Gordons, rushed up to meet the German.

'*Majoor* Johann Sattler, at your service,' the German bowed elegantly after the Highlanders gave introductions. He had a genial air about him, firm-jawed with bright brown eyes. He seemed bemused by their strange uniform, then saw their half-shadowed fierce faces staring back, so he kept his thoughts to himself. 'How goes the battle?'

Campbell explained the events so far from what he had seen. 'We've survived an artillery bombardment from hell and thousands of French cavalry. I've never seen a battlefield like it,' he admitted. 'Flame and smoke and dying. It's hell on earth.'

Sattler studied the Highlanders as he listened, noticing their red coats and faces black with powder residue so that they looked like chimney sweeps. 'May I ask your presence here?' Sattler enquired, as faint lances of slanting sunlight through trees brightened the eastern embankments and giving it a lurid glow.

Campbell explained their task in full. 'So you see, *Majoor*,' he said, summing up, 'we are here to assist you and to secure the hamlet of Smohain and push back the Frogs from the farms and heights.'

Sattler's face set hard. 'My men have not given ground so easily,' he said in a tone that his men were being slighted because the Highlanders had been sent. A French ball had torn a hole through his French-style shako and his face was grimy with sweat, powder and mud, proving he had been in the thick of the fighting too. 'It has been quite severe.'

'I have seen you Nassauers fight and I know that you would have challenged the Frogs with every step,' Campbell said with genuine praise. 'Can you help us with the terrain?'

Sattler considered that, then nodded and pointed a hand up towards the left bank. 'Up there is the farm of La Haye,' his hand flicked to the right, 'and over there is Papelotte. Both buildings are now occupied by my countrymen. Beyond La Haye the road twists east, then runs south to Smohain. To the east of the hamlet there is a large château called Frischermont. Both are in French hands.'

'Nae for long,' MacDonald growled.

'Frischermont doesnae concern us, Donald,' Campbell's reproach was softly spoken.

'Beware of Smohain,' Sattler warned. 'The ground itself is flooded from the rains and the French have artillery guarding the streets and the woods beyond the hamlet. They have also barricaded the roads with what they could, as well as the houses. It will be a hard fight. I know because I have been there. I came back to order the last of my reinforcements forward.'

Suddenly a roundshot screamed through the air, crashing through an oak tree and sending green boughs and bark down onto the bank to the right of the 42nd. The ball disappeared into the fields towards Papelotte.

'The French have turned your flank, sir!' MacDonald fumed.

'They can't have!'

472

Sattler turned and clambered up the verge. Campbell, MacDonald and Bannerman followed. The Nassau officer quickly pulled out his telescope and trained the lens on the eastern fields thick with tall crops.

'It's the Prussians,' Campbell exclaimed using his own scope. He frowned, wondering why they would be firing artillery at the Germans, then as Sattler swore, he studied his uniform realising the Nassauers were being mistaken for the French.

A shell, fired by an unseen cannon, exploded to the left of La Haye and two men went down screaming. Bannerman heard another two guns discharge and heard the impact further south, where the Nassauers skirmished on the outskirts of Smohain.

'They're killing my men!' Sattler protested.

'We have to let them know we're here too, sir,' Bannerman blurted.

Campbell stared at the dark-clad Prussians one more time, then snapped the lid shut. 'We'll advance on Smohain and then use the heights by La Haye to send a signal or send a man back to brigade and get them to send an Aide to our allies.' A roundshot smashed into a hedge scattering a group of Nassauers sheltering from French musket fire north of the hamlet. 'You'd better tell your lads that we're here, *Majoor*. I dinnae want to lose any of my men to friendly musketry.'

Sattler nodded vigorously and ran ahead of the grenadiers. The Highlanders marched off down the road glimpsing the walls of La Haye as they passed it. They couldn't see Papelotte, but that was not their destination. It was Smohain and where the 42nd followed the road east, then south, the air was dense with cannon-fire and musketry. Campbell halted the men just at the roads bend to scrutinise the area.

A company of Nassauers were skirmishing from the grassy embankments and woods leading into the hamlet. Over the stone bridge, where an overflowing brook spilled onto the banks, a makeshift barricade had been thrown up between white-painted buildings to block the road towards Frischermont that would eventually curl west to a village upon the French right flank called Plancenoit. The hamlets cobbled streets were also blocked with barricades. A Prussian roundshot plummeted down through the woods to the east into boggy ground and doing no damage. Bannerman could see many bodies on the bridge, where blood trickled to mix with the slow-flowing brook, and at the edges of the houses. French and German dead. The buildings walls were pock-marked by musketry. A few stragglers of wounded men made their way towards La Haye. Sattler shouted at them to go west to Papelotte for fear of the blundering Prussian guns killing them.

473

A volley of musketry crashed out from straight ahead, but no Nassauers went down to French bullets. A drummer was tightening the instruments drum skin, then gave a little flurry with his sticks. A crouching NCO with a bandage wound tight around his head watched Sattler approach him and went to stand, but the officer waved him down. The two spoke beside the shoulder of grass. Another volley sounded and this time a green-coated German gasped and fell forward into the brook. He scrabbled, blood diluting from a shoulder wound and cried out in pain when a comrade rushed over and hauled him by his wounded arm back onto muddy ground. Sattler pointed at the Highlanders and the German NCO, having lost an eye at Quatre Bras to a French Lance, rubbed underneath the grimy bandage and then examined the contents on his finger. A shell landed near the eastern barricade, whirling around and exploded harmlessly. Bannerman heard the balls strike stone.

'We need to shift those bastards!' MacDonald pointed at the barricades and had to yell as a Prussian ball hit the Nassauers near the bridge, taking an arm off one lad who looked fifteen or sixteen-years-old, and a foot off a man who was running with spare ammunition.

'We need to stop those Prussian guns,' Bannerman suggested. 'We're caught here between two attacks.'

The German teenager was sobbing for his mother and was helped away by two men. Both looked eager to depart and Bannerman couldn't blame them. The man with the severed foot, with the help of a companion, hobbled away using his musket as a crutch, leaving the haversack stuffed with cartridges for another to take his place. A young officer hefted the deep-yellow Nassau flag at the French to show that their resolution was still as firm as ever.

Then Bannerman had an idea. 'Permission to try something, sir,' he said, black eyes blazing. 'I think I can stop their artillery.' He didn't wait for Campbell to reply and led the two ensigns of the Colour party towards the eastern heights above stunted trees, sodden with brackish water. Midges buzzed about the ears. 'Up here!' he called, unceremoniously pulling the last ensign to the crest. 'The Prussians are over there and think we're the enemy,' he said to the stand-bearers. 'We're going to give them a shock.' He picked out several blocks that denoted the guns and saw figures moving besides them; the Prussian artillery battery. 'Unfurl them fully and wave them,' he ordered. The ensign holding the King's Colour had difficulty in using his strength to wield the heavy standard back-and-forth, so Bannerman tore it from his hands and waved it like a madman. The battery disappeared behind smoke and roundshot whipped down into the hamlet. A ball skidded along cobbles. A man shouted, but it seemed no one had been hit. 'Come on, you bastards!' Bannerman bellowed. 'Look this way! We're allies!'

It was dusk and the falling sun was gilding the east, rifting clouds scarlet and gold, but the mounted Prussian artillery officers watching saw the two flags, their red coats and understood their grave error. Bannerman, sweating, watched the artillery limber up, men and horses moved away, and he breathed a sigh of relief.

Campbell slapped his back on his return. 'We're going left to take the first defence, and the Gordons will take the central one. We'll link up at the last barricade and rush the bastards westwards. The bulk of *Majoor* Sattler's men will remain here, but he's accompanying us with three companies; one being *jägers*.'

Whistles blew and the two Highland Light Companies ran forward to join the battered Nassauers who took up positions to then join the other elite company; the grenadiers in the assault. The flankers were big men, tall and strong and they were suited for this work. The skirmishers hammered shots at the barricades, throwing down a *chasseur* who was aiming from a doorway.

'Watch the windows!' Campbell ordered, scanning the upper levels for enemy marksmen.

As the shots rained in on the defences, the grenadiers from the Gordons darted across the bridge and in the act of, a concealed gun from the central blockade, roared to life. The French gunners had timed it well and the tin can exploded to obliterate a half-dozen Highlanders. One minute they were running and the next churned to bloody offal in an instant. MacDonald was furious and led the remaining grenadiers over the blood-splattered stone, with bayonet-tipped muskets, at the barricade. Blades stabbed, muskets flashed, boots kicked and revenge was sworn.

French muskets traded fire and Bannerman saw one of Captain Reid's men, slide back down the bank, blood pumping from his shattered skull. The Black Watch's grenadiers, under Lieutenant Pinkerton, were making similar progress, but the defences were holding and this whole attack had been a risky strategy. The wet ground was a death-trap and the French had positioned the barricade in a way so that it would be suicide to try to cross the mire rather than attack the defences. Bannerman watched a grenadier stumble from a bullet in the marshy ground and another took a pistol shot to his face.

'Permission to assist them, sir?'

Campbell gaped, twisted to stare at the grenadiers, and then turned back to him. 'Granted, RSM.'

'Thank you, sir.' Bannerman rose to his feet and jogged over to join Pinkerton. He felt his palms slicken, and wiped them instinctively on the red wool of his coat. A musket banged, and the bullet fluttered past him. He pulled a wounded private aside, then swung his pole-arm straight down to cleave through a length of timber making an ear-splitting crack. A bayonet jabbed at him, but it was off balance and missed. Bannerman moved another grenadier aside and chopped down through a thick branch cut from the trees by a *sapeur's* axe earlier in the day, and suddenly the barricade shuddered. A gap appeared and Pinkerton rammed his sword into it and was rewarded with a scream. A musket flashed and it snatched at the red vulture plume in Bannerman's bonnet, an item once given in honour to each man after the battle of Geldermalsen in 1795, during the Flanders Campaign. The Highlanders had charged the French, bloodily repulsed a counter-attack that caused the enemy horrendous casualties, and recovered two captured field guns. Now the air was misted with charred bits of red fluff.

The Highlanders heaved and kicked at the barricade and Bannerman brought his unfashionable pole-arm down a third time that sheered through a Frenchman's hand, cutting off all his fingers, and thudding into a large beam where the blade stuck fast. Bannerman tried to wrench it free, but a gap-toothed Frenchman thrust a bayonet over the beams at his chest. He let go of the haft, dodged aside and the blade knocked his bonnet off. He could smell the man's fetid breath. A grenadier seized the enemy's weapon, but Bannerman recovered and clasped the Frenchman with both hands and dragged him over the falling defences and into the press of Highlanders. Two bayonets thrust deep into his chest and Bannerman stamped on his face, breaking his remaining teeth.

The barricade shuddered and collapsed. Scotsmen cheered and the grenadiers clambered over the barrels, branches, crates, boxes and lengths of timber. A score of Frenchmen had fought there and most were fleeing. Bannerman tripped on a body, ignoring the enemy at his knees who was sobbing from his mutilated hand, and put a boot to the wood to free his ancient halberd. A knot of Frenchmen offered defiance, but Highland blades killed them. A French officer had fled towards a door and Pinkerton was on him like a terrier on a rat. The Frenchman had to fight desperately, but he was no match against Pinkerton who was rumoured to have been a bastard child of a wealthy Edinburgh fencing instructor. Pinkerton parried a cut, turned his opponent's blade aside and skewered him straight through the heart in the time it takes a man to draw a cartridge from his ammunition box.

Pinkerton led Bannerman into the house, half-expecting resistance, but it was empty. Through a long passageway that smelt of herbs and cooked meat, there was a door leading from the kitchen, a room crossed by heavy beams. Bannerman slowly edged to it, hearing French voices outside. He saw them through a gap in the wood and grinned. Pinkerton understood and sent word for the grenadiers to follow.

The door burst open and Bannerman charged out first. The halberd almost decapitated the nearest Frenchman who had been reloading his pistol. Blood sprayed across and up to the next house. A short man with a tanned face came at him. He thrust his sword hoping to cut Bannerman's gullet, but it was a wild swing, and Bannerman dodged, kicked the man between the legs feeling something give, and brought the halberd's haft across his face. The officer crumpled, nose broken, but fell down without a sound. Pinkerton killed two men before they even knew he was there. The French defenders turned and saw that the enemy now threatened their rear. Highlanders poured from the doorway, snarling and crowed, teeth bared like a pack of wild dogs scenting the kill. Muskets flashed and one grenadier was torn back, but MacDonald's men hacked and pounded the barricade, which wavered under the strain. The French scattered as best they could but were caught between the Scotsmen. Men threw down their muskets and put their hands up, but Highland blood was up and none were given quarter.

The grenadiers searched the houses by bayonet point, whilst the Light Companies ran up the cobbled roads, skirmishing with fast retreating *voltigeurs* who fired and retired in pairs. Sattler's green uniformed *jägers* joined in with the attack. Armed with hunting rifles and sword bayonets, they expertly used all available cover to throw the French back westwards, away from the farms where they could make bastions to threaten Wellington's flank, or cause havoc to the Prussian advance.

Bannerman kicked a grenadier out of a house for looting, then saw that Campbell and the rest of the Gordons were now streaming across the bridge, ready to retake Smohain. He followed Pinkerton towards the next house where the street was at its widest. Musket smoke hung in the air. Blood trickled slowly between the cobbles. There was a steaming manure heap that stank. Bannerman heard French voices and edged around the corner of the house. Two Horse Artillery guns were positioned well so that they faced the main thoroughfare. An enemy charging would have to cross fifty feet of open ground where the guns would likely fire grape or canister to turn any attack into a massacre.

'We'll never make the distance,' Pinkerton hissed.

'We won't need to, sir,' Bannerman replied with a grin.

Sattler's *jägers* trained their rifles on the gunners from windows, doorways and walls. He gave them just one command: 'Make your shots count!'

The rifles crashed their brass butts into shoulders made raw by the day's skirmishing. Dirty smoke fogged Smohain, but the rifle fire had been accurate. Bannerman saw the two teams destroyed in an instant. An officer, hit by two bullets, nevertheless managed to wheel his horse west and gallop away unscathed from any further shot at his retreating back. Pinkerton led his grenadiers to the guns to find a man jerking and dying on the road and another trying to crawl away. The rest were all dead. One of the artillery horses was on its side, bright blood pumping from where a ball had pierced its throat. Bannerman put it out of its misery. The other horses, whinnied, but remained in their traces and harnesses.

With the gunners eliminated, Sattler took his men through the woodland to Frischermont, appearing moments later to tell Campbell that it was in fact deserted and that he would garrison it with a company and order the remainder of his men west to fall on the French right. Campbell was worried that there was French cavalry and artillery behind the grassy heights that overlooked the hamlet. However, there was a fierce sound of musketry coming from Plancenoit and so he considered that what French was once there, had now possibly been pulled away to protect the Emperor's rear from the increasing Prussian advance.

'I'll take my rogues up there,' MacDonald pointed the ridgeline with the tip of his broadsword, then back to the two farms across the Smohain brook, marshland and westbound road, a mere track, up ahead that linked the farms. 'Secure the line with your men at La Haye and the Germans at Papelotte. From there we'll spot any Crapaud movement.'

'And if needs be, we'll have the high ground and the farms to fall back on,' Campbell said, agreeing to the plan. 'And then what?'

MacDonald grinned wolfishly. 'What say we go hunting?'

'Ware cavalry!' Bannerman suddenly warned, as a troop of green-coated horsemen appeared past the road. They were unmistakably French Hussars and wore fur busbies with red plumes denoting they were men of that particular regiment's elite company. They saw the Highlanders and drew their sabres.

'Battalion - fix bayonets!'

The Highlanders hauled their seventeen-inch blades free of their scabbards and slotted them onto their muskets.

The Hussars formed into a grim battle line.

For France. For glory.

*

Beth opened her eyes. They were wet with tears. She had dreamt of Ran and her husband was dead. She saw him lying on straw, bloodied and lifeless. When she stirred, she realised she had been sleeping on a straw bed and that made her weep.

She had no idea what the time was, but the gunfire was still intense revealing that the fight was not over, yet it was after dusk.

She shared the food Madame Rademaker had provided with Robbie. A flurry of hooves and urgent shouts got her attention. She craned her head to see green-coated cavalrymen who were trying to thread through the mass of traffic on the road to Waterloo to the north. They looked frustrated at the difficulties of passing the obstacles as well as desperate and afraid.

'The battle is lost!' An officer was shouting loudly in accented English. Beth thought he sounded German, rather than Dutch or Belgian and they were certainly not a British regiment. A line of bedraggled wounded limped past. 'You see!' The officer pointed at them as though they backed up his blustering 'Bonaparte has won! You must warn everyone! You must flee!'

A British Staff Officer, fiery-cheeked, sweat-stained and flecked with mud, rode up to the man, and seized his bridle. 'Colonel Von Hacke,' he said in a Scottish accent. 'His Grace asks that you return to your post forthwith.' The cavalry officer tried to pull the bridle from the Staff Officer's gloved hands, which seemed to anger him. 'Immediately, sir!' he bellowed. 'You must understand the regulations of warfare. You must understand that any further withdrawal will be seen as a direct act of cowardice. Do your duty, sir! Return to your post forthwith!'

But the green-clad cavalryman ignored the threat, yanked free the leather bridle, and kicked his spurs back. The Staff Officer cursed, shook his head, and then wheeled his horse around to head back to the battle lines.

And Beth had an idea.

It was desperate. It was deadly and it was selfish.

But it was the only thing she could do.

*

Both sides watched each other, but neither the Hussars nor the Highlanders moved.

Gunfire thundered and in the distance the château Hougoumont was a blackened shell withering in an inferno of red fire, yet still held by the British Guards. Shells burst like fiery ink spots in the darkening sky above the valley.

'It's proved to be a thorn in the Emperor's fat arse,' MacDonald said of Hougoumont.

There were perhaps seventy Hussars and the Highlanders considered that they would not charge home. The redcoats had been ordered into column of companies so that both battalions blocked the trail into Smohain.

'If there are more Frog cavalry behind the trees,' Bannerman said to Campbell, 'and they somehow evade the Nassauers in the château, then they could threaten our rear, sir.'

Campbell chewed his bottom lip. 'Agreed, RSM,' he said, and immediately sent back two companies to guard the approach. 'That should give us a fair warning.'

The Hussars had still not moved and Bannerman was beginning to think that they were still weighing up the odds. This was a deadly game. As far as he could comprehend, that if they decided to attack, they would lose. The Highlanders would fire a volley, form a defensive stance with bayonets and there was little manoeuvring for cavalry to pass their flanks by the heights and the boggy ground running alongside the water-cleaved channel.

'What the bloody hell are they waiting for?' Campbell said tensely.

Then Bannerman saw why the Hussars had not moved. French infantry, a battalion strong, advanced to the lip of tufty grass. The horseman had been waiting for infantry support all along and now combined, they presented the Highlanders with a potentially fatal decision: to retreat or to stand firm.

French skirmishers ran forward in loose order and Bannerman knew if MacDonald and Campbell sent their Light Companies to challenge them, the Hussars would cut them down.

The slope dotted with smoke and the French muskets found targets. Bannerman saw the Hussars edge closer, as if anticipating the Highlanders' disorder. The Gordons didn't move, they simply endured the onslaught of musketry. The *voltigeurs* came forward. Bullets hissed and thrummed. Bannerman saw Pinkerton stagger, blood cascading down his face. More bullets hit men, killing and wounding.

Then Bannerman saw movement at La Haye. Green-coated men, with orange cockades on their shakoes. Nassauers, and he smiled. Sattler had seen the danger and sent his men to the farm walls and trees. MacDonald saw them too and let out a whoop. He ordered his leading company to fire a volley, which threw down the closest skirmishers, then before the French battalion had even formed for the attack, he sent his regiment up the slope in a wild bayonet charge. Drums hammered the assault and the Scotsmen, like devil-beasts unleashed for a blood-letting, screamed and yelled unearthly sounds.

The French fled. They bolted in sheer panic and the attack dissipated like morning dew in sunshine. The Highlanders hacked and stabbed at the *voltigeurs* unable to get away in time and the slope was splashed with blood. The Hussars decided to charge the Gordons. They came on slow, curb chains jingling and sabres drawn, but were then blasted by enfiladed musket and rifle fire from the Nassauers and horsemen were shot dead in their saddles. The rear ranks turned and fled, but some still milled about in confusion and when the last of the Gordons had cleared the road, the Black Watch fired a wicked volley and the last of the elite horseman were killed in a maelstrom of blood, steel and dying horses.

MacDonald, on his return, was smiling victoriously and clasped Campbell in a tight embrace. Both officers then waved a thank you to Sattler who saluted them with his sword.

'My God, what a victory!' Campbell exclaimed.

'Beaten the bastards with Highland resolve and cold steel,' MacDonald said. He had lost seven men and as many wounded, but the bayonet charge had won this fight.

The French could still have returned. They could have summoned courage and marched back to those heights for vengeance, but they chose to abandon them. They knew the grim Highlanders would pour volley fire into them, retreat and taunt them, inviting them to attack where they would die on Scottish blades already crusted with French blood.

Bannerman heard a new sound; a rhythm of voices and beat of drums. It made his skin prickle. The officers shared perplexed looks, then climbed the heights to see several French battalions marching down the southern ridge towards the allied centre. Even from this distance, it was impossible not to see who they were. They were big men, made taller by their huge bearskins and broad at the shoulders by their bulky epaulettes.

'Christ,' Campbell exclaimed. 'Boney's sending in the Guard.'

'That means nothing,' MacDonald dismissed the comment.

The Emperor's Imperial Guard marched with bayonets fixed. The sun loitered in great rifts between the swells of dark cloud, yet its light glinted from the hundreds of blades. There were seven battalions in total who were supported by their own Horse Artillery. This was not like the day's earlier attack, when the four infantry columns tried to smash their way through the allied lines, this was an assault by the elite. These were the unbeaten victors of Europe. They were veterans. They were legends. And Bannerman wondered if it was his imagination, or did the Eagle standards gleam yet more boldly in the rays of the diminishing sun?

The undefeated Guard climbed the battered ridge, over the mounds of dead and wounded, over the hundreds of spent roundshot that had pummelled the lip of land and they cheered because victory was close.

The Guard had never failed.

The Emperor, it seemed, had won.

'What are your orders now, sir?' Bannerman asked Campbell in the gathering twilight. His mouth was saltpetre-dry and his wounded arm was stinging like a viper's nest. He knew he had to change the bandage soon, it was beginning to reek, but it would have to wait.

'We return to our post with the rest of the brigade,' the major said hurriedly, thinking that the British army was nothing but a ragged line of weakened battalions who were lying in the trampled crops and mud, and trying to survive the French gunfire that still pounded the ridge. And now they faced the feared Immortals.

'We won't make it in time to beat those bastards,' MacDonald said, watching the Guard advance up the Mont St-Jean ridge.

'So what do you suggest, Donald?'

Bannerman couldn't see MacDonald's face, but felt that he was smiling. 'I say we advance on their flank. Stir things up for them. Kick them hard in the balls.'

'We dinnae have orders for that,' Campbell said.

MacDonald said nothing.

'Sir!' A voice called from behind and Bannerman turned to see Lieutenant Anderson jogging up the road. 'Prussian cavalry at the rear, sir! They know we're allies. The Nassauers have alerted them to our presence.'

The Highlanders parted the narrow roadside as dragoons clattered through Smohain and slewed to a halt. *Majoor* Sattler and two of his officers appeared from the farms and a quick exchange was given in German. Behind the dragoons were horse artillery, more cavalry and behind them columns of infantry. There were thousands of them ready for the attack.

'This is *Oberst* Sommer,' Sattler said of the leading cavalryman. He was clean-shaven with a strong-boned face and eyes as clear as glass. His horse was white, dappled with grey touches and was mud-spattered from hard riding. The Prussian spoke to Sattler in a loud voice as though he was used to giving orders. The Nassau officer grinned. 'He says that he and his men would be proud to fight alongside the Duke of Wellington's men.'

Campbell lifted a dirty hand, noticing the Prussian's stained uniform and scarred boots that marked him out as a man who knew his business. 'Tell him,' he started as Sommer took his proffered hand, 'that he fights with Wellington's best, and that it would be our honour indeed.'

MacDonald grinned.

And so after a further exchange of news and strategy, it was agreed that the two Highlander battalions would advance on the Prussian right with the Nassauers as they speared the Emperor's flank. Sommer was impatient, declaring his men wanted the honour of capturing Bonaparte for the terrible loss at Ligny.

The sun was just above the horizon now, a dazzling red orb suspended in the summer sky. Its dying glow threw its light on the Prussians that advanced on firm ground between Papelotte and the southern heights. French bugles and drums beat and the survivors of d'Erlon's attack turned to face a new threat. Already more Prussians were streaming to join Wellington's left wing so that the weary and shrunken battalions were able to bolster the centre where the French Guard were advancing under heavy fire.

The Black Watch surged forward with the Gordons on their left and the Nassauers on the right. Bannerman could see and hear volley-fire raking down the flank of a Guard column past La Haye Sainte. Behind the last column were cavalry and infantry waiting for the Grumblers to smash apart Wellington's line. But it was the screen of infantry that had his full attention. Skirmishers ran out to meet the two British battalions and at fifty yards, the Highlanders came to a halt.

Campbell drew breath into his lungs. 'Present!'

Seven hundred heavy muskets came up.

A pause. Four French battalions were advancing towards them.

Bannerman saw French faces light up, a mere heartbeat in length caused from the flash of the muskets before the world was obscured by a vast, roiling cloud of rotten-egg smelling smoke in the dusk-light. He heard the sound of the balls hitting targets as the volley's struck home.

'Load!'

A few French fired back, and a handful of Highlanders went down, as ramrods rattled in fouled musket barrels as the Scotsmen thrust down balls and wadding. A weaker volley exploded to the right as the Nassauers targeted the nearest enemy battalion and Bannerman saw an officer topple from his horse. There were bodies littering the ground, but the French outnumbered them all three to one.

'Fire!'

Flames roared out of the Scottish muskets, sparking pans turned to tongues of malevolent fire. The Black Watch's volley tore into the French just as they halted. The ranks shook and men tumbled to the churned field.

'Have we won?' A voice asked.

'Aye,' Bannerman said to Sergeant Weir who was dying with a bullet to his belly. He held the NCOs hand. 'We've slaughtered the bastards good and proper.'

'Good,' Weir said, tears making channels in the grime on his face. He breathed once more and was gone.

Bannerman stood in time to see a thick line of dark enemy muzzles pointing at the regiment. He grimaced as he instinctively waited for the explosion, but none came. He gazed down the ranks and suddenly the French seemed to twist away.

The Prussian dragoons, led from the front by the steely and vengeful Sommer, suddenly appearing through the powder bank, charged into the French lines. Swords sliced and hacked ruthlessly as the French were scrambling desperately away from the nightmare. They died in their scores. Bannerman saw a Prussian flense the face from a French officer protecting the regiment's Eagle and snatch the standard from the man's wavering hands.

'*Rächen!*' The Prussian officers chanted.

Revenge.

The French infantry were cut to bloody ribbons. Swords chopped down and came back red. Some French muskets crashed and dragoons were killed, but the lines had crumbled and the horses charged over broken bodies to pursue and slaughter the remainder. A battery of Horse Artillery rode up to the heights, unlimbered to pour fire into the French, followed by the grim Prussian infantry who marched with bright bayonets.

'Look up there!' Campbell said, voice made hoarse with emotion at the victory. 'The Guard are fleeing! We've beaten them, lads! Nosey has beaten the bastards!'

Bannerman blinked with astonishment at the great tide of the enemy flooding away like rats fleeing a sinking ship. Against the dark uniforms of the French a thin ragged line in red pursued them. All across the valley the Prussians were swarming and the French nerve broke. The Highlanders gave a parched cheer and spat malice at the routed enemy. Reid danced a jig, Anderson thrust his sword up at the sky screaming triumph and even Gray, a bullet in his shoulder taken from the last volley, shouted with unabashed joy.

Bannerman couldn't speak. His lungs felt like they'd been scoured with sand, but he dipped his head and gave a silent prayer. When he lifted his head, there were tears in his eyes.

For the Emperor's last gambit had utterly failed and the battle was over.

*

485

The air was humid and smelled bitter and sulphurous as Beth and Robbie clambered down the damp fields toward where the British battalions had just an hour or less earlier, beaten the Emperor's Guard by stubborn and well-practised musketry. She had been delayed at the farmhouse of Mont St-Jean, where the wounded and the dying were waiting for the surgeons to patch them up or saw off a shattered limb. It was an awful sight and after seeing a British gunner who had lost both arms at the elbows, stooping and ashen as though he was moments from bleeding to death, she could not look another in the face. A British officer and six privates had put her with three other women in the farm's cattle byre rather than let her go any closer.

'I have to see my husband,' she had implored at the officer who barely looked old enough to shave.

'Madam, please,' he had said with as much confidence as he could muster. 'I am under strict orders to apprehend all wives and...' he couldn't finish what he was thinking.

Beth rounded on him. 'I am a sergeant's wife. I'm on the company books. I have my papers, Lieutenant.'

The officer who had been thinking that she might be a whore or looter was taken aback by her attractiveness, however muddy, grime-stained and shattered she might look. He thought the other women looked like hogs in dresses compared to this one. 'I'm sorry. Orders are orders. I'm afraid you will have to stay here until such time to release you. It's for your own safety.'

Beth had cursed which caused the enamoured lieutenant to shudder, and so had sat down with the other huddling women and waited.

Now, she had found out where the regiment had gone from an officer serving the brigade as an Aide and plunged into the valley where the moon was silvering the land and the trees cast hard black shadows. She could hear murmuring all around her. Horses whinnying and men crying out. Her boots seemed inordinately loud as she fast walked. Her feet were swollen, painful and Robbie seemed to weigh more with every step, but all she could think about was Ran. How the dream of his death seemed so real. She shivered not out of cold but a chill dashed up her spine at the thought of being a widow and Robbie fatherless. Nevertheless, she pulled her shawl into her body.

It was oddly quiet, eerie in the tangle of monochrome tracks and made suffocating by the tall and imposing hedge banks. She was not scared of what might lurk out here. She had lived with soldiers all her life and had been a looter on occasion so knew the dangers. She carried a long-bladed dirk on her ever since aged sixteen two redcoats had tried to rape her. Ran and Bannerman had saved her and beaten the men to bloody pulp, but ever since then she always went armed.

There was a flicker of light, an orange glow that was haemorrhaging into the shadows. It was a campfire lit by the survivors and she smiled. She hurried on, the muscles in her legs and back strained and ached, but she saw men in kilts and she gave a cry of relief.

'Halt! Who goes there?' A sharp Scottish voice suddenly called out from the shadows.

Beth stumbled because it had caught her off guard. 'It's Mrs Grant. Sergeant Ran Grant's wife,' she said. 'You are the 42nd, are you not?'

There was a pause. 'Step forward please,' a different voice said. She obeyed and her face fell into moonlight. There was another pause. Leather boots creaked and footsteps thudded slowly towards her. Suddenly a tall man was in view, resplendent in Highland uniform and she beamed. She recognised him instantly and gave a great sigh of pure relief. 'Thank God, it's you. My husband, is he alive?'

Captain Neil Darrow regarded her at first with a wan smile, then beckoned her towards him warmly. 'I shall be honoured to escort you to him right now, Mrs Grant.'

*

Bannerman ran a hand over his stubble-shrouded chin and then through his thick hair. He arched his back slowly, revelling in the gentle pain of stretching muscles. He was conscious suddenly of how exhausted he felt, the rhythmic pounding of his heart now present in his ears as if to remind him of the need to rest. The battalion had simply collapsed with fatigue, some men unable to stand to take a piss. Head counts and the ammunition count would wait until the morning, although most had two or three cartridges left in their pouches out of the sixty at the start of the day. The men were battle-stained, blackened and frayed things; faces and hands caked in mud and soot. They smelled to high Heaven. The Prussians still came in the dark, although most avoiding Smohain's narrow roads so the area was mostly clear of allied troops. The Nassauers had fallen back to the ridge and would send burial parties out like everyone else in the morning. As the bivouac fires were lit and men snored against the embankments, trees and furrow-haunted field, Bannerman had returned to Smohain. The sky was clear so that moonlight cast sharp shadows from the edges of the walls and roofs of

487

the houses. The hamlet was an empty and silent place, where dead Frenchmen lay in gutters, sniffed by scavenging dogs.

It wasn't until he checked on the picquets to the north of Papelotte that the heady mixture of exhilaration and weariness was beginning to take its toll. He rubbed his tired eyes, yawned and wondered if his legs could carry him any further. Bats wheeled over the farm's high walls that were pock-marked by French grape-shot that had scoured the ramparts of Nassauers earlier in the day. The farm was deserted, but there were still bodies piled against the stonework from the fighting.

There was a soft cry. A voice that might have been a fox, Bannerman considered. He raised his head. A pistol shot echoed from the valley, no doubt putting a horse out of its misery, or to ward off the persistent looters. It was common enough and Bannerman had heard so many he thought skirmishers were still fighting. Idle moments passed and he went to move when he heard a murmur that turned into a shriek, followed by the sound of a child crying. It was coming from the farm. This was no animal. Weariness forgotten, he dashed back; his old leg wound making him limp, to the roofed main gate leading into the courtyard when a dull click sounded behind him. He twisted around to see a redcoat emerge from the shadows levelling a musket at him.

The scarred face of Sholto Burrell broke into a sneering grin.

'This is for my brother,' he said and pulled the trigger.

It was the sound of Robbie whimpering that stirred Bannerman. Sharply followed by pain. Everywhere. He opened his eyes, one of them was closed over. He drew a hand up to the eye, the flesh was swollen and pulpy. His ribs hurt, a shuddering pain that seemed to pulse, bringing waves of fresh agony with each breath. Sholto had shot him and then beaten him savagely. There was an overpowering copper taste in his mouth. He lifted his head, face laced with clotting blood.

'He's alive!' Beth said. She was holding Robbie close to her. There were two figures over him. The nearest one kicked him.

'What are you doing here?' Bannerman asked her, sounding incredulous.

'I came to find Ran,' she trilled tearfully.

The other man tutted. 'Still alive, RSM?' Darrow said, breaking into a laugh, the sound mirthless and bitter.

'Let them go,' Bannerman said, spittle and blood hanging from his lips. They were in a barn, lit by a single bright lamp hanging on the nearest wall.

'Och, I intend to,' Darrow replied. 'After a wee while,' he added wickedly, causing Sholto to snigger.

The corporal wiped an arm across his lips that dribbled wine through yellow-brown teeth. 'After I've had some fun with Mrs Grant,' he said, sucking on a wineskin. He gave her a wet smile as he rubbed his manhood, and Beth shuddered.

'You'll nae touch her,' Bannerman said, moving to face the twin.

Sholto screwed up his scarred face. 'I'll put that bitch on her back and show her what a real man can do.'

'You touch her and I'll kill you,' Bannerman said, sitting up.

Darrow laughed again and Sholto aimed a kick at Bannerman, which missed, so the corporal stood closer and gave a series of brutal kicks. Bannerman shielded his wounded side from the assault by bringing his legs up, but the kicks hurt.

'Enough!' Darrow exclaimed. Sholto turned an aggrieved face at him. 'I need him alive a wee longer,' Darrow explained as though Sholto was Robbie's age. 'Then you can have your fun.'

'Bastard,' Bannerman muttered, heaving his bruised and bloodied body over to face his attacker.

'Adam, they said Ran is dead,' Beth said, tears running down her face. The soft glow of the light made them appear like tracks of silver.

Bannerman nodded and swallowed hard. 'I'm so sorry, Beth.'

'And now it's time for you to join your friend, RSM,' Darrow said with relish. 'If only you had taken my generous offer, then you would live,' he said, shaking his head as if Bannerman had insulted him. 'Now you and a family will die, because of your ridiculous principles.' He turned to Sholto who was scratching his groin. 'You have unfinished business with the RSM.'

'Aye, sir.'

'Then finish it now.'

Sholto flexed the muscles in his neck before glaring at Bannerman. 'It's a pity that I'm going to kill you first. I really wanted you to see me hump the shite of Mrs Grant and then strangle the bitch and the weakling afterwards.'

'And to make this completely fair,' Darrow brought up a pistol, 'let the corporal have the first blow, RSM.'

'You killed my brother,' Sholto rasped. 'I shall revenge him.'

'You'll follow him to a grave,' Bannerman said, despite his injuries. His own retribution would not come, and it made him want to weep and vomit both at once. Since learning of Ran's murder, he had thought of the moment when he would crush Sholto and Darrow into bloodied gore. And now, it was all over. He had failed.

But he would not go without a fight.

Then a figure moved in the shadows behind Darrow and suddenly bright steel flashed in the half-light.

'I think you should let the RSM fight how he wants to fight,' Lieutenant Anderson said, his sword's tip pressed against the base of Darrow's skull.

Darrow narrowed his eyes, but did not move a muscle. Sholto did not take his gaze from Bannerman. 'I'm going to rip your head off and shite down your throat,' he said.

'Come and try.' Bannerman spat a gobbet of blood at his face and before he could stand, Sholto came forward, growling and aimed another kick at him. Bannerman rolled away from the assault, body screaming out in pain. Sholto's kicks missed him, or were blocked by his arms, but then one slammed into his jaw where teeth gashed the inside of his cheek. Bannerman was knocked flat onto his back. The twin raised his foot to stamp down on his face, but he seized the foot and gave it a sickening twist. Bones snapped like old wood and the corporal yelped. It was an odd sound to come from a man. Sholto shook himself free and tried to remain standing, but lost his balance and collapsed sideways. Bannerman spat more blood. He crawled over to the corporal and his big hammer fists slammed into Sholto's ribs, groin and face. The twin tried to kick, but his good leg was being crushed by Bannerman's weight and his other felt like it was on fire. He beat with his fists but one of Bannerman's hands clasped him by the throat and started to squeeze. Sholto, choking for breath, tried to haul the muscled forearm away, but Bannerman was too strong and it was like a man trying to push aside an oak tree. The fingers closed and the corporal began to twitch and flap like a landed fish. Then, Bannerman clambered over his body and clasped a hand over Sholto's purple face, covering it, and lifted it up to smash it down onto the floor. He did it again and again. Sholto's hands tried to protect his head, but then his head made a dull wet crack and they fluttered. Bannerman went on crashing it against the stone until there was nothing left but a shattered skull oozing red fluid and brain matter.

Bannerman stood, pain and exhaustion flooding every fibre of his body. 'Thank you, sir,' he said to Anderson.

'I'm sure the wee bastard deserved a fate worse than that,' Anderson said, face in half-shock at the brutal death. He turned to face the back of Darrow's form. 'And you, sir.' His eyes, glanced at Beth and Robbie, to see if they were unharmed. 'I watched you sneak here with that creature. I wondered what mischief you were up to. Looting perchance? I dinnae know the full story, but it's enough to know you're up to no good. You disgust me. After what the battalion has been through today. Better men who did their duty lie dead out there. You're a disgrace to the regiment!' He spat. 'I think it prudent to give me your pistol. Now!' The sword pressed further against Darrow's flesh.

Darrow had showed no flicker of emotion. 'Careful what you wish for, Lieutenant,' he said, quickly swivelling on his heels. The pistol flared and Anderson was hurled backwards by the close-range blast.

Beth screamed and Bannerman snarled, but Darrow's sword flashed towards their throats, the long blade glinting with lamp-light. He moved the blade towards Robbie, who Beth was trying to shield.

'Take a step further,' he said to Bannerman, 'and I'll cut the boy's head from his shoulders.'

Bannerman gazed over Anderson's lifeless body, the coat around the bullet wound was smouldering. 'I'm going to kill you,' he told Darrow. 'I swore that I would kill you both and I've been right so far.'

The Surgeon laughed. The sword nevertheless flicked towards Bannerman.

'Beth,' Bannerman said, 'did he tell you who killed Ran?'

Beth wiped her face. 'No. He said Ran died fighting.'

'What are you doing?' Darrow asked.

'He was stabbed in the back,' Bannerman said.

Beth gasped.

'Stabbed by this coward,' Bannerman kicked Sholto's skull, which made a slight-hollow sound.

Beth blinked, shook her head and tears flooded her eyes again.

Bannerman was staring at her. 'He was murdered and it was this man who ordered his death.'

Darrow whipped the sword up to Bannerman's neck. 'That's enough from you!'

Beth blew out her cheeks and shook in a mixture of fury and agony. Darrow glanced at her, but twisted to Bannerman who was the threat. And just as both men snarled at each other, Beth screamed as she plunged her hidden dirk into Darrow's back. The captain's mouth worked silently as his sword arm went limp, and the other tried to pull the blade free.

Bannerman swotted the sword from his hand and grabbed Darrow's head with both hands, forcing the man down onto his knees, where he began to push his head around. Darrow tried to resist by feebly tugging his forearms, but Bannerman, wounded and bleeding, still had enough strength in him to twist until Darrow's breathing became frantic rasps.

'Dinnae look,' Bannerman grunted, and Beth turned herself and Robbie away.

Bannerman kept turning until Darrow's throat was too constricted to make any sound. His head was facing Beth, a grotesque look of sheer terror on his thin face, but Beth spat at him. Then there was a grating noise and a sharp crack and his eyes disappeared up into his skull and his body went limp. Bannerman let it drop to the ground.

'It's over,' he said.

'Beth turned and glanced at the bodies. 'Adam...' she started, but words failed her.

'Did they hurt you?' Bannerman asked, his voice was distorted from the blood in his mouth.

'No,' she replied and, clutching Robbie, ran to him where he held them in his arms for what seemed an aeon.

'I'm so sorry,' he said over and over. When she moved back to cuff the tears away from her eyes, he produced Ran's letter. 'He wanted you to have this.'

She took it, unfolding it with great care, and lowering her head read it. More tears spilled onto the crinkled paper. 'Thank you for keeping this for me,' she said. 'What happens next?' She stared at the bodies. 'What do we do now?'

'Dinnae worry about a thing,' he said, soothing her. He clasped his side that suddenly lanced with pain. The bullet had winged him, probably on purpose so that Sholto could inflict more pain whilst he was alive.

'The captain and him,' Beth jutted her chin at Sholto's corpse.

'Food for the beasts,' Bannerman replied, stroking Robbie's head. 'Nasty men tried to hurt you,' he told the boy. 'Now they're gone. You and your ma are safe now.'

'The lieutenant,' Beth said at Anderson's body.

'I know,' Bannerman said sorrowfully. Anderson had saved them and paid with his life. His sacrifice might be explained by a lie about catching looters who killed him, but Bannerman thought his friend was owed a more heroic death.

'Do we tell anyone?'

And that was the problem. Reveal Darrow's crimes and there would be a long painful enquiry. With the Burrell twins dead, along with Ran and Anderson, there were no witnesses and no one who could corroborate the events. Campbell was unaware of events, so it was best to keep this dark secret safe. 'We cannae tell a soul, Beth.'

She bobbed her head, understanding. 'What do we do now?'

'We slit the captain's seams for gold, take anything of value, along with anything from that piece of shite,' he doubted Sholto had anything on him, but whatever wealth there was would go to Beth and Robbie. She would get a pension, but it wasn't much. 'You can keep it all.'

'Adam,' she started, but hesitated. Her freckled face was strained by the sadness, but it was still a face that stole his breath.

'What?'

'I dreamt Ran was dead,' she said, knowing that it sounded odd, but she wanted to confess it to Bannerman. 'Somehow I knew it – it was expected. But I still cannae believe it.' She sighed and gazed up at Bannerman's ravaged face. 'You need to have you injuries looked at.' Dark blood was seeping through his ragged coat.

'I will,' he said, pain and fatigue all coming at once. He winced and staggered to the doorway. 'But for the moment, let's get some air.' He didn't want Robbie to witness the horror. 'Does Robbie understand what's happened to his da?'

Beth shook her head, the boy still hidden in her frayed skirts. 'I dinnae think so.'

'If you want me to tell him, I will.' He wanted to tell her that Ran had said he was to care for them, but it was too soon. He stared out into the darkness and felt Beth's hand squeeze within his and he gazed round at her, weeping inside for the loss of his friends, but hoping with all his heart that she would decide to stay with him.

They stepped outside the farm to a country gutted by war and bleeding in its aftermath. A small insignificant place where the wounded sobbed, the dead stank and the surgeons plied their trade by guttering lights.

It was a land of shifting, melding shapes of grey, like a world dominated by wraiths, and where still bodies slept eternal peace.

Bannerman held Beth's hand tightly, because the battle was at last over, and the world as they knew it had changed.

Historical Note

Death is a Duty, is not about the one hundred days' campaign, because writing of the Black Watch from the sunrise of the 16th June to the final moonlit minutes of the 18th/19th was a very difficult process for me. I had no trouble writing of Jack Hallam's adventures in snowy, war-torn Holland in *Blood on the Snow*, or Lorn Mullone during the rebel assault on New Ross in *Liberty or Death*. But in *Death is a Duty*, the bloody battles of Quatre Bras and Waterloo took hold like a bird of prey's grasp. It almost became a novel in size. I had a lot more than a novella's worth, so I had to trim about 40k words off. The series is entirely comprised of novella's - so perhaps I'll revisit the campaign again someday for a novel.

So as it's impossible to include all of the events for a standalone novella, I've tried to put myself in where the brave Highlanders fought and marched during the 16th-18th as best I could. Sometimes I veered off course, most notably in the late afternoon during the battle of Waterloo, where Bannerman could see things that probably, from the battalion's position, he couldn't have. I couldn't help myself and proclaim artistic licence. For those enthusiasts and researchers of the campaign I humbly apologise for that and for any other erroneous details.

Why write about the Black Watch? As war-gamer, writer and devotee of the period, the regiment stands head and shoulders with some of the more notable regiments of the Peninsular War and indeed the British army. I was inspired by the painting of the Black Watch by William Barnes Wollen – which I've used as the cover for *Death is a Duty* – being charged at Quatre Bras by the French lancers.

The events of the campaign unfolded much as I have retold. The 1/42nd landed in Ostend, early May 1815, and then marched to Brussels where it was brigaded with the 1st , the 44th, and the 92nd, with Sir Denis Pack as Brigadier. It formed part of the 5th Division under the command of Picton on 15th May. Picton received movement orders around 2 am on the 16th, at which time the troops began forming to depart the city. Picton inspected his division around 4 am and had them on the road where it marched as far as the vicinity of Waterloo until noon where it was acting as an operational reserve in case the French probed west on the British right wing. At noon, the division

494

received orders from Wellington to march to Quatre Bras; a march of twenty-two miles, which it reached around 2pm, as detailed in the story.

The British regiments immediately formed for action and as the 42nd was advancing through a rye-field, it was charged by a body of lancers before it had time to form square. The two flank companies suffered most severely as the wings attempted to close, and perhaps twenty-forty lancers entered the square through the gaps. It was then in the bitter fighting that Colonel Macara was killed by a lance thrust. The regiment really did lose their two majors and so the command went to senior Captain Campbell, who was promoted brevet-major later that day.

As the wounded and dead lay in and around the square, the regiment was then charged by cuirassiers which it savagely repulsed, angered by the death of Macara and their comrades. The regiment beat off more French skirmishers, but as more and more British arrived on the field, Ney could not hope to take the cross roads and so as evening fell, the French withdrew. The regiment was mentioned by the Duke of Wellington in his public despatch, and did indeed suffer approximately three hundred casualties.

At the time of writing this revised edition (October 2015) I had the fortune to join many thousands commemorating the bicentenary in June 2015, where I visited the battlefields of the campaign. Sadly, there wasn't any event on the anniversary of Quatre Bras. The farms are all there in some form, or another, most impressive of all is the farmhouse of Gemioncourt. Bossu Wood is long gone and the farmhouse at the crossroads, which became the hospital, is a weed-haunted derelict. In fact, the plaque commemorating the battle had been wrenched from the building and stolen. There is talk of a fund to save the crumbling walls from demolition. I sincerely hope they do. Quatre Bras is a vacant, sad place of ghosts now, but one can still see the undulating ground that rolls and swells from the crossroads, and imagine the tall crops concealing whole battalions of infantry and cavalry of that blood-weeping fight.

At Waterloo the shrunken 42nd remained on Wellington's left flank where it helped destroy d'Erlon's infantry assault, but then played little part except by standing resolutely behind the reverse slopes being a solid anchor of support. They did not assist the Nassauers with retaking the farms around the hamlet of Smohain, or advance with the Prussians – but I had to give them something to do to enable Bannerman's final showdown with the dastardly Captain Darrow and Sholto Burrell. Incidentally, the Nassauers did suffer from Prussian artillery bombardments; mistaking them for French troops, but the Germans retook the buildings, particularly Papelotte, after continued assaults which kept the French right busy throughout the day.

I visited the farms of Papelotte, La Haye and the village of Smohain, (now named La Marache) and are worth seeing. Frischermont, not to be confused with nearby Fischermont (a convent), was once a walled-chateau on the scale with that of Hougoumont, but now is lost to time. Only rubble and earthen banks where it once stood remain. My good friend Adam (who this story is dedicated to) and I spent many hours searching for it on foot and in his ancient Rover. That car took us to far across the battlefields and more, and never let us down. Maybe I should have included it in the dedication, for upon its return to Blighty, the poor thing died and had to be scrapped.

There was no Captain Darrow whose treachery could have tarnished the regiment, but acts of violence for which he was involved with did exist. Wellington prized order above almost every other battlefield virtue. Order made men stand under withering fire, manoeuvre calmly when enemies assaulted and order allowed the British musketry to withstand and beat French fire. He once remarked that his army was 'the scum of the earth' and he was talking of when that vaunted order was broken. At the Battle of Vitoria, when the British captured the huge baggage train that contained their plunder of Spain, discipline was stripped raw and was gone in an orgy of looting and murder. Thus Darrow became one of those wretched men.

Sadly, Adam Bannerman is a figment of my imagination. So too are Boyd Anderson, the Burrell twins and Beth and Robbie. *Majoor* Sattler did command the Nassauers, and Major Donald MacDonald was the senior officer of the Gordons at Waterloo, another Highland regiment to have also suffered high casualties at Quatre Bras.

For more reading about the Black Watch I heartily suggest Archibald Forbes' *The Black Watch: The Record of an Historic Regiment* and A.G. Wauchope's *A Short History of the Black Watch (Royal Highlanders)*.

I self-published *Death is a Duty* very close to the anniversary. There was so much new interest in the subject that recommending books on the campaign proved to be very difficult and even harder for me to decide which ones to take with me on the momentous journey. However, 'David Howarth's *Waterloo*, Mark Adkin's *Waterloo*

Companion: A Complete Guide to History's Most Famous Land Battle, and David Buttery's *Waterloo Battlefield Guide* have all been indispensable.

Acknowledgments

The Soldier Chronicles were written sometime between 2008-2010, when I had finished writing a story about the British liberation of Egypt, 1801. Some of the main characters jumped off the pages of that book, quite selfishly to be honest, and demanded their own stories. These preludes have now formed companion pieces to that planned series of works which haven't been completed at the time of this publication.

In 2014, I finally got around to having the first of the five stories printed and self-published (originally going to be called The Union Flag Chronicles - harking to the English, Irish, Scottish and Welsh characters of the series, but then wondered would people think they were about the American Civil Wars.) To avoid any confusion the series became *The Soldier Chronicles*.

And it all became very real with the help of some very lovely people.

I'd like to thank Catherine Lenderi for her editorial work. I wish to thank all those beta readers that provided so many positive replies that really helped me fine tune the stories. Thank you to the Napoleonic groups on social media sites that have provided more knowledge than I've found in books on the subject. Thanks to Angharad Evans for her assistance with Arthur Cadoc's Welsh, a feat I really struggled with, and Matthew Harffy for those extra Spanish tips.

Debbie Liggins designed *Liberty or Death*'s cover with a scene from the rebel attack on New Ross. Green Door Designs couldn't quite get the British Marine feel of Gamble's story for *Heart of Oak* that I wanted for various reasons, but I still think they did a fantastic job nonetheless.

Many thanks must go to Jenny Q who brought *Fire and Steel*'s jacket cover to life with her incredible flair for design. I have had many compliments since publication. Jenny also designed the covers for *Blood on the Snow*, *Marksman* and *Death is a Duty*.

While I have attempted to make the stories as true to history as humanely possible, there will be the odd inaccuracy hidden somewhere. For this, and any other glaring errors that haven't come to my attention, I do apologise.

Thank you to my author/book friends - you really do make me smile. Finally, much love and appreciation to my family. An author's life is a lonely job. I do value the opportunity you give me to do something I really enjoy.

You can find more information about me and my books here:

@davidcookauthor
www.facebook.com/davidcookauthor
http://thewolfshead.tumblr.com

Made in the USA
Middletown, DE
07 December 2020

26497649R00298